TERRI BLACKSTOCK

#1 bestselling suspense author

Evidence of Mercy

SUN COAST CHRONICLES 1&2

Justifiable Means

ZONDERVAN®

ZONDERVAN.com/
AUTHORTRACKER
follow your favorite authors

ZONDERVAN®

Evidence of Mercy
Copyright © 1995 by Terri Blackstock

Justifiable Means
Copyright © 1996 by Terri Blackstock

Requests for information should be addressed to:

Zondervan, *Grand Rapids, Michigan 49530*

ISBN-10: 0-310-60954-2
ISBN-13: 978-0-310-60954-4

Published in association with the literary agency of Alive Communications, Inc., 7680 Goddard Street, Suite 200, Colorado Springs, CO 80920.

Interior design by Susan Vandenberg Koppenol

Printed in the United States of America

07 08 09 10 11 12 • 18 17 16 15 14 13 12 11 10 9 8 7 6 5 4 3 2 1

Evidence
of Mercy

This book and all those to follow it
are lovingly dedicated to
The Nazarene

ACKNOWLEDGMENTS

Special thanks to Chip Anderson, of Anderson's Optique in Jackson, Mississippi, for showing me his magic; to Carla Nowell, physical therapist at Methodist Hospital in Jackson, Mississippi, for helping me find authenticity; to Ellis Warren, pilot, for talking me through my landing; to Larry Morgan, aircraft mechanic, and Lane Smith, general genius, for helping me create my disasters; to the Cockrells and many others at First Baptist Church in Jackson, Mississippi, for their powerful prayers; to Greg Johnson, for sharing the vision; to the Phillips-Corry class, for leading me to the brink of awakening.

And to Ken, my spiritual leader, for helping me decide where to go from there.

PROLOGUE

He had waited for a new moon, for he needed the cover of darkness. Tonight was perfect. Dressed in black, he knew it would be virtually impossible for anyone to see him. The airport guard who patrolled the small building in the wee hours would never notice that anything improper was going on right beneath his nose. Not as long as he was swift and quiet.

Checking once again to make sure no one was near, he crept across the tarmac, past the private planes lined up like a military fleet, squinting to read the number and name on each fuselage.

Solitude was the fourth from the right, just as he'd expected.

With one more quick look around, he bent down and duck-walked under the plane, found the wheel well, and shone his small flashlight to find the spot he needed. Calmly he pulled the tool he'd brought out of his pocket, made the necessary adjustment, then flicked off the light.

It had taken less than thirty seconds to create the catastrophe that would finally make things right. Grinning, he hurried quietly back across the tarmac then broke into a jog for a mile beyond the airport until he reached his car. He'd parked it far enough away so he wouldn't be heard back at the airport as he cranked it. He pulled into the street, keeping his lights off. Laughing out loud, he headed home, eager for the satisfaction he would feel the next time *Solitude* was flown.

Then there would be one less obstacle between him and his prize—and one more victory to show who was really in control.

CHAPTER ONE

olitude—the perfect name for the toy that defined Jake Stevens, not because he liked being alone. He didn't. He'd always found it better to be surrounded by the right kind of people, and Jake had a knack for collecting friends just like he collected brandy snifters from the cities he'd traveled to. But the only way to be completely autonomous was to be unattached. It was a credo Jake lived by, and it meant that he knew the value of his own solitude. At the top of the pyramid that was Jake's life, there was only one person—the one he smiled at in the mirror every morning. At thirty-nine, he was just where he'd wanted to be at this point in his life. Unfettered and financially fluid, he had the world by the tail, and today he was going to bag it and take it home.

Ignoring the doorman who greeted him, he trotted down the steps in front of the Biltmore. At the bottom of the steps, his red Porsche idled as the valet got out. "Hey, put the top down, will ya?" Jake called down.

The kid, who looked no more than eighteen, knew exactly how to do it, and as the top began to buzz back, Jake's attention was snatched away by the blonde on her way up the steps. She was college aged, probably twenty years his junior, but he'd never found that to be a problem. Tipping his sunglasses, he gave her that engaging grin that had always worked for him before.

She smiled back, as they always did, and slowed her step as he came toward her.

"I'm not usually this blunt, Ma'am, but I've learned over the years that if I let an opportunity slip by me, I sometimes never get it again. And you are, by far, the most beautiful woman I've laid eyes on since I pulled into St. Clair yesterday."

She laughed, as though she'd heard the line before, but it didn't seem to hurt his chances. "I'm Sarah," she said. "Are you staying in the hotel?"

"Yes," he said, "and if I had time, I'd turn around and escort you right back inside. But alas—" He threw his hand dramatically over his heart and sighed heavily as she laughed again. "I have to be somewhere—to look at a plane I'm thinking about buying." He waited a beat for her to be sufficiently impressed, and when her eyebrows lifted slightly, he went on. "Now, I don't want you to think I'm the kind of guy who hits on every woman he sees, but do you think, by any chance, you'd care to meet a lonely transplanted Texan for drinks later? I can call you when I get back."

He knew he wasn't imagining the sparkle in her eye, for he'd seen it many times before. "I'm in room 323," she answered. "But if I'm not there, I'll probably be out by the pool."

The pool, he thought with a grin. *Perfect.* "I'll call as soon as I get back."

"You haven't told me your name yet."

"Oh, yeah," he said. "Jake. Jake Stevens."

But already he'd forgotten hers. The room number was all that really mattered. Waving, he trotted the rest of the way down the steps. Tossing a five-dollar bill at the valet, he slid behind the wheel.

Florida was great, he told himself as he pulled onto Highway 19. Opportunities everywhere he looked. It was pure luck that he'd gotten transferred here. He only wished he could spend less time house hunting and more time playing in the few days he had left before he had to report to work.

He pulled up to a stoplight and leaned his head back on the headrest, letting the morning rays of sunlight beat down on his face. The wind was picking up, haphazardly blowing his hair. *I should stop somewhere and get a haircut*, he thought, glancing into his mirror. But it didn't look so bad a little longer, and the women seemed to like it. Idly, he decided to wait.

The stoplight didn't change, and he started to get irritated. Traffic often made him feel out of control, and there was nothing he hated worse.

He glanced around at the billboards that dominated the four corners and saw one for his favorite cognac, another for a restaurant near Honeymoon Island, a third for the outlet mall, a fourth for a television station.

The light still hadn't changed, and he began to perspire. He flicked on the air conditioner, knowing that it would do little to combat the heat with the top down, but Jake had never been one to let logic interfere with his quest for comfort.

When the light flashed green, Jake stepped on the accelerator and flicked on the radio. The wind in his ears made it impossible to hear, so finally he turned it off and tried to concentrate instead on the new toy he was going to buy—a Piper Arrow PA 28. Just what he needed to make life complete.

Once he had it, he would finally have everything he wanted.

The wind was too strong for a leisurely afternoon test flight, and Lynda Barrett wished she'd scheduled it for another day … another month … another year. But this fellow Jake Stevens was her first potential buyer, and she had already delayed showing him the plane as long as she dared; she didn't have the luxury of waiting any longer. The maddening thing about listing something for sale is that, sooner or later, someone will buy it.

Lynda stood on the wing of the Piper, gently polishing the name she'd had painted on the side when she'd bought it two years ago. *Solitude.* This plane was her escape, her refuge from the pressures of her job as an attorney. She would rather have sold her home, her father's home, and everything else either of them owned than the plane.

But she had tried selling both houses, and there hadn't been any buyers. Now the only way she could see to get a start on paying off the enormous debts her father had bequeathed her was to sell her favorite possession—the only thing she had that anyone seemed to want to buy.

The wind picked up, blowing an empty paper cup across the tarmac. Her eyes followed it—until she saw Gordon Addison leaning against the wall of the hangar, smoking a cigarette. He was watching her the way he always did, with that narrow-eyed look that gave her chills. He hadn't spoken to her in weeks, not since she'd come up with her fifth excuse not to go out with him. He was the one thing about this airport she wouldn't miss when she sold her plane.

Moving to the other side of the wing so he couldn't see her so easily, she looked into the wind and ran her fingertips over the cold, smooth metal of the fuselage. She remembered the day she bought *Solitude*. It had meant that she'd finally risen above the humdrum existence of her parents—whose lives consisted of "Jeopardy" and macaroni-and-cheese. Lynda had had a plan—to have more, to do more, to *be* more. Buying the plane had meant that she had finally arrived.

As her love for the plane had grown, she had begun casting off friends, as though they exceeded the weight limit of the baggage she could carry. She had shaken off her hobbies, her clubs, and her church in order to free up more time to spend in the cockpit. The cockpit she was about to sell. Where would she anchor herself once the plane was gone?

Shaking off her quicksand depression, Lynda went back to polishing the plane. The prospective buyer would be here any minute, and she supposed she should be practicing some kind of sales pitch. She did need the money after all. But somewhere in the back of her mind, she knew she was still hoping some miracle would keep her from having to go through with the sale.

She heard the sound of a car and turned around. Across the tarmac, a red Porsche was weaving through the parked planes, as if the driver had a perfect right to drive wherever he pleased. Lynda stopped polishing and watched as he made his way toward her.

The man who got out was in his late thirties and sported a dark tan and designer clothes that mocked his attempt to look casual. He grinned up at her, a cocky grin that set her instantly on guard. "This isn't a parking lot," she called down.

"It's okay," he said. "I parked here yesterday when I looked at the plane, and nobody objected. I'm Jake Stevens."

The confidence with which he uttered his name riled her, and she resisted the urge to say, "Oh, *well*. Since you're Jake Stevens—"

Climbing down, she eyed him more closely. He was too good-looking, too self-assured, and probably had too much money. The combination made her dislike him instantly.

Grudgingly, she extended her hand. "I'm Lynda Barrett."

"I figured as much," he said. "Did Mike tell you I came yesterday?"

"Yes. He said you'd want to take a test flight today."

"I wanted to take one yesterday, but he had a problem with it."

"He runs the airport," she said, "but he doesn't own this plane. I do, and I was in court."

"So he said." He took off his Ray Bans and dropped them into his shirt pocket, as if by showing her his "mesmerizing" eyes he might soften her mood a bit. "No problem, though. Today's as good a day as any."

"Not really," she said, looking into the breeze. "The wind's a little stronger than I like."

"Not for me. I can handle it."

The ego behind his words made her grin slightly. "Of course you can. So, Lindbergh, any questions you wanted to ask about the plane?"

He cocked his head at her barb. "No, but I might have a few about its owner."

"Such as."

"Such as, where you get your attitude?"

"*My* attitude?" She breathed a laugh and shook her head, her comeback forming on the tip of her tongue. But something stopped her. *No need to make him angry*, she told herself. *Unfortunately, this is business.* Sighing, she took a stab at honesty. "Look, I guess I'm just having a little trouble with this. I'm not looking forward to selling my plane."

"I don't blame you." Walking under the Piper, he checked the wing flaps and glanced back at her. "I looked it over pretty well yesterday. You've really maintained it."

"I spend all my spare time taking care of it," she said. She watched him drain a little fuel from the wing sump and fought the proprietary urge to tell him to keep his hands off her plane. "Did Mike let you see the log books?"

"Yeah, and the maintenance records. He was able to answer most of my questions, but he didn't really know why you were selling it."

Lynda's stomach tightened. "Financial reasons."

"Your law practice isn't doing well?"

"My practice is fine, thank you."

Frowning, he turned back to her. "Excuse me for asking, but before I sink a wad into a plane like this, I need to know the real reason you want to sell."

"I told you the real reason."

"Okay, okay. Don't get so hot. Save it for something worthwhile."

It was his type that she hated she finally realized, and this guy fit every macho stereotype she could think of. "You're pretty sure of yourself, aren't you?"

"Sometimes." Grinning, he checked the engine sump and the oil, and Lynda watched, shaking her head at his arrogance.

The attitude, she thought. Her attitude was coming back again, filling her with bitterness, and somehow she had to fight it. Taking a deep breath, she tried to change the subject. "How long have you been flying?"

"About twenty years," he said. "Right now I fly a 747 for TSA Airlines."

Lynda raised her eyebrows. "Then why would you want your own plane? I'd think you'd be tired of flying when you aren't working."

Jake went to the propellers and ran his hands along the blades. "Flying for work and flying for pleasure are two different things. There's nothing like leaving the world behind and being up there all alone without anybody telling you where to go."

Lynda looked up at the sky and realized that, finally, they had found common ground. "It's a sanctuary," she said quietly. "If my church could blueprint that feeling, they'd pack the pews every Sunday."

He looked around the prop, eyeing her narrowly. "Oh, no. You're not one of those, are you?"

"Those what?"

"Those flower-selling, tract-passing, baloney-flinging religion junkies."

She couldn't decide whether to be offended or not. "Do you mean Christians?"

"Whatever they call themselves," he said, turning back to the plane. "I attract them, you know. They flock to me in airports like I'm wearing a sign that says, 'Try me. I'll believe anything.'"

"I've never sold flowers or passed out tracts or flung baloney, and you certainly don't attract me. At the moment, the only thing I'm trying to sell you is my plane."

Chuckling slightly, he touched the name painted on the side. "I like what you named it. *Solitude*. It fits me. I think I'll keep the name."

"You haven't even decided to buy it yet."

"No, but I'm really interested. It's the best I've found for the money."

"You'd better fly it first. It's a big step down from a 747 to a single engine."

"No kidding."

"You might not like it."

His grin returned. "You're trying to talk me out of it, aren't you?"

"No, of course not."

He stepped up onto the wing, opened the door, and turned back to her. "Come on, get in. Let's see what she can do."

Reluctantly Lynda followed him up and slipped into the seat next to him. She attributed the feeling of dread taking hold of her heart to her despair that she might have to surrender the plane today.

CHAPTER TWO

A m I making you nervous?" Jake glanced at her as he pitched the plane downward then pulled back up, like a Thunderbird performing for his fans.

"I always get nervous when my life is in the hands of a psychopath." Gripping the edge of her gray vinyl seat, she closed her eyes as he dove again. "You know, you won't get a good feel for the ride if you keep showboating."

He laughed and brought it back up. "I'd forgotten how much lighter this feels. I love the hands-on quality instead of everything being so automatic. The pilot is in complete control."

"I knew you were one of those control types."

He laughed. "Don't tell me you're not. You wouldn't own a plane like this if you didn't like being in control."

She looked out the window and saw the airport growing smaller below them. "I don't fly for control," she said quietly.

"Then why do you?"

"Because unless I'm in the company of an aspiring stunt pilot who asks a lot of questions, I can think up here. Reflect."

"So how long have you been hiding up here in your Piper?"

She shot him a look. "I've had the plane for two years if that's what you mean. The best two years of my life."

He chuckled. "You almost sound like you're talking about a husband."

"Oh, no. A plane can give a lot more pleasure than grief. Not like a husband at all."

"Those are the words of a bitter woman. You must be divorced."

His presumptions amazed her. "Actually, I've never been married. And I'm not bitter. Just smart." Her eyes trailed back out the window, and she wished he'd hurry and land so they could get this transaction over with.

"Me either," he said. "I try not to strap on anything I can live without."

Lynda laughed out loud, surprising him. "You've got to be kidding. You could live without that Porsche you drove up in or that Rolex on your wrist or that diamond cluster on your finger? Those are not the trappings of a man who likes to keep things simple."

"Hey, I never said I don't like a little self-indulgence now and then. Besides, we were talking about spouses, not possessions."

"We were talking about keeping things simple," she said. "I'm just pointing out your contradictions."

He was getting annoyed, and something about that pleased her. "It's not a contradiction to want a few material things. I'm a firm believer in going after whatever makes you happy."

"Is that what all those things do? Make you happy?"

"Don't I look like a happy guy?"

She smiled, unable to help herself. "But owning a plane would make you happier?"

"You got it, darlin'. It made you happy, didn't it?"

"Yeah," she whispered. "It did most of the time." That melancholy fell over her again, and she tried to steer her mind from imagining what life would be without *Solitude*.

"I'd like to close the deal as soon as possible," Jake said, cutting into her thoughts. "When we land, we can discuss the particulars."

She sighed. "I guess the sooner the better. Are you ready to land now?"

"Sure," he said. "I've seen what I need to see."

Taking the radio mike from its hook, she held it to her mouth. "St. Clair Unicom—Cherokee 1–0–1–2 Delta. We're ready to land, Mike."

Mike's voice crackled in their headphones. "All clear, Lynda. No traffic reported. Runway 4."

She glanced at Jake as he began to fly parallel to the right side of the runway. "I'll land, if you want me to."

"I've got it," he said.

She watched out the window as he boxed around the airport and began his descent, and her heart grew heavier. Absently, her fingertips stroked the soft gray cloth of the seats that were so comfortable to her, and she wondered if she'd ever find another sanctuary that was quite as fulfilling. Jake was getting a real bargain, and she was the big loser. She almost wished she hadn't cleaned the charcoal carpet last week or polished the instrument panel or vacuumed the cloth ceiling. All those things only contributed to the comfort and luxury of the quiet cabin. If it had been dirty or ragged or badly maintained, maybe he wouldn't have wanted it.

Jake reached for the lever to release the landing gear, and a short whirring sound followed as it started lowering. But the sound was too short, and Lynda shot a look at the instruments.

"Is there something wrong with these lights?" Jake asked.

Lynda checked the gear indicator lights. According to them, the landing gear hadn't gone down. She leaned up and grabbed the lever. Nothing happened.

"I heard them go down before," Jake said. "Didn't you hear it?"

"It didn't sound right," Lynda said. "Either they're jammed, or the light's not working. Pull up."

She waited as Jake aborted the landing and climbed again. "I'll check the circuit breaker," she said. "Keep trying the lever."

Jake tried again and failed, as Lynda pressed on the circuit breaker marked "gear."

"It seems okay," she said, maintaining her calm. "Let me pump it down manually."

Gripping the hand pump between the seats, she tried to pump it down by hand, but the light still wouldn't come on.

"Here, let me," he said, trying to move her hand.

"Something's wrong," she said, surrendering it. "The pump moves too easily, and nothing happens."

Jake tried it, his face growing tense. "It has to be a busted hose, or there'd be more resistance."

"No," she argued. "It can't be. It just can't."

But she couldn't think of anything else it could be, and as panic began to rise inside her, she tried it again.

There was nothing Mike Morgan hated worse than a hotdogger playing with a plane as though it were a paper kite. Aggravated, he watched out the window as the plane feigned a landing, then pulled up at the last minute.

It couldn't be Lynda flying, he told himself, sitting in his makeshift control tower that looked more like a concession booth. Lynda had too much respect for her plane. It had to be the arrogant guy who belonged to that red Porsche. Grabbing his microphone, he called up to the plane to put a stop to this.

"Cherokee 1–2 Delta—St. Clair Unicom. What's with the touch-and-go's, Lynda?"

He waited for an answer, and when he didn't get one, he pushed the button again. "Lynda? Do you read me?"

Finally, he heard her voice. "We're having a little problem with our landing gear, Mike. We're not sure whether it's down or not."

"Oh, no," he said to himself then glanced out at the plane circling overhead.

"Mike, we're going to do a flyby. Could you come out and see if the gear's down?"

Mike grabbed his binoculars with his left hand and pressed the button again with his right. "Affirmative, Lynda."

Then dashing through the glass doors, he tried to see just how much trouble they were really in.

Cherokee 1–2 Delta—St. Clair Unicom. You reading me, Lynda?"

"1–2 Delta." Bracing herself, Lynda looked over at Jake, whose temples glistened with perspiration. "How does it look, Mike?"

"Worse than we thought, guys. The landing gear is only partially down, and one looks like it's down further than the other."

Jake swore, and Lynda closed her eyes and tried to let the news sink in.

"We can't even do a smooth belly landing if it's *partially* down!" Jake said. "And if it's not locked all the way down, it could squirrel all over the place."

"Even if it's locked where it is, we'll land lopsided," she said. "We'll lose a wing and cartwheel."

Jake grabbed the microphone out of her hand. "Mike, could you see any oil?"

"I was just getting to that," Mike said. "It looks like there could be oil streaming down the belly behind the gear. Did you try to pump it manually?"

Lynda and Jake exchanged worried looks, and Lynda took the mike back. "We tried, Mike. It has to be a loose hose."

Jake snatched the microphone again. "Mike, we're gonna have to take our chances and land with what we've got."

"No!" Lynda shouted. "We could crash! My plane would be destroyed."

"Not to mention its passengers!" he shouted back at her. "But there isn't enough fuel for us to stay up here long enough for a miracle, so unless you've got any better ideas...."

Viciously, Lynda tried the hand pump again and then the automatic lever, as if the plane might have healed itself in the last few minutes.

Finally giving up, she took the mike back. "It won't go up *or* down, Mike. He's right. We don't have any choice."

"I'm so glad you agree," Jake said caustically.

Lynda ignored him.

"I don't see any alternative either, Lynda," Mike admitted. "This could be bad. The wind isn't gonna help any. This crosswind could be a nightmare."

"Yeah," she said, "and if the gear isn't down all the way, then our brakes aren't working, either. And the fire hazard...."

Jake jerked the mike back. "If we had a choice, Mike, we'd sure find another way. But we don't. Are you ready for us or not?"

"No, not yet," Mike said. "It'll take some preparation. Just stand by, and I'll get back to you."

Silence followed, and Jake set the microphone back on its hook and continued circling the airport.

For a moment, neither of them spoke.

It was the closest Lynda had ever been to death, yet she didn't feel the peace she had always thought she'd feel. She wasn't ready to die—not mentally, emotionally, or spiritually. Wasn't there supposed to be a warning so good-byes could be said, apologies made, and affairs put in order? She just wasn't supposed to take off into the sky on a morning test flight and then never come back down.

"I hope somebody moves my Porsche," Jake said, eyeing the small airport below them.

Again, Lynda was amazed. "We're about to crash, and all you care about is your car?"

His expression betrayed his growing anger. "You're the one who cared more about your plane surviving than the people in it."

"Hey, *I'm* in it. I'm not crazy about the prospect of death either!"

Wiping his forehead with the back of his sleeve, he said, "Look, we don't have time for this. We have to get ready, whether we like it or not. I'll land the plane. I have more experience with emergencies."

"You don't have experience with *this plane*, Lindbergh. The weight's different, and you don't have a feel for it. You might bring it down too hard, and with this crosswind—"

"How many real emergency landings have you ever made?" he cut in.

"None. But I know—"

"I've had two," he said. "*I'm* landing the plane."

"This is no time for ego!"

"You're right. It's not."

Livid, they stared at each other neither wanting to back down. Suddenly, the cabin seemed too small for both of them, and she wished she could put more space between them. If she could just breathe....

On the verge of tears, she said, "All right, maybe you *are* more experienced. You land it, and I'll cut off the engine and the fuel. We'll need to shut everything off before we touch down. This is gonna take both of us."

Cursing, Jake tried the pump again, his hands trembling. When it was obvious how hopeless it was, he sent another expletive flying and slammed his hand into the instrument panel. "Piece of trash! Don't you ever check your landing gear?"

"Of course I do," she said. "I've never had any problem with it at all! I just had an annual three months ago, and everything was fine."

"A pilot should know every inch of his plane!"

"I didn't notice *you* sticking your head up the wheel well on the preflight!"

"It's *your* plane." He wiped his forehead again. "Are you sure you weren't just trying to unload it on some poor soul before you had to foot some major repair bills?"

Her mouth fell open. "I didn't even want to sell it! If my father hadn't died and left me a mountain of debts, you wouldn't even be here!"

"Lucky me."

Again, thick silence filled the cabin, and she told herself she wouldn't cry. She couldn't do what had to be done if her eyes were blurry with tears. "Look, we have to try to get this plane down without either of us getting killed. Now, if we could just—"

"Cherokee 1–2 Delta," the radio cut in. "St. Clair Unicom."

Lynda took the microphone. "1–2 Delta. Go ahead, Mike."

"We're trying to clear the runway, but we need a little time to clear the tarmac, too, so no other planes are damaged. Just hang on for a few minutes. You have plenty of fuel, don't you?"

"Enough to blow us to kingdom come," Jake muttered.

She sighed and checked the gauge. "About forty minutes' worth."

"Well," Mike said, "it won't hurt to burn some of that off to cut down on the fire hazard. While we're waiting, is there anyone either of you would like for us to contact? Jake?"

Jake hesitated for a moment, racking his brain for someone who would care. The little blonde on the steps came to mind, but he only remembered her room number, not her name. He thought of his boss, but in case things came out all right, he was afraid of the conclusions the airline might draw about the crash landing.

Dismally, he realized that there really wasn't anyone.

"Jake?" Mike prompted. "Do you read me?"

Jake took the mike. "Nobody, okay? I don't want you to contact anybody."

He couldn't escape the long look Lynda gave him.

"Lynda?"

Jake handed the mike to her and saw the emotion pulling at her face. "Yes," she said quietly. "Contact Sally Crawford at 555–

2312. Tell her to cancel all my appointments for this afternoon. But you don't have to do it now, Mike. Wait until … afterward, so she won't have to sweat this out."

Jake gaped at her. "Cancel your *appointments?*"

Her face turned rock hard, and she didn't answer him.

"Don't you have a mother or a lover or somebody?" he asked.

"No."

"So the closest person to you is your secretary? That's pretty pathetic."

Her face reddened. "Who do you think *you* are? At least I had somebody to call. What about *your* mother or a close friend or even an enemy or two? Surely you must have a couple of women somewhere who'd be interested in knowing you're about to buy the farm!"

His jaw popped. "Both of my parents are dead. And I'd rather admit there was no one than to hide behind some secretary and all those important appointments."

"If I wanted someone, I could have someone. There are plenty—" Her voice cracked, and she cut herself off, unable to go on. Tears came to her eyes, making her angrier, and she struggled to hold them back.

"But right now there's no one who cares that you're probably about to die. You're just as alone as I am."

"There are worse things than dying alone!" Lynda threw back at him.

"Are there?" His voice softened by degrees, and as he looked out the window at the activity on the tarmac below them, he said, "Right now it seems to me that the worst thing in the world is…."

"What?" she asked. "What is the worst thing in the world?"

"Dying with a total stranger."

The reality of that concept knocked the breath from her, and she fought the conflicting feelings assaulting her. As her first tears fell, they were both quiet, embroiled in battle with their own raging thoughts.

Her tears softened him, and finally, he let out a long, weary breath. "You're right, you know. There're at least three women who would like to see me burn."

"They probably have good reason," she whispered.

"Yeah, probably. I guess if you condemn a man for not wanting to tie himself to one woman for life, I deserve what I get."

"Life isn't really that long, though, is it?"

"Not lately," he said.

He looked out the window, searching the area around the airport. "If we could just find a pasture or something to land in. If we landed in the dirt, it would cut down on the fire hazard."

"The joys of flying in this part of Florida. Nothing but pavement and swamp. And the swamp has too many trees for a water landing."

"It might not be so bad if the gas tank weren't so low. I think I could get us down on the belly, maybe without cartwheeling, but the sparks could start a fire."

"Maybe they won't," she whispered with her last vestige of hope.

"Maybe not," Jake whispered. "I've still got a lot of living to do."

CHAPTER THREE

On the ground, Mike looked at the plane through his binoculars again, wishing for a miracle. But the landing gear was still unevenly dropped and only partially down. Dropping the binoculars around his neck, he waved an arm, directing the planes that were moving, one by one, from their parked positions on the tarmac. The red Porsche sat right in the way, and for a moment, he thought of driving it out to the middle of Runway 4 so that Jake would have to run over it himself. It would be poetic justice.

Then he quelled the thought and checked to see whether the keys were in the ignition. Waving to one of the men nearby, he said, "Get this car out of the way, will you?"

Sirens drew closer, and he ran to the end of the building and parted the growing crowd of spectators to direct the fire trucks onto the tarmac. Three of them whizzed past him, lights flashing. Then there were the ambulances—one, two, three, four—and he realized with a sinking stomach that they were preparing for additional casualties on the ground.

He started back to the planes taxiing out of the way and saw a van pull in behind him. It was a media van with the call letters *WTTV* on the side. The van slowed beside him, and a reporter he recognized from the six o'clock news jumped out. "We heard on the police radio that there's a plane about to crash." He pointed up to the plane circling overhead. "Is that it?"

"Stay back," Mike ordered as he kept walking. "Don't get any closer to the runway and move the van."

"Man, I need it right here."

"I'm telling you, when that plane hits the ground, it's liable to blow from here to Montana. Don't say I didn't warn you!"

"Have you been in contact with the pilots?" the reporter asked.

But Mike didn't answer. He had too much work to do.

The trees beyond the airport were greener than Lynda thought they should be in September, probably because they'd had so much rain this summer. She wondered now why she hadn't noticed that stark, clear color before. Only now was she even aware that those trees existed. Of course, this landing was different. This time the plane might not stop until it reached them.

Between two lines of those trees, one on either side of the street leading to the small airport, she saw a convoy of vehicles that looked as small as toy cars heading to the gates. A shiver went through her. "Are those fire trucks?"

"And ambulances. Just waiting for us to hit bottom."

"Don't be so cynical. They're there to help us."

"There may not be anything left to help." He tore his eyes away from the small square airport and checked the gauges. Lynda followed his eyes and noted that they'd used up half of their fuel already.

"If you've already given up, maybe I should land the plane after all."

"No. If there's a chance of getting us out of this alive, I'm the one who can do it."

Disgusted, she gaped at him. "Has it ever occurred to you that you're not the final authority in all this?"

"No? Then who is?"

"Oh, that's right," she said. "You don't believe in God. You've got the world all figured out."

"I'm not into myths," he said. "I like facts. And what is there to figure out, really? You're born, you live, you die. End of story."

"It's *not* the end of the story," she said. "There's an afterlife."

He laughed then and shook his head. "Wouldn't that be convenient?"

She bristled. "Convenient?"

"Yeah. Tell yourself a little lie just before you crash, and maybe you'll feel better about giving it all up."

She opened her mouth to argue but changed her mind and wearily leaned back. "Believe what you want. You're not worth trying to convince."

The steady, muffled hum of the engine became the only sound in the cabin again, and their eyes strayed to the concrete square below them where mechanics, pilots, and staff ran up and down the tarmac. Half of the planes had been moved already, and the other half taxied out in a single stream of traffic, like toy planes strung together and dragged by a toddler. It looked orderly and peaceful from here, not at all like a rushed attempt to prepare for a tragedy.

The air seemed thinner now than she remembered it being before, and she longed to roll a window down as she would in a car. But even if that had been a reasonable thing to do at 10,000 feet, moving 100 miles per hour, the windows weren't built to budge. The vessel that had once been her refuge was now just a cage.

Jake seemed to be struggling with his own thoughts. Swallowing, he wiped his brow and glanced at her. "So how long since your father died?"

Wondering where that question had come from, Lynda reluctantly answered, "Three months."

"I'm sorry," he said quietly.

It was true that losing her father had been tough, but she couldn't say it was the death itself that had grieved her. Instead, it was the "what-might-have-been's" that had assaulted her when she'd buried him. The relationship they could have had. The one she had been too busy to maintain.

"You don't want to talk about it," he said quietly. "No problem. I'm just trying to get our minds off this."

She shook her head. "It's all right. I just can't think right now. It's so quiet up here—so *normal*. The engine's running like a charm; everything's intact. It's hard to believe that this landing is gonna do us in. But look at them down there. *They* know it. That's why they're hurrying around, getting ready for the worst case."

"Yeah," he said, "and none of them knows the first thing about us."

She turned back to him, and saw the first trace of vulnerability she'd seen. "Would it make any difference if they did?"

"There might be some comfort in knowing there was somebody down there who had a stake in whether we made it through this."

"It wouldn't help us land any smoother," she whispered.

"I don't know," he said. "It might."

Why his words frightened her, she wasn't sure. "Are you saying you'd take more care in the landing if you knew someone cared about you? That just because neither of us has close attachments, it doesn't *matter* if we crash?"

"No! I don't have a death wish."

"Well, that's the second time you've said something pretty negative about our landing. I'm starting to get really scared that you might just give up and let us die. Is that what you're saying?"

"Of course not! I don't *know* what I'm saying, okay? I just wish...." His voice trailed off, and he found it difficult to center his thoughts. "I mean, doesn't this make you feel ... something? Incomplete? Regret?"

A still, small voice reminded her what she knew—or what she had once known—about completion, about regret. The memories were vague from lack of use, and she couldn't share them with him for fear that he would mock her and throw the words back in her face.

"You *must* feel that way," he said. "I mean here you are in a busted plane called *Solitude*, telling your secretary to cancel your appointments. Not the makings of a full life."

The voice in her heart died, and she let her old, human voice speak instead. "You have a lot of room to talk."

"I know. Maybe I'm thinking that if I can figure you out, I can figure me out."

"Hey, there's nothing wrong with me. I'm a loner, okay? I have everything I need."

"Do you?" he asked.

"Yes. No surprises, no letdowns. No one to disappoint me."

"So you've eliminated the lows. But that also means there are no highs."

Those words might have been her own. But the ego part of her, the part that held pride to her breast like a shield, dismissed them. "That's why I fly."

"A woman who spends all her free time alone in an airplane strikes me as someone who's hiding from something."

"Oh, brother," she groaned. "You've got a lot of nerve, you know that? Driving up in your yup-mobile with your diamonds flashing and your arrogance dripping off you like cheap cologne— How dare you make any judgments about me?"

"I'm not. I'm making an observation."

Furious, she jerked the microphone off its hook. "Come in, Mike. This is Cherokee 1–2 Delta. I'm ready to land right now! Do you read me?"

Jake grabbed her arm. "What do you think you're doing?"

But Mike's answer came quickly. "Negative, Lynda. We're not ready."

"How long are you going to keep us up here?"

"Until we've taken every precaution! Do not land until I give you the go-ahead! Do you read me?"

Lynda wiped away another tear. "Loud and clear."

Slamming the radio down, she covered her face and told herself to calm down. She was letting this man dig at her in the painful, bruised places she'd been shielding for so long, and suddenly she wished she could just be alone to face her life—and her death.

"Look, I'm sorry," Jake said quietly. "I didn't mean to send you off the deep end."

"Just shut up, will you? You're not making this any easier. If you're so interested in figuring someone out, maybe you should do a little *self*-analysis. Why are *you* all alone in the world?"

He hesitated only a moment, and his voice was flat when he answered. "Simple. Because I'm a selfish pig."

"Now, there's an unexpected revelation. I guess fear of death brings out the truth."

"Too much maybe," he said sullenly. "Too late."

She let those words sink in and wondered if *she'd* gotten to the point of honesty yet. Had she missed the chances she'd had to face the truth? Would she get another chance?

That small voice prompted her again to tell him it wasn't too late, but the voice was growing more distant and easier to ignore.

"We're going to make it, you know," Jake said. "Together, we can do this. We're both experienced pilots, and neither of us wants to die."

She tried to imagine the plane landing carefully, easily, and without incident, but the possibility seemed too remote. "But neither of us has tried to land metal to pavement with no brakes in a crosswind."

"Talk about looking at the bright side," he muttered. He glanced at her. "You're shaking."

"So are you," she pointed out.

"I'm scared."

Lynda wasn't sure why those two matter-of-fact words, uttered by such a tough, hard man would shake her so, but she wilted and surrendered to her tears. "I'm scared, too," she whispered.

He reached over and took her hand, and something about that touch comforted her. Their eyes met, a moment of connection, where she thought she knew him, and he thought he knew her, a moment when they ceased to be strangers.

"Cherokee 1–2 Delta—St. Clair Unicom. Come in, Lynda."

Jake let go of her hand, and she grabbed the mike, bracing herself. "1–2 Delta. Go ahead, Mike. Are you ready for us?"

"Affirmative. You can land now, guys," Mike said softly. "Just watch that crosswind, and be careful. I wish I could offer you something in the way of advice, but you know what to do. I'll be praying for you guys down here."

Lynda swallowed and wiped her eyes. "Yeah. Thank you, Mike."

She put the radio back on its hook and looked at Jake, who was staring dully out the window. His face was empty, drained, and for a moment she thought he might cry too. She wished he would so that she could fully surrender to her own emotions and wilt outwardly the way she was wilting inside.

Finally, he looked at her, reached across to touch her face, and whispered, "Are you ready?"

"Yeah," she said. "You?"

"As ready as I'll ever be, I guess." He checked the gauges, then said, "Once we're on short final and know we've got the runway made, kill the engine and cut all the switches. And if you can, unlatch the door so we can get out fast."

In a gesture that surprised her, he leaned over and tested her seat belt then checked his own. "All right," he said. "Here goes."

The plane descended smoothly like any other craft coming in on any other day, but Mike knew that the moment it touched down the problems would begin. He eyed the rolling cameras and the reporter with his microphone in hand, waiting to get every gory frame.

The ambulances were in place, ready to speed to the scene, and the fire trucks were standing by. Mike felt a wave of dizziness and shook it away, telling himself this was no time for panic. There was too much that had to be done.

He brought the binoculars to his eyes as the plane narrowed the distance between the sky and the runway, and under his breath, he prayed for a miracle.

The plane touched down, sending a spray of sparks as it scraped down the runway—too fast, like a speedboat on an open sea. When it fishtailed, Mike dropped the binoculars.

For several seconds that stretched into eternity, the plane cartwheeled across the runway, rolling and sliding, breaking a wing here, losing the tail there, leaving pieces in its wake, until it finally rolled to a deadly halt on its side.

The ambulances and fire trucks launched across the runways. Stricken with dread and terror, Mike ran toward what was left of the plane.

CHAPTER FOUR

cross town in the law offices of Schilling, Martin and Barrett, Sally Crawford rushed to type the three motions that Lynda needed ready for court the next morning. As much as she managed to accomplish each day, it was clear to her that Lynda needed a second secretary. Sometimes things moved so fast that she had to run just to stay in place.

But it was tough convincing a workaholic that you were working too hard. As long as Sally's fingers flew across that keyboard, and the phone calls were answered, and the motions were filed, and the appointments were made, and the office ran smoothly, Lynda was happy.

She shouldn't complain, Sally admitted as she punched in the command to *print* then swiveled in her chair and began stacking the papers that had to be ready before the mail boy came around to empty the "out" baskets.

The phone buzzed; she picked it up. "Lynda Barrett's office."

"Sally, there's a Paige Varner here to see Lynda."

"Lynda's not in," Sally told the receptionist who intercepted visitors as they came in. "Take a message, and I'll have Lynda call her." Hanging up, she saw that the printer was finished, and she pulled out the pages.

The phone buzzed again. "Lynda Barrett's office."

"Sally, she says she's left messages, and Lynda hasn't called. She's pretty upset—"

Sally moaned. "All right. Send her back. I'll talk to her."

She hung up and sat for a moment, staring at the phone, wondering what excuse she'd use to cover for Lynda this time. The plain, simple truth was that Paige Varner's was a *pro bono* case, and it wasn't exactly one of Lynda's top priorities.

She saw the elevator doors open, and Paige bolted off, clutching her three-year-old daughter, Brianna, on her hip. Paige's eyes were swollen and red as she cast Sally a frantic look and started toward her.

Sally got up to meet her. "Hello, Paige. Lynda's not here."

"I've *got* to talk to her," Paige said, starting to cry. "We've got to *do* something. He tried to kidnap Brianna!"

"Who?" Sally asked, leading her to a chair and making her sit down. Brianna's feet hit the floor, but Paige pulled her into her lap, unable to let her go.

"Her father," she said. "Do we have a court date yet? If we do, I can make plans to leave the state, so he won't know where we are—"

"Calm down," Sally said, stooping in front of her. "Now start over. Take a deep breath and tell me what happened."

Paige didn't want to take time to start over, but she tried. "Her day-care teacher called me at work and told me that Keith was there claiming that I told him to pick her up."

"Wait a minute. Don't you have a restraining order?"

"Yes!" Paige cried. "But it's *worthless!* We're not safe here! I have to talk to Lynda. If she can get us a court date, then I can get that over with and get out of town, before he takes her, or comes after me again, or—"

The phone rang, and Sally stood up reluctantly. "I'm sorry, Paige. I have to get that."

Paige covered her eyes and nodded.

Sally went back to her desk and grabbed the phone, praying it was Lynda. "Lynda Barrett's office."

"Is this Sally Crawford?"

Sally glanced at Paige. Brianna was wiping her mother's tears, and Paige was whispering to her. "Yes."

"This is Mac Lowery. I'm a mechanic at the St. Clair Airport. I'm afraid there's been an accident."

CHAPTER FIVE

For a moment, as the fog slowly cleared, Lynda lay still, trying to find some clarity to hang her thoughts on. The plane had hit belly to pavement, she remembered, and had slid for what had seemed like miles, breaking into fragments, crumpling, shattering, rolling—

Now the plane was on its side, and she hung sideways in her seat, still clamped by the seat belt that cut mercilessly into her shoulder and hipbones. Trying to get her head upright, wincing at the stab of pain in her ribs and the cracking pain in her head, she released the latch and slid from her seat against the back of the one next to her.

Pain seared through her, and she looked down to find the source of it. Shards of glass had lodged in her arm, her thigh, and her stomach. With bloody hands that seemed to belong to someone else, she tried to pull one out.

But then she saw him.

All clarity returned as she reached for Jake, still strapped into the bottom of his seat, which had broken off from its back. Twisted, unconscious, and soaked with blood, he lay limp under the bashed instrument panel.

"Jake!" Her voice sounded hollow and distant, as if it came from someone else as she tried to reach for him. "Jake, are you all right?"

But he didn't stir.

Panic shook her as the first hint of smoke reached her senses—then, with dim relief, she heard sirens. But they sounded too far away, and there was no time to wait!

Forcing herself to move despite her pain, she managed to free Jake from his seat belt then grabbed under his arms and, with all her might, slid him two feet back toward the door. Praying that it would open, she disengaged the latch. The door swung down, providing a hatch no more than a yard above the ground.

The smoke was growing thicker as the sirens came closer. Lynda half-fell out the opening. Then with every ounce of energy she could gather, pulled Jake behind her, ignoring her own fuzzy thoughts about his limpness and the blood soaking into her clothes.

The moment he dropped onto the pavement, she struggled to her feet beside the plane, grabbed his arms, and dragged him across the dirt as far away from the plane as she could before collapsing beside him.

She heard tires screeching and people yelling; suddenly she was aware of movement around her. Closing her eyes, she surrendered to the paramedics as they lifted her onto a gurney then ran with her like war medics taking her out of the line of fire. A vague protest formed in her mind that they should leave her and save Jake, but that thought evaporated as a loud, vacuum sound—*whoosh*—split the air.

She opened her eyes—her plane was engulfed in quiet flames that spread to cover the place where she and Jake had lain only moments before. *It should be loud,* she thought, *like a lightning bolt from God.* Instead, this explosion had been a quiet one, almost gentle, as it worked its violence on the plane.

As the paramedics hurried her along, she glimpsed another group of medics carrying Jake. He was still limp on the gurney, and blood glistened on that expensive shirt and those slacks that had been so perfectly creased such a short time ago. The paramedics set her down and, blocking her view, bent over her with stethoscopes and an IV. "No!" she cried, trying to move them out of her way. "Help him! He's bleeding!"

"So are you."

"No, take him first! Please!"

"He's in good hands," the lead paramedic said in a steady voice, trying to calm her. "*You're* my concern right now." He took her vitals, barking out numbers that meant little to her. Still, she strained to see around him. "Is he—is he—alive?"

They were busy attaching the IV, talking to each other over her, shouting and exchanging orders.

And then she saw the urgency on the faces of the other group of paramedics, and someone shouted, "Talk to him! He's going into shock!"

"Jake, can you hear me?" someone asked him. "Jake, you've got to hold on. We're getting you to the hospital."

"We're losing him!" one of the others shouted.

"Oh, no, God, please!" She lost sight of him as the EMTs crowded around him, desperately trying to bring him back. She saw someone bring the defibrillator, and heard the desperate counting and the "Clear!" then the shock that jolted his body.

She lost sight of him again as her paramedics loaded her into the ambulance, and she tried to sit up to see through the doors before they closed them. "Please! I've got to know if he's—"

But the doors shut, and the ambulance accelerated away.

Lynda didn't remember when she had lost consciousness, but when she woke, she was in a hospital room, the cold antiseptic smell stirring her back to life.

A woman she didn't know stood over her, shining a light in her eyes. "How are you feeling?"

Lynda squinted against the light and jerked her face away. "Am I in the hospital?"

"That's right," the woman said. "You just got out of surgery."

"Surgery?"

The woman nodded. "And judging by what you've been through, I'd say you're extremely lucky. You're scratched and cut up pretty good, and you broke a couple of ribs, but you're going to be fine." The woman patted her shoulder gently then said, "I'll go tell the doctor you're awake."

Lynda squeezed her eyes shut and tried to find some clarity. Images rushed through her mind: the plane hitting the ground; the horror of impact after impact; the sight of Jake strapped in his seat … Jake drenched in blood … Jake not responding.… He was dead. It was her punishment, she told herself—although she wasn't sure at the moment what she was being punished for. A thick, smothering shroud of guilt draped itself over her.

Tears oozed from her eyes. She squeezed them shut and, under her breath, tried to bargain with God for Jake's life.

The door swung open. Two doctors came in, followed by the nurse, who rushed to Lynda's side when she saw her tears. "Lynda, you're going to be all right," one of the doctors said gently. "You had some internal bleeding, and we had to remove your spleen. I know it's been traumatic for you—but try to understand this: You're going to be okay. Please try to calm down."

Hiccuping her sobs, she reached up and grabbed the doctor's coat with her good hand. "Is he ... dead?"

"Is who dead?"

"Jake!" she shouted.

"Doctor, the other crash victim," the nurse said. "He was brought in with her."

The second doctor took her hand, and she gripped it with all the urgency she felt as he leaned over her. "I just left him, Lynda," he said. "He's still in surgery. His condition is critical, but—"

"He's alive?" she asked, almost sitting up. "Jake's alive?"

"We almost lost him," he said. "But we think he's going to pull through."

"Oh, thank God," she cried, wilting back down.

The doctor checked the monitors attached to her then whispered a few instructions to the nurse as Lynda tried to catch her breath. When she was able, she grabbed the doctor's coat again. "I want to see him. The minute he's out of surgery I need to see him."

"That won't be possible today," he said gently. "And even tomorrow, if he regains consciousness, he'll be in ICU. That means no visitors."

"Please," she said. "You can bend a few rules, can't you? Let me see him for five minutes. That's all."

The two doctors exchanged looks, and finally, one shrugged. "We'll see what we can do. No promises. But right now there are several people out in the waiting room anxious to see you. Are you up to any visitors?"

She covered her face with a hand and tried to stop her tears. "Uh, who's out there?"

The nurse pulled a pad from her pocket, flipped a few pages, and said, "Mike somebody. And Sally—she said she's your secretary.

And your pastor and a few people who said you used to go to their church...."

"Um, I'd like to talk to Mike first," she whispered.

"All right," the nurse said, "but just for a few minutes, okay? You don't realize how weak you are, but you will as soon as you start seeing people."

Lynda already felt too weak to talk, but there were things she needed to say to Mike. Things that couldn't wait.

CHAPTER SIX

The police station smelled like stale cigarettes and three-day-old sweat, and the noise level was worse than the day-care center where Brianna spent each day. Paige bent and picked up the child, holding her close and felt that familiar surge of shame that she hadn't been able to shelter her from the ugly realities of life.

"It's okay, Brianna," she whispered, kissing the child's forehead. "We're going to get one of these policemen to help us."

"Are they putting Daddy in jail, Mommy?"

Paige hesitated. "I don't know, honey. We'll see. Do you want them to?"

"Yes," she whispered with timid honesty.

Paige made her way to the big desk where people waited in line to file complaints, trying to blink back the tears that threatened her eyes again.

A plane crash. It couldn't be real, yet it was. Lynda had been in a plane crash.

She closed her eyes and tried to fight off the abject terror that her lawyer could die—or might, in fact, already be dead. Sally had said that Lynda was still alive, but she'd been in such a panic that Paige wasn't sure it was true.

The person at the front of the line left the desk, and Paige counted the people in front of her. She was fourth in line. Any minute now it would be her turn, and someone would tell her what to do.

Brianna laid her head on Paige's shoulder, and Paige realized that the child hadn't had her nap today. She was tired. She should be home, safe in her own room, resting to a Barney tape, instead of waiting in a police station to find a way to keep her father from getting close to her.

Lynda had known ways and had made lots of promises, but Paige couldn't depend on her now. Those tears surfaced again, and she told herself that she should stop thinking so much of herself. Lynda's plane crash was a tragedy, but Paige could only deal with one tragedy at a time.

At last her turn came, and she tried to steady her voice as she faced the uniformed woman behind the desk. "My name's Paige Varner. I have a restraining order against my ex-husband, Keith Varner, but today he tried to take our daughter from her day care. I went to my lawyer first, but she was in an accident today...." Her voice trailed off, and she waited for a response.

The officer casually dropped her pencil and leaned forward, elbows on her desk. "Mrs. Varner, we can't arrest someone for violating a restraining order unless we witness the violation."

"What do you mean, witness it? Who has to witness it?"

"You're supposed to call the police when it happens, and when they arrive, they have to see him there. If he leaves, it's out of our hands."

Paige gripped Brianna tighter, incredulous. "But that's ridiculous! I wasn't there! The restraining order is supposed to keep him away from her, too."

"You should have had the teachers call 911. Next time, you need to call us as soon as he shows up, and if the officers get there while he's still there—"

"Next time?" Paige shouted. "There's not supposed to *be* a next time. You people are supposed to protect me from that!"

"We can only do what the law allows."

"Then what's the use in having a restraining order? He can still do anything he wants!"

"You do have recourse," the woman said, as if talking to a child. "You need to file a motion for order to show cause."

"A what?"

The woman sighed. "Mrs. Varner, did you say you have a lawyer?"

"Yes, but—" She stopped, pinched the bridge of her nose, and tried to temper her voice again. "I can't reach her right now.

And no one else will represent me because I—I don't have much money. Do I have to have a lawyer to do this?"

"It would help. Then a judge would review it and decide whether to arrest him or summon him back to court. But usually, if there was no violence involved, and if he didn't threaten you in any way, the judge doesn't opt for jail time."

"Threaten?" Paige asked. "You don't think it's threatening for him to show up at her school and tell her teacher that I told him to pick her up? Do we have to wait until he attacks one of us again or until he kidnaps her and takes her so far—"

"I'm just telling you your options, Ma'am. Now, if I were you, I'd contact my lawyer right away."

"But if there's no guarantee he'll even be put in jail...." Frustrated, she half turned away. "You don't know my husband. He'll just get madder and then come after me. And he's smart. He probably already knows that he can't be arrested unless he's caught. That's why he's getting so bold."

The woman behind the desk softened a little. "Look, I can give you the name of a shelter for battered women. We could get you in there tonight if you want."

Paige thought about that for a moment. Her mind was too muddled, and she couldn't think.

"Mommy, I want to go home," Brianna said.

"Just a minute, honey." Wiping her face, she tried to take a deep breath. "He knows where the shelter is. He told me that if I ever went there, he'd drag me out."

"But he *can't* know, Mrs. Varner. It's a very well-kept secret. He was probably just trying to scare you."

"You don't know him. He has ways of finding things out."

"Mrs. Varner, every woman in that shelter has an angry man looking for her. You just have to trust the staff to know how to handle these things."

"I can't trust anyone," Paige said dismally.

"Well, here's the number anyway if you change your mind." The officer handed Paige a piece of paper. "Good luck, Mrs. Varner."

But as Paige carried Brianna back to their car, she realized she was going to need a lot more than luck. What she really needed now was Lynda.

I have to tell you," Mike said as he approached Lynda's bed, "for a few minutes there I didn't think I was ever going to see that smile again." He pulled a chair up to her bed and sat down. "So how do you feel?"

"Like I've been spared," she whispered.

He leaned his elbows on his knees and rested his chin on his hand. "It *was* a miracle, you know. When I saw that plane hit the ground, I didn't see any way in the world either one of you would make it. Who could have believed you both would?"

"Jake's not even out of surgery yet, much less out of the woods."

"Yeah, but he has a lot of people praying for him out there."

"Really?" she asked, sitting partially up. "Who?"

"Some of the people here from your church."

"My church." Wearily, she wilted back down. "I'm surprised they remember me; it's been so long since I darkened the doorstep."

She looked at the man she had known for the last two years, the man with whom she had talked airplanes and flight reports and weather, the man who was as close a friend as she had. Only now did she realize how little they really knew about each other.

"Mike, I want to thank you."

"For what?"

"For offering to pray for us today," she whispered.

Tears came to his eyes, and he struggled to blink them back. "What else was I gonna do, Lynda?"

"Oh, I don't know. Stay busy. Throw up your hands. All I know is that I wasn't doing much praying up there. Yours are the ones that got answered."

As long as he was still breathing, Jake figured he was alive, even if he couldn't manage to open his eyes or move an inch or speak.

There was something in his mouth impeding his speech and something else holding his eyelids down.

Panic struck him, and he wanted to sit up, cry out, run away, but his body wouldn't cooperate.

He could hear quiet voices around him, a steady beeping of machinery, and he felt hands probing....

The crash, he thought. He had survived the crash.

Or had he?

Panic seized him, and he opened his mouth to cry out, but something in his throat choked him. Concentrating all his effort on the task of clearing his mouth, he lifted his hand—but he moved it only an inch or two before he felt something sting and someone laying it back down.

"Calm down, Jake," a soft voice said. "You're going to be okay. Just rest."

He struggled to open his eyes but failed. Once more he tried to cry out, but the voice was back again. "Don't try to talk, Jake. There's a tube in your throat. Tomorrow you can talk if you want."

But Jake's panic needed answers, and it needed answers now. He tried to formulate a question to ask but found that his mind was too fuzzy. Then the voices seemed to fade farther away, as numbness crept like mercy through his limbs.

And soon he forgot about those questions and surrendered instead to the darkness.

CHAPTER SEVEN

The rain began as Paige drove home from the police station, her brain reeling from the injustice of the system that left her entirely on her own. But it wasn't the first time she hadn't known where to turn.

She turned on her windshield wipers and tried to concentrate on the slippery road. The last thing she needed now was an accident. Lynda's was bad enough.

Then again, maybe a four-car crash on the highway was just what she should expect. Maybe she deserved all she'd been going through. Maybe, as Keith had said so many times, Paige was petty and selfish and stupid. Maybe she had brought all this misery on herself.

Lightning flashed, followed by a quick clap of thunder, and she touched Brianna's knee to reassure her. What did it really matter what Paige deserved, she argued. It was what Brianna deserved that mattered. Brianna deserved peace and she deserved safety and she deserved security and stability. She didn't deserve a father who could sing her a lullaby one minute and crack her mother's jaw the next.

The child was just drifting off to sleep as Paige turned onto their street and glanced ahead to her house halfway up the road. It would be good finally to get home, make Brianna a bowl of soup, and put her to bed for her nap.

Then she saw it: Keith's car in the driveway.

Slamming her foot on the accelerator, she flew past the house, skidded around the corner, and headed as far away from the neighborhood as she could.

Her breath came in gasps as she watched her rearview mirror for a sign of him. Terror clutched at her heart. Where could she go to be safe? Not home—he was there, sitting in her house, waiting for her.

Trembling, she pulled into a Walmart parking lot and groped for her purse. Grabbing out two quarters, she circled to a pay phone on the edge of the lot. Afraid to get out of the car, she inched as close as she could to the phone then rolled her window down. The rain poured in, soaking her arm as she reached for the receiver. Quickly she dialed 911.

"You've got to help me!" she cried when the dispatcher answered. "I have a restraining order against my ex-husband, but he's in my house waiting for me right now. You have to send an officer out immediately. They have to see him there!"

She rattled off the address, then restated the urgency. When she'd hung up, she tried to catch her breath.

She'd go back, she told herself. She'd go back to make sure they got him. If he was still there, maybe she'd go in and try to reason with him. Maybe that would hold him there until they came.

But what if it didn't? What if he took Brianna?

No. She couldn't risk it. Instead, she would drive by the house to make sure he was still there. Then she would watch from the corner, and when the police came, she could follow them into the driveway.

The rain pounded harder against the roof of the car, and the wind whipped more viciously, but Brianna stayed asleep as Paige, weeping softly, made her way back to the neighborhood and turned up her street. Holding her breath, she peered through the rain-blurred windshield to see if his car was still in her driveway.

He was gone.

Slamming the heel of her hand against her steering wheel, she cried harder. This was *hopeless!* He was out there somewhere, looking for her....

And the women's shelter would be the first place he'd look if she didn't come home. He'd told her more than once that he knew where all of them were, and if she ever went there, he'd go after her and make her sorry.

Leaving the street as fast as she could, she went back to the Walmart parking lot and dug through her wallet for money. She had thirty dollars and an ATM card. There might be fifty more in her account if her checkbook balance were right. That was enough for a hotel room, she told herself, trying to calm down. It would get her through until tomorrow.

She took a few deep breaths, trying to calm down, scanned the roads nearby to make sure he was nowhere in sight, and then pulled back into the street. *Don't even think about tomorrow right now*, she cautioned herself. *All you can deal with is one day at a time.*

CHAPTER EIGHT

The creak of her hospital room door woke Lynda from her shallow sleep. Squinting her eyes open, she watched the plump nurse come in, her nylons making a brushing sound as she walked and her white Reeboks squeaking on the floor. It was the same nurse who had attended to her the last time she'd awakened—Jill something—and Lynda watched her set down her tray of medications and flick on the dim light over Lynda's head.

"How are you feeling?" the nurse asked in a voice loud enough to wake the comatose patients on the floor above her. "Any pain?"

"Some," Lynda mumbled.

"Well, that's expected." Pulling a thermometer out of her pocket, she covered it with plastic and shoved it into Lynda's mouth. "If I had as many stitches in me as you have, I'd be hurting, too. The doctor said they pulled half the plane's windshield out of you." She took the thermometer, made a notation on Lynda's chart, then adjusted the IV. "We've given you something for pain, but if it's worn off, I can give you more."

Lynda moaned. "No wonder I've slept most of the day. No, I don't want any more." She watched the nurse wrap the blood pressure cuff around her arm. "Jill, do you know if Jake is out of surgery yet?"

Jill stared at her watch for a few seconds then slipped the cuff off again. "As a matter of fact, he is," she said, making another notation. "He's still critical, though. I don't have any of the details."

Lynda tried to sit up. "I want to see him."

"Sorry." The nurse gently pushed her back down. "He's still in ICU. No visitors."

"But I'm not a visitor. I was in that crash with him. It was my plane."

Jill snapped her chart shut and put it back in the pocket at the foot of Lynda's bed. "He isn't even conscious yet. Wait until tomorrow, and we'll see if we can get you permission to visit him. But not tonight, Lynda. Besides, you're still too weak to get out of bed."

"No, I feel fine. I just want to make sure he's all right."

"I'm sorry, Lynda. You'll just have to take our word for it tonight."

Lynda closed her eyes as the nurse left and tried in vain to steer her thoughts to something besides Jake's life. What weren't they telling her? Critical. What did that mean?

She tried to turn over, but a cut down her leg made it uncomfortable, so she shifted to her other side. The sheets were rough beneath her skin, and she wondered why they couldn't manage to get sheets that covered the whole bed, instead of those stupid half sheets that folded halfway down, overlapping another one that covered the end. It made changing the beds easier, she supposed, but that didn't help the patient's comfort any, especially when the patient was covered with cuts and scrapes. She longed for her own smooth sheets and the big bed she had shopped for a month to find.

She was so uncomfortable she might *never* fall back to sleep, and what good was lying here when Jake could be dying? If she could just see him, maybe she could relax tonight and let go of the guilt that was causing more pain than her broken ribs. If the only way to see him was to sneak through the halls and slip into ICU, she was willing to give it a try.

Making the decision almost as quickly as the thought came to her mind, she sat up and moved her feet over the side of the bed. The checkerboard floor was cold beneath her feet, and she felt a wave of vertigo as she sat up. Fighting it, she stood slowly. Her muscles strained, and she touched the place on her abdomen where her spleen had been removed. The pain in her head got worse, and she stood still a moment, waiting for the dizziness to pass.

Steadying herself with a hand against the brick wall, she put one foot in front of the other, stepping carefully until she reached the door. Already she felt soul weary, but she knew that ICU was just one floor up. If she could just get to the elevator....

Opening the door, she peered up the corridor. A visitor was going into another room, but she saw no one else. She closed the door behind her and took a barefoot step up the hall.

Miraculously, a wheelchair sat parked against the wall. Mumbling a "Thank you, Lord," she dropped into it. For a moment, she tried to catch her breath, but then, fearing she'd be caught if she didn't hurry, she grabbed the wheels and tried to push herself along.

Her left arm was stiff and sore, and pain stabbed through her ribs, making her perspire, but she pushed on nonetheless, passing the nurse's station without being noticed. She made it past the waiting room, where two or three people sat watching television, and breathed another "thank you" that none of them knew her.

Waiting anxiously beside the elevator, Lynda glanced up the hall. Nurse Jill stepped out into the hall from someone's room, and Lynda turned her head away. The elevator doors opened, and quickly she rolled on.

She pressed the button for the next floor up and waited, trying to fight the pain sending clouds circling through her head. The elevator stopped and she got off, careful to avoid the nurses clustered at the coffee pot near the elevator.

She was growing fatigued, and she pushed more slowly, wondering whether she'd made a mistake. But the doubts fled when she caught sight of the glass doors to the Intensive Care Unit.

A sign warned against unauthorized personnel entering ICU, and she knew that in the wheelchair she'd never get through that door and to Jake's bed. Taking a deep breath and bracing herself against the pain, she got to her feet.

Slowly, she opened the door and slipped inside.

A nurse was on the phone, and another one bent over a monitor. Stepping carefully, and battling the dizziness threatening her again, she made her way past them.

A little girl lay in an oxygen tent behind one curtain, and further down she saw an old man. She reached out to steady herself against the wall and checked a file on a door. Heather Nelson and then Lawrence Sims—

She froze as she came to the next room. Inside was a man with a bandaged face lying still on his bed, tubes and wires attaching him to the monitors and machines that hummed and beeped.

She searched for the name on the file on his door.

Jake Stevens.

A sob choked her, and she stumbled into the room. He was as still and pale as death. A bandage covered one eye and half his face, and large patches of skin were scraped from his arm, his hand....

"Jake?" she whispered.

He didn't stir. Muffling another sob, she stood over him, thinking how carefree and healthy he had looked this morning, driving up in his Porsche and irritating her with that lethal grin.

"Jake, I'm so sorry." Clutching the bed rail, she leaned over him. "I don't know how—"

"What are you doing here?"

The voice startled her, and she swung around and saw one of the nurses she'd seen outside, a black woman, standing in the doorway. "How did you get in here?"

"I—I had to see him," Lynda wept. "I had to."

Instantly, the nurse was at her side. "It's all right, child," she said, putting her arms around her and guiding her back to the door. "You're the lady who was in the crash with him, aren't you?"

Unable to speak, Lynda nodded her head.

"Honey, I'm so sorry," the nurse said, taking her to her wheelchair and lowering her into it. "But you shouldn't be out of your room. You should be in bed. Jake will still be here tomorrow."

"Will he?" Lynda asked, looking up at her. "He looks like—like he may not make it."

"Looks can be deceiving," the nurse said. "I don't know you, but I'd say you've probably looked better yourself."

"But he's still ... unconscious. What if he doesn't wake up? And what's wrong with his face? It's all bandaged."

"He was in a plane crash, darlin'. His face is the least of his problems."

Lynda grabbed the nurse's arm and started to stand, her face pleading for the truth. "Just tell me if—if he's expected to die."

The woman gently lowered her back to the chair. "I can't lie to you. It could go either way. But if he makes it through tonight, I'll feel a lot better about his chances tomorrow."

Finally leaning back, Lynda wailed into her hands.

"I'm gonna take you back to your room now, darlin', and tomorrow, if he wakes up, I'll make sure you get to see him. My name's Abby, and you can call me anytime tomorrow to get a report."

Lynda couldn't talk as the nurse rolled her back to the elevator.

CHAPTER NINE

Paige lay still as she heard a car door slam in front of her motel room. Footsteps passed her door, and then she heard the door to the next room open and a woman's shrill laughter.

It wasn't Keith. She turned onto her side and looked at her daughter, sleeping only in her underwear since they hadn't brought any extra clothes with them. The child slept soundly. Why not? She feared her father, but she didn't understand that her father was stalking them, threatening to take her from her mother and make her little life one nightmare after another, just as Paige's marriage had been.

What was he doing right now? Was he still waiting at her house, expecting Paige to breeze in and confront him? Or was he at his own apartment, devising another way of getting close to Brianna, inventing more lies about Paige's being an unfit mother, a child abuser, and a general danger to society?

"What am I gonna do?" she whispered to the darkness.

Brianna muttered a string of nonsense words under her breath. Turning on her side, Paige pulled her daughter against her. "It's okay, sweetheart," she said softly. "Mommy's here."

Brianna's breathing settled back into a peaceful rhythm, and Paige checked the clock. Only three hours before she had to be at work, she thought. What was she going to do with Brianna? She couldn't take her to day care again. Keith could come back and intimidate Brianna's teachers into handing her over. No, she couldn't take that chance. But she couldn't call in sick, either. She'd used up all her sick days earlier in the year when Keith had broken her arm and blackened both eyes. The shame of going to work like that had kept her home until makeup could disguise her bruises. But there were no sick days left.

There was no choice, she told herself. She would take Brianna to work with her. Brianna could sit on the floor and color as Paige typed; maybe if she explained it to her boss, he would understand. Maybe, just this once, fate would have a little mercy on her.

CHAPTER TEN

Someone had driven a stake through his temples, Jake thought as he opened the eye that wasn't bandaged. And if his pain was any indication, that someone had done the same through his cheekbone, his neck, down his arms, and across his shoulders.

Had some woman's angry boyfriend or husband beaten him to a pulp? Had he been in a car accident?

He opened his eye, and a cruel, blaring light forced him to close it. Confused, feeling the beginnings of panic, he squinted the eye open and tried again to orient himself. Before his eye was able to make out the room, his other senses detected the smell of iodine and alcohol, a soft beeping, and the electrical hum of machinery. Focusing, he saw the white walls of intensive care, the camera in the corner with which he was monitored, and the impressive machinery around his bed.

Yes, he thought through the haze in his brain. He'd been in an accident. But not a car crash.

A plane crash.

Catching his breath as the horror of his landing came back to him, he tried to sit up, but something held him down, and the pain stabbing through his face and head warned him not to try again.

His throat felt as if he'd swallowed a bucket of sand. He needed a drink, he thought desperately. He needed a drug. He needed to die.

"He's waking up!"

He looked up to see a pale, skinny nurse standing over him on one side, and a man with a stethoscope on the other.

"Jake, can you hear me?" the man asked in a voice so loud it thundered through his brain. "Jake, you're in the hospital."

No kidding, he thought, but when he tried to speak, his throat rebelled. The nurse set something cold against his lips, something wet—ice chips—and he opened his mouth gratefully and let the cold water ooze into his throat.

"How long?" he asked in a raspy whisper.

"Since the crash?" she asked. "Almost twenty-four hours. How do you feel?"

He thought of the worst hangover he'd ever had and decided it was a mere annoyance compared to this. "My head," he said, raising a lead-heavy hand to touch the bandage covering his eye.

"You have a gash down your face, Jake," the man said gently. "Your eye was pretty badly injured."

Jake looked up at him with horror. "My eye?"

"Yes. Do you have any feeling in your legs yet?"

His legs. There was no pain in his legs, he realized for the first time. They were numb. He tried to slide his leg up, to feel his toes, but it wouldn't move. Closing his eye, he wished he could block this out, that he could have stayed asleep, never to wake up and face the ways his body was failing him.

"Jake?"

"Tell me about my legs," he whispered, looking up at them with dread.

The doctor laid his hand on his shin. "Can you feel me touching you, Jake?"

"Yes!" he blurted, as if that proved that things weren't as bad as they seemed. "I feel pressure. Weight."

"That could be a good sign," he admitted weakly. "We need to run some tests." He started listing orders for the nurse, but Jake grabbed the sleeve of his coat and stopped him.

"What's broken?" he asked desperately. "My legs? My neck?"

It was obvious the doctor wasn't ready to be pinned down. "No broken bones, Jake, but you have deep lacerations in several places. The numbness is probably a blessing, considering the pain you might be feeling."

"I don't need any blessings like this," he bit out. "Besides, my head is enough to do me in."

"Well, if you need a stronger painkiller—"

"Yes," he cut in. "I need it."

"All right." But he didn't rush off for a hypodermic, as Jake had hoped. "Jake, your chart says you're new in town and no relatives have been notified. Is there anyone we could call for you?"

He thought of the one relative he still had, the one he'd woven stories about to make his past sound charmed, the one he had pretended was dead. "No," he said finally. "The last thing I need is people crying over me, waiting like vultures to see if the new me will have any resemblance to the old one."

"It wouldn't be like that, Jake," the nurse said. "You need the support of people who love you."

"I've never needed it before," he whispered as he closed his eye to dismiss them. "And I'm not about to start needing it now."

If you'd wanted a vacation, Lynda, all you had to do was say so." Sally Crawford pulled a chair up to Lynda's bed and set the bag she'd brought on the table in front of her. "I could use one, too, but you don't see me crashing a plane to get one."

Lynda was tired—her sleep last night had been restless and plagued with nightmares—but she managed to smile at her secretary. "Looks like I'm gonna get a longer vacation than I need. That blasted doctor said I have to stay out at least a month. Honestly, I feel like I'll be as good as new in a few days, but—"

"Lynda, you have injuries you can't even see. You have to let yourself recover. Besides, I'll be in the office taking care of the day-to-day stuff."

"But I have cases pending. Court dates...."

"Some of them can be postponed, and the ones that can't are going to be divided among the partners and associates. We went over all of them this morning. Your cases are in good hands."

Lynda sank back onto her pillow. "Well, I guess that's something."

"There's just one thing."

Lynda looked up. "What?"

"The Paige Varner case. No one wanted it."

"No one?" she asked.

"There's no money in it," Sally reminded her. "And it's a real shame because she came in yesterday all upset because her husband had shown up at her daughter's day care and tried to take her."

Lynda closed her eyes. "It's my fault. I've been putting her off."

"You've been busy. When you reach for a handout, you have to wait your turn."

That had, indeed, been her philosophy, Lynda admitted, but hearing it now, she didn't like the way it sounded. "She can't help not having any money. And that man. The restraining order obviously hasn't scared him at all. I was afraid it wouldn't. He's fearless. He'd *have* to be—he's suing *her* for custody, claiming *she's* the one who's abusive."

"She's anxious to get the case resolved so she can leave the state."

"I know. The judge has ordered her to stay in town until after court. Do you have her file with you?" Sally reached for her briefcase and pulled it out, and Lynda took it. "So nobody wanted her, huh?"

"I'll just tell her she'll have to find another attorney."

"No, she's tried." She studied the file for a moment, then glanced at Sally again. "Sally, am I really that mercenary?"

"How mercenary?" Sally asked, not following.

"So mercenary that I would push this case to the bottom of my priority list just because the hours I spent on it weren't billable?"

"Lynda, you did what anybody would do."

Lynda sighed and closed the file. "I'm keeping this case," she said. "I'll handle it."

"But Lynda!"

"It'll be all right," she said. "Just call Paige and tell her to come by to see me here."

Sally held back her protest, but her disapproval was apparent. "All right, Lynda. If you say so. I'm gonna go now. You look like you need some rest. A lot of it."

Lynda dropped the file onto the table next to her. "You think *I* look bad. You should see the other guy." But the words weren't said in humor, and that haunted look passed over her eyes again. "At least he's alive. I've been calling ICU every hour. As far as I know, he's still not awake, though."

"They're saying he may never walk again."

Lynda snapped a look back to Sally. Slowly, she sat up. "What? Where did you hear that?"

"On the news," Sally said. "Last night they did a report about the crash. Apparently he has a spinal cord injury, and he lost one eye."

Lynda brought her hands up to cover her face and sank back into her pillow. "Abby said his face was the least of his problems, but I didn't know...."

"All things considered, Lynda, he's lucky to be alive."

Lynda tried to take in a deep, cleansing breath and slid her hands down her face. "Yeah," she whispered. "I guess we have to look at it that way. I just don't understand."

"Understand what?"

"Why *I* wasn't hurt worse. My legs are fine. I only broke a couple of ribs and lost my spleen. He almost died, and it wasn't even his plane!"

"Lynda, stop beating yourself up. If you'd been hurt worse, do you think it would have taken away from his injuries?"

Sally didn't understand, Lynda thought dismally. Nobody could understand.

Sally seemed at a loss for anything else that would comfort her, so she opened Lynda's bag. "Well, anyway, I got you everything you wanted from home. If you need me to go back, I'll be happy to."

"No," she said, without even checking the bag's contents, "this should be enough. Thanks, Sally."

Sally slapped her thighs. "No problem. I'll get in touch with Paige as soon as I can. And you call if you need me. Everything will be back to normal in no time, okay?"

"Yeah," Lynda whispered, but as she watched Sally leave the room, she wasn't sure that normal would ever be good enough again.

Jake wished he'd stayed asleep.

And frankly, he didn't know why he hadn't. What was the use in waking up, just so he could listen to the doctor tell him again of the gash that had maimed his face and destroyed one eye? And that was just the beginning.

"Tell me about my back and my legs, Doctor. Tell me why I can't move."

Dr. Randall—a man in his mid-fifties who had more lines on his face than a street map of Tampa—leaned wearily over Jake's bed rail and seemed to consider his words carefully. This was going to be a tough one, Jake thought. When a doctor grew that thoughtful and hesitant about giving a prognosis, the most obvious question was, "How soon should I buy my burial plot?" But Jake feared the news might even be worse than death.

"You have lower lumbar compression, Jake, due to the impact of the crash, and that's led to a condition called spinal shock," the doctor said carefully. "It's caused paralysis in your legs. You can count yourself fortunate, though. If the compression had been higher, you wouldn't have use of your arms, either."

"So I'm supposed to breathe a sigh of relief because I'm a paraplegic and not a quadriplegic?"

The doctor accepted his cynicism with patience. "Let me finish, Jake. The paralysis could be temporary. You have a gash on your back, too, and a lot of swollen tissue. The steroids we're giving you are to keep the swelling down so it won't cause any more nerve damage. And until we get that swelling down, there's no way to tell how much of the damage is permanent."

Jake fought the furious tears burning his eyes. "Bottom line, Doc. Am I ever gonna walk again or not?"

Dr. Randall rubbed his eyes, leaving them red. "We can't know that for several days. Maybe longer."

"But what do you *think*?"

The truth seemed to take more out of the doctor than he had to give. "I don't know, Jake. We've been successful with a drug that we think regenerates the nerve cells, and we've started you on it today, in your IV. It all depends on the extent of the nerve damage. We just have to be patient and hope for the best. Meanwhile, you'll start working with the physical therapist and occupational therapist this morning to keep your joints and muscles working."

"I can't move," Jake scoffed. "How can I work my muscles or joints?"

"They'll do it for you. But Jake…." He touched Jake's arm, forcing him to look up at him. "As hard as your therapy is going to be, you have to cooperate. Those therapists are going to get you functioning as well as possible, but you have to work really hard. Harder than you've ever worked before."

"I don't want to work at being a functional invalid," Jake countered. "I'd rather just give it all up."

"Well, that's not one of your choices," Dr. Randall said, still kindly. "You flat-lined in the ambulance, but the paramedics brought you back. And later, when the worst part of this is behind you, you're going to be glad they did."

"They should have let me die," he said through dry, cracked lips. "I don't want to be here. I don't want to do this."

"No one ever does, Jake," the doctor told him. "But you're going to."

"What about *her*?" he asked. "The plane's owner. Did she make it?"

"Yes, she survived," Randall assured him.

"Is she paralyzed, too?"

The doctor seemed to know where this was going. "No. She broke some ribs, damaged her spleen, but she was lucky."

Jake's face reddened. "Terrific," he bit out. "And I'm lying flat on my back." Gritting his teeth, he slammed his fist on the bed. "It wasn't even my plane!"

"There'll be anger, Jake," the doctor said. "But you'll get through it. You'll need support. Call all of your family and friends to rally around you. Don't underestimate how much they can help."

Jake didn't respond, for the tears were blurring the one eye he had left, constricting his throat, making him so angry he could have killed someone if he'd just had a weapon.

Family, he scoffed bitterly. Friends.

Didn't the doctor realize that he didn't want anyone to see him like this?

Dr. Randall left him then with the monitors and machines humming in his room, with the IV dripping through a tube in his arm, with the nasogastric tube in his nose draining the bile that kept rising.

Who would have believed it when he'd gotten up yesterday morning, all enthusiasm and hope?

He wished he'd never decided to buy a plane of his own; he wished he'd never picked up the aviation magazine that had advertised the Piper in its classified ads; he wished he'd never met Lynda Barrett.

It seemed like a year ago that he came bouncing down the steps of the Biltmore, introducing himself to the blonde—now he couldn't even remember her room number—and riding off in his Porsche. He wondered whether anyone had contacted the manager of the Biltmore to get his stuff or called the moving company about storing his furniture. Was anyone watching his car?

But who? It wasn't as if he had anyone here he could call. He was new in town and completely alone. Flat on his back or not, he was on his own.

The thought sent rage spiraling up inside him, anger that he didn't know how to direct. Why had this happened to him? Why not her? *She* was the one who'd taken *him* up in a busted plane.

As if in answer to his thoughts, the nurse who'd been hovering over him all morning came to his door. "Jake, is it all right if Lynda Barrett visits you for just a minute? If you're not up to it, I'll send her away."

Jake looked at the door with his remaining good eye, welcoming the opportunity to feed his anger. "Yeah," he said bitterly. "Send her in. She might as well get a good look."

The nurse hesitated a moment, then disappeared. In a few moments, she was back, wheeling Lynda in a wheelchair. He gave her a once-over—she was stitched and bruised, too, but both eyes were intact, and her legs, crossed at the ankles, looked as healthy as his had looked yesterday.

"Hi, Jake," she whispered almost timidly. "How do you feel?"

He looked at the ceiling. "How do you think I feel?"

She took that gracefully. "Probably pretty bad." She watched as the nurse stepped out of the room to give them some privacy, then wheeled herself closer to the bed. "Jake, I'm so sorry."

"Not as sorry as I am."

She swept her eyes down his body, and they lingered on his legs. "We didn't know if you'd make it. I prayed all night that you would."

"What for? So I could lie here like a vegetable for the rest of my life?"

"I know how you must feel—"

"Do you?" he asked with exaggerated surprise. "Do you really? Tell me how you know how I feel, Lynda. Have you ever been paralyzed? Have you ever had the sight cut out of your eye? Have you had your face maimed beyond recognition? How do you know how I feel?"

She only gaped at him for a moment, and her fragile expression crumbled. "Okay, I don't know. But you survived, Jake. Just like I did. We both could have died in that crash, but we didn't."

He turned his head to look at her now. "Are you kidding me? I'm supposed to be happy that I'm useless as a human being instead of dead?" Disgusted, he looked at the ceiling again. "Why did you come in here anyway? What do you want?"

For a moment, she couldn't speak. "Just . . . I just wanted to see if you were all right."

"Well, I'm not. Satisfied?"

It was clear that she hadn't expected this reaction from him, and he wondered if she'd expected them to bond from the trauma. Were they supposed to be best friends now and compare notes on what they remembered of the crash and eat lunch together and play cards? Didn't she realize that the very sight of her made him lament the day he'd laid eyes on her?

She covered her mouth and started to cry. "I guess I shouldn't have come. I'll go now."

"Yeah," he said. "You need to nurse those poor cracked ribs. I'd call the nurse, but I can't move."

At that, Lynda sprang to her feet. He watched her reach unsteadily for the rail, and with a look of furious determination made softer by the tears on her face, she grabbed the remote control with the nurse's call button from his bed table and thrust it into his hand. "That's one less thing you can feel sorry for yourself about," she said. Then, grabbing the handles of her chair, she walked carefully out of the room, pushing it in front of her.

Jake watched her go, his bitter anger at her for surviving intact fading as his indignation at her attitude grew.

Abby, the nurse who had found Lynda in Jake's room the night before, came upon her again, sitting in her wheelchair in the hall of ICU, weeping bitterly into her hands. Stooping in front of her, Abby tried to raise her face.

"Are you all right, child?"

Sucking back her sobs, Lynda looked up at her. "Jake just said some things—"

"He's hurtin', darlin'. Don't put any stock in what he says. When people hurt, they say all sorts of things."

But her assurance didn't help. This was bigger than words. "You want me to push you back to your room, honey?"

Lynda couldn't answer. "I went there to comfort him, and he just made me so mad—" She broke off and covered her face again. "I told him he felt sorry for himself. How could I *say* that?"

"You're human," Abby said. "Girl, I've been spit on, slapped, kicked, cursed, screamed at, puked on—and as much as I pride myself on keeping my cool, I have been known to say some nasty things, just because I'm human. You aren't even getting paid for listening to it. You can't expect to grit your teeth and smile through it. That takes something bigger than either one of us."

Reaching into her pocket, she pulled out a tissue, and Lynda wiped her eyes.

"You know where I go when I can't take much more, and I feel that old dark side of Abby taking over?"

"Where?"

"The chapel. It's on this floor. I'll take you there if you want me to, child. Maybe you'll find some peace there."

Lynda nodded. "Yes, that's where I need to go."

"Fine." Abby got to her feet and pushed her out of the ICU doors. "When I get off tonight, how 'bout I come by your room and wash your hair? I'll bet you're a pretty brunette when you don't look like you've lost a fight with a grizzly."

Lynda managed to smile under the tissue. "That would be great. I have trouble lifting my arms."

They reached the double doors to the small chapel, and Abby pushed her inside. The room was dimly lit with candles at the corners of the altar, and it was only big enough for three small pews on either side of the wide aisle.

Abby rolled her to the front and then in a more reverent voice, said, "There's a phone here at the back, honey. You call me when you're ready—extension 214—and I'll have someone come get you."

"Thank you," Lynda whispered.

Abby smiled, then closed the doors on her way out.

Lynda sat still for a moment, staring at the cross behind the small lectern and then behind that, at the stained glass window. A white dove was etched into the glass, flying down to the shoulder of a silhouette kneeling in a pool of water.

This is my son, in whom I am well pleased. God's words echoed through her mind, their very praise an indictment of her own actions.

Tears stung her eyes, and she sat before the altar, wishing to be judged, ready to be condemned. "I don't know what to say to him," she confessed aloud. "I don't even know what to say to you."

It had been too long since she'd had a serious heart-to-heart with God, too long since she'd sat in his presence. Now she felt her inadequacy like a verdict.

Awkwardly, she tried to thank him for her survival, but Jake's injuries limited her gratitude. And then she thought of the plane she had loved so much, destroyed in a matter of minutes, leaving her to face the solitude of her life without it.

As her own thoughts condemned her, she looked up to the window again.

… in whom I am well pleased …

It was from the New Testament, she thought quickly, but she couldn't remember where. It had been too long since she'd read her Bible, and now she wasn't even sure where she'd put it.

But she didn't have to recall the reference to know what it meant to her.

God wasn't pleased with *her.* How could he be when she'd made a god of an airplane, an altar of her job, and an idol of her own ego? How could he smile on her when she'd spoken to a sick man the way she had today or when she'd ignored the needs of a poor battered wife who depended on her?

The truth was that she'd just quit caring. She hadn't cared about her relationship with God or her friends or her family. She hadn't cared about anything except her job and that plane. Not in a long time.

Like Peter after he'd denied Christ, she wept bitterly, brokenly, not expecting God to recognize or comfort her, not expecting his peace—

But suddenly it came.

Her tears slowed, her sobbing stopped, and she looked up at the dove on the window and felt his slow, warm, forgiving embrace welcoming her home.

Instead of remorse, she felt hope. Instead of shame, she felt purpose. It *wasn't* too late.

For a moment, she sat still in her wheelchair, her head bowed, her eyes closed. For the first time in she couldn't remember how long, she listened.

And God spoke.

In that still, small voice that could be so easily ignored, so quickly forgotten, so often dismissed as nothing more than an idle thought, he reminded her to whom she belonged.

And with that reminder came a flood of determination finally to do something about it.

But what?

She thought of Abby, offering to wash her hair after working a twelve-hour shift, because she couldn't lift her own arms. That was faith in action, wasn't it? It was giving of yourself when you got nothing back. It was stretching out of that comfort zone, even when you got cursed at.

The new Lynda would do better, she promised as she sat before that altar. She would stretch. She would grow.

And filled with a renewed spirit and a peace that gave her strength, she felt a sudden urgency to go back to her room and get started.

CHAPTER ELEVEN

She wasn't dead.

He had been there when the plane crashed. He'd been standing at the fence, watching like a curious spectator as the plane circled overhead and the ground crews scurried around in a panic. It had made the news on all three local channels and even got a mention on CNN.

He had watched as the plane descended at the end, had held his breath as it had spun. He'd seen both wings breaking off, metal flying, glass breaking—and he'd been sure that he'd succeeded, that it was impossible for anyone to survive that.

But the paramedics had moved too quickly, and when the plane had ignited, she was out of its range. He had watched, troubled, as the ambulances blared past him, carrying both passengers to the hospital.

Still, he'd seen the blood, and he had believed that the injuries would be too great, that she would die en route or on the operating table or later in her room.

But no. She was not only still alive, but she was also doing well. No lasting impairment. No permanent damage.

It was a failure. But it would not be repeated. Next time, she would not escape.

All he could do now was bide his time and wait until the right moment. It would come soon enough. And then his problems would be over.

Then he could finally get on with his life.

CHAPTER TWELVE

The orderly who came to get Lynda from the chapel had a cautious, compassionate demeanor, and Lynda wondered with some embarrassment if Abby had warned him of her emotional state. As he wheeled her toward the elevator, he made light conversation.

"It's gonna rain again today, looks like. And, of course, I left my umbrella in the car. Isn't that always where it is when you need it? But I don't get off till three. Maybe I'll miss the storm."

The elevator doors opened, and he wheeled her on. "Oh, I was supposed to tell you that there's somebody here to see you. She's down in the first-floor lobby."

"Who?" Lynda asked, straining her sore neck to look up at him.

"I didn't get her name," he said. The doors opened, and he rolled her off. "She couldn't come up because she has a kid with her. They won't let her past the first floor. I told her you would call down when you were back in your room."

Paige. Lynda grabbed the wheel to stop the chair and looked up at him. "I have to go down," she said. "I have to go see her."

"Are you sure you're up to it?" the orderly asked her. "You look tired."

"I'm fine," she said. "Really. It's important."

An alarm sounded, and two nurses bolted around the desk, running toward an emergency. "I can't take you," he said. "I have to help with this."

"It's okay. I can make it. Go ahead."

The orderly rushed off behind the nurses, and quickly Lynda rolled back onto the elevator, ignoring the pain in her ribs when she used her arms. One crowd of people on the cramped elevator commiserated about a grandfather and a heart attack; another couple at the back cried softly and whispered together. *Pain all around me*, Lynda thought. *Pain and desperation. How can I have floated through it for so long, not seeing any of it?*

The moment the doors opened, she saw Paige across the plush maroon-and-gray lobby and pushed toward her. She was sitting on the couch, rocking Brianna back and forth gently. Her clothes were rumpled and wrinkled, and her eyes were swollen, as if she hadn't slept in days.

"Paige?"

Paige looked up quickly. "Lynda!" She sprang to her feet and rushed to help her. "Oh, I didn't expect them to send you down here! I was going to call you when you got back to your room. Oh, I'm so glad you're alive! I didn't see how you'd survive, and when I called Sally today, and she told me—"

"It could have been so much worse," Lynda cut in, smiling at the child whose thumb had gravitated to her mouth at the sight of the bruised, cut-up woman wheeling toward her. "I'm really doing pretty well. How are you, Brianna?"

The little blonde girl took her thumb out of her mouth. "Fine. Did you hurt yourself?"

"Yes, a little. But I'll be better soon."

"Did you fall down?"

"Way down."

"Did it hurt?"

"Bad. But I'm okay."

"But you look ... terrible," Paige said. "I mean, not really terrible. ... Just ... "

"Like I've been in a plane crash? That's okay, Paige. I'm just happy to be alive."

Tears came to Paige's eyes, and she sank to the couch again. "I'm happy you are, too, Lynda. For really selfish reasons."

"What's wrong?"

Using her fingers, Paige combed her fine blonde hair back from her face and held it in a ponytail. "Keith was at my house when

I went home last night," she blurted. "He was in there waiting. I saw his car in the driveway, and I kept going. I haven't been back."

"Did you call the police?"

She let the ponytail go, and her hair fell around her face again. "I called, but he was gone before they got there. I can't believe they have to catch him violating the order. Do they think he's stupid enough to be caught?"

"Where did you go, Paige?"

"To a motel. But I don't have much money left, and then this morning—" Her voice broke off, and she covered her mouth. Sensing her mother's despair, Brianna climbed onto Paige's lap and put her arms around her mother's neck to comfort her. The sweet gesture only made Paige wilt more.

Lynda pulled Brianna gently away. "Honey, see that book over there? Why don't you go get it and look at the pictures?"

"The Winnie the Pooh one or the Barney one?" Brianna asked.

"Barney," Lynda said.

The child considered that for a moment. "No, Pooh."

Lynda smiled faintly as Brianna gave her mother one last look, then scurried to the table with the books. Paige watched her every step of the way.

"Then what, Paige?" Lynda asked. "What happened this morning?"

"I couldn't take her back to day care, because he had been there yesterday. I was afraid he'd take her, Lynda, so I took her to work with me. And my boss came in and saw her, and he—he fired me."

"You lost your job?"

"Yes," she cried softly. "I might have all of forty dollars left to my name, and I'm afraid to go home." She looked at Lynda, her eyes pleading. For what, Lynda suspected even Paige didn't know.

Lynda took Paige's hand. "Sally told you that I'm keeping your case, didn't she?"

Paige nodded. "Yes."

"As soon as I get back to the room, I'll call her and get her to file a motion to get us before a judge so we can tell him Keith violated his order—"

"No," Paige cut in. "That won't do any good. It'll just make him mad."

"It doesn't matter, Paige. If he realizes he won't get away with it—"

"*If* they put him in jail, he'll get out in a couple of days. He'll come after me, Lynda. I'm afraid of him. All I want is my court date so we can get the custody hearing over with and have his visitation denied so I can take Brianna someplace where he'll never find us—"

A man walked past the place Brianna sat reading. Springing from her seat, Paige dashed to her daughter. "Brianna, honey, bring the book and sit by me."

"Okay." Brianna followed her mother back to the couch and climbed up next to her. Paige put her arm around her, as if only by touching the child could she be assured of her safety. Weary, Lynda realized that a court date could still be weeks away, and the woman had no livelihood and was living in terror. If Lynda hadn't left so much of her case to chance, it might have been over by now.

Lynda dropped her head into her hand, wrestling with the emotions she knew were on her face. "Paige, I hope you'll forgive me for letting you down."

"Letting me down?" Paige asked. "You haven't let me down. You're the only lawyer who would take me."

"No," Lynda said. "I *have* let you down. I could have pressed for a court date earlier. I could have paid more attention to your case."

Paige was silent for a moment, obviously confused about what to say.

"I want to make it up to you," Lynda whispered. "I've just been in the chapel, trying to sort things out, and I'm starting to see that I haven't been a very nice person."

Paige shook her head adamantly. "No, you're the greatest, Lynda. I don't know what I would have done without you."

"That's sweet," Lynda said, but she wasn't buying. "I want to help you for real this time. Somehow I feel like if I do, I'll be helping myself, too."

"But you *are* helping me."

"No," Lynda said. "Not really. But that can change. I want you to stay at my house."

Paige caught her breath. "No, I couldn't. Lynda, representing me for free is enough of an imposition."

"It's not an imposition. It's a favor," Lynda said. "Please, I want you to. My house is just sitting there, and Keith will never think to look for you there. I'll get Sally to get you some money out of my account, so you won't have to worry about your job *or* about Keith until we get into court."

Paige was stunned. "But that's too much, Lynda. You don't have to do this."

"Yes, I do," Lynda said. "Please, Paige."

"But why? I'm just a client. You hardly even know me."

Lynda paused and tried to find the right words. "Because your hair doesn't need washing."

Paige breathed a laugh. "What?"

"It's something I can do, Paige. Something besides sitting here and worrying about you. Please."

Paige stared at her for a moment as fresh tears came to her eyes. "I can't believe you'd do this."

"Then it's yes?"

Paige shrugged and looked down at her daughter. "Yes, I guess so."

"Then I'll go call Sally right now. She has a key, and she can let you into the house. There's food there, but she'll get you some money out of my account, so you can get anything else you need. Meanwhile, I'll make some phone calls. We'll get someone to go to your house and get your clothes and whatever else you need. Just don't tell anyone where you are. If anyone needs you, they can go through me or Sally." When Paige still didn't respond, she asked, "Does this sound all right to you?"

Paige surrendered and relaxed, her gratitude evident on her face. "Yes," she whispered. "Thank you."

As Lynda rode the elevator back up to her room to call Sally, she told herself that she should have offered Paige this kind of help weeks ago. It wouldn't have hurt her at all, and it would have made a world of difference in the young woman's life.

She only hoped she had the fortitude now to finish what she was starting.

Two hours later, Lynda was still on the phone when Sally came into her room. She whispered that she was on hold, and Sally set her hands on her plump hips and glared at her. "The nurse told me that she's calling the doctor to fink on you. She said you'd been either out of your room or on the phone all day. Lynda, if you don't stop this, you'll never recover."

Lynda put her hand over the receiver. "It takes my mind off my ribs. Did you get Paige situated?"

"Of course I did," she said. "I got her the money and gave her the key. I put them in one of the guest rooms, in case you ever get out of here. But at the rate you're working, that's not looking good. Who are you holding for?"

"Steve McRae."

"Keith's attorney? Oh, good. He ought to be a big help. He's the one trying to take that beautiful little girl away from her mother."

"He needs a warning," Lynda said. The Muzak on the phone stopped as someone picked it up, and Lynda raised a hand to silence Sally.

"Lynda?" the attorney asked in a voice that seemed a little too cordial.

"Yes, it's me," she said. "I need to talk to you about your client, Keith Varner."

"What a relief to hear your voice," he said. "I saw the crash on the news last night. I have to admit, I thought it would be a while before I'd hear from you again."

"Sorry," Lynda said in a saccharine voice. "No such luck. I am still in the hospital, which gives me all the time in the world to work on Paige Varner's case. And I called to tell you to warn your client that his harassment has got to stop."

"What harassment?"

"For starters, he tried to take Brianna from day care, despite the restraining order, and he broke into Paige's home—"

"Give me a break, Lynda," the man cut in, dropping the cordiality. "You know as well as I do that he has a key. It was his home."

"*Was* being the key word. She was granted possession of the house in their divorce, and the restraining order stated that he wasn't to come near it. And as for Brianna, until we see him in court, he isn't to go near her either."

"Put yourself in his place," the man said. "He hasn't seen his daughter in over a month."

"You're right. Not since he bashed her mother's head into the wall and knocked her out."

"Her word against his. He contends that *she* knocked *him* out when he was defending the child from one of Paige's rampages."

Lynda saw now what she was dealing with. "I'll have him arrested, Steve. If he comes near her again, I'll use every resource I have to get him locked up. Tell him."

The man sighed. "Anything else?"

"Yes. I'm going to appeal to the judge for a court date as soon as possible. I won't let you keep dragging this out."

"No need," the man said. "I got a date this afternoon. Despite what you might think, we're anxious to bring this to a head, too. It's October 14."

"That's six weeks away!" she said. "We need it earlier."

"Too bad. That's as early as we could get it."

She sank back onto her pillow and closed her eyes. "Six weeks is a long time, Steve. Tell your client that he'd better be on his best behavior during that time because I plan to pull out all the stops when we get into court."

"Good luck," he said. "You're gonna need it."

She heard the phone click in her ear, and slowly she dropped it back in its cradle and collapsed into her pillow.

"Good going," Sally said. "You told him." She looked at the color draining from Lynda's face and said, "Now will you get some rest? Paige and Brianna are safe, you have a court date, Keith's hand has been slapped—All is well with the world. Please, just get some rest before the nurses convince the doctor to sedate you."

"All right, Sally," she said, already feeling herself slipping away. "Maybe for a minute."

That night, true to her word, Abby came down from ICU with a cart made especially for washing hair and had Lynda lie down with her head over the small tub full of warm water. Gently, carefully, she washed Lynda's hair, methodically pulling more tiny chips of glass from her scalp as she did.

"It's a wonder you could sleep with all this glass in you and your hair all matted like this," she said. "Wasn't it hurtin' you?"

"Sure, it was," Lynda said. "But I thought the pain was just from the cuts." She closed her eyes as Abby poured more warm water over her head. "I thought they got all the glass out in surgery."

"No, child," Abby said. "It's hard to get it all, and the nurses don't have that kind of time when they're on duty. But we'll get every piece tonight if I have to work on it till my shift tomorrow."

Lynda opened her eyes and gazed up at the woman. "Why would you do this?"

Abby smiled. "Because it needs doin'. We're supposed to wash each other's feet, but I figure washin' hair is just as good."

The tear that rolled from Lynda's eye disappeared into the water Abby poured over her hair.

CHAPTER THIRTEEN

There was little relief for Jake in being moved out of ICU to a private room on the orthopedic floor. He was still flat on his back, unable to sit up or stand, unable to take care of his own bodily functions without help, and his hope of being released from this place was as dismal as his hope for the rest of his life.

But the Clinitron bed they laid him in gave him some degree of comfort. For one thing, it reduced the likelihood of bedsores. It felt something like a waterbed, except that air was continually pumping through it, making it conform to his shape and weight. And this room had a television so that he could keep remembering what normal people's lives were like while he contemplated what he'd do now that his would never be normal again. And he had a phone—a reminder that he had no one to call.

At least no one in Florida.

He looked at it, wondering whether anyone in Texas had heard of his accident. He doubted it. As far as they knew, he was living it up, as he'd always done. If they could see him now.

He picked up the phone and tried to remember the number of someone—anyone—who might care what had happened to him. What about Sheila—red, flowing hair, big green eyes. She'd been in love with him forever and had followed him around like a devoted puppy, even when he'd shunned her. He'd broken her heart, finally, and sent her on her way. But she would never get over him. She would want to know about this accident.

He dialed her number and waited as it rang, wondering what to say to her. Would she be glad to hear from him? Would she fly to Florida to visit him?

Quickly, he hung the phone back up. She might. He couldn't take that chance. He couldn't let her see him like this. *No* one could see him like this. Not yet. Not until the bandages came off and he could see how extensive the scarring was. Then he would decide.

Loneliness filled him like a disease, further darkening the black places in his heart. Jake Stevens wasn't used to being alone. What he wouldn't give for someone he *could* talk to without fearing how that person would see him.

And then he thought of that little truck stop in Slapout, Texas, where Doris waited tables each day, always naively hopeful that one of the truck drivers who came through would be the one to rescue her from her own loneliness and shame, make an honest woman of her, and provide her with the white picket fence and the little pink house that she had done nothing to earn on her own.

He wondered if she'd found her dream man yet among the regulars who came and went. He wondered if she'd been able to forgive him for running away from her himself, putting her behind him like forgotten garbage. Maybe she'd realized somewhere along the way that he'd had a life to make for himself and that he'd had to make it without letting her pull him down.

Maybe *she* would care that he lay here now, unable to run anymore.

He reached for the phone, called information, and got the number of the truck stop. With a trembling hand, he punched in the number.

"May I speak to Doris, please?"

On hold, he waited long, threatening moments, wanting to hang up. Finally, he heard her familiar voice, though it had grown raspier and deeper from cigarette smoke and booze.

"Yeah, hello?"

Jake swallowed, almost hanging up, but finally forced himself to speak.

"Mama? It's me. Jake."

Silence.

"Did you hear me, Mama?"

"I heard you," she said. "What do you want?"

If it was possible for his heart to fall further, it did. "I know it's been a long time. I've just been real busy, and—"

"Busy gettin' rich," she said. "I know why you haven't called. It's because you were afraid you'd have to let go of a few bucks if you talked to me. What made you call me now?"

He thought of telling her that he was lying in the hospital, that his charmed world hadn't been so charmed, that it had all come crashing down, that he didn't know if things would ever be the same. But something told him it wouldn't make any difference. He had never been there for her, though he could have been. Why did he expect her to be here for him now?

"Answer me, Jake. What do you want?"

"I just wanted to see how you were."

"Oh, I'm great," she rasped. "I just got a secondhand stove put in since mine has been out of commission for ten months. And my trailer is fallin' apart, but hey, at least it's a roof over my head. May not be a fancy condo like you've got ..."

He didn't know whether to offer her money or an apology, but that old anger that he'd nursed since childhood began to fill him again, keeping him from offering either.

"Look, I'm sorry I bothered you. You might as well get back to work."

"Yeah, I think I will. I can't afford to miss any tips. It's not like I have anybody to take up the slack if I can't pay my rent, is there?"

The click in his ear startled him, and for a moment, he held the phone to his ear as the dial tone hummed out its indifference. Then, as his face reddened, he hung up and lay glaring at the ceiling, trying hard to push the stark self-recriminations out of his mind. He'd been good at it before, but that was when he'd had life to keep him busy. There was always a party somewhere. Always a woman. Always a drink that could make him forget.

Until now.

He flung the telephone across the room, and it crashed with a final, protesting ring. There would be no parties now and no relief from his despair. But he didn't need his mother, and he didn't need his friends. They would all only let him down in the long run.

Mommy, is this gonna be our house?"

Paige smiled at her daughter, who sat on the floor playing with some of the blocks a police officer had gotten from their

81

house, along with most of their clothes. "No, sweetheart. We're just staying here for a while."

"Until that lady gets well?"

She left the spaghetti she was cooking and bent down to her daughter. "Maybe. I don't know how long we'll be here. But it's nice, isn't it? It's a lot better than that old motel room."

"But why can't we go home?"

"Because...." She lowered herself to the floor to put herself at eye level with the child and met her big, innocent eyes. There was so much Brianna didn't understand, and Paige didn't know how to explain it to her. How could she tell her that her father was a threat to them, that she feared for her life around him, that she feared for Brianna? "Because it has bugs," she said finally.

Brianna's face twisted. "Bugs? What kind of bugs?"

"The gross kind," Paige said. "A man's spraying so they'll go away, but it's gonna take a while."

"You mean spiders and stink bugs?"

Brianna might never want to go back into the house if she made it sound too horrible. "No. Roly-polies and grasshoppers. But this man is getting them out."

"Oh." Brianna got quiet, and Paige could almost see the wheels turning as the child imagined her bedroom full of roly-polies and grasshoppers. She hoped it didn't give her nightmares. She got up and went back to the spaghetti sauce simmering on the stove.

"Mommy?"

She looked back at Brianna.

"Can I keep just some of them? In a jar with holes in the top?"

She laughed out loud and realized it was the first time in weeks. "Yes, sweetheart. You sure can."

Jake, are you up to seeing that insurance guy?" Beth, Jake's nurse in orthopedics, asked him later that day. "I told him it was your first day in the private room and that you weren't up to seeing anybody, so if you don't want to, I'll nix it right now."

Jake looked irritably at her. "What insurance guy?"

"Something about the plane."

Jake had nothing better to do, and he'd grown so tired of being alone that he had actually been lying here wishing Lynda would come by. But after the way he'd treated her yesterday, he didn't really expect her back.

"Yeah, all right," he said. "Tell him to come in."

Beth disappeared, and Jake waited until a man in a dark suit came into his room and introduced himself as Rick Malone, investigator for the company that covered Lynda's plane.

"I just want to ask you a few questions," Malone said.

"About the crash?" Jake asked. "I would think the condition of the plane pretty much tells the whole story."

Malone consulted his notes, disregarding the comment. "Mr. Stevens, could you tell me if you or Miss Barrett did a preflight inspection of the plane?"

"Of course," Jake said. "I did it myself. I never fly without a preflight."

"And everything looked fine?"

"It looked perfect. And the day before I had really given the plane a once-over. I checked everything. I was thinking of buying it, you know. I wanted to make sure I wasn't missing anything. It was the best-maintained plane I'd ever seen for its age."

Malone plunked down, as if too tired to stand. "Is there anything you could tell me about Miss Barrett's behavior that day? Did she seem nervous, jumpy?"

Jake frowned. "What are you getting at?"

"I just want to know how she acted, Mr. Malone. Did she seem to behave normally?"

"How do I know if she was normal? It was the first time I'd met her. But yeah, I'd say she was pretty normal. She wasn't crazy about selling her plane. That was obvious."

"Did she suggest you test fly it alone? Or balk at going up with you?"

Jake thought for a moment. "No. She mentioned something about the crosswind, but I really don't think she would have let me go up alone."

"Did she mention her financial condition?"

Jake stared incredulously at him. "You don't think *Lynda* had anything to do with this."

Malone shifted in his seat. "We've been on the site since the crash yesterday," Malone said. "And we've found evidence that a hose was partially cut so the hydraulic pressure would pull it completely apart as soon as the landing gear was lowered."

Jake sat silently for a moment, trying to make sense of that. "It could have torn—"

"There's more. We've gone over all of the airport's security videos, and on the night before the crash, it caught someone tampering with that plane."

"Who?"

"We can't tell exactly," Malone said. "All we were able to make out was a penlight around the wheel well and the vague shape of someone under the plane. We can't rule out that the plane's owner might have set up the crash to collect the insurance."

Jake was getting angry. "Let me get this straight," he said. "You think she would sabotage her own plane and stage her own crash just to get the money when she could just as easily have sold it to me for full market value?"

"Maybe she didn't plan to fly with you," Malone said. "Or she didn't anticipate such a dangerous landing. After all, she did survive."

Jake gaped at him for a moment, unable to believe what he was hearing. "That is the most ludicrous thing I've ever heard. Lynda Barrett had nothing to do with that crash. She was as surprised as I was when the landing gear didn't go down. And she was scared to death. She could easily have *died* in that crash. What good would the insurance money have done her then?"

"All we know is that somebody did it."

"Then stop trying to pin this on her and find out who really did it and why." He struggled to sit up, but dropped down, defeated. "And when you do," he said through his teeth, "you tell me who they are. If it's the last thing I do, I'll make sure they pay."

CHAPTER FOURTEEN

I don't *believe* this." Lynda sat in a vinyl chair that hadn't been made for comfort, watching the parking lot below through her hospital room window as the insurance investigator cut between the cars. "He thought *I* had something to do with the crash."

"Don't sweat it," Mike said from where he sat by Lynda's bed. "Between Jake and me, we convinced him you didn't. But the question is, who did?"

She turned back to Mike, the light from outside casting a shadow on one side of her face. "Why would *any*body want to sabotage my plane, Mike? Wouldn't they know that the next time I flew it—?"

Mike only looked helplessly at her.

"That's it, isn't it? Someone was trying to kill me."

"Maybe. Maybe not. It could have been a random act."

"Were any of the other planes tampered with?"

"No. We've inspected all of them and checked back over the videotapes for anything out of the ordinary. It looks like it was just your plane."

She leaned back in the chair and looked out the window again. "How could I have made such an enemy and not known it?"

"I can't believe you did," Mike said. "Maybe it *was* random, Lynda. Random acts of violence happen all the time. People break into houses randomly, shoot at passing cars—"

"Some world we live in, huh?"

"You're right; it's not a pleasant thought—but it's better than thinking someone tried to kill you."

"What if they're still trying?" she whispered. She felt fear rising inside. "I mean, they failed, didn't they? What if they haven't given up?"

Mike got up and came to lean against the windowsill. "Think, Lynda. Is there anyone in your life who hates you enough to want to kill you?"

"Well, I didn't *know* there was, but obviously—"

"Not so obviously. I mean, yes, there's somebody out there who was trying to get his kicks, but that doesn't mean he's after you."

"Kicks?" she whispered. "Causing a plane crash gave him his kicks?"

"There's a lot of evil around us, Lynda. We don't have to let it consume us."

"What if we don't have a choice?" she whispered. "They're probably going to let me go home tomorrow. Am I gonna be a sitting duck? And what about Paige and Brianna? They're staying in my house."

"If he'd wanted *you*, whoever it is, he could have found you at home before, don't you think? That's what makes me think it's random."

Lynda shrugged, unconvinced.

"Anyway, the two cops who are working on it are planning to come by and talk to you today. If there *is* someone after you, they can get to the bottom of it." He leaned over and pressed a gentle kiss on her forehead and wiped a stray tear off her cheek. "It'll be okay."

"I just need some time alone to think about it, I guess."

"I'm going," he said. "But first, I want to tell you that the cops who are investigating this are Tony Danks and Larry Millsaps. Larry's a buddy of mine from church. I've known him for years. You can trust him."

She felt some comfort in that. "Thank you, Mike," she whispered.

The two people assigned to rehabilitate Jake—Allie Williams, a 120-pound dynamo who approached occupational therapy with a determination that rivaled Jake's determination to sink into depression, and Buzz Slater, a former paraplegic who'd become a physical therapist after learning to walk again himself—didn't seem to care that Jake's head was still on the verge of bursting with pain or that nausea was hiding just below the surface, waiting to assault him at any given moment. Since he awoke from the accident, their hands had been all over him, poking and prodding, flexing and massaging, despite his venomous verbal resistance.

Nothing he said daunted them, no insult offended them, at least not enough to make them leave him alone. Every two hours they came in and turned him over, massaged him, and bent him this way and that until finally he'd vowed to learn how to turn *himself* over just to get a little peace.

"That's not all you'll learn to do today," Allie said brightly as she wheeled a gurney into the room. "Today you're going to the tilt table in the rehab room. We're going to get you sitting up, so you can get out of bed."

That sounded easy enough, and Jake was almost hopeful as they wheeled him down the hallway, flat on his back to the big room where a dozen or more people like him worked—on mats, in a pool, on parallel bars, with walkers.

He didn't object when they transferred him to the flat table, but when they began strapping him down, he got worried. "What are the straps for?"

"To keep you from sliding off, Jake," Buzz said. "You've been flat for three days. We have to get you upright gradually. You may have some problems."

But Jake couldn't imagine ever having problems being upright. "Try me," he said.

They finished strapping him on then slowly began to tilt him up.

He felt a cold sweat prickling his skin; his head pounded. Though the table inched upward at a snail's pace, he grew increasingly dizzy, nauseous, weak....

"I'm gonna pass out!"

Instantly, they lowered him flat again.

"That's all right, Jake," Allie said. "You made it to thirteen degrees."

Jake looked at her. "That's all? Why did I react like that?"

"It's called orthostatic hypotension. You've been lying down for a while, so your circulation is weak. Your blood pressure drops when you're upright. We just have to keep trying it, getting a little higher each time, until you get through it. Ready to go again?"

He wanted to scream out that he wasn't, but instead he said, "No. I'm thirsty."

"We can give you some ice chips," Allie said, "but you won't be able to keep anything else down."

She put an ice chip in Jake's mouth, then allowed a few seconds for it to melt. "Ready now?"

Jake cursed as the table tilted again. As the blood drained to pool in his feet, the world threatened to turn black.

"Just get through this, Jake," Buzz said when he was flat again. "After this, we'll start you on traction."

Two hours later, they wheeled him back to his room in time for the bland lunch that awaited him, the lunch he couldn't eat. His skull felt as if it had intercepted the pain from all the places on his body that he couldn't feel. His stomach was empty but still threatened to turn on him, and the worst part was that for all his work, he'd only made it up to twenty degrees on the tilt table. At this rate, he'd be flat on his back for the rest of his life.

And the traction had been another nightmare. They had hooked him to the pulleys and turned the machine on, making it pull for twenty seconds, then release for five, then pull again....

Jake's hope as he endured the pain was that the pulleys would relieve the compression in his spine, free the nerves to function again, and bring the feeling back into his legs. But when the exercise was over, he was as numb from his hips down as he had been when he'd gotten here. It would take time, Buzz told him. Lots of time.

And time was something he had more than enough of. He had all the time in the world and absolutely nothing to do with it but endure more torture, more terror, more disappointment.

Yanking at the sheet the nurse had laid over him, he tried to fling it off the bed, but it was attached somewhere. Instead, he grabbed a glass of watery tea and hurled it across the room. It shattered and left a stain on the wall, but that did nothing to appease Jake's rage.

Lynda heard a crash as she reached the door of Jake's room. Stepping out of her wheelchair, she pushed the door open. A tray of food flew against the wall, and plates and food and a cup went crashing to the floor.

"Jake! What are you—?"

She ducked out of the way of the plastic pitcher.

Jake's face was red, and his bandage was wet with tears. Randomly, he reached for something else to throw. The phone book sailed across the room and then the tissue box. When he grabbed the phone he had already broken the other day and tried to yank off the cord, she dove for him.

"Stop it!" she cried, wrestling the phone from him and grabbing his flailing arms. "Jake, stop it!"

He fought for a moment more, and then, sobbing and cursing, finally gave up and let his arms fall across his face.

Lynda stood next to the bed, staring down at him, feeling helpless. Where were the people who loved this man? Where were the ones who could fight this battle with him? Was there really no one?

But there *was* someone, Lynda thought, succumbing to her own tears. *She* was here, and Jake needed her probably more than he'd ever needed anyone in his life.

She leaned over him and slid her hands to his shoulders. Somehow as he sobbed and shook and wailed, she got her arms around him, and suddenly he was clutching her like someone hanging from a cliff, about to fall to his death.

Maybe she was the only one who could pull him back.

He held her while he wept out his last ounces of strength while she cried against the bandage on his face.

"It's okay, Jake," she whispered. "I promise it's going to be all right."

But they were empty words. She could make no such promises.

When his grief had run out of strength for the moment, he loosened his arms.

Slowly, she let go of him.

He looked like a little boy in a broken man's body, she thought as she stroked his hair back from his damp forehead. Tears still rolled slowly down his temple, but he was too exhausted to wipe them away.

She stroked his forehead until his wet eye finally closed, until she felt the last ounce of fight seep out of him, until she heard his breathing settle into a relaxed cadence.

When she was sure he was sleeping, she went to get someone to clean up the mess he'd made.

But she didn't leave him until someone from her floor came and forced her to.

For it was only now that she realized just how alone he was. As much as he might hate her, she was all he had.

CHAPTER FIFTEEN

He fingered the newspaper photo of the crashed plane, still amazed that anyone had survived. It should have been a sure thing. He'd snipped the hose with such precision, leaving it partially intact so that it wouldn't be noticed on the preflight. When the landing gear engaged, the pressure in the line was certain to tear it the rest of the way. The gear would go partially down without locking—a deadly combination of problems. They should have been the last ones she would ever encounter.

But Lynda Barrett had a way of getting around sure things.

He clenched his jaw in frustration as he picked up the phone and dialed the number he had memorized for the hospital. He'd gotten daily updates on her condition, posing as a reporter one day, an uncle the next, a deacon another. The nurses had been unusually forthcoming, probably because her injuries were so minor. She'd be going home soon, he'd been told. Now he just had to find out when.

He asked for the nurse's station on her floor then waited as he was transferred. After a few rings, someone answered.

"Third floor nurse's station. Sarah McNair speaking."

"Sarah!" he said as though he knew her. "How's it going?"

She hesitated, trying to place his voice. "Fine."

He grinned. He loved throwing people off guard.

"Listen, this is Bob Schilling, Lynda Barrett's law partner. I just tried calling her room, but the line was busy. I wonder if you can tell me yet if she's had any word on when she might be released?"

"Uh … just a second. I'll check."

He waited as she left the phone. She was back in just a moment. "I'm sorry, but there's no word yet. We may keep her a couple more days. Would you like for me to transfer you to her room?"

"No need. I'll drop by to see her this afternoon. You gave me what I needed for now. Thanks a lot, Sarah."

He hung up, frowning, and wondered whether he should make his move now, rather than waiting until she returned home.

But how?

He checked his watch. Three hours before he had to be at work. Time enough to pay the hospital a visit, check out the possibilities, and formulate a plan. If he played his cards right and caught her while she was sleeping, he might even be able to get into her room to see if she is on an IV. Maybe he could inject it with something—aspirin to thin her blood, maybe. Or he could grind up some of his blood-pressure pills. Maybe enough to make hers crash. Maybe this crash she wouldn't survive.

One way or another, he was going to get her out of his way. Lynda Barrett's luck was about to run out.

CHAPTER SIXTEEN

H e knew they were cops the minute he spotted them. It was probably the sports coats that tipped him off, he thought; cops always wore coats to cover the guns strapped under their armpits. Or maybe it was the way they walked, with that quick, arrogant stride, as though they didn't exist on the same plane as everyone else. Then the radio blaring in their unmarked car confirmed it.

Were they here to talk to Lynda? he wondered. Had they realized yet that the crash was not an accident?

Curious, he sped up to join the two men where they waited for the elevator. Rubbing his hand over the slick hair he'd combed back, he tried to assess them over the frames of his glasses.

One of them, the dark-haired one who stood at least four inches above him, flashed him a smile. He hoped they'd never seen his picture before. The last thing he needed was to be identified before he even got to her room.

The elevator doors opened, and he followed them on.

"Which floor?" the blonde cop asked the other one.

"She's on three; he's on four. You want to talk to her first?"

"Might as well," he said, punching the button. "How about you? Where are you going?"

For a moment he didn't realize they were addressing him. "Uh ... three."

"We may not be able to talk to him," the tall one said. "They're saying he's in pretty bad shape."

"We need to, man. Our hands are tied until we do."

The bell rang, and the number three flashed above them. The doors opened, and they all stepped off.

He looked both ways up the hall, as if trying to figure out which way to go. The two cops headed for the nurse's station. Taking out their badges, they flashed them to the first nurse they approached.

"Hi, Ma'am. I'm Larry Millsaps, St. Clair Police Department. This is my partner Tony Danks. Could you tell us Lynda Barrett's room number, please?"

He made a mental note of their names. He might need to know them later.

"Lynda's in 413. Down that hall and to the left."

"Thanks a lot." They started in the direction she was pointing.

He stepped into the waiting area and watched as they disappeared into her room.

What were they up to? Until now, the crash had been ruled an accident, at least according to the television. They couldn't know that someone had sabotaged the plane, could they? No—they were here for something else.

He eyed the room next to her; there was a name on the door. But the room on the other side of hers appeared to be empty. Checking behind him to make sure no one was watching, he went into the vacant room.

The bathroom door was on the side adjacent to Lynda's room. The door was closed. He remembered being in a hospital once that had rooms that adjoined through the bathroom, and carefully, he turned the knob.

The door opened quietly, and he peered in. Another door was on the other side. It must open into Lynda's room.

Grinning, he went in and pressed his ear against the door. He couldn't hear, so he hesitated a moment weighing the risk and then turned the knob.

The door opened silently, and he heard her voice.

Perfect. If he could get this close, he could wait until she was alone. Maybe he could wait until she slept, then put a pillow over her face. That way he wouldn't have to worry about IV's and blood thinners. He could take care of her with his bare hands and make sure that he did the job right this time.

Then, as quickly as the thought had come, he realized how absurd it was. The cops had seen him. If she were found smothered in her bed, wouldn't they consider everyone who'd been on the floor a suspect? Of course, they'd still have to find him and identify him, but it was too risky. When he finally took her out, he needed an alibi. He needed to be far enough away that they could never pin it on him.

For now, just listening was enough. Maybe he'd hear what he needed to hear.

CHAPTER SEVENTEEN

Y ou're the pilot," Larry told Lynda as she sat up in bed, all bruised and scraped and stitched, like a mad scientist's experiment. "Maybe you can help us figure out what kind of person might know enough about planes to cut exactly the right hose."

Lynda shrugged. "A mechanic, I suppose. I'm not sure *I* would have even known which hose to cut."

Tony paced to the window and looked down on the parking lot. "What we're trying to determine is whether we're dealing with someone who's very familiar with planes or someone who didn't know what he was doing and just got lucky."

"Lucky, huh?" Lynda said in a dull, flat voice, and Larry wished Tony had chosen a better word.

"See, Lynda," Larry threw in, "it was difficult to determine if there was anything else tampered with, since the fire destroyed so much, but from what the NTSB can tell us, that was the only hose that was cut. It seems pretty deliberate. Calculated. Like someone who knew planes well had done it."

Lynda agreed. "It would have to be someone who's done a lot of work on airplanes."

Larry shot Tony a look. "So I guess that narrows down our hunt to someone with a background in aircraft mechanics or maintenance or maybe someone who had built planes."

"Did you interview all the guys who work at the airport?"

"We're in the process of doing it now. The problem is, we aren't having any luck finding anyone who has a vendetta against you."

Pulling her robe tighter around her, Lynda got out of bed and went to the dresser across the room. "I've been racking my brain since yesterday to think of anyone who might hate me. Maybe people whose cases I lost or didn't get along with or people I've been rude to." She let her voice trail off and tried to blink back the tears as she pulled a small notebook out of the drawer. Pulling out a piece of paper with a short list on it, she handed it to them. "These people wouldn't put me on their top-ten list of favorite people. But I can't see *any* of them doing something so deadly. I felt guilty even putting their names down."

"Anything would help at this point," Larry said, examining the list. "So who's this first guy?"

"Jack Gild. A client whose business was being sued, and I lost the case. He had to file bankruptcy, and he lost his home. He was really angry."

"What kind of business was it?"

"He repaired medical equipment. He was real mechanical, but I don't know if he knew about airplanes."

"What about this one? Doug Chastain?"

She sighed. "That was a client I dropped because he was so hard to get along with. I should have stuck it out, but I cut him loose before we went to trial, and it might have hurt his case."

"Did he make any threats?"

"No, not to my face. He really didn't seem like the violent type. He just had an attitude."

"What were his charges?"

"Arson. He and some friends got drunk and set a girl's yard on fire, just for kicks. Unfortunately, the house caught fire, too."

"How old is he?"

"Maybe twenty."

"What's he doing now?"

She shrugged. "I don't know. He served a little time, but I haven't kept up with him. And that third name, Gordon Addison. Well, I feel silly even putting it down. It's a pilot who's asked me out several times, but I didn't go. He has a tremendous ego, so I thought maybe...."

"That he might try to get even for his hurt pride?"

97

She winced. "Actually, it's ridiculous. Just mark him off. Talk about egos. I'm as bad as he is if I could imagine him being that torn up over my rejecting him."

"We'll just question him like we're questioning everybody. He won't know you gave us his name."

"All right." She sank back down on her bed. "This is the hardest thing I've ever done."

"It might save your life. Try to think of more names, Lynda. It's possible that your plane was picked randomly, that all of this had nothing to do with you specifically, but until we can determine that for sure, I think we have to assume it was someone going after you."

She went back to her bed and sat back on the pillows. "It's just so unbelievable."

"It always is when something like this happens."

"But who would want me dead?"

"Like he said," Tony suggested, "it may not be you at all. In fact, it's occurred to us that it could have been someone after Jake."

"But it wasn't his plane."

"Maybe someone knew he was looking at it. We're going to talk to him next."

Lynda's face changed. "I don't know if that's a good idea."

"Why not?"

"He's ... having a real hard time. He's depressed. Really depressed. I don't know if he can take any pressure right now, especially if you're planting the seed in his mind that someone may have done this to him deliberately."

"It's a long shot," Larry said. "But we have to ask. Don't worry. We'll try to be sensitive. But sometimes it's helpful for someone in his position to have a chance to brainstorm with us. It gives them back a little control. If they know something's being done—"

"But nothing really *is* being done, is it?" she asked quietly. "I mean, you don't know who it is, so you can't do any more than I can."

"But we can keep digging until we reach the bottom," Larry told her. "And that's exactly what we intend to do."

Lynda stared into space for a while after they had left, wondering whether, indeed, someone wanted her or Jake dead and why. It was crazy. It was amazing. It was unlikely.

Yet it had happened.

She heard a knock and thought the detectives had forgotten something. "Come in."

Gordon Addison, one of the men whose names she had put on the list, stepped inside.

"Gordon!" she said, every muscle in her body tensing.

He smiled—which may have been, she realized, the first time she'd ever seen that expression on his face. "I didn't know if it was appropriate for me to come," he said stiffly. "But I wanted to bring you some flowers and tell you you're missed at the airport."

Her heartbeat accelerated as she took the flowers wrapped in tissue paper and tried to look grateful. "You shouldn't have, Gordon. But thanks. That's so sweet."

"How do you feel?"

"Better," she said. "I'm expecting to get out soon."

"Great. That's good news."

An awkward silence settled between them, and she looked down at the flowers, as if studying the petals.

"Well," he said, finally. "You look tired. I'll go. I just wanted to bring those by."

She swallowed. "Thank you. Really."

She watched as he left the room, and when the door closed behind him, she let out a deep breath and wilted back on her pillow. She should be ashamed, she thought. All he'd ever done to her was ask her out then act hurt because she wouldn't go. He wasn't a killer. Didn't the flowers prove that he was only trying to be nice?

But *someone* had tried to kill her. Someone who'd gotten into the airport. Someone who knew airplanes. Someone who had a vendetta. That made it hard to be anything less than suspicious of someone like Gordon, who met those criteria as well as anyone.

Finally, she picked up the phone, hoping she could catch Larry and Tony in Jake's room.

J ake was so relieved to have visitors that forced his therapists to postpone his torture for an hour that he would have told the cops anything just to keep them there.

But for the life of him, he couldn't come up with the name of anyone who might want him dead.

"Think," Larry said. "You had looked at the plane the day before. Who knew about that?"

Jake shrugged. "Well, a few people. There's the first officer I fly with sometimes. We had a few drinks the night before while he was laid over. And there was the woman I met in a club that night . . . and some of her friends. . . ."

"Can you name them?"

He moaned. "The pilot is Frank Adkins. But as for the others, I can't even remember the name of the woman I was with. I'm not very good with names. Besides, why would someone who'd just met me want me dead?"

"You tell us," Tony said.

Jake was getting tired of this. "Nobody wants me dead, okay? It was *her* plane."

"Well, that's what we're thinking, too," Tony said. "But we just thought we'd try. If you think of anybody, maybe you could give us a call."

"Sure," Jake said, watching him set his card down on the bedside table. "If I come up with any valets I didn't tip enough or any gas-station attendants I might have offended, I'll let you guys know."

"And we might call you, if we think of any questions you might be able to answer."

"I'm not going anywhere," Jake assured them. "Look, you find that guy, okay? You find whoever it is and tell him what he did to me. He may not have wanted me dead, but you can sure bet that I'd love to see *him* dead. And if I ever get the chance—"

"We have to find him first," Tony said.

The door opened, and Abby stuck her head in. "Jake, Lynda was trying to call your room, darlin', but the phone wasn't working."

Jake glanced at it sitting cracked and lopsided on his table. "What did she want?"

Abby came in further. "Are you gentlemen from the police department?"

"Yes," Larry said.

"Well, she said to tell you that as soon as you left, one of the guys she put on her list visited her. Gordon somebody. He just left."

Tony and Larry looked at each other. "We'd better go," Tony said.

"Yeah." Larry patted Jake's arm and mumbled, "Take care."

Abby followed them out, and Jake watched the door close behind them then let out a labored breath. He wondered if the cops' questions had frightened Lynda. She was probably scared to death, and he couldn't really say he blamed her. He wondered if the guy who'd done this to them would really have the guts to show up here.

She'd given them a list, they'd said. Her paranoia about people she'd insulted, offended, or defeated almost amused him, but it really wasn't funny. She was struggling to think of people who had reason to be irritated with her since she couldn't think of anyone who hated her outright.

On the other hand, there were plenty of people who hated him. Women whose hearts he'd broken, men whose women he'd stolen, people he'd walked on, stepped on, kicked in the teeth—

Even his own mother.

He shoved the thought out of his mind.

Frustrated, he tried to sit up and move his legs, as if he could jump off the bed and run as fast as he could from his own thoughts, but they wouldn't budge. Finally, he gave up in a sweat and collapsed back into the pillows.

Why hadn't he just died?

Maybe it wasn't too late. Maybe if he just kept his eyes open for an opportunity, he would find a way to do just that.

If there was a hell for people like him, it couldn't be any worse than this.

Lynda saw the vacuous look in Jake's eye when she came to his room hours later. It was a haunting look, a look that spoke of defeat and self-loathing, that said he would throw the towel in if only he had a towel and knew where to throw it.

He seemed unwilling to look her in the eye now. She wondered if he were beating himself up for holding her and crying against her yesterday. He was probably surprised she had let him, after the way he had treated her. He had just finished throwing things at her, for pete's sake, as if doing her further harm could somehow relieve him of his own injuries.

But Jake Stevens didn't seem like the type to let anyone see him so unveiled, so vulnerable. And she could tell he didn't like it.

"Did you talk to Larry and Tony?" she asked.

"The cops? Yeah, I talked to them. Did they catch up with the guy who visited you?"

"I don't know," she said. "I never heard."

"They seem to know what they're doing. Maybe they'll find whoever did this. I just wish I could get out and look for him myself. You don't know how many times I've dreamed of getting my hands around his throat and showing him just what he did to me."

The words startled her, but then she realized that she had had the same fantasy. "I just want to know why he did it. What if we had died?"

She saw the raw pain growing more pronounced on his face. Covering his bandage with his wrist, he lay quietly for a moment. "Funny," he said finally. "I've been more concerned with the consequences of living."

He was back, she thought, that man who had been broken, vulnerable, and honest yesterday. Taking a chance, she reached down and touched his hand and moved it away from his face to make him look at her. "What do you mean?"

When he looked up, she knew the barrier was gone. This was Jake, the man so full of pain that he couldn't contain his grief or his rage, the man she liked more than the one he often pretended to be. "I mean if I'm paralyzed, I'll lose my pilot's license. Even in the best-case scenario—if my legs do start working again—I've still lost an eye. Which means I'm out of a job. There's disability, of course, or I could take a desk job. But TSA has a policy against keeping pilots who are damaged goods. And did I mention the fact that my face has a gash the size of the San Andreas Fault? The Elephant Man didn't have anything on me."

When she couldn't find the words to take his pain away, she squeezed his hand. And he squeezed back. It was something, she thought.

Trying to lighten the mood, she said, "No, but what's *really* wrong?"

He shot her a look that said she was crazy, but when he saw the grin in her eyes, he began to laugh softly. "Maybe I just need a hobby," he said facetiously.

"Sure," she teased. "You should take up woodworking or something."

"I'm actually thinking about taking up jogging. I hear there's a great running track on the roof of this building. And if running doesn't boost your spirits, you can always jump."

Her grin faded. "That's not funny."

His smile died as well. "No, it isn't. Don't mind me. I'm just fantasizing."

"You don't need to fantasize about suicide, Jake. That's not the answer."

She saw the mist welling in his eye as he looked away. "Then what is? The doctors told me I'll never take a step again. So tell me what good physical therapy will do me."

"None," she admitted, "if you go into it determined to fail. Besides, I know they've told you that there's a chance you could walk again. I've asked them myself."

"All right," Jake conceded. "A slim chance. A next-to-nothing chance. And judging by the way my legs are lying here like limbs on a corpse, I'd say the chances are even slimmer than that."

"And what odds would they have given either of us for surviving that crash? Probably none, Jake. And they sure wouldn't have bet on my being able to go home tomorrow, less than a week after the crash."

"They're letting you out?" he asked, his gears suddenly shifted.

She wondered at his choice of words. Did he consider this a prison? "Yes. Only because I have someone at home who can help me out."

"Yeah? Who's that?"

"A client of mine who needed a place to stay. But my point is that—"

"Well, if that's the criteria, I guess I'll grow old here."

She forgot what she was saying, and for a moment, just looked at him. "You're going to be all right, Jake. And if you need anything—I could go by your hotel room and bring you all your things. Or go to the store for you. I could sneak you in a hamburger...."

Jake looked up at the ceiling, his face expressionless. "Get off it, Lynda. You're gonna leave here without looking back, just like I'd do."

"No, I'm not," she said. "I'm going to visit you every day."

He moved his angry eyes back to her. "Why?"

"Because, I . . . I want to."

He let go of her hand. "I don't need your pity," he said as his lips began to tremble. "And I don't need your visits. We hardly even know each other, and we sure don't owe each other anything."

"Jake, there's no way I'm going to forget that you're lying in here. And pity is the last thing I feel for you. I'm not the one moaning about how you'll never walk again and how you need to get to the roof so you can jump off."

"What if I don't want you to come?"

"Tough," she said. "I'm coming, anyway."

For a moment, he seemed at a loss for a reply. Finally, he muttered, "I'll believe it when I see it."

"Good."

There was a thick silence between them as they stared at each other, and finally his eyes softened infinitesimally. He reached for her hand again and held it in front of his face, as if examining it. "Are you sure it's safe for you to be at home?"

Instantly her courage deflated, and she felt like a broken, injured, frightened woman again. "I hope so. Mike seems convinced that no one's after me personally, that it was just some random act, that it could just as easily have been one of the other planes on the tarmac that night."

"And what do you think?"

She sighed. "I think I'll go along with his theory. I have to go on with my life, after all. And if there is someone after me, maybe having the police snoop around will deter him."

"Pretty optimistic, considering what you've been through."

"Yeah, well …" She looked down at their hands, clasped on his chest and felt a surge of warmth that there was someone who cared. "I'll be okay." Taking a deep breath, she redirected her thoughts. "Anyway, back to my offer. Do you want me to do anything for you when I get out?"

He considered that and realized there wasn't anyone else he could ask. And there were loose ends of his life to be tied up. Loose ends that he'd tried to handle by phone until now. "Yeah," he admitted finally. "There are a few things you could do once you get on the outside."

CHAPTER NINETEEN

The light assaulted Jake with jackhammer force as Allie, his occupational therapist, threw open his drapes the next morning.

"I like them closed," he muttered.

"Don't be silly. You can't lie here in the dark all day. You need sunlight to motivate you."

"Motivate me to do what? Roll over? I've gotten real good at that already."

"Nope," she said. "You're going to sit up today. We're gonna get you in a wheelchair if it kills you."

"It might," he said, getting angry. "We've only gotten to twenty degrees without me passing out or puking all over the place, remember?"

"Buzz is bringing a special wheelchair that reclines. We'll move you up as slowly as we need to. And to help with the circulation, I brought you these TEDS."

She held up a pair of stockings, and Jake moaned. "Forget it. I'm not wearing those. There's got to be a limit to the humiliation."

"Oh, yes, you are." She uncovered his legs and began to work a stocking over one foot. "And then we're going to wrap the legs tight with Ace bandages. It'll help you fight the orthostasis, so we can get you sitting up." As she spoke, she worked the tight stocking up his calf then propped his foot on her shoulder as she pulled it over his knee. "Tonight we're gonna start you on sequential compression stockings to keep the blood from pooling in your legs while you're asleep."

"If I could kick, I'd send you flying," he gritted as she got the stocking up his thigh.

"If you could kick, none of this would be necessary."

He lay on his back, miserable, as she fought the other stocking up then began wrapping both legs so tightly that he imagined his face turning red. He was almost glad he couldn't feel them.

"I have this theory about Mary Poppins," he told her through his teeth.

"Mary Poppins?"

"Yeah. You remind me of her. I hated her even when I was a kid. I've always thought she was a child abuser, leading those kids into all sorts of danger, introducing them to bums and no-accounts, playing with their heads. She was probably an occupational therapist before she was a nanny."

Allie looked undaunted. "Well, I did finish Torture 101 at the top of my class."

She finished wrapping just as Buzz came in followed by two orderlies, pushing a black monstrosity on two wheels.

"Hey, Jake," he said, just as cheerfully as Allie. "You ready to go for a ride?"

"You people are crazy. If I don't pass out in the first ten seconds—"

"When you start feeling faint, we'll lay you back for a few minutes," Buzz said. "This chair reclines to whatever angle we need. It'll be slow going, but we've got to get you sitting up before we can get on with serious therapy."

There was nothing he could do to stop them, so Jake braced himself as they surrounded his bed.

"All right now, on the count of three," Buzz said. "We're going to lift you carefully into the chair, lying flat. Our goal is just to get into it for a few minutes. Are you ready?"

Jake couldn't answer, but it was just as well. At the count of three, they lifted him into the chair.

Allie was all business now as she adjusted the recline of the chair and moved his foot rests to elevate his feet then carefully positioned them. Then she gave Buzz the signal to begin raising him up. "Easy, easy ... How do you feel, Jake?"

He couldn't find words to describe the agony of dizziness and nausea. Sweat dripping from his chin, he muttered, "Sick."

"He's pale. Let him down," she said, and they lowered him flat again.

"Imagine how bad it'll be when it's moving," he whispered.

"You'll get over it, Jake. Come on now. Let's try it again."

He groaned as they pulled him back up. "Talk about motivation," he said, breathing hard. "I'm starting to feel some. I'm wanting real bad to move these feet so I can ram them through your teeth."

Buzz suppressed his grin. "Well, we all have to have goals. But if it's any consolation, I've been there. I was in a bad car wreck when I was nineteen, and I had injuries real similar to yours." He held out his hands, as if he might burst into a shave-and-a-haircut routine. "And look at me now."

"Yeah, well, I'm not nineteen, and they told me I may never walk again."

"They told me that, too, man. But with hard work, I overcame it. That's why I went into physical therapy. I'm gonna do everything I can for you, too. Trust me. You do what we say, try really hard, and I promise you, if we don't have you walking within a few months, you'll at least be able to function within your disability."

Jake looked down at the wheelchair beneath him and realized for the first time that he truly was disabled now. He was one of those people he got impatient with in stores because they took up too much room in the aisles and slowed him down. He was one of those people who had to be boarded first on airplanes and needed special attention getting off. He was one of those people he had always looked at with an air of superiority, an air that said, "Sorry you're disabled, pal, but you're in my way."

Disabled. The word hung in his heart like a fish hook, and that familiar, fighting anger spread through him like an infectious disease.

"After we get you up higher," Allie said gently, "I can take you for a ride. You're probably ready to get out of this room on something besides a gurney, aren't you?"

He had seen a Stephen King movie once where a deranged nurse had wheeled her victim into walls, down stairs, and dumped him out into a heap on the floor when she was finished with him.

"No thanks," he muttered.

As if in punishment, they began raising him up again until his stomach churned.

By the time they had worked him up to forty-five degrees, Jake was exhausted.

"I—I think we damaged something," he grunted after they moved him back to his bed. "My head feels like it's about to burst."

"That's normal, Jake. At least now you know that you don't have to lie on your back all the time. You can sit up, and you can get out of bed. We may get you all the way up tomorrow. And before you know it, we can change you to a lighter-weight chair, and you can get in and out of it by yourself. After that, we may be able to send you home."

Home, Jake thought with a sinking heart. Where was that? He'd sold his condo in Houston, and everything he owned was here, except his car, which he couldn't drive. He didn't have a job, a place to live, or any friends to speak of.

And he might as well not have any family.

As Allie and Buzz left, he dropped his head back on the pillows. Home, he thought. What had once been such a given, such an expected element in his life was now something he didn't have. He was not only disabled, but he was also homeless. He didn't even want to think of all the biases he'd once had against homeless people.

He had no idea where home would be when he was released from here. At least he wouldn't be released for months and months. But that thought, his greatest comfort, was also his greatest fear.

CHAPTER TWENTY

Y ou didn't have to come get me," Lynda told Paige the next morning when she met her in the lobby. "I could have had Sally bring me home."

"Well, that would be silly," Paige said. "Sally has plenty of work to do, and I'm just sitting there in your house."

Lynda looked down at the child sitting on the lobby floor, playing with a puzzle. She looked so safe today, so secure. "Paige," Lynda said with a heavy sigh, "we need to talk."

Paige's face took on a guarded look, and she started twisting her hair into a pony tail. "Okay."

Lynda sat down on the couch and glanced around, making sure no one could overhear. No one sat nearby. "Paige, they've found out that someone sabotaged my plane and caused my crash."

"How awful!" she said.

"Yeah, it's pretty awful," Lynda said. "But the really awful part is that this person might have been trying to kill me. We don't know."

Paige twisted her hair harder. "Do you know who it could be?"

Lynda shook her head dolefully. "I've thought and thought. But the bottom line is, if someone is out to get me, then anyone with me is also in danger."

Paige let her hair fall. "You want us to move out."

"No, that's not what I want. I just wanted you to know the danger. You have to know that living in my house might be putting you and Brianna in jeopardy."

Paige considered her child for a moment, then brought her gaze back to Lynda. "Are you scared?"

Lynda tried to find honest words to express what she felt. "I think ... that maybe ..." She failed and tried again. "I don't know. It could have been just a fluke that he picked my plane. But that's really just what I want to believe. If I'm wrong ..."

Paige sat slowly back down on the couch, the look on her face telling Lynda that she couldn't take much more. "You don't need the stress of having us around anyway."

"I'd love to have you around, Paige. You know that's not it. And if you still want to stay, you can. You just had to know."

For a moment, she watched Paige's big blue eyes wrestle with the decision. Other visitors waited on the couches or milled through the lobby. The elevator bell kept ringing every few seconds, and on the intercom doctors were paged and codes were recited. In the corner across the room, a television was on, and a few children sat transfixed in front of it.

When Paige finally brought her eyes back to Lynda, Lynda fully expected Paige to thank her, then say that she would find another place to stay. But Lynda had underestimated the girl's desperation.

"Well, Lynda, I guess I see it like this. If I go home, I'm in absolute, inevitable danger. And if I stay with you, I may be in danger—but I may not. And since I don't see any other possibilities right now, I think Brianna and I will stay."

Lynda hadn't realized how much she had hoped Paige would say that until she heard the words. "Good," she said. "I'm glad." She reached out and squeezed Paige's hand. "We're in God's hands, Paige. I believe that. We're going to be all right."

And as they left the hospital, Lynda believed it more than ever.

CHAPTER TWENTY-ONE

Today. She was going home today. Thanking the nurse who'd given him the information, he hung up the phone, leaned back, and laughed.

So much for patience. He didn't have to wait even one more day.

But he had a lot of work to do if he was going to take care of things tonight. He'd heard every word that she'd said to the police that day in her hospital room, and the knowledge empowered him, even while it created a new urgency. He had to do this quickly before they managed to stop him.

Grabbing his car keys, he dashed out of his apartment, his spirits higher and more hopeful than they had been since the day of the crash.

CHAPTER TWENTY-TWO

The airport looked just the same as it had the morning of the crash, and as Paige pulled her car into a parking place facing the fence—and beyond that, the runway—Lynda found herself reliving that morning. It had been windy, like this, and she remembered thinking she should have postponed the test flight. If only she had. But that wouldn't have helped, would it? The crash would have happened anyway the next time she took the plane up, and she might not have survived the landing if she'd been alone.

"Are you all right?" Paige asked quietly.

Lynda shook herself out of her reverie. "Yeah. Fine. It's just kind of weird, coming here after what happened."

Paige crossed her arms over the steering wheel. "Is it really necessary? I mean, I'm sure Jake's car is fine."

"I just have to get his hotel key out of it," she said. "And I want to get Mike to move it someplace where Jake doesn't have to worry about it."

Paige checked the back seat where Brianna was sound asleep in her car seat, and she patted Lynda's hand. "You go on in and do what you need to. I don't want to wake her up. Take your time, okay?"

"Okay." Wincing against the pain in her ribs when she twisted, Lynda got out of the car and went inside.

The small airport was just as she remembered: the blue couches forming a square in the middle of the floor; the line of vending machines against one wall; the posters of exotic places; the rest rooms; the tall desk that looked like a concession stand but was really Mike's version of a control tower.

Mike sat there now, sipping on coffee and going over paperwork. He looked up when she started toward him.

"Lynda!" Spilling his coffee, he blotted it up quickly then came around the desk to meet her. "What in the world are you doing here?"

She hugged him, careful not to test her ribs, and he led her to a seat and made her sit down. "They sprang me this morning."

"You should have called me," he said. "I would have picked you up. Are you okay? Do you need a wheelchair? I have three."

She couldn't help being amused. "Mike, relax. I'm fine. I may look like Frankenstein's daughter, but I'm really okay."

"But you aren't supposed to drive this soon after your surgery, are you? And shouldn't you be at home—?"

She touched his arm to stem his rambling. "I didn't drive. I have a friend out in the car waiting for me. I just came to make some arrangements about Jake's car and get some things out of it for him."

"Oh. Well, okay. I have it parked in the hangar."

Getting to her feet, she tried to look stronger than she was. "Do you have the keys?"

"Yeah. He left them in the ignition that day. I locked it up and put the keys in my safe." He hurried around behind the desk and unlocked the safe.

"Here they are." He handed them to her. "I'll walk out to the hangar with you."

"No," she said. "It's okay. You need to stay here. Who knows? Somebody's landing gear might fail."

He hesitated then looked at the controls behind his desk and realized she was right. "All right," he said. "Are you sure you'll be all right?"

"I'll be great."

She pushed through the glass door of the airport, and the wind immediately whipped her hair into her face. Shoving it back, she peered across the concrete to runway 4. She wasn't sure exactly where her plane had ended up—the crash was such a blur to her now—but she remembered waking up and seeing Jake crushed and twisted and bleeding, and she remembered sliding him to the door. . . .

Shivering, she started to the hangar.

It was open, as it usually was this time of day, and planes sat lined up, waiting to be flown. There was a big space where she had occasionally parked *Solitude*, and tears came to her eyes. But she reminded herself that she hadn't come here to mourn, and she blinked the tears away. She had things to take care of.

She saw the red Porsche parked at the back of *Solitude's* empty space, and slowly she started toward it.

"Lynda? How are you doing?"

She looked up; one of the mechanics was standing on the wing of a plane. "Hi, Mac. I'm great."

"You sure look a lot better than I expected you would after I saw that plane hit."

She smiled. "It'll take a lot more than a little ole plane crash to get me down."

He laughed. "It's good to have you back."

But her smile faded. She wasn't back. Not really.

She went to Jake's car and unlocked the door, but as she did, she heard footsteps behind her. She turned and saw Gordon Addison.

Though she waved, a shiver went through her again; quickly, she got into the car and locked it shut. Trembling, she looked back at him through the windshield, wondering whether he knew she had given his name to the police or whether they'd caught him leaving the hospital and interrogated him about why he'd come. He was standing half in the shadow of his plane, staring at her as if surprised to see her. That look frightened her, and she found it hard to breathe. She had to calm down. He probably wasn't the one who'd done this to her, and she had no reason to be frightened. Besides, there were witnesses all around them here in the hangar—mechanics and maintenance people, other pilots—and he couldn't do anything to her here.

When he disappeared behind his plane, she calmed down. He wasn't going to approach her. She was just being paranoid.

She tried to relax in the sleek interior of Jake's car, smelling the spearmint scent of the gum he kept on the dashboard. Opening his glove compartment, she found the hotel key just where he'd told her it would be. She pulled it out, along with the hairbrush he kept there, the sunglasses, and the ID tag that identified him as a TSA employee.

Putting them into the bag she'd brought with her, she looked around for anything else he might like to have. There was an aviation magazine on the passenger's seat—probably the same one in which he'd seen her classified ad—and she stuffed it into the bag to throw away. She flipped down the visor over the driver's seat and saw his checkbook. Slipping it out of the pocket that held it, she dropped it into the bag, and looked around for anything else. Only the gum, she thought, and he might like that.

She got out, opened the small trunk, and saw some of the bigger items he'd put there during his move—things he'd decided to bring to Florida himself rather than turning them over to the movers since he might need them before he found a place to live— and she took out what she thought she could carry and made a mental note to ask Mike to unload the other things and take them to Jake. The more personal items he had around him, the better he would feel.

Taking one last inventory, she reached for the trunk, wincing at the pain in her ribs, and closed it.

She jumped, startled—Gordon Addison stood leaning against the car, staring at her with his arms crossed. "You scared me, Gordon."

"What did you tell the police?" he asked.

She swallowed and looked toward the plane where Mac had been working. He was gone.

"What do you mean?" she asked, starting to back away.

He stayed where he was. "They came here this morning asking all kinds of questions. Where I was the night before the crash, what my relationship with you is, why I came to the hospital yesterday—"

"Well, they interviewed everybody here. They weren't singling you out."

He pushed away from the car then, the frown on his face revealing a deeper anger than she could hear in his voice. "I want to know what you told them."

"I told them something about everybody here, Gordon. Not just you." Again, she searched around for Mac or one of the other mechanics, and though she could hear some of them on the other side of the hangar, none was in sight.

"If you think I had anything to do with that crash—"

"Of course not," she cut in. "What reason would you possibly have?"

As if he turned that question over in his mind, he left it unanswered.

Lynda started to walk away. She half expected him to catch up with her, grab her, and stop her, but as she stepped out into the wind again, she turned back. He hadn't moved from where he was standing, and he was watching her.

With more energy than she could spare, she walked faster until she was all the way to Paige's car.

Later that night after Paige had cooked her the best meal she'd had since her mother died, Lynda walked outside to sit on the massive deck attached to the back of her house. The cool night air felt good on her face as she lay on a white wicker chaise lounge chair and gazed up into the stars. Somewhere, under these same stars, an enemy lurked with deadly intention. God knew who it was.

Maybe it wasn't Gordon Addison at all, she thought. Maybe it was some kid caught in a game, and now that he'd seen the results of his actions, he was remorseful and repentant. Maybe it *was* just an accident.

Or maybe not.

But the face of Gordon Addison, angry and pensive, staring at her in the hangar today still chilled her.

Across the deck, a cricket chirped, and she could hear the sound of the leaves in the oak tree whispering over her head. The breeze had grown cooler while she was in the hospital, but she knew it wouldn't stay that way for long. Soon the temperature would rise, and it would feel like summer again. Summer didn't let go easily in Florida.

The back door opened, spilling light out, and Paige looked startled. "Oh, I'm sorry. I didn't know you were out here. I was just going to take the garbage out, but I'll do it later."

"No, it's all right," Lynda said. "I was just thinking."

Paige set the garbage bag in the vinyl can next to the deck and took a step toward the chair. "Really, if you want to be alone ..."

"Sit down, Paige," she whispered. "Brianna's asleep, everything's put away—you deserve to rest."

"Oh, I'm not tired. Really. I love doing household things. And I'm so thankful that you've given us a place to stay."

"You don't have to wait on me hand and foot just because you're grateful. I think I'm getting a lot more out of this deal than you are."

Paige was quiet for a moment. "I just want you to see that I'm ... decent. I don't want you to think I'm just trash."

"Why would I think that?"

Paige had trouble meeting her eyes. "I don't know. That's what people think about women who have to hide from their ex-husbands. Things like this don't happen to 'nice people.'"

Lynda touched her hand and made her meet her eyes. "I've *never* thought you were trash, Paige. If anyone is, it's me, for not giving your case the priority it deserved."

"Well, why would you? I couldn't pay—"

"That doesn't matter," Lynda said. "You needed help, and I just became another problem."

Paige walked out to the railing of the deck and leaned back against it. She sighed and rubbed her eyes wearily. "Sometimes, I look back on the dreams I had growing up and all the promises I made myself, and I can't figure out how I got into all this."

"What promises, Paige?"

Paige turned her back to Lynda and looked out over the night. "Promises that I'd have a different kind of life when I grew up." She laughed softly, but there was no joy in the sound. "You know, the picket-fence promises. The ones about the knight in shining armor who would protect me instead of threatening me."

Lynda tried to listen beyond Paige's words. "Paige, did you come from an abusive home?"

Paige was silent for a while, and Lynda wondered if she'd heard her at all. When she finally spoke again, her evasion told Lynda what Paige couldn't. "Keith seemed like just the kind of man I needed. Strong and smart—have I told you that he has a genius IQ?"

The turn in the conversation surprised Lynda, but she tried to follow it. "Really?"

"Yeah. But he still keeps failing. He's a computer whiz, but he has trouble keeping a job because of his temper. I think he expected to really be somebody. But his IQ hasn't helped him much. That only adds to all that anger boiling inside him. I really don't think he means to let his temper blow up the way it does. He's just so used to being in control. Every time I leave him, it just sends him into a rage."

"You've left him before?"

Paige turned back. "Yeah, a few times."

Lynda sat up. "And you went back?"

Paige turned to the night again. "He convinced me to, every time. Told me how sorry he was, that he'd change, that he'd never lay a finger on me again. He really did love me, Lynda. I know he did. And I worried about him. Nobody understands him like I do."

Lynda got up then and went to stand beside Paige. She turned Paige to face her and saw Paige's tears. "You sound like you still love him."

Paige shrugged. "I just get so mixed up. Sometimes I hate him, and sometimes...."

"But he hurt you, Paige. He hurt Brianna. How could you find any rationale for that?"

"He never means to, Lynda. It just ... happens."

Lynda tried hard to keep her expression from revealing her amazement—or her judgment. "Paige, abusive husbands kill their wives all the time. They kill their children."

"I know that," she said. "That's why I'm here. That's why we're divorced. I'm just trying to explain to you why I'm in this position. I'm not stupid, you know. Things happen to people sometimes that are out of their control."

"I know that more than anyone." She reached out to stroke Paige's hair and wished she had the wisdom that Paige needed right now. "But Paige, you did what you had to do to protect yourself and your daughter. It took a lot of courage, but you did it. Don't back down now."

"I'm not," she said adamantly. "Besides, Brianna's scared to death of him. Whenever I get weak and think of going back, I remember that."

Lynda stared at her, wanting to blurt out that she was crazy if she'd even considered going back to Keith, that she needed to go to counseling and get help, and that she needed to step back and start looking at things realistically.

But then she realized that Paige didn't need to be condemned right now. She needed patience and understanding. And she needed someone she could count on. Maybe that was the reason God had forced Lynda to rearrange her priorities: so that she'd be here for Paige. Not as a judge but as a friend.

She only hoped she had the grace to put friendship ahead of her own personal biases.

CHAPTER TWENTY-THREE

The five-gallon bug sprayer was perfect for the job. He screwed off the top, pulled the sprayer cord out, and dropped in the funnel he'd brought. Then, careful not to spill any, he poured the gasoline out of the can with the "J.R.'s Auto Repair" logo on the side.

That should be enough gas, he thought, checking his watch. It was after midnight. Lynda should be asleep by now since it was her first day home from the hospital. She was probably zonked out, what with those internal injuries and those painful broken ribs. She should thank him for putting her out of her misery.

He loaded the bug sprayer and the empty gas can into his car and drove across town to Lynda's house; he had located it days ago by simply looking up the address in the phone book. Turning down the exclusive street lined with groomed palm trees and extravagant homes, he did a drive-by, checking out the lights in the neighbors' houses, making sure there were no late-night walkers, no dogs liable to bark, no policemen staked out in parked cars.

He slowed when he reached Lynda's house, a two story Tudor style that reminded him of a miniature castle, and he thought how ironic that she had that whole house to herself when there were entire families living out of cars. She deserved whatever he gave her.

And it looked like the perfect night. No lights had been left on. The garage door was closed, and even the porch light was off. It would be easy to steal through the shadows and do what he had to do.

He drove the car around the block and parked at a vacant lot he'd found earlier. Quietly, he got out, pulled the empty gas can and the sprayer full of gasoline out with him, and cut through the trees separating the yards.

Her backyard was the third from the vacant lot. He slipped into her yard and saw the deck that would be the first to ignite. Quietly, he laid the empty gas can in the grass, close enough to the house to be found later but far enough away to escape harm. Stealing closer to the house, he began pumping the trigger on the sprayer and doused the side of the deck with gas.

The fumes reached his nostrils, satisfying him, and when he finished the deck, he ran a stream along the walls of the house, then turned up the side between the house and the garage, and kept spraying.

He sprayed until he ran out of fuel, and still there was no sign that Lynda had awakened. It was all falling perfectly into place.

Reaching into his pocket, he pulled out the matches he'd brought. All he had to do now was light it.

And then his problems would go up in flames.

CHAPTER TWENTY-FOUR

cross the street, Curtis McMillan, an eighty-year-old retired judge, awoke from a sound sleep. It happened more and more often these days, this middle-of-the-night wake-up call, when he knew that going back to sleep would be next to impossible.

Careful not to wake Lizzie, who didn't have that problem and had slept like a baby since he'd met her his senior year of high school, he reached for his robe and slippers and padded into the kitchen.

Without turning on the light, he got a glass out of the cabinet and scuffed to the sink for water. Next to the sink were his glasses; shoving them on with his free hand, he brought the glass of water to his lips.

His eyes focused on the night outside the window and the shadows of windblown trees dancing on Lynda Barrett's house across the street. Poor woman, he thought. Bless her soul. He hoped she was recovering quickly and would be home soon. The crash was such a tragedy.

He set the glass down and started to head toward the den to see if any late-night movies worth watching were on, but as he turned, a movement outside caught his eye.

It was different from the shadows of trees. It moved more deliberately, more methodically, and he cupped his hands on the glass and peered out more earnestly.

It was a prowler, he thought, someone trying to break into Lynda's house.

His heart began pounding, as if he'd climbed that flight of stairs at the courthouse, and calling out, "Lizzie!" he reached for the phone.

He heard his wife stirring as he punched out 911. Just as the dispatcher answered, the perimeter of the house went up in flames, draping the walls like neon paint.

And he couldn't see the prowler any more.

By now, Lizzie was in the kitchen, and the dispatcher was waiting.

"It's a fire at 422 West Evan Street," Curtis blurted, and Lizzie looked quickly out the window and threw her hand over her mouth. "It's arson," he said. "I saw a prowler, and then it went up in flames."

"Oh, Curtis!" Lizzie shouted.

"It's okay," he said then to both the dispatcher and his wife. "Thank God nobody's home."

Lynda rested more soundly that night than she had since her plane crashed, tucked in her own bed on the second floor of her own home. The soft percale sheets on her queen-sized bed were a wonderful contrast to the hospital sheets, and as she snuggled down under her Laura Ashley comforter, she felt welcomed by the items around her she had grown to love: the antique furniture she had collected a piece at a time, the finely crafted vases with silk flower arrangements, the oriental rug on her hardwood floor, the small baskets of potpourri scattered around the room, and her favorite art hung in strategic places on her papered walls.

She had worked hard for these comforts, and as she slipped into the depths of sleep, she had a sweet contentment that all would be well.

But sometime just after midnight, a whining sound outside startled her. Disoriented, she sat up, looking around, hearing it more clearly. A siren ... no, two or three sirens, right here on her street. She scrambled out of bed, but the moment her feet touched the floor she felt the heat and caught the faint smell of smoke.

"Paige!" Grabbing the pillow from her bed and holding it to her face, she ran down the hall to the guest bedroom where mother and daughter slept. "Paige, get up! There's a fire!"

Paige sat up and rubbed her eyes. "What?"

"The house is on fire! Get Brianna!"

As though a light had come on in her brain, Paige grabbed the child and began to cough. The smoke was more dense on this side of the house; Lynda was choking on it as well. Grabbing another pillow and wrestling it out of its case, she tossed the case at Paige. "Here, cover Brianna's face with this!"

"The floor's hot!" Paige shouted, and Brianna started to cry.

"We've got to get out!" Lynda cried as Paige followed her into the hall.

Lynda reached the top of the stairs in a half-dozen frantic strides then immediately jumped back; long, reaching flames were climbing the carpeted stairs and lapping against the wall. "We'll have to go out the window!" she shouted, pushing them toward the other end of the second floor. "Hurry, before the floor collapses!"

Two of the windows they passed were engulfed in flames from the outside, but at the far end of the house, the flames hadn't yet taken hold. Lynda threw open the window. "Climb out there on the roof. Hurry!"

Brianna's screams went up two octaves as she saw the flames licking their way up the side of the house. But holding her tightly, with the pillowcase pressed over the child's face, Paige climbed out and ran to the edge of the roof. Lynda followed her, ignoring the pain shooting through her ribs, pulling at her stitches, but she couldn't fight the dizziness beginning to take hold.

"How will we get down?" Paige screamed.

Only then did Lynda see the flashing lights of three fire trucks in front of her house. Someone shouted, "There's someone on the roof!"

In seconds, a ladder had been elevated to lift them down, out of the grasping hands of the flames.

They hadn't even reached the ground when the roof they'd been standing on caved in.

And so did Lynda. Covering her face in horror, she got off of the ladder and slid down to sit in the dirt, watching through her fingers as her house and everything she owned surrendered to the fire.

Brianna's wailing only echoed what was in Lynda's own heart as paramedics rushed to examine them. Lynda was just too tired and too stunned to express it herself.

"I'm so sorry, Lynda," a voice said above her as the paramedics put her on oxygen. She looked up into the troubled eyes of Curtis McMillan from across the street, who stood over her in his slippers and robe. "I didn't know you were home! I thought you were still in the hospital—I should have checked. I should have called."

She pulled the oxygen mask away from her face. "What are you talking about?"

"I woke up around midnight and happened to look out the window. I saw him start the fire, so I called the police, but I told them you weren't in there. I didn't know—"

"Wait a minute," she said. "You saw someone start the fire?"

"Yes," he said. "I thought it was a prowler at first. He was sneaking around your house, and the minute I had 911 on the phone, I saw him light it. The house went up in flames, but I didn't even check to see if you were in there."

"Did he go *into* the house, Judge?" she asked in a shocked whisper.

"I didn't see it if he did. But he must have doused it with gas because the fire caught instantly and circled the house—"

The paramedics were checking her vitals, prodding under her clothes, checking her incisions and her ribs. Impatiently, she shoved them away and got to her feet. "Judge, did you see his face? The color of his hair?"

The old man shook his head with distraught frustration. "He was more or less just a shadow. I only saw him for a second."

Smoke fell like a cloud around them as the flames devoured her house. Waving it away so she could breathe, she grabbed the old judge's arm. "I have to talk to the police," she told the frustrated paramedics. "I'm fine, really. Just let me go."

"But you probably need to go to the hospital! You need to be examined at least!" one of them said.

"In a minute," she said.

Lynda pulled the judge toward one of the trucks to find someone in authority. But as she did, she saw a car approaching, and Tony Danks and Larry Millsaps got out.

Still pulling the judge behind her, she met them at the car. "It was *arson!*" she blurted before they could even get out. "This is Judge Curtis McMillan, my neighbor. He saw the man who did it."

Larry shook the man's hand then somberly studied the house. "Thank God you got out."

"Only because he called." Lynda's face glowed with the orange reflection of the inferno as she gazed back at it. "He called 911. The sirens woke me up." Turning back to Larry, she said, "It's official now. Someone's trying to kill me."

Larry opened his arms and she collapsed against him, crying out her rage and terror as everything she loved burned down behind her.

CHAPTER TWENTY-FIVE

So what's next?" Lynda's voice was weary as she looked across Curtis's kitchen table to the two detectives who had spent the last hour questioning the old couple.

"We follow up on the leads we've got until we apprehend the right person," Tony said.

"You don't *have* any leads," she said in a hoarse voice. "You don't really have a clue who he is, do you?"

Larry leaned forward on the table, meeting her eyes directly. "Here's what we know, Lynda. It's probably a man, between five feet eight and five feet ten, around 180 pounds. We know that he has at least a working knowledge of airplanes—"

"And we have the gas can he used with the name of an auto repair shop on it, even though he didn't leave any fingerprints."

"And you know he wants me dead."

"Yes," Tony admitted. "That does seem to be his goal. Now all we have to do is find someone with a motive. We still need your help for that."

But Lynda couldn't help. Wearily, she got up and went to the same window through which Curtis had seen her house catch fire, and she peered at the smoldering pile of rubble that had once been such a source of pride. Next to the pile the garage still stood, unscathed except for the black scars from the fire that had just begun to penetrate the structure when the fire trucks arrived. Lizzie, who had been tending to a fresh pot of coffee, slid her arm around Lynda. "It'll be all right, honey. These young men aren't going to let anything happen to you."

Lynda didn't respond. Instead, she ambled into the living room where Paige and Brianna sat in a rocking chair. Brianna was asleep, and Paige's smoke-stained face looked numb with shock as she leaned her chin against her daughter's head and stared blankly in front of her.

"Well, I guess the thing to do now is figure out where we're going to go," Lynda said. "At least our cars survived."

"I was just thinking how glad I am that *we* did," Paige whispered, bringing her dull eyes back to Lynda's.

Lynda shook her head, feeling gently—and, she was sure, unintentionally—reproved. What were her lost treasures compared to her life? And Brianna's? "You're right. Once again for some reason, God spared us."

Lizzie squeezed Lynda's shoulder again. "Honey, I've already made up the guest rooms for you. You're going to stay here tonight, all three of you."

"No, Lizzie. That's sweet of you, but I can't do that."

"Why not?"

Her face reddened, and she hugged herself as a shiver ran through her. "Someone's trying to kill me," she said. "I'm not safe. And if I'm in your house, *you're* not safe. I shouldn't even be here now."

Lizzie's eyes drifted to her husband's. Curtis took the baton. "Lynda, don't you think you're safe enough tonight? I mean, he wouldn't dare come back, and besides, how would he know you were here?"

"It's okay," she said, waving off the questions. "I've got an idea. I still have my father's house on the other side of town. I've been trying to sell it, but I'll just have to live there until I can rebuild. It should be safe. Only a few people even know I have that house. If I don't tell anyone where I am ..." She met Paige's eyes, and saw the despair on her face, the indecision. "Paige, I know you won't want to come with me, but I can give you some money so you can get by until he's caught. You could stay here or get a hotel—"

As if she'd spent the last hour holding them back with a paper-thin wall of resolve, Paige's eyes filled with tears. "Maybe I should just take my chances and go home."

"No," Lynda insisted. "You can't. Paige, we've come this far. Don't let this make you drop your guard."

Paige pinched the bridge of her nose and tried to steady her voice. "I can't keep taking your money, Lynda. I've got to start handling things myself."

"Not until after we go to court, you don't." Lynda stooped in front of her, making Paige meet her eyes. "I know this was traumatic tonight, but don't give up just because some lunatic is out to get me. That has nothing to do with you."

Larry, who had been jotting notes on a pad, looked up at Paige. "What do you mean, take your chances? What's the risk in going home?"

"My ex-husband." Paige swallowed, and a tear dropped from her cheek onto the top of Brianna's head. "He's abusive, and he's suing me for custody of Brianna. Lynda's representing me."

"She's not safe at home," Lynda cut in. "Despite our restraining order, he's tried to take Brianna, and he's broken into her house. That's why she's staying with me."

"I see." Frowning, he got up and paced across the kitchen. "And you don't have anyone else you can stay with?"

Paige shook her head. "My family is in Arizona. But the judge ordered me to stay in town until this court thing is settled."

Tony frowned and stared thoughtfully at Paige, as though flipping through possibilities in his mind. But it was Larry who had the solution. "Listen, Lynda, what if I guaranteed that we'll have someone guarding your father's house, at least for the next couple of days? That way Paige and Brianna could go with you, and you could feel safe. If it isn't common knowledge that you have that house, chances are you'd be okay there anyway."

Lynda was skeptical. "Larry, I know how the police department works. They're not going to waste a man guarding me twenty-four hours a day."

"I'll take care of it," Larry promised. "Even if Tony and I have to take turns on our off-hours, I know I can at least get them to agree to somebody the rest of the time."

Lynda glanced at Tony, who was gaping at Larry, but Larry ignored him. "You both need protecting. You might as well be in the same place so we can kill two birds with one stone."

Lynda smirked. "Somehow that cliché isn't very comforting to me right now."

"Sorry," Larry smiled. "So what do you say?"

Lynda turned her worried eyes back to Paige. "Paige, this is up to you. I can't ask you to put your life and your daughter's life in jeopardy to stay with me."

The turmoil on Paige's face told Lynda what a struggle this was. Then Paige wiped her eyes and settled her troubled gaze on Lynda. "Who'll take care of you if I'm not there? I promised. You just got out of the hospital. The doctor said—"

"Paige, I'll be fine. For heaven's sake, I just scaled the roof and got out of a burning house. I can take care of myself. I've done it for a long time."

Paige dropped her head back on the chair. "This nightmare just keeps getting worse."

They waited for her decision, not prodding her, and finally, she took a deep breath and tried to steady her voice. "I guess we'll stay in a hotel. But … I swear I'll pay you back someday, Lynda. I know it's hard to believe, but—"

"It's not hard to believe, Paige. But I don't care about the money right now. That's not important."

"I feel like I'm letting you down or taking advantage of you, and you've been so nice to me."

Stooping down in front of the rocking chair, Lynda stroked Brianna's sleeping head. "You aren't letting me down, Paige," she said softly. "You're protecting your daughter. I think you've made the right decision. And when they catch this guy, you can stay with me again."

Paige turned her worried face to Tony and Larry. "Do you promise you'll guard her? You won't let anything happen to her?"

"I promise," Larry said. "And we'll take you to the motel tonight to make sure you get there safely."

Tony didn't look too happy about all the promises Larry was making on his behalf, but he didn't argue.

Lynda's father's house sat at the end of a dead-end street; a thickly wooded area separated it from the other two houses back up the road. Looking out the living room window, Lynda realized that she'd never thought of her parents' house in terms of safety before. She had only seen it as too small, too old, too mundane for an up-and-coming young lawyer.

The furniture was worn and faded, hopelessly outdated. From the rickety rocker in the corner to the recliner that had provided the only comfort her father had been able to find in his last days, she had been ashamed of it all.

Now it was all she had.

And coming here from a position of vulnerability and fear, she found some comfort in that it was so secluded and so familiar.

Larry touched her shoulder, and she jumped. "Sorry," she said, embarrassed. "I guess I'm a little jumpy."

"Can't say I blame you." Stepping closer to the window, he peered out. "Well, one thing's for sure. No cars will be coming here by accident. If anyone comes this far up the street, they're looking for something."

Lynda glanced across the street; in the moonlight, she saw only one edge of the empty car backed into the wooded lot where Larry would be spending the rest of the night.

Turning away from the window, she looked back over the stale-smelling house she hadn't walked into in weeks. "It's pretty dusty in here. No wonder it hasn't sold."

Larry looked around. "It's homey. I like it."

"I used to hate it," she said pensively. "I couldn't wait to get away from here. My folks turned the garage into a little apartment for me when I started college since we couldn't afford for me to live on campus. It was a little more freedom, but I still felt so trapped here."

For a moment, she let melancholy creep in as she surveyed the living room where her parents used to spend so much time—her mother crocheting, her father reading the paper and watching "Jeopardy" at the same time, each occasionally blurting out an answer that often was right. The standing joke around the house was that someday her father's ship would come in by way of a stint on "Jeopardy," where he was certain to win. But he'd never made it.

Shaking off her thoughts, she sank wearily onto the gold-and-green plaid couch.

"Where's the linen closet?" Larry asked.

She gave him a questioning look. "At the end of the hall. Why?"

"I'm going to make a bed up for you," he said. "I don't think you want to sleep on a bare mattress."

"No, I can do it," she said, getting up. "Really."

"Sit down," he ordered gently. "I've had broken ribs before. And you're not in any shape to be up at this hour, much less dressing beds. Now, which bedroom do you want?"

She looked toward the hall for a moment, trying to decide. "The guest room. I don't think I can sleep in my father's room yet."

"How long has he been ...?" The word fell off, and Lynda took a deep breath.

"Just three months."

"I'm sorry," Larry said. "Looks like a run of bad times for you."

"It could be worse," she whispered. "I thought it was bad luck that I hadn't sold this house, but now I see that God was saving it for me."

"No subtlety there, huh?"

Remembering what Mike had told her about Larry being a believer, she smiled as he left the room, and she heard him in the guest room, shaking out sheets and blankets, stepping around the bed. Was changing beds a part of his job description?

After a few minutes, he came out. "All done. You get some sleep now, and I'll be right out there in my car. No one's gonna get past me, so just relax. And tomorrow, I'll take you to the doctor to get checked out, just to make sure you didn't hurt yourself getting out of the house."

"I'm fine," she assured him, "but I need to go by the hospital anyway. I need to visit Jake."

"Then you can do both." He picked up the cellular phone he'd made her bring in from her car. "Now since you don't have a phone hooked up here, use this if you need to call anyone. I've got one in my car, too, and I've punched my number in here already. If you need me, all you have to do is punch the memory button and the number 1."

"Okay," she said, taking the phone. "Thanks."

He looked reluctant to leave her, and she knew it was because she looked so fragile. Lifting her chin and trying to look a little tougher, she said, "You don't have to worry about me, Larry. I'm really fine."

He sat down across from her, fixing his soft, green eyes on her. "You know, Lynda, you've survived two really narrow brushes with death in the last few days. You've seen two pretty obvious miracles, so maybe we'll get a couple more to help you out."

Lynda sighed. "I'm starting to wonder."

"About what?"

She swallowed, knowing that the thoughts raging through her mind bordered on blasphemy. "I just ... sometimes wonder if God's really working in this. I mean ... it's just all so bizarre. Why is he letting this person do these things to me? Is he trying to teach me something, or is he just turning his head, or is it Satan?"

"I personally don't like to attribute a whole lot to Satan," Larry said. "I believe God is in control. And he's working on this. I can tell."

She got up, trying not to cry, and turned her back to him. "Then why doesn't he just strike this person dead and keep him from terrorizing me anymore?"

"Because God doesn't work that way," Larry said. "If he did, Tony and I would be out of a job."

Lynda tried to laugh, but it didn't come easily. Taking a deep breath, she turned back around. "Thank you for watching over me, Larry. I feel better knowing you're out there."

"No problem," he said, getting up. "Call if you need me."

Lynda could only nod mutely as he went out the door and locked her in.

Across town, in a hotel room that was nicer—because Lynda had insisted on it—than the cheap motel Paige had stayed in just days before, Paige lay next to her sleeping daughter and stared up at the ceiling.

She heard the elevator ring, and her stomach tightened as she listened to the doors open and the footsteps in the hallway and then a door opening halfway down the hall. Relieved, she let out her breath.

Too many noises, she thought. Too many strange people around her. Too many reasons to be afraid.

She got up, went to the window, and peeked out between the crack in the curtains. Down in the parking lot, a trucker with a cigarette in his mouth walked around his eighteen wheeler, a huge rig that took up the whole back edge of the lot.

Everyone was suspect. Anyone could have set that fire. Anyone could have almost killed her and Lynda and Brianna tonight.

It was ironic that she had been staying with Lynda only to get out of danger in the first place.

Helpless, she dropped down onto the bed and closed her eyes against the tears assaulting her. How was she ever going to find peace in her life again? Would she spend the rest of her life running with Brianna, relying on the kindness of others? Even if she proved that Keith's allegations about her being an unfit mother were a lie and was allowed to keep custody of Brianna, wouldn't she still have to fear him for the rest of her life? Wouldn't he be able to track her down wherever she went?

Seeking comfort, she mouthed a clichéd prayer that she feared fell on deaf ears. "God, if you're listening—please help us."

Brianna jerked, and her face twisted in her sleep. As she muttered something incoherent, Paige began stroking her daughter's forehead. Was she dreaming about fire? Or about her father? Or was it some new nightmare, the next one, that her little mind was working through?

"It isn't fair," Paige whispered, not certain if she still addressed God or the black space around her. "She's too little to fear for her life. She's just a baby."

Brianna rolled over, found her mother, and snuggled in next to her.

And as Paige held her closely, that powerful maternal love that could fix boo-boos and scare away monsters washed over her, and she knew that whatever happened—whatever she had to do—she would protect her daughter.

CHAPTER TWENTY-SIX

S till flat on his back, Jake stared mindlessly at the television screen as Harry Smith interviewed someone in Washington about a bill being debated in the Senate. It didn't affect him, he thought, touching the bandage on his eye that had been changed this morning. Nothing affected him any more—he didn't have a job or a home or a life. He might as well not even exist for all the hope he had.

CBS broke for a commercial. After a detergent ad, the local news came on for an update. He reached for the remote control to change the channel as the anchor told about a fire in the exclusive Willow Heights area last night.

"Police suspect arson. The home belonged to local attorney Lynda Barrett, who—"

Jake dropped the remote control and tried to raise himself up. Dizziness assaulted him, and he dropped back down, straining to listen.

"—was involved in the plane crash at St. Clair Airport earlier this week. Sources told Channel 16 News that there is evidence that the crash was the result of foul play, and that this may have been a second attempt on Barrett's life. Barrett and two houseguests escaped the fire, but we have no word yet on whether they sustained any injuries."

Amazed, Jake groped for the buzzer to ring for his nurse. In moments, she was in the doorway. "What is it, Jake?

"Do you have Lynda's number?" he asked.

"No, but I can look it up."

"You can't look it up!" he threw back. "Her house burnt down last night! Do you have her number at work?"

"Her house burnt down? Are you sure?"

"I saw it on the news," he said, breathing hard. "Was she—was she brought in here last night?"

"Well … I don't know. I can go check." She walked further into the room and peered at the television screen. "Do you think somebody's really trying to kill her?"

"Without a doubt," Jake said. "Just—get me a phone book. And a phone that works. I'll pay for the one I broke. And see if anybody knows anything."

The nurse hurried in, pulled the phone book from the drawer in Jake's table, and handed it to him. "Who are you calling?"

"Her office. Maybe her secretary can tell me where she is."

"I'll go see if she's checked in here," she said, scurrying out of the room.

CHAPTER TWENTY-SEVEN

Curtis McMillan sat at his kitchen window, looking across at the neighbors clustering in Lynda's yard, marveling at how thoroughly, and how quickly, the fire had destroyed her home. He had watched all morning, trying to remember exactly what he'd seen, so that some detail that could help the police might come back to him. But there were no details. It had been too dark and had happened too fast.

He saw a car drive by, slow down in front of the skeleton of the house, then pull over on the side of the road. Curtis wondered if he was another reporter—there had been so many around early this morning. But as he got out, he saw that he didn't carry a camera or a notepad, and for a moment, he just stood and looked at the structure, as if stricken by what had happened. Then, slowly, he headed toward one of the clusters of neighbors.

"You should come away from that window, Curtis," Lizzie said. "You're getting obsessed with it."

Curtis glanced back at her over his shoulder. She was knitting—something for Brianna, he suspected. She had really taken to that little girl last night.

"It's not obsession, Lizzie," he said. "It's just that I don't remember when there's been this much excitement around here. People coming and going ... Investigators, fire inspectors, reporters ..."

His eyes strayed out the window again, and he saw that the man was questioning the neighbors, and one of them was pointing toward the McMillan's house. Was he asking who had reported the fire? Or something about Lynda?

The man started to cross the street toward his house, and Curtis stood up. Something about his walk looked familiar ... and he was the right size ... but he couldn't swear it wasn't just his imagination groping for the culprit, trying to make up for what he hadn't seen last night. But in all his years on the bench, he'd had many cases where the perpetrator of a crime had been caught returning to the scene. Could this be ...?

The doorbell rang, and Lizzie jumped up. "I'll get it. Probably another reporter."

But Curtis didn't think so. He went to stand behind her, and she opened the door slightly. "Yes?"

The man flashed a smile that made Curtis uncomfortable. "Excuse me, but I'm John Hampton, a close friend and coworker of Paige Varner, the woman who was staying with Lynda Barrett. I saw her and her daughter on the news this morning—that they were in the fire. I wanted to check on them, and one of the neighbors told me you might know where I could reach them."

Lizzie stiffened and started to close the door. "I'm sorry. I don't know where they are."

"Well, you must have heard them discussing it last night. Didn't they mention anybody they could stay with?"

Lizzie stepped aside, and Curtis came to the door. "Paige and Brianna are fine," he said. "No one was hurt."

"Well—are they still with Lynda?"

"I wouldn't know," he said. "Who did you say you are?"

"John Hampton, sir." He reached out and shook the old man's hand. "Don't you know where either of them is?"

"I'm afraid I can't help you." Curtis started to close the door, and the man backed away.

"All right," he said. "Well—thanks, anyway."

He backed down the steps, but Lizzie and Curtis kept staring at him through the narrowing opening in the door.

Lizzie closed it all the way and locked it. "Get the tag number, Lizzie," Curtis said as he headed for the phone.

Lizzie rushed to the window and squinting, whispered the numbers out loud as the man drove off down the street. Then, quickly, she scribbled them down. "Do you think he's the one you saw last night?"

"I can't say," Curtis told her, dialing the police station. "All I know is he's the right size. He could be the one. We'll just let the police decide."

Larry's eyes felt like sand by ten o'clock that morning, and he hoped his third cup of coffee would finally clear his fatigue. He poured it into the styrofoam cup, then went back to the table where Tony sat with their captain, going over the few things they did have on the Lynda Barrett case.

"I'll make sure she has a round-the-clock watch for at least a few days, but I can't do it indefinitely, guys. We just don't have enough manpower."

Larry pulled up a chair and sat down, rubbing his eyes. "Well, maybe he'll slip up soon."

The door opened, and one of the uniformed officers stuck his head in. "Call for you guys. It's Judge McMillan. Says he has a lead on the Barrett case."

Larry slid his chair back. "That's Curtis. He's our eyewitness," he told the captain. "I'll take it."

He closed the door behind him and went out to his desk. Picking up the phone, he said, "Millsaps, here. Whatcha got, Judge?"

"A man was just by here looking for Paige and Lynda," Curtis said. "He said his name is John Hampton, and he insisted that he had to know how to reach them. Now I may be jumping to conclusions, but I thought you—"

"You didn't tell him anything, did you?"

"No, of course not."

"John Hampton, huh?" Larry asked, jotting down the name. "Can you give me a description?"

"About five-eight, 180 pounds," Curtis said. "He may be just what he said he was, of course—a concerned friend—but one can never be sure. Lizzie got his license number just in case."

Larry sat back hard in his chair, smiling. "Tell her if I were there I'd kiss her. What's the number?" He wrote it down. "Thanks, Judge. If he comes back, you call me. Meanwhile, we'll find out who this sucker is, and if he's involved, you can bet we'll pick him up."

He hung up, tore off the page with the license number, and turned to the computer on his desk. "Lucy, go in there and get Tony," he said, punching the numbers onto the keyboard to start a search. "Tell him I may have something."

He waited a few seconds as the computer searched, and just as the license number surfaced, Tony reached Larry's desk.

"What is it?"

"A guy showed up at Judge McMillan's house, looking for Paige and Lynda. They got his tag number."

He watched as the information scrolled down the screen then finally stopped on a name. "Well, he lied about his name. That's a bad sign."

"Who is it?" Tony asked, leaning on the desk.

"Says the car belongs to Keith A. Varner."

"Varner. Isn't that Paige's name?"

"Yep." Punching a command on the keyboard, Larry started a cross-search for any information he could find on the man. "That's her exhusband, all right. We show a restraining order against him."

"But that doesn't make sense," Tony said. "Paige wasn't anywhere near that plane. And last night their daughter was with her. Would he deliberately burn down a house with his child in it?"

"He would if he's a nut case." Larry pressed the button for a printout, then tore it out of his printer. "Happens all the time. I say we pick him up."

"For what?" Tony asked.

"For questioning. We can't prove he was there when the house burned, but we can at least find out where he was and why he's looking for Paige when he's not supposed to go near her."

"All right," Tony said. "Let's go."

K eith Varner wasn't used to being told what to do, and when Larry and Tony found him sleeping in his apartment and insisted that he come with them for questioning, he hadn't taken it well. Now he sat in the interrogation room waiting for his lawyer, trying to be a little more cooperative since he was beginning to see that he had no choice.

"I was looking for my little girl," Keith told Larry. "There's no law against that, is there?"

"No, but there's a law against arson, pal."

"I told you I was at work last night. Ask anybody."

"We did. We found out that you work alone on the bank's computer system. You're not that closely supervised. You could have left at any time and come back."

Keith dropped his face helplessly into his palm. "What would you guys do? You're sitting at home watching the news on television; you hear about some fire, and all of a sudden you see your only child right in the middle of the whole thing." He looked up at them. "I freaked, okay? I didn't care about that stupid restraining order. I just cared that my Brianna was okay. And I *still* haven't found out if she is."

"She's fine," Larry said. "And your concern is moving, especially considering that her mother feels the need to hide from you to protect that same child."

"Give me a break!" Keith shouted, slapping the table and springing to his feet. "It's the oldest trick in the book. There's probably a restraining order and an abuse accusation for every custody case that's brought to court. You guys have been around. You know how things work!"

Tony glanced at the notes he'd found in Paige's and Keith's files. "Says here that Paige called just the other day because you had broken into her home. She also alleged that you tried to take the child from her school."

Keith sat back down and leaned forward, fixing his eyes on theirs as if they could understand. "I just had to know she was okay. I wanted to see her, make sure she was clean, didn't have any bruises, that sort of thing. Paige may come across as a sweet, mousy little thing, but she can be violent when you cross her, and she tends to be real selfish. She's neglected my daughter before. And if I broke into her house, why didn't I get arrested?"

Neither Larry nor Tony made any response.

"It's her word against mine. You won't show one violation of that restraining order against me. Look in the file. Do you see one?"

"That just means the police department didn't catch you in the act."

He leaned his elbows on the table. "As I recall, you're innocent until proven guilty. I'm telling you, boys, this is a war. She'll stop at nothing to keep me from getting custody, so she's going around staging crises to make her look like the victim. She deserves an Oscar."

The door burst open, and Keith's lawyer, a spit-and-polish yuppie who'd been too successful for his own—or anyone else's—good, rushed into the room. "What's going on here, gentlemen?"

Larry shot Tony a look that said the production was about to begin. He'd never liked Steve McRae, first because he was a smart aleck who thought he had all the answers and expected everyone else to acknowledge it, and second, because he'd gotten too many criminals off on technicalities, after the police department had spent hours of legwork making an arrest. With a bored, markedly unimpressed expression, Larry muttered, "We were just questioning your client about his whereabouts last night."

"They think I torched the lawyer's house," Keith said, like a kid telling his mommy of all the wrongs done against him. "Can you believe that? I wouldn't be surprised if Paige gave them the idea herself. Great strategy. Make me out to be the culprit, and it'll still be in the judge's head by the time we have the hearing."

McRae set his briefcase down on the desk but didn't sit. "Is my client under arrest?"

Larry glanced at Tony, knowing there wasn't cause. His restraining order didn't prohibit him from going to the site of a burned-down house, and as far as they could document, he hadn't gone near Paige or Brianna. At least not today. "Not at this time, no."

"Then I'd suggest you release him immediately, gentlemen."

"We could get a warrant. Search his house. Lock him up."

"Not without evidence," his attorney said. "And unless I've read the report wrong, the only evidence you have is that he asked one of the neighbors where his daughter is. Am I missing something?"

Larry rolled his eyes and breathed a heavy sigh.

"He fits the description of the arsonist," Tony said. "We have a witness, you know."

"No way," Keith said.

All eyes in the room turned back to him. "What's that?" Larry asked.

What Larry had at first thought was fear instantly became indignation. "I said, *no way*. Did someone tell you they saw *me* there last night? Could they pick me out in a lineup? Could they describe what I was wearing?"

Neither of the cops answered, and after a moment, McRae began to chuckle. "You know, if you guys would stop wasting time bringing in innocent fathers, you might get a little police work done. Now, if you're finished with him ... "

Tony swept his hand in a be-my-guest gesture, indicating that Keith was free to go. Keith got up and with a mocking grin, extended his hand to Larry for a facetious handshake. Larry made no move to take his hand. "It's been fun, guys."

"Hasn't it, though?" Larry muttered.

Keith headed for the door. Still within hearing range of the two cops, he said, "If somebody's really trying to kill that woman, and Paige is still staying with her, that means she's putting my daughter into direct, unnecessary danger. Isn't there something I can do about that before this guy tries again?"

"There sure is," McRae told him. "We'll go back to my office now and put our heads together."

Larry waited until the men were gone, then glanced back at Tony. "I think he's lying."

Tony shook his head. "I don't see it, Larry. He could just be a father who cares about his little girl."

"His wife is hiding from him. Doesn't that tell you something?"

"It tells me that both their stories are convincing, and either one could be a lie. When custody of a child is involved, sometimes the parents take desperate measures. You know that."

"Sometimes they will," Larry agreed. "Even to the point of killing her lawyer?"

"Why her lawyer?" Tony asked. "Why not Paige herself?"

"He almost did, last night."

"Well, the crash had nothing to do with Paige. Your theory is kind of scattering all over the place, Larry. I say we get back to the facts. Stick to what we know for sure."

"All we know for sure," Larry said, "is that there was a crash and a fire, and Lynda almost died in both of them. And that if we don't do something soon, chances are, there's going to be another attempt."

"Then let's get out there and find the guy," Tony said.

CHAPTER TWENTY-NINE

The physical strain of the night before had taken its toll on Lynda as had the stark loneliness. Outside, a policeman whom she hadn't met guarded her house in Larry's place. Fighting soreness and fatigue, she got up and went to the washer to drop in the pajamas she had worn here last night, the only clothes she had escaped with. Today, she wore an old T-shirt of her father's and a ragged pair of her old jeans that she'd found in one of the closets.

She wondered what Paige and Brianna were going to do for clothes. Mrs. McMillan had given Paige a housedress to wear last night, but it wasn't something Paige would want to be seen wearing in public. And Brianna had nothing but the big T-shirt she'd worn to bed last night for pajamas.

Larry had left a note under Lynda's door before he'd left that morning with the phone number and room number of the hotel where Paige was staying. Now Lynda dialed the hotel, hoping she'd catch Paige there.

"Hello?" Paige's voice was soft, tentative.

"Paige? It's just me."

"Lynda!" she said, breathing more freely. "How are you feeling?"

"A little tired and a little sore. But very much alive."

"Yeah, me, too. I keep trying to be thankful."

"I was thinking," Lynda said. "We all need clothes. Do you think it would be too much trouble for you to take my credit card this afternoon and buy us all something to wear?"

"I'll be glad to go shop for you, but we're fine," Paige said. "Really. We don't need anything—"

"Come on, Paige," Lynda insisted. "Everything was burned. You can't wear the same thing every day for the rest of your life."

"But it isn't your responsibility to pay for replacements. I can go to the Salvation Army or something."

Lynda moved her phone to the other ear, as if that would help her make her point more clearly. "My house was insured, Paige. I'll get compensated for it. Please. I want you to buy enough clothes for several days for both of you. Socks, underwear, shoes, clothes—everything."

Paige still wouldn't budge. "I still have some things at my own house."

"Not enough. Admit it, Paige. Most of your clothes were at my house."

Paige hesitated. "Okay. I guess they were."

"Come on. Let me do this. Help me assuage some of this guilt."

"Guilt? What do you have to feel guilt for?"

"Everything," she insisted. "Don't make me recite the list. Just buy some clothes."

"All right," Paige said with a chuckle. "Maybe just a few things."

Lynda smiled weakly. "Good."

"So what time are you due for your doctor's appointment?"

"Three o'clock," Lynda said. "They said Larry or Tony will take me." She breathed a soft, sad laugh. "Isn't this amazing? I'm practically trapped here in this house that I've been trying desperately to get rid of and can't go anywhere without police protection." Her voice broke off, and tears filled her eyes. Her voice betrayed her despair as she whispered, "Who would have ever thought I'd be in this position?"

"It's gonna be okay," Paige said, too quickly and without conviction.

And as Lynda surrendered to the emotions she'd been storing up, she realized how ironic it was that this woman whom she had vowed to comfort and protect was now comforting her instead.

An hour later from the offices of Schilling, Martin, and Barrett, Sally Crawford dialed the number of Lynda's cellular phone.

"Hello?"

"You're not going to believe this," Sally blurted. "Are you ready?"

Lynda hesitated, and Sally realized with a tinge of guilt that Lynda couldn't take many more surprises. "What is it?" she asked in a hoarse, hollow voice.

"Keith Varner just filed a motion with the court to get temporary custody of Brianna pending the hearing"

"What? That's ludicrous! He's wasting his time."

"I don't know," Sally said. "He's basing it on the fire last night, Lynda. He saw Brianna and Paige on the television coverage, and now he's saying that Paige has put Brianna in jeopardy."

"You've got to be kidding."

Sally wagged her head, as though Lynda could see her. "The hearing's tomorrow. If you're not up to meeting him in court, maybe Bill or Andy can fill in."

"No," she said quickly. "I'll be there."

"Are you sure, Lynda?"

"Dead sure," she said. "Call me back if you need me. I'm keeping the cellular close by."

"Are you sure you don't want to tell me where you are, Lynda? I could do some shopping for you, or whatever. You know you can trust me."

"Of course I do. But knowing could put you in danger," Lynda told her. "It's best if no one knows. Besides, I'm not sure the office phone isn't bugged. If you need to give me something, I'll meet you somewhere. And be careful, okay? This lunatic might follow anyone who knows me, hoping they'll lead him to me. I don't want you getting caught in the crossfire."

"Reassuring thought," Sally said. "Maybe I need to get a gun. So have there been any leads yet?"

"None that I know of." She paused. "Sally, you're the one who has to deal with the tempers of all the irate clients. Have there been any angry enough to kill me?"

"Not even close. Most of your clients are pretty happy."

"Well, one of them isn't. Would you do me a favor and pull up a list of all the cases I lost in the past—say, three years? Or even cases I may have won but didn't win big. You know, low awards, that sort of thing."

"Will do," Sally said. "I'll call you as soon as I get it. Hey, Lynda, take it easy, okay? You sound really tired."

"What can I say? It's been a rough week."

"Are you sure you're all right?"

"Well, I'm safe. I'm being guarded twenty-four hours a day, at least for a while."

Sally heard a doorbell ring on Lynda's end.

"Sally, I've got to go. Somebody's here."

The phone clicked, and Sally hung up, hoping that whoever stood at Lynda's door wasn't bringing more trouble.

Lynda saw Larry Millsaps through the peephole in the front door and let him in. "I thought it must be you. I'm almost ready to go."

"No hurry." Larry came in and closed the door behind him.

"Sorry about the outfit," she said, slipping on a pair of sandals. "I found these shoes in my old closet. They must be ten years old. And the clothes are my father's. All I had when I got here were the pajamas I was wearing."

"You look fine. Uh—before we go ... can I talk to you for a minute?"

Lynda stopped what she was doing and braced herself. "Sure. What is it, Larry?"

He looked dead tired, and Lynda realized he hadn't slept all night. "I thought you should know that Keith Varner was caught hanging around your house today, asking questions about where Paige and Brianna are. Apparently, he saw them both on the news."

"Oh, no."

"Judge McMillan called and reported it, and we picked Keith up for questioning. We had to consider the possibility that he could have set the fire."

"Keith? But that still wouldn't explain the crash—Paige wasn't anywhere near it," Lynda said quickly. "And besides, why would he try to kill his own daughter?"

"Good question," Larry said. "One that probably lets him off the hook. His answers were reasonable when we got right down to it."

"You let him go, didn't you?"

"Had to. That hotshot lawyer of his rode in on his white horse, and we didn't really have any evidence against him. And it's possible that he *was* just trying to make sure his kid was all right."

"You didn't tell him where they are."

"No, of course not. We didn't give him a clue."

Lynda pulled out a chair and slowly fell into it. "He's assuming she's still with me."

"How do you know?"

"Because I was just on the phone with Sally, and she told me that his lawyer has filed a motion for a temporary hearing to get custody of Brianna pending the final hearing. He thinks she's in danger."

Larry plopped into a chair and rubbed the stubbled jaw that was in desperate need of a shave. "I thought this might happen. He was already talking about it when he left."

"He won't get her," Lynda assured him. "I'll be there myself. I have all of Paige's medical records already, showing fractures and injuries that he caused. Oh, if only formal charges could have been filed against him for violating his restraining order, so I'd have something concrete to mention in court."

"Sorry. So far, all he's guilty of is looking for his daughter. We can't arrest him for that. Chances are that's all he's done."

Lynda shook her head. "Except beat and terrorize his wife. I don't know how much more Paige can take." Lynda took a deep breath and tried to think like a lawyer. "Part of this is probably his attempt to draw her out or make me tell in court where she is. If he accuses her of putting Brianna in danger by staying with me, then he thinks I have to tell him where she is to prove she's not. But it won't work. I know every judge in this town. If I tell them she's not staying with me, they'll believe me."

"Problem is, McRae knows them, too." Larry gestured to the phone. "You want to call Paige and break the news before we go? I can talk to her if she has any questions."

"She's not there," Lynda said glumly. "I asked her to do a little shopping for us. I'll take the phone with me. She's supposed to call when she gets back to the room."

CHAPTER THIRTY

J ake had tried all day long to reach Lynda or find out how she was, but the people at her office had been deliberately vague. Though he could understand their caution, he had been desperate for information.

Now she stood before him, keeping her promise to visit him even though she was on the tail end of her second trauma in a week—a fact that moved him more than he cared to admit. She looked pale and bruised and weak, but she was, nevertheless, one of the most beautiful sights he'd ever seen.

But it wouldn't do to tell her that, so he hid his feelings behind flippancy. "You look worse than I do," he said.

"Thanks." She walked closer to the bed and leaned on the rail to look down at him.

"Sit down, Lynda," he said quietly. "You don't need to stand for my benefit. I can see you fine if you sit."

Acquiescing, she pulled a chair across the floor and sat down. Her eyes were tired and dejected, and he longed to see in them the fiery spirit he had grown accustomed to.

Without thinking, he reached out and took her hand. Closing her eyes, she brought his hand to her face and squeezed it. For an instant, it made him feel needed, as if his existence gave her strength, as if he had some purpose other than lying flat in this bed. "You're in trouble, Lynda," he whispered.

"Tell me about it."

He could see from her eyes that she wasn't taking this lightly. "What did the doctor say?"

"He said not to do any more leaping from two-story buildings for a while."

"I'm serious."

She smiled. "I'm okay. Just tired and sore. He told me to get plenty of rest and try not to exert myself."

"So, what are you doing in here?"

She closed her other hand over his and looked down at it. "Visiting a friend."

He wanted to tell her how much he appreciated it, how it changed his day, but something inside him kept him from saying it.

"Have they found out who did this? Do they have any promising leads?"

"They're working hard on it," she said. "I guess I can't complain."

"But it could happen again. Are they protecting you?"

"Yes," she said. "Twenty-four hours a day. Larry's right outside."

As if to take the focus off her, she stood and leaned on his bed rail again. "So how are *you* doing?"

"Not so good today," he said. "I've had visions of you wasting away somewhere from smoke inhalation or living in some homeless shelter or making yourself an open target for some insane sniper."

He could see that his concern pleased her. "I should have called," she said. "I guess I didn't realize it was all over the news."

He grinned. "That's okay. My phone was kind of broken anyway, remember? They replaced it today."

She laughed softly, and he joined her as his eyes swept over her. It felt good having her so close, and he wondered if it were Lynda Barrett he was growing attached to or just the idea of having anyone he could touch.

To be honest, he really couldn't say.

"So how was physical therapy today?" she asked.

"Oh, peachy," he said. "My therapists are a laugh a minute. We're still working on getting me upright."

"You have to start somewhere, Jake."

He breathed a laugh. "What's the point?"

She thought about that for a second. "Don't you want to sit up?"

He shrugged. "I'm just trying to be realistic. It's such a simple thing, but when I try it, my system goes haywire." He fixed his eyes on the ceiling. "I'm trying to accept. That's what the shrink told me to do."

"You're not being realistic *or* accepting," she argued gently. "Realistically, you've got your whole life ahead of you. All you can do is work with what you have and make it the best it can be. And pray. Hard. I've been praying for you, Jake."

"No offense, Lynda, but if there is a God, it doesn't look like he's on your side."

Instead of the fight he expected, she wilted. The defeated look that crossed her face startled him, and he hated himself for putting it there. Lowering herself back into her chair, she said, "Maybe you're right."

He frowned. "So you're backing down from your beliefs now?"

She shook her head, and he saw the tears reddening her eyes. "No," she said. "I'm not backing down. I guess I'm just confused. Is God really dealing with me through all this? Maybe it's just a really loud wake-up call."

She saw the emotion cross his face, and finally, he whispered, "I'm sorry, Lynda. I didn't mean to upset you. I was just trying to rile you—to see some of that famous Barrett passion in your face again."

She kept those haunted eyes on him for a moment, but finally, the humor in what he'd said seeped in, and a rueful grin returned to her face. "I'm still going to pray for you, Jake. I'm going to pray that you'll stop being a jerk."

He smiled.

"I'm also going to pray for your therapy," she said. "Maybe if you get more mobile, you'll have a better disposition."

"Don't waste your time praying for me," he said. "I've got this under control."

"Is that why you can't sit up?" she asked. "Is it better to keep telling yourself that you'll never walk?"

That question irritated him, but she didn't seem to care. He let go of her hand. "Do you think I *want* to lie here like this?"

"No, I don't," she said, standing up again. "So don't do it. Work hard and do what the therapists tell you, and stop thinking how this is the end of your life. Start thinking of it as a beginning."

"The beginning of *what?*"

"The beginning of your learning how to be a human being." When he gave her a surprised look, she went on. "You know, you weren't my idea of a terrific guy when you had functioning legs and a flawless face."

"So you think being paralyzed is going to build character?" he asked, growing angrier. "Hey, I didn't need to have my world ripped out from under me to know how to be a human being."

She looked regretful. Setting her elbow on his rail, she dropped her forehead into her palm. "I'm sorry, Jake. I need to learn how to keep my mouth shut. I really didn't come here to lambaste you." She slid her hand down her face and lifted her brows as she gazed at him over her fingertips. "I was really just trying to get that famous Stevens passion back in your eyes."

He didn't find that amusing, as she had. For a moment, he was quiet, focusing his eye on the ceiling to keep from meeting hers. When he spoke again, his voice was lower. "I'm not a charity case. I don't even know why you're here. Tell the truth," he said glumly. "They hired you to give me an aerobic workout, didn't they? You come in here, get my blood boiling, then leave. It's probably covered under my health insurance."

"Right," she said with a wink. "It's all a clever conspiracy. And they wanted to find a lawyer to get your blood boiling because we're so good at it."

He smiled now. "I thought so."

"Oh, I almost forgot," she said. "I went by your hotel on the way home yesterday and got all your stuff and paid your bill and checked you out. Luckily, your things were still in my trunk when the fire hit. The garage was all that was left standing. Larry Millsaps left the boxes at the nurse's station since I'm not supposed to carry anything heavy. They'll be bringing them in later. Maybe you'll feel better having your own things."

"I don't know," he said. "I was getting kind of attached to these air-conditioned gowns." He smiled and squeezed her hand. "I appreciate your doing that for me. What about my car?

"It's been parked at the airport since the crash," she said. "It's just fine, locked in the hangar until you're ready to move it."

"Terrific," he said. "I hope it's safer than your plane was."

"We'll move it wherever you want."

Jake looked at her, his eye soft, searching. "Do you feel guilty about the accident or what? Why are you doing all this for me?"

"Because I care about you," she admitted with great effort.

"Why? You hardly know me, and what you knew before the accident, you didn't even like."

"I see a lot of potential there," she said with a coy smile.

He didn't find that amusing. "Well, I hate to disappoint you, Lynda, but crippled and half-blind, the only potential I'm likely to reach is the potential for suicide."

Her face changed. "That's the second time you've mentioned that, Jake. You don't mean it, and when you say it, I feel just as threatened as I felt after the fire last night."

"Why would that be a threat to you?" he asked.

"Because I've started getting attached to you, Jake, and I don't let go of my friends that easily." Tears came to her eyes, and she blinked them back. "I had you figured for a guy with at least a little bit of integrity," she said quietly. "The guy who landed my plane wasn't a coward."

"The guy who *crashed* your plane did what he had to do. But don't worry. It's not like I have a gun under my pillow or a knife in the drawer. I can't get out of bed to hurl myself out the window, and I don't have free access to the drugs they're giving me. I'm trapped here for now."

"If I can go out there and fight for my life, Jake, you can do it in here. And if you think I'm going to sympathize with your fantasy to rig up a noose, then you need to call a neurologist because you have brain damage, too."

Someone knocked on the door, but Jake only kept staring at her, his own misty eye taking seriously the fire he had restored to hers.

He heard the door open. "Sorry to interrupt. How are you, Jake?"

Finally breaking the lock he had on her eyes, Jake saw Larry and nodded.

"I'm gonna have to take you on home, Lynda," Larry said. "Tony has a suspect in custody. He thinks he might be the one who's been after you. I have to get to the station to question him."

"Really?" Lynda wiped her eyes. "Who is it?"

"One of the guys on your list," he said. "Doug Chastain."

"Doug?" she asked. "But—what evidence is there?"

Jake frowned. "Who is this guy?"

Larry checked the notes he'd jotted when Tony had called. "He's a mechanic who lives in the area, and he already has one prior arson conviction. We traced the gas can we found back to where he works."

"You're kidding," Lynda said.

Larry tried to hurry her to the door. "This might be the guy, Lynda."

Her face suddenly hopeful, she turned back to Jake. "I'll be back tomorrow, Jake," she said. "And I'll call you tonight and let you know what they come up with. That is, if you don't break your phone between now and then."

He nodded again but didn't speak until she was almost out the door. "Hey, Lynda? Be careful, okay?"

"You, too."

Jake got her meaning. He only wished he had a choice.

CHAPTER THIRTY-ONE

B race yourself," Tony told Larry as he rushed into the precinct. "He's in an even worse mood than he was when we interviewed him yesterday. He got a tad bit offended when I told him he was under arrest."

Larry watched the twenty-year-old kid through the one-way glass. Yesterday, when they'd interviewed him at home, Larry had been suspicious, but he'd talked himself out of considering the kid a suspect since he had no experience with airplanes. It was feasible that he could have started the fire, but could he have rigged the crash in such an expert way? "What have you got on him?"

"Besides his prior arson conviction and his mechanic experience and the gas can we found with the name of his employer on it, we found gas stains in the carpet in his trunk. Fresh ones. You could still smell the fumes. And his alibi is weak."

Larry stepped closer to the glass. There was a tattoo of a bald eagle covering most of Doug's upper arm, and his hair was doused with mousse and spiked to stand straight up on his head. He wore a black T-shirt with the sleeves rolled up to his shoulders and a general expression of readiness to curse the next cop who crossed him.

"So what's his alibi?"

"Says he was at home. No witnesses."

They opened the door, and the kid burst out of his seat. "You might as well let me out of here," he spat out. "I didn't do it."

Larry gave him a long, considering look as the kid sneered back at him. Finally, he reached across the table to shake his hand.

"I'm Larry Millsaps," he said, then withdrew his hand when the kid rejected it. "Why don't you calm down, Doug? My partner here can be a little gruff sometimes, but I just want to ask you a few questions."

"I already answered the main one," the kid said. "I didn't do it!"

"Didn't do what?"

"I didn't set her house on fire! They keep asking me if I had a grudge against her, if I was in the area last night, if I was near the airport when that crash happened—I'm telling you morons, I've never even been *down* that street, and I wouldn't know how to get to that airport. I was sitting at home last night. Reading."

Larry's eyebrows lifted. Somehow he couldn't picture this kid reading. "Reading what?"

The kid threw up his hands. "What is it? You don't think I can read?"

"You don't look like the type who stays at home and reads."

"Yeah? Well, you don't look like the type who gets out of work by pinning crimes on innocent people." He sat back and cocked his head arrogantly. "I was reading *Hamlet*. You got a problem with that?"

"Yeah? Who wrote it?"

"You tell me," the kid challenged. "You're the one with all the answers. What do you do? Go down the list of ex-cons in the area and assign one of them to each crime that comes down?"

"We found a gas can that belongs to your employer," Tony said less patiently.

"Yeah? Well, maybe *he* did it! Were my fingerprints on it?"

Neither Tony nor Larry answered, but they both knew that no fingerprints had been found on the gas can. The arsonist must have been wearing gloves.

"How do you explain the gas stains in your trunk?" Larry asked.

Doug mouthed a curse. "I mow yards on weekends, okay? I always take extra gas in case I run out. I'd have been more careful not to spill some if I'd known somebody was gonna be sniffing around trying to pin something on me."

"What do you carry it in?"

He looked from Larry to Tony then back again. "In a can, okay? Probably a J.R.'s Auto Repair can. We have them all over the shop. People stop by and borrow them all the time. Lots of people have them."

Larry only watched him as he rambled, giving him enough rope to hang himself.

The kid realized what was going on and crossed his arms obstinately. Flopping back into his chair, he said, "I'm not talking anymore without a lawyer."

"Do you have one?"

"Sure, man," he said facetiously. "Got one on retainer."

"You don't have one, do you?"

"So appoint one," the kid said through his teeth. "Only don't appoint that witch whose house burnt down because she'll string me along and dump me at the last minute. Besides, there's somebody out there still trying to kill her. I don't want to be around her."

Tony shot Larry a telling look, and Larry nodded.

The door opened, and one of the officers stuck his head in. "Tony, can I see you a minute?"

Larry watched his partner leave the room then turned back to the kid. "I'll have an attorney appointed, but he won't do you any good if you're not telling the truth."

"You don't want the truth, man. You want a scapegoat."

The door opened again, and Tony stepped back in. "I just got an interesting bit of information." He pulled out a chair and set his foot on it. Leaning on his knee, he looked down at the kid. "Seems somebody you work with called your house three times last night, and you weren't home."

"So I didn't feel like talking," Doug said, his face reddening. "I'm taking a night class at the college, and I had to read *Hamlet*. I swear. You can call and check. Search my house. You'll find my Shakespeare book."

Tony shot Larry a skeptical look.

Doug slammed his hand on the table. "Hey, man, last time I checked, it wasn't a crime to unplug your phone!"

"No, it isn't. And neither is going to the Monroe Street Lounge, where several people saw you earlier last night."

Larry breathed an incredulous laugh. "Still want to stick to your story about being at home reading?"

"You asked me where I was when the fire started. I was at home. So I had a few drinks earlier. That's no crime either."

"And it just slipped your mind?"

For a moment, Doug sat still, his face a study in belligerence and hatred, but finally, he leaned forward and clasped his hands in front of his face. "Go ahead and get that lawyer," he said. "I'm not saying another blasted word."

CHAPTER THIRTY-TWO

he radio news blared in the background as Keith Varner checked out the suit he would wear in court tomorrow. He would look like a competent businessman when he faced the judge, he thought, and Paige would play the role of a stringy-haired waif about to have a nervous breakdown. And the lawyer—he chuckled for a moment at the thought that she was going to appear in court to represent Paige. When he'd seen her on the news after the fire, she'd looked like someone who'd been beaten up. He could just see the judge's reaction to her propping herself up in the courtroom—complete with bruises and scrapes and the stitches that held her together—fighting for Paige. Her very presence would be all the argument he needed that she herself was in danger and, therefore, Brianna was in danger. By tomorrow night, he'd have Brianna at home.

He went into the empty bedroom in his apartment, kicked aside the piles of dirty laundry, and considered where he would put the child's bed. There, in the corner. Once the judge awarded him temporary custody, he'd ask him if he could get her bed from her home. That way she'd be comfortable with him. He just hoped she didn't cry all night like the last time he had her.

But that he blamed on Paige. She had filled the child's head full of lies, and until he got that woman out of his daughter's life, he would never get Brianna to bond with him. He had so many plans for them. She would learn to be dependent on him, to obey and respect him, to need him....

He went back into his small den, knocked the newspapers out of his chair and onto the floor, and flicked on the television. Maybe there was another hint about where they were. Maybe they'd have something about the sheriff department's pitiful hunt for the arsonist.

He listened through two murders, a rally for a local politician, a mail fraud scam that had been uncovered.

"—and in other news, an arrest was made today in the Lynda Barrett case—"

He leaned forward and turned it up, watching carefully as the film clip showed the mechanic being led through the precinct in handcuffs. Flopping back on his couch, Keith began to laugh. It was perfect. They were off his trail. They were hanging it on that poor bozo he'd heard Lynda name that day in her hospital room. It had been easy to find him, and using the gas can to lead them to where Chastain worked was ingenious. Now Lynda Barrett had a false sense of security. He loved it.

Now there would be another chance, he thought with a smile. If he didn't convince the judge to give him Brianna tomorrow, he could still make sure he got Lynda Barrett out of the way before the real hearing. It would take a host of angels to keep her alive the next time.

T he telephone rang, and Lynda pulled it out of her jeans pocket, which was baggy enough to carry several small appliances. "Hello?"

"I hope I didn't wake you."

It was Paige, and Lynda smiled at the sound of her voice. The house was getting awfully quiet. She abandoned the stack of books she'd been sorting through in the closet and sat down on the closest chair. "I just woke up a few minutes ago, and I've been sorting through some things to see if my dad left a Bible somewhere."

"Any luck?"

"No. I know he had one, though. He used to wave it at me all the time."

She could hear Paige's soft laughter. "I'll go buy you one if you want."

Lynda sighed. "No, that's okay. I'll get one the next time Larry or Tony takes me somewhere."

"Well, it doesn't look like that'll be necessary any more. The guy they picked up? Looks like he's the one."

Lynda caught her breath. "Really? How do you know?"

"They called me a little while ago. Larry said you were tired when he brought you home and were probably sleeping, so he asked me to give you a couple of hours and then tell you. They shot his alibi to pieces, found gas stains in his car—it's him, Lynda. We're home free."

Lynda leaned back in the chair. "No more guards? No more surprises?"

"Nope. They called the guard back to the precinct over an hour ago. Look out the window."

Lynda got up and pulled the curtain back. For the first time since she'd come here last night, there was no one watching her from across the street. A chill went through her, and she had the fleeting sensation of standing on the edge of a cliff, leaning, leaning, with nothing to catch her when she fell. "They're gone."

"That's right. You don't need them now."

Lynda allowed the news to sink in for a moment. "I knew he didn't like me when I resigned from his case, but I didn't think he'd come back to kill me."

"Well, at least he's behind bars. And we can come and go as we please. The only thing we have to fear is this hearing tomorrow."

Lynda pushed aside her uneasiness and tried instead to concentrate on tomorrow. "This is perfect, Paige. Keith's motion is based on your putting Brianna in danger by being with me. That whole premise has just been shot into a million pieces. Once I tell the judge that I'm not in danger any longer, his theory is shot. And then I'll tell the court that your whereabouts are confidential due to Keith's threats and leave it at that. In fact, if you want to check out of the hotel right now, you can come here. It's probably okay now."

"I don't know," Paige said. "He's assuming I'm still with you."

"But he doesn't know where I am."

"I told you, Lynda. He's smart. He figures out ways to get information."

"He's not *that* smart. He's just conditioned you to think so. But even if he did find out, he's not as likely to hassle you knowing I'm here as he might be if you were alone. I mean, I'm the one who's going to pull out all the stops when we finally get to trial. He won't want to give me any more ammunition to throw at him."

Paige hesitated. "Even if you're right, I still think I should stay here tonight. If for some reason the judge asks you point blank if I'm staying with you, you can say no."

Lynda sighed. "You're right, I guess. But how about tomorrow?"

"Are you sure you want us there?"

She heard the smile in Lynda's voice. "Of course I want you. I need company. I'm at my wit's end."

"Okay, then," she said. "Tomorrow. And about that Bible. Why don't I buy you one and bring it when I bring all the clothes I got for you?"

"Where's Brianna?"

"Watching Barney. It's almost over."

Lynda looked down at the junk she'd begun sorting through. "Paige, if you would do that, it would be such a lifesaver. Use the credit card I gave you last night. I'll call the store and find out what translations they have and tell them what I want. Just ask the clerk when you get there. By the way, do you have one?"

"A Bible? Well . . . somewhere . . . at home."

"Buy yourself one, too," she said. "On me. A little thank-you for taking such good care of me. And get Brianna something, too."

"Lynda, you don't have to do that."

"Yes, I do," Lynda whispered. "And you have to let me."

A few minutes later Lynda dialed her office number. "Do me a favor," she told Sally. "Go back a couple of years and dig up Doug Chastain's file. I need to refresh my memory about his case."

"I heard they'd arrested him," Sally said. "Thank goodness. You want me to bring it to you along with the other papers I need to give you for tomorrow?"

"Yeah," she said. "We can meet this afternoon."

"Are you going to tell me where you are yet?"

Lynda considered it a moment and realized she didn't yet feel safe enough to tell anyone where she was. "No, I'll just meet you somewhere. Call me on my cellular phone before you leave work today."

"Are you supposed to be driving?" Sally asked.

Lynda hesitated. "Well . . . no. But it can't be helped."

"Yes, it can. I can bring them to you."

"Just humor me," Lynda said. "I'll get over it. It'll sink in eventually that I'm not being hunted."

"All right," Sally said with resignation. "Do you want to come to the office?"

"No. I don't think I'm up to seeing everybody yet. How about the Jackson Street Post Office? Then I can just have Paige meet me there too with some stuff she's picking up."

Sally let out a ragged breath. "All right. But I'll be so glad when all this is over."

"You think *you* will."

Paige drove up just as Lynda finished signing some papers Sally needed her to sign. Saying good-bye to her secretary, she got out of her car and got into Paige's.

Paige handed her the Bible, still in its box. "They were expensive," she said. "You should have just ordered me a paperback one."

"I wanted you to have that one," she said. "Did they put your name on it like I told them?"

Paige opened her box and took out her leather-bound Bible. Running her hand across the name engraved in gold, she said, "Yeah, they sure did." Her eyes were misty when she looked up at Lynda. "That may be the sweetest thing anybody's ever bought me."

"Well, make it worthwhile. Read it."

Paige leaned over and planted a kiss on Lynda's cheek. "You're a real friend."

"I'm trying," she said. "But I've got a lot of catching up to do."

CHAPTER THIRTY-FOUR

A re you sure you should be here today, Lynda?" Judge Albert Stacey set his elbows on the conference table, assessing her with deep concern. Keith and his lawyer sat on one side of the table, and Lynda sat alone on the other.

She tried to smile, but it was difficult. The long walk through the building had been tiring, and she'd encountered several bouts with dizziness since she'd been here. Everywhere she went, people stared, especially those who knew her. She hadn't even tried to hide the bruises and scrapes on her face. "I feel fine, your honor. And I had to be here today. This motion Mr. McRae is filing is ridiculous and a waste of the court's time."

The judge turned to Keith's lawyer. "Well, I've reviewed the motion, and my understanding is that your client is concerned about the safety of this child since she was involved in the fire at Miss Barrett's the other night. Am I reading that correctly?"

"Yes, Judge. Mr. Varner feels that his ex-wife has deliberately risked the child's life by staying in the same home with Miss Barrett, even after so many attempts have been made on her life."

"Excuse me," Lynda cut in. "Be specific, please. How many attempts?"

McRae sat back in his chair with a look that said she was walking proof of his case. "You tell us."

Rather than telling him anything, she addressed the judge. "Your honor, there were two attempts made on my life. The first was the plane crash I was involved in last week, and the second was, obviously, the fire two nights ago. Paige was staying in my house while I was in the hospital, primarily because she became convinced that the restraining order she had filed against Mr. Varner was not going to stop him from breaking into her home or trying to remove their child from school. At that time no one realized that anyone was after me. It wasn't until after the fire the first night I was home that we realized that."

The judge turned back to McRae. "So what's the problem exactly? How did Mrs. Varner endanger her daughter's life? Are you saying *she* started the fire or knew it was going to happen?"

"Of course not, your honor."

Keith couldn't stay quiet any longer. "I'm saying that for all I know she's still staying with her, even though she's aware that someone's out to get her."

"Your honor," Lynda said, calling his attention back to her side of the table. "May I?"

He gestured for her to go ahead with her explanations, and she took a deep breath. "First of all, I can assure you that Paige Varner and Brianna are safe and that they have been in no danger—except perhaps from Mr. Varner—since the fire. In fact, they're here in the building as we speak but chose not to come into the hearing because she feared the child would be traumatized by seeing her father."

"Oh, for crying out—"

The judge's stern look silenced Keith, who gave a disgusted look at the ceiling, as if calling on some unknown entity in the plaster to come to his aid.

"Secondly," Lynda went on, "the police have a suspect in custody. They captured him yesterday, and he's in jail awaiting his own hearing."

"Really?" the judge asked, eyebrows raised. "Well, I know that's good news for you."

"Extremely good news, your honor."

Keith rolled his eyes. "So a guy was arrested. He could get out on bond within the week if he's the right guy in the first place. How can I be assured that my child is safe?"

Lynda answered the question for him. "Your honor, I can assure you that it's my priority to keep those two safe as well. In fact, that's why theirs is the only case I've kept since my accident and why I came here, against doctor's orders, to make sure the rights of Mrs. Varner and her daughter are adequately protected."

Judge Stacey studied the motion in front of him, and McRae seized the moment of silence to speak up. "Judge, my client is also concerned with the mother's neglect of the child, her inability to support that child, and her past abuses. Mrs. Varner has lost her job and left her home, and my client worries about her mental stability and her capacity to provide Brianna with what she needs. He's concerned about their whereabouts, as I'm sure you would be if your own children disappeared."

"Well, your honor, I can answer that as well," Lynda spoke up. "For the duration of this crisis—and it is a crisis, sir, whenever a battered wife goes into hiding—I am helping my client and her daughter financially. I won't allow them to go without. For the time being, I've recommended that she remain in hiding."

The judge sat back in his chair. "Well, I'm satisfied that the child is in capable hands and that she's being cared for. As for the allegations of neglect and abuse on either side of this case, that remains to be proven in the appropriate hearing. That's not what this hearing is about. I hereby rule that the child shall remain with her mother until the trial."

Keith cursed, and his lawyer grabbed his arm, trying to shut him up, but he burst out of his chair and started for the door.

Lynda waited until he was gone then turned back to the judge with a little smile, knowing he made note of the volatile temper. She hoped he was the judge assigned to the custody hearing. "Thank you, your honor."

Patting her hand, he got to his feet. "Quite impressive that you would come to court in your condition, Lynda. It speaks to your conviction that the child is in the right place." He leaned over the table and whispered, "And I trust you."

"I appreciate that, sir. Would you like to confer with Mrs. Varner?"

"No, that won't be necessary."

She watched him disappear through the door that led to his chambers and picking up the few papers she'd been able to carry in with her, she went back to the conference room where she'd left Paige.

Paige jumped when the door opened then wilted with relief when she saw it was Lynda.

"What happened?"

"We won," Lynda said. "I told you."

"Oh, thank God." She drew Brianna into a crushing hug. "Where is he? Is he still in the building?"

"No, he's gone. He rushed out cussing and ranting. I'm glad you weren't there."

"Me, too." Propping her chin on Brianna's head, she said, "Are you sure we can win next time, Lynda? He's not going to pull a fast one on us and trip us up, is he? He's always been able to do that with me."

The worry in Paige's eyes touched Lynda. "He won't trip me up, Paige. I'll have so much against him, he won't know what hit him. We'll get everyone who's ever seen him lose his temper into that courtroom. I'll have documentation of every trip to the emergency room, every neighbor who heard him yelling through the walls, every call to 911. I won't leave anything to chance."

Paige's lips trembled as she took it all in. "It's Brianna's life at stake here," she whispered, "but if I have to trust anyone to fight for it, I trust you."

CHAPTER THIRTY-FIVE

Keith cruised through the courthouse parking garage, looking for Paige's white car. He found it on the third level.

He stopped his car right behind it. The door-lock buttons were down, he could see. He glanced around to see whether there was anyone nearby who might see him when he got out.

Someone was pulling into an empty space a few cars down. And two people across the aisle stood talking beside one of their cars.

He took a piece of paper off the seat next to him, folded it to look like a note, and got out the switchblade he carried in his pocket. Leaving his car idling, he stepped out and glanced at the others in the garage. He still hadn't been noticed.

He set the blank note under her windshield wiper, so it would look as if that was his purpose then pretended to drop his keys. Bending over, he opened his switchblade then slashed her front tire. Still stooped, he went to the back one and stabbed it, too.

He drove around until he found a parking place on the other side of that level from which he'd be able to see her come to her car.

It would take more than a judge to keep him from being with his daughter.

CHAPTER THIRTY-SIX

Paige held Brianna's hand as they stepped off the elevator into the parking garage. Trying to remember where she had parked her car, she let her eyes sweep over the colors until she came to the white Chevette parked across the garage.

The car parked next to hers began to pull out as she approached, leaving the space next to her car empty. Her step slowed—through that open space, she saw that both tires on that side of her car were flat.

She froze.

She heard a car start across the garage and caught a glimpse of pastel blue pulling out—the color of Keith's car.

Her heart stopped and she dropped her purse, spilling out her car keys, a lipstick, some change. Abandoning it, she grabbed Brianna and bolted back toward the elevator.

Brianna started to cry, but over the child's sobs Paige heard tires screeching. The elevator was taking too long. She scanned the area for a door to the stairway. Quickly, she headed toward it and shoved it open. It clanged shut behind her as she tore down the stairs.

Above her, just beyond the door, she heard a car door slam and footsteps running. The door above her opened, and she heard the click of shoes taking the steps faster than she could move.

Her foot slipped, and she stumbled, skinning her shin against the metal railing. Brianna's screams went up an octave. Reaching out to grab the rail with her free hand, Paige steadied herself and took the next flight down.

But he was right behind her, closing in. "You can't get away from me, Paige!" he shouted, his voice echoing in the stairwell.

As if she only now realized what they were running from, Brianna's shrieks grew more piercing, reverberating through the stairwell. Her little arms tightened desperately around her mother's neck. Struggling to breathe, Paige threw herself at a door on one of the landings.

But just as her fingers grazed the handle, Keith grabbed her shirt and flung her against the wall. He reached for Brianna, but the child fought and struggled and screamed. Bracing herself against the wall, Paige kicked him with all her might.

He fell back, cursing, then rallied and grabbed her hair. He jerked her off-balance, trying to get his arm between her and the child. Then he shoved her back and kicked her feet out from under her. Losing her grip on the child, Paige fell back, stumbling down four stairs and landing on her back.

"Mommmmeeee!" The child's terror rang through the stairwell, echoing off the walls. Keith grabbed her, and she bit his arm and kicked him with her sharp little shoe. He recoiled long enough for her to reach her mother again and attach herself in another strangling grip.

Suddenly the door one flight below them burst open. Startled, Keith let them go and took a step backward, then turned and fled back up the steps.

"Help me!" Paige cried, stumbling down the stairs. She fell into the building and collapsed as a crowd formed around her, Brianna still screaming at the top of her lungs, clinging for dear life to her mother.

It took twenty minutes to quiet the child's screaming, but she trembled for the next two hours as Lynda and Larry sat with Paige and Brianna, trying to calm them both.

"I searched the whole garage and all around the courthouse, Paige," Larry said. "He's gone."

"Can't you—can't you arrest him?"

"We have to find him first."

"What if he finds *me* first?" Paige shouted. "Who would have ever thought he'd try to snatch her out of my hands right here at the courthouse?"

"He's getting desperate," Lynda said. "He's liable to do anything."

"He'll go to every hotel in the city until he finds my car—if I can manage to drive it again after what he did to my tires. He'll find us. I know he will."

"No, he won't," Lynda said through her teeth. "You're coming home with me. I'll send someone to change the tires, and we'll get your car later. But you don't need to be alone."

"What's happening to us?" Paige cried, sopping her tears with a wadded tissue. "Everywhere I turn, there's danger. How am I ever going to protect her? Feel her. She's still shaking."

Lynda laid her hands on the child and felt the shiver. "She must have been pretty scared when she saw him."

"Well, what do you expect? To have him burst out of nowhere like that and start grabbing her—What is he trying to do to her? Doesn't he realize that a child shouldn't ever have to be that afraid?"

Lynda stroked back Paige's hair where it was matted to her wet face. "It's going to be okay, Paige. Come on. Larry's following us home now."

Wearily, Paige got up, shifted Brianna more securely to her hip, and with a troubled, miserable expression, regarded Larry. "You have a gun, don't you?"

"Of course I have a gun. I'm a cop."

"But—you would use it if you had to, wouldn't you?"

"That's my job, Paige. Don't worry. I'm not going to let anything happen to you."

Her face was pale as they started out of the room. "Larry, do you think I should get a gun?"

Lynda watched Larry's face, for she had wondered the same thing herself. "No, Paige, I don't. Too many accidents happen. Too many people rely on them when their tempers flare. Too many people die because there was a gun too readily available. And I sure don't recommend it with a child in the house."

"That's what I thought you'd say." But as they walked to Larry's unmarked car, Paige whispered to Lynda, "If I had the money, I'd buy one anyway. And the next time Keith sprang up out of nowhere, I'd be ready."

Larry was quiet later that day as he and Tony prowled St. Clair in their unmarked car, working on a cocaine case that they were close to breaking. The sheriff's department was too small for any of its detectives to specialize in one area, so Larry didn't know from one week to the next what kind of crime he'd be assigned to.

It gave the job some diversity, which he supposed was a plus. But the minus was that they slapped a file closed so quickly the moment they had someone booked that he was never able to get a sense of closure.

"What's on your mind?" Tony asked, glancing over at him as he drove.

He shrugged. "I don't know. I was just thinking about that Doug Chastain kid. Did I tell you we found a Shakespeare book in his apartment?"

"Three times. Why is that bothering you so?"

He sighed. "I didn't say it was bothering me. I just stated a fact. He really is enrolled in night school. And his phone *was* unplugged."

Tony rubbed his chin in disbelief. "So you think a guy who reads *Hamlet* can't burn down a house? Is this another one of your bleeding-heart theories?"

"No," Larry returned. "But I don't want to assume somebody's guilty just because he has an attitude and a weird haircut. Especially when his alibi could be true."

"*Part* of his alibi. The other part was a lie. And what about his mechanic skills and the gas stains and the arson conviction and the gas can? You think some Shakespeare book clears up all that evidence?"

"No, I don't." He took in a deep breath and shifted in his seat. "I just feel uneasy about things. Like maybe we closed the case too fast."

"We have an assignment board full of unsolved cases, Larry. Neither one of us has time to dwell on long shots."

"Well, I'd feel better if we could pick up Keith Varner again. Slap an assault charge on him."

"There are deputies working on it, buddy."

Larry was quiet for a few moments. "You just should have seen how scared they were today. The little kid and Paige. Even Lynda. I wish there was something definitive we could do."

Tony only chuckled. "Lighten up, pal. They'll be fine."

CHAPTER THIRTY-SEVEN

P aige tucked her sleeping child into bed in the master bedroom then pulled back the curtain and peered out the front window.

The street was dark, and she wasn't sure she would even know if someone sat out there, watching, waiting. What if Keith had discovered where they were? What if he were just biding his time, waiting until her guard was down to pounce again and snatch Brianna from her hands?

She was getting crazy, she told herself, but she wished the police would go back to guarding the house again. But police never guarded battered, frightened mothers or abused children. They didn't consider the threats wrathful husbands made to be as serious as attempted murder. Paige didn't see the difference.

Sighing, she closed the curtain and went through the living room to the back door. Through the window, she saw Lynda sitting on the patio with her head resting against the back of her chair, staring up into the stars.

Quietly, she opened the door and stepped outside. "Lynda, are you okay?"

Lynda offered a weak smile. "I'm fine, Paige. Sit down."

"I don't know." Crossing her arms, Paige gazed across the yard to the woods behind the fence. "I feel too vulnerable out here. I think I'd rather stay closed up inside."

"I felt that way at first, too. But I love sitting outside at night, and I decided not to let Doug Chastain take that away from me. You shouldn't let Keith."

"All right." Still watching the shadows beyond the yard, Paige took the padded swing across from Lynda and began to move gently back and forth. "I've been so jumpy today since the run-in with him. It feels good to relax."

"It does, doesn't it?"

Crickets chirped in the yard, signaling that fall was approaching, and Lynda smiled. "Those crickets remind me of college."

"College? Why? Did you study them?"

Lynda laughed. "Crickets? No. But every fall, the library seemed to be full of them. Especially at night. I'd be there studying, and those crickets would be chirping as loud as you could imagine, and I'd look for them so I could throw them outside. I don't know why they bothered me so much."

Paige closed her eyes against the cool breeze whispering through her hair. "I always meant to go to college. When I married Keith, he promised I could. But every time I brought it up, he nipped it in the bud."

"Well, maybe you could try it now."

Paige shook her head. "No, I'd never make it through. I'm not smart enough."

"Smart enough?" Lynda asked. "Paige, you have as much upstairs as anyone I know."

Paige didn't seem to buy it. "Besides, now I have to worry about making ends meet. It's not easy supporting a child alone. The whole time we've been divorced, I haven't gotten one penny of child support from Keith. But I don't really want it. I don't want him having anything at all to do with Brianna." Hugging herself, Paige scanned the fence.

"I think God's with you on this, Paige."

Paige chuckled softly. "Oh, really? Why?"

"Call it deductive reasoning. You've come through more narrow escapes than I have. You do believe in God, don't you?"

Paige sighed. "I guess so. I wish I had as much faith as you."

"Where do you get the idea that I have more than you?"

Paige considered that for a moment. "Well, you live a real decent life, Lynda. You're a good example. Like you really believe."

"Why?" Lynda asked honestly. "Because I don't have a criminal record, I only let a curse word fly when I'm really mad, my name is on a church roster, and I have a pro-life sticker on my bumper? Is that my example?"

"No," Paige said. "Because you took Brianna and me in, and you gave us money, and clothes...."

Lynda sighed. "That's nothing, Paige. With my income, I should be ashamed for all I *haven't* done."

Paige was amazed. "Lynda, you just don't know. Other people aren't like that. Even family."

Lynda grew quiet for a moment, and Paige diverted her eyes, knowing she'd said too much.

"Paige, you never talk much about your family. Why?"

"Not much to tell," she said without conviction. "They live in Arizona."

"But have you contacted them to tell them what's going on? Do they know you're in trouble?"

"Oh, Lynda. They don't care."

Lynda sat up straighter. "Don't care? How do you know?"

Paige blinked back the tears pushing into her eyes. "Lynda, you have to know my mother. She's lived with my father for thirty years, and no matter how bad things get, she believes in sticking it out. No matter who gets hurt."

Lynda sat quietly, weighing the implications of what Paige had just said and decided to take a chance. "Paige, were you abused when you were a child?"

Paige looked into the trees for a moment, struggling to keep her face free of emotion, but it wasn't easy, and finally, she covered her face with a hand and squeezed her eyes shut, but the tears pressed out anyway. "I won't let Brianna live that way," she whispered. "I'm not like my mother. I can't turn my head, and I can't keep bouncing back."

Lynda moved across to sit on the swing next to Paige, reached out for her, and pulled her into a hug, and Paige laid her head against Lynda's shoulder and wept like a child.

"Is that why you married Keith? To get away from home?"

She nodded. "He ended up being so much like my father. I thought his temper was just normal because that's the way things always were at home, too. But it's not normal, is it?"

"No," Lynda said. "It's not normal. It's criminal."

Paige wept for a moment longer until she heard Brianna crying through the door she'd left open, and sucking in a deep breath, she got to her feet. "Brianna's crying," she said quickly, wiping her face. "I guess I'll go lie down with her." Paige could see the helplessness on Lynda's face, and she wished she hadn't burdened her with this. "Good night, Lynda."

"Good night."

Paige hurried into the master bedroom where Brianna, in the throes of a dream, cried out in her sleep. Lying down beside her, Paige stroked her face and comforted her. "Shhh. Mommy's here. Nothing's going to hurt you."

As she held her, she felt the terror seeping out of her.

For a while, she lay still in the dark, thinking about the fears that plagued her daughter, and that stalked her as well. They were real fears—fear for her life, fear of losing her child, fear of harm coming to either of them. She had never expected to live in such fear once she left her father's home.

Despair settled into her heart like a slow-moving disease, but as she drifted toward sleep, she thought she heard a voice: "*Shhh. I'm here. Nothing's going to hurt you.*"

And even as she sank into sleep, she realized that the voice, the promise, and the feeling of peace warming through her felt as tangible as that little girl curled up against her chest.

CHAPTER THIRTY-EIGHT

The crowd in the bar where Keith had decided to brood was thinning out, and men and women had begun to couple off with a frenzied desperation, as if going home alone was tantamount to social suicide.

But it wasn't his reputation that worried Keith tonight; rather, it was that he'd driven into the parking lot of his apartment building today to see three sheriff's cars. He didn't have to be Einstein to figure out that they were looking for him.

Never one to linger too long when trouble was brewing, Keith had turned his car around before they could spot him and had headed to this obscure bar across town where people knew him only by his first name.

He'd been drinking for hours, and his head had begun to throb. He needed to lie down somewhere.

Sliding off the bar stool he'd been propped on for the past several hours, he stumbled toward the door, catching the chairs as he passed to steady himself. He heard laughter outside as he fell out into the night and saw a couple of intoxicated men pawing at a woman who cackled loudly enough to wake the dead. Though they weren't looking at him, he suspected that the laughter was directed at him anyway, and he set his eyes on his car and concentrated on getting to it.

Again, laughter erupted behind him, and he swung around, letting a string of expletives tear from his mouth. One of the men cursed back at him and started toward him, and Keith opened his car door and fell behind the wheel.

He heard the man's fist hit his trunk, and groping to get his key into the ignition, he started the car. The man was banging on it now, and the woman's abrasive laughter split the night again.

Cursing because his hands were so maddeningly slow to cooperate, he got the car into gear and took off through the dirt.

Looking in his rearview mirror, he saw the man shouting obscenities at him. Keith rolled down his window and yelled back, "You can't touch me! I'm invincible!"

But that invincibility was meaningless if he couldn't prove it to someone. He wished he knew where Paige was tonight, so he could burst into her house, jerk her out of bed, and remind her who the man of the family is. He would show her what all her whining and running had gotten her. He would teach her how to show a little respect.

The idea became more attractive to him as he wove and zigzagged through town, heading toward the neighborhood where he had lived with her. Maybe she and Brianna were home. Maybe she had run out of money and been forced to go home, and he could walk in and surprise her....

The street was dark, and he chuckled under his breath and tried to focus his blurry vision on the house as he got closer. There were no lights on and no cars in the garage. Blast it all, she wasn't home. She was still hiding.

He thought about pulling into the driveway and going in, just to rest for a few minutes until his head quit hurting. But that voice inside his head that remained the slightest bit rational reminded him that a world of trouble would fall on him if he were caught here after what had happened today. No, he had to keep driving. He had to go home.

He ran over a corner curb making the turn off her street and felt his car bounce and screech as he accelerated. His eyes were growing heavy, and his head was hammering, but somehow he kept driving.

By rote he made his way home and pulled into his parking lot, making a cursory inspection through his blurred vision; he saw no squad cars. Satisfied, he pulled into a space. They'd forgotten about him by now, he thought with relief. That was the thing about the St. Clair Sheriff's Department. If you weren't there the first time they looked for you, chances were, they wouldn't be back. Not on a stupid charge like approaching his wife at the courthouse.

His parking job was crooked, but at least he didn't hit the car next to him. He cut off the engine and got out, stumbling toward his apartment while he searched his key chain for the apartment key.

When he heard a car door slam, he didn't bother to look. His head hurt too badly, and he had to find that key—

"Police! Hold it right there! You're under arrest!"

Keith cursed again and turned around, his hands limp at his sides as he glared at Larry Millsaps, who held a gun on him as if he'd just caught him robbing a bank. "You gotta be kiddin'."

Larry came up behind him and threw him against a car next to him, which wasn't difficult since he could barely stand as it was.

"What're the charges?"

"Assault, contempt of court, and whatever else we can hang on you."

Jerking him up, Larry threw him into the back seat of the unmarked car as he read him his rights, and Keith decided that he didn't care where Larry took him or for what reason, as long as there was a place there to lay his head.

There was no outside light to indicate that it was morning, but the sounds of echoing doors and yelling men sliced through Keith's brain with machete force. His head still pounded, but forcing himself to open his eyes, he looked around and tried to orient himself.

And then he remembered that he was in jail.

The reason escaped him, however, and clutching his head, he sat up on the side of his cot and tried to think. Had he gotten into a fight last night? Had they pulled him over for drunk driving? Had it been for driving by Paige's house?

Paige. It was something about Paige. The haze over his brain seemed to clear as he recalled the incident in the parking garage yesterday when he'd tried to take Brianna. What had Paige told them?

Fury rose up inside him, intense enough to propel him to the cell bars. "Hey!" he shouted up the corridor. "Hey! I want to talk to my lawyer!"

An inmate several cells down yelled for him to shut up, but he turned up the volume a few decibels. "I want a lawyer, do you hear me? I have the right to a lawyer!"

He heard someone coming then, a linebacker in a guard's uniform, and he backed a few steps away from the bars. "Are you gonna let me call my lawyer?"

The man leveled hateful, bloodshot eyes on him as he stuck the key in the lock and opened the door. "Come on, Varner."

Keith hesitated. "Are you—am I gonna call my lawyer now?"

The man smirked. "What do you think? That I'm gonna smash your face in as soon as you step over this line?"

Keith didn't like the question, so he offered no answer.

The man's grin faded. "Get out here, Varner. You're wasting my time."

He felt nauseous as he stepped out of the cell, and the guard escorted him to the telephone.

Two hours later, standing in front of a judge who might or might not let him out on bail, Keith did as he was told and let his lawyer do the talking.

"It was all a misunderstanding, your honor. My client and his ex-wife are in the middle of a custody dispute. She's tried pinning things on him before to stack the deck in her favor, but this takes the cake."

The judge didn't seem all that interested. "Says here that he vandalized her car, assaulted her, and tried to take the child against the orders of the court. Is that or is it not true?"

"No, your honor," McRae said. "All that happened is that they happened to be parked on the same level in the parking garage. He hadn't seen his child in over a month, and when he saw them coming across the garage, he was overcome with the desire to see her and approached her. He never dreamed she would interpret it as a threat right there in the courthouse parking lot."

The judge propped his chin in his hand, as if he'd heard it all a million times and didn't know if he could stay awake for one more.

"His ex-wife saw him and assuming incorrectly that he planned to take the child, took off running down the stairs. Unfortunately, she slipped and fell on the way down, and when my client heard her scream, he went to see if she was all right. She milked the incident for everything it was worth, your honor, and made it look as if he had assaulted her, which couldn't be farther from the truth. Judge, I ask that you drop these charges so that we won't waste any more of your time."

The judge studied the paperwork on his desk. "Is his ex-wife in the courtroom?"

McRae made a helpless gesture. "We weren't able to reach her or her attorney. My guess is that they are reluctant to stand before you with such a blatant lie."

The judge assessed Keith, who was tired and unshaven. "I'm divorced, myself, Mr. Varner, and I know how difficult it is to be without your children. But your ex-wife must have a restraining order for a reason."

"I told you, Judge. She's stacking her deck so she'll win permanent custody."

The judge rubbed his head, as if he nursed a headache of his own and then in a half-audible voice, said, "All right then. I'll give him the benefit of the doubt." He leaned forward then and pointed a finger at Keith. "But I won't do it again. If I see you back in this courtroom for any reason, Mr. Varner, you'll go to jail. Do you understand me?"

"Yes sir."

"All right." Banging the gavel, he moved on to the next case.

Trying to look humble and sincere, Keith left the courtroom. But inside he was dancing; he'd gotten away with it again.

His lawyer brooded as he drove him home, which aggravated Keith. He wasn't in the mood for this silent treatment. His head still hurt, and he wanted to take something and go to bed for a few hours before he had to go to work. When they reached Keith's apartment building, Keith started to get out.

"Hey, Keith," McRae said, stopping him. "No more antics, huh? You almost ruined your case."

"I didn't do anything," Keith said.

McRae breathed a disbelieving laugh. "This is me you're talking to. I know what you did, and it was stupid. And if you do anything like it again, you're going to have to find yourself a new lawyer."

"Okay, so it was stupid. I lost my head."

"Don't lose it again."

Keith got out then leaned back in the door. "Relax. It's going to be all right. We'll still win the case. Paige won't be able to fight back much longer."

McRae frowned back at him. "What do you mean by that?"

"Just that you should trust me," Keith said. "I've got this under control."

CHAPTER THIRTY-NINE

The maddening thing about having his own clothes in his room was that Jake couldn't put them on. Allie had told him that he'd have to be sitting upright before he could learn to dress himself, and even though she'd offered to do it for him, he'd declined. He liked the gowns, he told her. She believed him—which just proved how naive she was.

The truth was that he couldn't stand the thought of a woman doing something so personal as dressing him. Already Jake had little dignity left. The things they had to do for him were things he'd always taken for granted. Now he'd never take anything for granted again.

That morning they had put him in that monstrosity of a wheelchair again, and he'd persuaded them to leave him in it; the longer he sat upright, the easier it would become. He was up to sixty degrees now, and he was determined to conquer this particular obstacle. But it was taking too much time.

Rolling carefully toward the closet, he tried to reach a coat hanger, but it was just out of reach. Looking around in the closet where the nurses had put all of the things Lynda had gotten out of his hotel room, he found a tennis racket. Carefully, he slipped it into the triangle of the hanger and lifted it off the rod.

He dropped the racket then bent the hanger into a straight piece of wire with a hook at one end, and slipped it into the waistband of his sweat pants. If he could just hook that waistband over his foot and work it up to the point where his arms could reach, maybe he could actually get them on.

He broke out in a sweat as he maneuvered the pants with the hanger, trying to hook them over, missing, then trying again. The waistband of the sweat pants kept collapsing when it hit his feet, and the hanger offered little control, but he kept trying.

And trying.

And trying.

But it was too difficult, and finally, he gave up and flung both the pants and the hanger across the room. Slamming his hands down on the wheelchair armrests, he let out a raging curse.

A knock sounded on the door, and he cursed again, hoping it wasn't Lynda. It was bad enough that she saw him as a helpless invalid, but he didn't relish the idea of her catching him in this stupid chair, reclined back the way he was, wearing that degrading hospital gown that covered only his thighs, revealing the stupid stockings and Ace bandages wrapped the length of his legs.

The door opened, and Mike, the guy from the airport, stuck his head in. "Hey, Jake. Is it a bad time?"

Jake breathed a sigh of relief. "No, come on in."

Mike stepped tentatively into the room, wearing the same look of awkwardness most people did when they saw him. "I thought I'd come by and see how you are doing."

"Terrific," Jake said, throwing up his hands. "I'm great. How are you?"

Mike went to the chair across from Jake and started to turn it around but saw the sweat pants lying at the foot of it. Bending down, he picked them up. "You want me to hang these up for you?"

Jake swallowed. "You can throw them out the window for all I care."

Mike's eyebrows rose. "Tired of them?"

Jake laughed sarcastically. "Yeah, that's it. I'm sick of them."

Mike sat down and was quiet for a moment, and Jake knew he wasn't making it easy on him. "Thought you might want some of your stuff," Mike said, holding out a box of Jake's things that were in the trunk of his car. Lynda thought you might want it, but I thought I'd make sure. If you don't need any of it, I could just put it back."

Jake considered it for a moment, wishing that he had some means of taking care of these things himself. "Uh, just put it back in the trunk. It's okay."

"All right," Mike said. "You know, it's really good to see you sitting up."

Jake gave a dry laugh. "Not all the way up."

"You're getting there."

"Maybe."

Mike shifted. "When I think how close you came to going up in that plane's explosion—I still don't know how she got you out."

Jake frowned. "How who got me out?"

"Lynda," Mike said. "The plane was on its side, and you were strapped into your seat. Somehow, she unfastened you and pulled you through the door then dragged you away, even before we could get there. The plane went up seconds later."

"She did that? With broken ribs, spleen damage, and cuts all over her? How?"

Mike smiled. "I guess somebody was helping her. Maybe there was a reason you weren't supposed to die."

Jake couldn't exactly swallow that. "Well, if you think of one, you let me know. Right now, I'm not looking toward some great purpose. All I want to do is get my pants on."

Mike looked down at the sweat pants he was holding. "These? Hey, man, I could help you with these." He got up and came to stand at Jake's feet, but Jake shook his head.

"No, that's all right. I don't need them."

"But you'll feel a hundred times better if you don't have to wear that gown. No offense man, but I don't think that's your look."

Jake grinned, then eyed the pants again. "If you could just get them over my feet and up to where I can reach them—"

"No problem." Mike slipped the pants over Jake's feet and slid them up his legs. As soon as Jake could reach them, Mike let him take over.

It took some effort, but Jake worked them under his hips and all the way up.

"Would you look at that?" Jake asked. "I look almost normal now."

Mike went to the closet. "Which shirt do you want?"

"Give me that Far Side T-shirt," Jake said, pulling the gown off over his head and tossing it to the bottom of the closet.

Mike handed him the shirt, and Jake pulled it on and tucked it in.

He looked down at himself and smiled. "Man, that feels better."

"It sure looks better," Mike said.

Jake looked up at Mike, gratitude in his eyes. "I owe you one, buddy."

"Well, then, we may as well run up the tab. I can come by tonight and help you change again if you want. Or drop by on my way to work in the morning."

"No need," Jake said. "I'll ask my PT. He just wasn't here this morning, and my OT is a woman. I think I'll be fine. Either that, or I won't take these off again."

Mike laughed and relaxed back in his chair, feeling like he knew Jake better already.

CHAPTER FORTY

I can't believe my eyes," Lynda said later that day. "You're sitting up and dressed and everything."

Jake looked up at her from his wheelchair by the window, trying not to look quite so glad that she was here. "Yeah, but let me tell you. It's no picnic."

Lynda took the chair across from him. "When did this happen?"

"This morning. I got up to sixty degrees, so they left me here. I threw my usual tantrum, called them names, and threatened lawsuits, but they left me anyway."

He could see that she wasn't sure if he was kidding or not. "Don't you want to sit up?" she asked.

He shrugged. "It's not as simple as that, Lynda. Sitting up is a major ordeal. If I ever get all the way up, I'll never take it for granted again."

Her face softened. "I'm sorry, Jake. I didn't mean to be insensitive."

Now he felt like a heel. "It's okay. Actually, I asked them to leave me in the chair. I wanted to look out the window."

Lynda peered out at the parking lot below them. "So how is it?"

"Makes me feel more like a prisoner, frankly," he said quietly. "I'm stuck in here, and there's a whole world still out there."

"A whole bunch of cars, anyway. Oh, look. Is that a red Porsche parked over there? It looks just like yours."

Jake struggled upward to see it. "Where?"

"In that last row, off by itself."

Jake spotted it, and his face changed. "Yeah, it does look like mine. What do you know?"

"Me?" she asked with a grin. "Nothing. I don't know anything."

He looked up at her, his eye narrowing and saw her teasing grin. "Lynda, that wouldn't be mine—"

She nodded slowly. "I had Mike move it today. He said he came in and saw you."

Jake gazed hungrily down at the car. "He didn't tell me he brought my Porsche."

"It's a surprise," she said. "We were going to wait until you could see it out the window, but here you are."

His smile faded, and a look of longing came over his face—not for the car but for the life he'd had when he could drive it.

Lynda looked down at his chair. "Does this thing roll easily?"

"It's supposed to," he said.

"Then how about if I take you for a walk? We can go say hello to the car."

Jake grinned. "I'd like that. But what about your ribs? You're not supposed to push anything heavy, are you?"

"I'm doing a lot better," she said. "I'm getting my strength back. Don't worry."

"I don't want you hurting yourself for me, Lynda."

"Would I do that?"

"Of course you would. You already have."

"What does that mean?"

Jake's look was soft as he met her eyes. "Mike told me how you pulled me out of the plane. Nobody told me. I don't know how I thought I'd gotten out, but it never occurred to me that you'd done it."

"You would have done the same thing for me."

She started pushing him toward the door, and he mulled those words over. *Would* he have done the same thing? If she had been unconscious and he'd been the one awake, would he have risked his life to take the time to save her?

He doubted it. And if he *had*, he no doubt would have told her about it the moment she came to. He didn't like doing things he didn't get credit for.

But she'd done it and then hadn't mentioned it; she probably counted her heroism as such a natural thing that it hadn't occurred to her to tell him.

Shaking off the thoughts, he tried to be flip again. "So—has anybody tried to kill you today?"

She smiled. "Not today. I think it's all over now that they have Doug locked up. I'm starting to relax a little."

"So you feel pretty sure he did it?"

She was quiet for a moment. "Well—I still find it hard to believe. I mean, it's just weird that he would try something like that after all this time. But I guess things fester. Who knows what prison was like for him? Maybe he spent the whole time plotting his revenge on me."

As she spoke, she pushed him down the long hall and onto the elevator then to the first floor and through the courtyard where patients were scattered about under trees and strolled down sidewalks while the Florida sun shone down warmly and the autumn breeze cooled.

"How do you feel?" she asked after a moment.

Jake was smiling. "Fine," he said. "I'm feeling just fine."

"We can go back in any time you want."

"Not yet," he said. "I really do want to see my car."

She pushed him out onto the parking lot and through the rows of cars. He closed his eyes and let the sun beat down on his face and thought how good it was to be out of that controlled, air-conditioned environment.

When he opened his eyes again, he saw his car. Slowly, he smiled. "Not a scratch on it."

"No, it looks pretty good, for a Porsche."

He laughed as they got closer, and he touched the fender with featherlight fingers, as if greeting a cherished lover. "Man, what I wouldn't give to sit in it again."

Lynda's smile faded. "Well—I could go try to find an orderly who'd be willing to lift you in."

Jake shook his head. "No. I can't sit all the way up, remember? I'll save it for later."

The look she gave him was sweet and surprised. "Jake? Do you realize that's the first positive thing I've heard you say?"

"That I can't sit up?"

"No, that you'll save it for later. You know you're getting better, don't you?"

He sighed. "I guess so. I'm just not very optimistic about how much better I can get." He rolled to the window of the car, peered in at the plush, sleek seats that used to feel so natural beneath him. "Thanks for bringing it here, Lynda. It made the effort of sitting up worth it."

"Good," she said. "I'll leave it here for a while, so you can look out and see it any time you want."

He smiled. "That'll be good."

She wheeled him back to the courtyard where other patients and family members milled around. They found a shady place under a tree, and she sat down on a bench opposite him. Jake relaxed and looked up at the sky. It was cobalt blue, cloudless, a perfect day for flying. He wondered if he'd ever be able to experience that feeling again.

"Do you miss flying?" he asked her.

She nodded. "Yeah. I miss it pretty bad."

"What are you gonna do about your plane? Get another one?"

"No. I was going to sell that one, remember?"

He brought his gaze back to her. "But you loved it so much."

"Maybe too much. Anyway, I've kind of reconciled myself to giving it up for a while."

"What a waste," he said, his gaze returning to the sky. "You can fly and don't want to while I'd give my right arm to fly—and can't."

Lynda followed his gaze to the sky.

"They replaced me, you know," he went on. "I got flowers from my boss at TSA. I called him to thank him, and he said that he'd had to find a replacement. He said they were looking into a supervisory job on the ground if I wanted it, but I told him no thanks."

"Well, couldn't you at least consider it?"

"Right now, I'm not up to considering anything. I don't want to take a desk job, and I don't want to be on disability, and I don't want to be grounded for the rest of my life."

"You can get a medical waiver to fly with one eye, Jake, if you get use of your legs back. Maybe you can't fly for TSA, but you'll be able to fly again someday."

"But I loved my job." His voice caught, and he let out a heavy breath. "I guess I thought that maybe … by some miracle …" His words fell off, and she saw the tears gather in his eye as he shook the thought away.

After a moment, as if one dread reminded him of another, he spoke again. "We're having the unveiling Monday."

"What unveiling?"

He pointed to the bandage on his face. "The bandages. They're taking them off for good."

"Jake, that's wonderful."

Those tears seemed to well deeper. "Is it? I have a gash that goes through my eye to my cheekbone, Lynda. It was bad enough to blind me. I don't even know how many stitches I have. Do you honestly think I'm looking forward to seeing myself?"

"It'll be okay. You have good doctors."

"It doesn't matter how good they are if I have only one eye and a mug that would terrify children." He looked away, as though doing so could divert her attention from his tears. "You know, I was a good-looking guy. Women liked me. It was my greatest strength."

"I guess that's a matter of opinion."

"What? You didn't think I was good-looking?" he asked skeptically.

"Oh, there is no question that you were. But that wasn't your greatest strength. It never is. Maybe you needed to stop relying on your looks so you could find what you're really made of."

He felt his face reddening. "In other words, I was arrogant about my looks, so I needed to lose my face? Is that what you're saying?"

"No. What I am saying is that looks are just temporary, anyway. Don't you think it's time you go deeper into yourself to discover other strengths?"

"Wow," he said. "What did the doctor do? Ask you to prepare me for looking like the Elephant Man? Did he tell you to teach me to be beautiful on the inside?"

"No. Your face is going to be fine, Jake. You lost an eye. But you can still see. You're not blind."

"I'm blind enough to lose my job even if I get my legs back! What am I gonna do for a living?"

"Not everyone who works in the airline industry is a pilot, Jake—there are other positions, even at TSA. And if that doesn't appeal to you, you'll find something, Jake! You're an intelligent man. It's going to be all right."

Her reassurances seemed to make him angrier, and he looked off into the trees and shook his head dolefully. "Sometimes I wish I could have your kind of naivete."

"I'm not naive," she said. "In fact, I think I'm pretty savvy." She touched his hand, and he recoiled. "Jake, look at me."

He moved his disgusted gaze back to her. "What?"

"You're scared, but it'll be all right. In fact, I'll be here when they take the bandages off if you want. Do you want me to be here?"

He breathed a sarcastic laugh. "Yeah. You can give me another pep talk like this one after I see myself. You always make me feel so much better."

"I'm sorry, Jake," she said. "I haven't been trying to depress you, really. Do you want me there?"

His shoulders wilted, and he rubbed his forehead. "Yeah, I guess so," he said quietly. "I'll probably need somebody in my corner."

"Okay, I'll be here. And you'll see. You're probably even better looking now than you were before."

"Yeah," he said, not believing a word. "The scar will give me character, right?"

"Right. I happen to really like men with scars."

"Yeah, sure," he said. "I didn't notice any scars on that detective friend of yours."

She frowned. "Who, Larry?"

"Yeah, *Larry*."

For a moment, she stared at him blankly, and he hated himself for sounding like a jealous lover. He wasn't jealous. He was just ... curious. "So you two are getting pretty close, aren't you?"

She seemed to struggle with the smile creeping across her face. "There's something about having a maniac trying to kill you that makes you depend on the detective on the case. Call me crazy. I don't think I'll be seeing that much of him now, though, since they caught the guy."

She couldn't tell if Jake accepted that or not or if he even wanted to. Finally she stood up. "Are you ready to go back in?"

"Yeah," he said. "I have a hot date with Oprah. Can't miss that."

"Do you want me to bring you some books Monday? Or a radio? Or a hamburger?"

"Why don't we get these bandages off first, and then I'll decide if I have an appetite."

She looked down at him, wishing for the right words. "Are you that scared, Jake?"

He thought for a moment then said honestly, "Scareder than I was when we were about to crash. On Monday, I might just hit bottom."

CHAPTER FORTY-ONE

Wearing his shaded glasses and a fake mustache with his hair moussed back, Keith pulled into the parking lot outside the Schilling Building where Lynda worked and slowly drove through it, searching for her car. If only he could find it, he could wait for her to come out then follow her to wherever she was staying now. He could get her out of the picture once and for all and find Paige and Brianna in the bargain.

But her car wasn't there. It wasn't going to happen today. He tried not to let it discourage him.

But the clock was ticking, and recent developments hadn't helped his case any. If he knew Lynda Barrett, she'd find some way to use his arrest against him in court, even though he'd gotten off. She was slick that way. That's why she was dangerous. He never should have shown up that day at Brianna's school, but after the crash, he'd felt so sure he wouldn't meet with any resistance. If Paige didn't have a lawyer to run to, she would start feeling defeated and give in.

He'd always made her give in before. All those visits to the emergency room when he'd convinced her to tell the doctors that she had fallen down the stairs or been in a car accident or a dozen other creative stories he'd come up with, she had always complied.

Until Brianna had gotten hurt.

That, he admitted now, was his biggest mistake, but it wasn't as if it was all his fault. They'd been arguing, he and Paige, and she'd mouthed off to him, forcing him to crack her with a backhand across the face. Brianna had started crying—that loud, shrill, eardrum-piercing screaming that drove him up the wall—and someone *had* to shut her up.

It was his duty as a father to teach her to control herself.

But, as usual, Paige had gone off the deep end. And Lynda Barrett had empowered her to leave him, once and for all, and take his little girl.

But if he could get rid of Lynda now, he knew he could reason with Paige again. She *knew* he was a better parent. He made more money and could give Brianna nicer things. He could teach her self-control, teach her right from wrong. He could discipline her much more effectively than Paige, who let her run wild most of the time. And he was certain that he loved her more.

All he had to do was catch up with Lynda. She would have to report to work sooner or later, and when she did, he would be waiting. What he would do then he wasn't sure, but he knew something would come to him.

For a while, he drove around town—as he did every day before he reported to work—looking through parking lots of hotels and apartments, driving through neighborhoods and parks, looking for Paige's or Lynda's car, searching for his daughter's tawny head among the children at playgrounds.

He had even called Lynda's secretary, pretending he was an insurance investigator looking for her, but the woman wouldn't tell him a thing. When he'd asked her when she expected Lynda to return to work, she'd said maybe another week or two, possibly sooner.

He thought as he drove: What *would* he do when he finally caught up with her? She had escaped the crash and the fire, so this time his attack needed to be swift and vicious. And certain.

A bomb.

A slow smile came to his face as he flipped through the possibilities. It was easier to buy dynamite than a gun, and he knew enough about engines to rig it to her car. All he needed was a few ingredients and a window of time to plant it in the right place. Then it would be all over.

Turning the car around, he headed for the interstate. He'd have to buy the dynamite out of town, so the cops couldn't trace it to him after the fact. While he was at it, he should probably get a gun, too. Then if he discovered where they were all staying before Lynda returned to work, he could try one more time to get her out of the way.

One more time was all he would need.

The big church that had once been like a home to Lynda was still warm and welcoming, but in many ways she felt like the Prodigal Son, covered with mud and pig slop, starving and remorseful as she returned to her Father's house.

At her side was Paige, holding Brianna on her hip, looking a little awkward and nervous as they stepped through the side door of the church and entered the hallway where the Sunday school classes were.

Paige's step slowed, and Lynda saw the trepidation on her face. "I hate to leave her. I know this sounds crazy, but what if somehow Keith found out we were coming? Or sees our car here? He's smart, Lynda. What if he comes to her class and takes her?"

Lynda knew she couldn't promise that nothing would happen, not when Paige had encountered so many surprises already. "I really wanted you to come to the adult class with me, Paige," said Lynda, "but I understand your fear and wanting to stay with Brianna."

"I think it's more important right now for *her* to be in Sunday school," Paige said. "Do you think they'd let me stay with her? I could help with the other kids."

She had half-expected Paige to flee back home. This idea was at least better than that. "I'm sure it'll be all right," she said. "They always need help in the preschool area." She followed the signs to the class for three-year-olds and looked inside. A few children were already there, playing with blocks, coloring, and banging on the piano in the corner of the room. Lynda didn't know the teacher, and sadly she realized that a whole new group of people had become family members in the church in her absence. Maybe it wasn't even her family any more.

The teacher welcomed Brianna with delight and immediately interested her in some Play-Doh, and Lynda waited as Paige explained that she didn't want to leave her.

The teacher embraced Paige as an answered prayer. "My assistant just had a baby, and I didn't know how I was going to handle the class today. Come on over here, and you can help me get the glue out for the projects."

Satisfied that Paige was welcome, Lynda left the room and drifted back up the hallway, wondering if her class was still meeting in the same place. Despair and humility fell over her as she went up the hall, against the crowd beginning to get thicker and realized that the few people she did recognize didn't notice her.

And then she saw Brother Tommy, the pastor who'd once had such faith in her, the man who'd come to visit her in the hospital, who'd started a prayer vigil for her the moment he'd heard of the crash.

Like the Prodigal Son, she was transformed by the joy in his eyes, and he cut through the crowd, arms outstretched to meet her.

"It's so good to see you, Lynda." He hugged her carefully, as if he feared breaking her. "I've been waiting for you to come back."

Sadly, she looked around her. "I don't even know anyone any more."

"Sure you do," he said. "Come on. I'll go with you to your class. They'll be glad to see how their prayers have been answered."

The class met in the same place it had for years, and by the time the hour was over, Lynda felt accepted back into the family. When she met Paige and Brianna outside the sanctuary before the worship service, she felt so full of God's Spirit that she had no doubt some of it would spill over onto Paige.

CHAPTER FORTY-THREE

A cross St. Clair, Keith Varner worked at his kitchen table with the background noise of a broadcast church service filling the dead air in his apartment. He had all the ingredients laid out on the table in front of him: fuse wires, needle-nose pliers, ten pounds of Power Prime Dynamite, a blasting cap—everything he would need to blow Lynda to kingdom come.

All he would need was a few minutes under her car, and he could tape the bomb to her gas tank, wire it to the starter, and then get back and wait.

He could see it now. The explosion, the fire, the ambulances that would get there too late, and the media reports. And then he'd get a call from his lawyer saying that the court date had been postponed until Paige was able to find another lawyer. Only she wouldn't be able to get another lawyer because she had no money, and then she'd have to make a choice: either go into court to represent herself or give Brianna to him without a fight. And if she chose to represent herself, it would be a joke. Paige was not an articulate person, and she froze whenever she had to speak in front of a crowd. She would stutter and stammer and hem and haw, but she wouldn't make her case as clearly as he and his attorney would. It wouldn't take anything for the judge to rule that Keith was the better parent to have custody of his daughter. It was practically a done deal.

All he had to do was make sure that—once he caught up with Lynda Barrett—she would be taken out of the picture once and for all. And if he could get her when she was parked in her office parking lot, maybe she would have Paige's file and all of the evidence against him in her briefcase. That, too, would go up in flames.

He heard the choir on television singing the "Hallelujah Chorus," and with a round of laughter, he joined in.

He had an awful lot to be thankful for.

CHAPTER FORTY-FOUR

J ake was sitting upright in bed when Lynda got there on Monday morning, and she stopped and smiled at him before coming all the way into the room. "You look like sitting up comes more naturally now, Jake," she said. "Are the nausea and dizziness gone?"

"Yes, thanks to those two sadistic slave drivers who wouldn't let me rest until I was upright." He grinned slightly then and added, "Actually, I'm pretty thankful for them."

"So am I."

She came further into the room and set down the bag of magazines and books she'd brought him. "So have you heard from the doctor yet?"

His grin faded. "I'm told he's in the building, but he hasn't made it by yet." He breathed a sardonic laugh. "Amazing. Getting this bandage off seems like a matter of life and death to me, and to him it's just routine."

"It's going to be all right, Jake. I know it is. Have they prepared you at all? I mean, you've seen yourself when they changed the bandages, haven't you?"

"They wouldn't let me. The hospital shrink convinced the doctor that I couldn't handle it. When they took my eye out after the crash, they put in an implant and attached it to the muscles. They told me it doesn't look like an eye at all. In fact, they said it looks like the inside of my mouth. Talk about bloodshot."

Lynda stepped closer to the bed, realizing that this might be more grim than she'd expected. "I guess I figured they had already put an artificial eye in."

"No, they can't do that for another three weeks or so. Most of the swelling has to go down. Plus, they have to make the eye. The guy who makes them and installs them is coming by this morning, too, to fill me in on the gory details."

"The guy who makes them puts them in?" she asked, cringing. "Is he a doctor?"

"Nope. An optician."

"An optician in the operating room?"

"Apparently there's no surgery involved," he said. He glanced up at her and noted the dour expression on her face. "Hey, if you don't want to stay, I understand. In fact, I'm not too thrilled about anybody seeing this but me."

"I'm staying," she said firmly. "You're going to need somebody here. It's just—I didn't realize they did it that way."

Groping for something to get both their minds off the dread, she glanced at the untouched breakfast tray beside his bed. "Aren't you going to eat?"

He shook his head. "Can't. I don't have much appetite today."

"But Jake, you're losing so much weight."

"And you think that'll detract from my good looks?" he asked sarcastically.

"Well, it won't help your therapy. You need your strength."

"I can't eat," he bit out. "Period. So give it a rest."

"Fine."

He reached over to his bed table and pulled out the mirror he shaved with. As he gazed into it, Lynda realized that the bandage allowed him to imagine his eye still intact and his scars perfectly healed. After it came off, however, there would be no imagining.

"Did you know I was in a calendar once?" he asked quietly.

"A calendar? What kind?"

"It was a calendar that the Chamber of Commerce in Houston put together—Houston's eligible bachelors. I was August. For a couple of years, people recognized me wherever I went. I had women lined up. I even got fan mail."

She wasn't impressed. "And are you better for the experience?"

He thought for a moment. "All I know is I didn't have a scar down my face, and my baby blues were intact. Small things, I know, but they meant a lot to me."

The catch in his voice reminded her how hypercritical it was for her to pass judgment on his vanity, when she had lost so little in comparison. "They're not small things, Jake," she whispered. "It's got to be a trauma. But you know, don't you, that no matter what your face looks like under that bandage, they can do plastic surgery? They're doing great things now. And artificial eyes look real."

"Yeah," he whispered without conviction. "I keep telling myself that."

She was about to name all the celebrities she knew who'd had false eyes when the door opened, cutting off her thoughts.

"Good morning, Jake," the doctor said, coming into the room followed by an entourage of others. "Are you ready to get that bandage off?"

"Ready as I'll ever be."

"Great." The doctor was too cheerful, and Lynda wished he would make this a little easier, acknowledge Jake's suffering, offer him reassurances. As the doctor approached, she started to step away from the bed, but Jake caught her hand.

"No. Stay here."

"Okay," she said.

The doctor sat on the edge of the bed and got the scissors out of his pocket. "Jake, I'd like you to meet Dan Cirillo. He's the one who's going to be making your eye."

Jake shook his hand.

"Have they explained to you that you shouldn't be shocked when you see your eye, Jake?" Dan asked.

"Yeah, they warned me."

"It's not going to be pretty, but we'll put a patch over it until we can put a prosthesis in. After that, you'll be almost as good as new."

"Unless TSA has changed its policy about pilots having vision in both eyes, I won't be good as new." Turning back to the doctor, he said, "Let's get this over with."

Lynda held her breath as the doctor began to work the tape off Jake's face. She felt his hand tightening, and she squeezed back, wishing there were more she could do.

The doctor got the tape off and slowly began to peel the gauze away from Jake's face.

She saw the gash down his eyebrow, the black, blood-caked stitches that had been cleaned and sterilized with yellow iodine whenever the bandage had been changed. Now it was clear just how deep the gash on his face had been, deep enough to require several layers of stitches, and deep enough to destroy his eye.

"Yes, that's healing nicely," the doctor said in a pleasant voice as he worked the bandage further down. "When I saw that gash originally, I didn't know how well we'd be able to repair it. But this looks very nice."

But Lynda knew Jake's heart was going to be broken. The doctor uncovered his damaged eye, and she saw the small scar down the center of his eyelid, where it had been severed.

"Can you open that eye now, Jake?"

Jake opened it slowly, and it came only halfway up. In the socket was a pinkish-clear implant that looked nothing like an eye.

Perspiration beaded on her temples, and she tried to fight the tears threatening her. She couldn't cry. Whatever she did, she had to be positive. She had to smile.

The rest of the bandage peeled down easily, and finally, the doctor rolled it up and handed it to a nurse. Then, leaning in, he examined the gash. "Let me take these stitches out before I let you have a look," he said, reaching for another pair of scissors the nurse handed him. As he snipped, he kept talking. "The healing looks good, Jake. If you opt for plastic surgery later on, after it all heals, you can do a lot to get rid of this scar. For now, though, it looks like you lost a bad fight."

He finished snipping the stitches, pulled them out, and then cleaned the scar. "What do you think, guys?" the doctor asked. "Better than we expected?"

The others in the room concurred with scripted enthusiasm, but Lynda was silent.

The doctor got up, and Dan took his place to examine the eyelid.

Jake's hand still clung to hers.

"Most of this swelling should be gone in a couple of weeks, Jake. When that happens, you can come by my office, and we'll make you a new eye."

Jake looked up at him. "Come by your office? Will I be out by then?"

"Oh, you'll be going home in a few days, Jake," the doctor said as he made a notation on his chart. "You're doing fine. You're sitting up now, so there's no reason we should keep you here. You'll have to come back every day for therapy, of course, but there's no reason you have to stay here."

Ambivalence was written all over Jake's face. "Doc, I can hardly get around in that chair. Do you really think I'm capable of going home and taking care of myself?"

"Dr. Randall seems to think so, and he's ordered Allie to start concentrating on that a lot in the next few days," he said. "And we certainly don't mean to send you home alone. You'll need someone with you at first, to help you, and of course, you can't drive yourself back and forth to the hospital for therapy."

Lynda saw the emotional struggle on his face.

"So this is it?" Jake said. "You're accepting that I am like I am for good? You're not going to give me any more hope of getting better—or any more help?"

"There's plenty of hope, Jake, and we'll be helping you every day. We haven't given up on you."

She saw how desperately he struggled not to let go of his tenuous emotions, and finally, he looked up at Dan again. "So is this eye gonna wander all over the place? Are people going to know which eye not to look at when they talk to me?"

"It shouldn't," he said. "Artificial eyes have come a long way, Jake. They tend to move pretty well, especially if the initial surgery is done right. It looks like this was."

"*Pretty* well?"

"They satisfy most people who have them," he said. "But there are some methods to get more precise movement with the other eye. Most people don't think they need them after they see how well the eye moves, but for people who are on television, or say, models, we might go that extra mile and install a peg in the back of the eye that helps kick it around. Either way, the eye is going to be very similar to your other one. Most people won't realize you have a prosthesis."

Jake wasn't buying any of it, and Lynda had to admit that she wasn't either.

"So—are you ready to see?" the doctor asked.

Jake let go of her hand and took the mirror the doctor offered him. Slowly, he brought it to his face.

For a moment, he showed no expression as he saw the scar cutting down his face, the still-swollen socket where his eye used to be, the red conformer in the place of his eyeball, the black-and-blue bruising covering his forehead and most of his cheek.

"Not bad, huh?" the doctor asked.

Jake couldn't speak.

"It's not finished, Jake," Lynda whispered. "You have to give it time."

She saw the tear forming in his swollen eye, and felt some relief that he could still make tears. His face began to redden, and she realized that he was about to break down. She turned back to the doctor and the others. "Can you give him a little time alone?"

"Sure," the doctor said, patting his leg. "Jake, you give us a call if you have any problems. Lynda, here's the eye patch. It's easy to put on. Ring for a nurse if you have any problems with it."

Jake stayed silent as they left and kept staring blankly into the mirror.

"Do you want me to go, too, Jake?"

He didn't answer her, but his face grew redder, and he began to tremble.

"Jake?"

His face twisted, and his knuckles turned white as he gripped the mirror's handle. Suddenly, he hurled it across the room. It crashed against the wall.

"Stop it, Jake!" Lynda shouted.

But he didn't stop, and when he reached out and turned over the table beside his bed sending a cup of water, a plastic pitcher, a box of tissues, and the telephone crashing onto the floor, she covered her ears. "Jake, I know you're upset, but—"

His face still raging red, he scooted to the side of his bed, pushed his legs off, and acted as though he would stand on them and walk out on sheer anger.

"Jake, stop it!" she said, trying to hold him back, but he shook her away. "You know you can't do that! Jake, you'll fall!"

Gritting his teeth, he tried with all his might to stand on his feet, but they only hung there limply, brushing the floor without life.

The rolling tray of food sat next to his bed, and he swung his arm and sent it toppling over, too, his breakfast spilling onto the floor with a crash that reverberated throughout the room. Righting it, Lynda began to cry. Finally, she swung around to him, her hands in fists at her side. "Who cares about your stupid face!" she screamed.

He froze then and brought his tormented gaze up to her, staring at her with greater, deeper pain than she'd ever seen in anyone. Catching her breath, she cried, "It's not what matters, Jake! There's so much more to you!"

"That's easy for you to say," he said through his teeth. "Your face was only bruised!"

"And yours has a scar! It's not the end of the world, Jake! Your face has nothing to do with who you are!"

"Get out of my room," he said, trying to pull his legs back up. She reached over to help him, but he pushed her away again. "Just get out!"

Muffling her sobs, she ran from the room, not knowing what to do, where to go, how to help. For now, any help she offered was futile. Jake was hitting bottom, and there was nothing she could do to pull him back up. Not now. Not yet.

Instead of going home, Lynda found refuge in the prayer room and prayed that Jake's heart, so freshly broken, would start to seek God's face, instead of his own.

Jake couldn't remember weeping as hard as he wept that day. Now he knew the meaning of "gnashing of teeth." His teeth were gnashing, his heart was bleeding, and he didn't know where to turn.

No one could comfort him. No one. He would never be comforted again.

He wept over his distorted face and the legs that refused to move and his life that had been so prosperous and busy and content before. He wept over his loneliness, his isolation, despite how self-inflicted it was. And he wept over having no place to go even though he would be released in a few days. Where would he go when he couldn't even walk, and his face might frighten strangers? Was there a halfway house for maimed invalids?

Not for the first time he wished he'd died in the crash.

Jake Stevens, who always had so much control over his life, who was unfettered and uncommitted, who had all the money he needed, and who won friends and influenced women wherever he went, was now broken, alone, and homeless.

And there was no hope.

From the depths of his despair, from some place he didn't know existed inside of him, he cried out to God in fury. *I don't even know if you're up there, God, but I need a miracle.*

Did God hear him? He didn't know. But in that faithless moment of brokenness when he'd been sure that he was talking to thin air, he decided to believe that God had indeed heard him. He had no other choice.

CHAPTER FORTY-FIVE

J ake wore the patch the next day, even though he was despondent and still refused to eat. He put forth little effort in therapy. He had determined that he was going to die even if it took every ounce of the strength he had remaining. Nothing mattered any more.

When Lynda knocked on his door, he was surprised. After yesterday, he had expected never to see her again. "What are you doing here?" he asked.

She stayed in the doorway, leaning against the wall. "I wanted to see how you are. I worried about you all night."

"I'm still here," he said. He swallowed and struggled with the apology on the tip of his tongue. "I figured I scared you off yesterday. Thought you wouldn't come back."

She started slowly toward him. "I never even considered staying away," she said. "You're not going to run me off just because you have a bad day."

"All my days are bad," he said.

She came to his bedside where he was sitting up. "You know, the way you reacted yesterday wasn't surprising. I might have done the same thing."

"Would you?" he asked sarcastically but without much fervor. "I would have thought you'd take it real philosophically. It's just a face, they're just legs, it was just my life."

"No," she said. "I wouldn't have felt that way at all. I'd be as mad as you were. I might not have the strength you had to throw things and knock things over, but I'd have been just as mad. You

213

know, for somebody who has to stay in one spot, you sure did a lot of damage."

"Yeah," he said without humor. "Funny how much strength you can come up with when you don't care anymore."

"You do care, Jake. You know you do."

He fixed his sight on the ceiling. "Nope. That's where you're wrong."

Crossing her arms as if warding off his chill, she got up and stepped closer to the bed. "Well, anyway—I kind of like that patch. It gives you an air of mystery."

He kept staring at the ceiling. A tear fell to his cheek and rolled to his chin. "I'm gonna give little kids nightmares and old ladies heart attacks everywhere I go."

"No, you're not, Jake. They'll be fascinated, especially when you tell them the scar is the result of a plane crash."

He met her eyes directly for the first time that day. "Do you think the artificial eye is going to look just like mine?"

"I think so, Jake. They said it would."

"How can it?" he asked helplessly.

"I don't know how, but it can. Trust them."

He wiped the tear off his face and looked at the ceiling again. "I wonder if this is as good as it gets."

"Of course not. There are still several layers of stitches in there. There's a lot of swelling." She reached out and touched his injured cheek with her fingertips. "It'll go down," she whispered. "When these bruises clear, you'll see."

He took in a deep breath and caught her hand in his fist. Another tear dropped out, and he whispered, "No one back home would even recognize me. Not even my mother."

Lynda was confused. "Didn't you say your parents had both died?"

He let go of her hand then and covered his face, and a sob overtook him, then another, and another, until he wilted against her.

She sat next to him on the bed and held him, and she felt his arms closing around her, felt the despair, the loneliness, and the regrets wash out of him as he wept.

"I have a mother," he whispered. "I lie about her. But I have one."

"Jake, why haven't you told me? She should be here. I would have called her."

"She wouldn't have come," he said with certainty. "There's a lot of bad blood between us. She hates me."

"She can't hate you," Lynda said. "Mothers don't hate their sons."

"They do when their sons go years without seeing them, pretend they don't exist, and are too stingy to give a dime to help them out." He caught another sob, and his body shook with the force of it.

She pulled back to search his face. "But, Jake …"

"I'm being punished," he said, pointing to his injured face. "That's what all this is about. Before the crash, there was a lot of ugliness inside of me. Now I'm wearing it on the outside, too."

Lynda just held him tighter.

"I'll call your mother for you, Jake," she offered softly. "I'll talk to her. Does she know you're here?"

He shook his head. "She doesn't know anything about the crash. As far as she knows, I'm still living high, looking good, and trying to forget where I came from."

Someday she wanted to know just where that was, where Jake Stevens came from, but for now she was more concerned with where he was right now.

"Don't call her," he said. "I've got enough scars to last me a lifetime. I don't need any more."

"You need your mother, Jake. I'd give anything if mine were still alive and could be here with me one more time. There's so much I'd say to her."

"She *won't come*, Lynda."

"She needs to have the chance to decide that for herself."

"Fine, then," he said. "Call her. You'll see. She's the only Doris Stevens in Slapout, Texas. Just don't get your hopes up. Her tongue can slice right through you."

"I've survived worse," she whispered. "And so have you."

He crumpled in tears again and breathing a deep sob, shook his head viciously. "No, I haven't. I haven't survived. Not at all."

And as they clung to each other, Lynda searched for a way to make Jake see that it wasn't the end, it wasn't the worst, and he wasn't alone.

She would be here for him no matter how bad things got because in a strange way that she wasn't able to understand just yet, his despair had become her own. And she was determined to find a way to change it into joy.

May I speak to Doris Stevens?"

The woman who had answered the phone didn't respond but just put the phone down, and Lynda hoped that she had gone to get Jake's mother. It hadn't been easy to track her down. First Lynda had called information, only to find that they didn't have a listing for Doris Stevens, so she had tried the Slapout post office. The postal clerk knew Doris and had explained that she was listed in the phone book under her initials, H. D. Stevens. Graciously, she gave Lynda the number then told her to try Grady's Truck Stop if she wasn't home. That was where Doris worked, she said.

Now she waited, listening to the noise of the crowd in the background, and hoping that Doris would be able to hear her. She had practiced all the way home from the hospital what she would say, but now that the moment had come, she had forgotten all of it.

"Hello?"

Lynda's heart skipped a beat. "Is this Doris Stevens?"

"Yeah, who wants to know?"

"My name is Lynda Barrett. I live in St. Clair, Florida. Ms. Stevens, I've gotten to know your son, Jake. He's here and—"

"Whatever he's done, I had nothin' to do with it."

Lynda hesitated. "Ms. Stevens, why do you think he's done anything?"

"Because he's got a heart of ice, that's why. I ain't seen the man in eight years. He got to be a big-shot pilot, and now he's ashamed of me. Well, you know what? I don't care. I'm ashamed of him, too."

This was harder than Lynda had imagined. "Ms. Stevens, Jake's been in an accident. A plane crash."

"What?"

The voice came through louder, clearer now, and she imagined the woman clutching the phone tighter. "That's right. About three weeks ago."

"Three weeks?" She hesitated, and then in a softer voice said, "That's about when he called me. He didn't tell me nothin' about no plane crash."

Lynda didn't know what to say to that. Why would Jake have called her and not told her that he was lying in the hospital? "He was injured badly, Ms. Stevens. He has a bad back injury that has caused paralysis in his legs."

"He can't walk?"

"No. There is a possibility that the paralysis will go away, though. They think when the swelling goes down, the feeling may come back. But there's no guarantee. And he also had a severe cut to his face and lost an eye."

Doris muttered an expletive then asked in a wobbly voice, "So what do you want from me?"

The question took Lynda by surprise. "Nothing. I just thought you'd want to know that your son is in the hospital in a lot of pain. Ms. Stevens, he's absolutely alone. He apparently doesn't know many people here—"

"What is he doin' there, anyway? I thought he lived in Houston."

She couldn't believe that Jake hadn't told his mother he was moving. "He was in the process of moving here when this happened. Ms. Stevens—he needs you."

She laughed then, a bitter, cold laugh. "Oh, yeah? Well, where was he when I needed him? Huh?"

"I don't know."

"Yeah, well, neither do I. Is there a lawsuit involved here? Is he suin' somebody?"

Until now, the thought had never occurred to her that Jake could sue her. Deciding against telling her that it was her plane and that she had been in the same crash, she said, "No, not that I know of."

"Then there's no money involved?"

"No. I haven't heard him suggest suing, at all."

"Then there's no need in my comin', is there?"

She didn't want to believe that Jake's mother was mercenary enough to see dollar signs in Jake's accident, so she chose to believe that it was a question of how she would finance the trip. "Uh—if you don't have the money, I'd be happy to send you a plane ticket."

The woman hesitated. "I wouldn't have a place to stay."

"I'd pay for your hotel, too," she said. "Will you come, Ms. Stevens?"

Again a pause. "What's the weather like there this time of year?"

"It's fine. Nice."

"Nice enough to go to the beach?"

She closed her eyes. Surely she wasn't looking at this as an opportunity to take a free vacation. "I don't know, Ms. Stevens."

"How close are you to Disney World?"

Reality began closing in on her. "I would think your time would be spent with Jake. Don't you care about his condition?"

"Let me tell you something," the woman spat back. "I raised that ingrate by myself with no help from anybody. I was there for him until the day he skipped town without lookin' back. When I was strugglin' and needed a hand, he wasn't there for me. So now, when he can't walk and can't see, I'm supposed to welcome him back with open arms so I can wait on him hand and foot? What's in it for me?"

For a moment, Lynda was quiet. "Maybe the knowledge that you did everything you could for your son?"

"I already did that," she said. "I don't owe him nothin' more."

Slowly Lynda set the phone back in its cradle and rested her face on her palm. No wonder he had lied about his mother. No wonder he hadn't visited her. Their relationship was an endless cycle of blame and selfishness and anger, a cycle that Lynda wasn't wise enough to break.

But what would she tell Jake? That his mother wouldn't come unless there was a monetary settlement involved or a trip to Disney World or nice weather for sunbathing?

How could a mother have such contempt for her son?

"Are you crying, Miss Lynda?"

Lynda turned around and saw Brianna standing in the doorway, looking up at her with big, curious eyes.

"Come here."

Brianna came slowly toward her. "Why are you crying?"

"Because somebody just made me real sad." She pulled Brianna into her lap, and the child kept gazing at her.

"Did somebody hit you?"

"No."

"Did they try to take you?"

She realized then that Brianna was going down the list of things that made her sad, and Lynda felt a twofold rush of sorrow. Closing her eyes against the tears, she dropped her face to Brianna's crown. "No, Brianna, no one tried to take me. I'm sad for someone else."

"So they won't have to be?" she asked, as if trying to understand this new concept of surrogate sorrow.

She smiled. "Something like that."

Brianna laid her head against Lynda's chest, as if she knew that sitting still might be of some comfort to her, and finally, she looked up at her again. "Do you like to color?"

Lynda smiled. "Yeah. Yeah, I do."

Brianna slid out of her lap. "Come on, then."

And Lynda realized that the child's simple therapy might be just what she needed right now.

CHAPTER FORTY-SIX

I t felt like a burning, tingling sensation, just on the outside of his big toe. Nothing to get excited about.

But Jake got excited anyway. He jerked the sheets off his legs and peered down at his feet.

He'd been so exhausted when he'd gotten back from rehab today—where they'd forced him to work despite his indifference—that he had almost forgotten the scar and his eye. Maybe now he was just imagining the sensation. Maybe he just wanted to feel it so badly.

But it felt real, and his surprise gave birth to a fragile hope.

He started to call the nurse but changed his mind. What if he told the nurses, and they assured him it was just a side effect from the traction they'd had him on in the rehab room? What if he found out that it was nothing?

He focused all his concentration and every ounce of his energy into that big toe, willing it to move. But it lay still, dead, not getting the messages his brain was sending.

Was this no different than the pressure he felt when he was touched or pulled? Was it without meaning?

He heard Lynda's familiar rat-tat-a-tat-tat knock on the door and called, "Come in."

She came into the room all cheer and sunshine, and he debated whether to tell her what he felt.

"Hi," she said.

"Hi." He kept staring at his foot.

"How'd your rehab go today?"

"Good."

She followed his gaze to his toe. "What are you looking at, Jake?"

He didn't answer for a moment then finally looked up at her. "My toe," he said. "I've been feeling some pain in it. Kind of a burning."

She caught her breath and with wide eyes, went to stand at the foot of his bed. Touching the toes on both feet, she asked, "Can you feel this?"

His eyes grew wider. "Just on that toe. But I feel you touching that toe!"

She was trying to hold back her excitement, just as he was. "Have you tried to move it?"

"I was trying," he said. "It hasn't budged."

"Well, try again. Come on, Jake. Move it."

Silence fell over the room as he found his concentration again, and as though he could telekinetically move the toe, he stared down at it.

"Was that a twitch?" she asked finally. "I thought I saw a twitch!"

Jake wasn't sure. He tried again, and this time the toe moved an eighth of an inch.

"You did it!" Lynda cried, jumping up and slinging a fist through the air. "Oh, Jake, you moved it!"

He started to laugh, and she ran around the bed and hugged him.

"Call somebody before I forget how," he said.

With trembling hands, she found the button that called for the nurse.

It was definitely cause for celebration, Dr. Randall said when he finally made it to the hospital to examine Jake. It might mean that Jake could get his legs back.

But for all his newfound hope, Jake couldn't escape the doctor's qualifier that it didn't mean he'd get all his feeling back, or get movement in his leg or the rest of his foot. But this was something.

Torn between exhilaration and frustration, he asked Lynda to take him out of the hospital.

221

Glad to be asked for anything, she wheeled him outside where night had already descended, and the stars lit up the sky with a magnificent brilliance. Jake leaned his head back and looked up, taking it all in.

Lynda had gotten quiet, and he could see that something was on her mind. Maybe there was something she didn't want to tell him. When they got to a small park near the hospital, she locked his wheels and sat down on a bench facing him.

He met her eyes squarely. "What's wrong, Lynda?"

"Nothing. Why do you think something's wrong?"

"I could read it in your mood swings today," he said. "As happy as we got, something kept bringing you down."

He studied her face for a moment. "She won't come, will she?"

Lynda couldn't deny it. "No."

He took in a deep, ragged breath. "It's okay," he said, trying not to look crestfallen. "I told you it would be that way. What did she say?"

He saw the turmoil on her face and realized that it must be bad, too bad for her to relate to him. He almost wished he hadn't asked. "She's just ... busy right now."

Jake looked into the breeze and thought about the last time he'd seen his mother. He wondered if she had changed, or if the years of hard work, cigarette smoke, and nights spent in the truck stop flirting with the patrons had aged her. "When you told her about my injuries ... What did she say?"

"She was shocked," Lynda said. "She said you had called her since the crash, and you didn't say anything about it."

"She didn't seem all that receptive." He could see by her face that she knew what he meant. "There's a lot of water under our bridge, Lynda," he went on. "I haven't been proud of where I came from, and I haven't been particularly proud of her. I've said and done some hateful things. She has a reason for hating me."

As he spoke, he felt exposed, open, as transparent as he'd ever been in his life. But Lynda had already seen farther into him than anyone else ever had. "I think you're changing, Jake."

He breathed a laugh. "Oh, yeah? You think so?"

She smiled. "I don't think the old Jake would ever have admitted guilt."

"Well, I've had a lot of time to think about it over the last few weeks."

Her smile faded. "Have you been thinking about going home, Jake?"

He averted his eyes again and studied the trunk of the tree next to him. "Home where? I've thought of going back to Texas to finish my therapy there. There are people there I could probably stay with. That is, if they aren't too repulsed by me. I haven't even told them I've been hurt."

She wasn't sure why that disappointed her. "Is that what you want to do?" she asked.

He sighed. "I don't know. It honestly feels like I'm somebody else now. Like the Jake Stevens they all knew is dead. And here I am in his useless shell, trying to figure out who I am now. And nothing against all my friends, but most of them are kind of—self-centered. I can't see them wanting to help out an invalid."

"You're not an invalid," she said. "You're just in transition. You need time."

Something about that sweet declaration made his heart soften, and he smiled at her. She leaned forward, her big, round eyes drilling into his, and he wondered how she had managed to make him risk more honesty with her than he'd ever risked with anyone else. Even himself.

"I had an idea," she said. "But I don't know how you'll feel about it."

"What?"

She averted her eyes and studied her hands. "I've been staying at my father's house, and there's a garage apartment there that used to be mine. It's got a small kitchen, a refrigerator, and a bathroom, and it's pretty comfortable." She made herself meet his gaze. "I was thinking that ... maybe when they release you ... you could stay there. I could take care of all your meals, transport you back and forth to the hospital for your therapy every day, and help you in whatever way you needed. But you'd still have your privacy."

A lump the size of Wyoming formed in his throat, and he gaped at her, not believing that he'd heard her right. "I couldn't, Lynda. That's too much of an imposition. You're recovering, too. The last thing you need is somebody like me in your way."

"You won't be in the way. You'd have your own place. You won't have to worry about rent or food or anything for a while. I have someone else staying with me, a client of mine and her daughter. She's hiding from her abusive ex-husband until we can get into court. Between his shenanigans and the stuff that's already happened to me, we're both a little paranoid. It might be nice to have a man around the house."

The word "man" shook him, for he hadn't thought of himself as a man in a long time. "Not that I'd be of any use if anything happened," he said. "I guess I could run over somebody in my wheelchair, but it's not like I can defend you."

She smirked. "I don't know, Jake. You were pretty dangerous the other day. If you had something to throw—"

He took it as it was intended and chuckled softly.

"Besides, we don't need defending," she said. "Her ex doesn't know where we are, and the guy who was after me is still in jail. Your presence will just lend a little stability."

She didn't mean it, he thought. She was just saying that to make him feel needed, but he had to admit he appreciated it. She was giving him the option of keeping his dignity, his masculinity. She was offering him a home, temporary though it might be.

It was better than any other option he had.

She saw his reticence. "Come on, Jake. Say yes if for no other reason than to appease my conscience. It was my plane that crashed. Let me make it up to you as much as I can."

Tears came to his eyes, and he struggled to hold them back. "You don't have to buy my forgiveness," he whispered after a moment.

"That's not what I'm doing," she said. "The truth is neither your feet nor your hair needs washing, so I can do this instead."

"What?"

She smiled. "Never mind. Just say yes."

He sighed. "You're going to regret it."

"No," she said with a smile. "I don't think I will."

CHAPTER FORTY-SEVEN

The sound of his heels echoed through the old, musty judicial building as Keith checked the sign on each door, looking for the county clerk's office. He was tired of waiting. He'd spent most of several days watching the parking lot at Lynda's law firm, but she hadn't been there yet. Then he'd tried to get her forwarding address by sending something to her old address with a note to the post office to return it with her new one. But the address they had returned was to a post office box. He had even tried staking out the post office, but he hadn't been able to be there all the time, and if she'd checked her box, he'd missed her.

But he wasn't stupid. He had resources, and he knew how to use them. And he was going to start with public records. It had been worth the drive to St. Petersburg where the county records were kept, and though he didn't know what he was looking for, he was sure he'd know when he found it. His goal for now was to find every public record that existed on Lynda or her family. Something there would have to give him a clue.

He found the office and went into the dimly lit room that looked as if it could use a good electrician to update the wiring. A young couple was there getting a marriage license. Smirking, he leaned on the counter and thought of telling the poor guy to save his fifteen bucks and run like the wind. But the kid was young—too young to be reasoned with, old enough to make mistakes that would ruin his life. Just like Keith had been when he and Paige had stood there, giggling like this couple and anticipating the life they were planning together.

But that was before he'd learned what a shrew she was.

Now, on the battleground of their marriage, his daughter had become the spoils. Didn't Paige realize what her obstinance was going to cost her? Didn't she understand that when he got through with her, she'd have nothing left? Least of all Brianna.

The couple blushed over their finished license, and Keith flashed them a saccharine, congratulatory smile then winked at the lady behind the desk. "Cute kids," he said as they left the room.

"Yes, they are," she said. "I hope everything works out for them."

"I'm sure it will," he said. "We've been married for ten years now, and we're as happy as the day we came in here to get our license."

"Oh, that's nice."

"Yes. Course, I realize that not everybody is as lucky as I am, but we work at it, you know? Teamwork. It's the only way."

He could have sworn her eyes were twinkling as she smiled up at him. "That's so rare these days. Frankly, I worry about every couple that comes in here. I pray for them."

"Good for you," he said. "Good for you."

She cleared off the papers she'd had them sign and stuck them in the appropriate bins. "Now, what can I do for you?"

"I need to look up some public records."

"All right," she said, grabbing a form out of another bin. "Just fill this out, and I'll show you how to find them. What exactly are you looking for? A person or a property?"

"A person, but that might lead me to real estate."

"That's fine. And what is the last name of the person you're looking for?"

He almost gave her Lynda's last name then realized that there had been too much publicity about the attempts on her life. "Barnett," he said finally. "Frank Barnett."

"All right," she said, taking the form back and checking the fake signature. "Just follow me. We have A through J in this room."

She took him to a huge room full of volumes of public records for Pinellas County and led him to a computer where she showed him how to find the name of the person he was looking for, see the list of documents the county had on that person, and determine what volume the record was in.

He thanked her profusely then waited as she left him alone.

The moment he typed in Lynda's name, two listings came up. Quickly he jotted down where to find her birth certificate and the documents pertaining to her property. There was no record of a marriage license or a divorce or any judgments against her or any other documents.

Leaving the computer, he found the book with her birth certificate and flipped through it until he found her name. There she was.

As if he'd found some crucial bit of information, he stared down at it with a smile and quickly jotted down both parents' names and her birthdate in case he ever needed it.

The documents on her house would be useless now; the house was burned, so she wouldn't be going back. He went back to the computer and typed in her mother's name.

A list of records emerged, and he jotted down the number of the book that had records on her property. He scanned the list again, looking for anything else he could use and saw her death certificate.

Dead end, he thought, clearing the screen.

He punched in her father's name. Again, he jotted down the property book and came across another death certificate.

Frustrated, he sat back in the chair.

All right, he told himself, *don't give up yet. There's got to be something here.*

Looking down at his note paper, he noticed a connection. One of the numbers on the list of Lynda's properties matched the book number for the property on both of Lynda's parents. Had she inherited their home? If so, it surely wasn't the one that had burned down—that one had been far too new and expensive.

He flew to that book, pulled it out, and shuffled through the pages until he came to what he was looking for—A house on the other side of town, bought forty years ago; ownership had been transferred to Lynda three months ago upon the death of her father!

He banged his fist on the table then waved it over his head in exhilaration. This was it! It had to be. She was staying in her father's home, and he had found her! Paige and Brianna were probably there with her!

He slammed the book shut but didn't bother to put it back. Quickly, he went back to the computer, cleared the screen so no one would link him to her, and headed out without another word to the clerk.

CHAPTER FORTY-EIGHT

It had been months since the garage apartment had even been opened and years since it had been used for more than storage. With Paige's help, Lynda cleaned all of the junk out of it then set about scrubbing. A thick layer of dust had settled over every piece of furniture, and the bedspread and sheets and curtains all smelled musty. She gathered them all up to wash while Paige vacuumed the mattress and couch, the recliner, and the carpet, which really didn't look so bad considering how old it was.

"Does this Jake person know about me?" Paige asked in a slightly troubled voice as she worked.

"Yes. I told him last night."

"Mmmm." She coiled the cord on the vacuum cleaner then got her bucket from Brianna, who was sitting in the empty bathtub, "scrubbing it" with a dry brush. "So you say he's paralyzed? He can't walk?"

"No, he can't. What's the matter, Paige?"

Paige shrugged. "I don't know." She started to say something, stopped then tried again.

"What is it, Paige? What's on your mind?"

Paige leaned back against a wall and looked down at her feet. "I was thinking. Maybe it's time we went on home."

"Home? Are you serious?"

"Well, yeah. I mean, Jake's coming, and you won't be alone any more."

"But Paige, what about Keith?"

Paige thought that over for a moment. "He's probably cooled down by now. His rages don't usually last that long. He's probably feeling real bad about what he did, and when he gets like that—sorry and all—he can be okay. Maybe I don't have to be afraid of him."

Lynda wanted to scream at her that she was being stupid, but if her time with Jake had taught her anything, it was that she had to learn diplomacy. "Paige, if you go back home and have any contact with him at all, it could ruin our case. And it could get you killed."

When Paige covered her face with her hand, Lynda stepped closer. Removing Paige's hand and making the young woman look at her, she said, "Paige, what's really wrong?"

"I don't know. Maybe I'm just homesick. And with Jake coming—I don't know; I'm just not very comfortable around men."

"But you weren't uncomfortable with Larry or Tony."

"I didn't have to be *alone* with them much. Besides, I knew they were protecting me."

"Well, think of Jake as protecting you, too. And you're not really going to be alone with him. I'll be here."

"Yeah, but you'll be going back to work soon." She caught herself and tried to rally. "I'm sorry. You're helping me, so you have every right to help him, too. It's awfully nice of you. I'm sure he needs help. I'll get over it."

"But will you get over it here or at home?"

Paige met Lynda's eyes, and Lynda saw the struggle there. "You'd hate me if I went back home, wouldn't you?"

"No, Paige, but I think *you* would hate you."

"But I'm not considering taking him back. Not at all. I just miss things being familiar."

Lynda sat down and studied the carpet for a moment, trying to find the right words. "Paige, familiarity has a lot of power. That's why you went back to Keith all those times before. It probably had a lot to do with familiarity, didn't it?"

Paige nodded.

"And if you let familiarity cause you to put yourself in danger again, don't you think that when—not if, but when—Keith shows up, he'll be able to convince you one way or another to take him back for that same familiarity?"

"Maybe, but—"

"Paige, he might take Brianna this time and go so far that you'd never see her again. The court date isn't that far off. He's bound to be getting desperate."

Paige's face changed, and she glanced into the bathroom at Brianna, who was singing the theme from "Barney." When she looked back at Lynda, she whispered, "You're right. Absolutely."

Lynda got up and faced Paige head on. "Paige, Jake's paralyzed. Why would you be worried about what he might do?"

"That's the crazy part. I know he won't hurt me if he's your friend, and I know he couldn't if he wanted to. But—men are so unpredictable to me. I never knew what to expect with Keith. Just when I thought I had all my bases covered, he'd show me that I didn't."

"You have them covered now, Paige. Right?"

Her sigh suggested she wasn't sure. "Maybe being around Jake is what I need now. Maybe he'll restore my faith in men."

Lynda wished she could say that was possible, but she wasn't so sure. "Well—he's a little scary-looking right now. He has a patch over his eye and a big scar down his cheek, and he's not the most pleasant person to be around because he's so angry about his injuries. But I've watched him change since I met him. In big ways. And he's going to keep changing. He'll have to if he's going to make it. But he'd never hurt you or Brianna. More likely, he'll keep absolutely to himself, and you won't see him at all except to take him meals."

Paige regarded Brianna, still sitting in the empty bathtub. "I guess I should realize how lucky I am," she said. "I have my legs, both eyes, and I have Brianna." She smiled and turned back to Lynda. "And I have you. So does he. Because of that, I promise to make him feel welcome here."

"Thank you, Paige. I knew I could count on you."

CHAPTER FORTY-NINE

K eith knew better than to drive down her street; it looked like a dead end. Instead, he parked his car a couple of blocks away in a small church parking lot and walked into the thick woods that lined one side of the street, except where it had been cleared for houses. There were only about three houses on the street, two right at the entrance and one secluded down at the dead end. He worked his way quietly through the woods, trying not to be seen.

There was someone outside at the first house he passed, a man working in the garden, so he assumed that wasn't the house. He crept forward until he had a clear view across the street and read the numbers on the opposite house. That wasn't it, either.

So it must be the one at the far end of the street. He stole through the trees and came up to the cyclone fence that defined the property. But there was no sign of any of them. He needed to get around front to see if he could identify one of their cars.

He was just about to risk stepping out of the woods when the back door opened. Keith froze.

He saw his little girl bounce out, and his heart melted.

It had been so long since he'd seen Brianna happy. The last few times she'd been screaming her lungs out, after all those ideas Paige had put into her head about him. But once he got her, he would manage to erase those ideas and turn them back on Paige. Then Brianna would be just as happy with him as she was now without him.

He trembled with anticipation as she walked out into the yard, talking to her doll as she went, and he poised himself to act the moment she came close enough. He could reach over the fence, grab her, and have her out of here before Paige even knew she was gone.

He wished he'd brought some candy or something to keep her quiet until they got away.

But then Paige came out with a broom and started sweeping the back porch. That was her, always cleaning, as if she couldn't stand to sit still.

Well—too bad. He would grab Brianna anyway, whether Paige saw or not. Maybe he could get out of there before she could get to the phone—

No. That was ludicrous. He'd be arrested before he got his car started. And he'd probably wind up in jail. This time, McRae would probably wash his hands of him, and he wouldn't have an advocate in court, and that lady lawyer would convince the judge that he was dangerous.

Quietly, he sat down on the ground behind a bush and watched, waiting for Paige to go back in and for Brianna to come near the fence. His only hope was to take her when Paige wasn't watching, so he'd have a head start in getting away.

But that wasn't going to happen today.

Paige said something to the child, and Brianna turned and frolicked in behind her mother. The door closed.

He didn't move. Maybe they would come back out. Maybe Brianna would stray out here alone....

He heard another door close, one he couldn't see from this position and then a car door. In seconds, he heard the car in the driveway starting.

They were leaving!

Jumping up, he ran through the trees back toward his car parked at the little church, hoping to catch up with them and follow them. But by the time he was behind the wheel, they were nowhere in sight.

Cursing his luck, he slammed his hand against the wheel. Didn't it always happen this way? Fate just kept working against him.

But it wouldn't forever. Sooner or later, something had to give. He thought of the possibilities, now that he knew where they were living. He couldn't set this house on fire because Brianna might be hurt. And if he installed the car bomb here, Brianna might be in the car or nearby when it blew up. No, he couldn't do anything that might put her in danger again. But he could watch the house; he could follow Lynda and, when she got to where she was going, fix a little surprise in her car. Or, if he kept watching, sooner or later Paige would take her eyes off Brianna and he could grab her. Either way, when the chance came, he would be there.

Time was running out, and he was getting anxious. But he was several steps ahead of the game already.

And he intended to win.

CHAPTER FIFTY

The morning Jake was to be released Lynda gave the garage apartment one final inspection. It was clean now, and she'd moved things around to accommodate his wheelchair. While the room wasn't as luxurious as he was probably used to, it was certainly better than a hospital room. She sat down in her father's recliner, which she'd asked Larry to move out here for Jake, and looked around at the small rooms her father had so lovingly built for her.

She had never forgotten the ribbon-cutting ceremony her parents had had for her the day she'd moved into the room. Her father had made a little speech in which he told her that while this room signified her independence from her parents, its proximity to the house symbolized that no matter how independent she grew or how far away she moved, she would always belong to them. Always.

As she sat here now, breathing the familiar scents and absorbing the warm colors and textures, she missed her parents. As much as she'd wanted to believe she was independent when she'd moved into this room, she had been far from it. Her parents had helped her to take her first leap out of the nest gracefully. They had made it easy for her, until she'd learned to fly on her own.

In many ways, Jake was like she had been then. She would have to teach him that he could be independent and that he could make it on his own. But she also wanted to teach him who he belonged to. And she surprised herself—she who had been so long without darkening the doorway of a church—with the fervency of her desire that Jake understand this.

She bowed her head and whispered a heartfelt prayer that this room would be blessed and that God would change Jake here. Then she got out the Bible she had bought especially for him and slipped it into the drawer of the end table beside the recliner. She wouldn't mention it; he would have to discover it for himself. She only hoped she would be able to help him understand the truth of its message.

She couldn't preach to him or force him. All she could do was pray for him.

Jake's life—both physical and spiritual—was in God's hands.

Allie walked beside Jake's wheelchair as he left the hospital, letting him push the wheels to move it along. He couldn't believe they were sending him home like this, still unable to walk. Oh, Allie had taught him how to function well enough in day-to-day activities, and now that he could sit all the way up and had this smaller, more maneuverable chair, he was much more capable. But he still didn't like it. Hospitals are supposed to heal people, not teach them how to cope with their brokenness.

But the alternative—*staying* in the hospital—was worse. He'd rather be going away somewhere, even if it wasn't home.

Lynda had brought the car to the front entrance. She had dressed up for the occasion, he saw, and had pulled her hair up in a loose chignon. He wondered why she'd bothered.

"Do you need help getting in, Jake?" she asked.

He wasn't sure whether he did or not but decided not to accept it anyway. "I can do it," he said, sidling his chair up to the open car door.

"You can do it, Jake," Allie said, not offering a hand to help. "Just use your arms and your stomach."

He could feel them all holding their breath as he got his arms into position then slid his body onto the car seat.

As if he'd just completed some Olympic feat, they all congratulated him. He felt like a toddler who'd just gone to the potty by himself, and the idea of such pathetic enthusiasm worsened his mood.

Lynda closed his door and got into the driver's side, but Allie came to his window. Jake lowered it.

"Just because you're going home doesn't mean you can neglect your therapy, Jake. I want you back here at nine tomorrow, and Lynda can just plan to leave you for six hours or so. We'll see if we can get some more of your toes to burn."

He smiled in spite of himself; he liked the sound of that. "I'll be here."

And as they drove away from the hospital, Jake wasn't sure whether to consider it a beginning or an ending. To him, it seemed as though he left the old Jake back there in the morgue, and he didn't yet know who the new Jake was.

A butterfly lit on Keith's shoulder, and he waved it away and peered between two bushes to the yard where Brianna played. Paige had set up a little tea party for her, and she had all her dolls in attendance. He smiled as she talked aloud to her friends and herself like a little princess to her courtiers.

But as always, Paige was right there, hovering over her. Calculating the distance to his car, which he'd parked on the closest street behind Lynda's house through the woods, he tried to decide whether he should chance jumping the fence and grabbing Brianna. Sweat broke out on his forehead, and he wiped it on his sleeve. He would have the advantage of surprise. Paige would probably be stunned long enough for him to get Brianna. It would probably take less than ten seconds to get back over the fence and maybe another thirty to get back to his car. By the time Paige stopped screaming and got to the phone, he would have blended into the cars on the main road a mile or so away.

The butterfly flitted across the fence and lit in some wildflowers growing in an old, untended garden. Keith watched Brianna laughing with one of her dolls and then pouring more invisible tea and offering it a cup.

He heard a car pull up in the front, and his heartbeat accelerated. "Lynda's home," Paige said as she got up. "I'll be in front, okay, Brianna?"

Brianna nodded indifferently as Paige went around between the garage and the house, and a slow smile came to Keith's lips. Was Brianna really alone?

He straightened and stepped through the bushes, watching his child with hungry, anxious eyes. He watched the butterfly flit over to the table where she sat.

"Mommy, it's a butterfly!" she said, her voice soft so that she wouldn't frighten it away.

It fluttered off, and Brianna got up and followed it. It lit in a piece of grass, and she bent over, trying to coax it onto her finger, but it flew a little further. As if it were in cahoots with Keith, it led her closer, closer, closer to the fence until she was almost close enough to reach.

Keith stepped into her view and touched the fence, whispering, "Brianna."

She looked up at him, stunned. The butterfly flew away.

His heart hammered, and his hands shook; there was so little time before Paige came back.

"Come closer, honey," he whispered, leaning over the fence. "Come give Daddy a kiss."

Her bottom lip began to tremble, and she backed away, farther out of his reach.

"Brianna, I said to come here," he said more firmly. "Now."

She started to cry and looked around for her mother, who was nowhere in sight.

He was getting angry now. This wasn't working out like he'd planned. Gritting his teeth, he whispered, "Brianna, I told you to come here right now! I'm your daddy!"

He started to lunge over the fence, but Brianna screamed and lit out across the yard.

Cursing, Keith realized he'd gone too far; he'd never catch her before she made it to the front yard. Afraid of being caught, he tore back through the woods to his car.

Lynda had just gotten Jake into the apartment and introduced him to Paige when they heard the scream.

Paige dashed outside and found Brianna almost to the garage apartment already, shrieking.

"What is it, honey? What's wrong?"

"Daddy! Daddy! He's gonna take me!" she screamed.

239

Paige stepped back into the doorway, looking helplessly at Lynda. "No, honey. Daddy can't get you here."

"It's him!" Brianna screamed.

"It's me, isn't it?" Jake asked. "She saw me coming in, and I scared her."

Paige wasn't sure. "Honey, that's not Daddy. That's a nice man named Jake. Remember I told you he was going to live here? Remember we got the room fixed up for him?"

Hiccuping her sobs, Brianna refused to look up.

Paige looked apologetically at Jake. "She's—terrified of men. If you knew her father you'd know why. I'm so sorry."

"It's all right," he said. "I make a pretty scary first impression."

"I'll take her in," Paige said and quickly hurried back toward the house.

The silence in their wake was palpable, and Lynda turned back to Jake, trying to find the words that would make him feel less like an intruder. "Not exactly the welcome I had planned for you. I'm sorry, Jake."

He tried to take it philosophically. "Hey, I told you I'd frighten little kids. It's no surprise. Look, if this is gonna be a problem, they were here first."

"It'll be all right," Lynda assured him. "She's just been through an awful lot lately. Her father tried to fight her out of Paige's arms at the courthouse just a few days ago. It was terrifying to her. It's not the way you look, Jake; it's the fact that you're a man."

But Jake wasn't buying it. "It's okay, Lynda. Really, I can handle this."

She sighed. "We're having dinner at seven. Paige has been doing the cooking. She made a special dinner just for you."

"Maybe I'd better just eat here."

"Out of the question. You have to have dinner with us tonight."

"It might spoil your appetite," he said sardonically. "That is, if it doesn't send the kid into hysterics again."

"She'll be all right," Lynda said. "Come on. We all need to get used to each other."

"Bet you never dreamed you'd have a houseful of wounded souls, did you?"

"Recovering souls," she amended with a smile. "And I couldn't be happier to have all of you here. It's about time I had someone besides my secretary in my life." It seemed like so long ago that they'd had the argument in the plane about the emptiness in both their lives, but Jake remembered and smiled slightly.

She went to the portable intercom she had bought just for him. "I haven't had the phones hooked up yet. I'll get someone here eventually, I guess. I'm just a little jumpy about having strangers here. Anyway, if you need anything, just press this button, and I'll hear you in the house."

"I won't need anything."

"Well, the kitchen's stocked, the refrigerator's full, there are towels in the bathroom.... Oh, and I had some special rails put into the tub, so you shouldn't have any trouble getting in. I can't think of anything else."

"It's real comfortable, Lynda," he said softly. "Thank you."

Her smile was genuine. "I'll see you at seven, Jake. And if you don't show up, I'm coming after you."

Brianna was still crying when Lynda went back into the house. Paige held her close and rocked her, but the child hadn't calmed down at all. "Is she all right?" Lynda asked.

"She's scared to death," Paige said. "She's shaking worse than she was at the courthouse."

Lynda sat down next to them and stroked the tiny child's hair. "Do you think it was Jake?"

"I don't know, Lynda. I think she must have caught a glimpse of him after he got out of the car. She probably thought he was Keith for a split second, and it freaked her out."

"Brianna, were you afraid of that man we were with?"

Brianna hiccuped another sob. "It was Daddy."

"No, honey," Lynda said. "That was Jake. And he might look a little scary with that patch over his eye and that wheel chair, but he's a really nice man. You're going to like him."

But Brianna was still trembling and crying softly, and Paige tried to loosen the child's clutch so she could see her face. "Honey, you didn't finish your tea party. Do you want to go out and get your dolls?"

241

"No!" Terror twisted the child's face, and she threw her arms more tightly around Paige's neck. "Daddy's there!"

Paige sighed with frustration and glanced at Lynda. "No, he's not, sweetheart. That's just Jake, and we have to be nice to him because he needs our help."

But the child couldn't be convinced. "I'll go out and get her dolls, Paige," Lynda said. "She'll be all right. She just has to get to know him."

"Yeah," Paige said, though her voice lacked conviction. "Look, we'll give it a try, but if she goes off the deep end when he comes over for dinner tonight, I think I'll just take her to McDonald's or something."

"Of course," Lynda said. "I don't want her to be afraid."

She went outside, feeling more despondent than she had hoped to feel on Jake's homecoming day. She gathered up the dolls then dropped down wearily on the porch swing with her arms full.

What was she going to do? The last thing Jake needed was for someone to be afraid of him, reinforcing the fears he had of being too repulsive to go out in public.

And the last thing Brianna needed was more terror in her life. They had all been through enough. Lynda just wondered when the ripples of all this tragedy would finally settle down.

In the apartment, Jake rolled around in his chair, unpacking the few belongings he'd brought with him from the hospital. Lynda had already brought over most of his things in the past few days, and they had been all neatly put away.

Quietly, he opened each drawer in the big room, exploring the contents, taking mental inventory of where she'd put his socks, his shirts, his underwear. Then he came to the end table with the Bible.

He smiled as if he had expected as much but closed the drawer without taking it out.

He rolled to the window and looked out at the driveway, to the red Porsche that Lynda had moved here from the hospital just yesterday. It had been well protected; there wasn't a scratch on it.

Rolling to the door, he went outside, hoping the child wasn't anywhere near a window; he didn't want to frighten her again. But he needed to get to his car, to smell the leather of the seats, feel the wheel in his hands....

He rolled down the driveway, opened the driver's door, and aligned his chair so that he could pull himself into the seat.

It felt different than he remembered—cramped, tight, but he put his hands on the wheel nonetheless and imagined himself driving through town that day he'd gone to the airport. He'd been on top of the world. He hadn't realized then how far he had to fall.

But it wasn't the car that was different now. *He* was different.

And now he couldn't drive this car. He might never be able to again. Even if he could by some miracle have it redesigned so that a paraplegic could drive it by hand, it wasn't big enough to fit his wheelchair into. Besides that, it was a look-at-me car, a car that screamed that an eligible bachelor was inside, looking for a good time.

He didn't want anyone to look at him now, and he didn't feel so eligible any more, and he had more important things on his mind lately than having a good time.

Like an old girlfriend who didn't fit into his life anymore, the car felt uncomfortable, awkward, useless.

Grief washed over him, grief at the things he was leaving behind. The car, the job, the fast friends, the money ...

And what was left of him was something he couldn't quite relate to, something he couldn't quite identify.

"If I'd known I was going to be left with just my character," he whispered to no one, "I'd have worked harder at building some."

But there was none there, at least none that he could put his finger on. He was helpless and hopeless and heartless. And he didn't want to be any of those things.

Cursing, he pulled himself out of the car and back into the chair, slammed the door, and went back inside.

He should count his blessings, he told himself sardonically. At least he *had* a Porsche, even if he couldn't drive it. And a houseful of great furniture, even though it was in storage and he had no place to put it. And a little black book full of names of women he couldn't call.

His anger faded as his despair grew, and he found himself grasping for the real positives, the ones that might add up to just a little bit of hope.

He was able to sit up.

He could still see out of one eye.

He could move his toe.

He had a temporary place to live.

Little things. But they were all he had. And he'd better get used to them, he thought, for he would probably never have the big things again.

CHAPTER FIFTY-TWO

When Brianna had cried herself to sleep, Paige laid her down on the couch and went to help Lynda prepare dinner. She watched as Lynda bustled around nervously, looking distraught, too preoccupied to notice Paige's help. Whenever Lynda passed the kitchen window, which looked out toward the garage apartment, she peered out, as if to catch a glimpse of Jake.

"What's wrong, Lynda?" Paige asked finally.

"Nothing," Lynda said. "Why do you think something's wrong?"

"Well, you've been awfully preoccupied."

Lynda stopped what she was doing and looked out the window again. "I saw him go out to his car and get into it," she whispered.

Paige frowned. "He can't drive—can he?"

"No. He just went out and sat in it for a while. You'd have had to know him before to understand. He loved that car. When we were in that plane knowing we were about to crash, he was actually worried about who would take care of his car."

"You were going to crash, and he was worried about his *car*?"

"Yeah. And it was so sad to watch him roll out there just to sit in it. Maybe I shouldn't have brought the car here."

Paige didn't know what to say. It seemed so silly to her to grieve over a car when there was so much else to mourn. "So—do you think he'll come over at seven?"

"I don't know," Lynda said. "I hope so. He needs to be around people."

"But the thing with Brianna—I wouldn't blame him if he stayed locked in there forever after that. That was so embarrassing."

"I still don't understand it," Lynda said. "I mean, he has that scar and everything, but it's not that bad."

"That's because you're used to it," Paige cut in. "We're not. It's the whole picture. The scar, the patch, the wheelchair. It's going to take some time."

"But he's still a man. Inside he's just like you and me. Just because of a scar on his face—"

"You're right," Paige said. "Absolutely right. But this isn't a rational thing. It kind of took me by surprise, and it obviously jolted Brianna. I'm ashamed of myself for saying that, Lynda, but I'm going to get over it. I'm sure once I get to know him I won't even notice those things."

Weary from the emotional toll the day had taken on her, Lynda sighed and dropped into a chair. "Maybe when he gets his artificial eye it'll be easier."

"Oh," Paige said, "I'm sure I'll get used to him before that."

"I mean other people," Lynda said. "I want him to be able to go out in public—to the store, to a movie, to church—without people staring at him." But Lynda knew that if it were up to Jake, he might not ever count himself healed enough to blend normally with the public.

"Does he go to your church?" Paige asked.

"No. In fact, I just met him the day of the crash."

"*Really?* All this time I thought the two of you had known each other forever. I mean, the way you kept visiting him, and the way you took him in—"

"No. He's all alone. He doesn't have anybody. You know, almost dying with somebody is quite an intimate experience. It bonds you somehow."

"Yeah." Paige smiled. "I've had that experience myself."

Lynda realized that she referred to the fire, and she smiled. "Yeah, you have, haven't you? Then you understand. I can't help caring about Jake. Even if he's totally opposite from me, and he's belligerent and moody." She went to stir the pot on the stove and then wiped her hands on a towel. "I have a theory about Jake. I think maybe God is refining him."

"What does that mean?"

"Do you know how they used to refine silver?" Lynda asked.

Paige laughed. "No, not that I recall."

"Well, I heard it in Sunday school a long time ago. The silver-smith hammered the silver into little pieces and then melted them. And he stayed with it the whole time, making sure it wasn't damaged in the fire. But as the silver melted, the impure metals rose to the top. He removed it from the fire, scraped off the impurities, and saw a blurry image of himself in the silver. Then he put it back on the fire and did the whole thing again. He did it seven times, each time scraping off another layer of impurities, until he saw his clear reflection in the silver. God does that with us, too."

"Scrapes off the impurities?"

"Yes. But he also puts us through the fire. What you're going through with Keith is your fire, Paige. And what I'm going through. And what Jake's going through."

Paige tried to follow. "So you think he's making these things happen so he can get the impurities out of us?"

"Maybe he didn't *make* them happen, but he's using them," Lynda said. "And with each trial, we get stronger and purer. And he sees more of his reflection in us."

"But people don't always get closer to God when they suffer."

"True," Lynda said. "Sometimes we cling to those impurities, and we're impossible to refine. But I think God keeps working on us. And sometimes he has to take everything we've got to make us notice him."

Paige was quiet for a moment, and finally she looked up at Lynda. "Is that what you think he's done with Jake?"

Her eyes drifted to the window again. "I think that's what he's done with *me*," she whispered. "Whatever he's doing with Jake, that's between Jake and God. All I know is that whether God caused or allowed the crash to happen, it happened, and here we all are in this house together. And I don't think it's an accident."

Jake struggled to get himself into the tub and onto the bench that Lynda had left there for him so that he could take a shower. But once he got there and turned on the water, pleasure burst through him. He hadn't had a private shower since he'd gone into the hospital. An orderly had taken him into one in a wheelchair every day for the last couple of weeks, and he'd felt degraded and embarrassed to let a stranger help him with such intimate needs. Now he was on his own, and as difficult as it was, it was worth the effort.

Getting out, his hand slipped on the rail and he fell, but he quickly pulled himself back up into his chair. He could do this, he told himself. He could take care of himself. He didn't need nurses and aides and orderlies to wait on him hand and foot.

He rolled back into the bedroom and gathered his clothes from the drawer. Allie had been working with him to teach him to dress himself, but it was still difficult getting pants legs up, and putting the socks on was almost too much. He looked around, wondering where Lynda had put his Birkenstocks.

And then he felt it.

That burning sensation again, spreading *throughout* his toes and down the bottom of his foot!

He wiggled the toe that he'd managed to move the other day then concentrated on moving the other ones. For a moment, they resisted and just lay there, motionless. But he kept trying, kept focusing, kept watching—

His little toe twitched.

"Yes!" he shouted, feeling as if he could leap out of the chair and dance a jig on the coffee table. He moved the toe again and then with great effort, managed to bend the middle three toes slightly.

Tears welled in his eyes, and he looked up at the ceiling. "Thank you," he whispered brokenly. "Thank you."

He couldn't bear to put shoes on those feet, for he wanted to show Lynda what he could do. He glanced at the clock—almost seven. She probably wouldn't mind if he barged in a little early.

Humming a tune, he finished getting ready. Leaving his feet bare, he rolled out across the patio to one of the back doors of the house.

Lynda had seen him burst out of his apartment and race in his wheelchair across the concrete, and now, before she had even made it to the door, he was banging urgently.

She threw it open and saw the joy on his face. "I moved them," he said. "The other toes. I moved all of them. Look!"

She caught her breath and looked down at his bare feet and saw the infinitesimal twitch of his toes. A small movement but as significant as kicking the winning field goal in the Super Bowl. "Oh, Jake!" she said, throwing her arms around him. "Paige, come look! He's moving his toes!"

Paige came to the door and looked down at them, not sure what it meant. "Does this mean you'll be able to walk again?"

"It might," Lynda said.

"I'll walk," Jake told her. "I know I will. I'm gonna throw myself into my rehab and work with everything I've got."

"Do you have feeling in your other foot?" Paige asked.

"Not yet. But I will."

It was one of the first purely positive things Lynda had ever heard from Jake, so she didn't dash his hopes by reminding him that there were still no guarantees.

He came into the kitchen and closed his eyes as he breathed deeply of the smell of the turkey baking in the oven, the home-made dressing baking beside it, and the vegetables on the stove. "And to think I didn't believe in heaven. It was right here in this kitchen all along."

Lynda smiled. "Heaven smells a lot better than this," she said. "But I think you're gonna like it." She stirred the peas then turned back to him. "How are you doing over there? Is everything going all right?"

"I've hit a few rough spots," he said. "But all in all, it's good to be free of that hospital." He looked down at his toes again, wiggled them slightly and then threw his head back and laughed. "I can't believe this. I never thought I'd feel anything there again."

He saw Paige's face change from amusement to concern as she looked past him to the doorway, and quickly he followed her gaze. Brianna stood there, clutching her blankie to her cheek and looking sleepily into the kitchen.

For a moment, they all held their breath as she assessed Jake.

"Who are you?" Brianna asked calmly.

He glanced up at Paige then back at the child. "I'm Jake," he said in as calm a voice as he could. He extended his hand gently, as if coaxing a deer to eat out of it. "Who are you?"

"Brianna," she said, taking his hand and shaking it. As she stepped closer, she regarded the patch on his eye. "Are you a pirate?"

He laughed. "No. I just hurt my eye, and I have to wear this until it gets better."

"Like a Band-Aid?"

Lynda smiled; Paige just looked confused.

"What is this?" Brianna asked, touching the wheel on his chair.

"It's a wheelchair," he said. "I hurt my legs, too, and I can't walk. So I ride around in this."

Brianna's eyes lit up. "Is it fun?"

He smiled. "Well—"

"Can I ride?"

He looked up at Paige, surprised, and a slow smile came to his face. "Well, sure." Patting his leg, he said, "Hop up."

Brianna climbed onto his lap, and he began to roll her around in circles. She giggled as if she had a new toy then looked up at him and pointed to the scar. "How'd you get your boo-boo?"

He stopped and looked at Lynda again, his smile fading. "I had a real bad cut."

"I have a Band-Aid if it hurts. A Garfield one."

He smiled down at her. "It's not so bad."

"Can we ride some more?"

It was as if he'd been validated, accepted by the world and by life; he did not, after all, repulse this little child. As he rode her into the living room, Lynda looked back at Paige.

"Well, what do you think of that?"

Paige shook her head. "Weird."

"Well, I'm grateful. Children are so resilient."

"And so unpredictable," Paige whispered. "I don't get it. She was petrified this afternoon."

"Well, maybe the nap did it. Maybe she was just irritable when she saw him, and he took her by surprise."

"Guess so," Paige said. "But I never would have dreamed she'd warm up to him this fast." She watched, flabbergasted, as he tipped the chair back, almost making Brianna fall out, and she clutched him tightly and giggled with delight.

That night, Lynda led Jake out onto the patio as Paige put Brianna to bed, and they sat side by side, looking out over the yard.

"I told you you weren't repulsive," she said with a smile.

"That sure was one quick turnaround. I'll never understand children."

"Who knows what set her off today? It doesn't really matter now, though." She caught him looking down at his foot, wiggling the toes again. "I think you've gotten more movement just in the last few hours."

"I have," he said. "And unless I'm imagining it, I'm starting to feel that burning on the bottom of my other foot."

"Really?" she asked. "Jake, maybe the swelling's going down. Maybe the traction's helping. Maybe—" Her voice trailed off as she saw him look distractedly out across the yard and rub his top lip with his finger. "What's wrong?"

"Do you think I'm getting my hopes up too high? I mean, it's such a little bit of feeling."

"It has to start somewhere."

"But what if it doesn't go any further? What if—"

"Hey—I was just starting to enjoy the positive, upbeat Jake. Give yourself a chance to be happy before you start knocking yourself down again."

His smile returned like a gift, and he started to laugh quietly. "Who would have thought?"

"What?"

"That day when I looked at your plane, who would have ever thought that we'd be sitting here, actually friends?"

"I sure didn't."

He raised his eyebrows. "Was I that bad?"

"Pretty bad," she admitted. "I knew your type."

"Yeah, well, you were probably right." He looked up at the stars sprinkled across the sky. "Do you think I'll ever look normal again?"

She smiled. "When you get your eye, Jake, you'll probably start knocking the ladies dead again. I dread it, actually. I hate to see you revert to your old self."

"My old self seems a long way away," he said softly. "I don't know if I'll ever find him again."

CHAPTER FIFTY-THREE

K eith was glad there were no street lights on this deadend street; the darkness gave him the perfect cover. Ever since he'd left Brianna that afternoon, he'd been watching his back, waiting for a uniformed car to squeal up behind him, lights flashing.

Why it hadn't happened he wasn't sure, but he knew he didn't have much more time. The court date was fast approaching, and with every day that passed, Lynda Barrett would find more and more evidence against him. Already she had all of the medical reports, and she probably had records of all of Paige's calls to the police. And McRae had warned him that she was getting depositions from neighbors who claimed to have witnessed things. The idiots ought to mind their own business instead of sticking their noses into things they didn't understand.

He was getting desperate either to take Lynda out or grab Brianna and run. Either way would bring about the same result. All he wanted was his daughter.

He crept closer to the house and saw the cars in the driveway: a red Porsche that he recognized as belonging to that paralyzed pilot who was still in the hospital, Lynda's BMW, and Paige's old Chevette with new, unslashed tires. He smiled and laughed softly as he slipped his knife from his pocket. Releasing the blade, he started toward the car to slash the tires again—then caught himself. Not a good idea. If he didn't manage to get Brianna tonight, Paige would know he'd been here. As much as he'd like for her to know she hadn't bested him, he couldn't take that chance yet.

She'd figure that out for herself anyway—when he disappeared with Brianna.

He stole through the front yard, glancing from one window to another. All of the curtains were drawn, but he saw a light on in two of the rooms. One of them, he guessed, was the living room, but the other, dimmer one, probably came from a bedroom.

Knowing that Brianna always slept with a nightlight, he stole toward it and checked the screen to see if it was locked. It was, but it was plastic screen—easy enough to cut if he could be sure he wouldn't be heard. He wondered if the window was locked. From here, it looked as if it was.

The idea of cutting a section out of the glass big enough to slip his hand through and unlock the window was quickly discarded; the section he cut would likely fall in and shatter on the floor. No, he couldn't do anything that stupid.

Quietly he made his way to the front door, tested the knob, and found it locked. Not giving up, he went around to the side of the house, saw the garage apartment, and wondered whether it was empty. Maybe he could hide in there until he had the chance to catch Brianna.

He pulled a silver fingernail file from his pocket, preparing to try to pick the lock.

Voices.

He froze.

They were coming from the back patio just around the corner of the house. Two voices. A man's and a woman's.

For a moment he couldn't breathe, and he stood motionless like a bobcat caught in headlights, trying to decide which way to go.

Finally, he slipped around the garage apartment into the woods surrounding the fence. Once hidden by the bushes and shadows of the trees, he tried to figure out who was outside. But it was too dark; he could barely see the two forms on the patio. They were talking quietly. The woman was Lynda, he thought. Brianna must be inside, then.

But this man, whoever he is, certainly changed the equation a bit. Is he one of those cops who'd picked him up, here because Brianna had told them he'd been here today? Were they setting a trap for him?

Panic gripped him. Turning, he jogged silently back through the woods and came out on the block behind Lynda's house. Hurrying back to his car, he flipped through all the possibilities.

But by the time he'd settled in behind the wheel, he'd decided that he was just being paranoid. After all, even though he hadn't gone home today, they could have caught up with him at work if they'd been after him. Still, he'd better stay away for a few days, just until the heat died down.

Work, he grimaced, checking his watch. He had to get back before someone noticed he was gone. He needed to keep this job—at least until one way or another he managed to get Brianna. Then he could quit and flee the state before Paige caught up with them.

He would show her. He would show all of them. And somehow he'd make Paige sorry she'd ever filed those divorce papers.

CHAPTER FIFTY-FOUR

I 've got to get to the hospital fast!" Skidding his chair across the kitchen floor, Jake grabbed Lynda's purse and keys off of the table. "My left foot is burning!"

If not for the look of unadulterated joy on his face, Lynda would have been alarmed. "Jake, slow down. I'm coming."

"Didn't you hear me?" he asked. "The *other* foot. It's burning!"

She caught her breath and grabbed his chair, stopping him halfway down the driveway. He turned back to her impatiently. "Are you telling me that you have feeling in *both* feet now?" she asked.

"Yes!" he said. "Now come on! I want to get to the hospital."

Laughing, she grabbed her keys from him and ran to get into her car. By the time she'd started the engine, he was already inside, folding up his chair and slipping it in behind his seat. "Jake, do you think this means—"

"You bet it does. I'm gonna walk."

"But—are you sure?"

When he met her gaze, she realized how good hope looked on him. "As sure as I can be. I'm gonna walk, Lynda. I know it."

She was quiet as they drove to the rehab wing of the hospital, possibilities flitting through her mind. As they drove, she prayed that he wouldn't be disappointed, that his hopes wouldn't be shattered, that this new burning sensation did indeed mean that something was happening. Something permanent.

She got out of the car to help him when they reached the hospital, and when he was in his chair, he checked his watch. "You want me to give you a call when I'm finished?"

"That'll be fine," she said. "Do you think it'll be several hours?"

He nodded with certainty. "I'm gonna work today until either I stand on these feet or collapse trying."

"Jake, don't push it. You've come a long way. There's no need to get impatient now."

"Don't worry about it," he said with a grin and started inside. She caught up to him. "Don't you want me to take you in?"

"Nope," he said. "I can take it from here."

She stopped and watched him moving farther away from her. "Don't do anything stupid, okay?"

"Like what?"

"Like—throwing away your chair or something. You're going to give this time, aren't you?"

"As little as possible," he said.

She got back into the car and sat at the wheel for a moment, praying with all her heart that his expectations weren't in vain.

But Jake wasn't known for his patience or for his emotional resilience in the face of disappointment.

Buzz and Allie were pleased with the new sensations in his feet, but as Jake might have expected, his doctor was a little more reserved. "We've got to be patient, Jake," he said. "Don't expect too much too soon."

"But can't I expect anything at all, Doc? I mean, this all means *something*, doesn't it?"

Dr. Randall could have made a killing as a poker player, for his expression never betrayed a thought. "Well—your swelling has probably gone down significantly, which would help with the spinal shock. And the traction is, no doubt, helping with the compression. There's certainly cause for hope, Jake. But I have to emphasize that there are no guarantees."

"Give me odds, Doc. What are the chances that I'll walk again?"

The doctor wasn't about to go that far. "I can't do that, Jake. If I gave you terrific odds, and this is as much feeling as you ever get back, you'd never forgive me."

"But if you were inclined to give me odds, you're saying they'd be terrific?"

The doctor laughed. "I didn't say that."

"But they *are* terrific, aren't they?"

"They're hopeful, Jake. They're better than they were when you came in. But there still are no guarantees."

"Yeah, well, I can live with that," Jake said. "I've been through enough in the last few weeks to know that nothing comes with guarantees. Not life, not health, nothing. In fact, *you* could walk out of here right now and meet with a terrible accident and never walk again. So essentially, you and I have the same guarantee."

Dr. Randall smirked. "Thank you, Jake, for pointing that out to me. I appreciate it."

"No problem. I give as good as I get."

Dr. Randall laughed again and patted Jake's leg. Jake thought he felt it.

"Allie and Buzz are putting you in the pool today. It should be a nice change of pace."

"What will that do?" Jake asked. "Increase circulation? Help with motor coordination?"

"Well, it does a number of things. Today you'll just float and do some resistance exercises with your arms. The lack of gravity sometimes makes it easier for people to stand when they're ready, but you're not ready for that yet. We'll just take it a step at a time."

But Jake decided he *was* ready. When they took him to the pool and moved him from the chair into a harness seat that would lift him mechanically and lower him into the water by a chain, he saw the parallel bars in the pool and immediately knew what they were there for. People used them to balance ... to stand ...

To walk.

The water felt like liquid heaven, and as he slid into it, he let his upper body relax. Allie helped him float then ordered him to push his arms against the water.

She stood waist deep, and he tried to determine where the water would have come on him. He was six-two, and she was only five-seven or so. If it came halfway up her ribcage, it was probably waist deep for him.

He kept at the arm exercises the doctor had told him about for as long as he could but didn't want to tire himself out. He would need his arm muscles when he stood. "Can we go to the parallel bars?" he asked Allie finally.

Grinning, she shot Buzz a look. "Jake, we were just going to float today."

"Come on, Allie. Just let me see what my feet will do without gravity."

"I say we take him over there," Buzz said.

Allie's grin grew more mischievous. "Truth is, I have been wondering just how much function you might have in those feet."

"Then let's go."

They helped him over to the bars, and Jake grabbed one on each side of him. The weight of his legs made them float to the bottom, and for the first time since the accident, he was in a standing position, upright, his height towering above Allie and even above Buzz.

"Can you feel your feet touching the bottom?" Allie asked.

He barely felt the smooth bottom of the pool and looked down at his limp legs. "Sort of."

"Now, see if you can let your weight rest on your legs. Use your gluteus," Buzz said. "That's the trick. You have to hold your torso up with your glutes."

He felt his face reddening as he put every ounce of concentration he had into tightening his gluteals, and he looked down at his body. His legs weren't taking the weight, and his stomach was trying to arch outward. He tightened more and felt his body aligning more normally, but it was still only his arms that held him up. His legs were useless.

But Allie and Buzz didn't see the futility of it, and he saw that they were pleased by the smiles on their faces as they checked the alignment of his legs and feet to his torso.

"This is good, Jake," Buzz said, standing in front of him. "Real good. You have the muscular strength to stand, even if your legs aren't cooperating."

"What good are the muscles if I can't use them to do what I want?"

"You *will* be able to get them to do what you want, Jake. It's happening a little at a time, but we're seeing a lot of progress. So are you, and you know it."

He let his arms relax a little, and his body collapsed into the water. Allie caught him.

Defeated, he let her pull him into a float, but he feared the weight of his disappointment would drown him completely. And he almost didn't care if it did.

Something was wrong. It wasn't like Brianna not to want to go outside. But since the day Jake had moved in and Brianna had run in screaming that her daddy was trying to get her, she had absolutely refused to set foot through the back door, with or without her mother. Paige was getting frustrated; they'd been too cooped up in the house, and she wanted Brianna to get some fresh air.

"Honey, why can't we go out there? I'll be right there with you. There's a fence and everything. Nothing's going to happen to you."

Brianna's bottom lip puckered out, and she looked worriedly through the door. "No, Mommy. I don't want to."

"But why? Just tell Mommy why."

"Daddy's out there."

"He's not, honey. He doesn't even know where we are. How could he be out there?"

Brianna shrugged, but she didn't accept Paige's logic. Paige realized that regardless of what had originally triggered it, Brianna's fear was real, not imaginary, and she couldn't dismiss it. Stooping in front of her daughter, she got to eye level with her. "Brianna, tell Mommy why you think Daddy is out there."

"Because he is," she said, and big tears filled her eyes. "He's waiting for me."

"How could he be?"

The question confused the child, and she didn't answer, just wiped her eyes and smeared the tears across her temples.

"That day you thought you saw Daddy, it was Jake. He scared you, and you thought he was your daddy. But it wasn't him."

"Yes, it was," Brianna said. "I was chasing the butterfly, and he told me to come with him."

"The butterfly?"

"No, Daddy!" Brianna was getting upset now, and Paige pulled her into a hug.

"It's okay, honey. We don't have to go out. You don't have to cry."

Brianna hiccuped a sob and nodded her head, as though that would be fine with her.

But Paige couldn't understand what the problem was, and later that afternoon as Brianna napped, Paige stepped out into the backyard and looked around at the perimeter of the fence. There was nothing but woods that backed up to the fence and no trails. No one would be there by accident. If there had been someone there, he would have been there deliberately.

Had Brianna really seen someone?

She wanted to dismiss the possibility, as she had so quickly done when it had first come up, but she realized now that Brianna had never really demonstrated a fear of Jake except for that first meeting. And she wasn't entirely sure that Brianna had even seen Jake at that point.

Had Brianna been trying to tell her something all along, something that she had refused to believe?

She looked through the trees again, shivering with the sense that she was being watched, that someone was out there. Someone dangerous.

Had Keith found them? Had he approached Brianna in the back yard?

Starting to tremble, she backed into the house. Quickly, she bolted the door then ran to the front and checked the lock. In the master bedroom, she locked the door that opened to the patio.

By the time she was back in the kitchen, she heard a car door. Lynda was back with Jake.

Breathing a huge sigh of relief, she rushed outside.

Jake was getting into his wheelchair with a hang-dog look on his face, and Lynda was decidedly sober, too. But Paige hardly noticed.

"Thank goodness you're both home."

"What is it?" Lynda asked.

"Keith," she said breathlessly. "You know how Brianna keeps insisting that her father is in the backyard?"

Lynda waited for Jake to move away from the car door then closed it. "Yeah."

"Maybe he was."

Lynda stopped cold. "You think Keith was back there? When? How?"

"I don't know," she said. "But I'm scared. What if Brianna wasn't imagining it? What if he really was back there? I mean, she's obviously terrified of something, and it isn't Jake because she warmed right up to him that night. But she still won't go outside."

Lynda stood still, thinking for a moment. "Maybe we ought to give Larry a call."

Jake pulled the house key out of his pocket and quietly opened his apartment door.

"Jake?" Paige asked before he could go in.

He looked back at her over his shoulder. "Yeah?"

"Would you mind ... coming into the house for a while? Just for security. Until we hear from Larry? I'd feel better if there were a man around."

He looked stunned by the request. "Who are you worried about? Me or you?"

She didn't understand the question and glanced at Lynda for help. "I'm just scared, Jake. I was hoping—"

"So you think I need a couple of women to protect me?"

She looked stricken. "No. I wanted you to protect us."

"Nice try," he said, rolling over the threshold and pivoting at the door. "But I think I'll stay here."

He closed the door hard, and Paige jumped. "What's wrong with him?"

Lynda sighed. "He had these grand delusions of walking today, I think. It didn't happen. He's really depressed."

"But I really meant it, Lynda. I'd feel better with a man in the house. Why did he twist what I was saying?"

"Because he truly doesn't feel that he can offer us any protection. In his own mind, he's useless, so he thinks he's useless to everyone else, too."

"Oh, for heaven's sake." As if she had no more time to dwell on Jake's problems, Paige headed inside. "I need to go in and check on Brianna."

Lynda gave Jake's door one last glance then followed her in. "I'll call Larry," she said.

CHAPTER FIFTY-FIVE

K eith knew better than to come back, especially in the daytime, but the obsession that kept him from sleeping, eating, or thinking drove him to take chances.

In the three days since he'd tried to grab her, Brianna's face had haunted him day and night: the fear in her eyes when she'd spotted him; the way she'd backed away; the shrill scream that had startled him and sent him running through the woods....

She'd been brainwashed, and he had to put a stop to it. He couldn't allow her mother to poison her mind against her own father. It would take some time to get those thoughts out of her mind and win back her trust. But once he had her in his possession, he would have all the time in the world. He would tell her that Paige was dead, that she'd been in a car wreck or something. She'd get over it quickly; kids are like that. Resilient.

He moved quietly through the trees, again approaching the fence around Lynda's house. He had to be bolder if he was going to succeed. He hadn't gotten many breaks lately. Even his lawyer was turning against him.

He took his usual place, sitting on the ground against a tree, hidden behind two bushes, between which he had a clear view of the back door. He still seethed from the call he'd gotten from McRae that day, asking him whether he'd found where Paige was staying and whether he'd approached the child without permission.

"I don't *need* permission," Keith had said. "She's my kid. I'm her father, and no judge is ever going to tell me I can't see her."

"Does that mean you did show up at their place and threaten the kid?" McRae asked.

"How would I know where they're staying?"

McRae had thought about that for a moment. "You're a smart man, Keith. Did you or didn't you find them?"

He'd been amused at McRae's assessment of him; he always enjoyed it when people found out this night-shift employee had some brains. For a moment, he'd entertained the thought of telling him how he'd found Lynda's house, but then he realized that it wouldn't pay to brag. McRae was liable to resign from the case, and then where would he be?

So he'd lied and told McRae that he didn't have a clue where they were, but that if some guy had approached his daughter, he wanted the police to find out who it was. He'd even suggested filing another motion for temporary custody since she still seemed to be in danger, but McRae had rejected it. Court was only two weeks away, he said. He wasn't going back before the judge on Keith's behalf until the trial.

But Keith could see the writing on the wall. McRae was pulling back, losing faith in him. If Keith couldn't depend on him anymore, then he couldn't depend on the justice system to get Brianna. He could only count on himself.

And in just two weeks he would have to go into court and face Lynda Barrett. Unless something happened to her in the meantime.

So he was back here, waiting for a glimpse of Brianna, praying for another chance to grab her. This time he wouldn't botch it.

And if he couldn't reach Brianna, then he'd bide his time until he caught Lynda leaving and rush to his car to follow her.

He heard the side door open; he got to his feet, still crouched low, and moved until he could see who was coming out. It was Lynda, all dressed up, as though she was going to church, but she was alone.

Perfect. He took off through the trees. If he could make it to his car and follow her, he could plant his little surprise under her gas tank while her car was in the church parking lot. Talk about hellfire and brimstone.

Laughing breathlessly, he fired up his car and drove up the block and around the corner. He pulled over and waited.

Today was the day. Lynda would be taken out, Paige would be homeless and without representation, and his court case would be in the bag. Piece of cake. Even McRae would have to give him credit for working things out.

He saw the car come to the end of the street, stop, and then turn right. He waited until it was far enough away so she couldn't see him. Then he began to follow.

CHAPTER FIFTY-SIX

I thought you were going to invite Jake," Paige said as Lynda turned the corner.

"I did. Last night and again this morning. He wasn't interested."

"He should go anyway," Paige said. "After all you're doing for him ..."

Lynda looked at her thoughtfully. "Is that why you're coming with me? Because you feel you owe me something?"

Paige looked embarrassed, as though she'd just stuck her foot in her mouth. "No, of course not. I told you, I need to get Brianna back in church. You've made it easier. It's not always so easy to walk into a new church by yourself."

Lynda wasn't sure she believed her. "I didn't mean to strong-arm you into going with me or to make you feel guilty if you didn't. It's just that what they teach there is the most important thing in the world." She glanced into the rearview mirror as she merged into the next lane. "I just wish Jake would have come. He needs to hear that message more than anything."

Paige didn't respond, and Lynda wondered whether she agreed.

They pulled into the parking lot of the church, waiting behind a few cars looking for parking places as cars from the earlier service left. Three security guards in the parking lot helped to direct traffic. She glanced in her rearview mirror again to see if she was holding anyone up.

A pale blue car slowed at the entrance to the parking lot, hesitated, and then drove on. The car looked familiar, but many of the cars here looked familiar.

They parked and went into the church, and again, Paige opted to stay in Brianna's class with her. She was starting to learn where everything was and what was expected of her, and the teacher seemed glad to see her.

As she went to her class, Lynda hoped that Paige would also seize the chance to be ministered to. She wasn't sure that the foundation of Paige's faith was any stronger than Jake's was.

CHAPTER FIFTY-SEVEN

Outside, Keith circled the church, trying to decide what to do. He had seen Paige and Brianna in the car with Lynda, so he could forget about the bomb, at least for today. He wanted Lynda dead, and if Paige had to go, too, the more the merrier. But he didn't want his little girl to die.

Besides, even after the traffic died down, the security guards remained in the parking lot like sentinels guarding the cars.

Continuing past the church, he pulled into an empty space in the parking lot of a closed jewelry store. For a moment, he just sat and thought, trying to sort out the possibilities.

Brianna was in that church somewhere now. Probably since she was a visitor and the teachers didn't know the family, no one would protest if her own father showed up to get her.

On the other hand, if she went into hysterics and started screaming like she had the other day, they would call the police. And this time there would be witnesses.

Still, there was no harm in going in to check things out. Then he could make a plan. He reached into the glove compartment for the fake mustache and thick glasses he'd used the day he bought the dynamite. Then, walking at a brisk pace as though he knew where he was going, he went in the back door of the church, hoping to avoid the Christian "welcome wagon" that always seemed to be on the lookout for visitors.

He ducked into a men's room at the end of the hall and wet his hair so he could comb it back. It wasn't him anymore, he thought, looking into the mirror. It was someone else—someone who couldn't be identified.

He went back into the hallway. There seemed to be class-rooms further down the hall. He saw the babies through a glass window in the nursery nearby. The kids seemed to get older as he walked on until finally, he came to the three-year-olds' room.

He passed the door quickly without looking in for fear of startling Brianna if she saw him. But then he turned back and peered in from the side.

He saw his little girl working a puzzle at a table near the door. His heart began to race.

Just a few steps away, he thought. All he would have to do is wait till the teacher had her back to him, take a few steps inside the door, and grab Brianna before she had the chance to scream. He could have her in his car before anyone noticed she was gone.

He stepped closer, trying to see inside to where the teacher was. He saw two of them, and they both had their backs to him. It was perfect.

"I'm finished!" Brianna said, popping the last piece into the puzzle. "Mommy, come look."

He jumped back, startled, as the teachers turned around. One of them was Paige.

What was she doing here? Didn't they have classes for adults? Did they let just anybody teach these children?

His heart sank, and he quickly found the closest door and jogged back to his car.

When he got in, he hit his steering wheel and let out a loud curse.

Today wasn't going to be the day after all, he thought, crank-ing his engine and screeching away. But tomorrow had to be. Time was running out.

CHAPTER FIFTY-EIGHT

I f there was a bright side to a boring Sunday, it was that Paige had cooked a meal fit for a prince. Jake sat quietly at the table, reminded of his days as a child when one of his friends—Jimmy Anderson—used to go to church every Sunday then come home and eat a big, sit-down meal with his parents. Jake had envied him. Doris always used Sunday mornings to catch up on her sleep, and then they feasted on sandwiches or canned ravioli on paper plates. At the time, Jake had believed that it was the meal he envied, but now he realized that it had been more than that—it was the good mood everyone seemed to bring home from church, the structure of having a reason to get all dressed up, and the camaraderie of sitting down together at the table. He'd shared that meal with the Andersons a time or two when he'd shown up to play at exactly the right moment, but when Doris had found out, she'd forbidden him to go anymore.

"They look down their noses at us," she had said. "And when you eat with them, it's like saying that your own mother won't feed you. You can eat at home if you're hungry."

Well, his mother couldn't stop him now.

But the conversation today was awkward, and he could see that Lynda was struggling to pull him out of his melancholy. He admired her for the attempt; he just wasn't sure that anyone could do it. Even though he'd spent the night wallowing in depression, he'd still hoped that when he woke this morning, he'd have more feeling in his feet and legs than he'd had yesterday. But he'd been disappointed again.

"Brianna likes her Sunday School class," Paige said. "Don't you, Brianna?"

Brianna nodded and finished her mouthful of potatoes. "Are we going back tonight?"

Paige gave Lynda a questioning look.

"If you want to," Lynda said. "I'm going, and I'd love for you to go with me."

"Can we go every day?"

Paige laughed. "No, honey. They don't have it every day."

Brianna looked perplexed at that.

"So what did they teach you in there?" Jake asked for the sake of conversation.

"About Jesus making people well." Her eyes brightened, and she began to get excited. "And there was this guy like you, Jake, and he couldn't walk, only they didn't have wheelchairs then—"

"She asked," Paige interjected with a smile.

"But he was lying down by the beautiful gate, the man was—"

"The name of the gate was Beautiful," Paige clarified.

"And you know what happened?"

"What?" Jake asked, getting uncomfortable.

"Some of Jesus' friends came and told the man to stand up, only he couldn't stand up, but they took his hand like this—" She slid down from her chair and went to take Jake's hand to demonstrate. "And he said—what did he say, Mommy?"

"Rise and walk," Paige said.

"Yeah!" Brianna said. "He said, 'Rise and walk,' and you know what the man did?"

Jake withdrew his hand and took a deep breath. He didn't want to know what the man had done. He didn't care because it had nothing to do with him. But the child waited beside him, bursting with excitement, and he knew she wouldn't back down until he took the bait. "What?"

"He got right up, and he could walk!"

Jake glanced at Lynda, who was smiling proudly at the child's enthusiasm, and he wondered if they'd rehearsed it in the car. He didn't like being talked about behind his back, and in his opinion, the story they'd chosen was particularly cruel. He didn't appreciate it.

"That story is in Acts, isn't it? And who gave him the power to do that, Brianna?" Lynda prompted.

"Jesus!" she said. "Jake, why don't you do it?" When he didn't answer, she shook his arm. "Jake?"

"I heard you," he said, staring down at his food. "I heard every word." He looked up at Lynda and Paige. "Nice try. If I recall, there are stories in there about people's eyes being gouged out, too. You want to lay one of those on me?"

"Jake, come on," Lynda said. "We didn't plan this."

Jerking his napkin out of his lap, he threw it on the table and started to back out of his place.

"Jake, what's a matter?" Brianna asked in her high-pitched voice.

"Nothing's the matter," he said, glaring at Lynda again. "You know, it's reprehensible to use a child to deal a low blow like that."

Lynda's face showed the full force of her anger. "Oh, right. Riding home in the car today, I asked Paige what we could do to really twist the knife in you. We came up with that story, and Paige said, 'I know! Let's use Brianna!' It was a clever plan, Jake, only you're too smart for us."

Confused at the exchange, Brianna sat back down, still looking at Jake, and said softly, "I asked Jesus to make you walk. Didn't I, Mommy?"

Paige put a protective arm around her daughter. "Yes, honey. You sure did." Her voice hardened, and she leered at Jake. "She told the whole class about you, Jake, and we all prayed for you. I don't know how you can turn this into some kind of conspiracy."

A host of emotions did battle on his face. "I don't need your prayers."

"Well, you're getting them anyway," Lynda said. "Powerful ones. Jesus said that children's angels always see the face of God." She looked at Brianna. "That means that God listens extra carefully to the prayers of children."

Jake, too, looked at the baffled child staring up at him with those big, questioning eyes.

"If that's the case," he said, "then where was God when her dad was abusing her? If God's paying special attention to the children, why do so many of them have to suffer?"

And Lynda knew that they weren't just talking about Brianna any more. They were talking about Jake.

Trying with all her might to fight her anger instead of Jake, she lowered herself back into her chair. "God got her out of there, didn't he? He used her mother to protect her."

"Why didn't he protect her before anything ever happened?"

She hesitated. "I don't know. There's a lot of evil in this world, Jake. God didn't cause it. And we don't know how he's working in suffering children's lives. We don't even know how he's working in our lives."

"Then you're contradicting yourself again, Lynda. Out of one side of your mouth, you tell me this beautiful idea about children having angels with access to God. And out of the other side, you say that it really doesn't make that much difference because God can't protect us from evil."

"I didn't say that he couldn't. God can do anything."

"Oh, I see. He just won't."

Paige's hand came down hard on the table, startling them all. "That's not what she said, Jake, and you know it!"

"It *is* what she said."

Lynda started to speak, but Paige stopped her. "You have a lot of nerve, you know that?" she said. "All she's done is take care of you, be a friend to you, feed you, give you a place to live—and you still keep throwing her kindness back in her face!"

"Paige, it's all right," Lynda said quietly.

"No, it isn't!" she said. "And as for God, he *has* protected Brianna. He's protected me, too. He gave us Lynda, and a place to live, and a means to get away from Keith. And he even made it so I didn't have to worry about money or a job or anything while I'm waiting to go to court. And I know he's going to take care of that, too. I know because he's taken care of everything else." Tears choked her, and she stopped, trying to steady her voice. "You know, you're not just blind in that one eye. You're blind in both eyes if you can't see that God is providing for you, too. If he didn't care, you'd still be in the hospital right now, and everybody would be trying to figure out what to do with you!"

Brianna started to cry. Picking her up and hugging her close, Paige went on. "Or worse. You could be just like you were before the accident, walking around on two good legs with two good eyes, worshiping that Porsche of yours and in all your vanity and arrogance, be even more blind and crippled than you are now!"

Lynda collapsed back into her chair and covered her face, uttering a silent prayer that whatever happened, the outcome of this wouldn't be as bad as she anticipated.

Paige stormed from the room, carrying Brianna, and silence fell over them as Jake sat motionless in his wheelchair, avoiding Lynda's eyes.

She rubbed her hands down her face and looked at him over her fingertips. "Jake, I'm sorry."

He started rolling his chair toward the door. "I think I'd better go now."

"But you didn't finish eating."

"I'm not hungry," he said quietly and left the house.

Back in his room, Jake pulled himself onto the bed and lay flat, looking up at the ceiling. Tears rolled down his temples, and he wondered why he felt as if he were drowning in that waist-deep pool with legs that served only as cement weights to pull him under. Why did he try to pull everyone else down with him?

Restless, he sat up, wiped his face, and pushed his legs over the side of the bed. His eyes strayed to the drawer in the table beside his chair where she'd put that Bible. He pulled it out and began flipping through it.

Acts, she'd said. He found the book then turned the pages, looking at the topic headings for the one about the crippled man being healed. He was almost surprised when he found it.

He began to read the third chapter aloud:

One day Peter and John were going up to the temple at the time of prayer—at three in the afternoon.

Now a man crippled from birth was being carried to the temple gate called Beautiful, where he was put every day to beg from those going into the temple courts.

When he saw Peter and John about to enter, he asked them for money.

Peter looked straight at him, as did John. Then Peter said, "Look at us!"

So the man gave them his attention, expecting to get something from them.

Then Peter said, "Silver or gold I do not have, but what I have I give you. In the name of Jesus Christ of Nazareth, walk."

Taking him by the right hand, he helped him up, and instantly the man's feet and ankles became strong.

He jumped to his feet and began to walk. Then he went with them into the temple courts, walking and jumping, and praising God. When all the people saw him walking and praising God, they recognized him as the same man who used to sit begging at the temple gate called Beautiful, and they were filled with wonder and amazement at what had happened to him.

Jake stopped reading as tears dropped onto the pages of the Bible, and he wondered why that passage affected him so. It was just a story. But it was *his* story. He could have been the man who'd "been put" at the gate to beg. In many ways, he was "put" here to beg from Lynda for the food and the shelter he needed. His pain was the same as that of the man who was so desperate, so alone that he had to cry out to everyone who passed to help him.

Funny how quickly pride could vanish when you were desperate.

His eyes strayed out the window to that red Porsche sitting like an indictment in the driveway, and he knew that Paige was right. In some ways, he had been just as crippled before the accident as he was now. He clenched his teeth. He'd rather be figuratively crippled than physically crippled any day.

He looked back at the Bible. Why had Peter and John cared about the man? Why hadn't they just stepped over him and forgotten him? Why hadn't they averted their eyes? Why hadn't they just thrown money at him?

He didn't know the answer, any more than he knew why Lynda had helped him. And Paige was right. He continually threw her kindness back in her face. It was a hobby, challenging her beliefs, but he'd learned already that he wasn't going to shake them. Lynda knew what she believed. He, on the other hand, didn't have a clue.

But as the afternoon passed, he continued to read. Maybe he would find out.

When someone knocked on his door two hours later, he'd already finished the entire book of Acts and had turned back to Matthew. But he didn't want Lynda to know it yet. Closing the book, he stuck it back into the drawer then went to answer the door.

Paige stood there, her arms crossed in front of her, and she gave a stab at smiling. "Hi."

"Hi," he said.

She swallowed and looked down at her hands. "I just came to tell you I'm sorry. I shouldn't have blown up at you like that."

"Yes, you should have," he said. "You were absolutely right, and it needed to be said. I owe you an apology."

For a moment, she seemed unsure if he was mocking her. "Really?"

"Really," he said. "It's all right, Paige."

She laughed softly. "And I was so nervous about coming over here. I figured you'd never speak to me again, but I wanted you to come for supper. It's just leftovers, but you liked what we had today. It was cut a little short, but—"

"I'll be there," he said. "Is Brianna up?"

"Yeah," she said. "She just woke up from her nap."

"Maybe I'll come over in a little while and play with her. Let her know I'm not a total jerk. Maybe thank her for praying for me."

"She'd like that."

He closed the door and sat for a moment, surprised at how good it felt to make someone smile.

Maybe the day wasn't turning out so badly after all.

CHAPTER FIFTY-NINE

The burning had spread partially up Jake's calves by the next morning. Allie and Buzz didn't want to put him in the pool again so soon, but when he managed to move one foot at the ankle, they gave in to his pleading.

Determined that he would stand this time, he moved between the parallel bars, got his feet into place, and tightened his gluteals.

"That's good," Allie said. "Real good."

"Just watch the knees," Buzz told him. "Keep the stomach from bowing out. Easy now."

Focusing hard, Jake got his knees to lock. It took a moment for him to realize that he was standing. He looked up at them with something close to terror in his eyes.

"I'm doing it. I'm standing!"

He would have paid money for the look on Allie's face as she realized that he really was.

"Buzz, he is. He's standing!"

"All right, Jake. Let's see how long you can do it."

Already he felt the energy seeping out of him, and he knew he couldn't hold the position for long. "I feel so heavy," he said. "And wobbly." He looked up at the joy in both their faces. "But this is the beginning, isn't it? I'm gonna walk again."

"Looks like it, man," Buzz said. "I'd bet money on it."

His PT's confidence was what Jake had waited weeks to hear, but now that he had, exhaustion kicked in, and he deflated like a balloon losing its air.

"That's okay," Allie assured him. "You were up for about thirty seconds. That's great."

"But you're sure it means I'll walk."

"It means you'll be able to get around on your legs. You might need crutches or a cane or walker, but—"

"No," Jake cut in. "I'm going to walk on my own. You'll see. It's gonna happen."

No one tried to dampen that enthusiasm as he worked toward doing that for the rest of the day.

Jake decided not to tell Lynda about his progress; he wanted to surprise her when he took his first steps. When the doctor declared that Jake's eye was healed enough to have his prosthesis put in, he decided not to tell her about that, too. It would be more rewarding to see the surprise on her face. After she dropped him off at the hospital for therapy, he got Buzz to drive him to the optical center where he'd be fitted for his eye.

He was mildly surprised as he wheeled himself into the shop with hundreds of pairs of glasses on the walls and posters that advertised contact lenses. "I thought this place would seem more—medical," he told the receptionist. "I didn't know you could pick up an eye like you'd get a pair of lenses."

"Well, there's a little more to it," she said, pushing his chair into the back room where Dan Cirillo, the optician, waited. "But probably not as much as you'd imagined."

He wasn't expecting to have the eye made while he waited, but that was Dan's intention. After they'd taken the impression of his socket, Jake waited for the wax model of his eye to be made, and sat in front of the optician and allowed him to use his other eye as a model while he painted a little disk to match Jake's iris. When that was done, the wax model was ready to try on, and Dan checked its fit.

Jake thought it odd that he couldn't feel it. Pulling it back out as easily as he would a contact lens, Dan said, "Okay—go on back to therapy for a few hours, and by the time you're done, your eye should be ready."

Buzz brought Jake back that afternoon, and Dan greeted him with a plastic, painted model. "So what do you think?" he asked.

Jake cringed. "No way. That's not gonna look normal."

"Wait and see."

Dan put the eye in, then tested the movement. "It's perfect," he said. "It moves right along with your other one. I think you're really gonna be happy with this."

He handed Jake a mirror, and bracing himself, Jake brought it to his face. The eye looked identical to his other one, and he felt a rising sense of relief that the man in the mirror looked more like the Jake he used to know than he had since the crash.

He blinked, testing it and then moved his eyes back and forth to see how it felt.

"What do you think?"

Jake's smile spoke volumes. "I think I'm amazed."

Jake wasn't wearing his patch when Lynda picked him up that afternoon, and she gaped at him as he got into the car. "Jake, why didn't you tell me?"

His grin almost split his face. "I wanted to surprise you."

She couldn't stop staring. "Look at me. I can't even tell which eye is false. It looks just like your other one!"

Still grinning, he leaned over and planted a quick kiss on her lips. The look on her face told him she was stunned, and he began to laugh. "It's back. The old mesmerizing charm. I hypnotized you with my baby blues, didn't I?"

"Well, I—"

He kissed her again. "See? I've still got it."

Shaking her head, she started to laugh. "It's like a whole personality change."

"It's hope, darlin'," he said, leaning back in his seat. "Just pure, colorful hope. I might just wind up with a life after all, now that I don't make people cringe when they look at me."

Still laughing, she started the car. "So are there any other surprises?"

"You mean, am I gonna lay one on you again? I don't know," he teased. "If I were you, I'd keep my guard up."

He enjoyed the pink color that faded across her cheekbones as she drove and realized what a joy it would be when she finally did learn of the other surprise he hadn't told her. He had stood outside the pool this afternoon on both feet without holding his weight up with his arms. He was ready to walk, he thought. It was just a matter of time. In a very few days, maybe he'd be able to walk out to the car when Lynda came to get him. The look on her face would almost make all the misery he'd gone through worth it.

CHAPTER SIXTY

W hen Lynda announced that she was going back to work on the following Monday to prepare for Paige's deposition a few days later, Paige was concerned. Lynda still had yellow bruises on her cheekbone and forehead, and last night Paige had caught a glimpse of Lynda dressing. Black bruises still colored her ribcage, and Paige could only imagine the pain that Lynda had been suffering without complaining since the crash.

"You know, I could go with you and help you," Paige said as she worked on getting breakfast ready, so at least Lynda wouldn't have to leave on an empty stomach. "I could bring Brianna something to occupy her, and—"

"Paige, what do you think I have Sally for? She can help me."

"I'm just worried about you. It's too soon to be going back."

"The doctor said it's all right. Besides, we go to court in two weeks. I have to be ready."

"But you could prepare for the deposition at home. Why do you have to go in?"

"There are things I can do better there, Paige. I want to document every infraction Keith has ever had in his life, and I need to be there to get it all put together the way the judge likes it. McRae's had some run-ins with this judge, which may play in our favor as long as I don't do anything to neutralize that advantage, so I'm going to do everything I can to please him in court. I have to contact all of the witnesses and meet with them. With time running out, I can't afford not to be on top of this."

Paige felt like a heel for being the cause of this.

"But are you sure you feel up to it?"

"I'll be fine, Paige."

"All right," Paige said, giving up.

"Will you be all right here with Jake?"

"Yeah," Paige said. "I don't know what it is, but his mood seems to be changing lately. I think we'll get along fine."

CHAPTER SIXTY-ONE

F inally!" Keith whispered to himself when he saw Lynda's car pull into her parking space beside her office building. He had figured that she'd probably be back to work today since it was Monday and she had to prepare for the hearing. He'd been sitting in his car across the street for a couple of hours already, waiting for her to make her appearance. His homemade bomb, wrapped in a leather pouch, sat on the seat next to him.

He had already decided that her personal space was in the perfect location—far enough to the side of the building that the security guard couldn't see it easily. Besides, as Keith had noticed for the past two hours, the guard stayed in his little office inside the building most of the time, watching television and talking on the phone. Keith could slip under her car, plant his package, and rig some wires, and the guard would never know. He could do it quickly; he'd been practicing.

Then all it would take was one turn of the key.... Keith made an exploding noise and then laughed as Lynda got out of her car and headed into the building.

He waited until she'd had enough time to get on the elevator then grabbed his package and got out of his car. The security guard was nowhere in sight. Looking down and walking fast, as if he knew exactly where he was going, he reached her car, looked around casually to make sure no one was watching and then got down on the ground and slid under it.

On his back, he unwrapped the bomb, pulled the duct tape out of his front pocket, and peeled off a long piece. He tore it off with his teeth, taped it to the gas tank, and then peeled off some more. When the bomb was taped securely enough to stay put, he inched forward on his shoulder blades and wired the bomb to the starter.

The guard still hadn't resurfaced when Keith stood up slowly beside the car. He hurried to the sidewalk, then slowed to a leisurely pace and cut across the street to his own car again.

Should he get out of the area or stick around and watch? The temptation was too great. He got back into his car, got comfortable, and prepared to wait as long as he needed to see the result of his planning and cleverness.

CHAPTER SIXTY-TWO

The wall of noise that assaulted Lynda when she got off the elevator startled her into a near coronary—until she realized that it was just her co-workers shouting "Surprise!"

Pressing her hand over her heart, she stepped back onto the elevator, and Sally grabbed the doors to stop them from closing. "It's a welcome back, Lynda!"

Lynda covered her mouth then and started to laugh, allowing Sally to pull her into the circle of her friends and associates. "You guys wouldn't do that if you knew how many surprises I've had in the last few weeks!"

Barraged with welcomes and pats on the back, she let them sweep her to the staff lounge where they had donuts and drinks and a "Welcome Back, Lynda" cake.

When the celebration was over and she wound up back in her office with Sally, she settled back in her chair and relaxed. "Gosh, it's good to be back."

"We're just so glad you're alive," Sally told her.

Lynda pulled Sally into a tight hug. "You've been a life-saver, holding down the fort the way you have. I really appreciate it."

Sally took a deep breath. "Well, it'll be nice helping you get caught up. I'll admit, it's been a little hard juggling everything. Are you ready to dive into this mess?"

Lynda looked over the stacks of mail, messages, and papers on her desk. "I really need to get some things done on Paige's case first. Then we'll tackle the stack."

"All right." Sally shuffled the papers around and pulled out her pen and notepad. "Shoot."

And as Lynda started doing what she did best, she felt as if the world were realigning itself, and things were on their way to getting back to normal.

Jake helped Paige with the breakfast dishes as Brianna sat on a stool at the sink, "washing" the plates but getting more suds on herself than she did on the dishes.

He'd been quiet ever since Paige had told him that Lynda had gone to work today, but he couldn't pinpoint what bothered him about it the most. That she might not be physically ready to dive back into work yet? That she hadn't told him? That she wouldn't be the one to drive him to the hospital for therapy today? Or was it simply that she wasn't here, and he missed her?

"As soon as you're ready to go, I'll change Brianna's clothes and take you," Paige said.

Jake shrugged. "No hurry. Buzz and Allie don't expect me today until ten o'clock." He rolled his chair up to Brianna's stool and asked, "Why don't you and I go outside and get some fresh air, Brianna?"

Brianna's little smile faded, and she shook her head and kept scrubbing a plate. "No."

Paige stopped what she was doing and shot Jake a look.

"Why not?" Jake asked.

"Cause." It was a simple answer, but in Brianna's mind, it probably covered it all.

"Cause why?"

"Daddy might come."

"She just insists that he's been out there," Paige said quickly. "That day you got here, when she started screaming, I thought she was just mixed up. That she thought you were her daddy ..."

"But she sure wasn't afraid of me later."

"Yeah, that's been bothering me, too." She walked to the back door and peered out the window into the back yard. "Maybe he really was here."

To Jake, that seemed unlikely. Why would anyone take that chance? It would be crazy, coming here and talking to Brianna. If he were caught, it would show everyone, including the judge, that Keith lacked any kind of judgment, that he was willing to break the law, and that he was unpredictable—and dangerous. "Hey, Brianna, what if I go out there with you?" he asked. "Your mom and I want some fresh air. We could all go. Nobody's gonna take you with all of us out there."

From her stool, Brianna looked down at him then thoughtfully considered her mother. When her eyes moved back to Jake, she said in her borderline baby voice, "You won't leave me? Even if he comes, you won't let him get me?"

"Of course not," Jake said. "But your mom will never let him get you, either."

"He's strong," she said matter-of-factly as she slipped off the stool. "He can push her down."

As Brianna scurried through the house to find her shoes, Jake and Paige exchanged troubled looks.

In seconds, Brianna reappeared with her shoes.

Paige's eyebrows rose. "Are we going out?"

"Only if Jake comes."

"I'm coming, kiddo." But as Brianna put on her shoes, he looked up at Paige and asked, "Why would that make her feel safer?"

"Because you're a man," Paige said. "I guess she thinks Keith is more of a threat to me than he is to you."

As Jake let that sink in, Brianna ran to get her dolls. They followed her out the door, then watched as her gaze gravitated to the back corner of the yard. Timidly, she took a few steps into the grass.

Paige followed her gaze to the area beyond the fence where it would be easy for anyone to hide.

"What's on the other side of those woods?" Jake asked behind her.

"A street with a few houses." She glanced back at him. "You think he was here, too, don't you?"

"I don't know, Paige."

Feeling sick, Paige settled onto the swing as Brianna set her babies around the picnic table and began talking to herself.

"I can't believe this," Paige whispered. "When I married him, I thought he was a dream come true. I thought he was my escape. But three days after we got married, his temper exploded, and I found out I'd just traded one nightmare for another."

"Did he hit you that soon?"

"No. If he had, I probably would have left. But he broke things and yelled a lot. I started trying to walk on eggshells just to keep from setting him off. But it's like he doesn't think straight. There is no reasoning with him. Keith has a whole different way of viewing the world than most people."

"So why did you stay with him?"

She considered that for a moment. "You have to understand him. He had been this brilliant kid raised in foster homes with no one who ever really got that involved with him. He had never had anyone of his own or anyone he could trust, and I had this stupid idea that if I just proved myself to him he'd settle down."

"When did he start hitting you?"

"When I was five months pregnant with Brianna." Her eyes filled, and she blinked back the tears. "And there I was with this little baby on the way ... and my only real option was to go back to my family—which wasn't an option at all. Besides, I wanted Brianna to have a father. And I wanted to give her a home. I kept thinking that once he saw her, he'd love her so much that he'd change. If not for me, for her."

"Did you ever leave him before now?"

"Sure I did," she said. "Several times. But he always talked me into coming back. You have to understand; we were in the military. He wasn't home half the time, so I told myself that I could manage the times he was. When I'd leave him, we'd be stuck in some town where I had no friends, no help." She swallowed. "I owe a lot to Lynda. If she hadn't been willing to take my case and give me advice, I don't know if I would have had the courage to leave him for good, even after he hurt Brianna. I don't know why it's so hard for me to stick to my guns."

Jake's eyes strayed to the child playing at the table then scanned the trees on the perimeter of the yard. "Did you say he was in the military?"

"Yes. The Navy."

"No wonder he was gone so much."

"Yeah. He'd be out on that aircraft carrier for weeks at a time. I wouldn't even hear from him. It was so peaceful."

"Aircraft carrier?" Jake cut in. "What did he do?"

"He was an aircraft mechanic," she said. "On the ships, they—"

"Wait a minute." Jake stopped her and sat straighter. "Did you say he was an *aircraft* mechanic?"

"Yes. He…" Her voice trailed off as she saw his reaction, and she realized what he was thinking.

"Does Lynda know this?"

"Well, she knows he was in the Navy. I don't think she ever asked what he did there. Jake, you don't think—"

"Paige, was Keith ever a suspect in the plane crash?"

Paige gaped at him. "I don't know. But anyway, they caught the guy who did that."

True, Jake thought, they had. Yet he couldn't dismiss the uneasy feeling that had gripped him. "I'm just saying—what if they were wrong? What if they got the wrong guy? I mean, if Keith knows airplanes, he would know exactly what to do to sabotage Lynda's plane. The cops may have overlooked it because you don't think of airplanes when you think of the Navy."

"But why would he do that? To get Brianna, he would have to get *me* out of the way, not Lynda—and I wasn't anywhere near Lynda that day." She thought back to the day that had erupted so horribly, starting the bizarre chain of events that had brought her to where she was now. "As a matter of fact, he went to the day care that morning trying to get Brianna. That's when this whole thing started."

"Doesn't that seem coincidental? That Lynda and I crashed the same morning that he started aggressively trying to take Brianna? Whoever sabotaged our plane did it the night before the crash. He could have been anticipating that Lynda would be out of the way, so that when he kidnapped Brianna, you'd have no one to help you."

Paige's face slowly drained of its color. "No, it can't be. Keith would do a lot of things. Sinister, mean things. But I can't believe he'd kill somebody."

"When they questioned him about the fire, you thought he could, didn't you?"

She got up, unable to sit still. "No. I mean yes. I was confused, but—Brianna was in that house. Of course, he didn't know that at the time." She turned back to Jake. "Keith *can't* be the one. He can't be. Because if he is, then the guy they've got locked up is the wrong guy. And Keith is still loose."

"Waiting to hit again."

The thought chilled her. Rushing across the grass, she picked Brianna up. "Come on, honey. We're going in." Abandoning the dolls, she took her into the house.

"Mommy, I want to play!"

"No, honey." She stepped back as Jake followed them in. Then she let Brianna down, closed the door, and bolted it. "We have to come in now."

"Paige, I think it's okay if she plays—"

"No!" Paige ran her trembling hands through her hair. "Brianna said he was here, and he was, Jake. He found out where we are, and he's been watching us! He's going to do something! I have to stop him!"

He watched her run frantically around the house, looking for something. Brianna stood watching her, not moving, and her thumb gravitated to her mouth. "Lynda took the cellular phone, didn't she? We haven't gotten a phone hooked up yet, Jake. Can I use the one in your car?"

"Sure," he said. "Who are you calling?"

She was out the door before he could get an answer. Pulling Brianna onto his lap, he rolled out after her.

She was already in the car dialing. After a moment's wait, she said in a shaky voice, "This is Paige Varner. I need to speak to Larry Millsaps, please." She closed her eyes and shook her head, apparently not liking the answer she received. "Then I'll speak to Tony Danks. Well, when will they be back? Do you know how I can reach them?"

She wilted and covered her face. "No, they can't call me back. Look, this is an emergency. Tell them to come to Lynda Barrett's house as soon as possible. And tell them I think they've got the wrong guy!"

Hanging up, she breathed a quick sob. "I'm going there."

"Where?"

"To the police department. I'm going to wait there until they get back. We're not safe here, Jake. You come with me."

"No," he said. "I'll stay in case Lynda comes home."

"Oh, no!" Paige wailed. "*She's* in danger, too. If he would mess up her plane and burn down her house, he'll do anything. If she's at work, she's a sitting duck. He knows where to find her!"

"All right," Jake said, trying to calm her. "I'll stay here and call her, and you take Brianna and go to the police station. Don't worry. I'll make sure Lynda's careful, and Tony and Larry will take care of the rest."

Sucking in a deep breath and wiping her face, she carried Brianna to her car.

Jake was dialing Lynda's office before Paige was out of the driveway, but the receptionist put him on hold for what seemed an eternity. When she came back, she told him that Lynda's line was busy. Would he like to hold, call back, or leave a message?

"Let me try her secretary," he said.

"Her line's busy, too. But she could call you back."

"Look, have her call me, but tell her it's an emergency. Tell her not to move until she talks to me. Did you get that?"

"Yes, sir."

"I mean it. This is very serious. Tell her to call me on my car phone at this number. Do you have a pen?"

He rattled off the number, and the woman jotted it down. "I'll give her the message, Mr. Stevens."

Jake cut the phone off and sat still a moment, wondering whether Paige had overreacted, and whether his own concern had caused her to. If this were all just a wild tangent....

Somehow, he didn't think it was.

He sat beside his car for twenty minutes or so, waiting for Lynda to call him back, and finally he dialed the number again.

"She's in a meeting, Mr. Stevens," the receptionist said. "I gave her the message, but—"

"Did she see it, or did you just put it on her desk?"

"Well—I gave it to Sally and told her it was urgent. But she was already in the meeting."

"How could she be in a meeting if she was on the phone before?"

"I guess she hung up and went before I could get back there."

He wanted to reach through the phone and throttle the woman. "Look, I don't *care* if she's in a meeting. Get her out."

"I can't do that, sir. It's a partners' meeting, and I've been given instructions to—"

"Then transfer me to Sally!"

He waited as he was put on hold, realizing what Paige must have gone through all those months before she was one of Lynda's priorities.

"Lynda Barrett's office."

It was Sally, and he breathed a sigh of relief. "Sally, this is Jake Stevens."

"Jake, I got your message. What's going on?"

"It's a long story. Is there any way you can get Lynda out of that meeting for an emergency?"

"Well, I suppose I could, but—"

"Then do it! Tell her to call me ASAP! I'm sitting out here by my car so I can take the call. Here's the number."

When he hung up, he waited, his heart racing. If only he could do something besides sit. If he could just get into this car and drive to her office.

Minutes ticked by, but the phone didn't ring. And he had no intention of going inside until it did.

Lynda couldn't have been more relieved when Sally got her out of the meeting. The sheer act of sitting still was making her ache all over, and her head throbbed from all the questions her partners and associates kept flinging at her about the cases they had taken over for her. And it was all time she could have spent working on Paige's case or catching up on her correspondence.

Sally gave her a once-over as she came out, laden down with papers. "Are you feeling okay? You look pale."

"I'm a little tired. What's wrong?"

"I got you out because Jake has been calling. He says it's an emergency. You'd better call him. He's waiting at his car. Here's the number."

Frowning, she took it. "Did he say what's wrong?"

"Nope."

"Okay, I'll call him," she said, heading for her office. "Hold all my calls."

She hurried into her office and dialed the number. Jake answered on the first ring.

"Hello?"

"Jake, it's Lynda. What's going on?"

"Lynda, Paige and I were talking, and we hit on something I think you should know about."

"What?"

"Did you know that Keith Varner used to be an aircraft mechanic?"

She caught her breath. "No he wasn't!"

"Yes, he was. In the Navy," he said. "He worked on airplanes on an aircraft carrier."

"Are you sure?"

"Dead sure. Paige said it herself."

There was a moment of silence, and finally, Lynda blew out an unsteady breath. "Jake, they had him. After the fire and again after the assault. They had him twice, but they let him go. It was him all the time."

"Yeah. Some poor guy is sitting in the slammer right now for something he didn't do, and this lunatic is still out there. Probably waiting for another opportunity. Or at least we have to assume for your safety as well as Paige's and Brianna's, that that's true."

She felt dizzy, and for a moment, she considered asking him to hold while she splashed cold water on her face.

"Where's Paige? How's she taking this?"

"The way you might expect, just short of hysterical. She decided to take Brianna and go to the sheriff's department to talk to Larry and Tony."

"Good. That was smart."

"But I'm worried about you."

She swallowed and reached for her car keys. "Frankly, *I'm* worried about me. Look, I'm coming home. I'm not feeling that terrific anyway. I'll just call it a day."

The relief was clear in Jake's voice. "All right. I'll see you soon. Lynda?"

"Yeah."

"Be careful, huh?"

She sat for a moment after he'd hung up, trying to organize her thoughts. She wasn't going to panic.

Picking up the phone, she buzzed Sally's desk. "Sally, would you get me all those files I need to look at for Paige's case? I'm going home, and I'll take those with me."

"Sure thing."

She looked up the number of the police station, dialed it, and asked for either of the two detectives.

Neither Larry nor Tony was in, and they couldn't be reached.

As she sank back into her chair, Sally breezed in with the files. "Lynda, are you sure you're all right?"

"Yeah. Sally, Jake's just run across some information that makes him think Keith Varner caused our crash and that he burned down my house."

Sally's eyes widened. "Paige's husband?"

"Yeah. And to tell you the truth, I think he's right. It all makes sense." She was trembling as she got to her feet. "I'm going home, but if Larry or Tony calls, tell one or both of them to call me on the cellular phone. I have to talk to them."

"Okay."

Lynda reached for the stack of files that contained the depositions from all the witnesses, all the emergency-room reports, and all the police complaints and stories from neighbors. But Sally put out a hand to stop her.

"This is too heavy for you," she said. "Give me the keys, and I'll go drop them in the car for you so you won't have to carry them."

Lynda managed a smile. "That would be great." She tossed her the keys. "I have a few other things I need to do before I leave."

"I'll be right back," Sally said and flitted out of the room.

Lynda sat and thought for a moment then decided not to wait for Larry and Tony. She would go straight to the DA, even before going home to Jake. Picking up the phone, she dialed the district attorney's number and told him she was coming right over.

Preoccupied, she got on the elevator and rode it down, hoping to intercept Sally in the parking lot.

The security guard was waiting just outside the elevator door when she got off.

"Sally said she'd bring your car up to the door, Miss Barrett, so you wouldn't have to walk."

Lynda smiled wanly. "That was sweet of her. All I wanted her to—"

A sound like the end of the world shook the building, breaking out the front windows and knocking her to her knees. The security guard threw himself against her, covering her from the flying glass with his body.

"No!" she screamed as she hit the floor, but it was too late. She'd already seen the glow that bathed the parking lot in a weird, unearthly light and the smoke that billowed across the lot as if shot from a hose. She knew without the slightest doubt that a car in the parking lot had just exploded.

And she knew without looking whose car it was.

CHAPTER SIXTY-THREE

Struggling to her feet, Lynda crunched across the shattered glass and through the ruined door toward the flames, but the security guard caught up to her on the sidewalk.

"You have to stay back!" he shouted.

"But Sally's in there!" She tried to push him away, but he held her more tightly, and finally, the fight turned to mourning as she collapsed into his arms, covering her face with her hands, watching through her fingers as the flames devoured the car.

Already a crowd was spilling out of the building, and she heard sirens.

"They've got to get her out!" she cried.

But the guard wouldn't let her go. "She's dead, Miss Barrett. There's no way she could have survived that."

Lynda shook free of him again. "But it was my car! It was meant for me!"

She collapsed on the ground and immediately friends surrounded her as the parking lot filled with emergency vehicles.

Paige paced the floor at the police precinct, waiting for Larry or Tony to come back in or call. She couldn't just stay here, she told herself. Keith was still loose out there. He could try to hurt Lynda or even Jake again. He could burn the house down—or worse.

Grabbing Brianna from the dirty floor where she'd been looking at a book, she went back to the precinct desk and tapped the arm of the uniformed deputy who had helped her earlier. "I have to go," she said. "Please tell Tony or Larry when they come in that Keith Varner is the one who's been after Lynda Barrett. Please. They have to arrest him."

The man had already checked Paige's situation out in the computer. He knew that she'd complained about her ex several times. He also knew they were embroiled in a custody battle, and he'd seen enough to know that such spouses would do whatever it took to discredit the other. He jotted down the note disinterestedly then slipped it in a stack. "They'll get the message."

Paige could see that he wasn't counting it as urgent. "I'm telling you if you don't do something, somebody might die. He's out there."

"Call us if anything comes up," he said.

Cursing under her breath, Paige gave up.

"Where are we going, Mommy?" Brianna asked as they headed out the door.

Paige sighed. "I don't know. Maybe to Lynda's office."

"Good. I like Miss Lynda's office."

"Okay," Paige said. "That's where we'll go then."

Brianna was quiet as they drove, as though she knew that her mother needed time to think.

But the moment Paige turned onto the law firm's street and saw the fire trucks and police cars surrounding the parking lot, her heart leapt in fear. Forced to stop in the line of traffic, she rolled down her window and stretched as far out as she could to see what the problem was.

A car alongside the building was on fire.

Terror ripped through her, and she covered her mouth, muffling a scream.

Brianna started to cry. "What's the matter, Mommy?"

But Paige didn't answer, for as the traffic began to move, she saw the car that was burning.

Lynda's car.

Trembling, she pulled out of the line of traffic, did a quick U-turn, and headed back to the house as fast as she could, trying with all her heart to fight the certainty that Lynda was dead.

CHAPTER SIXTY-FOUR

Keith had watched and waited from three blocks away, knowing that the moment the car went up, he'd know it. And he'd been right.

He hadn't expected it to happen so soon. He'd figured he would have to spend a few more hours sitting in his car watching, but she had made it easy on him.

He laughed now as he drove to the house where his wife and daughter were hiding. Paige was defenseless now, both in court and out. Brianna was his. All he had to do was tie up these loose ends.

Boldly, he turned down the street that he hadn't dared to drive down before and passed the trees he had hidden in as he had stalked them over the last week.

But Paige's car wasn't in the driveway. Only the red Porsche sat there—the car that hadn't been moved since he'd first noticed it.

Disappointed, he turned around at the dead end and left the street. Okay. So he would park and watch for her to come home, then. And the moment she did, he would grab Brianna before Paige could get inside. There would be nothing she could do. Absolutely nothing.

CHAPTER SIXTY-FIVE

I t's Keith Varner." Lynda's voice was dull and without inflection. "He did it."

Larry had just shown up on the scene after getting the urgent message from Lynda—one that had to be delivered by another detective since he and Tony had been working on an undercover case in which they couldn't carry their radios. "What?"

"He was an aircraft mechanic in the Navy. It's him, Larry. He's the one who's been trying to kill me. I thought you had the right guy behind bars! I never would have let Sally go out there if I'd known—"

"You didn't know. You couldn't have known. You don't even know now."

"Then explain this!" she screamed at him. "Something seems to go up in flames everywhere I go! If the guy you've got in jail is the right one, then why did this happen? I'm telling you, it's Keith! He's crazy!"

Larry looked up at the other officers who were filling out reports. "Put out an APB on Keith Varner. If he did it, we'll know it soon enough."

"Do you honestly think you're just going to go get him? He's not sitting at home waiting for the police!" Lynda shouted.

"We'll find him. Just calm down."

"I *can't* calm down! My secretary is dead in my place! She was my friend!" She collapsed in tears, then shook her head, trying to pull herself together. In a cracked, high-pitched voice, she said, "I have to tell her family. They can't hear this from just anyone."

"Well, you'd better do it soon," Larry said. "Before the authorities tell them."

"Would you—would you take me?"

"Sure." He took a deep breath, then walked her to his car and set her inside. Then he turned and gave a few more instructions to the deputies still on the scene.

As they pulled away, Lynda glanced back at the crowd that had formed around the parking lot. Another gruesome sight they would never forget. Another incident Lynda Barrett had escaped.

She didn't know how many more she could take. Especially not at this cost.

CHAPTER SIXTY-SIX

eith got tired of waiting and decided to park his car in his usual spot on the street behind Lynda's house and cut through the woods. Then he would sneak up on the back of the house, look through the windows, and find out whether anyone was home.

He made his way to the fence enclosing the back yard, the same place where he'd talked to Brianna just a few days ago. Satisfied that no one was near, he climbed the fence and cut across the yard.

Boldly, he crossed the patio and peered into the kitchen window. The lights were off. He moved past the back kitchen door and looked through the living-room window. No one was there.

Stepping quietly, he made his way down the length of the house to the other back door, the one that went into the master bedroom. Peering through the glass pane in the door, he saw that the bed was made and the lights were off.

So they were gone. He tested the door that led into the bedroom. Locked. Going back to the kitchen door, he tested it, too.

The house was empty. When Paige came home, it would be just the two of them—and Brianna. He found a comfortable seat behind the house and waited for Paige.

Jake heard the screeching tires as Paige pulled into the driveway; as quickly as he could, he pushed himself out of the recliner and into his wheelchair. He rolled to the door—but even before he could turn the knob, he heard Brianna scream.

Through the door's window, he saw that a man had grabbed Brianna out of Paige's car and that Paige was fighting and clawing and kicking him with all her might.

His heart jumped, and he twisted the knob, ready to burst through the door and defend her—until he was hit with the crushing realization that there was nothing he could do. He couldn't walk or fight or defend anyone.

For a moment, he sat stunned, watching Paige fight for her life, watching as the man—he assumed it was Keith Varner—held Brianna roughly around her waist with one arm, and with the other pulling Paige by the hair to the door, making her unlock it. "You have ten minutes to pack everything she has here," he said through his teeth. "And then I'll decide what to do with you."

Jake roused himself, knowing that regardless of his limitations, Paige and Brianna needed his help. Flying back to the small kitchenette, he pulled the biggest knife he could find from the drawer, set it in his lap, and headed back to the door.

He heard the house door slam. He hoped that, with all the screaming inside, Keith wouldn't hear him if he went out and tried to reach his car phone. Jake guessed that they were in the bedroom at the back of the house, getting Brianna's things.

As quietly as he could, he opened the door and rolled out onto the driveway.

Paige's screams still sounded from inside the house, and something crashed. Jake's hands trembled as he opened his car door as quietly as he could then slipped inside. Pulling the door shut, he checked to make sure that Keith had not heard him. Apparently he hadn't.

He dialed 911 and keeping his voice barely above a whisper, told the dispatcher that Paige and Brianna were being held hostage inside the house and that Keith was dangerous. When he told them it was the home of Lynda Barrett, the dispatcher hesitated.

"Barrett? The same woman whose car blew up today?"

Jake clutched the phone. "What?"

"Is it the Lynda Barrett who works in the Schilling building?"

For a moment he couldn't find his voice. "Yes," he said. "What happened to her car?"

"Uh—there was an accident. An explosion."

Trying to steady his breath, he said, "Was she—was she killed?"

"There was one death in the accident," the woman confirmed hurriedly. "Do you think the person in the house could be a suspect in the explosion?"

Jake felt as if he were falling, falling, and there was nothing he could grab to stop his fall.

"Sir? Can you hear me?"

"Yes," he breathed. "Yes, it's him. Hurry, or he'll kill them."

He punched the end button on the phone then sat still, trying to grasp everything she had said. Explosion. Lynda's car. One death.

For a moment, he considered putting his key in the ignition, turning on the car, and ramming it headfirst into the house. Maybe he could get rid of Keith and himself in one quick action.

It was too much.

Not Lynda. She couldn't be dead.

He covered his face with his hand, too shocked to weep or scream. It had to be a mistake. She wouldn't die on him just like that. She would fight and survive. Somehow she'd make it.

So caught up was he in the turmoil of his raging thoughts that he didn't hear a car pull into the driveway behind him. But he jumped when he heard the car door slam and wrenched his neck to see. Lynda was walking toward the house, and a car was backing out of the driveway.

He flung the door open and almost fell out. "Lynda! You're alive!"

She looked pale, and there were red circles under her eyes. "Yeah," she said, and tears came to her eyes again as she reached for him. "Sally's dead."

He wanted to fling himself at her, hug her, but there wasn't time. "He's in there, Lynda. He has Paige and Brianna."

"What? Who?"

"Keith! He caught her getting out of her car and dragged them in. I've called the police."

Lynda stood shocked for a moment, then turned frantically toward the street, lifting a hand—but the car was already gone. Jake pulled himself into his chair then rolled around a corner of the house where Keith couldn't see him if he looked out. Lynda followed him.

"That was Larry who dropped me off! I should have made him stay, but he had a lead on where Keith was—" She looked around for a weapon then saw the knife Jake clutched in his hand. "But surely the dispatcher will let him know—"

"We can't wait," Jake said. "We have to do something! I think they're in the bedroom getting Brianna's things. If we can figure out where they are, when the police get here they can go in another door and surprise him."

Lynda nodded. "I'll go look."

A shadow of frustration crossed Jake's face. He wanted to go. But he couldn't.

"Be careful," he said.

Lynda crept along the side of the house. Peering around the corner nearest the bedroom, she saw them.

Keith stood in front of the screen door that opened to the patio. He held Brianna with one arm while he pointed a gun at Paige. She was on her knees, throwing clothes into a suitcase. Lynda could hear Brianna screaming. And through it, their voices.

"Please," Paige begged. "Just put her down, Keith. Let her go!"

"Shut up," Keith snarled. He grabbed Paige and pulled her up. "Now, where's the rest of her stuff?"

"The living room," Paige choked out. "Her dolls are in the living room."

As soon as they were out of sight, Lynda dashed back around the house to where Jake waited.

"They're headed for the living room," she whispered.

Something else crashed inside the house, and Lynda jumped. Brianna's blood-curdling scream cut through the air.

"He'll kill them," she whispered loudly. "He's insane. What are we going to do?"

"First, we're gonna calm down," he whispered. "And we're gonna think."

"I can get in through the back way," she whispered. "The door to the master bedroom."

"And do what? You don't have a gun. And even if you did, you couldn't use it."

"Then what do you suggest?"

"Let me go in that way," he said. "You wait here then create a diversion at the front of the house when the police get here."

She looked at his functionless legs, at his wheelchair. "No, I can't let you do it."

There was another crash, and Brianna's screaming stopped short. From the house came nothing but dead silence.

"That's it! I won't let him take another of my friends!" Throwing down her purse, she sprang toward the kitchen door.

"Lynda, stop!" he said in a loud hiss.

But she burst through the door before he could reach her. "Stop it!" she screamed. "Let them go and take me instead! I'm the one you really want!" The door slammed shut behind her.

For a moment, Jake sat frozen. He thought of going in after her, giving the fight everything he had. But that wouldn't help anyone. In the distance, he could hear sirens, but they were still too far away. Lynda's purse lay on its side on the ground; he reached for it and dug for her house key. Gripping the knife, he rolled around the back of the house, through the dirt so he wouldn't make noise. As the sirens got louder, he unlocked the master bedroom door and rolled inside.

He heard Keith cursing at Lynda, and Paige starting to scream again; things crashed and fell. Outside, the sirens seemed to have disappeared; had they gone the wrong way?

What if it was all up to him?

Grasping for help, Jake closed his eyes. *If you're up there, God, I could use a hand. Just make my body function well enough to help them.*

In the living room, Lynda tried to breathe, but Keith's arm was brutally tight against her throat. Paige's face was bleeding where he'd hit her, and Brianna sat hunched under a table with her arms covering her head.

"At least let Brianna go," Paige was crying. "Please, Keith. She's your *daughter!* If you really loved her you wouldn't make her watch this!"

"You don't know the first thing about love," he bit out. "She needs to know what kind of a tramp her mother is. She needs to see how weak you are. And she needs to see you dead, so she won't keep expecting you to rescue her when I take her. That way we can start a new life together, and she can depend on me, and I can clear her mind of all the brainwashing you've done."

Lynda struggled to loosen his hold on her. "You won't get away with this," she said. "You think they'll let you keep that child after you've killed two more people? They'll never let you out of here with her."

"Who won't?"

"The police!" she shouted, but Keith just grinned down at her insanely.

"The police are idiots. They already had me twice, and they let me go."

"Don't you hear the sirens?"

For the first time, he listened. The sirens were loud now and sounded as if they were right outside the house. Venomous rage reddened his face. "Then I have nothing more to lose, do I?"

Throwing Lynda down, he grabbed Paige's hair and put his gun to her head.

The doorbell rang, and a loud banging followed. "Police department! Open up!"

The gun fired, and Paige collapsed. Lynda screamed and dove for Brianna, who clung desperately to her, shivering. Keith kicked Paige, and when she recoiled, it was clear that she hadn't been shot. Thankful, Lynda tried to catch her breath and whispered to Brianna, "She's all right, sweetheart. Mommy's all right."

"The next shot goes through the door!" Keith shouted. "And then I'll kill both women!"

"We just want to talk to you, Varner!"

Lynda recognized the voice outside the door—Larry. She prayed that he hadn't come too late.

"Where's the phone?" Keith asked, sweat beading on his face as he looked from one side of the room to the other. "I can talk to 'em—negotiate."

"We don't have one!" Lynda threw back. "We used the cellular phone in my car, but you blew it up!"

"Shut up!" Keith bellowed and kicked over the table they sat under.

It didn't take another gunshot to tell Jake that there was no more time. If he were going to act, he had to do it now. Opening the bedroom door as quietly as he could, he wheeled into the hallway, holding the knife in his fist.

Keith picked up Paige again by the hair and arm, and as she struggled to free herself, Keith's hold tightened and Paige let out a muffled scream.

"In the name of God, let her *go!*" Lynda cried. "Think of Brianna. Look what you're doing to her!"

Jake silently wheeled to the corner where the hall joined the living room. Staying as far back as he could, he saw Brianna crouched beside Lynda. Keith stood nearby, still holding Paige with both arms. He let her go, and she fell to the floor. Bending down, he reached out to touch Brianna.

Curling into a tighter ball, she strained away from him.

"Brianna, it's just Daddy," he said in a quiet voice. "I'm not gonna hurt you again. Don't you believe me?"

Jake's gaze narrowed to the revolver hanging in Keith's hand, muzzle toward the ground, as he reached for Brianna with the other.

Slowly, Jake came out of the shadows and began to move across the carpet.

Tears started down Keith's face as he touched Brianna's hair. She hunched her shoulders higher, and her mouth grew even wider in terror, but her heaving sobs were silent.

First Lynda then Paige caught sight of Jake moving across the carpet in his wheelchair, and they froze, not certain what to do.

"It's not too late, Keith," Lynda said, keeping her timbre steady and low, trying to draw Keith's attention. "You can change your life. You can be the father she needs. Just let her go for now."

Keith dropped his head and began to weep; the gun slipped slightly in his loosening grasp.

Jake pushed his wheels gently one more time, easing closer to Keith's side, holding his breath to avoid any sound that would give him away—

And swung his arm with all the strength and speed he could muster. He hit the gun, sending it bouncing several feet away across the carpet, then swung back to grab Keith's wrist and twist it behind his back, forcing him to his knees. "Didn't know I was here, did you, pal?" Jake asked through gritted teeth. "Recognize me? I'm the guy you maimed in the plane crash."

Keith couldn't move; the strength Jake had built in his arms over the past few weeks was overpowering. "Let me go!" he screamed, but Jake forced him forward until his face rested on the floor. Paige scrambled after the gun and stood up, aiming it at her ex-husband.

"Take her out, Lynda!" Paige shouted. "I don't want her to see me kill her father."

Lynda grabbed Brianna and rushed for the kitchen door. Paige waited until they were out of the room before she pulled the hammer back. "I could pull this trigger right now!" she said through her teeth, "and they'd call it self-defense. I'd be a hero for ridding the world of you. And my daughter could finally learn what it's like to live without terror."

Keith struggled against Jake's grip and tried to look up at her. "You won't do it. Brianna would always blame you—"

"Shut up!" she cried.

There was the sound of splintering wood, and the front door burst open. Larry lunged into the room then stopped when he saw Paige holding the gun on Keith.

"Paige, give me the gun," he said.

Paige shook her head. "Stay back. Jake, move away."

Reluctantly, Jake let Keith go and slowly rolled backward.

Her face was red and streaked with tears. "If I blew you away," she said, her voice trembling, "it would be for all the pain you've caused Brianna. All the nightmares. All the trauma. It would be for her peace of mind." The gun began to shake.

"Send him to jail, Paige," Jake said carefully. "Don't let him die knowing he finally broke you."

Her face twisted as she struggled between the emotion of the moment and the hope of the future. Finally, she breathed in and out deeply, her breath catching as her tears flowed anew. "He's right, Keith," she said. "You're not going to break me. You're just going to rot in prison."

When she lowered the gun, the house filled with deputies. Larry handcuffed Keith, jerked him to his feet, and took him away.

CHAPTER SIXTY-SEVEN

As low as Lynda's life had gotten in the past few weeks, she was certain that Sally's funeral was the lowest point yet. As if even God mourned her passing, the sky opened up with torrential rains that morning, and it stormed throughout the day. Lynda sat between Paige and Jake, holding hands with each of them, trying to rein back the tears that had controlled her since the day of the explosion. Even Keith's confession and guilty plea to felony murder had not relieved the pain.

She watched Sally's parents weep over their daughter. Sally had been close to them, even though they lived several hours away.

"At least she didn't leave a husband and children," Lynda heard someone whisper behind her.

Lynda quelled the urge to turn around and tell them that Sally had had many people who'd loved her, that she'd had as much of a family as most people had, and that her being single didn't make it any easier to say good-bye.

The car ride home was quiet, and when they had been back at the house for a while, Paige came out of her room with her bags packed.

Lynda had known they were going back home today, but she'd tried to put it out of her mind. Now there was nothing she could do but face it.

Dropping the bag, Paige reached out to hug Lynda. As they clung together like sisters, Lynda realized that, for the first time in her life, she didn't feel like an only child.

"I'm gonna miss you," Lynda whispered.

Paige wiped her tears. "Me, too. I don't know how I'll ever thank you for what you've done for us."

Lynda tried to smile. "Well, for starters—I need a new secretary." Tears rushed into her eyes again as she got the words out. "And frankly, I don't think I can get used to someone new right now. How about taking Sally's job?"

Paige seemed confused, wary. "Do you really mean it?"

"I sure do."

"But how do you know I'm qualified?"

"You can do anything," Lynda said. "I have a lot of faith in you."

Again, they embraced, then Lynda stooped to kiss Brianna. The child had been quiet and withdrawn since the scene with her father, but she'd already expressed her wish to go back to "school" soon. Paige thought it was a good idea to get her life back to normal as soon as possible.

Jake offered Brianna a final ride on his lap as they hurried through the rain to the car, and Lynda smiled sadly as he hugged the child who had brought him so far, gave her a quick kiss on the cheek, and then helped her into the car.

The rain poured harder as the car pulled away, but neither Lynda nor Jake made a move to go inside.

"Are you all right?" he asked when the car was out of sight.

Lynda was still gazing in the direction they had gone as raindrops mixed with the tears on her face. "I was just thinking."

"About what?"

"That day in the plane," she said. "When they asked us if we had anyone to contact. Neither of us had anyone, really."

"You had Sally."

"Sally the secretary," she whispered. "But not Sally the friend, not then. I didn't really have any close friends then. I thought I was happy, all alone."

"We've both come a long way."

She looked down at him, saw how wet his hair was getting, how soaked his clothes, but he didn't seem to mind. He wasn't the same man who had gotten out of his Porsche that day wearing his designer clothes, expecting crowds to part and women to swoon. "I like having people to love," she said.

He nodded, swallowed, and she knew that the mist in his eyes had nothing to do with the rain. "I like it, too."

For a moment, they smiled at each other as the rain dripped down their faces, and finally, she said, "It's going to be awfully quiet around here without them."

"Well, I'll see what I can do about making a little more noise."

She wiped her tears. "You'll have to eat my cooking now."

"I've been keeping it a secret, but I'm a pretty talented cook myself," he said. "As a matter of fact, I was thinking of making my special Texas stew for you tonight. Paige left all the ingredients in there. I already checked."

Slowly, the despair left Lynda's eyes, and she began to smile. "Then we'd better get busy peeling potatoes. You do have potatoes in your stew, don't you?"

"Among lots of other things, which shall remain secret."

"Well, I've survived four brushes with death in the last few weeks. I guess one more won't hurt me."

His smile faded. "That's not really funny," he said softly. "Matter of fact, it's downright chilling when you think about it."

"You're telling me." Looking around at the trees surrounding her house, she rubbed her arms and shivered. "Let's go in before we get sick and your chair starts to rust."

"I'd better change clothes first," he said. "If I don't, I'll ruin your kitchen floor."

"All right," she said. "I'll meet you in the kitchen."

She went back into the quiet house and felt the assault of silence again. But it wasn't so bad because she knew Jake was coming. Quickly she changed out of her wet clothes and towel-dried her hair.

When she went back into the kitchen, he was already at the table, peeling potatoes.

The sight of him there stirred her. Feeling awkward, she pulled out a chair and sat next to him. There were things she needed to say, things he needed to hear.

"We haven't talked much about that day," she said. "It's been kind of busy, and Sally's been on my mind. And we were all worried about Brianna...."

"Yeah. There hasn't been much time for reflection, has there?"

She looked down at the table, tracing the pattern of the wood grain with her fingertip. "I've been meaning to thank you."

"For what?"

"For coming to the rescue when Keith was here. My bursting into the house was really stupid. If you hadn't come in when you did—"

"I got lucky," he said. "If he had turned around and seen me coming, things could have turned out a lot differently."

"No, I think you would have been able to defend us even then. I didn't realize how strong you are, Jake. Even without your legs, you overpowered him. He couldn't fight you."

He smiled, but that smile quickly faded. "I just kept remembering that morning, when Brianna agreed to go outside because I was with her. I realized that she *expected* me to protect her. My legs weren't a factor to her. If I was to help her, then they couldn't be a factor to me, either."

She leaned on the table and faced him squarely. "Did you learn anything from that, Jake?"

His smile was subtle, but it reached all the way through her. "I think I did."

He didn't have to explain. She already knew that whatever he had learned, it was miles ahead of where he'd been before the plane crash.

"The important thing," he said, returning to his work, "is that that slimeball is behind bars." He finished peeling a potato then grew still for a moment, staring down at it.

"What's wrong?" she asked quietly.

He shrugged. "I was just thinking. That day when I called the police about Keith being in the house. They told me about the car blowing up, and said there had been a death."

Stillness.

"You thought it was me."

His facial muscles shifted with emotions he could not have named. "I was so glad when you walked up."

For a moment their eyes locked, and she wanted to reach out and hold him, cling to him. She had done it before when he'd needed comforting. But this was different.

This was more dangerous.

This was more important.

He reached out and took her hand, and squeezing it tightly, brought it to his lips. "You're a miracle, you know that?"

Coming from a man who didn't believe in miracles, that statement overwhelmed her. She saw the way his eyes misted as he gazed openly at her without the barriers of pride or humor, with only the honest glisten of pure affection.

Was he going to kiss her? Did she want him to?

She wasn't sure.

When he let her hand go and picked up his paring knife again, she breathed a sigh of both relief and disappointment. For as much as she'd feared that moment of truth between them, she regretted that it was over before it even started.

CHAPTER SIXTY-EIGHT

David Letterman was almost over when Jake started getting ready for bed. Turning off the lamp and leaving only the light of the television, he glanced out the window to see whether Lynda's light was still on. It wasn't.

Was she sleeping? Or was she lying awake, struggling with her grief, needing the same kind of comfort she'd offered him more than once?

And then he saw movement in the darkness on the patio and realized she was sitting out there alone, her feet pulled up and her arms hugging her knees. Moonlight played on her hair and touched her face, and he wondered why he hadn't been struck by how pretty she was the first time he'd met her. She was beautiful to him now.

Wanting to be close to her, he rolled out his door. Lynda looked up at him as he came around the house.

In the moonlight, he could see that she'd been crying. How did one soothe a grief like this one? How did you offer comfort when there was none?

"Need company?" he asked softly, rolling up beside her.

She smiled. "Yeah, I could use some."

He remembered the old days when he would have eagerly held a woman with tears on her face—but it would only have been so that he could use his hundred-dollar-an-ounce charm to work her vulnerability to his favor. It had been so easy for him, then, to make them trust him, count on him, believe in him—then to walk away without looking back the next morning.

Things had changed. Nothing was that easy anymore. He knew that all the introspection of the past weeks had given birth to something new in his life: a conscience. And he didn't think of Lynda the way he'd thought about any other woman in his life.

"I was just thinking about Sally," she whispered.

"Not beating yourself up again, I hope."

She looked out into the shadows of her yard. "I was thinking how unfair it is that she should die because of Keith's vendetta against me."

He turned his chair to face her, then reached out and took her hand in both of his. "Well, call me selfish if you have to, but I'm not going to feel guilty for being glad you weren't in that car."

"What could make a man want to kill?" she asked. "How could he have believed it would set anything right? Didn't he understand that he lost Brianna because of his violence in the first place?"

"He must by now, or he wouldn't have confessed and pled guilty."

Lynda shook her head. "No, I don't think he did that because he understands. I think he did that because McRae dropped his case, and he wasn't getting a lot of sympathy from his public defender."

Jake thought about that for a moment. "Not to mention the little fact that he was caught red-handed holding you all hostage, and he'd admitted, to all of us, that he'd done the other things."

"I think it was more a matter of defeat than regret," Lynda said. "He knew he couldn't win."

"Well, I guess our revenge is in knowing that he's behind bars and that he'll probably never see his daughter again."

She shook her head slowly. "I'm not supposed to want revenge."

"Why not?"

She looked up into the stars as new tears rolled down her cheek. "I'm supposed to pray for my enemies. I'm supposed to love them."

"Yeah, well, 'supposed to' is a long way from being able to. Look at all he did to you. Look what he did to me. I can't forgive him for that. I don't want to. But if I ever get the chance to meet him alone—"

"You won't," she whispered. "He'll probably get the death penalty. Unless I do something … say something…."

"Lynda, you can't."

Her sudden surrender to her tears surprised him, but without giving it a second thought, he gathered her up and pulled her against him. She closed her arms around his neck and wept against his shoulder, and he found himself weeping with her—*for* her. And he remembered how *she* had held *him* when he'd wept, how right it had felt, how much it had comforted him, how it had seemed like light seeping into the darkened chambers of his heart. That, more than her heroics in the plane, had probably saved his life.

"I came out here to pray for him," she whispered. "I made up my mind that I would. But I'm having trouble. It's the hardest thing I've ever done."

She wilted against his chest, and he stroked her hair. "It's okay, Lynda. It doesn't matter."

"It *does* matter."

"Why? Tell me why it matters."

She sat up then, breaking his hold on her and looked him squarely in the eyes. He reached up to wipe her tears away with the back of his fingers.

"It matters because Christ forgave me."

"Forgave you for what? What terrible thing have you ever done?"

"Oh, Jake," she cried. "I do terrible things all the time. And the morning of the crash when we were in that plane, knowing we could die the minute we landed, I just sat there. I didn't care what would happen to you if you'd died. I didn't even try to tell you what I knew. What could save you. But he didn't turn his back on either of us. He forgave me and let me start over. He let me see—"

"Lynda, you couldn't have saved me if you'd tried. I thought I had all the answers. Maybe I still think that. I was a creep then, and I'm probably still a creep, and you were justified in how you felt about me in that plane."

She shook her head. "You don't think it's important because you don't believe. But I do. And I want to obey now, but if it means forgiving Keith …"

"Keith Varner hasn't asked for your forgiveness."

"That doesn't matter. I still have to forgive him. And I hate myself for not being able to do it."

Later that night, when she had gone back into the house and lay awake in bed, staring at the ceiling and wrestling the monsters of memory and despair, Lynda tried to tell herself that she *could* forgive Keith, that maybe she already had. But as she drifted into a shallow sleep, she dreamed about cars blowing up and planes crashing and houses burning and about that panic that comes right before death between realizing it's going to happen and surrendering to it. Like a running theme through those images, Keith appeared here and there, laughing, cursing, escaping....

She awoke in a cold sweat and looked around at the room full of distorted shadows; she had left the lamp on. Trembling, she reached for her radio and turned it on. Maybe the noise would block out the fears, override the terror.

But her heart was beating too wildly for her to go back to sleep, so she got up and wandered around the quiet house. What if the dream were a warning? He is smart, after all. What if he *had* found some way to escape?

She went back to her bedroom; the dresser mirror caught her reflection as she passed, and she stopped to study it. She wasn't the same person she'd been before the crash. She was different. More fragile in some ways, tougher in others.

Would she ever stop being afraid?

Sitting down on the end of her bed, she pressed her face into her hands and tried with all her heart to pray for peace of mind. But the words wouldn't come, and she found herself unable to pray, unable to ask for help, unable to surrender.

She thought of going to Jake's door and waking him up, but the idea seemed crazy. She would have to wait until morning. And then, perhaps she'd look into counseling. Maybe she needed professional help. Maybe she needed her preacher to teach her to pray again. Maybe she needed a gun and a security system and a bodyguard.

Maybe none of this was really over yet.

CHAPTER SIXTY-NINE

I wish I'd killed him."

Paige's words would have surprised Lynda if she hadn't struggled with the same thought herself. Paige sat at her new desk—Sally's desk—with dark circles under her eyes, indicating that she hadn't been able to sleep either.

"I had the chance," Paige added quietly.

"Don't say that," Lynda whispered without much conviction as she sank into the chair across from Paige's desk. "You did the right thing. The only thing you could have done."

"Brianna's still having nightmares."

"Aren't we all?"

Paige's tired eyes met Lynda's, and she shook her head. "The DA asked me to testify at Keith's sentencing. It's amazing that he confessed and didn't even try to negotiate away the death penalty. I think maybe he really wants to die."

"The DA called me, too," Lynda said.

"So I guess, indirectly I have another chance." Paige propped her chin on her hand. "I keep having visions of sitting up there in front of him, telling the judge to give him the chair while he watches me with those persuasive, hurt eyes. He'd be so shocked that I went through with it."

"So are you going to?"

Paige shrugged, despair evident on her face. "I don't think I can."

Lynda was quiet, not questioning, for she knew the dilemma.

"He's Brianna's father. I don't want her growing up with that kind of stigma. And I guess when I come right down to it, I don't want that guilt. I don't even know if I believe in the death penalty."

Lynda was quiet for a moment. "I used to be against it right across the board. But now I'm not so sure. I've never been the victim before." She thought that over for a moment, hating herself for not being able to choose one side of the line or the other. "I guess it's time I decided what I really believe."

"Are you going to testify?"

"I don't know," Lynda whispered. "The judge's pre-sentencing investigation has already probably told him all he needs to know. My testimony wouldn't make that much difference." She sighed. "Maybe I'm just wimping out. I don't know what to do."

Paige accepted that. "Jake probably will."

Yes. That would be his way of getting some measure of revenge. She almost hoped he did.

But the reality of that hope only drew her deeper into a pit of depression that seemed impossible to escape.

Lynda didn't sleep for the three nights before the day she was to testify at the sentencing, and that morning as she drove Jake to the courthouse, she still wasn't sure whether she would even go in when she got there.

Her dejection hadn't escaped Jake's notice, and reaching across the seat, he stroked her hair. "You don't have to do this, you know."

Lynda nodded. "I don't know if I will." She glanced over at him. "Do you think I'm a coward?"

"No, Lynda. When I think about you, a lot of different words come to mind, but coward isn't one of them. I don't think it's fear that's keeping you from wanting to testify."

"Then what is it?"

"Indecision, maybe? Those people in there want to know how we, the victims, feel about what should happen to Keith Varner. And you can't really tell them if you don't know yourself."

She reached the courthouse and pulled into a parking place then sat there for a moment, making no move to get out. "But you're sure, aren't you, Jake? You think he should be put to death."

Jake's face hardened slightly. "I'd do it myself if I could."

She dropped her head back on her headrest and stared at the courthouse—the same building where Keith had attacked Paige and tried to take Brianna such a short time ago. She remembered Brianna's terror that day—and on another day, cowering under a table....

"Let's go in," she said quietly.

Jake shot her a surprised look. "Really? You're going to testify? What are you going to say?"

"I'll decide when I get in there," she said.

Jake got his wheelchair out of the back and slipped into it, and she followed him in. The building seemed too warm, and she found it hard to breathe. At the entrance, a few reporters rushed toward them with questions about their testimony, but they both threw out "No comment," and kept walking.

By the time they reached the courtroom, Lynda felt as if she might hyperventilate. Jake glanced back at her and noticed the perspiration on her temples and above her lip, and he handed her a handkerchief. "You okay?"

She sat down next to him. "Yeah. Fine."

The DA spotted them and came toward them. At the same time, the door at the front of the courtroom opened, and the bailiffs brought Keith in.

His eyes were bloodshot and he hadn't shaved. He searched the room frantically. Lynda knew he was looking for Paige, but when his gaze rested on her, her heart jolted.

All her anger rushed back in a tidal wave of memory, and she thought again about Brianna and Sally. Yes, he deserved death. And he deserved to hear her say it.

Why then did she still feel so divided? Could she really get up there and say what the DA wanted her to say?

Standing up, she pushed past the DA and Jake. "I'm sorry," she said. "I can't do this."

Jake caught her arm, and the DA looked crestfallen. "Lynda, what's wrong?"

Tears came to her eyes, and she glanced back at Keith, whose back was to her now. "I just don't know what I believe anymore," she whispered harshly. "And I can't sit up there and say something if I'm not sure." She looked down at Jake, expecting condemnation, but all she saw was concern. "You do what you have to do, Jake. Call me when it's over, and I'll come back to get you."

And before he could respond or the DA could talk her out of it, she shot out of the room.

At home, Lynda sat in the quiet, trying to decide why she was so angry with herself. Was it because she thought she'd wimped out or because she hadn't? Or was it even deeper? Did it have to do with this forgiveness issue that had plagued her since Keith's arrest?

Praying for her enemies had always seemed so logical, so easy—when she'd had no enemies. Loving had been a breeze—when she'd never really hated.

Now she was being tested. She had been tested before, but those other tests she had failed, and God had taught her through that failure how fruitless she was to his kingdom. How useless.

And if she'd learned anything in the past few weeks, it was that the only true joy she'd found was in being obedient to him. Maybe that was why her heart was so heavy now. Maybe it was because she was resisting.

Pulling her feet up onto the couch and wrapping her arms around her knees, she dropped her head into the circle of her arms and tried to pray again.

But this time, instead of praying for her fears and her trauma and her decisions, she prayed for Keith.

And as she did, his tremendous guilt became real to her, as did his grief. He had lost his wife and his daughter. Even though he'd caused those losses, that didn't change the level of pain he suffered. She didn't pray for his release or for some miraculous acquittal—for she knew that God was a just God and that crimes held consequences. Instead, she prayed for a change of heart, for light in his darkness, and for his salvation.

And she prayed that God would help her find a way to forgive him.

The moment she ended the prayer, she felt a great weight lifted off her, and peace replaced it.

A car door slammed. Through the window, she could see Jake getting out of a car. The car backed out of her driveway, and Jake rolled toward the door.

She opened it before he knocked. "Who brought you home?"

"One of the guys from the DA's office," he said. "Are you all right?"

She smiled, probably for the first time since Sally's funeral. "Yeah. I think I am."

Jake came inside, and he gazed at her for a long moment. "I was the last witness to testify, so they gave it to the jury right afterward. They agreed unanimously on the death penalty. The judge accepted their recommendation, Lynda. He got death."

She pulled out a chair and sat down slowly. "I figured he would." She let out a long breath. "It sure didn't take long."

"No, the jury wasn't out very long," he said. A slow, gentle smile changed his expression. "You really are better, aren't you? What happened?"

"I had a long talk with the Lord," she said. "And we got a few things straightened out."

"That's good." Then, as he gazed at her, he saw the pain return to her eyes. "What is it?"

She let out a deep, ragged breath. "I have to go see him," she whispered.

"What?"

"You heard me," she said. "I have to."

He rolled closer, as if by touching her he could chase away this madness. Taking her hand, he said, "Lynda, you can't. No one expects you to do this. Probably not even God."

"You're wrong," she whispered. "I think God does expect it. And I'm going."

"What will it prove?"

"I don't know," she said. "Maybe nothing."

Jake looked out the window, and she saw the intense struggle on his face as he groped to understand. "This is crazy, Lynda. I want you to think about it."

"I already have," she said. "I'm going tomorrow, before they transfer him to the state penitentiary."

He gaped at her again, his face a study in disgusted bewilderment, but after a moment, that look faded, and he sank back in his chair. "You can't be talked out of this?"

"No," she said. "If I could, I would have talked myself out of it already. It's not something I *want* to do, Jake, believe me; it's something I *have* to do. I was going to let a man die unsaved once before—I can't do it again. That's as clear to me as it was to you when you testified today."

Silence screamed out between them as he stared at her, and finally, he broke it. "All right," he said finally. "But I'm going with you."

Back in his apartment that night, Jake searched the New Testament for the reasons Lynda might have chosen to pray for her enemy, to visit him in prison. As he read through Matthew, Mark, Luke, and finally John, he saw it there over and over. This was why, then, she felt that God wanted her to go, why it was so important to her.

When she'd left the courthouse that day, she'd been confused about what she believed. She must have come home and decided. And tonight, rather than depressed, she seemed centered, peace-filled, and eager to do what she'd decided to do.

He lay awake for a long time that night, thinking back over Lynda's active concern for him and for Paige and Brianna, her determination to do God's will even when it meant sacrifice, and the way she had made him feel less like a shell of a human and more like a man with a spirit. A man with a soul.

And as he reflected on those things, that slow, deep, burning ache began to spread farther up his legs.

He lay there, knowing what it meant, knowing that maybe it would help him to finally take that first step....

Tomorrow, he thought. Maybe he would do it tomorrow.

But first, he would keep his word to Lynda. First he would go with her to see Keith.

Because Keith had not yet been transported to the state penitentiary—that event was scheduled for the next day—the visitation room at the St. Clair Correctional Institute was not the maximum security sort where plexiglass separated them. Instead, Lynda used her attorney's credentials to meet with him on a day that wasn't a visiting day, so the room was empty. The fact that she and Jake were his victims complicated things somewhat—but Lynda had known the warden for years, so he allowed the visit to take place with the stipulation that two of his burliest guards would stand watch over them, just in case Keith tried anything.

It was clear from the disappointment on his face as they brought him in that Keith probably had expected Paige and Brianna. His face twisted in a vile sneer at the sight of Lynda in the chair across the table from him, and Jake in his wheelchair beside her. Muttering a curse, he pulled a chair out and dropped into it.

"You've got a lot of nerve coming here."

Lynda had gotten up early that morning and prayed that God would give her the words she needed when she came face-to-face with Keith, but now she found her courage faltering. "I know we're the last ones you expected to see, Keith. But we're not the reasons you're in prison. You're the reason."

"I did what I had to do for my kid!" he said, hammering a fist on the table. "And if you weren't such a bleeding heart fool, you'd see that Paige drove me to this, and you helped her. You're as much to blame for that plane crash and that woman's death as I am!"

"Wait a minute, Varner!" Jake blurted, but Lynda touched his hand to quiet him, and he flopped back, rubbing his temple and gritting his teeth. Jake had had enough. It had been all he could do to come in with a facade of civility, but Lynda knew he was aching to hurl himself across the table and shut Keith up once and for all.

"I didn't come here to answer your accusations, Keith," she said. "I don't even care what you think of me."

"Then what *did* you come for?"

Looking at this angry, hostile, deluded man, his face rigid with hate, Lynda suddenly felt a deep compassion for him, a compassion that she couldn't explain, for it wasn't something she had pulled out of any human part of her. She leaned on the table, getting closer to him. "I came here because you're going to die, Keith. But I wanted you to know that you don't have to die alone. It wasn't too late for the thief being executed next to Christ on the cross, and it isn't too late for you."

Reaching into her bag, which the guards had thoroughly searched at the door, she withdrew the Bible she had brought for Keith. "This is for you, Keith. I hope you'll read it."

He stared down at it, raw but undefined emotion tugging at his face, and for a moment, she thought he was going to take it. But suddenly that stricken look changed to potent rage, and he ripped the Bible out of her hands, spat on it, and flung it hard against the wall.

The guards rushed to grab Keith, and fury shot through Lynda as she sprang to her feet. For a second, she thought of rushing around the table and unleashing all the rage she'd been harboring for weeks. But she held herself still, and soon a quiet and unexpected peace fell over her. The rage vanished, and instead she felt a deep, abysmal sorrow for him. "I'll pray for you, Keith," she said.

Then she turned and strode from the room.

Jake had been ready to lambaste Keith Varner, the man who had crippled him, with every curse he knew. But seeing Lynda's reaction, he felt suddenly humbled. Without another look at the prisoner, he turned his chair around and followed her out.

When they were back in the car, Jake touched her shoulder and made her look at him. "Are you all right?"

"I'm fine," she said. "Really. I feel good."

He couldn't quite understand that, for he had expected her to be crushed. "But you hoped for a turnaround, didn't you? I mean, didn't you at least go in there thinking that he'd take the Bible?"

She thought about that for a moment. "That was between Keith and God. All I know is that I did what I was supposed to do." Sighing, she started her car. "Maybe he'll pick that Bible up and take it with him, after all."

"But probably he won't."

She smiled sadly. "But he had the chance, Jake."

Jake thought he understood that on some primitive level. She had given Varner the chance to change, even though he didn't deserve it. In that way, she had been like Christ to him.

Just as she had been like Christ to Jake.

"Have you forgiven him?" he asked, amazed.

She thought about that for a long moment. "Let's just say I'm working on it."

Silently, he watched her face with appreciation and deep contemplation as she drove. Self-conscious, she finally shot him a questioning look. "Why are you staring at me like that?"

He sighed and leaned his head back. "I was just thinking. God and I aren't on real familiar terms. Maybe you could pray for me that I'd get my legs back all the way."

"I thought you didn't believe," she said.

He hesitated then said, "Yeah, well. I've seen a lot of evidence lately. Maybe I'm changing my mind."

She smiled. "I pray for your legs all the time, Jake."

"But tomorrow is going to be a real important day. I haven't told you this, but I've been standing."

She almost ran off the road but managed to pull over. Gaping at him across the seat, she asked, "Really? By yourself?"

"Well, I used the parallel bars, but I've been standing on my legs. I'm getting more feeling every day."

"Why haven't you *told* me?"

"I wanted it to be a surprise," he said. "I had this fantasy of ambling out to the car one day when you came to pick me up. But I'm really nervous about tomorrow. I'm going to try to walk, and I couldn't keep it to myself anymore."

"Oh, Jake, can I be there? Can I watch? What time are you planning to get on the bars?"

He almost told her then faltered. He couldn't take the disappointment if he failed in front of her. So he lied. "Probably around ten. They'll put me on traction for a while first and then warm up my muscles."

"I'll be there at ten," she said. "Oh, Jake, this is wonderful!" Reaching across the seat, she hugged him, and he closed his eyes and held her a moment longer than he needed to.

When she pulled back, their eyes locked, and for a fleeting moment, he realized that he would be willing to give up the opportunity to walk tomorrow in exchange for the courage to lean over and kiss her like he had the day he'd gotten his eye. But he'd just been playing then, and this was serious.

Something stopped him.

Fear? The great Jake, who had never met a woman he couldn't charm? The same Jake who had once practiced womanizing with as much devotion as Lynda practiced her faith?

He let her go, and she drove back to the house in quiet. When they pulled into the driveway, she cut off the engine and sat still for a moment. "Well, I guess I'll see you tomorrow."

He caught her hand as she reached for the car door, and she turned to look at him. Her face was expectant as he held her gaze, and his heart sprinted wildly in his chest, anticipating, hoping....

Finally, he leaned forward and kissed her. And at the gentle, sweet touch of her lips, he felt the world settling back on its axis, righting itself and everything around him falling into place.

When he broke the kiss, she looked up at him, soft, humble, surprised.

He touched her face, as if it were something precious, priceless. "Good night," he said quietly.

She leaned forward then slowly and pressed a soft kiss on his scar. He closed his eyes and found her lips again, and this time the kiss was more startling, more telling. When at last it ended, he pulled back and gazed at her, seeing the emotion clearly written on her face.

"Good night," she whispered.

He sat still as she opened the door, slipped out, and started to the house. But before she went inside, she looked back at him.

And there was a sweet, unguarded smile on her face.

Jake found it hard to sleep that night. What had happened between them haunted him—and not in a completely positive way. It didn't make sense. In his "old life," if he'd been attracted to a woman for this long, he would have had more than a passing intimacy with her by now.

This was the first time he'd stopped at just one kiss and the first time he had ever lain awake thinking about one. It was the first time he'd felt such a dependence on another human being, a painful but sweet, heartrending need for her smile, her touch, her presence.

It was frightening. It was frustrating. It was exciting. And it was hard to believe, for no one he knew had had more experience than he had with women. But strangely, he felt as though this was his first experience. As though only now, at age thirty-nine, he was learning the true value of a woman.

As he was learning the true value of himself.

He lay in bed, fighting the searing pain growing more pronounced in his calves—the pain they told him was temporary—

and told himself that maybe some good had come from the accident after all. Maybe he was discovering the powerful essence of life, now that the trappings had been taken away.

He sat up in bed, too restless to sleep and thought about tomorrow. What if his legs rebelled and refused to cooperate with him? What if the progress he'd made was as far as he'd ever go? What if he remained a paraplegic for the rest of his life?

For the first time since the crash, Jake admitted that if that happened, he could live with it. He was alive, after all, and things were looking pretty good.

He got into his wheelchair and rolled around the tiny apartment for a little while then restlessly went outside. It was late, and he could hear the crickets chirping and the toads croaking. The wind was strong, whipping through the trees and ruffling his hair, and in the distance, he heard an owl hoot.

It was beginning to feel more like autumn; the wind was brisk and cool as it whispered through the leaves. It never got very cold here, he'd been told, and he wondered what it was like in Texas right now. Was it cool? Were the leaves falling?

He wondered whether autumn was still his mother's favorite time of year.

The moment Doris Stevens came into his mind, his optimism deflated, and he was confronted with all the unfinished business of his past. Before he could clean up his present life, he suddenly realized he would need to clean up his past one. He had skeletons to lay to rest, dirt to wash away, and peace to make.

Going back into his apartment, he picked up the phone that had at last been connected and dialed the number he remembered from so many years ago, the number that had been his in Texas when he'd been nothing more than a poor waitress's illegitimate son. How far he had run to escape that image.

He put the phone to his ear and waited as it rang once, twice, three times....

"Hello?"

The voice was the familiar one he'd had such contempt for before, with its nasal twang and its hoarse brusqueness. Now, it just sounded pleasantly familiar.

"Mama?"

She was silent as he held his breath, then finally said, "Jake?"

That she didn't reject him immediately, as she had so many times before, gave him hope.

"I know it's late, Mama, but I thought you might still be up."

"I just got in from work," she said carefully.

Silence again.

"I heard about your legs. That woman called me."

"Lynda," he said, smiling. "Yeah. She's been looking out for me."

"So ... how are you doing?"

"I'm fine," he said. "I'm out of the hospital. I'm getting a little feeling back, and I've been able to stand some. I'm gonna walk again, Mama. I know I am."

He could hear the tinge of emotion in her voice when she whispered, "That's good."

Encouraged by the few words, he decided to say what he'd called to say. His voice trembled. "Mama, I know I've been a pretty crummy son all these years. I don't blame you for feeling the way you do about me."

Quiet again and then, "What is it you want from me, Jake?"

Tears misted his eyes. "Your forgiveness."

"My what?"

"I want you to forgive me, Mama. I turned my back on you."

"You were ashamed of me."

"I was ashamed of me, too," he whispered. "Where we came from, where we lived—"

"I *still* live here," she said.

He closed his eyes. "I know, Mama. But I'm not ashamed anymore. I just want to start fresh. I want to do what's right."

"And what would that be, Jake?" his mother asked.

He wasn't sure, and as a tear rolled from his eye and down his scarred cheek, he floundered for some gesture that would make it right. But he had nothing now. Not a job, not a home of his own, not even a plan.

Yet he had a greater sense of the rightness of the direction in his life now than he'd ever had when there was more money in his bank account than he could spend.

"My car," he said suddenly. "I want to give you my car. It's a Porsche, Mama. You probably don't want a Porsche, but you could sell it."

The idea seemed absurd almost the moment he'd said it, but Doris wasn't laughing. "You'd give me your car?"

"Sure," he said. "It's paid for, and it's fairly new. You could get a lot for it."

"But—what if you start drivin' again?"

"I *will* start driving again, sooner or later. But when I do, I won't want to drive that." He hadn't realized that he felt that way until the words were already out of his mouth.

She was quiet again. He knew that this was as awkward for her as it was for him. He was paying her off, in a sense, or at least it seemed that way—as if the Porsche were a bribe to accept him as her son again. But that was all right. It was a start.

"All right," she said. "I'll take it."

He smiled and restrained the urge to laugh. "Okay, Mama. I can either send you a plane ticket, and you can drive it back, or I can sell it here myself and send you the money."

She thought about it for a moment. "I'll come there and get it. Who knows? I might like to drive it a while."

His eyes welled deeper. "Good. I'd like to see you."

"I'm not being greedy, you know," she said quickly. "I'm thinkin' of this as punitive damages. For all the grief you've given me. And all the years I gave to you before you threw them back in my face. Do you understand that?"

"If I didn't, I wouldn't have made the offer."

"You're not gonna back out now, are you?"

"No, Mama," he said. "I'll have the ticket delivered to you tomorrow. One way. Maybe you can stay awhile, on me. I have someone here I'd like for you to meet."

CHAPTER SEVENTY

Since she'd dropped Jake off at the hospital that morning, Lynda had been praying. She had pled with God, arguing how vital it was that Jake walk again, that he needed a miracle to nudge him along, that he needed to see God working in his life, that he needed to know he had a future.

But as she drove back to the hospital at ten to be there when he tried to take his steps, she realized that God was aware of all of that already. Jake was in God's hands, and God knew much better than she what he needed.

Still, she held her breath as she made her way to the rehab room, where a dozen patients worked on several levels of therapy, each deeply engrossed in the torture required to make one tiny bit of progress.

Jake wasn't in sight.

She looked around for Allie or Buzz but didn't see either of them.

"Excuse me," she said, catching a therapist as he passed. "I was supposed to meet Jake Stevens here. Have you seen him?"

"Yeah, he was here," he said. "I don't know where he went."

"Well, where are Allie and Buzz?"

"In a meeting, I think. Jake probably took a break."

Lynda was confused. Wasn't ten o'clock supposed to have been his big moment? Had they changed his schedule at the last minute? She went back into the corridor. Jake was nowhere in sight.

Maybe he'd gone to say hello to the nurses in orthopedics. Or maybe his morning therapy hadn't gone well; maybe he'd gotten discouraged and had decided not to make the attempt to walk today. Maybe the doctor had stepped in to postpone the attempt for some reason. Maybe something was wrong.

She had worked up a fair amount of anxiety by the time she decided to go to the fourth floor to see if he'd gone to say hello to his nurses. Abby, the nurse who had cared for him in ICU, was waiting for the elevator when the doors opened.

"Abby, have you seen Jake?"

Abby set her hands on her hips, as though offended. "That's it? No hello? No nothing?"

Lynda laughed softly and hugged her. "I'm sorry. It's good to see you."

Abby pointed up the hall. "He's in the chapel, baby."

Lynda glanced toward the prayer room then brought her troubled eyes back to Abby's. "Is everything all right?"

"I don't know," she said. "I just caught a glimpse of him goin' in. He didn't speak to anybody up here. Just rolled right to that room."

Lynda started toward the prayer room, but Abby stopped her. "Lynda, he's doin' okay, isn't he?"

Lynda didn't know how to answer that. "I don't know, Abby. We'll see."

She hesitated outside the chapel door, bracing herself for whatever she might find inside. Slowly she opened it and stepped into the dark room lit only with candles.

Jake was sitting in his chair near the front row, looking up at the cross on the wall behind the small pulpit.

When she approached him, she saw that his face was tear-stained. "Jake, what's wrong?"

His smile was heavy with emotion. "Nothing's wrong," he whispered.

"Then why are you in here? I thought you were going to the parallel bars at ten. I thought—"

"I lied to you," he said quietly. "I didn't want you to see me fail. I've already been there."

Compassion for his disappointment washed through her, and she sank down on the end of a pew. "Jake, I'm so sorry. But it was just the first try."

He started to laugh then, and she frowned, confused.

"What is it?"

"I did it," he whispered. "I walked."

She drew in a sharp breath. "You did?"

But Jake's smile twisted at the corners as a new wave of emotion came over him; new tears welled in his eyes and rolled down his cheeks. "Four steps, Lynda. I took four steps!"

"Four steps?"

"Yes," he said. "They said I'll be able to get around with a walker soon. Then crutches ..."

"Oh, Jake," she whispered and reached out for him.

He accepted her embrace and clung to her tightly, laughing softly into her ear as his tears wet her hair.

"But why did you come in here? You looked so sad when I came in."

He drew in a long, shaky breath and looked at that cross again. "I had somebody to thank," he whispered.

She pulled back to look at him, afraid to make any assumptions, yet hoping....

"It wasn't just the walking," he told her. "I'm grateful for that. But it's the other things."

"What other things?"

"The way he reached out and chose me and worked on me and even broke me, just to get me to the place where I could start really living." He wiped the wetness on his face and moved his wet, red eyes to hers. "And for his forgiveness that didn't cost me anything—not even a Porsche."

As he smiled through his tears, she leaned back into the pew, weakened by her glad amazement over what she was hearing.

"And I had to thank him for you," he whispered.

He pulled her against him again, and this time they wept together, for joy, for sadness, for the future, for the past.

It was a while before Jake could speak again. "Do you think God really spared me because he had a plan for me?"

She felt as certain of that as she'd ever been of anything in her life. "I know he did."

His arms tightened around her, and as he looked back at the cross, he laid his head on hers. "If it was just to give me one moment like this, it would all have been worth it."

And though Lynda closed her eyes and thanked God, too, for this very moment, she knew in her heart that there was much more in store for them.

So much more.

AFTERWORD

A year or so before I wrote this book, I became convicted that my Christian walk had been useless. I had never been available to God, though I had called on him often to get me through my crises (usually self-inflicted). My problem was trust. I thought I believed, I said I believed—but I did nothing to put the belief into action. I was neither hot nor cold, but lukewarm, and absolutely fruitless. One day, someone called to my attention something that Jesus had said: "Not everyone who says to me, 'Lord, Lord,' will enter the kingdom of heaven, but only he who does the will of my father who is in heaven. Many will say to me on that day, 'Lord, Lord, did we not prophesy in your name, and in your name drive out demons and perform many miracles?' Then I will tell them plainly, 'I never knew you. Away from me, you evildoers!'" (Matthew 7:21–23).

These words startled me. Was I one of those whom Jesus didn't really know? I finally realized it was only through my knowing him that he would know me as one of his own. And to know him, I needed an ongoing, active, intimate relationship with him—the kind of relationship I would have with anyone important to me. I don't ignore the people I love, and I don't neglect them, and I don't forget them. I talk to them every day, and care about pleasing them, and work hard to be the person they need me to be. If Jesus Christ is real to me, then I have to treat him as a real person.

Once I recommitted myself to making Christ the center of my life, I decided to make myself available to him in every area of my life. That's when the idea for this book came to me. The characters interested me because their own spiritual battles were so much like my own: Lynda, a lukewarm Christian who would let someone die without witnessing to him; Jake, an agnostic who couldn't give up the pilot's seat in his life until it was taken from him; and Paige, a spiritual infant on the verge of belief, who lacked the faith to make the final plunge. I was interested in their awakenings, their spiritual growth, their lessons, and I hoped their struggles might be something others could relate to.

Fortunately, I've finally begun to learn from the lessons God has taught me. I've learned that true Christianity is about going to him on my knees and asking him to fill up all the empty places inside me with his Holy Spirit. It's about asking him to forgive me and cleanse me of all the things that will destroy me—things like greed, apathy, anger, bitterness, fear, malice, and selfishness—so those places can be filled with him, too. It's about deciding what I *really believe*, then relying on it, totally, completely, in every area of my life. This, I discovered, has little to do with sitting in God's house on Sunday mornings. It has everything to do with *being* God's house, every day of the week.

Justifiable Means

*This book is lovingly dedicated
to the Nazarene.*

ACKNOWLEDGMENTS

Special thanks to all of my AOL friends who shared their expertise with me. I am so grateful for the help of Florida attorneys Michael Cohen, James Mays, Mike Gotschall, and a certain judge who wishes to remain anonymous. Also, many thanks to the cops who answered my endless questions—Lou and Pat and others who didn't want their names published. And a huge thank you to Cathy Logg, Washington state crime reporter, who continues to be a wonderful resource.

I also thank my children—Michelle, Marie, and Lindsey, for not taking it personally when my preoccupied "Uhh-hmms" don't really answer their questions—and my husband, Ken, for keeping the family going even when I'm buried in the pages of another world. Without his powerful prayers, his support, and his constant encouragement, I'd have found an easier job long ago.

But most of all, I thank the One who called me and set me apart, and turned my writing into something that has purpose. He truly is a God of second chances.

CHAPTER ONE

The lights from the squad cars were still flashing in the night, illuminating the modest apartment building in alternate shades of blue and black. Larry Millsaps pulled his unmarked Chevy to the curb and glanced at his partner. "So much for having a night off."

Tony Danks nodded bleakly as he scanned the crowd forming on the sidewalk. Officers were already questioning some of the neighbors, and other uniformed cops came and went through the building's front door. "This hasn't happened in—how long?"

Larry grabbed his windbreaker from the backseat and pulled it on over the 9 mm he had holstered under his arm. "Almost a year since the last one."

They got out of the car and pushed through the crowd, not bothering to flash their badges since all of the cops in the small St. Clair Police Department knew the two detectives by sight. They made their way through the crowd into the building. "One a year is too many for me," Larry said. He'd been plagued by the trauma on the young girl's face the last time. There was a look that rape victims wore, a waiflike, haunted look that spoke of violation and soul-deep despair. This one probably would be no different, and he started up the stairs reluctantly, past the other tenants who were watching the open door of the apartment with fascination and dread, waiting for bits and pieces of the drama to be revealed.

There were four cops inside the apartment, two with cameras and one with a camcorder, recording the crime scene just as they'd found it. Lamps were broken, tables overturned, glass shattered . . .

Larry spotted the victim then, sitting alone on a chair in a corner, cocooned in a blanket, her blonde hair wet and stringing in her face and around her shoulders, her pale blue eyes raw and swollen from crying. One of the cops handed him a clipboard with her report on it, then turned his back to her and, in a quiet voice, said, "She showered before she called."

"Figures," Tony whispered.

Larry looked back at the young woman and felt that familiar, unwelcome stirring of frustration and compassion as she glanced hopefully up at him with big, blue, tearful eyes, as if he might offer her some comfort, some hope, some . . . *something*. Her showering would definitely make it tougher to get the evidence they needed, but Larry couldn't say he blamed her. She had been defiled, desecrated, dehumanized, and he couldn't imagine any victim of such abuse *not* wanting to wash the filth away.

"Is she hurt?" he asked.

The uniformed cop nodded. "He had a knife. She has a pretty deep cut on her leg. The ambulance should be here soon."

Larry stepped over the broken glass, the lamp shades on their sides, and skirted around the overturned table until he stood in front of the woman. "Hi, I'm Detective Millsaps." He glanced over his shoulder and saw that Tony was right behind him. "This is my partner, Detective Danks. Are you all right?"

She swallowed hard and whispered, "Yes."

Stooping down to get eye level with her, Larry glanced down at the report the other officer had handed him. "Your name is Melissa Nelson? May I call you Melissa?"

"Yes," she said again.

"Good," he said in a don't-spook-the-victim voice. "And you can call me Larry. He's Tony." He scanned the information the first cop to the scene had compiled, and saw that she was twenty-three years old. He looked into her face again. "Melissa, I know that you've already given your statement, but would you mind telling it one more time? Tony and I will be the ones trying to find the man who did this to you. We really need to hear it firsthand."

A stark, determined look filled her reddened eyes. "Yes. I'll tell it over and over until they catch him," she said through clenched teeth. "I don't care how many times I have to tell it."

"Good. First, could you start with a description of him?"

"I can do better than that," she said, smearing her tears away with a trembling hand. "I can give you his name."

"You know him?" Tony asked, sitting down on an ottoman near her chair.

"Yes. I work with him. His name is Edward Soames, and he lives in some apartments on Fresco Street on the north side of town."

Larry jotted down the street. "Have you given this information to anyone else?"

"Yes," she said. "The first officer I talked to is calling it in." A sob broke her voice, and she gave in to it, then tried to recover. "He probably thought I wouldn't tell anybody, that I'd be too ashamed. That I'd just sit here and deal with it."

Tony took his notepad out of his coat pocket and clicked his pen. "Was this someone you were dating?"

She shot him a disgusted look. "Of course not. I was just sitting here watching television, and he knocked on the door. When I opened it, he pushed his way in. He grabbed me, and . . . I started fighting him with everything I had . . . but it didn't stop him . . ."

"I understand he had a weapon?" Larry asked.

"Yes," she said. "A knife. A switchblade, I think." She opened her blanket, revealing the shorts and T-shirt she wore, and lifted the bloody towel she'd been pressing on her leg. "I thought he was going to kill me."

Larry winced at the sight of the cut. "That's deep. You're going to need stitches. The ambulance should be here soon."

"It just all happened so fast," she went on. "And then he was gone . . . and . . . I didn't know what to do. I was so disgusted, so repulsed . . . I didn't think about the evidence. I just wanted to wash it all away . . . but it's not going to go away . . ."

She was trembling, and Larry feared she was going into shock from loss of blood. He made her press the towel back over the wound. Outside, sirens sounded. He hoped it was the ambulance.

"He . . . he touched that table. His fingerprints are there. And they're on the doorknob. And he had my blood on his shirt when he left . . . it was a . . . a T-shirt with some cartoon on it. And if he's not home, if you need to identify him, there's a picture of him in his office at work. We both work at Proffer Builders, over on

345

Haynes Street. He has a recent picture of himself on his desk, catching a fish or something. You could use that to identify him. My boss, Henry Proffer, could let you in. He's in the book."

Tony jotted rapidly as she spoke, and Larry was amazed at how easy it was to get information out of her. Victims of such trauma were usually confused, disoriented, and too upset to remember details.

"Has he ever threatened you before?"

"No," she said. "Oh, he's come on to me, but I just blew it off. I didn't know he was capable of this."

They heard the paramedics running up the stairs. "Melissa, we'll talk to you later. You go get that leg stitched up and let the doctor examine you."

Larry started to stand up, but she grabbed his coat and looked up at him desperately. "You won't just let this go, will you? You're going to go pick him up, aren't you?"

"Of course. Someone's probably picking him up right now."

The paramedics hustled in, but she kept clinging to Larry's coat. "But what if he didn't go straight home? He probably wouldn't. He would know that someone might be looking for him. You have to find him! He's dangerous, and he'll come after me again."

"We won't rest until we have him behind bars," Larry assured her. "You have my promise. Now show them your leg. She needs stitches, guys, and she's lost a lot of blood."

"Let's get you onto the stretcher," one of the EMTs said, coaxing her out of her chair onto her good leg.

"But behind bars isn't good enough!" she pled through gritted teeth, eyes desperate, in obvious pain as she stood. "You have to keep him there. You have to get a conviction."

"We will."

She glanced frantically around the apartment as they tried to put her on the stretcher. "My word won't be good enough. You'll have to have enough evidence. You can't forget anything!"

Larry frowned. "Our police officers are trained, Melissa. They know what to do."

"But will they dust for fingerprints? Will they look for hair follicles, to prove he was here? They can't just stop with my identification of him!"

346

The paramedics began to carry her out, even though she hadn't yet lain down. "Please don't let them miss anything," she said. "Find the officer I talked to first. I gave him more details—you need to know them."

"We will, Melissa," Larry said. "Just try to relax. We'll talk to you after the doctor examines you. And I'll let you know the minute we pick him up."

But the look on her face as she finally lay down told him that she would believe it when she saw it. Larry watched the paramedics carry her out. Slowly, he turned back to his partner.

Tony looked pensive, perplexed. "Well, she sure came out of her shell. Coaching us on police procedure? That's a first."

Larry shook his head. "Maybe we just underestimated her because she looks so fragile. She's obviously pretty sharp. And let's face it—botched investigations make headlines. You can't blame her for being careful."

Tony stared at the empty doorway for a moment longer. "Yeah, but careful is one thing. There was something more than careful there. Doesn't feel right."

"You're not suggesting she's lying."

"No," Tony said thoughtfully. "Not exactly. I'm just saying that something doesn't ring true. It was all too easy."

"You could look in her face and tell she was raped," Larry said quietly.

"Unfortunately, facial expressions don't hold much water in court."

"Give me a break, Tony. Are we gonna make a broken, violated woman tap-dance and stand on her head to prove that what she described really happened? There's no reason anyone would want to put herself through all this if it didn't really happen."

"Put herself through what?" Tony asked.

"Through *what*? Are you kidding?" Larry asked. "You think this is fun for her? The interrogations of cops who don't believe her, lawyers who drag her through the mud—"

"Okay, okay," Tony cut in. "Maybe you're right. Obviously, there's plenty of evidence here."

"And there'll probably be a lot more when we find this guy."

"We'll see, buddy," Tony said. "I hope you're right."

Two hours later, after being photographed, stitched, examined, and interrogated by the doctors and social workers who claimed to want to help her, Melissa sat alone in the examining room. She had turned the lights off; now she watched frantically out the window into the parking lot for some sign of Edward Soames.

He's going to kill me, she thought miserably. *If they don't lock him up, he'll kill me.*

But they hadn't locked him up. So far, according to the social worker who'd made some phone calls for her, he hadn't even been picked up. He was still out there somewhere, driving around, no doubt looking for vulnerable women to attack.

She had begged the doctor not to release her—not until Soames was off the streets and in police custody. She was too terrified to stay in that apartment by herself, too plagued with memories—she would get no rest. If she could just stay here overnight, long enough for them to find him, then tomorrow she could face going home.

Reluctantly, the doctor had agreed, but told her that, before they admitted her, a police detective would need to talk to her some more. She didn't know why. She'd already given them more than enough information to find him and arrest him. She'd left nothing to chance. Instead of talking to her, they ought to be out looking for him.

She heard footsteps coming up the hall and looked toward the door. Her doctor ambled into the room, studying her chart. "Okay, Melissa," he said, still in the soft, cautious voice that made her want to scream. "We're going to move you to a room now. Are you sure you want to stay?"

"Will it have a guard?" she asked.

"I'm afraid not. But I'm sure you'll be safe here. They'll have this guy picked up in no time, and you won't have to worry."

She sighed and looked out the window again. A car had just driven up, and a tall, slender man was getting out. Was that him? No, she thought with relief. Not yet.

She stood up, wincing at the pain from the stitched gash on her thigh, and the doctor made her sit back down. "An orderly is bringing a wheelchair. You need to stay off that leg for a while. You don't want to break the stitches. Oh, and I've prescribed something for pain, if you need it."

Her eyes strayed out the window again. "No, I don't want it. I need to stay sharp, just in case." The orderly wheeled the chair in, but she didn't take her eyes from the window. "Does that room have a window over the parking lot?"

The doctor glanced at the orderly. "I don't know. Does it?"

The orderly thought for a moment. "Yeah, I think it does. I can change her to a room that doesn't, if she wants—"

"No," she cut in, getting up on her good leg and transferring her weight to the chair. "I want to be able to see the parking lot. I need to see who's coming."

The doctor shot another look at the orderly. She realized that they thought she was suffering from paranoid delusions, but she didn't care.

The orderly wheeled her out, and the doctor stayed beside her. "Oh, Detective Millsaps called and said that he might not be able to come back by tonight. He said it might be morning before he could make it."

"No," she said quickly. "Tell him to come tonight. Please. I don't care what time it is. I don't think I'll do much sleeping tonight."

"We could give you something to help you."

"No," she said again. "I told you, I need to stay alert. Tell him to come no matter how late it is. Have they found Soames yet?"

"He didn't say."

Tears sprang to her eyes again, and she scanned the hallway as if he might jump out of one of the rooms at any moment. "He's still out there. He's too smart to get caught."

"If he's in St. Clair, they'll find him."

"And what if he's not? What if he's already left town?"

"Then you're safe. You don't have to worry."

But his logic was lost on Melissa, and as they pushed her onto the elevator, she tried not to panic. This was just the beginning, after all; it was too soon to jump to conclusions. Larry what's-his-name had seemed competent. Maybe he would catch him. Maybe Soames would finally be taken off the streets. Maybe women everywhere would be safe from his violence.

It had taken two hours to get the warrant they needed for Soames's arrest, as well as a search warrant to check out his apartment, car, and place of business. Though the paperwork had taken longer than he wanted, Larry had been confident that the uniformed officers would find and apprehend Soames even before the warrant was in Larry's hand. But Soames had managed to evade them so far.

As they walked rapidly between the police squad cars in the parking lot toward their own unmarked car, Tony said, "You have that look on your face, Larry."

"What look?"

"The look that says you know exactly where we're going to find Soames."

"Wish I did, pal. I was thinking we should probably go by his office first and get that picture Melissa told us about. Then we could start with the bars in town. See what turns up."

Tony climbed into the passenger seat and checked his notes as Larry started the car and pulled out into traffic. "Let's see. We have the name of the business owner. We could ask him to meet us there to let us in."

"That's what I was thinking. Meanwhile, if Soames is stupid enough to go home, we have people there waiting for him."

"Sure would help if we had a tag number."

"Yeah. Kind of weird, don't you think? A man that age not having a tag registered to him?"

"Maybe he uses somebody else's car."

"Or maybe he drives a stolen car."

Tony grinned and nodded toward a pay phone coming up on their right. "Pull over. I'll call her boss."

Larry watched, chin propped on his palm, as Tony made the phone call. He tried to calm the rising tide of urgency he felt. But that woman sitting with wet hair stringing around her shoulders, trembling as she hugged her bloody knees to her chest, had gotten under his skin, and he wanted, badly, to give her some peace—right now.

Tony got back into the car. "He said he'd meet us there. Sounded helpful. He said he had the guy's tag number in a file at the office, too."

"Great. Let's go."

CHAPTER TWO

enry Proffer, a short man with Hulk Hogan arms and a ruddy complexion from years under the harsh Florida sun, was waiting when Larry and Tony reached the small office of Proffer Builders. "Is Soames all right?" he asked. "He didn't have an accident or anything, did he?"

"There was a rape tonight," Larry said as he followed the man in and waited for him to flick on the light. "Another one of your employees—Melissa Nelson. Edward Soames is a suspect."

The man's face drained of color. "Melissa—raped? When? Was it here?"

"No," Tony said. "In her apartment. She said there was a picture of Soames on his desk. We need to use it and look around a little."

Looking disturbed, Henry led them down the hall to a small office. He turned on the light, then stepped back as they walked into the immaculate room. "She said *Soames* raped her? You sure that's what she said?"

"Absolutely. When's the last time you saw him?"

"Well . . . today. Around 4:30 or so. It was just an ordinary day. He's my best architect. He's not a rapist!" Distraught, he watched as they took the picture, studied it, and deposited it in a paper sack.

"Can you tell us anything about Soames? What kind of man he is? Where he likes to go after work? Any abnormal behavior you've noticed with women?"

Henry lowered himself into a chair and raked a hand through his hair. "Well, he seems like a decent guy. He does good work. I've

351

never gotten to know him that well, but I've had no complaints about him." He frowned as he looked up at them again. "Uh . . . what were the other questions? Oh, yeah. Women. Well, he was kind of a flirt. But then, so am I. No crime in that. I wouldn't think he'd have to force himself on anyone. I mean, he never had trouble getting a date. Women like him."

"What about Melissa? Did he ever show any interest in her?"

"Well, sure. I mean, so did I. She's a cute girl. A little too serious, sometimes. She's kind of hard to get to know. Doesn't talk much. Kind of high-strung. You know—jumpy. She's only worked here about a month, so none of us knows her very well."

"She get along with Soames?"

"Well, yeah. I mean, I guess so. I kind of thought she might have a crush on him, tell you the truth. She acted funny around him. You know, tense. Clumsy. That kind of thing."

Larry gave Tony a troubled glance. "You said you had his tag number?" Tony asked.

"Sure," Henry said. Popping out of the chair, he rushed down the hall. Larry followed him.

"This is too much," Henry said when he reached his own office. "I mean, what am I gonna do tomorrow? Is Melissa gonna be back? Is Soames? We're working on a big bid for a new office complex on Highland Drive. I can't do without either of them." He pulled out the file he'd been looking for and flipped through it. "Here it is." He got a pen and jotted the number down. "He drives a dark blue Cherokee. Couple of years old. Oh—and you asked where he liked to hang out. He has a favorite bar over on Triumph Street—you know, over by the Kash 'n' Karry. Steppin' Out, I think it's called."

"Thanks." Taking the paper from him, Larry hurried back up the hall to where Tony was still looking through Soames's things. "Come on, Tony," he said. "I think we've got him."

It took only a few minutes to run the tag number through the police computer.

"Edward J. Pendergrast?" Tony jotted the number down. "What do you think, Larry? Is it someone else's car, or did this guy change his name?"

Larry grabbed the radio mike. "Do me a favor, Jane," he told the desk cop who'd done the search for him. "See what you've got on that name."

The radio crackled. "Will do."

A few minutes later, Jane radioed back. "Hey, Larry. Are you ready for this?"

"Yeah, go ahead."

"Edward J. Pendergrast has a rap sheet. Two rape charges, as well as breaking and entering, and assault with a deadly weapon. In the first case, the grand jury acquitted him of all charges due to lack of evidence. The second one never even got to the grand jury because the judge released him on a technicality. Something about an illegal search and seizure."

Larry glanced at Tony. "You believe this?"

"He obviously changed his name. Got to be him."

"Let's get him," Larry said.

Steppin' Out was a popular bar where young professionals came to mingle and drink and dance after work each night. The parking lot was full of BMWs and Mercedes, Jaguars and Infinities. When they found the dark blue Cherokee, they checked the number. "That's it. That's the number," Larry said, trying to control his rush of adrenaline. "He's inside."

"Did you get a good enough look at that picture to recognize him?"

"I think so. Let's go."

They double-parked behind the Cherokee so that their suspect couldn't make a run for it, then went in and tried to blend into the crowd. The mingling aromas of two-hundred-dollar-an-ounce perfume, cheap aftershave, booze, and cigarette smoke wafted on the air, and the music from the band sent a deafening roar over the voices and laughter around them.

"And they really come here to relax after work?" Larry asked his partner facetiously as they wove through the crowd.

"It's really not such a bad place. You should try it sometime when you're not on duty."

"No, thanks, pal," Larry said. "I prefer to breathe clean air and have a little peace and quiet when I relax."

Tony grinned. It was no secret that Larry never darkened the door of any of the bars in town unless he was on duty and looking for someone. Tony, however, didn't mind stopping in now and then. "Great place to meet women."

"I meet plenty of women," Larry said.

"Right," Tony muttered with a smirk. "At church. That's a surefire setup for disaster. Get involved with Judy Churchgoer, and you've automatically got to start giving up stuff, making commitments, acting like the Pope. No, I'd rather meet someone in a place like this, where nobody really expects anything."

Larry had heard it all before. He concentrated on scanning the faces of the people at the bar.

"See anything?" Tony asked.

"Not yet. You?"

Tony shook his head, then checked the faces at the tables—men with their most seductive smiles, women with their faces tipped up in anticipation. A soft haze of smoke gently floated over their heads, as if it held some magic that would cast a spell on each of them.

"There." Larry grabbed Tony's arm and nodded toward the back corner of the room.

It was the face they had seen in the picture, though it wasn't as happy as it had been when photographed catching a twenty-pound bass. He seemed to be sulking as he sipped on his drink and watched a group of women at the bar. His striped pullover shirt was clean and freshly pressed, as were his khaki trousers. He'd obviously gone home to shower after leaving Melissa's—he must have been quick, since he hadn't been home when they'd tried to pick him up.

"Here goes." They wound their way between tables. Soames saw them coming toward him and straightened.

"Edward Soames?" Larry asked, extending his right hand as if to shake.

Soames looked from one man to the other, then accepted the handshake. "Yeah, that's me."

Larry snapped his handcuffs on Soames's wrist. "I'm Larry Millsaps, with the St. Clair Police Department. I have a warrant for your arrest. Would you come with us, please?"

Soames sprang out of his chair and tried to wrest his hand away. "For what?"

"You're being charged with the rape of Melissa Nelson. You have the right to remain silent . . ." As he rambled off the words that had become second nature, he jerked Soames's other arm in front of him and snapped the second cuff.

Even in the darkness, Soames's face was visibly reddening. "Wait a minute! I didn't touch her! What did she say?"

"If you cannot afford an attorney, one will be appointed . . ."

"This is crazy!" Soames shouted. "I never laid a hand on her! She invited me over, then changed her mind and said she was sick or something. I left! That's all there was to it!"

"That's not what *she* says, pal."

"Then she's a liar! I didn't *do* anything!"

The band stopped playing midsong, letting the chorus die a slow death. The crowd in the bar had already grown suddenly quiet. As Tony frisked him, Soames cursed and searched the faces around him. "Hey, McRae!" he shouted. "I need a lawyer, man! Help me!"

Larry groaned as Steve McRae, a lawyer he had had run-ins with before, hurried through the crowd. "I'm his lawyer. What's going on here?"

"They're arresting me for rape!" Soames whispered harshly. "*Do* something!"

"Do you have a warrant?" the lawyer asked the detectives.

"We sure do, McRae," Tony said, pulling it out of his pocket. "We also have one to search his car and his apartment."

"They're trying to pin a *rape* on me," Soames whispered so that the crowd wouldn't hear. "A rape that never happened."

McRae raised one finger to quiet him. "Don't say a word," he ordered. "Not one word. Calm down and just go with them, and we'll get this all straightened out."

Soames cursed again. His face reddened as they pulled him through the crowd, with McRae following.

"Put him in the car," Larry told Tony. "Radio it in, and I'll start searching his car." He turned back to Soames. "Give me your car keys."

"I'm not giving you anything!" Soames spat out.

"Fine. Then I'll bust a window and unlock it myself."

Soames kicked at some invisible object. "They're in my pocket," he said. "I'm cuffed, remember?"

But before Larry could reach into the man's pocket, Soames slid his own hand in, fished the key chain out, and flung it at him. "You're not gonna find anything in there," he said as Tony pushed his head down and guided him into the unmarked car's backseat. "I'm telling you, she's crazy. You'll find that out yourself. I didn't touch her, man. She started freaking out on me, even pulled a knife on me, and I got out of there."

McRae, the lawyer, leaned into the car. "If you want me representing you, Soames, you're gonna have to shut up, *now*! You and I will talk when you get to the station. You're not gonna tell them anything until I give you permission."

"But I didn't *do* anything, man. I have nothing to hide!"

"That shouldn't be too hard to prove."

Soames wilted back on the seat.

A squad car pulled up, and patrons of the bar spilled out onto the parking lot as Larry got his flashlight and began his search of the car. He checked the glove compartment, handed the registration papers to Tony, then released the trunk latch so that Tony could check inside. Then he bent down and shone his light under the seat.

"Bingo," he said. He stood up and pulled a pair of rubber gloves out of his pockets, slid his hands into them, then bent down again. "We've got something here, Tony."

"What is it?"

"Oh, just a bloody shirt," he said. "With a cartoon on it. And look. A knife."

Tony leaned through the back door, astounded. "You mean he just stuffed them under his seat?"

Larry opened the knife. "Blade's got blood on it. What do you bet it's hers?"

"Why would he be that stupid?"

"Maybe she was right. He banked on her being too ashamed to tell anyone." Larry dropped the shirt into a bag, then the knife into another one. "Is there anything back there?"

"No," Tony said. "The trunk's coming up empty."

Larry slid out of the car and went back to his own. Soames sat in the backseat, his teeth gritted, waiting. "Tell me something, Soames. Why would your car be registered under the name Pendergrast?"

Soames shook his head. "I'm not telling you a thing until I've cleared it with my attorney."

"Fine," Larry said. "Then I guess it's going to be a long night for all of us."

When Soames was booked and locked up, they headed for his apartment. Several tenants came outside at the sight of the fleet of police cars in the parking lot, and Larry assigned one of the officers to question them about Soames. They used his key to get in, then began searching for any sign that a rapist lived there.

The apartment was immaculate, with plush, unblemished furniture and cherrywood tables. Nothing was out of place. The bed was made, all the shoes were put away, and the bathroom was spotless. If there was anything telling here, it would be hidden, Larry decided.

He went through the drawers in the kitchen, looking for anything out of the ordinary. When he found a stack of snapshots, he flipped through them. They were low-quality pictures of women who looked as if they hadn't known they were being photographed, coming in and out of doorways, getting into cars—all photographed from a distance. Carefully, he studied them. A vague reflection on some of them made him wonder if they'd been taken from inside a car.

"Larry!" Tony called from the other room. "Come take a look!"

Larry found Tony in the bedroom closet, where the police photographer was taking pictures of something they'd found on the shelf. "What is it?" Larry asked.

"A bag," Tony said. "It has a pair of binoculars, another knife, and a camera with a night lens."

Larry brandished the stack of photos. "And here's what he was taking pictures of."

Tony glanced through the pictures and looked up at him. "His prey?"

"Could be. Found anything else?"

"Yeah. Our man seems to be into pornography. There's magazines up here that would curl your toes. And videos, too."

"Tag 'em. We'll take 'em all."

When they'd labeled everything that seemed to have any significance for their case, they talked to a few of the tenants standing outside. All of them considered Soames a quiet, secretive kind of guy who went out a lot at night and didn't come in until the wee hours of morning.

When they'd finished searching and removed all of the evidence, they drove back to the precinct. "You ready to hear what he has to say for himself?"

"Sure," Tony said. "This ought to be good."

CHAPTER THREE

Melissa didn't feel the pain in her leg until she got the phone call from Larry Millsaps, telling her that Edward Soames had been picked up, and that they'd found the bloody shirt and knife under his seat. They had also discovered, Larry said, that Soames had been charged with rape before, under another name. He wouldn't be going anywhere for a long time, Larry predicted.

Only then had Melissa been able to relax enough to notice the stinging pain of her cut and stitches, or to realize how her head hurt and how exhausted she had become. Even so, her mind was still reeling. What if something about the search had been illegal? What if they'd forgotten to read him his rights? What if the doctor's report was too ambiguous? What if some idiot judge let him out on bail?

She almost wished she had taken the painkiller or the sedative the doctor had offered so that she would be able to rest tonight and have her wits about her tomorrow, when she would need them. It wasn't too late—she could still call the nurse and ask for something. The social worker had urged her to take something to help her sleep, so that her mind could release what had happened. But Melissa couldn't afford to release it. She had to keep her facts lined up in her mind, like exhibits in a trial. She had to review them, over and over, so that she could make sure everyone else did their job. Otherwise, something might be overlooked. Someone might drop the ball.

Reluctantly, she moved away from the window, where she'd been watching the parking lot, and lay down on the bed. But sleep didn't come. Morning would be here soon enough. And then, maybe, she could breathe. Then she could make sure that morning was something Edward Soames would never again experience outside a jail cell.

W hy did you change your name?" Tony asked Soames, who sat slumped in a chair at the end of the table.

McRae nodded to him, and Soames said, "I didn't think I could get a job if someone found out about my record. I was falsely accused, and I was found innocent. But the stigma of the arrests would have followed me here."

"You weren't found innocent," Larry said. "You were never tried."

"If I wasn't found guilty, I was found innocent," Soames said. "It's in the Bill of Rights."

"You have an interesting history of similar false accusations," Tony said sarcastically. "What a poor, misunderstood guy."

Soames leaned on the table, intent on making them understand. "The first one was some married woman who had a crush on me, and when I rejected her, she came up with this crazy story to get attention. The second one was a girl I'd broken up with. She was trying to get even."

"And this one?"

His lawyer leaned forward. "Tell them what you told me about her invitation today."

Soames nodded. "It's weird. Most of the time, she acts like she doesn't even know I exist. Won't look at me, hardly answers me when I talk to her, gets real nervous around me—"

"A real challenge, huh?" Larry asked.

Soames ignored it and went on. "Today, after my boss leaves, she comes into my office and asks me if I'd like to come over for dinner tonight. She seemed real nervous, but I thought it was cute, you know? And I had plans, but I canceled them. I told her I'd come."

"*She* invited *you*," Larry repeated doubtfully. "You're sure about that?"

"She *did*, man. I was surprised."

"Were there any witnesses?"

Soames thought for a moment. "The bookkeeper in the office, Gretchen, was still there, but I don't know if she heard it or not. Melissa was talking real low, like she didn't want to be overheard."

Tony wrote the bookkeeper's name down. He couldn't wait to ask her. "So—what time did you tell her you'd be there?"

"I said seven. She said okay, and then went home. Then, I show up about 7:15 or so, and she meets me at the door looking real agitated, and tells me that she's not feeling well. She wants to cancel. I thought she was mad 'cause I was late, so I apologized, but she tells me to leave. I got a little ticked off, since I had canceled a date to come over there, and I thought the least she could have done was call—"

"Ticked off?" Larry cut in. "How ticked off?"

"Just a little hot. Hey, I didn't touch her! I just said something about her jerking me around, that I didn't appreciate it. Next thing I know, she's pulling a knife on me—one of those long carving knives like for a turkey—and waving it at me and screaming for me to get out. So I went. That's absolutely all there was. I never laid a hand on her. I didn't even come more than four feet into her apartment."

"Another false accusation?" Tony asked with mock sincerity.

"That's exactly what it is! And I have no idea why she's out to get me. Why she'd call the police and lie like that."

"You're totally in the dark about this, huh?"

Soames turned his palms up, arms spread wide. "Absolutely. I mean, if we'd gone out or something, and things hadn't gone well, and she wanted revenge . . . well, maybe. But it's like she planned this or something."

"What about the shirt under your seat?"

"What shirt?"

"The shirt with the Far Side cartoon on the front."

"It isn't under my seat," Soames said. "It's in my closet at the office. Sometimes I get dirty on the site, and I change clothes." The perplexed look on his face seemed genuine. "You found it under my seat?"

Tony stared, not missing a nuance of Soames's expression. "So you're saying you didn't put it there? Tell me, how do you explain the blood on it? Or the knife wrapped up in it?"

"What?" Looking astounded, Soames turned to his lawyer. "Man, I'm being framed. I noticed my knife missing from my office this afternoon. She must have taken it."

"So let me get this straight," Larry said. "You're saying that she took your shirt out of your office closet, took your knife, opened a vein to get blood all over it, then stuffed it under your car seat so that when you raped her, she'd have evidence?"

"I didn't *touch* her! She had this planned out before she even invited me to dinner. Don't you see? It's starting to make sense. I still don't know why she'd do it, but she did. Isn't it obvious to you morons?"

"It's not obvious to me," Larry said facetiously, glancing at Tony. "Is it obvious to you?"

"Sounds a little far-fetched," Tony agreed.

Soames was beginning to sweat, and he wiped his forehead with the back of his wrist. "Okay, look. If you just think about it— was the blood dry on the shirt? 'Cause if it had just happened, the blood would be wet."

Larry shook his head. "We didn't pick you up until a couple of hours after she reported it, and she didn't even call until a half hour or so after it happened. The blood would have had time to dry."

"Man, you got to believe me. I'm being set up. The woman's out to get me."

"Just like the other two were?"

Soames slammed his hand on the table. "Yes! Just like the other two. It happens, man. One person falsely accuses you, and then you're easy game for the next one who wants to get even."

"You said she didn't have anything to get even for."

"She doesn't! Hey, I don't know any more than you do what's going through her head. But I do know that she's accusing me just as falsely as the others did."

"Then I'd say you have real bad luck with women," Tony said.

The door opened, and one of the uniforms stuck his head in. "Larry, Tony, there's a call for you. Dr. Jasper. Says he's returning your call."

"I'll take it," Tony said, getting up.

Larry watched Tony leave the room, then got up himself. "We found some interesting things in your apartment, Soames. Wonder if you could explain them to us."

Soames looked uncomfortable. "I got nothing to hide."

"Right. So you have a good explanation for why there were binoculars, a camera, and a knife in a bag in your closet."

"I take them to ball games," Soames said. "I can see better with the binoculars, and I like to take pictures."

"Is that why the only pictures we found were of women who didn't know they were being photographed?"

Soames laughed then. "They were my friends. They all knew I was taking their pictures."

"Yeah? Then you won't mind giving us their names, will you, so we can talk to them."

Soames got quiet again.

"Come on, Soames," Larry said. "What are their names?"

"I'm not gonna subject my friends to your gestapo tactics."

"Do you *know* their names, Soames?"

"His friends have no relation to this case," McRae interjected.

"No, but his prey have a lot of bearing on this. And if he can't give us the names of these unsuspecting women he photographed from his car at night, then we have to make our own assumptions."

Soames turned to his attorney, beseeching him to help him out, and McRae leaned forward. "Okay, you've got your statement from him. I don't think he needs to say any more."

Tony came back in, his face glum, but before he could sit down, Larry said, "Fine, I think we've got enough. Maybe a night in jail will help him get his story straight."

"Steve," Soames pled, "can't you get the arraignment moved up? I don't want to stay in here."

"It's just one night," McRae said. "Tomorrow we can probably get you out on bond."

"I wouldn't hold my breath," Larry said. "When the judge sees the evidence and your record, he's gonna want to throw away the key. 'Course, if you came clean and told the truth, he might cut you a little slack."

"I *am* telling the truth, man!"

"Fine. Stick to your story. It's kind of a hobby of mine, shooting stories like this all to pieces."

Soames was still yelling when Larry and Tony closed the door behind them and walked through the noisy precinct. Several gang members just brought in shouted at the officer who had booked them. Across the room, an abusive husband let out a string of obscenities as he struggled to break free of his handcuffs. Somewhere a baby cried incessantly.

"So what do you think?" Tony asked.

"I think he deserves an Oscar. What do you think?"

"I don't know. I mean, yeah, the evidence is pretty clear, and his record doesn't leave much room for doubt."

"But?"

Tony hesitated, looking out over the chaos of the room. Finally, he brought his eyes back to Larry. "On the phone, that was the doctor who examined Melissa Nelson."

"Yeah, I know. What did he say?"

Tony combed his fingers through his sandy hair. "He says that, based on his examination of her, he can't confirm for certain that a rape occurred."

Larry stared at him for a moment. "Did he say it didn't?"

"No, he couldn't say that. Not for sure."

"Well, we knew that evidence was going to be flimsy because she showered. But what does he call the cut on her leg?"

"Assault, maybe, but not rape."

Larry backed up a step, glaring at his friend. "So what are you saying? Just because some doctor says he can't find evidence, it didn't happen? You *saw* the evidence in this guy's car. You saw his record. You heard what he said in there."

"That's just it," Tony said. "What if it happened just like he said?"

Larry gaped at him. "I can't believe you. You want to make this poor woman regret she ever called us."

"I just don't want to accept either one of these stories at face value," Tony said. "We might be getting a little truth from each of them. It just feels like there's something else going on here, like we're not getting the whole story."

"Well, if anybody's hiding something, we'll find out. This guy's not walking out of *this* jail on a technicality."

CHAPTER FOUR

M elissa left the hospital the next morning before the doctor had even come in. In the bright, revealing light of morning, the apartment she had left last night had a look of absurdity: tables still overturned, broken glass still scattered across the floor, the bed still rumpled and unmade.

She stood near the front door, slowly perusing the signs of struggle, the evidence laid out so distinctly, the story it all told. Stepping over the broken, overturned lamp, she went into the bathroom, where bloody towels lay crumpled on the floor. Her eyes strayed to the bathtub, then flitted away, then gravitated back again.

The memory of another bathtub flashed into her mind, and quickly she turned away, bending over the sink to splash cold water on her face. Straightening, she grabbed the hand towel and looked into the mirror. The face staring back at her was tight, as it often was, with worry, urgency, and grief. The worry was something that came and went, alternating with a death-defying courage that sometimes propelled her into decisions she had trouble carrying out. But the grief was ever present, always deep, smothering, sickening, something she could not escape. Maybe there would be an end to it now.

Turning, deliberately keeping her eyes from the bathtub that had ignited those memories, she limped into the bedroom she usually kept so neat. She found something else to wear and quickly changed, careful not to brush the cut on her leg. Then, brushing her long blonde hair with little attention to how the soft waves fell, she flipped through the phone book and found the number of the police station.

Larry Millsaps wasn't in, she learned, and neither was Tony Danks. Edward Soames was still in custody, but his bond hearing was at ten.

Fear burst through her, fear that he would somehow convince the judge that this was all a mistake, that he deserved to, at least, be released on bond. She needed to talk to someone, to find out if one of the prosecutors would be there, or if this was one of those hearings where just the defendant and his lawyer would be present. The court *had* to understand the seriousness of the crime he'd committed! Quickly, she found the number to the DA's office and asked for the attorney working on the case.

No one had even been assigned to it yet.

"But his hearing is scheduled for ten this morning! Won't anyone be there from your office? What if they release him?"

"Judges generally won't release a man charged with rape, Miss Nelson. There's really nothing to worry about."

"He'll come after me if he gets out!" she said, her voice rising. "I'd say there's very certainly something to worry about. I've seen people released on technicalities before. I've seen the justice system fumble. I don't want to be the victim of somebody's mistake!"

"I told you, we'll have someone there."

"But I need to talk to whoever it is. They need to see what he did to me, what he did to my apartment. They need to hear—"

"I'm sure we'll have the police report soon. You gave them a statement, didn't you?"

"Yes, but that's not enough! If I could just talk to someone, so you could see how important it is to keep him locked up!"

"I've got your name and number, Miss Nelson. Once the case is assigned, I'm sure they'll be contacting you. Please relax." The voice on the other end paused, then changed to a softer cadence. "Look, I know you've been through an ordeal. I have the number of a terrific counselor who specializes in rape victims. Why don't you call her this morning and talk to her?"

"I don't need a shrink!" she cried. "I need some peace of mind. I need to know it isn't going to happen again just because he managed to charm some judge into letting him go!"

"Please, Miss Nelson. I know it's hard, but you really have no alternative right now except waiting. I promise someone will contact you."

Melissa slammed the phone down and wiped at the tears forming in her eyes. She couldn't just sit here and wait. She had to go somewhere, do something. She couldn't just let it go.

She searched through the phone book for the name Millsaps, then scanned down the page until she came to Larry. Quickly, she dialed the number, then waited as it rang once, twice, three times ...

Finally, it was picked up, dropped, and then a rumbly, groggy voice said, "Hello?"

"Uh, Detective Millsaps? This is Melissa Nelson. From ... last night?"

"Yeah, Melissa," he said. "Are you all right?"

"Yes ... well, no. Look, I'm sorry I woke you. I wouldn't have, except ..."

"That's okay. Melissa, what's wrong?"

"It's the bond hearing. It's at ten this morning, and it hasn't even been assigned to anyone in the DA's office yet, and I'm worried he might get out."

Larry sighed. "He won't, Melissa. No way. They have your statement, and I stayed late last night making sure all the paperwork was in order. It's all there."

She brought a trembling hand to her forehead and shoved her bangs back. "It's just—so hard for me to trust the justice system."

His voice was waking up now, and she had the feeling he was sitting up. "I understand why you're jumpy. I probably would be, too. Are you still in the hospital?"

"No, I'm at home," she said. "You know, I'm thinking about moving. Maybe I need a new address. Maybe I just need to leave town until this comes to trial."

"That's up to you," he said, "as long as we can reach you. Are you planning to go in to work today?"

"No," she said quickly. "I don't think I can go back there. It would be too hard to face anyone. And his office is there ..."

Suddenly she realized that she was babbling like a crazy person, and she had awakened him to do it. "Look, I didn't mean to wake you up. Or, maybe I did, but I shouldn't have. I'm sorry. I'm just a little fragmented. Would you—would you call me when you get to the office today? I'd like to talk to you some more."

"Sure," he said.

"All right, good-bye." But she held the receiver in her hand for a few moments before finally setting it back in its cradle. Then, going to her favorite chair, still stained with a few drops of her blood from last night, she curled up on it and tried to think what to do next.

Larry lay in bed for a while after he hung up, wishing there was something he could do to help this distraught woman. He'd seen the way a crisis like this ate at people, how it tore at the fabric of their security and ripped away their trust in all that was good. She needed an anchor.

He rolled toward his bedside table, fighting the fatigue still clinging to him, and dialed information. Then he sat up and punched in Melissa's number.

"Hello?" Her voice was soft, apprehensive, yet hopeful. He wondered who she'd been expecting.

"Uh, Melissa? This is Larry again. Listen, I was just thinking—would you like to have breakfast somewhere? You obviously need to talk, and I've gotten all the sleep I need."

"Are you sure?"

"Well, yeah."

He could hear the relief in her voice, that someone was taking her seriously. "Yes, that would be great. When?"

"How about an hour? I don't live far from you. I could pick you up." But as quickly as he'd said that, he kicked himself. The last thing a rape victim wanted was another man coming to her apartment. "Or if you'd rather just meet somewhere—"

"No, that's fine," she said. "You can pick me up."

A little surprised, he said, "Okay. I'll see you then."

This time, she didn't sound quite as forlorn as she said good-bye.

CHAPTER FIVE

arry wasn't sure he would have recognized her if Melissa hadn't been standing in the door of the same apartment where he'd met her the night before. Her hair had been wet and matted then, and she had been curled up in a blanket most of the time, her eyes raw and red, her skin pallid.

But today her hair, a soft baby blonde color, waved down to her shoulders. Soft bangs covered her eyebrows. The skin around her eyes was still red, but their soft blueness was striking even though she wore no makeup. Melissa Nelson wasn't a woman who needed much help from cosmetics, Larry decided. They would only cheapen the effect of the beauty she'd been gifted with.

He noticed also how small she was, no more than five-feet-five against his six-two, and he hated the image that crossed his mind of Soames overpowering her. He supposed they should be thankful that she hadn't been left dead.

"You ready?" he asked.

"Yes," she said. "Come on in. I have to get my purse."

The apartment looked just as he'd left it last night—tables overturned, glass shattered, liquid spilled and congealed on the floor. From the doorway, he could see into the bedroom; nothing had been changed on the bed. Not a pillow had been moved, not a sheet disturbed.

"I—I didn't know if the police had gotten all the evidence they needed," she explained, stepping over some glass and still favoring her left leg. "I thought I'd better leave everything alone until I was sure."

He shook his head. "We finished last night, Melissa. We have film and video of the whole scene, and we got fingerprints and a lot of other routine evidence. I don't think we missed anything."

"But are you sure? If I clean it all up, and you think of something you forgot to look for, it'll be too late."

"Have you found anything you think we missed?" he asked, confused.

"No. I'm just saying there could be something."

Gently, trying not to make her feel stupid, Larry said, "Melissa, it's really okay to start putting things back together. I could help if you want, after breakfast. You can't keep living in this mess, with all these reminders. It would drive you crazy."

"I'm willing to take that chance, if it'll ensure that he gets put away."

"I know you are. You're very brave. But you really have to start thinking of yourself. You may not even know this yet, but you've been traumatized. You need to talk to people who know how to deal with this—even some people who've been through it. It would really help you adjust."

"I'll adjust when I know for sure they aren't going to let him go," she said. She started out the door, limping slightly, and Larry followed her, locking the door behind him. Every case was different, he thought as they went down the stairs. The last rape he'd worked, the woman had not only showered before she'd called the police, but she'd cleaned up her apartment, trying to wipe away any sign that the man had ever been there. But she hadn't been able to scrub away the horrible memories, and finally, she had called the police.

It was odd that Melissa, who had also showered to clean away any bodily memory of the man who'd violated her, had chosen to keep the apartment just as he'd left it. Whether she was incredibly strong, or incredibly paranoid, he wasn't sure.

"How's your leg?" he asked.

"Fine," she said. "It really doesn't hurt much."

Incredibly strong, he decided, with a very high threshold of pain.

At the bottom of the stairs, he noticed a tiny old woman peering through the crack of her partially open door. Dismissing her as a neighbor still curious about last night, he stepped out of the building and pointed to his car parked on the street. "It's not much, but it's paid for."

She smiled, and he realized that he'd never seen that expression on her before. It changed her face, softening the lines around her mouth and eyes.

He opened the door for her, and she got in, careful not to hurt her leg.

"So what do you like to eat?"

"Anything's fine," she said. "I didn't really come to eat."

He cranked the car and pulled out into the traffic. "We'll go to this place I know a couple of blocks away. They have great omelets."

"Fine," she said.

He glanced at her occasionally as he navigated his way through the traffic. She was pretty, he thought, but he had realized that last night. Her eyes gave her face a startling softness and depth. Left alone, undisturbed, what did she think about? What did she like to do—before last night, that is. And how long would it take for her to heal?

"Do you have family around here?" he asked quietly.

She shook her head. "No. My parents live in Pensacola."

"Have you—told them?"

The turmoil in her eyes grieved him. "No, I haven't. I'm not going to. Maybe they won't hear about it."

"Well . . . if this goes to trial, it will be in the paper, and since he's had arrests in other counties, the coverage might reach across the state."

She grew quiet, and her eyes strayed out the window.

"Why don't you want them to know?"

She drew in a deep breath, then let it out slowly. "I don't think they can take it. It would kill them."

"Well, maybe you could get someone to help you tell them. Do you have brothers or sisters?"

She hesitated for a moment, and he saw the tears filling her eyes. "No," she said finally, quietly.

"Well, I could help you, if you want. I'm used to breaking bad news to people."

She brought her eyes back to him. "That must be awful."

371

He frowned and thought about it for a moment. "It used to be. I used to dread it, and wish someone else would do it for me. But then I realized that not everyone can bring bad news with any sense of compassion. I can. I finally decided that if somebody had to tell them horrible things, it might as well be me. At least I could know it was handled right."

"And what's the right way to tell a couple that their daughter has been raped?" she asked in a monotone.

"Well, I'd tell them first that you were all right. That the man is in custody. Those things should give them some peace. Then I'd let them cry and yell and cuss, if they had to. And then I'd tell them what I do in times of deep tragedy, when I don't know where to turn."

She gazed at him for a long moment. "What do you do?"

"I pray," he said. "I turn to God. And instead of asking 'why,' I ask God what he wants me to do."

Those tears resurfaced again, and she looked down at her hands. "If you've never asked why, it's because you've never experienced a tragedy so deep that it shakes the foundation of everything you've ever believed in your life. Sometimes you *have* to ask why."

"And if there are no answers?"

"Then you make some," she said.

They pulled into the parking lot of the little diner. Neither of them spoke as they got out and went inside. He was a little surprised when she ordered; he hadn't expected her to be able to eat. He was glad she could.

Finally, when the waitress brought their food, he got back to the subject they'd started in the car. "I've been thinking about what you said. About making your own answers. And I thought how convenient that would be if it were possible. But I've found that my own attempts to resolve things never work." He studied her for a moment as he sipped his coffee. "Tell me something, Melissa. Do you pray?"

Her eyes seemed to glaze over, as if she were deep in a memory from years earlier. "I used to," she said. "I used to pray all the time."

"What made you stop?"

"I don't know," she whispered. "Anger, maybe."

"Anger at what?"

She seemed to shake out of her reverie at his question, and looked at him again. "Personal things. Things that went wrong, without any reason. Things that didn't make any sense."

"And you haven't prayed since?"

She hesitated. "Some. But I don't think they were heard. Finally, I gave up."

"I can assure you they were heard."

She shrugged. "Well, maybe they were. They just weren't answered."

"Sometimes the answer is 'wait.' Sometimes we don't want to do that. Sometimes maybe we'd rather trust in our own strength."

"Maybe," she whispered. "Maybe so."

The food came to the table, and he watched as she ate, picking at her food, looking distracted.

"So do you want me to talk to your folks?"

She shook her head. "No. I appreciate it, though. If they hear about it, I guess I'll have some explaining to do. But maybe they won't hear, and then they'll never have to suffer through this. I want to protect them from this if I can."

"But you need their support, Melissa. You can't get it if they don't know."

"I'll be all right," Melissa whispered. "I can do this alone."

He shut up then, realizing that she was not only strong, she was stubborn. And she'd made up her mind.

After a few minutes, she moved her plate away and folded her arms on the table. "Detective Millsaps—"

"Larry," he interrupted. "Please, call me Larry."

"Okay, Larry. I wanted to talk to you about the evidence. What's being done with it?"

He set his fork down and leaned back. "What do you mean?"

"I mean, you're not going to just blow off the hair and fingerprints and everything, and assume that the shirt and knife in his car were enough, are you?"

Larry shook his head. "Of course not. It'll all be used in court. Every bit of it."

"And, you did have a warrant when you arrested him, didn't you?"

Larry nodded. "Search warrants, too." Her questions bothered him. He wasn't used to getting the third degree from a victim. She looked at her watch, and he knew that she was calculating how much time before Soames's bond hearing.

"Will the judge make an immediate decision about whether to release him or keep him?"

"Yes," he said. "And I guarantee he'll keep him. He'd be out of his mind to let Edward Soames back out on the streets."

"Yeah, well, I've seen judges out of their minds before. Outrageous decisions are made in court every day."

"That's one of the hardest things about being a cop. I take 'em in, and they let 'em go. But we have too much evidence on this guy. You really don't have to worry." He hoped he sounded more confident than he felt.

He paid the check, and they went back to the car. "I meant it about helping you clean up your apartment," he said. "I can help you right now."

"No," she said. "I don't want to go home."

"Where do you want to go?" he asked.

Her eyes were determined as she faced him. "I want to go with you to the police station, or you can drop me off at the courthouse."

"The courthouse? Melissa, you don't want to be there. You don't want to see this guy—"

"I have to know," she said. "I have to know that they're not releasing him. Either I can sit in the courtroom and watch the hearing, or I can wait with you until you hear something."

"Or I could take you home and call you when I hear."

"By the time you call me, he could be at my apartment banging my door down," she said. "I won't feel safe until I know for sure."

Larry sighed. "All right then. I guess you can come to the precinct. But I can't stay there all morning. I'll probably get called away."

"That's fine," she said. "I won't bother anyone. I just need a safe place, until there's a decision."

Larry moaned inwardly, anticipating what Tony would say. But he didn't have the heart to force her to go home. He'd already taken this much responsibility for her; he might as well finish what he'd started.

CHAPTER SIX

T he precinct smelled like a locker room when Larry walked Melissa through, trying to find a place to put her while he worked. The waiting area was filled with what looked like a gang, no doubt waiting to post bail for one of their members. Putting her there would be like throwing a lamb to the wolves. She'd already been through enough.

So he grabbed an empty chair and dragged it around to his desk. "Here," he said.

"Thank you." Checking her watch, she sat down. Larry saw on the wall clock that it was almost ten.

He tried to recover last night's train of thought as he sifted through the paperwork he'd left on his desk. He needed more information on the other rape charges against Soames. Names of women. Circumstances. Maybe he could determine his MO, whether he only went after women he knew, or if those pictures found in his apartment were pictures of potential victims. He needed to get a job history, affiliations, a credit report, anything that would help him trace Soames's steps for the past few years. There might be other women who had been attacked and hadn't reported it—women who might come forward if they knew someone else had filed charges.

Whatever it took, he needed to make sure that the system didn't let Melissa down. She was already, for some reason, very distrustful of it.

"Hey, how're you doing?" It was Tony's voice behind him, and Larry looked up and saw that his partner was addressing Melissa.

"Fine."

"Is, uh, Detective Millsaps here helping you?"

Larry grinned. Tony didn't recognize her. "Tony, this is Melissa Nelson."

Tony's eyebrows shot up. "Oh. From last night?"

"Yeah," Larry said. "She's just waiting here for word about Soames's bond hearing."

"What about it?" Tony asked.

"Whether he's released on bond."

Tony almost laughed, but caught himself. "They're not letting him out."

When Melissa didn't answer, Larry spoke up. "She didn't want to wait at home, just in case. Listen, I need to talk to you about some things."

He excused himself and whisked Tony into the interrogation room.

"What's going on?" Tony asked. "Was she waiting here for us?"

"No. I picked her up."

"You what?"

"She called me this morning, all upset, worried he was going to get out and come after her. I took her to breakfast—"

"Oh, brother," Tony said, shaking his head. "You're nuts, you know that? Larry, you can't go getting involved with victims in the crimes you're investigating. That's crazy!"

"I'm not! She's just scared and paranoid right now. If sitting at my desk makes her feel better, it's fine with me."

"You can't work with her sitting there."

"Watch me." With that, Larry flung the door open and stormed through it.

"All right," Tony said, fast on his heels. "But if she's here, I'm not going to tiptoe around her. She's going to have to answer some questions."

"Ask away," he said. "She'll tell you anything you want to know."

But Tony didn't ask. Instead, he busied himself at his computer, punching the keys hard and deliberately, as if to vent some of the frustration he felt. Larry tried to ignore him, doing his own work on the computer, tracking down the work history of Edward

Pendergrast, the names of the other two alleged victims who'd pressed charges against him, and any other information he could find.

After a while, Melissa got up and wandered toward him. "Are you working on my case?" she asked.

"Yes." He gave her a distracted glance, then hit the "print" button. "It seems our man has a couple of other arrests. For the same thing."

Melissa didn't look as surprised as he'd expected. "Can that be mentioned in his hearing? Should you call the DA?"

Larry looked fully at her now, studying her face. "You didn't happen to know his background before, did you? Is that why you're so afraid of things falling through?"

She grew stiffer then, but kept her eyes clearly focused on his. "Of course not. How could I have known? I've barely had a complete conversation with him."

As she talked, Larry noticed Tony behind her. Tony stared at her, glanced back at his computer screen, then shot a look at Larry. "Excuse me a minute," Larry said. "I need to talk to Tony."

"What if your phone rings? What if someone calls about the hearing?"

"I'll hear it," he said. "Don't worry." He crossed the room to Tony's desk. "You have that look on your face," he said quietly. "Like you've got something."

Tony glanced up at him over his shoulder. "I thought I'd check out our little lady. Just to get a better take on her. Take a look at this."

Larry leaned over him and read the skeleton history he'd come up with. "She's got a degree from Florida State. Changed her major to criminal justice after her sophomore year. Graduated summa cum laude. My question is, how did a criminal justice whiz wind up here working as a secretary?"

Larry frowned. "Why would she do that?"

Tony shook his head. "Why don't we ask her?"

Larry straightened. "I will."

The phone was ringing when he got back to his desk, and he snatched it up. "Millsaps."

He listened as the secretary in the DA's office relayed the decision in the hearing. "Thanks. I appreciate it."

He hung up and leaned forward on his desk.

"Did they let him go?" Melissa asked.

He shook his head. "No bond. He's staying."

Relief washed over her, and she leaned back in her chair, finally relaxed. "I can't believe it. I was so worried."

"I know you were." He set his chin on his palm and looked at her for a moment. "Can I ask you something, Melissa?" She was smiling, and he hated to ruin it, but he had to. "We had to do a little research on you, just as a matter of routine. And we were looking at your educational background."

Her smile faded, and she fixed her eyes on him. "What about it?"

"Just seemed odd to me, that's all. You have a degree in criminal justice, of all things."

"Why is that odd?" she asked.

"Well, because you're not working in that field. In fact, I wondered why you'd take a job doing secretarial work."

She glanced away then, avoiding his eyes, and shrugged. "I worked for the FBI for three months after I graduated last spring. Three months was long enough. Now I'm a secretary, until I find something better."

"Why didn't you mention this earlier?"

Her eyebrows shot up, and she gaped at him. "I've been a little bit distracted. The subject didn't come up!" She glared at him, as if trying to determine if he was suggesting that she had covered up, then finally, she came to her feet. "Do you have any more questions for me, Detective? Like why I drive a red car instead of a green one, or why I chose exactly the apartment complex I did? I'm familiar with how a rape case often gets turned on the victim. As you pointed out, I spent a lot of time studying things like that. So go ahead! Take your best shot."

His eyes remained locked with hers, but finally, he shook his head. "I'm not trying to interrogate you, Melissa. I just have to ask about things that seem out of sync."

"And since my job is out of sync, maybe what happened to me last night is too, right?"

"I didn't say that."

"You didn't have to. Call me if you come up with anything else that's out of sync. I'll see if I can explain it to you." With that, she started to limp away from his desk.

Larry lunged out of his chair and caught her arm. "Melissa, I'll take you home. Just wait a minute."

"No, thanks," she said. "I'll get a cab."

He stood there as she hurried from the room, and it was a moment before he realized that Tony was standing next to him.

"She didn't like the question, huh?"

"No, she didn't," Larry said. "And now I feel like the kind of pond scum that makes rape victims sorry they ever report the crime."

"If she can't take the heat—"

Larry spun around, his face furious. "If she can't take the heat, what, Tony? Who really *can* take the heat? Could you? What if you were attacked on the street, and when you reported it, all of a sudden your life and your history became suspect? Would your record stand up to our kind of scrutiny? Would *you* be able to take the heat?"

Tony rolled his eyes. "Man, you've got it bad."

"Give me a break!" he shouted, and some of the others in the busy room stopped what they were doing and looked at him. "I would like to think I have a little compassion for any victim I deal with, so don't go accusing me of preferential treatment just because she's a woman!"

"What are you so hot about?" Tony flung back.

"I'm hot about putting an innocent, wounded, violated woman on the defensive, Tony! That kind of thing always gets to me! I don't know why it doesn't get to you."

"Maybe it's because my gut is telling me that things just aren't fitting into place here."

"So who are you gonna believe? A guy who's been accused of rape before, who's being accused now, who had evidence up to his ears in his car and his apartment—or a woman whose only crime is to be overqualified for her job and who had the audacity to get raped?"

Tony threw his hands up. "All right. You got me. You're right. Now can we please get back to work?"

Larry plopped back down into his chair and turned to his computer. This day was going from bad to worse. And he hadn't had enough sleep last night to deal with any of this.

A couple of hours later, as Larry and Tony were returning from investigating a missing persons report on two seventeen-year-old girls who had apparently run away—and for good reason, judging from the neglectful homes they'd each come from—Larry's mind wandered back to Melissa Nelson. He thought about her indignation that morning, then about their conversation at breakfast. Something had been bothering him about that, something she'd said . . .

"*. . . you're not going to just blow off the hair and fingerprints . . . and assume that the shirt and knife in his car were enough, are you?*"

The hair. That was it. How had she known that they would find follicles of Soames's hair on her bed? Just an assumption, based on what she would have looked for, had she been investigating?

He shoved the question out of his mind. Tony's suspicions—of what, he still wasn't sure—were affecting him. Rubbing his eyes, he glanced at Tony, who was driving. "Did I tell you I ordered the police file on Pendergrast from Santa Rosa County?"

Tony shook his head. "No. I was going to do it this afternoon."

"I asked them to rush it. They said it would be here by tomorrow."

"What's the rush?"

"Well, the grand jury will be hearing the case soon."

"So the DA will ask for it."

Larry breathed a laugh. "Yeah, well, you and I both know that the more we lay the case out for the DA's office, the better chance we have of conviction. I just want to make sure."

"What are you looking for?"

"I don't know," he said. "Anything I can find on the previous arrests. Who the victims were, his MO, exactly why he walked. That kind of thing."

Tony glanced over at him. "Larry, you look like a zombie. How much sleep did you get last night?"

"Couple hours," he said.

"Why don't you go on home? I'll fax the info about these runaways to some other PDs across the state and see what I can come up with. Get some sleep. You're not worth a plugged nickel when you're this tired."

"Thanks a lot." They pulled into the PD parking garage. "I think I'll take you up on it, though."

"Sure you can drive?" Tony asked with a grin.

"Hey, I've functioned with less sleep before. Remember the Barrett case?"

"Yeah. I almost killed you, man. Volunteering us to stake her place out all night after we'd been on duty for over twelve hours already."

"Hey, I did it myself."

"Yep. Another case of a lady in distress. You do dumb things for women, Larry."

"It was dumb to stake out her house?" he asked irritably. "Are you telling me there was no threat?"

Tony grinned and shook his head. "Okay, okay. But breakfast this morning? I don't think that was within the call of duty, pal."

"Just don't worry about it. I'm going home."

"Good," Tony laughed. "And don't come back until you have a better disposition. Or I just might have to kill you after all."

Larry grinned as he headed across the garage to his own car.

A knock at the door woke Larry a few hours after he'd fallen asleep. He stumbled to the door. Tony stood there, the setting sun at his back, grinning as if he enjoyed waking Larry. "Rise and shine! We've got work to do."

Larry shuffled into the kitchen, and Tony followed. "What is it?" Larry asked, measuring out some coffee for the pot.

"A witness in the Nelson case."

Larry swung around. "Really? Who?"

"A woman who lives downstairs. She gave a statement last night that she heard things crashing upstairs in Melissa's apartment. I thought we should talk to her."

"Yeah, okay. Just let me change."

A few minutes later, Larry followed Tony out to the car, wondering whether the appearance of this witness would make Tony give more credence to Melissa's story. "So what else have you been doing today?" he asked.

"Well, I interviewed the people she worked with."

"Who worked with?"

"Your friend Melissa."

Larry shot him a look. "*My* friend?"

Tony grinned. "Well, you seem to be her champion. Anyway, you're not going to like what I found out."

Larry waited. "What?"

"That bookkeeper who was still there when Soames says Melissa asked him to dinner? She confirmed it."

"That she was there?"

"No. She confirmed that Melissa asked him. She heard it. She's apparently a real busybody, and she admitted that when she saw Melissa go into his office, she listened outside the door to see what they were talking about. She heard everything."

Larry tried to absorb that. "You believe her?"

"I don't know. What do you think?"

"Well, she could have a crush on him herself, and want to help him. Maybe he paid her. Who knows?"

"Yeah, well . . . I'm just telling you what she said."

Larry stayed quiet as they approached the apartment building where they'd found Melissa last night. Things looked radically different tonight, without flashing lights everywhere and a crowd of people on the street. "Who are we going to see?"

"A Matilda Berkley," Tony said. "She lives in the first apartment as you come in the door."

"Yeah, I saw her peeking out this morning."

Larry followed Tony in. Before they had even reached her door, it opened. The little old lady Larry had seen that morning stuck her head out. "Hello, officers. I've been expecting you. Won't you come in?"

She seemed delighted to have company, and Larry couldn't help smiling. They introduced themselves, accepted the coffee and cake she'd prepared for them, and sat down, anxious to get to the point. Finally, Larry jumped in.

"Mrs. Berkley, you told the police officers last night in your statement that you heard things crashing upstairs. Could you tell us exactly what time that was?"

"It was seven-thirty, because I was baking, and the timer went off right about that time."

Larry nodded. "Did you see anyone leave the apartment after that?"

Her eyebrows shot up. "No, and I kept waiting. I had my door cracked with the chain still on it, and I was watching the stairs to see who would come down. But until you officers came, nobody came out of that apartment."

Larry frowned. "Are you sure? You didn't just miss him?"

"No. I pretty much see almost everyone who comes and goes in this building. I know everyone here, and I like to make sure the people coming and going are *supposed* to be here. Especially with Melissa—she's such a lovely girl. She's been so sweet, always checking to see if I need anything, bringing me things from the grocery store when I can't get there myself. I feel kind of protective of her. And last night, after that first gentleman left, I heard all that crashing—"

"Wait a minute," Larry said. "What gentleman?"

"Well, the one who was here to see Melissa. I opened my door and looked out when he came into the building, and he asked me which apartment was hers. He seemed like a decent young man, and I was happy that she had a date. She has so few visitors, you know."

Larry was getting impatient. "Did you or didn't you see him leave?"

"I certainly did. He came down rather quickly and slammed the door going out. I was so disappointed, because I had hoped that maybe he was a suitor. She's a very lonely girl, I think—"

Tony tried this time. "But you say you heard the crashing things *after* he left?"

"Yes. I could tell that something was wrong, and I thought someone must be up there, but I hadn't seen anyone else go up. I guess I should have called the police myself, but I just wasn't sure whether anyone was there with her. It's possible that they had come when I hadn't been listening, so I waited and waited for them to come down, so I could decide what to do. But no one ever did. Not until the police began coming. Would you like some more cake?"

"No. Uh, thanks." Larry turned his troubled eyes to Tony.

Tony sighed. "Mrs. Berkley, are you sure you didn't just get the events mixed up? I mean, maybe you heard the crashing, and *then* saw him leave."

Her chin came up with indignation. "I'm telling you the way it happened. There must have been someone else up there. That first gentleman wasn't there long enough to do anything. I'd say maybe five minutes. But if there was someone else, maybe he went up onto the roof, or got into another apartment..." Her eyes grew round as she imagined all the places a culprit could have hidden.

"All the other neighbors were interviewed," Tony explained. "None of them saw anything like that."

She sat back hard on her couch. "Then it doesn't make any sense, does it? It's just downright peculiar. How did he get in and out?"

Tony pulled a picture from his shirt pocket. "Mrs. Berkley, was this the man you saw coming to see Melissa last night?"

She took the picture of Soames that they'd used to identify him last night, and nodded. "Yes, that's him. Nice-looking young man, like I told you."

"And you're sure that he's the same man you saw leaving?"

"Oh, absolutely."

"Did he have anything in his hands?"

"Like what?" she asked.

"Anything at all."

The woman thought for a moment. "No. I don't think so."

"Did he look angry?"

"Well, yes, he did."

"And what did he have on?" Larry asked. "Mrs. Berkley, this is very important. Can you remember what he had on when he arrived?"

"Well, the same thing he had on when he left. One of those striped pullover shirts, like a golf shirt or something, you know? It had red and green and navy stripes that went this way . . ."

Larry glanced at Tony. The same shirt he'd been wearing when they'd picked him up.

"And you're sure he was wearing that when he left?"

"Yes," she said adamantly. "Like I told you, he wasn't up there more than five minutes. He looked just the same when he came back down."

No cartoon T-shirt, Larry thought with confusion. So where had the bloody T-shirt come from?

They finished questioning her, thanked her, and left.

As he settled in behind the steering wheel, Tony asked, "Am I the only one who notices that something is a little tilted about this case?" He pulled the car back out onto the street.

"The woman has to be eighty years old. Maybe she's imagining things," Larry said.

"Did she imagine the shirt he was wearing when we picked him up?"

"Well—" Larry sighed, looked out the window, then brought his gaze back to his partner. "Well, how do you explain the crashing *after* Soames had left? Melissa didn't tell us anyone else was involved."

Tony shook his head. "I'm not sure Melissa is telling us the truth, Larry. I know you don't want to hear that, but I'm telling you, things aren't fitting together here."

Larry couldn't deny it. "I just don't get it. What really happened?"

"There's no telling," Tony said. "But the only story we've heard that we've been able to corroborate with witnesses is Soames's story."

Larry rolled his eyes. "Oh, come on. You saw his record. You saw the things in his apartment, the pictures, the bloody shirt under his seat—"

"That's right," Tony said. "I saw them. I'm not saying that he's not a scumbag. I'm just not sure what he really did in this case."

He pulled into a parking space near Larry's apartment and let the car idle for a moment. "Look, what do you say we just sleep on it, and tackle all this fresh tomorrow?"

"Yeah, okay." Larry got out and headed back toward his apartment. But before he reached it, he turned back and walked to his own car. He couldn't just let it go; he wouldn't be able to rest haunted by the possibility that Melissa was lying. He had wanted to check on Melissa anyway, to make sure she was all right. Tony would say that he was obsessing—that if she wasn't a blonde with soulful eyes, he wouldn't be giving this case such attention. But Larry hoped that wasn't true. He'd been on the police force for nine years now, and while many of his colleagues had gotten jaded, he'd worked hard not to. He liked to think that he would always stand up for justice, fairness, and the rights of the victims—especially the more vulnerable victims who needed someone to stand up for them. As tough as Melissa's facade suggested she was, he suspected that she was as vulnerable as any victim he'd ever encountered. Even if there were things about her story that didn't make sense.

He drove back to her apartment building and tried to be quiet as he walked in, to see if anyone could get past Mrs. Berkley without being noticed. But the first stair squeaked beneath his foot, and suddenly the door peeped open, still attached with the chain lock. Mrs. Berkley peered out. He waved. "Hi, Mrs. Berkley. I'm just checking on Melissa."

She pressed the door closed, unlocked the chain, then opened it further. "Good. She's up now. She slept most of the afternoon, but I've heard her moving around up there in the last few minutes. Enjoy your visit."

He smiled uncomfortably and continued up the stairs. A television blared from one of the other apartments on the first floor, and a baby cried in another.

The walls were paper-thin, he thought. Thin enough for Mrs. Berkley to hear everyone who came and went—thin enough to know whether Melissa was alone.

He knocked on Melissa's door. He heard footsteps, then waited while, he assumed, she looked at him through the peephole. After a moment, she opened the door.

"Hi," she said.

She couldn't be lying about this, he thought. Not someone with such pure blue eyes, such porcelain skin, such fine blonde hair ... "Thought I'd come by and check on you," he said. "See if you were all right after our questions this morning. I felt kind of responsible for making things worse for you."

She sighed wearily. "Is that an apology?"

"No. Actually, we were just doing our job," he said. "I just regret how it made you feel."

"Well, I'm fine." She stepped back and invited him in.

He looked around, and saw that the furniture had been turned upright, the toppled lamps were settled back on the tables again, and the broken glass had been swept into little piles.

"I guess I shouldn't have run out like that," she said. "It just got to me a little. If I hadn't been so tired, I probably would have realized that you had to ask. You're supposed to. I wouldn't expect either of you to just take everything at face value."

He glanced into the bedroom and saw that her bed was unmade and the covers pulled back, as if she'd been sleeping in it. "I hope I didn't wake you."

"No," she said. "I just woke up. I was trying to clean up a little. When I came home this morning, I started to, but I was so exhausted I decided to finish later. So I climbed into bed and fell asleep."

Odd, he thought. Most rape victims wouldn't have gone near the place where they'd been violated, yet Melissa had slept there all afternoon? She was tougher than he'd thought. Either that, or . . .

He tried to shove out of his mind the thought that she might not be telling it all exactly as it had happened, that she was leaving something out, or maybe making something up. Seeing the trouble in her expression, the fatigue on her face, he just couldn't believe that. She'd been traumatized. That much was clear.

"I'll help you, if you want," he said finally.

"Are you sure?"

"Sure," he said, rolling up his sleeves. "Have you eaten?"

"I was thinking of ordering a pizza."

"Great," he said. "My treat. You order it, and I'll see if I can get the rest of this up before it comes."

The misery in her expression lightened as she smiled and limped to the telephone. "You're a lifesaver, Larry. I didn't think I could tackle this myself."

It didn't take him long to scrub the stains out of the carpet and sweep up the rest of the glass, but as he did he kept remembering Mrs. Berkley's insistence that she'd heard the crashing lamps and tables *after* Soames had left.

"Melissa," he asked later, over the pizza, "did you have any other visitors last night, other than Soames?"

"No," she said. "And he wasn't exactly a visitor."

"Someone else from the apartments, maybe? Did a neighbor next door stop in? Anybody?"

"No. Nobody."

He studied the pepperoni on his slice again. "Did I tell you I met Mrs. Berkley?"

Melissa smiled. "She's a sweet lady, isn't she?"

"Tell me about her."

Melissa set her pizza down and wiped her fingers on her napkin. "She's been like a grandmother to me. It's been nice to have her around, since my parents are so far away. She's always baking me cakes and cookies, and telling me wild stories about all the neighbors."

"Wild stories? How do you mean?"

She shrugged. "Oh, you know. She doesn't really have much to do all day, so I think she spends a lot of her time imagining what everyone else is doing. And like anyone who lives in their imagination, she gets her facts mixed up. Just last week, she swore that my next-door neighbor in 2B—a forty-eight-year-old widow—had given birth to a little boy. I told her she couldn't have, that she wasn't pregnant, but Mrs. Berkley insisted. Later I found out that the niece of one of the neighbors on the first floor had a baby boy, and she's been visiting. So someone had a baby, all right; it just wasn't who Mrs. Berkley thought it was."

I knew it, Larry thought. The woman wasn't a competent witness. She was mistaken.

"So what did she tell you?" Melissa asked. "Did she see Soames last night?"

"Yeah, she saw him."

That tense look worked back over Melissa's face. "I thought so. She sees everybody."

"Yeah." He felt sorry now that he'd doubted her, that Tony's suspicions had infected him. Something definitely had happened to her. That haunted look in her eye had come from somewhere. And anyway, he couldn't believe that she would simply make up a story like this and put herself through this ordeal for no good reason. She had studied criminal justice; she had to know what this would cost her in emotional stress once it went to trial. No one would subject themselves to that unless they were telling the truth.

She ignored her pizza now, and he wished he hadn't brought the subject up again. Quiet settled over them, and that sad, grieving look in her eyes touched him. There must be some way to assuage that, he thought.

"Listen," he said, sighing. "You need to get out of this place. Just relax a little. Get your mind off things. What if I took you to a movie?"

She smiled softly. "Is that part of your job description?"

He shook his head. "Consider me off duty. This is just pleasure."

Her smile found its way to her eyes, and it was like sunshine reaching a chilled heart. "I'm assuming you aren't married, Detective?"

He shook his head. "You're assuming right."

"Then I guess it would be nice."

Mrs. Berkley was watching at the bottom of the stairs as they left. "Did you find a baby-sitter for the baby tonight?" the little woman asked her.

Melissa looked confused, then amused. "I'm not the one who had the baby, Mrs. Berkley. Remember? It was Mrs. Jasper's niece."

"That's right," the woman said. "Well, you two go on and have a nice evening, now. And be careful."

"We will," Melissa said. "And Mrs. Berkley, please keep your door locked."

"I always do," she said, though it stood wide open at the moment. "Good-bye, Detective."

Larry waved good-bye, feeling relieved that their witness's word wasn't worth much. If only he could convince Tony of that.

He could see that the movie had done her good. For two hours, she had been allowed to forget her problems, dismiss Soames from her mind, and pretend that she was someone else in another life. Now, as they flowed with the crowd toward the exit doors, he saw the shadow creeping back over her face, and how she glanced from side to side, as if expecting Soames to come out of nowhere.

Feeling protective, he reached out and took her hand. It was small, ice-cold, trembling slightly. Trying to decide what would help her right now, he asked, "Would you like to go get a cup of coffee?"

"Sounds good," she said.

He took her to a little café with lush plants spilling from windowsills and cascading down walls. A man with a goatee and a ponytail played an acoustic guitar in the corner, and they sat in a booth near the back and talked about the movie, then about favorite movies they'd seen growing up.

"My sister and I used to spend every Saturday afternoon at the movies," Melissa said. "Half our allowance went for that each week. We would laugh and cry—and when we cried, neither of us would look at the other, because we knew not to destroy the mood. Sandy was good about that."

Larry was confused. Hadn't she said she had no siblings? "Where's Sandy now?" he asked carefully.

Her smile faded, and she seemed to grow even paler. "She died. About three years ago." Tears welled in her eyes, turning the rims red as she looked away. Quickly, she changed the subject. "Do you come here a lot?"

Though she tried to look bright, the tears were still in her eyes, making her look even more fragile. "No, I don't come here much. I work a lot at night. It's nice, though."

"My father plays guitar," she said, watching the man in the corner as he strummed. "He used to play and we'd all sing with him. He taught me how to play the ukulele when I was little, but I only knew one song. I tried the guitar, but wasn't willing to practice."

Her rambling reminded him of a hamster on a treadmill, running as fast as it could without moving an inch. It was as if one moment's silence would break her completely. Even so, he listened carefully; each rambling revelation provided another clue to the woman who fascinated him.

"Do you play anything?" she asked. She had skillfully blinked back her tears by now, and she didn't look quite as forlorn. Trying to lighten things, he said, "I play softball. But no instrument."

"Softball, huh? For a team?"

"Yeah. A church team, during the summer. I can't make every game, because I have to work so much. We're not a very good team. We manage to snatch defeat from the jaws of victory pretty regularly."

She smiled—a distant, pensive smile. "I played for a while last summer, when I worked for the FBI."

The subject of her job with the FBI had seemed taboo earlier in the day when he had asked about her criminal justice degree, but now he seized the opportunity to ask the question that had been plaguing him. "Why did you quit? That sounds like an ideal job for a criminal justice major just out of college."

She breathed a laugh that said he was naive. "I was at the very bottom of the totem pole. It was drudgery. Mostly clerical work, and the pay stinks. I hated the job, and when I looked around me at the career FBI agents, I just decided that that's not what I wanted to do for the rest of my life." She looked up at him then, her eyes locked with his, and she smiled a little. "No offense, but criminal justice was a mistake for me. So I quit and took a job doing something else until I could decide what I really wanted to do. I should have just answered your question this morning, but I was upset."

"Why did you move here, though?"

She was getting tense again. "I was having trouble living in Pensacola, with all the memories—I missed my sister, okay?" Her voice cracked. "I thought if I started over someplace else . . ."

"But you graduated from Florida State, in Tallahassee. Why didn't you just stay there?"

"I wanted someplace completely new," she said. "St. Clair seemed like the perfect little town."

"It can be." He made his voice gentle and soft as he reached across the table and touched her hand. "You're not on the witness stand, Melissa."

"I know. It's just—" She smiled slightly, then brought those big eyes up to him again. "You've been so nice to me today, so I wanted to explain. I really don't know if I could have gotten through the day without you. It's weird, too. I mean, this morning, you showed up exactly when I needed you to, when I was about to lose it. And then again tonight, facing that mess—I can't believe you showed up when you did."

"I had you on my mind. I thought you could use a friend. You seemed pretty alone."

She seemed troubled by that thought. Letting go of his hand, she folded her arms across her stomach, looked away, and said, "I haven't had time to make many friends since I moved here."

"Why not?" Larry asked.

"Because . . ." Her voice quivered, and she cleared her throat and tried again. "I guess it's hard for me to get close to people."

He believed it. Melissa seemed like a loner who didn't like to be alone. Much like him.

"I've always found church to be a good place to make friends. It takes a while, but the friends I've made there will last my whole life."

She struggled against tears. "I don't belong in church. Sometimes I'm pretty sure that God is disgusted with me."

"Why?"

She wiped her eyes, smearing her tears. "What's the verse I learned when I was a kid in Bible school? 'He is of purer eyes than to even look upon iniquity.' Sometimes God turns away."

"But why would he turn away from you, Melissa? What happened last night wasn't your choice."

"I know he has, though." Struggling to fight her tears, she said, "There are things that happen, Larry. Horrible things. If God was there—if he was watching, he would stop them. When he doesn't, then I know he isn't even watching."

Larry only stared at her, feeling moisture in his own eyes as his emotions responded to hers. To tell her that she was reacting inappropriately to her own suffering would be insensitive. Who was he to say? He had never been violated in the way she had. He said nothing, unable to find words that weren't trite and pat.

"There was something that happened in my family," she whispered, covering half her face with one hand as she uncovered part of the horror that lay hidden inside her. "Something terrible. And I wanted so much to believe that God would take care of it. But he didn't."

Larry could think of no way to break the silence as he watched her struggle with her grief.

"Maybe I'm the one hiding from God," she said finally. "Maybe I've just moved too far to ever get back. There does come a point when you've moved too far."

Larry reached across the table and pushed back a strand of her hair caught in her tears. "I hope I'm around when God proves to you that you're wrong."

"I wish . . ." she started to say, but her words broke off.

She looked down at her hands as more tears fell; finally, she drew in a deep, cleansing breath. "Can we go now?"

They were quiet as they drove back to her apartment, and when they got there she was out of the car before he had even cut the engine off. Larry hopped out and caught up to her. "Let me walk you up."

She nodded and slowed her step then, and he put his arm around her and escorted her up the steps. Mrs. Berkley's door was open an inch or so as they walked by.

Melissa reached into her purse for her keys when they got to her door, but those tears were still coming, and Larry didn't know what to do for her. He took the key from her hand, opened the door, then stood in front of her for a moment, wondering what he could offer her to relieve the pain. "I know things look dark now," he whispered, "but they're going to get better. And if you need to talk, day or night, you can call me. Remember that."

She wilted as he pulled her into a crushing hug, and her arms closed around his neck. For a while, he just held her there, trying to give her support and hope and help as he felt the force of her sobs shaking her body. Some part of his heart wept with her, and his own eyes filled with tears.

When she pulled back, he touched her face. "Are you going to be all right?"

"Yes," she whispered. "Thank you for the shoulder."

"Anytime. That's what it's there for."

She drew in a long breath and looked up at him. "You make me feel safe."

"Good," he said. "That's my job."

"You do it very well." She smiled and almost laughed then, the kind of laughter that often follows weeping, and took a deep breath. "Good night."

He wanted to kiss her but knew it wouldn't be appropriate. Not the night after she was assaulted, not the moment after she'd found comfort weeping on his shoulder. Instead, he whispered, "Good night."

She went inside and closed the door, and he stood listening as she locked two bolts. He started down the stairs, then stopped and pulled one of his cards out of his wallet. It already included his extension at the precinct, so he turned it over and jotted his home and cellular phone numbers down. Then he went back to her apartment and slipped it under her door.

When he reached the bottom of the stairs, Mrs. Berkley was still peering out of a one-inch opening in her door. "Good night, Mrs. Berkley," he called.

"Good night, Detective Millsaps," she replied with perfect clarity. "Be careful driving home."

Larry frowned all the way out to his car, wondering how she'd remembered his name. Maybe she flowed in and out of confusion, sometimes getting things right, sometimes not. Still, it disturbed him.

Tony was going to hit the ceiling anyway, when he heard what Larry had done with his evening.

CHAPTER EIGHT

Y ou're losing your edge." Tony plopped into the extra chair at Larry's desk.

"What?"

"You heard me. I went by Mrs. Berkley's again today. I wanted to ask her a couple more questions, and she told me something very interesting."

Larry knew where this was going. He leaned back in his chair and waited. "Yeah? What?"

"She told me that you took Melissa Nelson out last night."

"It wasn't a date. And Mrs. Berkley is loony. She floats in and out of reality. We can't count on her story at all."

Tony wouldn't let him change the subject. "Did you or didn't you take Melissa Nelson out last night?"

He shifted uncomfortably. "I went by to see her, okay? I helped her clean up. And she needed to get out of the apartment, so I took her."

"On a date."

Larry stacked some loose papers on his desk. A telephone at the next desk rang. He wished it were his. "Call it what you want, Tony."

Tony leaned forward, fixing his eyes on his partner's. "Tell me the truth, Larry. You were disturbed by what Mrs. Berkley told us, right? And also by the stuff we found out yesterday about Melissa's job. You wanted to get to the bottom of it, and that's why you went to see her last night."

Larry dropped the papers and began rubbing his temples. "Okay, yeah. And I did get to the bottom of it. She didn't like criminal justice, once she started working in it. That happens. She decided to take a job doing clerical work until she could figure out what she wanted to do. And her sister had died, she was having trouble with the memories, and that's why she came here."

"A sister, huh?" Tony pulled a pad out of his pocket and jotted that down.

"What? Do you think she's lying about that, too?"

"Just gonna check," Tony said. "By the way, we have to testify for the grand jury day after tomorrow. Did you know that?"

"Yeah." Larry looked at him again. "And what are you gonna say, Tony? You gonna go in there and tell them that, despite what you saw that night, despite all the evidence we found, you think she's lying?"

Tony breathed a laugh. "Man, I'm telling you again. You're losing your edge. When's the last time I sat on a witness stand and told them whether I thought someone was lying or not? I'm being called to talk about the evidence, not my gut feelings."

"Good. Because your gut feelings are wrong."

A police radio on the hip of an officer nearby blared, adding to the grating noise of a teletype printing out a report.

Tony got up and looked down at his friend. "You're getting involved with her, buddy. And that's a big mistake."

"I don't do things the way you do, Tony. You've known that for a long time. I don't have to account to you or anyone else on this force for my personal life."

"Fine," Tony said. "I hope you don't have to eat those words."

Larry watched Tony go back to his desk, then stared for a while at his blank computer screen. Things had been tense between them ever since they'd met Melissa Nelson, but that wasn't his fault. Tony wanted to victimize the victim, and Larry wasn't going to let him. It was as simple as that.

Still, he thought, it probably would be better if he didn't keep seeing Melissa. Though he would never admit it to Tony, she *was* getting under his skin, and that wasn't good. Later, after the case was laid to rest, maybe he could explore those feelings again.

He got up and went into the interrogation room, the only quiet place in the building. He stared out the window at what he could see of downtown St. Clair. He watched as citizens walked by on the sidewalk, trusting the officers in this building to keep them safe.

Was Tony right? Was he slipping? Was this protective feeling toward Melissa compromising his police work?

Maybe it was, he admitted reluctantly. Starting now, he had to put it behind him. He wouldn't call Melissa Nelson again.

Melissa was trembling, two days later, as she sat on the witness stand in front of the grand jury that would decide whether Edward Soames would stand trial. Under oath, she told them her whole story—the way he'd shown up unexpectedly and shoved his way in, the struggle that had ensued as she'd tried to defend herself, the knife with which he'd cut her, his ultimate violation of her. She cried as she spoke, thankful that he wasn't in the courtroom, since defendants weren't allowed in a grand jury hearing. If he'd been sitting there, it would have been so hard . . .

But his attorney was there, and as he cross-examined her, she tried not to back up or stumble, tried not to sway at all or deviate from what she'd told them at first. When he suggested that she'd had a crush on Soames, she knew her repulsion was apparent on her face. He'd then gone on to badger her about inviting him to dinner—apparently Gretchen at work had testified before her—but his merciless bullying of her had only made him look like another monster, and her a victim suffering further abuse.

By the time they dismissed her, she was weak and exhausted. And the first person she saw outside the courtroom was Larry.

Needing his strong shoulder, she wilted into him, and he slid his arms around her and let her cry. "Are you okay?"

"Yeah," she whispered. "It was just . . . I don't know if they believed me. His lawyer was putting so many lies into their heads." She wiped her eyes and stepped back. "Will you wait with me until they give the verdict? I don't think I can stand to be by myself right now."

"Sure," he said, unable to deny her such a simple and heartfelt request. "I'll wait."

It was a couple of hours before the DA came out of the court-room and found them sitting together. "Well, we have some good news and some bad news," he said.

Melissa looked up, bracing herself. "Was he indicted?"

"Yes, he was," he said. "But the bad news is that the judge let him out on $100,000 bond, pending trial."

Melissa sprang up. "He did *what*?"

"I'm sorry, Melissa. I tried my best to convince him that it would be dangerous to let him out, but he said that it could take a year for it to come to trial, and he didn't want to lock him up for that amount of time."

"He's getting out? When?"

"Probably today," he said.

Feeling as blindsided as she did by this, Larry stood up beside her. "Melissa," he tried, "you know he'd be crazy to come near you. He knows what the consequences would be."

"He *is* crazy! Don't you people get it? He's going to come after me!"

"No, he won't," the DA said. "The judge laid down very spe-cific instructions. He told him he'd throw him back in jail if he so much as thought about you."

"This man doesn't care what a judge told him!" Melissa insisted, starting to cry. "I'm telling you, this is a big mistake! He could kill me the next time!" She headed back toward the court-room. "Where's the judge? I have to talk to him!"

Larry grabbed her arm. "Melissa, you can't. There's nothing you can do. But I agree with Sid. I don't think he'll bother you."

"You don't *think*?" she shouted. "Well, what if you're wrong?"

Jerking away from him, she turned and ran toward the door that would take her into the parking garage. Helpless, Larry just let her go.

She spent the rest of the afternoon hunting for a new place to live, then packing all of her belongings and moving. The move would wipe out her savings. And she hadn't yet found another job. But it was the only way she could evade the man who would kill her if he found her.

Now, in her new apartment in a building several blocks away from her old one, she found herself still uneasy. As night had fallen and she'd made the last trip from her old apartment, she'd had the uneasy, panicky feeling that someone was watching her.

She locked the dead bolt, checked every window, then sat on the couch, her back straight, eyes darting about. It *was* safer, she told herself. Much safer. Too afraid to sleep in her bed, which sat right below a window, she tried to sleep on the couch, curled up in a fetal position.

And all night, she clutched a knife in her hand.

CHAPTER NINE

Across the street, in a phone booth that gave him a perfect view of the second-floor window of Melissa's new apartment, Edward Pendergrast, alias Soames, dialed the long-distance number he'd gotten from information. Keeping an eye on the window, he waited for it to ring once . . . twice . . . three times.

"Hello?"

It was the just-awakened voice of an older woman, probably in her fifties, and he got a mental picture of her right away—martyred, long-suffering, self-righteous. It pleased him to death to bring her in on this now.

"Hello?" she said again.

"Mrs. Nelson?" he asked.

"Yes."

"Is this the Mrs. Nelson who's the mother of Melissa Nelson?"

"Yes," she said tentatively. "Do you know my daughter?"

"Do I know your daughter." He chuckled then, and looked back at the window. "Yeah, I'd say I know your daughter. Listen, I need to get in touch with her. Can you help me?"

The woman hesitated. "Well, I'd be happy to give her a message for you."

"I'd rather call her myself," he said.

Again, hesitation. "Would you like to leave a message? I'll get it to her tomorrow."

He grinned. She probably didn't know that her daughter had just moved. Wouldn't she be surprised to hear why? "Yeah, okay. Give her a message. Tell her an old friend called. She'll know who it is."

"Uh—may I tell her your name?"

"Just tell her that," he said. "Tell her I've been looking for her."

"Would you like to leave a number?"

He smiled. "She knows how to reach me."

He hung up then, and laughed out loud at the conversation that was probably taking place between Melissa's parents. Her father would probably grill her mother over and over on what had been said, then convince her that it had no significance. It was just some prankster. Within minutes, they'd roll over and try to get back to sleep.

But they wouldn't get a lot of sleep tonight.

His grin faded as he stepped out of the phone booth and crossed the street. If there was a weakness in that building, he would find it. And tomorrow, he'd have a huge new surprise for her.

The phone rang again, startling Nancy Nelson awake for the second time that night. She looked over at her husband, who was squinting to read the clock. "Three A.M.," he said.

She reached for the phone. "Hello?"

"Hi. Me again."

It was the voice of the man who'd called earlier—the old friend of Melissa. Covering the phone, she whispered, "It's the same person."

Jim sat up.

"Did you give Melissa my message?" the deep voice asked.

"No," she said. "It was late. I'll tell her tomorrow."

"That's okay," he said. "I've found her."

Something about the way he said that sent chills down her spine. "What do you mean, you've found her?"

"If you talk to her, Mrs. Nelson, tell her that she can't hide."

She caught her breath, and Jim snatched the phone away. "Who is this?" he shouted. "What do you want?"

"Ask Melissa," he said. "She knows what I want."

They heard a *click*, then a dial tone.

Jim got up and turned on the lamp.

"What are you doing?" Nancy asked, getting out of bed and reaching for her robe.

"Calling Melissa," he said.

"But it's three A.M. You'll wake her."

"I don't care," he said. "Something's wrong. She needs to know about this call."

Nancy went to sit beside him on the bed, and he reached for her hand and held it in a reassuring grip as he waited for Melissa to answer.

The ringing was interrupted by three ascending tones and an operator's voice. "I'm sorry. The number you have dialed has been disconnected . . ."

He slowly lowered the receiver. "Disconnected," he said. "Where is she?"

Nancy raked her hand through her hair. "Jim, you don't think—"

Jim got up and went to the closet, flicked on the light. "Get dressed. We're driving down to St. Clair."

"But it's 400 miles!" Nancy said, reaching for the phone. "I'm calling the St. Clair police. She may need help now."

Jim nodded. "If only we knew some of her friends to call. People she works with."

He waited as she got the St. Clair police on the phone and asked them to check on Melissa. When she hung up, she was just as troubled as she had been when she'd called.

"What did they say?" he asked.

Nancy shook her head as she began to get dressed. "They said they'd go check on her and ask her to call us. And they advised us not to make the 400 mile trip until we'd tried to reach her at work. But tomorrow's Saturday, and even if she does have to work, she won't be in for another five hours. Something could happen to her before that."

Nancy threw some clothes into a suitcase while Jim closed and locked the windows. Keys in hand, Jim grabbed the suitcase. "We'll stop at a pay phone and call home every hour or so and see if the police have left a message on our machine," he said.

"Okay," Nancy agreed. Grabbing her purse, she dashed out behind him to the car.

CHAPTER TEN

The next day, tired from the fitful sleep of the night before, when she'd stirred at every noise—ever aware that she had no phone hooked up with which to call for help if he somehow found her—Melissa went to a pay phone and had the telephone at her new address hooked up with an unlisted number. They gave her the new number and told her it would be on later that day. While she was at the pay phone, she called her parents to tell them her new number.

No one was home, so she left a message, explaining that she'd gotten aggravated at her landlord because of a leaky sink, and had moved to a new apartment. She had also taken a new job, she lied—to keep them from trying to reach her at work—and she'd let them know soon what that number was.

Then she set out to make truth out of her lie, checking the want ads for a job.

It was nine o'clock when the Nelsons pulled over to a pay phone for the fifth time since leaving home and called home for messages. Jim caught his breath when he heard Melissa's voice. "It's her!" he told his wife. "Listen."

Nancy put her ear next to his and listened to their daughter's explanation. Her voice sounded calm, not troubled, and everything made sense. She would be out this morning, she told them, but would call them tonight after her phone was turned on and update them on everything.

As Jim hung up the phone, they fell into each other's arms, laughing with relief. "She's okay!" Nancy cried. "She's fine."

"Now what?" Jim asked. "We're only a couple of hours away from St. Clair. Should we go on? Maybe she needs help moving."

"She didn't leave her address," Nancy said. "We wouldn't know how to find her. Besides, there's no need to let her know how badly we overreacted. Let's just go back home and wait until she calls tonight."

Jim thought that over. "I guess you're right."

The two parents got back into their car and headed back the way they had come.

Melissa managed to find a job doing clerical work for a chemical company, a job that didn't pay very well, but which seemed to be located in a safe place. It was a plus that they would let her start Monday. The sooner, the better, she thought.

It was almost dark when she got home and checked her phone to see if it was on yet. It was, so she dialed her parents' number, then cradled the phone between her ear and shoulder as she began to unpack one of her boxes.

"Hello?" Her mother's voice was always a sweet sound.

"Mom? It's me."

"Melissa, thank heaven! It's so good to hear your voice. We tried calling you last night, but the operator said your phone had been disconnected."

"Didn't you get my message this morning?"

"Yes, but until then . . ." She let her voice trail off and sighed. "Well, we're just glad you're all right. After those phone calls, we were beside ourselves."

Melissa frowned. "What phone calls?"

"Some man called last night. He was really kind of scary. At first he said he was an old friend, but I don't think he was a friend at all."

Melissa could feel the blood draining from her face, and she slowly sat down. "Mom, who was the man?"

"'An old friend' was all he said. We were going to come down and look for you, but then we got your message this morning. Melissa, are you all right?"

She clutched the phone so tight her knuckles were turning white. "Mom, what did he say?"

"The first time, he just asked us if we knew how he could get in touch with you. He said he was an old friend, but he was a little rude, calling so late. But we wouldn't give him your number. Then he hung up, and a little later he called back and told me that he'd found you. He said to tell you you can't hide. Melissa, do you know who he is?"

Melissa swallowed hard, and her heart began to race. He knew who she really was, she thought frantically. He had called her parents.

He had figured it out.

"Melissa?"

She tried to steady her voice. "Mom, it's this guy I worked with." She stopped, tried to regroup her thoughts and manufacture the story as she went. "He kept coming onto me, and when I wouldn't go out with him, he got a little hostile." She closed her eyes and tried to stop trembling. "He's harmless, really. Just annoying. Whatever he says, just ignore it."

"So hostile that you had to change your phone number, your address, your job?"

Her hand was trembling so hard she could hardly hold the phone. Maybe her explanation had been too frightening. She'd have to tone it down. "I told you why I moved, Mom. The manager wouldn't fix my sink. And the job . . . well, it just wasn't what I wanted. None of it had anything to do with him. Mom, did he say anything else?"

"No," Nancy said. "But, Melissa, what is this about your hiding? What was he talking about?"

Dizziness washed over her, along with an overwhelming feeling that she wasn't alone. She looked around slowly, warily, as if he were in the apartment somewhere, listening to this call.

"Melissa?"

"Yeah, Mom. Uh . . ." She tried to backtrack through the conversation, to give the response her mother needed. "I don't know what he was talking about. I told you, he's just some idiot. Probably drank too much and thought he'd get a good laugh." She knew her voice was trembling, and she was giving away too much, alarming her mother.

"Melissa, are you sure you're all right? Maybe you should come home for a while."

"No, I can't, Mom. I have to stay."

Her mother was crying now, and she could hear the subtle difference in her breathing, the grainy sound to her voice. "But this is how it happened before…"

As hard as she'd tried to shelter them from this, she was causing them grief anyway.

"Melissa?" Her father had taken the phone, and Melissa knew she couldn't hide anything from him without a Herculean effort. Trying to sound upbeat, she said, "Hi, Dad."

"Honey, I want you to tell me the truth. Is something wrong? Are you in some kind of danger?"

"No," she said. "Really. Everything's fine. I just moved yesterday, so my phone was disconnected. Dad, those phone calls—they're just a guy at work." As she spoke, she broke into a sweat. Slowly, she walked into the bedroom, looked nervously around, then cautiously checked the closet. "It's really no big deal. His pride is hurt because I wouldn't go out with him…" The bedroom was empty, so she walked out of it, crossed the living room, and went into the kitchen.

"Melissa, I got a recording device today. I'm going to tape the calls from now on. Maybe you should too."

"Just relax, okay? Stop worrying. I have everything under control."

"Melissa, does this person have something to do with why you moved so suddenly?"

She hated lying to her parents, but she had no choice. "No. I told you. My sink was stopped up, and the manager wouldn't fix it. I got fed up and moved. No big deal."

The kitchen was clear, so she headed for the bathroom. "Dad, I love you. Tell Mom I love her, too. And calm down. I'm sorry about the calls, but they really don't mean anything."

"All right, honey. But if we get any more calls, we're going to …"

She stepped cautiously into the bathroom as her father continued to talk. The shower curtain was closed, and she couldn't remember closing it herself. Her heart began to palpitate, and her

407

blouse began to stick to her. Clutching the phone tighter, she grabbed the edge of the curtain and jerked it open.

Empty.

Breathing a sigh of relief, she turned slowly around and leaned against the sink. This was crazy. He couldn't know where she was. He couldn't know *who* she was. It was just a coincidence. The caller was someone else.

"Melissa, did you hear me?"

"Yes, Dad. You said if you got any more call—"

Her voice stopped cold as she looked up and saw the writing on her mirror, big red letters made with the lipstick she had left on the sink that morning. She gasped and jumped back, and her throat constricted.

"Melissa? What is it?"

She couldn't speak, couldn't breathe, couldn't think. For a moment, she only stared at the words, bold and big:

Next time for real.

In a high-pitched, breathless, wavering voice, she managed to get the words out. "Dad, I've got to go. Bathtub—overflowing—"

She turned the phone off and dropped it, then grabbed her purse and her keys and fled the apartment.

CHAPTER ELEVEN

arry was eating a TV dinner and watching the news when a sudden banging on his door startled him. He grabbed his gun, which he'd laid on the table, and approached the door quickly but cautiously, sliding along the wall.

Through the peephole he saw Melissa and threw the door open.

Sobbing hysterically, she grabbed him and spoke so rapidly that he could barely understand her. "Help me! He was there. In my new apartment. I don't know how he found it, but he was in there. He wrote on my mirror, Larry! I'm not safe anywhere!"

He pulled her in and made her sit. Kneeling in front of her, he tried to calm her. "Tell me again. Who was there? Soames?"

"Yes!" she cried. "I moved yesterday, but he found me." She grabbed both of his arms. "He was in my apartment, Larry! He wrote in lipstick on my mirror. And he's been calling my parents! I don't know what to do. There's no place to go!"

Larry got up, pulled on his shoulder holster, slipped his gun into it, then put his windbreaker on. "All right, let's go back over there, and you can show me. What did he write?"

"He wrote, 'Next time for real.' I don't know what he means, Larry. But how could he have gotten in? Nobody knew where I was. Not even you!"

"All right. I'm gonna call Tony and have him meet us there. If we can find proof that he was in your apartment, we'll have him picked up again. This joker's going back to the slammer until his trial."

She was a wreck, Larry thought as they drove back to her building. What if he'd been in her apartment while she was home? What if he was still there now? Would he be that bold? That stupid?

Tony was waiting in his car when they drove up, and he got out and met them at the curb. Melissa was shaking and staring up at the window to her apartment.

"She says he was there," Larry said quietly. "Left a message on her mirror, in lipstick."

"Would he be that reckless?" Tony whispered.

"Looks like he was." He turned back to Melissa. "If you want to wait in the car—"

"No!" she said quickly. "I don't want to be by myself. I'm coming with you. I'll show you where it is."

They opened the door quietly and carefully—not wanting to disturb any fingerprints he might have left—pulled their guns, and went in. Melissa waited by the front door as they searched the apartment. Satisfied that he wasn't there, they came to the bathroom. "Was it in here?"

"Yes," she said, hanging back. "On the mirror."

There was a moment of silence, then Larry asked, "Did you clean it off?"

"What?" She abandoned the front door and went in to see for herself.

The mirror was clean.

"No, it was there! Right there, in big letters!" She gasped and backed out of the bathroom. "Oh, no—he was back! He came back while I was gone. Or maybe he was here all the time! Larry, you have to believe me! He's playing games with me. He was here! Dust for fingerprints! You'll see."

But she could see that Tony didn't believe a word, and Larry looked troubled and confused. "Melissa," Larry said, "are you sure you didn't clean it before you came over? You were upset. You might have—"

"No! I was on the phone with my father, and I dropped the phone. See? Here it is." She picked it up off the floor. "And then I ran out." She turned to Tony. "Please, I'm telling you—he was here. You have to pick him up. You have to get him back in jail, or he'll kill me."

"Is that what it meant—'Next time for real'?" Larry asked. "That he would kill you next time?"

"It must have," she agreed quickly. "And how did he get in here? The windows are all locked. I had the door dead-bolted. And how did he find this apartment? He must have been watching me when I moved out—stalking me."

Tony looked at the mirror again. "Is this the lipstick you said he wrote it with?"

She nodded, and Tony picked up the tube with a piece of tissue, opened it, and rolled the lipstick up. The tip was flat, as if it had been used for writing. Even so, Tony shook his head. "It doesn't make sense. Why would he risk coming back to clean it up? Why would he risk doing it in the first place, when he knows he's the first person we'd think of?"

Melissa felt herself trembling with fear and frustration. "Detective Danks, if I were lying about this, I'd have just written something on there myself, and it would still be there. And anyway, why *would* I lie about this? Why would I set myself up to look like a lunatic? I'm telling you, it happened. He came in, he wrote on my mirror, and then he came back—or maybe he was here the whole time. Only—I looked in every room before I saw the mirror. He wasn't here."

Larry left the bathroom and began looking around the apartment. After a moment, he said, "Tony, come look at this."

Tony and Melissa followed him. He stood at the far end of the hallway, pointing at a rectangular wooden door set into the ceiling. "It's an attic," Tony whispered.

Larry questioned Tony with his eyes. Could Soames be hiding there?

"Have you looked up there?" Larry whispered to Melissa.

"No. I didn't even know it was there."

"Do you have a flashlight?"

"Yes," she said, and ran to get it. When she came back, she saw that they were both preparing to open the ceiling door. "Stand back," Larry said, and pulled out his gun again. Tony did the same. Larry reached up and grabbed the hook on the door, and Tony held his gun aimed at it in one hand, the flashlight in the other.

In one rapid motion, Larry pulled the door down. They held their guns aimed for a moment, but nothing happened. Slowly, carefully, Larry reached up and unfolded the narrow ladder. Tony shone the flashlight through the black hole, revealing how small the space was.

Cautiously, Larry climbed the stairs, still aiming his gun, and stepped onto the board floor of the small crawl space. It was big enough for a man to sit in, he thought, though there was no sign that anyone had been here. He touched the floor, felt the dust, then had an idea. Stepping back onto the ladder so that only half his body intruded into the dark space, he shone the light around on the floor. A thick coating of dust covered it, but where he had just stood the dust clearly showed his footprints. He looked carefully around for any more disturbances in the dust.

There it was—the faint outline of the bottom of a sneaker. Beyond that was a wiped place, as if someone had slid across the floor.

"Tony, there's dust all over the place up here," he called down. "But in one place, it's wiped up. Like somebody was sitting there. And there's a shoe print in the dust."

"Let me see."

They traded places. "I see what you're talking about," Tony said, "but it could just be where the previous tenants had a box or something sitting."

"The edges aren't that clean," Larry said. "Looks to me like someone was sitting there."

Larry watched as Tony crawled farther into the attic, shining the light all around. After a moment, he came back to the opening. "Larry, come up here. You've got to see this."

Larry glanced at Melissa. She stood trembling at the end of the hallway, hugging herself and waiting. As Larry began to climb, she took a few steps closer to the ladder.

Tony was shining the light at a place on the attic floor. It was an opening around one of the inset lights in the ceiling of the bathroom. The plate that had been on the back was missing, as was the bulb, and

412

they could see through the glass covering straight into Melissa's bathroom, to the sink and mirror and the area in front of them.

"Still skeptical?" Larry asked.

Tony shook his head. "He was here, all right," he said in a voice too low for her to hear, "watching her discover what he wrote on the mirror."

"Let's dust the apartment for prints."

"Okay. But what about her? He'll be back."

"She can't stay here tonight," Larry said. "I'll think of something."

They climbed back down, then both hesitated to tell her what they'd found.

"Well?" she asked.

"It looks like he might have been up there while you were here," Larry said. "He probably left because he knew you were going to get help."

The color drained from her face. "But he'll come back! He'll come back!"

"We're going to call the ID techs to come dust for prints, Melissa. As soon as we run it through the computer and make a match, we can get him."

She waited, tense and quiet, as the apartment filled up with police photographers and ID technicians. As they dusted for prints, she sat like a little child waiting to be told her fate.

"He was probably wearing gloves," Larry said. "But maybe not."

"He's smart," Melissa said in a hopeless monotone. "He knows you need evidence. He knows what kind. So as long as he doesn't leave any, he can do whatever he wants."

"We'll pick him up anyway," Larry said. "For questioning. We'll put a little scare into him."

"But can't we just tell the judge he was here? Can't we tell him Soames called my parents?"

"It wouldn't help," Larry said. "Not unless we could prove he was here with a print match."

She ran her fingers through her bangs. "I can't stay here. I don't know where to go."

Larry looked at Tony and saw the censure in his eyes, as if he knew that Larry would jump in and rescue her. Larry didn't let it stop him.

"I could take you to a hotel for the night."

She thought for a moment. "I guess so. I'm just afraid that he'll find me there, too. I can't believe he found me this time, and so soon."

"Look, we'll send someone now to pick him up for questioning. We won't move you until we have him in custody. That way we'll know that he can't follow you."

"All right," she said. "But then what? I can't come back here."

"I'll talk to the manager about letting you put your own dead bolts on the door, so that there isn't an extra key anywhere. And we'll go around and reinforce the windows, make absolutely sure that they can't be broken into. Maybe even put up burglar bars."

"I never thought I'd wind up being a prisoner in my own apartment," she whispered.

"We'll put enough fear into him that he won't come near you. I'll even tell him he's being watched."

"You said that before. But he didn't care."

"He'll care this time. And who knows? Maybe tomorow we can find a witness who saw him around here. And the pattern of that shoe print was pretty distinctive. If we can find that shoe, maybe it'll be enough evidence to convince a judge he was here."

She nodded without much hope. "I'll go pack a few things," she said, and disappeared to the back.

Larry turned back to Tony. "All right, I know what you're thinking."

"She does have to have a safe place to stay," Tony conceded. "But try not to get too involved."

"Don't worry about it." Larry picked up the phone, dialed the station, and asked to have Soames picked up for questioning.

Melissa came back out with a suitcase, her expression strained and distracted. "You know," he said quietly, "maybe you should go home to Pensacola for a while. Spend some time with your parents."

"No, I can't," she said. "I don't want to drag them into this."

"Into what?" Tony asked.

"Into danger. If he comes after me there—" She stopped and tried to steady her emotions. "My parents still don't know about what happened to me. I can't tell them."

"But won't they hear when it goes to trial?"

She shook her head. "I haven't thought that far in advance. All I know is that they don't have to know yet."

"But if he's calling them, they already are involved."

"I told them it was a prank. I told them my sink was stopped up, and I argued about it with the manager, so I moved. That's all they need to know."

The phone rang, and Larry answered, instead of Melissa. "Yeah? You got him already? He was home?" He shot a look at Tony. "What alibi? Well, how long did she say she'd been there? Well, have you checked *her* out?"

He sighed and rubbed his temples. "Well, take them both in for questioning. And keep them separated, so they don't compare notes. Check her out, to make sure she's not lying for him. Oh, and check to see if she has a roommate or a neighbor, anybody who can confirm how long she's been gone.

"What kind of shoes does he have on, by the way? Yeah, I thought so. Get a picture and a print of the bottom of both shoes, will you? And keep him there until we get there."

He hung up, and Melissa sank down on the couch. "He has an alibi?"

"Some woman he was with. Says he's been with her there in his apartment for the last three hours. But it looks like he's got on our shoes. Anyway, they're keeping him until we can question him, so we have some time to get you to a hotel. He can't follow you."

"All right," she said, grabbing the handle of her suitcase, but Larry took it from her.

"I'll get this," he said. "Are you sure this is all you need?"

She looked around and shivered at the thought that he might have gone through her things. "No," she said. "I'm fine. Let's go."

Larry took her key and locked the door behind them.

CHAPTER TWELVE

W e've got to let him go," the officer who had picked up Pendergrast told Tony and Larry when they got back to the precinct. "The woman he was with confirmed his alibi."

Larry glanced into the room where the woman sat. She was several years older than Pendergrast, had garishly dyed hair, and wore cheap, tight clothes. She sat flipping through a magazine, swinging her foot with bored nonchalance and popping her gum. "She's not his type," Larry said.

Tony shrugged. "His type may be anything in a skirt."

"Well, I don't think he found her at that yuppie club you like so much. My guess is he's paying her to be his alibi." He turned back to the cop. "Did you tell her he's been indicted for rape?"

"Yep. She says he's innocent. It really didn't faze her."

"And she insists that he was with her? For how long?"

"Hours."

Tony leaned against his desk and thought that over for a moment. "We don't really know what time he wrote on her mirror. Even with the alibi, he still could have done that. But if Snow White here is telling the truth, he wouldn't have been there to wipe it off while she was coming to find you."

"He's lying," Larry said. "Pendergrast—Soames—whatever his name is, he's lying. And so is the woman."

"Probably. Now prove it."

"The shoe," Larry said, turning back to the cop. "You said his shoe matched the print in the attic?"

"Yeah, but I ran it by the captain. He said it was too weak. Lots of people have that shoe. It might be different if we'd gotten a match on the fingerprints. But just between you and me—" He lowered his voice and looked around to make sure he wasn't being overheard. "That lawyer, McRae, has been raising a huge stink about the department harassing Pendergrast. Says they're thinking about a lawsuit when this is over."

Larry chuckled. "Tell him to stand in line."

"Yeah, well. If it was anybody but McRae. That brutality suit he filed for one of his low life clients a few months ago cost the city a mint."

"Come on," Larry said, disgusted. "It was bogus and McRae knew it. Our guys were trying to restrain an addict so high on PCP he had the strength of a gorilla. That was by the book."

"But besides the money, the bad press hurt. The mayor already called the chief on this, Millsaps. He said if we lock Pendergrast up, it better be on something more than his shoe."

Larry groaned and glanced toward the two-way glass of the interrogation room. "Well, at least we can put some fear into him before we let him go."

McRae and Pendergrast sat talking quietly, their heads together, as Larry and Tony walked in. Pendergrast looked up at them with a smug grin. "Is there a problem, gentlemen?"

Larry propped one foot on a chair and leaned on his knee, fixing his eyes on the man who sat waiting for them to admit defeat. "We're not fooled, Pendergrast. Your little friend in there hasn't convinced us of anything."

"Fine," he said, throwing his arms open. "Then book me. What did you say the charge was? Breaking and entering? Stalking? You do have evidence, don't you? Evidence strong enough to override my alibi?"

Larry gritted his teeth. Ignoring the questions, he said, "We're gonna let you go, Pendergrast."

"Soames," the man corrected.

Larry dropped his foot to the floor and leaned over the table, putting his face inches from Pendergrast. "*I* know who you are, *Pendergrast*. You're a slimy nocturnal rodent who preys on innocent women, and I'm gonna see you put away if it's the last thing I ever do. In the meantime, leave Melissa Nelson alone. Stay away from her, or I'll personally see to it that you regret it for what's left of your pathetic little life. Got that?"

"Is that a threat?" McRae asked.

"You bet it is."

Too disgusted to stay, Larry left the room and headed for his desk. A Federal Express package sat on top of it, its return address from the Santa Rosa County Sheriff's Department. Still seething, he tore it open and pulled out the file on Edward J. Pendergrast.

Tony came out of the interrogation room, smirking as he headed for Larry's desk. "Larry, I think you hurt Pendergrast's feelings. He was downright wounded at what you called him. By the way, are rodents really slimy? I thought they were hairy, but—"

"Take a look at this," Larry cut in, unamused. "Pendergrast's file." Sitting down, he opened it.

Tony grabbed a chair and rolled it over beside him. "Took long enough."

"Yeah, but it's all here. Look at these pictures." Larry picked up one of a young woman with blackened, swollen eyes, a broken jaw, and split, bloody lips. He often saw gruesome pictures, and saw even worse horrors face-to-face at crime scenes, but he never got used to it. And brutality to women always turned his stomach.

He began reading the report. The woman who claimed Pendergrast had raped and beaten her had positively identified him. The report said that he'd been charged and questioned, but that he'd been released due to an illegal search of his apartment.

As if he'd been directly involved in the case, Larry struggled with the indignation rising in his chest.

The next photo showed a full body shot of a woman, her face bruised and cut, her eyes blackened, her lips swollen and bloody, and slashes and bruises up and down her legs and arms. Larry handed the picture to Tony and found the report. In this case, Pendergrast had been acquitted. Despite the victim's insistence that Pendergrast was the man who'd raped and beaten her, the grand jury had felt that there wasn't enough evidence to get a conviction. Anger reddening his face, Larry tossed down the report.

"How could they acquit him? Didn't they see the pictures? She gave a positive ID. How could they ignore that?"

"Apparently there were no fingerprints, no physical evidence at all that he was the one who had done it. Plus he had an alibi," Tony said, reading the report. "The only hard evidence was her identification, but they didn't believe she got a good look at him because it was dark."

"It's the way he looks," Larry said. "He looks too prosperous, too good-looking. If he were a scruffy-looking homeless man with a tattoo, he wouldn't have been acquitted." As he spoke, Larry flipped through the file and found a picture of the girl before the rape. She was pretty and blonde, smiling at the camera, looking nothing like the abused portrait after Pendergrast had made his mark. She looked like a happy young woman with a future. She had probably never even dreamed what would happen to her one day.

"Says here she killed herself shortly after he was acquitted," Tony said matter-of-factly.

"Killed herself?" Larry grabbed back the report, read of the suicide, and felt even sicker as he turned back to her smiling portrait. "What's her name?" he asked wearily.

"Uh . . . Sandra Hayden," Tony said. "She was married, no kids. About twenty-three when it happened." He looked over Larry's shoulder and studied the photo pensively. "I wonder if she killed herself because of the rape."

"Probably," Larry whispered.

Tony flipped further, until he came to the newspaper clipping of her obituary. "Married to Jack Hayden for six months," he read. "Buried in Pensacola where she'd lived all her life."

Larry looked up from the picture. "Did you say Pensacola?" He glanced at the obituary. "That's where Melissa is from."

Tony frowned, trying to put things together. "Pendergrast came from Santa Rosa County. Isn't that near Pensacola?"

"Next county over." Larry read on, intrigued but apprehensive. "Says Sandra Hayden had just started working at a department store in a mall. Noticed the guy following her days before he made a move. He broke in one night when her husband was working the night shift. He apparently beat her and left her for dead." He hesitated, swallowed, then forced himself to go on. "But she woke up after he left, showered and cleaned up everything, then passed out again from loss of blood. She never called the police. Her husband found her near death the next morning and took her to the hospital."

Tony flipped through the file, looking at the other documents. "Here's the police report of her suicide." Larry took it, scanned the contents, then shook his head and dropped it on the desk.

"What?" Tony asked.

Sometimes Larry wished he had a different job. "Her younger sister. That's who found her. She had slit her wrists in the bathtub."

"What a way to say good-bye," Tony muttered.

Larry glanced back at the room where they had interviewed Pendergrast moments ago. "We were too easy on him. He was working us. He knows the system too well."

"He must," Tony agreed. "I can't believe they let him go. We need to talk to Sandra Hayden's family. Find out anything that's not in the report. Anything about him we might need to know. Let me see the obit."

Still deep in his dismal, angry thoughts, Larry slid the newspaper clipping across the desk. "Okay," Tony said, poising his pen to jot down her parents' names. "Nancy and Jim Nelson, of Pensacola."

For a moment the name didn't sink in. It wasn't until Larry watched Tony write it that it penetrated. "Did you say Nelson?" Larry asked, reaching for the obituary.

Tony looked up, the significance of the name finally registering. "What are you thinking?" he asked.

A slow ache began at Larry's temples and spread to his forehead. He took the clipping and began to read. "Sandra was survived by both parents and her younger sister . . ." His voice broke off and the words just waited there like a live grenade.

Tony detonated it. "Melissa Nelson," he said.

Larry felt as if he'd had his body blown up from the inside out. His head throbbed, and he couldn't think.

"Oh, man," Tony said, staring at the words. "I don't believe this."

After a moment, Larry got enough control of his faculties to find his voice. "What does it mean?" he asked in a quietly desperate voice. "Pendergrast rapes and almost kills Melissa's sister. Then he comes after her?"

"Doesn't fit," Tony said, his voice growing less surprised and more excited. "*He* was here first, remember? *She* got a job working where he worked. How could he have orchestrated that?"

"Well, why would *she*?" Larry demanded. "You think a woman who'd seen her sister after she'd been left for dead by some guy would deliberately hang around with him afterward?"

Tony was in his element. This was the kind of mystery he loved to solve, the reason he had become a detective. "All right, let's look at what we've got. This happened three years ago, when Sandra Hayden was twenty-three. Melissa would have been twenty then."

"Right."

"So what *do* we know?" Tony went on, getting to his feet and pacing across the floor as he thought it all out. "We know that Melissa changed her major to criminal justice, right?"

"Yeah, so?"

"Well, maybe that was in response to the fact that the criminal justice system let her down. Or maybe it was out of anger. It's like a person with leukemia who decides to be a doctor. They want to fight the thing that has become their enemy."

Larry hated the high Tony was getting from this. And he hated even more where it was leading.

"So she gets out," Tony continued, "takes a job with the FBI, and uses the resources there to locate the guy who did that to her sister." Tony pointed at the photo.

"Now wait a minute." Larry said, resisting, getting to his feet to relieve his growing tension.

Tony shook his head. "No, listen for a minute. It's just a theory, but it fits. Let's say Melissa was obsessed with finding this guy and getting revenge. Now she knows where Pendergrast is working, what name he's using, everything. So she quits the FBI. You got to admit, that bothered us from the first."

"So you're saying she sought him out, so she could get a job working where he worked?" Larry asked angrily. "Why? To what end?"

Tony studied the picture of Melissa's beaten sister again, then brought his troubled eyes back up to Larry. "What if it was to set up another rape—one with so much evidence that he couldn't walk away from it this time?"

"You're out of your mind," Larry bit out. "She saw what he did to her sister. She would never put herself in the position of letting him do it to her."

"I didn't say she did. I said she set him up. It's the perfect revenge. He winds up getting tried for a crime that he really committed—just not to her—and gets put away. All she has to do is choreograph things a little—plant some evidence here, plant some evidence there. The truth is, this thing might have gone down just like Pendergrast said it did."

"Hold it right there." Larry leaned over his desk, seething. "Look at these pictures. This man is a monster, and you're making *her* out to be the criminal."

"Maybe they're both criminals."

"And what is her crime? Getting raped?"

"No. Lying about it." Some of the other cops were clearly listening, so Tony lowered his voice. "Look, it makes perfect sense." He got up and turned his chair backward and sat back down, but Larry kept standing. "To her, it's justice. He gets put away for something he's really done twice. She makes sure the justice system doesn't drop the ball this time. Just think about it. He probably terrorized her sister until she killed herself, and never served any time for it. Maybe Melissa wanted to set up enough evidence this time that he couldn't go free. Think about the night of the crime. She was so cooperative, so helpful. All the evidence was perfectly laid out—except for one thing. Even knowing all she knows, especially after her sister experienced all of it, she still showered before she could be examined. So that evidence was inconclusive. The doctor couldn't even say for sure there had been a rape at all!"

Larry kicked his chair, and it rolled into the desk next to his. The cop sitting there on the phone jumped. "So how do you explain the lipstick and the prints in the attic?" Larry demanded. "Do you think she set that up, too?"

Tony thought about that. "Probably not. I think Pendergrast may be after her now. If somebody set you up for something you didn't do, you'd probably want to get even, too. In fact, if he's been calling her parents, it sounds like he's put two and two together himself and figured out who she is. The 'next time for real' message could have meant that the next time, he'd really rape her. I'd say your friend is in a lot of danger right now."

Larry grabbed his chair and shoved it viciously behind his desk. "It's a theory, Tony. It's not fact. You have nothing to base it on. Just a feeling."

Tony shook his head. "I'd say, based on Melissa's relationship with one of Pendergrast's previous victims and the fact that she chose to withhold that crucial bit of information from us, I have probable cause for suspicion here. And I can get to the bottom of it, too—unless you're intent on standing in my way."

Larry clenched his jaw. "Hey, I'm in this for the same thing you are. To get to the truth."

Tony nodded. "But you're too involved with this woman. Look at you. Maybe you don't *want* to see the truth. In fact, I'd say this is disturbing you a lot."

"*You're* disturbing me!" Larry shouted. "I've never seen anyone so intent on proving the victim's the criminal. If this elaborate story of yours is anywhere close to the truth, I'll find out!"

"And how do you plan to do that?"

"I'm going to ask her," Larry said.

Tony laughed and shook his head. "Yeah. Like she's really going to confess it to you."

Larry rubbed his temples and started to pace. "I'll start with asking about her sister. She can't deny that. After that, she may tell a story that makes yours look ridiculous. Maybe it happened just like she's told us all along."

"Ask her," Tony agreed. "And then we'll measure her story against the facts, and see which one we believe."

Melissa couldn't relax or assume that Soames didn't know where she was. He seemed to know everything. He always had.

She lay in her hotel room bed, listening to the noises of people in the rooms on either side of her, their televisions blaring, their muffled exchange of voices, their footsteps going up the hallway, the ring of the elevators. All the while, she clutched a knife in her hand—and decided to buy a gun tomorrow.

As night turned into dawn, and her numb, exhausted mind registered the sun peeking between the blinds, she asked God if he was still out there somewhere.

Her only answer was silence.

"I hope I'm around when God proves to you that you're wrong." Larry had sounded so sure when he'd said that, but Melissa knew she *wasn't* wrong. There were some crimes too despicable to atone for, some people who weren't worthy of forgiveness—and she knew herself to be one of them. Not because she was evil, but perhaps because of the way she had *responded* to evil. Now she wished she didn't believe in God at all. It made the void too deep, the expectation of his wrath too dreadful, the separation from his love too gaping.

Even before that separation, though, she had lost all faith in God's ability—or willingness—to protect her. He had failed to protect others, and he would fail her as well. She needed protection, but she wasn't sure it was to be found anywhere. She was a target now—right at the center of the bull's-eye.

CHAPTER THIRTEEN

There was no answer when Larry knocked on the hotel room door, and for a moment he felt relieved. Melissa wasn't there. Maybe he could postpone this for a while. He turned to leave, then stopped. Where was she? She'd been terrified to leave the room, knowing that Soames would be back on the streets in a matter of hours.

He glanced up and down the hall, then stepped closer to the door. "Melissa," he called quietly, knocking again. "It's me. Larry."

He heard movement then, and the door cracked open. Over the chain lock, Melissa peered out. "Oh, thank goodness. You scared me to death."

She closed the door and opened the chain lock, letting him in. "I wasn't expecting you," she said. "When you knocked, I was sure he'd found me."

"We did have to let him go," Larry said.

Her skin looked pallid, and her blonde hair was mussed, as if she hadn't given it a thought all day. She wore no makeup, and her blue eyes seemed paler, more fragile. There were shadows under her eyes, and he doubted she had slept last night. He felt drawn protectively toward her, but he held back. "Have you eaten, Melissa?"

"No," she said. "I was afraid to go out, and I didn't want to open the door for room service."

"Why don't we go get something?" he asked. "You'll be safe with me."

She sighed and shoved her hair back from her face. "Well, I guess I can't stay locked up in here forever." She went for her purse and room key, then paused and looked around. "I'm running out of money, anyway. I'll have to go home soon."

He watched soberly, pensively, as she brushed her hair, then turned back to him. She looked so young today, he thought, so delicate, like a China doll precariously balanced on the edge of a shelf.

As they stepped off the elevator, she scanned the lobby. She walked very close to him all the way to his car, then she hurried to get in.

Larry was quiet as he drove her to a little restaurant where they could have some privacy and a corner table mostly hidden from the front door. Maybe she'd be comfortable there.

After they ordered, Melissa seemed to relax; he wondered how long it would last. "You've been a lifesaver, Larry," she said, clasping and unclasping her hands in front of her. "I don't know what I'd do without you."

"I'm just doing my job," he said, wanting to emphasize that before he asked what he needed to ask.

"And it's your job to take victims out to lunch?"

"It's my job to protect them." He looked down at his own hands, then added, "And to ask them questions."

She stiffened a little. "What questions?"

Larry didn't want to ask. He wanted to make her laugh instead, ease her mind, restore to her some peace. Instead, he was going to drag up the worst part of her past and dangle it in front of her like an accusation. But he had no choice. "We got the file on Soames this morning. It seems that he has a history in the Pensacola area."

He noted instantly when she averted her eyes.

"There were two other rapes," he went on.

Melissa's big, pale eyes moved back to his and locked there, waiting. Larry knew she expected what was coming, so he forced the question out.

"Melissa, why didn't you tell me that Soames had raped your sister?"

Melissa gasped—not the reaction he'd expected. "What?"

"Sandra Hayden. She was your sister, right?"

"Yes!" Melissa's face reddened, and she stared at him. "But that wasn't Soames. That was some guy named Pendergrast!"

The waitress came to deliver their food, and Larry stayed quiet until she was gone. Neither of them touched their meal. "Melissa, Soames and Pendergrast are the same guy. Are you trying to tell me that you didn't know that?"

Tears of indignation and horror filled her eyes. "Of course I didn't know that! How could I?"

"Hadn't you seen him? Didn't you know what he looked like?"

"The defendant isn't allowed in a grand jury hearing, unless he testifies," she said in a harsh whisper. "And he didn't. I never saw him in person. I saw pictures, but he had this beard, and he was heavier . . ."

That much was true, Larry thought. The mug shots of Pendergrast had looked different. Still . . .

"There are just some questions, Melissa. Like why you quit your job with the FBI to take a job as a receptionist in an office where your sister's rapist just happened to work."

Two tears escaped and ran down her face as she gaped at him. "What do you think? That I *planned* all this?"

He looked helplessly down at his food. "I just need for you to explain to me why it happened the way it did. *How* it could happen. And why you never told me about your sister."

"Because it's not the kind of thing I like to talk about!" She looked around at the other patrons, then lowered her voice as more tears ran down her face. Her lips seemed to grow redder as she got out the words. "Have you ever found your sister dead? Have you had to make that phone call to your parents? To her husband? Have you spent years wishing you could have helped her, gotten there in time . . ."

Her voice broke off, and she covered her face with both hands. Her shoulders rolled with the force of her quiet sobs, and Larry realized it had been a mistake to bring all this up in a public place. "Look, I'm sorry. I have lousy timing."

She couldn't stop crying, and Larry felt helpless. There was nothing he could do for her in the middle of a restaurant. He motioned for the waitress and asked for take-out boxes. Then, taking the bag with the boxes in it, he ushered Melissa gently out of her seat and back to his car. He set the bag on the seat, then nodded to the park across the street. "Wanna go for a walk and talk about this?"

She was still crying, and he hated himself. Doing his job had never been enough reason, he thought, for making a woman cry. He put his arm around her as they walked, and felt her shoulders shaking as more pain flooded back through her. When they'd reached a cluster of trees that surrounded a park bench, he made her sit down next to him.

"Please believe me," she cried, wiping her face with wet hands. "I didn't know that Soames and Pendergrast were the same person. How could I have known? I left Pensacola because I couldn't stand all the memories. I wanted to get away, and I thought St. Clair was a good choice. I had heard how clean the town was, how warm and friendly, and I thought maybe I could forget here."

"How did you know about the opening at that company?" he asked gently.

"It was in the paper," she said. "I answered an ad. And when I met Pendergrast, it never for a second occurred to me that he could be the same guy. Why should it? There was no indication. Maybe—maybe *he* orchestrated it somehow. He's like that. He stalked Sandy for weeks after they let him off. He drove her completely over the edge. Maybe he was following me, too, but I didn't know it. Maybe he put the ad in to lure me."

That was a stretch, Larry thought. A big one. "You weren't a secretary, Melissa. You had a degree in criminal justice. Why would he think that you'd apply for a job like that?"

"Maybe he talked to some of my friends from school. I had told them I would take a clerical job. Maybe he knew I'd gone to a couple of employment agencies looking for clerical work. I don't know."

Larry leaned his elbows on his knees. Propping his chin on his hands, he watched two squirrels darting up the trunk of a tree. It was so far-fetched, yet there was a gut-deep part of him that wanted to believe her. "You said you were a Christian, Melissa. I want to trust your honesty. I really believe that God put me on this case because you needed someone who wouldn't shoot first and ask questions later." He sat straight and looked her in the eye. "But if you're lying, this is very serious. You wouldn't take advantage of me that way, would you?"

She hesitated a moment, and he couldn't tell whether she was struggling with the lie, or devastated that he would question her sincerity. Either way, her expression grieved him.

"I'm telling the truth, Larry," she said in a dull voice. "If I'd known Soames was Pendergrast, I would never even have come to this town. I wouldn't have gone within a hundred miles of him. I'm scared to death of him. You should have seen what he did to my sister. How he destroyed her—"

She covered her mouth then and bowed under her grief, and Larry pulled her against him. This woman had so much pain inside her, he thought, more than he could imagine. To find her only sister dead, the way she'd found her—and now this.

"Tell me about Sandra," he whispered, hoping it would be therapeutic for her. "What was she like?"

"Sandy," she corrected, laying her head on his shoulder. "She was always happy. Sweet to everyone. She had been married just a few months, and they were delirious." She thought for a moment, then laughed softly through her tears. "We didn't always get along. When we were kids, we fought like sisters do. When I started wearing makeup, I was always 'borrowing' her stuff, and she could never find what she needed. When we got to be the same size, though, she started 'borrowing' my clothes. My poor mother— she was like a referee. But we always worked it out."

"Were you in her wedding?"

She smiled again. "Maid of honor. I'll have to show you the pictures. Sandy was beautiful. I always wanted to look like her. But after Pendergrast—"

Her voice broke off again, and she shook her head dolefully. "After it happened, she never looked the same. Not just the scars. I don't think I ever saw her smile again. There was this dullness in her eyes . . . like she was already dead."

She swallowed, then looked up at him, intent on making him understand. "Her husband worked nights, and sometimes she did, too. But she got off at ten that night, at the mall, and came home. She didn't know he was following her. When she opened her front door, he put a knife to her throat and pushed his way in."

Larry tightened his arms around her.

"Rick found her the next morning when he came home from work. She was almost dead from blood loss, and she had gone into shock. He got her to the hospital."

"Tell me about the hearing," he whispered.

She got that helpless look on her face again, and she stood up, paced a few feet, then leaned back against the tree the squirrels had gone up. "I'll never forget that day they decided to acquit him. Sandy fell apart. We practically had to carry her out of the courtroom. He was out on the street again, and she was petrified. Then he started making phone calls to her, laughing about getting away with it, telling her that he was free to do it again. She was so scared she quit her job, but she still saw him following her sometimes. After a while she didn't leave her house at all, just turned it into a prison for herself. She was locked in—but she wasn't convinced that he was locked out. And she just got more and more depressed, more and more terrified, more and more paranoid . . ."

"What about her husband?"

"Wonderful guy. Totally supportive, trying to help her through it," Melissa said. "He was scared, too, and started trying to prove that Pendergrast was making those calls, that he had followed her, that sort of thing, but Pendergrast was smart. They never could catch him."

A pigeon landed at her feet, pecked a little on the ground, then fluttered away, and her eyes followed it. "Sandy was a Christian, Larry, but toward the end, instead of turning to God, she just lived in fear."

Larry watched the pigeon's progress across the sky, then brought his eyes back to her.

"The attack changed her whole personality," Melissa said. She came back to the bench and sat down, wiping her tears. "Do you think a person who commits suicide can go to heaven?"

Larry looked down at the dirt, uttering a silent prayer that he'd give her the right answer. "I don't know, Melissa. I've never seen anywhere in the Bible where Jesus said that suicide was the unpardonable sin. If Sandy really believed—in her heart, not just in her head—if she truly had faith in what Christ had done for her—"

"She did," Melissa said unequivocally. "But sometimes I lie awake at night, just praying and praying that God has her with him. That there's no more pain for her. That the wounds are all healed. That she's forgiven." She stopped and stared off with a broken look. "But he has no reason to answer my prayers."

The last words were so softly uttered that they were almost inaudible, and Larry touched her chin and made her look at him. "Why not, Melissa?"

"Because I have my own sins," she whispered.

"And you don't think you can be forgiven?"

"Not for these," she whispered, averting her eyes again. "There are criteria for forgiveness, you know. I don't think I've met them."

"Just repentance," he said. "That's all."

"That's all?" she asked, almost laughing at the complex simplicity of it. "Well, that's the problem." She looked into the trees, where the wind was lapping against the leaves, and her hair began to blow into her face. Pushing it back, she said, "When I found her, I couldn't believe she had done it. That she had let him do that to her. That I let her do it to herself."

"Melissa, you couldn't have stopped her. What could you have done?"

"I was late," she whispered, fresh tears rolling down her cheeks. "I was supposed to have been there an hour earlier. But I stopped off somewhere. I didn't go when I should have. She had left the door unlocked for me. Maybe she wanted me to find her before it was too late. Maybe she didn't really want to die. If I'd just gone straight there . . ." She was sobbing now, and he pressed her head against his shoulder, wishing he could comfort her, but fearing that she would find comfort only when she was ready to receive it from God.

"Melissa, is that the sin that you think God can't forgive you for?"

"One of them," she cried. "Maybe I don't even want forgiveness. Maybe I don't even want to come close to God again. If I did . . ."

As a Christian, Larry had counseled many brothers and sisters. As a cop, he'd offered comfort before. But he'd never felt more helpless than he felt right now.

He did know one thing, though. No matter where this took him, he was ready. He just might be the only one who could point Melissa back to God.

CHAPTER FOURTEEN

Tony banged a fist into the wall of the interrogation room the next morning and muttered a curse. "You're losing it, Millsaps. You're totally losing your perspective. You need to take yourself off this case now before you get any more involved!"

"What!" Larry shot back. "Just because I'm not drawing the same deductions you are, I'm losing my perspective?"

"Listen to what you're saying!" Tony shouted. "She gives you some sob story about her sister and all these horrible coincidences, and you're buying it right down to the last word. I can't believe you! You really don't think she knew that Soames and Pendergrast were the same guy? You *really* don't think she deliberately got a job there, where he worked, so she could set him up?"

"I just think we need more evidence before we draw *any* conclusions," Larry said through his teeth.

Tony headed for the door, shaking his head, then turned back before opening it. "Know what I think? I think you're stalling. You're letting your feelings for some wounded woman interfere with your professionalism."

Larry slapped his open hand on the table. "That's not true! I'm open to any facts we can find. But the key word is *facts*. So far, all you've got is speculation. You're not open to listening to her side."

"Hey, I've got all the sympathy in the world for her," Tony said. "Her sister was brutalized and driven to suicide. I can imagine how she must feel. But she sat in front of that grand jury and told them that he raped *her*. Our job is to find out: Did he, or didn't he? And man, if he didn't, if she lied in an official hearing—"

Larry dropped into a chair and rubbed his forehead. "Look, I want the truth as much as you do. And we'll find it. We're both drawing conclusions—just different ones. You're wrong, Tony. I'm not getting too close to her, I'm not losing my professionalism—"

"Then why are you spending so much time with her?"

"Because whatever Pendergrast did to her, we know that he's probably done it to others, and we know he's dangerous. She's not safe."

Tony hesitated, then nodded. "All right, I'll buy that."

After a long moment of silence, during which neither looked at the other, Tony finally shook his head. "Well, this isn't the only case we've got on our plate. We'd better get back to work."

Reluctantly, Larry got up. But he didn't want to work on any other cases right now. Melissa's was the only one that mattered.

Melissa ventured back to her apartment the next morning, propping herself up with the hope that Pendergrast wouldn't dare come back now that he knew they were on to him. But then, that was his game. That was how he had played it with Sandy. He had always gotten around the police. He always had an alibi.

She wavered from panic to determination as she stopped on the way home and tried to buy a gun, but there was a three-day waiting period. From a pay phone, she called a locksmith to meet her at the apartment and had him change her locks. Then she had him add three more locks to the door and check out the windows. And before he left, she asked him if he'd look in her attic, just to make sure she was alone.

Looking a little perplexed, as though he were dealing with a lunatic, he did as she asked, and assured her no one was there.

The bill was more than she'd counted on, and as she sat in her living room balancing her checkbook after he'd left, she realized that her funds were almost depleted. The job she was supposed to have started today was too much of a risk, so she hadn't reported to work. Since she had gotten it on the same day that Pendergrast hid in her apartment, it was possible that he had followed her to the interview, too. Now she was faced with another job hunt, and she had to find something soon.

She changed clothes, then locked all the locks on her door and rushed out of the apartment that felt so frightening, so intimidating, and so unsafe despite the measures she'd taken. Breathing freer in the fresh air, she got into her car and headed for the nearest employment agency.

CHAPTER FIFTEEN

dward Pendergrast, alias Soames, watched from his car parked down the street as Melissa came back out of her apartment. She'd had a locksmith meet her there, as if that could deter him, and he'd laughed softly as the man had left. Did she think a new lock on the door was going to keep her safe from him, when moving to a whole different apartment hadn't worked?

She got into her car and pulled out into traffic, and he waited to let a few other cars pass, then pulled out behind her. She had gotten away from him for a couple of days, but he wouldn't let it happen again. He owed her big time.

And he always paid his debts.

CHAPTER SIXTEEN

rmed with a temporary job that started the next day, Melissa left the temporary employment agency, located in the St. Clair Mall. As she walked back through the mall toward the entrance near where she'd parked, she glanced frequently over her shoulder, feeling that someone was watching her. For a weekday, the mall was crowded. A group of teenagers—the girls dressed in black and the boys in white shirts and ties—clustered behind her, probably here to sing during the noon hour. Already, she heard another choir somewhere across the mall, singing some classical, doomsdayish song that made the hairs on her neck rise.

Determined not to let her panic drive her today as it had for the past several days, she stopped and got a hamburger, then found one of the few vacant tables and sat down to eat.

As she bit into her burger, she watched random faces in the crowd. No one seemed to be looking at her, pointing, staring. Everyone went about their own business, scurrying here and there, rushing back and forth, coming in and out.

And then she saw a man, his dark hair too familiar, his teal shirt even more familiar. She watched him walk around the food court, never looking her way. She twisted in her chair to follow him—and finally, he turned his head toward her.

Pendergrast!

Stifling the urge to scream, she grabbed her purse and pressed between the tables, toppling over a chair here and a chair there as she went, bumping into people, knocking packages out of hands. When she got to the mall exit nearest her car, she looked back.

He was gone.

She broke into a run and made it to her car. Her hands trembled as she jabbed the key into the ignition, screeched out of her parking space, and pulled back into traffic.

She searched her rearview mirror for a sign of him. Nothing.

Still, he was there, she told herself. He could see her this minute. He was nearby, somewhere, following, watching.

She headed for the police station, desperate to find Larry. Stopping in a no-parking zone, she slammed the gearshift into park and ran inside. The precinct was noisy with cops coming and going, angry prisoners, and telephones ringing on a dozen desks around the big room. She glanced toward Larry's desk but didn't see him.

Pushing to the front of the line, she asked, "Is Larry Millsaps here?"

"No," the desk officer told her. "He's out on a case."

"I have to talk to someone!" she shouted. "He's following me!"

"Who?"

"Pendergrast!" she shouted. "Or—Soames! Edward Soames. Please get in touch with Larry. He was at the mall, watching me—"

"Larry Millsaps?"

"No! Pendergrast!" She burst into tears, then, clutching her forehead, said, "Look, just ask a patrol car or someone to circle the block or something. Check out the cars in the parking lots around here. Look for his car—a dark blue Cherokee—and see if he's still following me. I'm afraid to go home."

She sat and waited for what felt like an hour. Finally, an officer told her that Pendergrast's Cherokee was parked in front of his apartment.

"Of course," she mumbled to herself as she hurried out to her car. He'd have known she'd go to the police station, so he'd have gone straight home, figuring that someone would be looking for him. But Larry would believe her.

Frantic, she drove to an electronics store and bought a caller ID device to connect to her phone, so that she'd know who was calling her before she answered. Then, from a pay phone, she called the phone company and asked them to hook her up to that service.

At least if he called her, she would have proof. If only she had access to some of the surveillance equipment they used at the FBI. But she didn't, and her money was running out.

She hurried home and locked herself inside the apartment, quickly hooked up the device, then grabbed a knife and sat on her couch facing the door, waiting for the knob to move or the floor to creak.

She had felt so relieved when the temp agency had given her a job to start tomorrow—she'd been so worried about her money running out. Now she wondered if she'd even be able to go. He was trying to terrorize her, just like he'd done Sandy. The worst part was—she was letting him.

I'm not going to let him get away with it, Sandy, she promised. *Even if it costs me everything it cost you, I'm not letting him get away with it.*

The phone rang an hour later, and Melissa checked the Caller ID and saw that the call came from the St. Clair Police Department. Quickly, she answered it. "Hello?"

"Melissa, it's Larry. I had a message that you'd been by. Are you okay?"

"He was following me," she blurted. "At the mall. I saw him."

"I talked to the officer who found his car in the parking lot of his apartment complex. It was the right car. Had his plates. And the engine was cold."

"Larry, it was him! I saw him at the food court. He's not going to leave me alone. I don't know what to do!"

"Is he still calling your parents?"

"Yes," she said. "He called a couple of times yesterday, and I keep trying to assure them that it's just a prankster. But I'm not sure they're convinced. My dad has him on tape. He express mailed the tape to me, and I should get it today. Then you'll see. Oh, and I got Caller ID. If he calls here, I'll know."

"Maybe. Caller ID can't identify calls that come from pay phones or car phones."

She sighed helplessly. "Well, what should I do? I came back here because I don't have enough money to stay in a hotel another night. I had all the locks changed. But I'm not sure that will stop him."

"He's not supernatural, Melissa. If anything happens, call me. I'll keep my cell phone with me just in case."

"Larry, I just want to lead a normal life. I have a new job to start tomorrow. It's just temporary, but it's money. If I don't get any sleep tonight . . ."

"Maybe I'll pay Pendergrast a visit. Put a little more fear into him. Let him know he's being watched."

"Can he be? Watched, I mean?"

"Off and on. But we can't spare the man-hours to put someone on him full-time."

"He knows that," she said, her voice falling to a helpless monotone. She sighed. "I'd appreciate your talking to him, Larry. It might help."

"Meanwhile, bring the tape as soon as you get it, and let me know if anything else happens."

Larry found Pendergrast's blue Cherokee in the parking lot, and he and Tony made their way up to the apartment they had searched just days before. They knocked, but no one answered.

"Now what?" Tony asked. "We can't break the door down. We don't have any evidence that he's done anything wrong."

"We have her word," Larry said.

Tony banged on the door again, waited. "He could be sleeping. Or just sitting in there refusing to answer."

"Maybe he rode somewhere with someone else. Maybe his alleged girlfriend." Larry glanced down at the Cherokee again. "Or maybe he has two cars."

"There aren't two registered to him."

Larry gave Tony a wry look. "Think that would stop him?"

Tony gave up on the door and looked back down at the parking lot. "It's possible. Maybe some of the neighbors have seen him driving something else."

"I'll take the downstairs neighbors," Larry said. "You take the ones upstairs."

Melissa hated to hear her mother cry. Worse than that, she hated to be the cause of it.

"Melissa, he's been calling over and over for the last two days. Hanging up in the wee hours of the morning, saying things like, 'Tell her I'll find her' or 'Someone has to pay.' I called the police last night, and today they found out that the calls have definitely been coming from your area. Melissa, what's going on?"

Her voice was weak when she got the words out. "Mom, he's just a jerk. I'll give him a call and tell him to stop. Maybe tell him I've given his name to the police."

"It's starting up again, isn't it? This nightmare. It's just like with Sandy. Melissa, we're worried about you. You're the only child we have left."

Melissa closed her eyes. "I know, Mom. But I'm fine. Really. I'll come home for a visit soon, and you can see for yourself."

"But you'd tell us if something was wrong, wouldn't you?"

For a moment, Melissa hesitated, wanting more than anything to share this burden with someone. But not at the cost of the pain it would cause her parents. "Of course, Mom," she lied. "Really, it's okay. Just let the machine get the phone for a while, and I'll see what I can do from this end about making him stop. Nothing to be worried about."

Her hand trembled as she hung up the phone. Edward Pendergrast had a plan, a plan that would start—and end—with her.

She went to the window and peered out at the street below, scanning the cars in the parking lot. She didn't see his Cherokee, but it could be anywhere, up the street, around the side of the building.

She checked her window locks again.

The phone rang, startling her. She checked the Caller ID, saw the words, "Out of area." Maybe it was her mother again. Her heart pounded as she picked up the phone on the second ring.

"Hello?"

"Were the windows locked nice and tight?"

She caught her breath and slammed the phone down, then looked toward the windows where she'd stood just moments before, looking down for him, checking the locks—

Trembling, she scrambled around for the note with Larry's cell phone number on it, but couldn't find it. It had to be here somewhere—

There was a sudden, metallic sound. She looked up—and saw the doorknob turning, shaking, heard the sound of some kind of gadget working in the locks. Wanting to scream but unable to find her voice, she grabbed a chair and almost leaped with it across the room, then jammed it under the doorknob. With strength she didn't know she had, not even conscious of the strain on joints and muscles, she shoved a heavy cabinet in front of the door.

Looking frantically around the room for her knife, she saw the piece of paper with Larry's number, lying where she'd been sitting. She snatched up the phone and dialed.

"Millsaps here," he said after the first ring.

"Larry, he's here," she whispered into the phone. "He's trying to get in!"

She heard the urgency in his voice. "Melissa, hang up, and call the dispatcher at 911. A squad car might make it before I can, but I'm on my way."

"All right." Melissa hung up and punched 911, but the phone went dead. Frantic, she punched some buttons and held the phone to her ear, but there was still no dial tone.

Pendergrast must have cut her telephone wire. She sat holding the phone in one hand, the knife in the other, waiting for him to come through the door.

CHAPTER SEVENTEEN

By the time Larry and Tony made it to her apartment, there was no sign of Pendergrast. But the scratch marks around one of her dead-bolt locks made it evident that someone had tried to pick it. After hearing Melissa's story—first with the phone call, then the noise at the door, then the cut telephone wire—Larry suspected that it had all been an attempt to terrorize her. If Pendergrast had wanted her, he could have caught her at the mall. And he wouldn't have warned her with the telephone call today.

But that didn't mean he wouldn't try something more dangerous tomorrow. And Larry and Tony had discovered, when they had questioned some of Pendergrast's neighbors, that one of them remembered seeing him driving an older-model gray Toyota now and then. Which strengthened Melissa's story about seeing Pendergrast at the mall.

Larry knew, now, that he couldn't leave Melissa here alone. She was terrified, and her fears were legitimate.

He paced across her apartment, watching her sit balled up in the same chair she'd been in the first night he'd met her. She'd been terrified then, too.

"She can't stay here," he told Tony.

Tony nodded, obviously concerned—something Larry found gratifying. "Melissa, why don't you go home to your parents? Lay low for a little while?"

"Didn't you hear what I told you?" Melissa asked him. "He knows where they live. He's been calling them. I'm no safer there, and I don't want to drag my parents into danger, too."

"She's right," Larry said. "She has to go somewhere where he can't find her. At least until we can catch him doing something and get him back behind bars."

Tony got up and rubbed his neck. "Shades of the Barrett case."

"What?" Larry asked.

Tony shook his head. "It just reminds me of the Barrett case." Lynda Barrett, a lawyer, had been pursued by someone as deadly, and as sneaky, as Pendergrast. In that case, too, Larry had gone beyond the call of duty to protect a lady in distress—which, as it turned out, had been necessary to save her life. Tony was beginning to agree that it might be necessary in this case, too.

"That's it," Larry said, stopping his pacing and turning back to Tony. "Lynda Barrett. I don't know why I didn't think of it before."

Melissa looked up. "Who's Lynda Barrett?"

Larry started to answer, but Tony cut him off. "What has Lynda got to do with this?"

"Her house," Larry said: "It's perfect. And she has room. We could ask her to let Melissa stay there for a while."

"Larry, you can't be serious," Tony said. "You can't call one victim and ask her to house another victim."

"Would you please stop talking around me like I'm not here?" Melissa demanded. "Who is Lynda Barrett?"

Larry sat down. "She's a lawyer who was being stalked a few months ago. Someone sabotaged the plane she owned, and she crashed—"

"Just the first of several murder attempts," Tony said, as if this proved how foolish Larry's idea was.

"And it almost succeeded," Larry continued. "But her father had died shortly before that, and he had this great little house on a secluded dead-end street. She hid out there."

"Does she still have the house?" Tony asked.

Larry nodded. "Still lives there." He picked up the phone, remembered it was dead, then hung it back up. "I'll call her on my car phone, Melissa. We'll see if she'll take you in for a while."

"But she doesn't know me. She wouldn't just take in a stranger, would she?"

Larry nodded. "She's been where you are. And besides that, she's a Christian."

"She kind of has a hobby of taking in strays," Tony threw in.

"Stray animals?"

"No. Stray people."

Melissa didn't appreciate that label. "Is that what I am?"

Larry smiled. "He's talking about Jake, the guy who lives in her garage apartment. It's a long story." He hurried to the door, then turned back. "Stay with her while I call Lynda, will you, Tony? Meanwhile, Melissa, start packing."

"How can you be so sure she'll take me in?" Melissa asked.

"Trust me," he said. "She will."

It was just getting dark when Melissa followed Larry's car onto Lynda's street. Between Lynda's house and the next one up the street was a long stretch of woods. Larry parked on the street, and Melissa pulled in behind the car in the driveway, then waited as Larry got out and walked across the yard to her car. "This house is secluded and safe," he said as she got out. "He'll never find you here."

The stress apparent on Melissa's face told him that the last thing she needed was to be thrust into a live-in situation with a stranger.

She looked toward the house. Lynda had left the porch light on, and mosquitoes buzzed around the bulb. "You won't have to be here long, Melissa," Larry said. "Pendergrast is going to screw up, and as soon as we can prove that he violated his bond, he'll be back in jail until the trial. Then you'll be safe."

"I just feel like such an intruder," she whispered. "Complete strangers, taking me in. I may even be putting them into danger."

"That's why I thought of Lynda," Larry said. "If anyone can understand your dilemma, she can. You'll see. Come on."

He reached into the backseat for her suitcase, and the door to the garage apartment opened. A tall man stepped out, leaning on two canes.

"Hey, Jake!" Larry said, laughing. "You're walking!"

"Yeah, Lynda didn't tell you?"

Larry stepped nearer to shake his hand, then looked down at his legs. "Well, she said you were a little, but I pictured a step or two now and then. I figured you were in the wheelchair most of the time."

"Nope. Got rid of the thing. I'll be jogging around the block in another month or two." Larry turned to Melissa, who seemed small, fragile, in comparison to the tall man.

"Jake, this is Melissa Nelson. She's going to be staying with Lynda, too, for a while."

"Lynda told me," he said, taking both canes in his left hand so he could shake. "Nice to meet you, Melissa. Tough times, huh?"

"Yeah," she said quietly.

"Larry probably told you we've been through them ourselves. My legs are a result of them. There was this little plane crash."

Melissa caught her breath. "You were in it?"

"Yeah. But there must have been a team of angels surrounding us, because both Lynda and I came out of it alive. Matter of fact, I'd say we both came out of it better than before."

The back door opened, and a woman with shoulder-length brown hair stepped out. Her eyes lit up at the sight of them, as if she welcomed an old friend. "You must be Melissa," she said, bypassing Melissa's extended hand and hugging her. "I'm Lynda. I was just making up a bed for you. Gosh, it'll be good having a roommate again."

"I really appreciate your taking me in like this," Melissa said.

"Have you eaten?" Lynda asked, looking down at Melissa's small frame. "Jake made a killer stew tonight. Larry, you stay, too. There's plenty for everybody."

Before Melissa could answer, she ushered them all into the house. Supper was already on the table.

An hour later, Larry could see that Melissa was relaxing. She'd been intrigued and reassured by Lynda's own story, told over supper, of being chased by a killer. Lynda explained, too, that she had housed another young woman and her child recently, and had been lonely since they had left. Even with Jake right next door, sharing meals and conversation, Lynda said she missed having a roommate. Larry knew it all made Melissa feel like less of an intruder.

Melissa walked Larry out to his car before he left. The smell of fresh-cut grass wafted on the October breeze, conveying a sense of peace and safety. Larry looked around at the trees, whispering in the night. If any cars came up this street, it would have to be deliberate and wouldn't go unnoticed. Melissa would be safe here.

"You're a genius, Larry," Melissa whispered. "Has anyone ever told you that?"

Larry laughed softly as he leaned back against his car's fender, his hands in the pockets of his windbreaker. "No, actually. They haven't. Why am I a genius?"

"Because I think I can feel safe here. I really do."

Taking her hand, he pulled her closer. "I want you to be safe, Melissa. And I want you to trust me. I'm going to get Pendergrast."

She looked away then, and he could see the weight of worry and fear she carried. It was hard for her to believe that the nightmare would *ever* end. Sometimes, he wasn't sure he believed that himself. Pendergrast had walked before. The system didn't always work.

Her blue eyes looked paler in the moonlight as she scanned the darkness. "It's kind of funny, isn't it?" she asked. "There are times like this, when the world seems so peaceful . . . so quiet . . . You can look around, and breathe in the serenity. You can almost believe that there's nothing evil out there. Anywhere."

"But then reality always hits, doesn't it?"

She sighed. "Under these same stars, Pendergrast is sitting somewhere. Or driving around looking for me. And if not me, then some other woman who thinks there's no evil out there."

He cupped her chin and made her look up at him. "Leave the evil to me, Melissa. You concentrate on the good for a while."

She drew in a ragged breath. "I don't know if I can." When he pulled her closer, she slid her arms around him and laid her head on his shoulder.

Something about that small gesture sent his heart reeling, and he touched her hair, stroking, comforting. What a feeling. This was something he'd been missing. Something he had occasionally prayed for, without expecting it to happen.

Was he losing his perspective, as Tony suggested? Or was he gaining something important? Something God had offered him?

"The truth is," she said in a whisper, "even after this is all over, and Pendergrast is locked up forever, I don't know if I can trust goodness again. I know too much."

"No," he said. "I used to think I knew too much, too. But evil is not going to prevail. That's a promise. It's in the Bible."

"But how do you see through the evil?" she asked, looking up at him. "How do you look past a sister's suicide? How do you look past rape? How do you look past that face that wakes me up in my sleep?"

"You let God fill your life with more of himself, so that he crowds Pendergrast out. You surround yourself with his goodness. When's the last time you went to church?"

She hesitated. "I haven't been since ... since before Sandy died."

"Will you go with me?"

She stepped out of his arms and turned her back to him. "I don't know if I'm ready for that."

"Why not?" he asked. "How do you get ready? There are no prerequisites."

"It's just that—I don't have anything to wear. And I haven't gone in so long."

Frowning, he turned her around, made her look at him. "Melissa, what are you afraid of? It's just church. It's a good place. It's God's house."

Again, she turned away. He waited for an explanation as she leaned back against the fender next to him. "Larry, what do you think it means to blaspheme?"

The question surprised him. "Blaspheme? Why?"

"I just—think about it sometimes. I remember reading in the Bible somewhere that blasphemy was one of the worst kinds of sins. Maybe *the* worst. And I wonder sometimes just what it is."

He shrugged, wishing he'd come more prepared. "Well, I guess it means denying the deity of Christ. What do you think it means?"

She shook her head. "I don't know. Mocking him, maybe?"

Larry tried to imagine where she was going with this. "Well, I guess that could be a form of blasphemy. Melissa, what does this have to do with your going to church with me?"

She hugged herself and took a couple of steps farther away from him, shaking her head. "I just can't, Larry. I don't think everybody belongs in church. Some people have no business there."

"The church should be open to everyone," he said. "No one should be excluded. Melissa, if you think you're tainted in some way, that God doesn't want you anymore—"

"I can't talk about this," she said, preventing what she sensed he was about to say. "Just—just accept that I'm not ready to go back to church. I can't do it. Not yet."

He let that sink in, then finally said, "All right." The curt tone of his voice made her look up at him, and the pain on her face looked so intense, so deep, that he couldn't help reaching for her again. "Melissa, I care about you. You have the most beautiful smile I think I've ever seen. It lights up my heart every time I see it. But I haven't seen it very often. I want to help you find your smile again."

She met his eyes then as tears rolled down her cheeks, and he touched her face gently and pulled her into a kiss.

It was soft, sweet, gentle, and it tasted of her tears.

When he broke it, he pulled back and looked at her again. "This isn't about police work anymore, Melissa," he whispered. "I'm taking this case very personally."

She smiled. "I don't deserve you."

He laughed softly. "Tell me about it. You probably deserve some hunk who can give you everything."

Her smile grew wider. "That's not what I meant."

He knew what she meant, and he kissed her again, this time sliding his arms around her, holding her as he had long wanted to do, only this time it wasn't for her, for her comfort. It was for him.

"I'd better go," he said finally, dragging in a deep breath and letting her go.

She smiled and looked down at her feet. "Yeah. Thanks for bringing me here, Larry."

"You'll be safe. He doesn't know where you'll be working, and he doesn't know where you live. You can relax a little. Just be careful."

"You, too," she whispered as he got into his car.

He watched her go back into the house before he started his car.

Lynda was putting the finishing touches on the master bedroom when Melissa came back into the house. "I think you'll be

448

comfortable here," Lynda said with a smile. "Paige was. She's the one who stayed here before you."

"But this is the master bedroom," Melissa said. "Lynda, I could just sleep on the couch."

"I don't sleep in here," Lynda said. "It was my parents' room. There are too many memories." She sat down on the bed with a sigh and ran her hand along the smooth bedspread. "My dad hasn't been gone long. Just a few months. I really miss him sometimes. Mom, too, even though she's been gone longer."

Melissa sat down across the bed from her, and looked around the room. On the dresser, there was a silver tray with a brush and comb, and an open box with a tie clip and a key ring. A tie rack hung on the closet door with her father's ties still carefully lined up. "You kept their things."

Lynda smiled. "Yeah. I haven't made myself get rid of anything yet. I used to hate this house and everything in it. I wanted more. And I got more. But when I lost it all, I started to realize how precious all my memories were. I guess I realized that *things* don't fill up your life."

"I have memories," Melissa said. "Of my family. My sister. We were so oblivious."

"Oblivious to what?" Lynda asked gently.

"To what was going to happen." She swallowed hard and cleared her throat. "Sometimes I wish I could go back and dwell on those memories. But the bad ones keep interfering. It's hard for me to be with my parents now, in their home. I keep remembering when my sister was there."

Larry had told Lynda most of Melissa's story, and she reached out and took Melissa's hand. "It's normal to grieve, Melissa. How long has it been?"

She shrugged. "About three years."

"Well, what's just happened to you has probably brought it all back. Stirred it all up." Lynda pulled her feet up beneath her on the bed and fixed her thoughtful, compassionate eyes on her. "It takes time, Melissa. Grief has a way of hanging on."

Melissa dipped her head, unable to meet Lynda's eyes with the intimacy of her tears.

"You'll never be the same," Lynda admitted softly. "The world will never be the same. You'll look back on your life before and it'll seem like some kind of surreal dream."

"It already does," Melissa said. "Like those fuzzy old reels of home movies. All laughter and no pain. Just a dream."

For a moment, there was a gentle silence between them, as if they knew each other well enough to share quiet together. "Larry brought you to Jake and me for a reason, Melissa. We've had to grieve, too. We've both had to plunge headfirst into a new era of our lives—whether we liked it or not. We've both survived."

Melissa wiped her eyes with both hands. "Maybe I'll be a survivor, too. Maybe there's hope."

Later that night, after she had gone to bed, Melissa lay awake trying to sort out all the thoughts in her mind. Why had God blessed her by bringing her here to Lynda, where she truly did feel safe, and cared for, and no longer forsaken?

The sweetness and mercy in it was almost more than she could bear, for she saw nothing in herself that merited it. God shouldn't even be able to look upon her, not after the shame of all the events that had brought her here.

In the darkness, she saw a Bible lying beside the bed, where Lynda had put it. Turning on the dim lamp on the bed table, she opened it. By memory—how long had it been since she had held an open Bible?—she turned to the Beatitudes in Matthew, a passage that had given her so much peace as a child. She had learned the whole passage in vacation Bible school once, but it had been years since she'd recited it, even longer since she'd read it.

Now her eyes fell on the one verse she needed to read tonight. "Blessed are the pure in heart, for they shall see God."

She closed the Bible, realizing how unpure her heart was, how far from seeing God she had come. Her heart had been tainted by events—many of them out of her control, true, but many of them well within it, and God could never be pleased with that.

Feeling the abyss of mourning and emptiness growing deeper inside her, she went to the door of the bedroom that opened onto the patio and gazed out into the darkness.

Lynda and Jake were sitting out there on a swing, snuggled up together, talking softly. It hadn't occurred to her that the two were a couple, but now, as she saw Jake lean over and kiss Lynda gently, she realized that something very special was happening between them.

Something she would probably never experience.

She went back to the big bed and lay staring at the tiles on the ceiling, remembering the way Larry had kissed her tonight. It was no longer just business, he had said. It was personal.

His interest in her sent a warm feeling spiraling through her, but she quickly quelled it and sent it away. She couldn't fall in love with Larry, and he couldn't fall in love with her. Nothing good could come from it. Only pain. Larry needed someone with a pure heart, someone like Lynda, who wasn't plagued with hatred and bitterness. Someone who didn't cling to her anger and injustice like an old, familiar—but lethal—friend.

When this was all over—when the trial ended and Pendergrast was behind bars for good—would she then be able to explore these feelings for Larry?

Something—that fatalistic voice that seemed to drive her these days—told her that she would never get that chance. Larry did have a pure heart, and the last thing he needed was someone like her in his life, separating him from God.

She turned over, adjusted the pillow, and tried to find sleep, but it wouldn't come. It wasn't the threat of Pendergrast that kept her awake. Tonight, it was the threat of what lurked inside herself. The threat of who she had become. How far she had strayed.

But that was why she was here. Lynda took in strays. Lynda, who loved Jake. Lynda, who missed her parents. Lynda, who had a pure heart . . .

There was something comforting in that, and finally, surrendering to her exhaustion, Melissa drifted into a troubled sleep.

CHAPTER EIGHTEEN

E dward Pendergrast watched her apartment until the wee hours of morning, then finally decided that she wasn't coming home. Like the other night, she had disappeared.

His mistake had been in trying to get in, but he hadn't been able to resist. Picturing the fear on her face when he had called to let her know he was watching her had spurred him to frighten her even more.

He chuckled now at the thought. When he'd gone to her door and tried to pick the lock, she'd really gone off the deep end. He had heard her calling that cop, just before he cut the line and took off. And while he was off setting up his latest alibi, she had left the apartment to hide from him.

Despite his frustration that he couldn't find her tonight, Pendergrast at least felt the satisfaction of knowing that she was terrified of him, and that she would be constantly, exhaustingly on alert, listening for sounds, vibrations, clues that he was near. He loved these mind games. If only he could see that fear on her face. That would make it complete.

Tomorrow, he thought, heading home. He'd find her tomorrow. She wouldn't be able to hide for long.

CHAPTER NINETEEN

The red Porsche that was blocking Melissa's car in had not been in Lynda's driveway last night. Melissa was sure of it. She stood at Lynda's kitchen window, dressed and ready for work, wondering who the car belonged to. The idea of someone new being here made her a little uneasy. Besides, she had to be at her new job in half an hour, and the car was blocking her way.

"Morning, Melissa. Did you sleep well?"

Melissa turned and saw Lynda, dressed in a blue business suit that completely changed her look from soft to professional. Now she looked like a lawyer.

"Yes," she lied. "I was really comfortable, thanks. You look nice."

Lynda smiled and set her briefcase on the table. "Thanks. I have to be in court this morning. I made biscuits. Are you hungry?"

Melissa shook her head. "No, I'm not hungry." She looked out the window again. "Is someone here? I mean, besides you and Jake?"

"Oh, yeah," Lynda said. "That car belongs to Jake's mother. I don't think she'll be here long. I can get her to move it if you need me to."

Melissa turned from the window. "Jake's mother drives a red Porsche?"

"Yeah, well, it's a long story." She glanced over Melissa's shoulder to the window. "Uh-oh, here they come."

Melissa looked out the window again. Jake was coming out of his apartment with an older woman with platinum blonde hair and black roots, and a cigarette in her mouth. "Brace yourself," Lynda said with a grin as she went to the door. "Doris is never dull."

Jake winked at Lynda as they came in, then he grinned at Melissa. "Hi, Melissa. I'd like you to meet my mother, Doris Stevens."

Melissa stepped toward her, extending a hand. "How are you, Mrs. Stevens?"

The woman shook with the tips of her fingers. "Oh, for heaven's sake, call me Doris," she said in a nasal twang.

"Mama's from Texas," Jake said with a slight smile. "She came to pick up her car, and decided to stay awhile."

"It's a beautiful car," Melissa said.

"My boy gave it to me," the wiry woman said. "And I got a job here, so I may not ever go back to Slapout. That truck stop is gonna have to get used to not havin' me to kick around anymore. I can be kicked around just as good here as I can anywhere in Texas. Besides, I been workin' on my tan."

Melissa didn't know how to answer; the woman's leathery complexion looked as if it had had all the sun it could stand. "It is nice here, isn't it?"

"Hot, though," Doris said. "Well, I'd love to stay and chat, but I have to meet somebody."

"Who, Mama?"

"A customer I met at the diner last night. He's takin' me to breakfast." She tossed a wave at Melissa.

"It was nice meeting you," Melissa said.

"Pleasure," the woman returned, then bounced out to the car.

They all watched through the window as Doris cranked up the sports car and sped out of the driveway.

"What was she doing here so early?" Lynda asked Jake.

"The usual," he said. "Wanted money." He opened the refrigerator door and took out a carton of orange juice.

"And you gave it to her."

He shrugged and reached for three glasses. "She's my mother," he said.

Lynda smiled and turned back to Melissa. "A few months ago, they weren't even on speaking terms. Jake doesn't want to admit it, but that Porsche was a peace offering."

"Not a peace offering," Jake said, pouring into the glasses. "Just an opening."

Melissa smiled and took the glass of orange juice Jake offered her. "I've been seeing a change in her, though," Lynda said. "Slowly but surely. I think the change in Jake has had a lot to do with it."

"Change?" Melissa asked, glancing at Jake. "You mean, your injuries?"

Jake shook his head. "Nope. She means my change of heart. A few months ago I had a lot of bitterness toward my mother. Frankly, I didn't care what happened to her, one way or the other. Now, I can actually say I love her. Of course, it makes her real uncomfortable when I tell her."

"So he told her with the Porsche."

He laughed. "I kind of thought she'd sell it and invest the money in a house or something. But she's had the time of her life driving around town in it. Truth is, it's been kind of good for me to have her back in my life. Humbling."

Lynda couldn't help laughing. "If you knew him before the accident, you'd know what an understatement that is. Jake, there are biscuits in the oven. Melissa, are you sure you don't want any?"

Melissa watched the Porsche pull out of sight, and she set her glass in the sink. "No, I really need to get going. First day on a new job."

Both Jake's and Lynda's expressions sobered, and they glanced at each other. "Listen, you be careful, okay?" Lynda said more seriously. "If you need me . . ." She reached into her purse for a card, and handed it to Melissa. "Here's my office number. Paige Varner is my secretary, and if I'm not there, she can help you."

Jake took the card and jotted his own number on it. "Or call me here. And if I'm not here, I'll be at the hospital in physical therapy."

Melissa blinked back the tears in her eyes. "You guys are so sweet. You don't even know me."

"But we know enough about you to worry," Lynda said. "You know, if you wanted to skip this job and just stay here for a while, you don't have to worry about money. Sometimes it's best just to hide out."

It sounded tempting, but Melissa couldn't forget the bills she had piling up. "That's sweet of you, but I really do need the money," she said. "Thanks anyway. And don't worry. I'll be all right."

But as she left the house, she wasn't sure that she really felt that way.

When Larry came in that morning, running late, he found Tony on the telephone, hunched over his desk with a somber look on his face. Larry had spent the past hour driving around the neighborhood of Pendergrast's apartment. He'd found several gray Toyotas that fit the description of the second car Pendergrast's neighbor had seen him driving, and he had written down the tag number of each of them. Now he was ready to check them all out.

Larry slid into his chair and turned on his computer just as Tony hung up, then looked down at his desk, obviously deep in thought. After a moment, Tony picked up the big manila envelope on his desk, pushed his chair back, and headed for Larry's desk. "What's going on?" Larry asked.

Tony looked down at the envelope he carried. "We need to talk," he said.

"Okay, shoot."

"In private," Tony said.

Something told Larry that this was going to be another one of those conversations he would regret, but he got up and nodded toward the vacant interrogation room.

Tony followed Larry in and plunked the manila envelope down on the table. It was a hot room, kept that way on purpose so that the suspects brought here would be uncomfortable. Now, Larry wished there was a thermostat they could turn down.

"What's that?" he asked, gesturing toward the manila envelope.

Tony sat down on the mahogany tabletop and looked at his friend. "It's some stuff I found out about Melissa."

Larry stiffened. "What kind of stuff?"

When Tony didn't answer right away, Larry picked up the envelope and pulled the contents out. "Her employment file at the FBI?"

"That's right," Tony said. "And her transcript from college. I ordered them a few days ago. Just came this morning. Since then, I've been on the phone with people who knew her."

Larry's face reddened as he pulled out a chair to sit down. "All right. Sounds like you have some kind of bomb to drop."

Tony slid off the table and dropped into a chair. "She's lying, Larry. Right across the board."

Larry felt his defenses swing into place. He shook his head. "Evidence," he said. "You'll need some substantial evidence to prove it to me."

"Okay." Tony reached for her college records and consulted the notes he'd taken. "I spoke to two of her professors in criminal justice at Florida State. They both said the same thing: She had an obsession with her sister's rapist. One of the professors pulled his file on her and described some of the papers she wrote for him. Check these out: One involved how to avoid dropping the ball on search and seizures in rape cases, another one was on forensic evidence to tie rapists to the crime scene. There was one on subsequent crimes of rapists who were set free; one analyzing statistical data on repeat crimes; one on profiles of known rapists, MOs, motivations—"

"Okay, okay," Larry said, getting up and walking to the two-way mirror. He stood in front of his own reflection, but didn't see it. "If your sister was raped and the guy walked, you'd be a little obsessed, too."

"One of her professors said that she showed a lot of promise," Tony went on behind him. "He's the one who helped get her the job at the FBI, and he was surprised when she up and quit just a few months later."

"She decided she didn't like that kind of work."

"He thinks differently."

Larry didn't like where this was going. He turned back to his partner. "Okay. What does he think?"

"He thinks now, and he thought then, that she had an agenda. That she was going to find this guy somehow and catch him at something. He told me all this, and I never uttered a word to him about her rape. Excuse me—about her *alleged* rape." Larry shot him a cutting look. "I just told him that she had been a victim of a crime we were investigating, and I needed some information on her."

"Still doesn't mean anything," Larry said.

"I'm not finished." Tony turned his notes around so that Larry could read them across the table. "This guy—Mark Sullivan. He was her supervisor at the FBI. She had a real peon job—

you know, entry level. He said that if she hadn't quit when she did, she probably would have gotten fired."

"What for?"

"She was caught using one of the computer systems when someone was away from their desk. Without clearance, she broke into a program that could track people by their Social Security numbers. Sullivan says he caught her himself, and asked her what she was doing. She tore off the printout, shoved it into her pocket, and told him that she had just borrowed the computer to type something up. She tried to turn it off before he could see what she was doing, but he saw the program and stopped her. Guess who she was doing a search on?"

Larry didn't want to know. He just waited for Tony to finish.

"Edward J. Pendergrast. Mark remembered because he had an uncle named Pendergrast, so it stuck in his memory. He volunteered it before I even asked. I hadn't told him anything about the case."

Larry was beginning to feel sick. "Did she find anything on him?"

"Oh, a thing or two. Like the name he was using now, where he lived, where he worked . . ."

Larry sank back down into a chair and covered his face with his hands. A siren outside blared as a squad car sped out of the garage and past the window.

Tony's voice softened as he said, "One more thing. She said she saw the job advertised in the paper. I called her boss today, and asked him. He said he couldn't remember if he'd advertised or not. He just remembers her coming in with a resumé and asking for a job. He gave me her starting date, though, and I called the news-paper. There wasn't a job advertised for that company anywhere around the time she started working for them."

"Then how did she know there was an opening?"

"He says her resumé was so diverse that she would have fit a lot of the jobs there. It just happened that someone had just had a baby and had resigned. She fit right in. Oh, and he faxed me her resumé. Here it is."

Larry took it. It said nothing about a degree in criminal jus-tice, or a job at the FBI. Instead, it listed bookkeeping, secretarial, and receptionist jobs in other towns. Jobs, he suspected, that could not be verified.

"You've been busy today," Larry said, looking at his partner with tired eyes.

"I felt an urgency," Tony said.

Larry sighed and shoved the papers back across the table. "And what urgency was that?"

Tony rubbed his tired face, putting off saying it. "Last night, when you were with her, worried about her, I could tell that this wasn't just any case. You've got feelings for her."

Larry couldn't meet his eyes.

"Now, I know that you're a Good Samaritan kind of guy, that you always go that extra mile. But I've never seen you so blinded by a pretty face. I've never seen a case where you haven't wanted to find the truth—but you just don't want to see the truth in this one. Not only are you buying into a lie, but you're letting her manipulate you."

Larry couldn't believe what he was hearing. "Tell me something," Larry said, finally meeting Tony's eyes. "Have you ever known me, in all the years we've been partners, to ever try to cover up anything?"

"Never," Tony said.

"And have I ever had a gut feeling about something, and been completely wrong?"

The door opened, and a lieutenant stuck his head in. Both detectives shot him scathing looks, and he shrank back. "Sorry," he said. "I thought the room was empty." He ducked out and closed the door.

Larry turned his angry eyes back to Tony.

"So what's your gut feeling here, Larry?"

Larry sighed. "That—that she's a good person. That she's been victimized. Violated."

Tony leaned forward, his eyes riveting into Larry's. "The question is: Was she raped?"

Larry hesitated again, perspiring a little. Phones rang on the other side of the wall, and printers buzzed. Another siren wailed by the window.

He wished he could be any place in the world but here. "So what do you want to do?"

Tony breathed a mirthless laugh. "What do *I* want to do? We're both go-by-the-book cops, Larry. It's not a question of what I want to do. If I had my way, I'd let Pendergrast go to jail for the rest of his life. With three rape arrests, the guy'll probably wind up there anyway, eventually. But we both know that's not the point here."

"Then what is the point?"

"The point is that perjury is a felony."

"No, it's not," Larry argued. "It's a misdemeanor."

"Not in a grand jury hearing, pal. It's a felony of the third degree. If Melissa Nelson sat on that witness stand and lied to a grand jury—"

Larry couldn't listen to the rest. "I'll find out."

"When?"

"Today!" he said. "Now."

"And what if you don't like what you hear?"

Larry shook his head helplessly, hopelessly. "I already don't like what I hear."

"Can you do the right thing, Larry? Because if you're in too deep with her, if your feelings are going to distort your thinking, I can take over from here. Completely leave you out of it."

"No," Larry said, swallowing back his emotion. "I can't be left out. I have to see this through." He looked up into Tony's eyes. "You don't have to worry about me doing the right thing."

But as he headed out of the interrogation room and back into the symphony of ringing phones, raised voices, and profanities flying from those being booked for assorted crimes, Larry had to ask himself: The right thing for whom?

And he prayed that God would enable Melissa to give him some answers that would clear all this up to both Larry's and Tony's satisfaction. Because if she didn't, he didn't think he'd be able to live with himself—regardless of what he chose to do.

CHAPTER TWENTY

The temp agency had assigned Melissa to a busy insurance company. She had been hired to collate and staple what seemed like thousands of booklets—a big step down from the jobs she was qualified to do. But she felt safe in her little cubicle at the back of the big room.

It wasn't quite eleven when her supervisor buzzed her. "There's someone here to see you, Melissa."

Clutching the phone to her ear, Melissa stood up and peered over her cubicle. "For me? Are you sure?"

"Positive," the woman said. "He's been waiting awhile because no one knew who you were. Listen, if you need to take lunch now, go ahead."

She hung up and tried to see over the cubicle again. There were too many people—she couldn't find him. But a terrifying certainty overwhelmed her as she reached for her purse.

Pendergrast had found her.

Was he waiting to surprise her in front of an office full of people? To cause her to react hysterically and to lose this new job? Was this part of his game?

She rushed out of her cubicle, looking for a back exit. Maybe there was one she didn't know about near the rest rooms. She started toward them, walking as fast as she could, rounded a corner in the hallway—and someone grabbed her arm.

She gasped and swung around.

Larry let her go as though she had burned him. "Melissa—it's me."

461

Tears sprang into Melissa's eyes as she fell into his arms. "Larry! I thought you were Pendergrast. I thought he had found me."

"Shhh. It's okay. How would he have found you?"

"The same way you did," she said. "How *did* you, anyway?"

"I went by your agency," he said. "But my badge carries a lot of clout. He doesn't have one."

She took in a deep breath and wiped her face. "You scared me to death."

"I can see that," he said. "I'm sorry. Come on. Let's go somewhere."

She held his hand and let him lead her back through the maze of cubicles to the front door.

The sunlight assaulted her, making her feel vulnerable and exposed. "I only have an hour for lunch," she said. "But I'm not very hungry." She looked up at Larry, and for the first time noted how sober he looked. "Is everything all right? Did something happen?"

He stared off into the breeze coming from the Gulf just a couple of blocks away. "Let's walk down to the beach."

They were both silent as they walked down the sidewalk that led from the insurance building to the park behind it. Ahead, Melissa could see the Gulf, blue-green and majestic. On the sand near the water, two little girls sat with their parents, giggling as they shared a picnic. They looked like Sandy and her, years ago, when there were still things to laugh about.

She looked up at Larry as they reached the edge of the beach and headed across the sand, their feet leaving indentations behind them. Larry took off his windbreaker and slung it over his shoulder, revealing his shoulder holster. He was pensive, squinting into the breeze coming off the water, watching the waves and the seagulls as though they might give him some peace.

"Larry, what's wrong? You didn't track me down at work for a walk on the beach."

Larry stopped then on a little hill of sand, and dropped onto it, setting his forearms over his knees. "I heard some things today. Things about you. They don't add up with what you've told me."

She didn't sit down. Instead, she stood stiffly over him, looking down with sad eyes. "What did you hear?"

He shook his head and avoided looking at her. "Melissa, Tony's a good cop. He digs. He doesn't leave any stones unturned. And he got some background on you. He talked to your college professors."

"So?"

"So, one of them said that you were obsessed with Sandy's rape. That that was the primary focus of all your studies. That all of your papers had something to do with what happened to her."

"That's true," she admitted. "I did try to apply everything I learned there to her case. It was my only point of reference. There were mistakes made in her case, and I didn't want to make those same kinds of mistakes when I got into law enforcement. I'm not trying to hide it, Larry—she was the main reason I went into criminal justice. The thought of things like that happening all the time was more than I could stand."

"Well, I can relate to that. I feel the same way. But—"

"But what?" She lowered herself onto the sand next to him.

"But that professor seems to think you had a plan. That you were going to get Pendergrast on something. That you were waiting to get even somehow."

Her gaze drifted to the waves lopping over the sand. "That was Dr. Jessup. He was worried about me. Thought I needed counseling."

"Maybe you did."

"No," she said. "I didn't need counseling."

"What did you need, then? Closure?"

The frown on her face betrayed her pain as she brought her eyes back to him. "What are you saying, Larry?"

He couldn't say it. Not yet. He looked away. "Tony also talked to your supervisor at the FBI. He said you were caught using a computer you didn't have clearance to use."

"Give me a break." She rolled her eyes and threw up her hands. "I sat at someone's desk and used their computer for a minute. I didn't break national security, for heaven's sake."

"He said you were looking up information on Pendergrast."

The indignant expression faded. "That's not true."

"Melissa, it is. Tony didn't ask him about Pendergrast. He volunteered it. He remembered the name."

For a moment she stared, incredulous, at him. "Oh, now I get it." Angry, she got up and started walking away.

Larry got to his feet and followed her.

"Melissa, I need answers! I need to know what you're doing."

"I reported a crime, Larry! And now people are digging into my past, trying to make sense of a few years there when nothing really did make any sense. I didn't do anything wrong!"

"Proffer hadn't advertised for that job, Melissa! How did you know about it?"

"I—I didn't! I put my resumé in a lot of places. He's the one who hired me."

"What other places, Melissa? Can you name them?"

"No!" she shouted. "I don't remember!"

"Why not? It's only been a few weeks."

She started to cry and began walking faster, but he kept up with her.

"Melissa, why did you leave your college degree and your FBI work off your resumé? Why did you make up all that book-keeping and receptionist and secretarial experience?"

"I didn't make them up, *Detective*," she said, spinning around to face him. "Tell your friend Tony he needs to dig a little deeper. I had several jobs in college. I included them all."

"But you didn't mention the FBI. Or your degree."

"I didn't want him to think I was overqualified!"

"But you *were* overqualified, Melissa. Why would you take a job like that in the same place where your sister's rapist worked?"

"Because I didn't know he was there!"

"According to your FBI supervisor, you did know. That's the kind of information you got off their computer."

She turned and began walking again, then, sobbing, she began to run. Larry kept up with her.

"Melissa, I have to know the truth. I've fought for you. I've defended you. I've taken care of you. Now you have to be straight with me!"

He grabbed her arm, stopping her, and she swung around to face him. Her face was raging red, and she smeared the tears on her face. "All right!" she shouted. "I did know he worked there. I did have a plan. I wanted to be where he was so I could watch him. No one else was doing it! I wanted to keep him from hurting anyone else!"

Trying to catch his breath, Larry took a step back and let her go. "Then why did you lie?"

"Because I knew what conclusions you'd jump to! I knew that you'd believe I set him up. I never dreamed he'd come after me, Larry. I thought I could take care of myself. I thought I was smarter than he was."

He remembered the classes he'd seen lined up on her transcript. "You *do* know how to defend yourself, Melissa. You don't get a law enforcement degree without that."

That guarded look returned, and more tears.

"Why didn't you use it on him?"

"He took me by surprise," she said. "I panicked. He had a knife."

Larry dropped his hands helplessly to his sides. "Melissa, someone heard you invite him over for dinner that night."

Crying harder, she turned away, shaking her head, one hand cupped against her forehead. After a moment, she turned back. "Larry, you saw me after it happened. You gathered the evidence. Are you trying to tell me you believe that I set all this up?"

"I think you could have," Larry admitted. "And I'm not sure I could even blame you. I'm not sure I wouldn't have done exactly the same thing, if I'd lost a sister because of some maniac."

"You think I'm lying."

He fought the tears coming to his own eyes, and looked out over the water again. The sun was directly overhead. "I don't know what to think, Melissa. I'm not judging you. I just have to know what really happened."

"I can't believe this!" She brought both hands to her head now, crying harder. "You're going to do it again, aren't you? You're going to let him go! It doesn't matter that he's followed me, broken into my house, threatened to kill me—you're going to let him keep walking free so that he can rape more women! How could you?"

One part of him wanted to shout that he couldn't, to pull her into his arms and hold her until her crying subsided. But that other part, that part that had been a cop for too long, that part that had sworn to uphold the law, battled with him. "Melissa," he said, his voice growing raspy with emotion, "if you set him up, you're denying his civil rights. That's a crime, too."

"As much a crime as *rape*?" she screamed. "What about *my* rights, Larry? What about my sister's rights, or the other woman he raped? Why is it that all anybody cares about is that monster's rights to go out and terrorize to his heart's content, over and over and over?" She dropped back onto the sand and covered her face with her hands, and Larry sat beside her.

After a moment of watching her cry, he put his arm around her and pulled her against him. She shook with the strength of her weeping, soaking his shirt, but he didn't care. He could understand some of what she felt. But he wasn't sure that understanding would change anything.

"Melissa, I'm not the only one asking questions," he whispered. "Tony's a good cop. A go-by-the-book detective, like me. I took a vow to uphold the law—and that means never covering up a violation of it, even when there was a good reason for it."

"So what do you want to do, Larry? See me go to jail? Is that what this is about? Put the victim in jail, so the criminal won't be harassed anymore? Some justice."

"No, of course that's not what I want. I just want the truth."

"The *truth* is that Edward Pendergrast is a malicious, brutal rapist and that he deserves to live the rest of his life in prison. That's the only truth I care about, Larry. Please don't help him get out of this."

That answer didn't satisfy him. He needed more than a rationale—he needed an honest denial. But he had pushed it as far as he could, considering that there was still a part of him that didn't want to know the truth if the truth would hurt Melissa Nelson.

"I need to go," she said, wiping her face and getting to her feet.

"We didn't eat," he said.

"I'm not hungry."

He got up then, brushing the sand off his pants. She didn't say a word as they walked back to the office.

The silence was devastating. Larry was afraid that this good thing, the thing he had thought was a gift, was fast being taken from him, and he didn't know what to do. He'd never been so confused.

When they reached the building, she went in without a word, without a backward glance. And Larry, feeling more dismal than he'd ever felt, went back to his car, trying to decide where he would go from here.

CHAPTER TWENTY-ONE

The building was hazy with smoke, and some wailing country song blared on the juke box. At the bar, several cops from Larry's precinct sat over their beers, commiserating about the day's events. Larry spotted Tony among them and wondered once again what his partner saw in this place.

He cut through the happy-hour crowd and reached Tony at the bar. The bartender looked up. "What'll you have?"

"Nothing," Larry said. "I'm not staying."

Tony glanced up at him. "Must be good, to get you in here."

"I was looking for you," Larry said. "What do you say we go have a bite? Talk."

Tony reached into his pocket, pulled out a couple of bills, and tossed them on the bar. Then, bidding good-bye to some of the others, he followed Larry outside.

The fresh air washed over them, and Larry took a deep breath. "That's real similar to how I picture hell," he said.

Tony chuckled. "You know what they say. One man's heaven—"

"They don't say that," Larry said irritably. "No one ever said that."

Tony got into the passenger side of Larry's car and waited for his partner to get in. "So what's going on?" Tony asked as Larry slipped behind the wheel. "I waited for you to come back all afternoon. Where were you?"

"I had some thinking to do," Larry said. "You could have reached me if you needed to."

Tony kept his eyes on his partner. "Did you talk to her?"

Larry didn't answer right away. Instead, he cranked the car and pulled out into traffic. For a moment, he was quiet.

"Bad news?"

Larry hesitated, then said, "Just suppose—"

Tony moaned. "Larry, police work is not about supposing."

"Yes, it is. To get where we're going, we have to start somewhere. Just suppose that Melissa did lie about part of it."

"All right. Which part?"

"Well, maybe she did know that Pendergrast worked there. Maybe she deliberately got a job there so she could watch him, follow him, that kind of thing. Maybe she figured she could put her law enforcement know-how to work."

"So her job was sort of like an undercover detective?"

"Yeah. Only she was her own client."

Tony's eyes narrowed. "Is that what she told you?"

"I told you, this is supposing. Can you just suppose for a minute?"

"All right," Tony said. "I'm listening."

"Suppose it backfired, and Pendergrast came after her. She expected to be able to defend herself if that happened, but she froze. This man, who had terrorized her sister and her family, who had become this huge monster in her mind, finally came after her, and she couldn't use any of what she knew."

"She knew she shouldn't shower. But she did. How do you explain that?"

"Trauma," Larry said, his face turning red. "Maybe she was so traumatized—"

"She wasn't too traumatized to tell us details about Pendergrast, where we could find the evidence we needed, and what we needed to do to make sure he didn't get off on a technicality."

Larry got quiet again.

"Besides, Larry, when she testified before that grand jury, she didn't tell them any of what you're suggesting. She never said he was the one who had raped her sister. She never said she had hunted him down to catch him at something."

"She wasn't asked, Tony. If this is what happened, she didn't lie on the witness stand. No felony was committed."

"No, it wasn't. *If* this is what happened. But if it's not—if she wasn't really raped, if she really set out to set him up by claiming he did, then she did lie. Did you talk to her or not?"

"Of course I did."

"And?"

"And I believe in my heart that he attacked her. I believe that she is telling the truth about that. And if she only lied about the other part, I guess the question is, what difference does it make? She wasn't under oath when she talked to us about her job and how she got it. She was afraid of how it would look to us if we knew the truth. She knew how apt we were to blame the victim."

"You should start writing screenplays, man. You've got a great imagination."

Larry slammed his hand on the steering wheel. "Why *couldn't* it have happened that way? Why are you so intent on making her out to be the criminal here?"

"And why are you so dead set on defending her?"

"Because I don't think she'd lie to me, Tony. I think when it came right down to it, she couldn't do it."

"She already lied to you, Larry. More than once. How do you know this latest story is the truth? I told you she was manipulating you. What did she do, Larry? Tell you she's in love with you? Make you think that you have a future with her, if you just overlook the obvious?"

"No!" Larry shouted. "As a matter of fact, she isn't even speaking to me right now!"

"Good. Maybe you'll have time to get your head clear."

Larry turned his car around and headed back to the bar where he'd found Tony. Pulling back into the parking space in front, he waited for him to get out.

"You're not going to let this woman ruin our partnership, are you?"

Larry didn't even look at his best friend. "That's up to you, man."

Without another word, Tony got out of the car and slammed the door behind him.

Justice, Melissa thought. Everything she'd done had been done in the name of justice. She lay in her bed in Lynda Barrett's house that night, staring at the ceiling and wondering what Larry was going to do next. Would he turn her in? Would he make her out to be the criminal, just because she had tried to set things right when no one else had cared? The police had let Sandy down, and then the court system had made a mockery out of the whole ordeal. They had torn the heart out of her sister, leaving her without even the will to live.

So Melissa had taken matters into her own hands. She had tried to provide justice when no one else was offering any. But they would never understand.

She got up and went to the glass doors overlooking the patio, and stared out into the night. Lynda and Jake had gone to a movie, and they weren't home yet. They had invited her, but she'd been too upset. This was eating at her, just as it was eating at Larry.

He had wanted her to go to church with him. Was that because he knew how far she'd drifted from God?

She stared up at the stars, searching them, as though she could see God's face, angry and dark, looking down at her. Shivering, she closed the curtains and went back to bed.

But she couldn't hide from him, and her sins shone out like neon signs under God's heaven.

She'd read, many times before, "'Vengeance is mine,' saith the Lord." But she hadn't trusted his vengeance, so she'd tried to provide it herself. Now she could neither face God nor hide from him. Now, when she needed him most. Now, when she was most afraid.

She hugged herself and hunched over, crying again. There had been a time when she could pray as if Christ sat in the room next to her, and he would answer. He had always answered. But after Edward Pendergrast stalked and terrorized her sister, Melissa's prayers had been answered with "No." At least, it had seemed that way. Pendergrast had simply walked away from punishment; what kind of vengeance was that? God had not struck him dead, or made sure that he was locked up. Sandy had been the one to die, instead.

She lay back on the bed, balled up and crying into the pillow. Would God ever forgive her for not trusting him, for taking things into her own hands?

Then she heard, whispering in the back of her mind, the question that reached to the root of the problem. Was she sorry? Would she repent?

No, she thought, sitting up suddenly and wiping her tears away. No, she couldn't repent. She couldn't face the consequences of that choice.

Nor, she realized, could she face having Larry turn her in. But if she left things as they had been this afternoon, he might. She needed to do something.

Maybe, if she just explained to him what she had done and why, he would understand. Maybe he would see that she was right to do what she'd done, and that he had to keep quiet and let things run their course.

Maybe he would even protect her.

Trying to calm herself, she stumbled to the phone and dialed his number.

"Hello?" His voice was deep, quiet, distant.

"Larry?" Her voice broke, and she tried to get control. "Larry, it's Melissa. I was wondering . . . could you come over here? To Lynda's? I really need to talk to you."

He was quiet for a moment. "I'll be right over," he said finally.

She hung up and got dressed again, then sat on the edge of the bed, waiting. *Please, God, let him understand*, she prayed, but then she realized the absurdity of her prayer. Even God didn't understand. She couldn't call on him to be her ally now.

Maybe he had turned his back on her forever.

I need you, anyway, Lord, her heart cried out. *Can you forgive me if I don't repent?*

The answer was clear, inscribed deeply into her heart from years of Sunday school as a child. God only required two things of his sinners. Confession and repentance. It was a simple thing, yet it had never held such dire consequences. She couldn't confess it to God, because if she repented, Pendergrast would walk. Instead, she would confess it to Larry, hoping to make him see the necessity in what she'd done.

Tell him the truth, explain it all—since he'd already figured it out anyway—and plead with him to keep quiet. He had feelings for her, she knew, just as she had feelings for him. Maybe he would support and protect her.

Before long, she heard his car in the driveway and met him at the door. Though Lynda had stressed over and over that she wanted Melissa to make herself at home, Melissa didn't feel right bringing her own company into the home when Lynda wasn't there. So she led him back to the patio and sat down across from him, aware of the look of anticipation in his eyes, the look of hope, as if he expected her to tell him the magic words that would make this whole nasty mess go away.

"I couldn't just leave all this hanging," she said finally, looking down at her trembling hands. "Too much isn't adding up, and you're not stupid. Neither is Tony."

She saw the look of dread fall like a shadow over his face, then she looked away as she said, "You were right. I did know that Pendergrast worked at Proffer Builders. I did deliberately seek him out."

Larry opened his mouth, instinctively wanting to help her, to give her an easy out, to tell her that he believed that she had been working "undercover" to catch Pendergrast at something, and that her plan had backfired when Pendergrast came after her. There had been a rape, and she had not been able to defend herself. Those facts would mean that she hadn't lied to the grand jury, and she would be cleared. But Larry the cop couldn't suggest those facts. Because if they weren't the truth, it would offer her another lie. She had to say it on her own. *Please say it*, he thought.

"I couldn't believe it when they let him go, Larry, and he still knew where Sandy lived, and he was calling her and our parents and saying things . . . Oh, we couldn't prove it was him, but we knew. And Sandy lived in fear. She saw him in crowds, in traffic, in every public place she ever went. And at night, she'd lie awake, listening for him. I don't think she had one good night's sleep after her rape." She stopped, tried to compose herself, then went on. "I found her on a Thursday afternoon, in the bathtub. It was . . . the most awful . . . sight I've ever seen. For six months, I was a basket case. I stayed out of school for a whole year, just grieving and trying to cope with what I'd seen. It still haunts me."

She looked fully at him now, saw the mist of tears in his eyes. "Larry, I had to *do* something. I promised her that day, as I sat there holding her limp hand while I waited for the ambulance." She breathed in a sob, and tried again. "I told her that if it was the last thing I ever did, I'd see that man behind bars for the rest of his life. And I set out to do just that."

She still hadn't incriminated herself, Larry thought. It could still turn out to be what he'd suggested to Tony. It could still be something he could deal with. He waited.

"But Pendergrast disappeared. Just moved one day, and left no forwarding address. I didn't know where he'd gone, and neither did anyone else. It was time for me to go back to school, so I changed my major to the thing that interested me the most—not because of the nobility of the profession, but because it failed so often. I wanted to find out why, and how those failures could be avoided. I knew that I'd get him one day, and when I did, I wanted the system to work. I couldn't allow any mistakes."

"I can understand that," Larry said.

"So I got out, and my first order of business was to find him. I was offered the job at the FBI, and it seemed like a good opportunity to track him down. As soon as I did, I quit and came here."

"And you got a job where he worked."

"That's right," she said weakly.

"Why, Melissa? What did you hope would happen?"

"I wanted to get all the evidence I needed on him—enough to put him behind bars for good this time."

"But he was acquitted. They weren't ever going to try Sandy's case."

"Exactly. So I had to make sure there was another one."

So you followed him and watched him? he wanted to prompt her. *You tried to catch him at something, only he came after you instead?* But he couldn't ask. He couldn't give her that story. If she would just say it on her own . . .

"What did you do, Melissa?"

She got up then, unable to look at him, and walked to the edge of the patio. "I decided to make myself the sacrificial lamb."

"No," he said, his heart plummeting. She didn't mean what he thought. She couldn't.

She turned back to him. "I knew the only way I could make sure I got everything on him I needed was to be his victim." Seeing the look of horror on Larry's face, she took a step toward him. "But it's not what you think. I wasn't really going to let him touch me. I just wanted it to look like he did."

"You did set him up." The words came out in a moan, and he stood and faced her squarely. "Is that what you're telling me?"

She was crying now, and her face twisted. She covered it for a moment, then dropped her hands. "Larry, I was desperate. You have to understand. It was the only way."

"How did you do it?"

"I—did invite him over—and I was terrified. I had planned to have him come in for a while, touch some things, get his fingerprints all over the place. But I lost my nerve, and when he got there, I told him I didn't feel well, and I'd give him a rain check. He got mad and pushed his way in—"

"By force." Larry latched onto those words, thinking maybe, just maybe, Pendergrast *had* done something. Maybe she hadn't lied about all of it. Not the important part.

"Well, not for long. I had a knife, and I threatened him with it. He finally just backed off and left."

Larry's stomach sank. "But your apartment . . ."

"I did all that," she said. "I turned over tables and furniture, broke glasses to make it look like a struggle."

He turned away. "What about the cut on your leg? What about the blood on his shirt in his car?"

She waited a long time before answering that one. "He had an extra change of clothes at work. I took his shirt that day, and got the knife out of his drawer. I cut my hand and got blood all over the shirt, then wrapped the knife up in the shirt and stuck them under his seat. And I got some of the hairs out of the brush he kept in his desk, and put them on my sheets. That night, before I called the police, I cut my leg. Then I showered. In case I was examined, I knew there wouldn't be any physical evidence, and a shower would explain that. And then I called the police, and as I waited, I started to cry, deeper and harder than I had even when I found Sandy dead. I don't think I've ever been more miserable in my life, but I also felt—I don't know—justice. That, finally, something was being done."

She clutched her head as the memory came back. "It was supposed to have been easy. They were supposed to arrest him, put him in jail, take him to trial. The evidence was so conclusive that no jury could have acquitted him. But I never counted on getting involved with a cop who could see right through my story."

Larry sank down into his chair and rested his face in his hands.

"Larry, it could work! Don't you see? He's raped two women, and one of them is dead—and those are only the reported cases, the ones we know about. If he goes to jail because of this, it'll be justice—finally."

Larry looked up at her with a helpless expression. "The defense will crucify you, Melissa. He knows you lied. He knows who you are now. He'll tell them everything you did. They'll find as much evidence as we have. You'll never get away with it."

"But I might!" She sank down next to him and touched his face with her trembling hand. "They won't believe him. Even his own lawyers won't. I'm not asking you to cover up, Larry. I'm just asking you to be quiet. Just don't tell anyone what you've found. Now that I've explained it all, you must understand. Haven't you ever had a case where the end justified the means?"

His face was a study in misery as he stared at her. "Melissa, if the police force operated with that philosophy, we wouldn't even have a court system. We'd just go around shooting everybody who looked guilty. I've always gone by the book. I believe in the system."

"That's because it's never failed you!" she shouted. "Your sister didn't *die* because of it! If she had, you'd have done exactly the same thing!"

He got up again, putting some distance between them, and paced across the patio, rubbing the back of his neck. "I understand why you did it, Melissa. But it's still wrong. You can't plant evidence. You can't lie to a grand jury."

"He had already raped, Larry!" she shouted. "They let him go!"

"But he didn't rape *you*!"

Silence screamed across the night, and she looked up at him with pleading eyes. "If you turn me in, Larry, *I'll* be the one punished, and he'll walk away scot-free. Again! Is that right? You swore to get criminals off the streets. Well, I'm not the criminal, and he's still walking the streets!"

His face twisted with pain as he looked down at her, and finally he sat down next to her and cupped her chin with his hand. "Don't you understand? Even if I did keep quiet, Tony's an inch away from going to the captain with what he knows. Everyone's going to figure it out."

"No, they won't!" she cried. "They may think they've figured it out, they may suggest it in court, but they can't prove it! The jury will just think they're grasping! Another case of the victim being made to look like the criminal." She rose up on her knees and grabbed his arms, making him look at her. "Larry, it could work. The man who raped my sister and caused her to kill herself could be convicted. All I'm asking you to do is *nothing*. Just leave it alone. And get Tony off the track. Come up with a story. You can do it."

He looked at her, saw the goodness, the determination, the torture in her eyes. He had vowed to bring her smile back, but instead he was threatening to send it fleeing forever. His convictions began to wane, and he wondered what would happen if he did just what she was asking—nothing. Maybe Tony would buy the story he'd already suggested tonight. Maybe no one would ever have to know.

God will know.

That voice inside him, the one that always warned him when he began to stray, startled him.

"I'm a Christian," he said. "I don't know if that means a whole lot to you, but it does to me."

"I know," she whispered. "But God promised that he would not leave the guilty unpunished. Maybe this is his way of punishing Pendergrast."

"You know it isn't," Larry said. "God never asks us to sin to accomplish his will. God didn't tell you to lie, or to set up a crime, or to pretend that you're a victim—"

"I *am* his victim!" she cried. "The day my sister died, I became his victim. God knows that!"

"You can't hide behind God on this one, Melissa. And I can't hide this *from* him."

"I'm not asking you to. This is between God and me. Leave it at that. This doesn't have to compromise your faith. God won't blame you for it."

"Melissa, if you believe that," he said sadly, "you're farther from God than I thought. If I lie for you, or cover up, or even withhold information, I'll be accountable. My relationship with Christ depends on *my* heart, not yours. And if I make a choice that I know is apart from his will . . ." His voice cracked, and he couldn't go on.

She covered her mouth again and caught a sob, and she rested her forehead on his knee. He touched the back of her head, then bent down to kiss it. Misery overcame him, blinding him, scorching him, and finally, he whispered, "I've got to go. I have a lot of thinking to do."

"Yeah," she whispered, raising her head. "I guess you do."

She followed him to his car, and before he got in, he lingered there for a moment, looking at her with sad, soft eyes. He reached up and touched her wet cheek, and she set her hand on top of his, held it there for a moment. Finally, he leaned over and kissed her, sweet, long, and sad.

"I'm sorry, Larry," she whispered.

"Yeah," he said, squinting against his own tears. "Me, too."

She watched as he got into his car and pulled out of the driveway. In her heart, she knew that he would never kiss her again.

CHAPTER TWENTY-TWO

Larry sat on the edge of his bed, staring at the floor as if the facts lined up on it like ceramic tiles.

Fact. He had sworn to get criminals off the street.

Fact. Pendergrast had been charged with two other rapes.

Fact. Pendergrast had managed to beat the law and was still on the streets.

Fact. Pendergrast had broken into Melissa's apartment, called her, and stalked her.

Fact. Pendergrast had threatened to fulfill the lies she'd told about him, and his history indicated that he would do just that.

Fact. Tony knew that something wasn't right in the case.

Fact. Melissa was guilty of lying before a grand jury.

Fact. The penalty for that lie was up to five years in prison.

Fact. Larry was falling in love with her.

That final fact made him cover his eyes with his hand and fall back onto his bed. Tony had warned him. He was getting too involved, too close. He was letting her influence him. Maybe he wasn't even thinking straight.

Even so—could he honestly take the chance of sending her to prison?

He fell to his knees beside his bed and cried out to God to help him with this lose-lose decision—this choice that shouldn't be a choice at all.

He had never meant to care about her, but she had seemed so alone.

He felt God's love, radiating through him like sunlight on a July day, and he knew that love was for Melissa, too. God had a plan for her. But what if it wasn't one that Larry could live with?

"She'll go to prison if I tell what I know!" he cried out to God. "With hookers and drug addicts and thieves. She's so little—she'll never survive.

"And Pendergrast will go free—again! He'll hurt others. You know he will, Lord. That can't happen. He raped Sandy. Lord, help me understand . . ."

His prayer went on into the night, pleading with God, reasoning with him, wrestling with him. The options, both his and God's, whirled through his mind, exhausting him with choices and possibilities, absolutes and shades of gray.

And by the time dawn intruded on the room, Larry had made the choice that he knew he shouldn't make, the choice that would protect the woman he loved. The choice that would be a lie. Wearily, he cried out to God again, "Please forgive me for what I'm about to do!"

But a shadow fell over the room as he spoke, for God wasn't listening anymore. Already, there was a barrier.

Already.

Feeling empty and angry, he got to his feet, exhausted, troubled, miserable, and tried to sort out what he needed to do. He would go to the station and tell Tony that Melissa had confirmed the "supposing" he had done last night. He would say that she had worked undercover to catch Pendergrast at something, but that the tables had turned and he had come after her instead. Her plan had backfired, and she'd been made a victim.

And then he'd call in every favor Tony had ever owed him to convince him to let Larry call the shots on this case. Tony would listen. He'd have to.

Melissa would only have to answer to the DA for not telling everything from the beginning. It would look bad for her, but it wouldn't land her in jail. And any jury would believe it.

Whatever the outcome, it was better than telling the truth.

He showered and got dressed, playing the story over and over in his mind. Tony would believe him. It would make sense. And

Tony would never in a million years think that Larry would lie. Not even for a woman.

His spirits remained deflated as he went around the apartment straightening up, keeping busy so that he wouldn't think about principles, or values, or his relationship with God. And then he saw his Bible, lying open on the table where he had been reading from it yesterday. The words were suddenly threatening, whatever they were, and he couldn't bear to see them. He closed it suddenly and set it on the bookshelf where it wasn't as likely to catch his eye.

He couldn't think about what he was doing. All he could do was act—quickly—before his own convictions forced him to change his mind.

CHAPTER TWENTY-THREE

M elissa, do you think suicide keeps you from heaven?"

"Why would you ask something like that? Sandy, don't even think that. We're going to put this behind us. One day, it'll all be over, and he'll be in jail, and we'll be able to laugh again—"

"He's not in jail, Melissa. He's still out there. And I feel so dirty."

"You have to trust. You have to have faith."

"Sometimes I just don't have the patience for faith. Prayers take too long to be answered. Maybe I have to take things into my own hands—"

"What do you mean? Going after him? Hurting him somehow?"

No answer.

And then the dream changed scenes, and there were ambulances, police cars, interrogations, coroners, the crowd around the house just like it had been on the night of the rape . . .

Drama upon drama . . .

Then the dream flashed back to little girls on the beach, romping in frothing waves, laughing and splashing each other. It changed to a ballet recital, when Melissa, in awe, had watched Sandy as the star soloist in the spring production, then afterward, when the family had gone out for ice cream, and Sandy had laughed and talked nonstop about all the catastrophes backstage.

Then Melissa stood over a baptismal, watching as her sister gave her testimony, then was baptized—then stepped aside as Melissa, younger but just as touched by the Holy Spirit, did the same.

"Do you feel different, Sandy?" she asked as they climbed the stairs out of the baptismal.

"I feel clean," Sandy said with tears in her eyes. "Reborn. Like this is a beginning."

And then the dream changed again, and the baptismal was a bathtub, and it wasn't the beginning, but the end, and Sandy wasn't born; she was dead.

Melissa woke in a cold sweat, shivering from the force of emotion that had assaulted her even in the dream. Throwing the covers back, she ran to the bathroom and threw up, then sat on the floor waiting for it to happen again.

"I feel dirty, too, Sandy," she whispered. Covering her mouth, she tried to muffle her sobs so she wouldn't wake Lynda. She *was* dirty.

And she was making Larry dirty, too.

She leaned back against the wall and looked up at the ceiling, as if she could see God through it. "Why did she have to die?" she asked.

She sobbed into her knees, hugging them tightly.

After a while, she got up wearily and washed her face, dried it, and looked in the mirror. She didn't like what she saw, so she turned away.

Opening the door that went from her bedroom onto the patio, she went outside and sat on the swing, hugging her knees and looking up at the stars as if being there brought her closer to the Lord. "I've asked Larry to do something horrible," she whispered to God. She covered her face. "How could I ask him to make a choice like that? Who am I, to do that?"

Her muffled sobs came harder.

"Oh, God," she whispered. "Can you ever forgive me? Can you ever make me new again, like when I first knew you?"

Slowly, a strange peace fell over her, as though some heavenly hand were stroking her hair, whispering to her that it would be all right. And for the first time since Sandy's death, Melissa began to feel that, someday, maybe it *would* be all right.

Sliding her hands down her face, Melissa cried out, "Lord, tell me what I have to do."

She wept some more, feeling all her energy draining out of her, but into her mind crept the answer she had sought. There was only one answer.

She had to set things right—for Larry, and for herself—no matter what the consequences were. There was no one left to depend on but God. And somehow, now, she felt that she had the patience Sandy had not had to trust him. He would take care of her. He would forgive her.

She really had no choice. She had tried to do it all herself, and she had spoiled everything.

She wiped her face, tried to pull herself together, and went back into the house. Tiptoeing up the hall, she peered into Lynda's room. Lynda was in her bed, but she was sitting up, looking back at Melissa as if she'd been waiting.

"Lynda?" The word came out hoarse, raspy, on the edge of a sob. "You're awake. I hope I didn't wake you."

Lynda pulled back the covers and patted the bed for Melissa to sit down. "I thought I heard you throwing up. I went to check on you, but you were crying. Something told me you needed to be alone. But I was praying for you."

Melissa breathed a laugh. "Well, that explains it."

"Explains what?" Lynda asked softly. "Melissa, are you all right?"

Though it looked as if she wasn't, Melissa nodded her head. "I'm going to be. But I need your help."

"What do you need?" Lynda asked. "I'll do whatever I can."

"That's good," Melissa said. "Because I'm going to need a lawyer."

CHAPTER TWENTY-FOUR

arry couldn't make himself go straight to the police station that morning. Instead, he drove by Pendergrast's apartment, looking for either of the two cars Pendergrast was known to drive. The dark blue Cherokee was in its place, and after searching the parking lot in front and back, he finally found the gray Toyota, too.

Larry put his car in park and let it idle as he stared up at the apartment where a rapist slept. Had he been out prowling all night? Was he sleeping now? Some part of him—some uncharacteristic part that he didn't recognize—made him want to kick down the man's door, grab him out of bed, and beat him to a pulp.

But he couldn't do that. He had no grounds, no warrant, no just cause.

He drove to a convenience store on the corner and found a pay phone at the end of the small building. He picked up the receiver and held it for a moment, letting his forehead rest against the phone. What would he tell Melissa? That she was off the hook? That he would lie for her?

His stomach played queasy games with him as he went over the words in his mind. Finally, he dialed Lynda's number. After a few rings, Jake answered.

"Hello?"

"Jake? Larry here. Has Melissa left for work yet?"

"Maybe," Jake said. "She and Lynda are both gone. They weren't even here when I came over for breakfast. Maybe they went out for breakfast."

Out for breakfast. His heart sank. He had been up all night, struggling with the decision to lie for her, and she had hopped out of bed and gone out to eat?

It didn't matter, he told himself. He had to stick to his decision to protect her.

His face was tired and somber when he reached the police station. As usual, it was an acoustical nightmare. Even at this hour, voices were deafening as burglary suspects and joyriders brought in hours ago waited to be booked. Printers were printing, phones were ringing. Tony's computer was on, but his chair was empty.

"Where's Tony?" Larry asked one of the other officers.

The officer held a telephone between his ear and shoulder and nodded distractedly toward the interrogation room.

Larry frowned. Who would he be interrogating this early?

He walked around the wall, to the two-way mirror that allowed him to look into the room.

And his heart plummeted.

Tony sat at the table across from two women: Lynda Barrett . . . and Melissa.

"Oh, no," he whispered.

Melissa was talking nonstop, and Tony was taking notes. He saw as she turned back to look at Lynda that she was crying, and Lynda was crying, too. Lynda reached out and took her hand, and he saw her tell Melissa to go on.

She's confessing! he thought. But why? She hadn't given him the chance. Had she believed he was going to turn her in? Had she been afraid of what he might do?

He bolted around the corner and burst into the room. "What's going on here?"

Melissa averted her eyes, but Tony and Lynda looked up.

"Larry, sit down," Tony said gently.

"No," he said. "I want to know what's going on."

Tony looked genuinely sorry as he got to his feet. "Melissa called me early this morning, Larry. She wanted to meet with me. She had something to say."

Finally, Melissa looked up, her red, wet eyes locking with Larry's, and he could see in her expression that she had told everything.

"I'm sorry, Larry."

He breathed out a sad, exasperated laugh. "For what?"

Floundering, she looked back at Tony. "Tony, can I have a minute alone with Larry? Just a minute?"

Tony seemed a little more humble than he had the last time Larry had seen him, and he closed his notes and took them with him.

"Do you want me to leave you alone, too, Melissa?" Lynda asked.

Melissa nodded. "It won't take long."

The two left, and for a moment Larry just stood there, staring at her. "You told him."

"I had to."

"Why?" he asked, pulling a chair to face her and dropping into it. "Last night, I told you I was going to think about it—"

"That's why. To keep you from having to."

The words came out on an overpowering wave of emotion. "But I wasn't going to!"

Her face twisted, and she touched his face as tears rolled down her cheeks.

"I never meant to put you in that position," she whispered. "God's been dealing with me, Larry."

He covered her hand with his, holding it against his cheek. "But I was going to protect you. I could have, if you'd just waited."

"And what would that have cost you?"

It had already cost him, but he didn't tell her that. "Melissa, what's it going to cost *you*?"

She tried to look stronger. "Lynda said there's a possibility that there won't be any jail time. It's my first felony, so there's a chance I could get probation, maybe some community service. And if I do get jail time, it may not be prison." Her voice cracked, and she lifted her chin. "Just the county jail for women."

He pulled her into his arms and laid his forehead on her shoulder. "I can't stand that thought," he said.

"I'll be all right," she whispered. "I have to trust God in this, like I should have from the first."

Larry wept harder, but he couldn't tell her that it was because *he* had chosen not to trust God, had in fact deliberately turned

487

away from him, deliberately disobeyed. The fact that he hadn't actually committed the act didn't matter. He had made the choice.

"I want to thank you, Larry."

"For what?"

"For reminding me who's in control."

"But Pendergrast is still out there!" Larry cried.

"I know," she whispered. "But I finally realized last night that Pendergrast can't hide his sins from God. Anymore than I can."

Larry gazed at her, his face twisted and reddening. "You can live with that?"

"I have to," she said, wiping her eyes. "Either I believe in God's power or I don't. Sandy didn't. Maybe it wasn't her fault. Maybe she had just gotten too weak—too tired. But I do, Larry."

He crushed her against him and held her so long that he thought he might never let her go. "I love you, you know."

She smiled through her tears. "Yeah, I think I've known that for some time."

Outside the door in the noisy precinct room where people came and went, Tony leaned against the wall, a baffled look on his face. "I'm amazed," he said. "I mean, I suspected things weren't right all along, but I never dreamed she'd just walk in and confess. Why did she?"

"I suspect it had something to do with Larry," Lynda said.

"But she could have told half the truth and gotten away with it."

Lynda studied his face. "You seem almost troubled that she confessed."

"Well," he said, shaking his head. "I have to admit that I wanted to get to the bottom of it. But now, when I think that she'll be punished, and that thug is going to go free . . . It almost makes me wish I didn't know anything about the law."

Lynda sighed wearily. "I know what you mean. When she told me, I came so close to telling her to stay quiet. But that wouldn't have been right, for either of us. This is between Melissa and God. And she feels she's doing the right thing."

"You see?" Tony said, grimacing. "That's what kills me. All these things you guys do in the name of God. Does she realize she'll go to jail in the name of God?"

"She won't be going in the name of God. She'll be going because of her own wrong decisions," she whispered. "Besides, the state may decide not to prosecute."

"But if they do, she'll probably go to jail. The people in that place—" He looked around the huge room and waved his hand toward some of the criminals being charged with crimes for which they deserved punishment they probably wouldn't get. "She may not even survive it."

"She just has to trust, Tony. If she had trusted God in the beginning, instead of taking things into her own hands, none of this would have happened."

Tony had to agree with at least part of that. His gaze shifting to the interrogation room, he asked, "Did *he* know?"

Lynda shrugged. "I honestly don't know. She didn't tell me, and I didn't want to know. I don't think you really do, either. It's between them."

He moaned and looked up at the ceiling.

"But I do know this much," Lynda said. "She didn't want him to be the one to turn her in."

"Or to cover for her." Tony crossed his arms and leaned his head back against the wall. "Under normal circumstances, nothing on earth would have made Larry lie about a case. But this is different. Something about that woman. Larry hasn't been himself lately."

"Maybe he's in love with her."

"Yeah," Tony said quietly. "Maybe he is." He looked back at Lynda, who looked as tired as he felt. He wondered whether she'd gotten any sleep last night. "Sometimes I wish I'd listened to my mother and become a dentist."

She smiled. "You, too?"

The door opened, and Larry stepped out, his eyes red and glassy. Tony pushed off from the wall, and for a moment, just stood looking at his friend.

"You okay?" he asked finally.

"Yeah."

"You want me to book her, or do you want to?"

Larry struggled with the emotion so clear on his face and rubbed his jaw with rough fingertips. "You do it. But go easy, okay? Don't make a spectacle out of her."

"You know I won't, buddy."

Larry touched Lynda's arm, making her look up at him. "Do what you can for her, Lynda. Don't let her go to jail."

"I'll do my very best."

His face was losing its battle with the feelings coursing through him, so he started briskly across the room.

"Larry?"

Larry turned at Tony's call. "Yeah?"

"Where are you going?"

His mouth trembled as he tried to get the words out. "Out. Something I need to take care of. I'll be back."

"All right, buddy."

And Tony and Lynda watched as Larry fairly ran through the precinct and out the back door.

CHAPTER TWENTY-FIVE

The pain raging inside Larry was inescapable and constant. His habitual instinct to turn to God for help, for peace, seemed foreign to him now. He was angry, and there was nowhere to turn.

The bell warning that his gas tank was dangerously low kept ringing until he finally pulled over into a small parking area along a beach. He didn't know how long he'd been driving, but he figured he was somewhere in St. Petersburg. The beach was bare, for the day was overcast, just as his heart seemed to be. He left his car and walked across the sand, staring furiously out at the clouds billowing over the farthest reaches of the Gulf.

She won't survive jail, his mind railed. *She'll never make it. She doesn't know what she's doing.*

He reached a long pier that stretched over the water and started walking toward the seagulls perched on the railing at the end.

It's too much—she'll be punished, and he'll go free.

He walked faster, his sneakers making little sound on the wooden planks. The cool wind whipped harshly through his hair and flapped at his jacket. Overhead, he heard the rustle of wings as a flock of egrets settled on the railing behind him.

He reached the end of the pier, scattering the seagulls, and looked across the water to the clouds beyond. It was majestic, beautiful, but it looked like anger coming home to settle on the water.

God's anger.

Larry's anger.

He began to weep, hard and loud, his anguish catching on the wind and flying off to some unknown place where it wouldn't be heeded. "Why?" he shouted. "Why?"

But there was no answer, just the loud drumming of the waves against the shore, and the ruthless *caw* of the seagulls soaring overhead.

He ran back down the pier, across the sand, and back to the car. He slammed the door and collapsed against the wheel, his head resting on his arms.

Forsaken. That was the word. He had been forsaken. His refuge was gone, and his peace had been shattered. He was alone, by his own choice.

Gritting his teeth against the rage that it had come to this, he started the car and pulled out into traffic, pushing his car to the speed limit and beyond.

But it would never be fast enough.

CHAPTER TWENTY-SIX

It was no surprise that the state decided to prosecute, nor was it a surprise that Melissa appeared for her arraignment that afternoon with a guilty plea. The judge wasn't interested, at this point, in why she'd done what she had done. All that mattered was that a crime had been committed. He ordered a presentence investigation by the Department of Corrections, then set the sentencing for a little over two weeks away.

All of the charges against Pendergrast were dropped.

As Melissa rode home from the arraignment with Lynda, she was quiet, preoccupied. "What are you thinking?" Lynda asked. "You're not having regrets, are you?"

Melissa thought that over for a moment. "Not about confessing. But I wish I'd found another way to get him." Her eyes strayed out the window as they drove through downtown, past the Ritz cinema and the hardware store and the newspaper office, all part of the town she had never really gotten a chance to know. "He's out there. He's going to hurt more women. Maybe even kill somebody."

"You're scared, aren't you?"

She moved her eyes back to Lynda. "Wouldn't you be?"

"Absolutely," Lynda said. She reached across the seat and patted Melissa's hand. "I've been there, remember?"

"Yeah." She sighed. "I just keep thinking how much rage he must feel toward me, knowing I lied about him and set him up. A man like him—he won't just sit still for that. He'll get revenge somehow."

"Well, you're more than welcome to stay with me as long as you want. Maybe he'll just let the court system get revenge."

"The court system," she muttered. "I'll go to jail, won't I?"

"Not if there's any way I can convince the judge not to send you there. But I have to tell you. This judge, L. B. Summerfield, is the toughest one I've ever dealt with. When the DOC interviews you for the presentence investigation, you need to tell them everything. Everything about Sandy's rape, how he continued to terrorize her, how he terrorized your family—"

"Does any of that really matter?" Melissa asked. "Everybody acts like it's only what I've done that matters." She looked thoughtfully at Lynda. "Won't the fact that I recanted and confessed have any bearing on his decision? Wouldn't he be more lenient because of that?"

Lynda sighed. "I wish I could say he would. But by law, you can't use recantation as a defense—at least, not in your case. There are some cases where you can—like if you recant during the same official proceeding where you lied—but it won't work for us now. The best we can hope is that your story will be enough."

"Will the DOC be interviewing Pendergrast, too?"

"Yes, thank God. And if they have any sense at all, they'll see him for what he is."

"No, they won't," Melissa said quietly, looking out the window again. "He's too smart. Too convincing. He'll make them think he's the victim."

"They'll look at more than his story, Melissa. They'll look at his history, too. You just have to have faith." She glanced at Melissa as they rounded a corner. "Are you going to call your parents?"

For a moment, Melissa couldn't answer. "I don't know. I guess I'll have to. I mean, I can't very well go to jail and keep it from them. Part of me wants to just wait and see how the hearing comes out. But if I'm sentenced to jail time, I might not get the chance to explain it all to them, to make them understand . . ."

"Tell them before the hearing," Lynda said. "Don't leave them out of this. You're their only child. They need to know."

Melissa wiped her tears away. "I'll think about it."

"Good." They reached the outskirts of her neighborhood. "Are you going to see Larry tonight?"

Melissa's mouth twisted, and she shrugged. "I doubt I'll be seeing him anymore. I mean, I don't blame him. It's not real good for a cop's reputation to be involved with a known felon."

"Melissa, the man cares about you. He's not just going to cut you off because of this. You saw how upset he was this morning."

"Exactly my point."

"Well, if I were a gambler, I'd bet that you're wrong about him. If I know Larry Millsaps, this isn't the end."

She turned down her long street, past the two houses on the corner. When her house, set alone at the end of the dead-end street, came into view, there was a small black Chevy parked in the driveway, and Lynda smiled slowly. "As a matter of fact . . ."

Melissa only frowned, afraid to get her hopes up as they pulled into the driveway next to Larry's car. She got out, looking for him, and in a moment, the door to Jake's apartment opened, and the two men walked out.

It had been a hard day for Larry, Melissa thought. His eyes were red, like hers, and she knew he hadn't gotten much sleep last night. He'd probably been up all night struggling with the decision she had given him to make. And this afternoon, in the courtroom, he had seemed to be in worse shape than she was.

She hated herself for putting him through this. If he'd never met her, if she'd never lied, he'd still be out there doing his job, arresting people and locking them up, going to his church, and enjoying his friends—rather than suffering because of something she had done. Yes, she hated herself.

But Larry cut across the driveway without a word and pulled her into a hug that crushed life back into her.

"It'll be all right," he whispered. "Somehow, it's gonna be all right."

She began to cry against his shoulder, and she saw Lynda and Jake disappear into the house, leaving them alone.

"We have to talk," she said finally, looking up at him. "See— you don't owe me anything. What I deserve is to have you just forget you ever knew me. I would be all right. Really."

He stepped back, framed her face with his hands, and gazed intently into her eyes. "Melissa, that's not going to happen. I'm going through this with you."

"But I don't want you to," she cried. "I don't want you to have to suffer."

"But I am suffering," he said. "I'm suffering because you are. I wish I could move the clock back three years and stop what happened to Sandy, for your sake, but I can't. All I can do is be here with you now. And you have to let me."

She wilted in his arms then, allowing herself to feel the peace and comfort and sustenance he offered, the support she didn't deserve, the grace she hadn't earned. Just like God's love, she thought. For she saw Larry as a gift, sent as a light in the darkness her life had become.

They spent as much time together as they could for the next two weeks, avoiding the subject of the hearing coming up, avoiding mention of the names Soames or Pendergrast, avoiding the topic of jail or hearings, avoiding the media, who had latched onto her story like hungry dogs to a bone. Because notice of her arraignment had appeared in the local paper, Melissa lost her job with the temporary agency. That was part curse and part blessing, Larry decided, since her mind wasn't on work right now, anyway, and she needed this time to prepare. Besides, her interview with the DOC had lasted for two whole days, and it had taken a few days after that for her mental and physical exhaustion from rehashing the whole story to fade.

Larry, too, was interviewed, along with Tony and some of the other cops who'd answered her call that first night. It was apparent to him that they were trying to determine just how much damage had been done with her lie, and how calculated it was. Melissa never asked what he had told them, and when he'd tried to tell her, she'd refused to listen. He didn't owe her an explanation, she told him. But whether they spoke of it or not, the clock was ticking.

He took some vacation days the week of her sentencing, and on that Tuesday, drove her to the beach. They took off their shoes and rolled up their jeans and walked barefoot through the gentle waves at high tide. The sun was just beginning to set, and a cool breeze swept in from the Gulf, whispering through Melissa's hair, the pink-golden rays of the sun making her hair look even lighter.

She slowed her step and kicked at a wave as it frothed around her ankles, then turned toward the breeze and watched the sunset fill the sky with a brilliant array of pinks and golds and yellows. "It's beautiful," she whispered. "Look, Larry. Isn't it beautiful?"

He put his hands on her shoulders and stood behind her, watching the sky. She felt so small beneath his hands. Her head barely reached the indentation of his neck. "Yes," he whispered, kissing the top of her head. "It's beautiful."

"Let's just sit here for a while," she said. "Let's watch it until it goes down."

She sat in the white, dry sand, and he sat beside her, holding her against him as the sun made its grand finale of the day. It took over an hour for it to disappear below the horizon, and in all that time, they didn't utter a word.

Finally, when the pinks and golds had given way to a grayish blue, Melissa scooped up some sand in her hand and watched it fall through her fingers. "I have to call my parents," she said.

"Good. I hoped you would."

"It's not going to be easy," she said, still watching the sand. "In fact, I can't tell them this over the phone. I need to do it in person."

"I'm sure they'll come."

She swallowed and looked up at him. "Will you help me, Larry? Help me tell them, I mean?"

"Of course. I'll tell them *for* you if you want."

"No," she said. "They have to hear it from me. But I'm just not sure I'm strong enough. And I'm not sure they are." Her voice broke off, and Larry pulled her against him.

When she finally pulled herself together and sat up straight again, she drew in a deep, rugged breath. "Let's go. I want to call them now. Maybe they can come tomorrow, and I can spend a few days with them before the hearing."

CHAPTER TWENTY-SEVEN

Melissa had trouble getting the words out over the telephone, but she managed to tell her parents that she was in trouble and she needed them. They were already frantic after not being able to reach her since her last vague, evasive phone calls, and the cursory note she'd sent them telling them not to worry hadn't helped. When she tried to tell them where she'd been, she couldn't go on. She handed the phone to Larry.

"Mrs. Nelson?" Larry asked. "This is Larry Millsaps. I'm a friend of Melissa's."

"Is she all right?" Nancy Nelson asked with a quiver in her voice.

"What's going on there?" Jim Nelson threw in from the extension.

"Well, she'd rather talk to you in person. I gathered from her end of the conversation that you're coming tomorrow?"

"Yes. We'll get the earliest flight. We can come tonight if she needs us to."

"No. Tomorrow will be fine."

"Mr. Millsaps, tell us—has she been hurt? Is she sick?"

"No, ma'am. She's not hurt or sick. She's fine."

"But she said she was in trouble!" her mother said.

"Does this have anything to do with—Edward Pendergrast?" her father asked.

Larry looked at Melissa, then closed his eyes. "Why would you ask that?"

"Because of the phone calls. The threats. The way she's been evading our questions. All the secrecy! It's so much like it was with Sandy. Does this have anything to do with him?"

Her mother was crying now. "We've just had a feeling all this time. When that man called us . . . I kept thinking I knew that voice."

Larry put his hand over the phone and whispered, "They want to know if it has anything to do with Pendergrast."

"Oh, no." She took back the phone. "Mom, Dad? Please. This is real important, and I need to talk to you in person. All I can tell you right now is that no one has hurt me. Can you just accept that and wait until we can talk?"

"All right, sweetheart." Her father's voice cracked. "All right. If that's how it has to be."

"Will you be all right until morning?" her mother asked.

"Yes, Mom. I'm in really good hands. I'm staying with a terrific person, a new friend. And Larry's watching over me, too. I didn't mean to scare you. This is not like it was with Sandy. My trouble is of my own making."

Perplexed, her parents were silent for a moment, then finally, her father said, "We'll see you early in the morning. Will you be at the airport?"

She wished she could say yes, but the airport was in Tampa, and she had been ordered not to leave St. Clair until her hearing. "Larry will be meeting you," she said. "He'll bring you to where I'm staying. He's a tall man, about six-two, with dark brown hair . . . good-looking . . ." She smiled slightly, and Larry couldn't help returning it. "You'll like him, Mom."

"Is he someone you're seeing?"

"Yes," she said.

"Well, why haven't you mentioned him?"

"I'll explain everything tomorrow, Mom."

Her mother didn't answer for a moment. "Melissa, I'm so worried about you."

"Please try not to worry, Mom. I'll see you both tomorrow."

Larry had made it a point to drive by Pendergrast's apartment several times a day to check for both cars. If one was missing, he would call Melissa and make sure everything was all right. It didn't appear that Pendergrast had yet figured out where she was staying. Larry had found Pendergrast's car parked at Proffer Builders for the past two days, so he assumed that he had gotten his job back. Everything was back to normal for him, Larry thought bitterly. Meanwhile, Melissa had to tell her parents that she might be going to jail.

Satisfied that Pendergrast was nowhere near Melissa, he drove an hour to the Tampa airport and walked the long walk to the gate where the Nelsons would be coming in. Melissa had described them to him, but somehow he felt that he would know them anyway the moment he saw them.

The plane was just landing as he reached the gate, and he stood by the window, watching, praying silently that they'd manage to take this well. It wouldn't be easy dealing with a jail sentence for their only daughter. God certainly knew it wasn't easy for him.

He watched the passengers come out of the tunnel, searching their faces. And then he saw them. The woman's blonde hair was pulled back in a bun, revealing a little gray around the temples, but it was clear from her blue eyes and the shape of her mouth that she was Melissa's mother.

They both looked younger than he had expected, probably in their late forties, and their eyes were troubled as they scanned the crowd for him.

Slowly, Larry worked his way to them. "Mr. and Mrs. Nelson?" he asked.

"Larry?" Jim Nelson returned.

Larry smiled and shook his hand. "It's nice to finally meet you. Do you need to go to the baggage claim?"

"No," her father said. "It's all in our carry-ons."

"All right. My car's this way."

They walked in silence for a moment. Larry glanced over at them. "Did you have a good flight, Mr. Nelson?"

"Jim," he said. "Call me Jim."

"And call me Nancy," Melissa's mother said. "You're obviously important to our daughter. There's no point in formalities. Have you known her long?"

"Only a few weeks," he said.

"Oh. From what she said last night, I thought it had been longer."

"It seems like longer," he agreed. They came to the escalator, and he stood back and allowed both of them to precede him.

Not much more was said as he led them to his car. When they were on their way, with Jim in front and Nancy in back, Larry could sense Jim studying him. "I know Melissa has something to tell us, and she wants to do it herself, but can you at least tell us where she's living? She has an apartment, doesn't she? Why isn't she in it?"

"She's just been spending a couple of weeks with friends," he said. "It wasn't a good time for her to be alone."

Her mother leaned forward on the seat. "Is she living with you?"

He glanced in the rearview mirror. "No, ma'am. Absolutely not. She's staying with a friend named Lynda Barrett."

Jim looked him over again. "What do you do for a living, Larry?"

Larry hesitated to tell him. "I'm a police officer."

Jim let the words sink in for a moment, then glanced back at his wife.

"How did you two meet?" her mother asked in a voice that was growing more raspy.

He swallowed. "I'll let her tell you about that, if you don't mind."

For the rest of the hour's drive to St. Clair, no one spoke. There was nothing more he could tell them, after all, without treading on Melissa's ground.

Lynda was at work and Jake was at physical therapy when Larry brought the Nelsons to Melissa.

Her parents looked apprehensive as they got out of the car and looked around at the modest little house. The side door to the house opened, and Melissa came out. "Mom. Dad." She ran into their arms, and for a moment, Larry stood back, feeling like an outsider. But he had promised her he would stay.

When the family hug broke, she led them all into the house, and into the living room. Her mother and father huddled together on the couch, waiting for the bomb to drop. "What did you want to tell us, Melissa?" her father asked gently. "Please don't make us wait any longer."

Melissa took Larry's hand and sat down across from them. "All right." She took a deep breath, and looked up at Larry, struggling to find the words. She'd practiced all night and all morning, but now that the time had come, all her scripted words escaped her. How would she tell them?

Mom, Dad, I may be going to jail.

No, she couldn't tell them that yet. She had to start at the beginning.

She cleared her throat. "You know when I quit my job at the FBI, and you were all upset and confused?"

"Yes," her mother said.

"I quit because I'd managed to locate Edward Pendergrast." Her mother gasped, and her father's frown grew deeper. "He was working here in St. Clair under another name," she went on.

"Oh, no," her mother cried, sitting back hard on the couch. "You came here to find him? Why? You should have stayed as far away from him as you could!"

Melissa blinked back the tears in her eyes. "I got a job working where he did."

"What?" her father asked in horror.

"I wanted to set him up," she said. She got to her feet, paced across the living room, and turned back to them. "I thought if I made it look like I'd been his next victim, then this time he'd get convicted. I'd make sure that there were no loose ends. That he wouldn't get off on a technicality this time. That he'd go to prison, where he belongs."

Her father stood slowly. "Are you telling us that you pretended he'd raped you?"

"Yes," she said. "That's exactly what I did. Larry was one of the detectives assigned to the case. He's a good cop."

Her mother was starting to cry. "Melissa, how could you do that? It could have gotten you killed! No wonder Pendergrast started calling us. He was looking for you!"

"Yes, he was," Larry agreed, "and they didn't keep him in jail after his indictment. He was out pending trial."

"Oh, Melissa! Is that why you kept moving?"

Melissa shoved her hair behind her ear. Her hand was trembling. "Yes. I caught him following me a couple of times. And he broke in."

"He was in your house?" her mother whispered.

Melissa nodded. "Nothing happened. I think he was just trying to scare me."

"I brought her here because I knew he wouldn't find her here," Larry cut in. "Lynda's a friend of mine."

"But—you lied, Melissa," her father said. "Is he in on this?" he asked, pointing to Larry.

"No, Dad. The thing is, I confessed two weeks ago."

Larry braced his elbows on his knees and propped his chin on his fist. Melissa kept her eyes on her parents.

"Why?" her father asked.

"Because it wasn't right. I had lied. And lying to a grand jury is a felony."

Jim's face paled, and he sank back down onto the couch. Her mother took his hand. "A felony?" she whispered.

"The actual charge is 'perjury in an official proceeding.' I could get up to five years."

"In prison?" her father asked in horror.

Her mother's face reddened. She covered her mouth, then asked, "What about him? What about that monster?"

Larry saw how Melissa struggled with that answer, so he spoke up. "They dropped all charges against him. They couldn't try him for something that hadn't happened."

"So he's still out there?" her mother asked on a sob. "And *Melissa's* the one who might go to jail?"

Larry nodded. "Unless the judge decides to go easy on her. The sentencing is Friday."

"Only two days from now?" Nancy gasped.

"Lynda's my lawyer," Melissa managed to say in a higher pitched voice. "She's hopeful that I won't have to serve any jail time. But there's no way to know for sure until we get into court. The judge will read all the testimony in the presentencing investigation, and he'll make his decision. All we can do is pray."

Melissa watched the pain distorting her parents' faces, and she broke into a sob. "I wanted you to hear it from me. I wanted you to be here."

Both of her parents got up and drew her into a hug. They all wept as Larry sat alone, wishing he could ease their pain.

CHAPTER TWENTY-EIGHT

hursday dawned with harsh finality—the last day of life as she'd always known it. Tomorrow was Melissa's hearing; tomorrow she would find out if she had a future. She had hoped to sleep late, but she woke just after dawn and lay awake staring at the ceiling.

Tomorrow she could be going to jail.

She closed her eyes and prayed for deliverance, but even as she did, she felt the shame of deserving what she was getting.

The funny thing about God's forgiveness was that the consequences still had to be paid. Not because God necessarily required payment—but because the state did.

Not for the first time, she longed to turn back time, to forget her obsession with making Pendergrast pay. If only she had put him out of her mind and gone on with her life, tried to forget. But such a big part of her hadn't wanted to forget. Feeding her vengeful hatred had somehow sustained her. Now it was doing her in.

Tears rolled down her temples and into her hair as she stared up at the ceiling. The image of Gethsemane flashed through her mind—Jesus weeping the night before his own arrest—the disciples sleeping through it all as Larry and Lynda and Jake all probably were. She closed her eyes and thought of Christ's prayer for deliverance. She, too, had asked for deliverance—had pleaded and bargained for it. But she feared that the price of her disobedience would still have to be paid.

Getting out of bed, she pulled on her robe and went barefoot down the hall. A light was already on in the kitchen, and quietly, she stepped into the doorway. Lynda was sitting at the table reading her Bible. In her white cotton nightgown with little blue flowers, Lynda looked like a little girl, rather than a successful attorney. "Hi," Melissa whispered.

Lynda looked up. "Did I wake you?"

"No. I thought you were still asleep. You don't have to be at the office for two hours, do you?"

"No." Lynda closed her Bible and pulled her knees up under her gown as Melissa sat down. "I'm thinking about taking the morning off."

"Why?"

"Because I'm ready for court tomorrow, and I think somebody needs to get your mind off things."

"I'm okay, really."

Lynda set her chin on her palm. "I'm not sure I am."

"This puts a lot of pressure on you, doesn't it? You're worried."

"I want to do my best for you," Lynda said. "I just don't know—"

Melissa touched her hand to silence her. "It's okay, Lynda. I know you'll do your best, and if things don't work out just right, it's not your fault. It's mine."

Lynda sighed. "I know how scared you are, Melissa."

Melissa couldn't argue.

"I've been scared, too," Lynda went on. "I was just thinking about it, trying to put myself in your place. The sense of dread, of uncertainty. And I kept going back to that morning when Jake was test-flying my plane, about to buy it, and we realized the landing gear wouldn't go down. We had forty minutes to burn fuel before we landed. That gave the airport time to prepare for a crash landing, and it cut down on the fire hazard. But it was the longest forty minutes of my life."

"I can imagine."

"I haven't flown since. It's weird, because I used to fly every day. The fact that I don't have a plane anymore has something to do with that, but I had planned to rent one every now and then and get back up there. It's just been kind of hard to get back in the saddle."

"How about Jake? Has he flown yet?"

"No, not yet," she said. "He hasn't been able to get a medical release yet. He still has a way to go before his legs are a hundred percent. But I don't think he's afraid of it. I think he misses it. Just the feeling of being up there in the clouds, looking down over the world . . . you can forget everything."

"Well, maybe when you're ready, you can take him up."

Lynda looked at her for a moment, and a slow smile dawned across her face. "I just had a wonderful idea."

"What?"

"What if we all went up today? I could rent a plane, if Mike— my friend who runs the St. Clair airport—has one available. It would be a great treat for Jake, and it would help distract you and Larry."

The thought didn't appeal to Melissa. "No, you and Jake go ahead. This should probably be a private moment for the two of you."

Lynda shook her head. "The more, the merrier. Come on. Let's make a memory today." When Melissa still hesitated, Lynda leaned forward, her eyes wide, as if a thought had just occurred to her. "Unless you're scared. Maybe you don't want to go up with me after what happened the last time I flew."

Melissa laughed softly. "I trust you, Lynda. Even in a plane. I'm not afraid."

"Great. Then let's do it. I'll go call Paige and tell her to cancel my appointments for the morning."

"Are you sure?"

"Absolutely. I'll be in the shower. If Jake comes over, don't tell him what we're planning. I want to surprise him."

"What if he doesn't want to go?"

"He will," Lynda was certain. "He's been chomping at the bit to get back in the sky. Even if he's not the one flying."

The morning air was brisk for Florida, and Jake thought maybe there was hope that he'd experience an autumn here, after all. This time of year, especially during his short morning walks, he missed Texas. He'd never thought much, before, about the colors the leaves turned, the piles of leaves in the yards, the way the wind felt sweeping through the stands at football games. He'd taken a lot for granted before, including his ability to walk without thinking about every step. But he was grateful he could walk at all. Not so long ago, he'd believed that part of his life was over.

Now he started each day with a walk up Lynda's street and around a couple of blocks. It took a long time, for he had to walk slowly, but lately he'd been relying on his canes less and less. His legs were getting stronger, and it was just a matter of time before he'd be a hundred percent. Already he'd come so far since the crash—and he'd come a lot further mentally and spiritually than he had physically.

He wished he could make Melissa see that this tragedy about to reach culmination in her life could be a beginning. That tragedies weren't always a curse. Sometimes they were a blessing. Through human eyes, they could look like the end of the world. But through God's eyes, there were forces at work, plans aligning, miracles taking place.

His breathing grew heavier as he passed the small church not too far from Lynda's street, then the house beside it with a bicycle and a pair of skates in the yard. He should get a bike, he thought, and try riding it for exercise. It would get him farther and help him to build up his legs more. Then maybe, finally, he'd be able to get his medical release and fly again.

His eyes strayed to the sky, clear blue and cloudless, and once again he found that melancholy sweeping over him. Yes, his tragedy had been a blessing. Yes, he realized God's sovereignty in all of it. Yes, he'd been given wonderful gifts as a result of his fall. He had met the woman God had chosen for him—the only woman he'd ever given serious thought to spending the rest of his life with—and that only because he couldn't stand to spend a single moment without her. But Lynda understood the emptiness that still ached inside him whenever he thought of flying. Would he never fly again? Or was God going to give that back to him someday?

He made his way up the street to Lynda's driveway, thankful that he could sit down for a while before he went to physical therapy. He wondered if Melissa was up yet. For her sake, he hoped she slept late, so she wouldn't have to deal with the unmitigated fear she must feel at the idea of what could happen to her in court tomorrow. He'd felt that way the weekend before they'd taken the bandages off of his face. In a way, he had feared prison, too. The prison of living the rest of his life with only one eye, with harsh scarring down his face that would frighten children. But now he could see that even that had carried with it blessings.

He saw Larry's car as he approached Lynda's driveway, and the cop came out of the house, dressed in a pair of jeans and sneakers and a pullover shirt—minus the windbreaker he wore to hide his weapon when he was on duty.

"Hey, Larry," Jake said, reaching for his hand.

Larry looked pale and tired as he shook, and Jake wished he would get some sleep. "How's it going, Jake?"

"Great. You take the day off again?"

"Yeah," Larry said. "I wanted to try to take Melissa's mind off things, but I'm afraid we're just going to feed each other's anxiety. Hey, you wouldn't happen to know what those two are cooking up today, would you?"

Jake glanced toward the window, and saw Lynda looking out. She smiled at him, something that never failed to brighten his day. "What do you mean?"

"I mean, Lynda's taking the morning off, and she's walking around the house like she's about to burst with excitement. She said it was a surprise."

Jake's breathing was returning to normal now. "Oh, yeah? Think it has to do with Melissa's case?"

"No, that was my first question, too. They just said it was a diversion."

"A diversion, huh?" He glanced back toward Lynda again in the window. "Then we're going somewhere?"

"As soon as Melissa finishes showering." Larry lowered his voice. "I told them I wasn't really in the mood for much—and frankly, Melissa doesn't seem to be, either. She's pretty down. But Lynda insisted that it wouldn't take more than a couple of hours."

Jake started for Lynda's door. "Well, I don't know what it could be, but I do know this. When that woman sets her mind to something, you might as well sit back and enjoy wherever it takes you."

An hour later, Jake still seemed confused at where, exactly, Lynda's enthusiasm had carried them. When they pulled into a parking space at the small St. Clair airport, Jake gave Lynda an uncomfortable look. He hadn't been back here since the crash, and it occurred to her that he might not be ready to see where his life had almost ended.

"What's going on?" he asked quietly.

Lynda squeezed his hand. "I was trying to think of a way to get Melissa and Larry's minds off tomorrow, something that would make a memory, and I thought of this." She leaned toward him on the seat, her eyes big, beseeching. "What do you think, Jake? Are you ready to get back into the sky again?"

For a moment, he stared at her, quiet, expressionless. Finally, he asked, "You rented a plane?"

"Just for the morning. Melissa needs to spend some time with her parents this afternoon. But I thought it was time."

Jake looked out over the tarmac, at the planes lined up, just as they had been the morning of their crash. He had driven his Porsche out onto the tarmac and parked beside the plane he wanted to buy, as if that Porsche gave him privileges that everyone else didn't have, never dreaming how final that short drive would be.

The wind had been blowing hard that day, just as it was today, only that day had been warmer. He remembered Lynda mentioning her concerns about the crosswind, but he'd assured her that he could handle it. He was a commercial pilot, after all. But no amount of training or experience could have prepared him for what happened that day. Now, looking back, he felt like Nebuchadnezzar, proud of how high he'd climbed, arrogant about his own status, believing he was invincible. God had showed them both, he and Nebuchadnezzar, just how dependent on him they were.

He looked at Lynda, remembering the conversation in the cockpit as they'd prepared to land that day. She had been trembling. He took her hand now, and felt the slight tremor again. "Are you sure you can do this? You're not afraid?"

She smiled with only a tinge of uncertainty. "I don't think anybody's out to kill me this time, Jake," she said, referring to the man who had sabotaged her plane. "I've really been wanting to do this. And I've wanted to take you. I can't forget that look you had in your eyes that morning when you were hotdogging in the sky like a Thunderbird."

"You hated me then. You thought I was the most obnoxious man you'd ever met."

"I was right. You were."

Jake grinned and looked at the two in the backseat, who listened with mild amusement. "She called me a psychopath."

"I sure did," she said proudly. "He was really being a jerk, showing off with all these loops and dips. But we had one thing in common. We both loved to fly." She squeezed Jake's hand. "And neither of us has done it since the crash."

Jake's hesitation diminished. Raising his eyebrows at the two in the backseat, he grinned. "Are you guys game?"

Larry shifted uneasily and peered out at a plane that was just taking off on runway 3, where he'd seen the jumbled, charred mass of Lynda's plane after the crash. "I don't know."

Melissa took his hand. "Come on, it'll be fun."

"Really?" he asked. "You want to do this?"

"Sure. It's better than moping around all day and playing all the different scenarios of tomorrow over and over in my mind. This might be my last day as a free woman. I might as well soar a little."

The shadows on Larry's face returned. "Melissa, don't say that. Lynda's a good lawyer."

Her eyes turning serious again, she touched Larry's mouth with her fingertips to hush him. "Anything could happen, Larry. I've cried until my eyes are raw, I've prayed until I've run out of words, and I've had so many regrets . . . I can't do anything about tomorrow right now. So let's just take advantage of today."

He leaned wearily back on the seat. "All right," he said without much enthusiasm. "Let's go fly."

Even though the flight was supposed to be relaxing, Lynda's hands trembled as she waited for Mike Morgan—the airport manager who served as air traffic controller in the small concessionlike booth inside the airport—to clear her to take off.

"Take it easy, now," Jake said, his eyes scanning the controls with some discomfort of his own. "We did a real good preflight check. Everything looked good. There's nothing to worry about."

"I know," she said. "I'm not scared to fly. I was just remembering . . ."

The radio crackled, and Mike gave them the go-ahead. The cabin was quiet except for the changing pitch of the engine as she accelerated down the runway.

The moment the wheels left the ground, Jake began to laugh like a little boy on his first Ferris wheel. "This is great!" he said. "Look how clear the sky is! Oh, man, I've missed this."

"I have too." Lynda relaxed as they gained altitude. She glanced to the backseat where Larry and Melissa sat close together, gazing out the window. "You two okay?"

"Yeah, we're fine," Melissa said quietly.

"As soon as I get my medical release—" Jake started to say, then stopped before he could get the rest out.

Lynda looked over at him, grinning. "That's the first time I've heard you say it so positively, Jake. Till now, you've seemed a little unsure if you ever would."

"I will," he said without question. "And when I do, we're buying another plane."

She looked over at him, her amused eyes searching his face. "We?"

"Yes," he said, returning her grin. "We."

Melissa grinned and winked at Larry. She had known Lynda and Jake were getting serious, but she hadn't known if they had discussed marriage. Judging by the pink flush across Lynda's cheekbones, and the smile on her face as she moved her eyes to the window, this may have been the first time they had.

Beginnings, she thought with a sigh as her smile faded and her eyes drifted back to Larry. Other people had beginnings. She had endings.

Larry noted the sadness that had fallen over her like a thick fog, so he slid his arm around her and pulled her tightly against him. She laid her head on his shoulder, wishing there could be a future for her with him. But that was too much to ask.

If they'd just met under different circumstances . . . If she'd just been more worthy of him . . .

But she knew that, if she had to go to jail, her relationship with Larry would be over. Cops didn't associate with convicts. He would forget about her; she almost hoped he would. He deserved happiness, and she would only bring him sorrow.

A tear dropped to her cheek and she quickly wiped it away. Larry saw her do it, and tipped her face up to his. She saw the trouble in his expression, the despair, the heartache. And she hated herself for putting it there.

Lord, please comfort him. Let him forget quickly. Let him find the person who can make him happy.

But it was hard to imagine any happiness replacing the sorrow in his eyes.

"You know, you were right, that morning we went up," Jake said softly to Lynda, breaking the silence in the plane. "This is a sanctuary. As reverent as a church."

"You have a different perspective now, don't you, Jake?" Lynda asked.

"Yeah," he said. "I thank God every day for that crash. Life has been a struggle since then, but I wouldn't trade a minute of it. Sometimes, you just have to go through hell to find heaven."

Was there a lesson there for her? Melissa wondered. She let the words sink in and tried to find comfort in them as her gaze drifted back out the window. Would there be a life after all this was over? Would there be a heaven at the end of her hell?

She knew that her life would go on, ultimately—but first, she would have to pay for her crime. She had to trust, she told herself. Like Jake, she had to believe that good would come out of it all.

She looked up and met Larry's eyes. He was going through a hell of his own, she thought. She was dragging him through it with her. Slowly, she began to withdraw. She lifted her head from his shoulder and sat straighter.

She saw his confusion as he loosened his hold on her, but he was demanding nothing from her today. He was here to give, and she received.

Thank you for letting him be here now, she prayed silently. Even if it was temporary . . . even if he forgot her . . . it was okay. God had given her this little interlude as a memory to take with her.

It was a memory that would remind her that she hadn't been forgotten or forsaken. God still loved her, in spite of herself. And he would see her through this, whatever happened tomorrow.

CHAPTER TWENTY-NINE

The harsh rap of the gavel intensified the headache that had plagued Larry since he woke in the early hours of the morning. Melissa, too, looked as though she hadn't slept. He sat next to her, gripping her hand.

Around them in the courtroom, others with criminal charges waited to be called—some who looked as nervous as she, others who'd walked this path many times before. In the midst of it all, Melissa looked like the lady she was. She held her head up, as if she'd come prepared to accept whatever the court decided, and Larry hoped the judge would see into her heart and give her a second chance. The agony of waiting until her case number was called was almost more than he could stand.

He had sat through many days in court in his career, waiting to testify in a case against someone he'd arrested, but it wasn't until now that he realized how coldly impersonal it was. There should be privacy when someone's future was being decided, he thought. There should be quiet, reverence. He thought of the injustice of Melissa's having to sit through all the ugliness, like one of these thugs who deserved what they were going to get.

He looked up as the doors opened, and saw Melissa's parents come into the room. Melissa got to her feet instantly and stepped past Lynda and Jake.

She placed her parents between herself and Lynda with whispered introductions, and Larry could feel the agony these two people felt. They had lost one daughter already, and now, in an attempt to set that right, their only remaining daughter had broken the law. It

515

would kill them if she went to jail, he thought. The brutal injustice of what continued to happen to their family was devastating.

The judge ordered a recess of fifteen minutes, and they all stood up. Melissa's parents embraced her tightly for a small eternity, weeping out their hearts. Larry stood back, feeling out of place, not sure where he fit in this circle of tears.

He tried to avert his eyes, tried not to watch the quiet display of emotion. The courtroom doors opened as people quietly came and went. Idly, Larry scanned the faces, wondering what their stories were, whether they were lawbreakers or hurting family members. A man came in alone and stood in the aisle with his back to them, looking for a seat. Slowly, he turned around.

It took a moment for the face to register in Larry's mind, but suddenly he recognized the one man he'd never considered might be here.

Edward Pendergrast.

Some cross of rage and anguish burst inside Larry's mind.

Pendergrast grinned as their eyes made contact, then, one by one, he regarded the faces in their row until he came to Melissa with her parents, the same parents he'd terrorized before.

Instead of taking a seat, he stood still at the end of their row, that smug grin on his face, that victorious expression of hardened pride, of invincible evil.

Melissa was stunned at the sight of him. Her parents slowly turned and saw him.

Pendergrast lifted his hand in a wave, as if they were all old friends, then slid into a seat across the aisle from them.

Larry's teeth clenched, and his breathing grew heavy. He bolted out of his seat and stepped around Melissa and her parents. Pushing out of the row, he headed toward Pendergrast. But Melissa caught his arm. "Larry, don't. Please—just stay here."

"I can't," he bit out, and kept going.

Pendergrast was enjoying this, and he beamed up at Larry as he approached. "Well, if it isn't ole gullible Detective Millsaps. Believer of beautiful women. Swallows their stories hook, line, and sinker. But all's forgiven, man. There is justice, after all." He held out his hand to shake, but ignoring it, Larry leaned over until his face was square with Pendergrast's.

"Don't talk to me about justice," he said through clenched teeth. "You don't have any business in here."

"*Au contraire*," Pendergrast said with a laugh. "As the victim of her little fantasy, I'd say I belong here even more than you do. I might even have something to say to the judge."

Larry's face paled, and he glanced back over at Melissa. She'd shown unbelievable composure until now, but since Pendergrast had entered her face had reddened and was twisted into a fragile, on-the-verge expression that made his heart ache. Her parents, too, looked as if they might come undone.

Larry pointed a finger in Pendergrast's face. "I want you to know something, Pendergrast."

"Soames. The name is Soames."

Larry wasn't daunted at his coolness. "I'm going to get you, *Pendergrast*," he said. "One of these days, I'm going to get you."

"I don't think so, Millsaps. Better men than you have tried."

"Watch me," Larry said. He stepped back across the aisle and bent down to Lynda's ear. "He says he's going to say something. Can he do that?"

She gave Pendergrast a troubled look. "I'm afraid so. The judge will listen to anyone who has something to say about this. The wronged party always has the right to speak."

"Then let me speak," Larry said. "I'll tell them what a good person she is, that she had good reason—"

"No," Lynda said, touching his hand. "I'm sorry, Larry, but I don't think it would help. You're the cop she originally lied to. It would be better if you stayed seated. Melissa does plan to address the court herself. I think that'll be enough."

"But you'll tell the judge about his past record, won't you? You'll tell him about Sandy?"

"It's all in the PSI, Larry. The judge has reviewed all of it."

"But maybe he hasn't made up his mind yet!"

She looked to the front of the room, and swallowed. "I'm going to do what I can, Larry. Please, just try to keep Melissa calm."

Miserably, he pushed further down the row, past her parents, and sat on the other side of Melissa.

Melissa was trembling worse now, and her palms were sweating. He didn't know how she would make it through this. Or how he would. "What did he say?" she asked.

"He's just trying to scare you," he said. "It's intimidation. Just ignore him."

Slipping his arm around her shoulders, Larry pulled her against him and pressed his mouth into her hair. Quietly, he prayed for her, not in words she could hear, but he knew that she knew what he was doing.

The gavel banged twice, making her jump, and the bailiff called out the case code. "Pinellas County versus Melissa Nelson."

Melissa got up, wobbling slightly, and Lynda slipped out of her seat with her files and led her to the judge.

Slipping into the seat she had previously occupied, Larry took her mother's hand, squeezed it. And then Jim Nelson, her father, reached over and took both of theirs. They drew strength from each other's touch as they watched Melissa take a seat at the table in the front of the courtroom.

"Is she going to say anything?" Jim asked him in a whisper.

Larry shook his head. "She wasn't sure when we talked about it, but Lynda wants her to, I think." He glanced over at Pendergrast, who had sat up straighter, as if preparing to go forward himself. Every muscle in Larry's body tightened.

The state attorney addressed the court in routine legalese concerning the findings of the presentencing investigation. When he recommended that the judge give Melissa at least two years in the state penitentiary, Larry closed his eyes.

"Your honor, before you rule on this, there's someone here who would like to address the court."

"Fine," the judge said. "Go ahead."

The state attorney turned back and nodded to Pendergrast. With a solemn look on his face—the look of a fine, upstanding citizen who has been deeply wronged—he made his way to the front of the room.

Melissa started to rise in protest, but Lynda made her sit back down and whispered to her as Melissa's face reddened and her eyes filled with tears.

"Your Honor," Pendergrast said, "I'm Edward Soames, the person this woman accused of raping her. I just wanted to say a few words before you decide on her sentence."

"All right," the judge said, taking off his glasses and fixing his full attention on Pendergrast.

Pendergrast cleared his throat and looked at his feet, looking for all the world like a clean-cut professional man who was nervous coming before the judge. "One day I was a successful architect with a lot of friends, just living life and not bothering anybody, and the next day, because of one lie that someone told about me, I'm branded a rapist, I lost my job, my friends won't talk to me—" His voice seemed to catch, and he stopped, swallowed, and started again. "You see, this all started because I didn't return her interest in me."

Across the room, Melissa's muffled cry interrupted, and the judge glanced at her. Lynda quieted her.

"So she got even," Pendergrast went on. "Now I have to live the rest of my life with this stigma following me around. Even though the charges have been dropped, my friends are still suspicious. She made a mess out of my life, and I didn't do a thing to deserve it." He seemed to get emotional, stopped, and pinched the bridge of his nose. After a moment, he looked up at the judge. "That's—that's all I have to say, Your Honor. Just think about that before you decide on her sentence. Women shouldn't be allowed to just go around ruining people's lives. They shouldn't get away with it."

The judge seemed moved. "Thank you, Mr. Soames."

As Pendergrast turned around to go back to his seat, he got that grin on his face again and glanced back at Larry. He was proud of himself.

Lynda stood up. "Your honor, my client would like to address the court herself. That is, if she can still manage to speak after that classic performance."

"All right," the judge said. "Proceed."

Melissa stood up, her knees shaking. She couldn't stop the sobs still overtaking her. "His name is not Soames," she said. "It's Pendergrast, and he's a liar. He killed my sister—"

The judge, looking disgusted, slapped his hand on the table. "Unless you have a murder conviction to back that up, Miss Nelson,

I suggest that you rephrase it. Otherwise I might be led to believe that you haven't learned your lesson."

She covered her mouth and tried to pull herself together. Finally, attempting to speak again, she said, "He caused my sister's suicide. He's a rapist, Your Honor. She wasn't the only one."

He shook his head and began taking notes, as if he'd already dismissed her for making false accusations again.

"Your Honor, I know what I did was wrong. I shouldn't have done it. But I was trying to right things. The court system let my family down, and he was still out there—you just don't know how desperate you can get, when you find your only sister dead in a bathtub, and the guy who ruined her life is still walking the streets, working, living like a normal person—"

She broke down then, covering her face, and collapsed back into her chair, unable to go on.

The judge looked up, waiting for her to go on. It was impossible to tell from his expression whether he was disgusted or sympathetic. "Do you have anything else to say, Miss Nelson?" he asked.

Melissa couldn't answer. She only shook her head and tried to muffle her sobs.

Lynda stood up, obviously shaken that Melissa's speech hadn't been more eloquent, and that she hadn't been able to finish what she'd tried so hard to say. "No, You Honor. She doesn't."

"Anyone else?"

She hesitated, then turned and glanced back at the three people huddled together in the back. "Yes," she said finally. "One more. Detective Larry Millsaps."

Larry sat still for a moment, not sure he had heard correctly. Finally, prying his hands away from Melissa's mother, he got up and headed to the bench.

Because it was an informal hearing, he stood in front of the judge and began speaking without preamble. "Uh . . . Your Honor," he said, "I've seen a lot of criminals in my day. I deal with them day in and day out. Melissa Nelson is not a criminal. She's an innocent young woman who's been deeply wounded by her sister's rape and suicide. I saw the pictures after Sandy's rape, your honor. They were brutal. And I saw Pendergrast's rap sheet. The very reason he changed his name is that he had these other arrests on his record. Yes, there was a stigma. There always is when one is charged with rape—not once, but twice. Yes, this third charge was false, but if you had lived through what Melissa and her family have lived through, and knew that a rapist was still out on the streets, waiting to terrorize more women, your state of mind wouldn't be the best in the world, either. As a police officer, I can say that Melissa is no threat to anyone. But if you send her to prison—" His voice cracked, and he looked up at the judge, his eyes pleading. "—with people who have committed horrible crimes for which they deserve that kind of punishment, I'm just not sure she can handle it, Your Honor. I'm not sure she'll survive it."

He looked at Melissa, still lost in her pain and grief, then brought his eyes back to the judge. "Look at her, Your Honor. How do *you* think she'll fare in prison? Will any justice really be served by sending her there?"

Unable to think of anything other than getting down on his knees and begging, he uttered, "Thank you," and went back to his seat.

The judge put his glasses back on and began to study his notes again. He scribbled something, frowned, then looked back up at Melissa. Setting his pencil down, he steepled his hands in front of his face.

"Well, we have two drastically different stories from three different people. While I do understand the emotional nature of this case, and perhaps even the reasons behind her actions, I can't condone anyone's calling the police on someone they don't like, for something that that party may or may not have done years ago to someone else. I can't condone anyone sitting before a grand jury and lying. Miss Nelson, this man has not been convicted of a crime. Citizens cannot pin crimes on innocent people, no matter what they may think they deserve, and get away with it. There has to be a punishment for that. I think six months in the Pinellas County Correctional Facility for Women should be enough of an example to anyone else who ever thinks of doing such a thing."

Despite her mother's muffled scream and Melissa's guttural sob, he banged his gavel again.

CHAPTER THIRTY

Six months. The words took a moment to penetrate into Larry's mind and sink down into his heart.

Had the judge really given her six months in jail?

Melissa sat stiff, stunned, as the judge continued reading his decision. He heard her mother's muffled, strangled cry. Across the aisle, Pendergrast was laughing.

The rapist was free. Melissa was going to jail.

It didn't compute, wouldn't sink in, and Larry found himself coming to his feet as the bailiffs came to take her away. They weren't giving her time to say good-bye, or to break down and cry, or to prepare for where she was going. She looked quickly back at her parents, then at Lynda, her eyes brimming with apology and remorse. Then her wet eyes connected with Larry's.

It can't be right, his eyes told her. *It's not over!*

But they all knew it was over, as the bailiffs ushered her out of the room.

Stepping on the feet of the people next to him, Larry hurried out of the row, then ran out of the courtroom and around through the back door where she would come out. His breathing came too hard, and he felt light-headed, as if he might pass out. He leaned back against the wall, his mind racing as he tried to find something that made sense.

The rapist free . . . Melissa in jail . . .

A sheriff's car drove up and idled at the door, and in a moment, the door opened. The two bailiffs came out with Melissa between them.

Fortunately, he knew one of them. "Al, let me talk to her for a minute. Just for a minute. What would it hurt?"

His friend glanced around at the sheriff and the others, and they all shrugged. "All right, Larry, but just a minute."

Larry looked at her for a moment, aware of the people standing around them. She was struggling to hold back her tears, but her chin trembled with the effort. Finally, he pulled her into a smothering embrace. "It's okay, Larry," she whispered in a fragile, broken voice. "Really, it is. I expected this."

"But Melissa—"

Her face changed, and her eyes fixed on some point across the street. Larry followed her startled gaze to the man standing there alone, leaning against the building opposite them, grinning and rubbing her nose in his freedom.

Something exploded inside him, and he almost launched across the street with his hands poised to grab Pendergrast by the throat. But Melissa stopped him. "Watch him for me, Larry. Catch him on something, okay? Something real."

He turned back to her. "I promise," he whispered. "And I'll come visit you. First visiting day. I'll be there."

"No, don't," she said. "I don't want you to."

"Why not?"

"Because—I don't want you to see me that way. You don't owe me anything." The bailiffs ushered her toward the back door of the car.

"I'm coming anyway," he said. When she didn't answer, he looked around one of the bailiffs at her car door. "Did you hear me, Melissa? I'll be there!"

She slid in and they slammed the door, and she looked at him through the window. Tears streamed down her face as they got into the front. As the car drove away, she looked down at her hands.

When the car was out of sight, Larry started to cross the street.

Pendergrast was gone, but it felt as if the evil lingered in his wake.

"I'll get him for you, Melissa," Larry whispered, looking up and down the sidewalk for a sign of him. "If it's the last thing I ever do."

CHAPTER THIRTY-ONE

he Pinellas County Correctional Facility for Women in Clearwater had been finished—after a flood of controversy over how much money the separate facility was costing the state—just six months before, not far from the jail that had housed both men and women for so long. Legislators had insisted that it was needed, due to the growing number of women being convicted of crimes. In her wildest dreams, Melissa had never guessed that it would be her home for six months.

The building still smelled like paint, and the floor down the long hall was polished, but she knew that that appearance of clean comfort was deceiving. Within these air-conditioned walls were other women who had committed crimes. Drug dealers, prostitutes, child abusers, thieves—the reports she'd read about the women imprisoned here had seemed like fantastic stories to her then, stories of dangerous women who'd surrendered to evil in their lives. Now Melissa was one of them.

The corrections officer who oriented her didn't care that hers had not been a violent crime, or that it had been designed to bring justice to someone who deserved it. To her, Melissa was only a number: 6324655. A faceless, nameless, colorless member of the inmate population, to be treated no differently from the women who'd been sent here for acts she couldn't even imagine.

Wearing her prison-issued orange jumpsuit with the words PINELLAS COUNTY CORRECTIONAL FACILITY in black block letters on the back, and carrying an armload of provisions—sheets, a thin pillow, a blanket, and the few things she had been allowed to bring from home in a small paper sack, which had been carefully searched—she followed the CO through the maze of locking doors and meandering hallways. They came to a wall of yellow iron bars. The guard pushed a few buttons, and the wall began to rise.

"You'll be in cellblock C," the big woman said, leading her into the cellblock. "We're putting you with Chloe."

"Chloe?"

"Yeah." The guard gave a cursory glance back at her. "If you start trouble, you'll be put in isolation. Trust me, you won't like it. If she—or anybody else for that matter—makes trouble with you, call a guard. Chloe likes to fight."

Melissa swallowed her terror and tried desperately to keep tears from filling her eyes. "Isn't there someone else, then?"

The woman seemed amused. "What are you looking for? A welcoming committee? Sorry, but our Welcome Wagon has four flat tires. Truth is, the other prisoners usually do harass the new ones, especially when they look as scared as you do."

With a loud bang that reverberated through Melissa's body and made her jump, the doors to cellblock C slammed shut behind them. "The cellblock doors are open certain hours during the mornings and at night, so people can get to their jobs in other parts of the facility. Most of the time, the cell doors are open, too, so inmates are allowed to go in and out of each other's cells. They're locked down at night, and if you want your cell locked during the day when you're in it, you can ask the CO. I wouldn't recommend locking Chloe out, though. She holds grudges."

Melissa followed her down a long hall with metal doors on either side, not at all like the cells with bars she had expected. Women she assumed were prisoners milled around the cellblock, smoking cigarettes and watching her make her way up the hallway.

"Most of the gals are working right now," the guard said. "They'll be back in a couple of hours. Some of them go early and get off early. Some of them play sick every day so they don't have to lift a finger. They get time added onto their sentence when they miss, but that doesn't matter to them, I guess."

Two women standing beside one of the cells turned to see the new addition to the block, and Melissa averted her eyes. Her arms were trembling, and she almost dropped her load. Stopping, she tried to get a better grip, but the CO looked back. "Hurry up, will you?"

She fell back into step behind the CO, breathing heavily and beginning to perspire. The guard stopped at a closed door, opened it, and peered in. A huge black woman who could have played linebacker for the Miami Dolphins lay on the lower bunk, and she turned to look at them as Melissa came in.

"Chloe, this is Melissa," the CO said brusquely. "She's your new cellmate."

"Hi," Melissa said, wishing the corners of her lips would stop trembling.

"I told you I don't want no cellmate."

"Well, you may have noticed that you don't call the shots around here, Chloe," the guard said. She pointed to the small table where Melissa could set her load, but Melissa only stood motionless, paralyzed.

"Oh, I've called some shots," Chloe smarted back. She gave Melissa the once-over, then sat up. "And you can't have the bottom bunk. This is my bunk."

"That's fine," Melissa whispered. "The top's fine." She turned back to the CO, her eyes beseeching her to reconsider and find her a smaller, more compatible cellmate, one who didn't terrify her.

But this was not a college dorm, and no one cared whether they got along or not.

The CO barked off a few final instructions that seemed to bounce around and echo in Melissa's head as she tried to take it all in—the bunk bed that was bolted to the floor, the small sink and toilet on the other side of a half wall, a wooden chair, two metal lockboxes. Beside the bed was a nightstand, also made of metal, with a small drawer. In one corner, Chloe had stacked some boxes that she used for shelves. Torn magazines lay crumpled on them, and a radio, and a little vase with some dead flowers.

"Well, do you?" the CO asked, breaking into her thoughts.

Melissa turned back to the woman. "Uh—beg your pardon?"

The woman smirked. "I asked if you had any questions."

"Uh ..." She struggled to find some just to keep the CO from leaving her alone with Chloe, but her mind was drawing a blank. "No. I guess not."

The CO left, and Chloe lay back down, ignoring her. Melissa set her things down on the dirty floor, slowly, quietly, carefully, then turned back to Chloe. What did one say to one's prison cellmate? *What're you in for?*

Though it was a pressing question on her mind, she didn't feel free to ask it. It might make Chloe mad, and she might take time to show Melissa how she got her fighting reputation.

"So what're you in for?" the big woman barked.

Melissa tried to think. "Uh—perjury."

"Do *what*? You didn't shoot nobody? Didn't rob nobody? Didn't steal nothin'?"

"No."

"And they put you in *jail*?"

"That's right."

"Abomination!" the big woman said in a voice so gruff it made her jump. "They really are tryin' to fill up this joint, aren't they?"

She turned over then, as if to go to sleep, effectively dismissing Melissa.

Quietly, Melissa got her sheets, pillow, and blanket and threw them on top of the bed, then grabbing her bag, she climbed up the steps at the end of the bed and sat down on her bunk, pulling her knees to her chest and hugging them with her trembling arms.

Tears started to flow immediately, but she bit back her sobs. *Sandy, I can't believe this is happening . . .*

And then she looked up at the ceiling, beseeching the Savior who had seemed so forgiving just a few days earlier, when she had decided to confess, when that feeling of peace had flooded her spirit. Had he left her now? Could he even find her here?

If there was good for her in this, or for anyone, she couldn't think what it was just now. Quietly, she opened her bag and pulled out her Bible. It had been dusty when she'd found it under the seat of her car, where she'd left it the last time she'd been to church. She'd have plenty of time now to catch up for all the years that she hadn't been reading it.

She heard the noise of the cellblock door opening down the hall. Voices echoed up the hall, voices of women coming back from their jobs and heading for their cells. She glanced at the open door, wishing she could close it. But it would make noise, and that might disturb Chloe, and she didn't want to have to deal with that just now. She didn't have the courage.

So she sat still, wiping her face and hunched like a little doll on her bunk, waiting for the next shoe to drop, for the next act in this nightmare she had written.

An alarm sounded when it was time to convene in the prison dining room. Melissa felt the bed shake as Chloe awakened and pulled herself up. As the woman stood, Melissa realized she had to be over six feet tall and weighed probably over 230 pounds.

Chloe gave her a cursory glance. "That's supper," she said.

Melissa glanced out the open door and saw the other women ambling by amid shouts, laughs, profane insults. "Uh . . . I'm not really hungry."

"So what you gon' do? Starve? Take it from me, honey. You gon' need your strength."

She felt nauseous at the thought of eating in this atmosphere. That would be all she needed, she thought, to throw up in front of everyone her first day here. If that wouldn't make her look vulnerable, she didn't know what would.

"Do I have to go?" she asked in a raspy voice. "I mean, is it required?"

"No, it ain't required. You can eat in your room, if you have something. But I don't see no food."

"Where—where are you supposed to get it?"

"Your family can bring it. Up to thirty-five pounds every two weeks. Or you can buy some things from the commissary, if you got money." Chloe went to the sink, bent over it, and tossed some water on her face. Drying it on her sleeve, she went on. "There's one hot plate per cellblock, and you got to stand in a long line for it. Ain't worth it, you ask me. I like my meals hot. You know, if you don't eat, you won't sleep tonight. You'll probably keep me up all night blubberin'."

It was true, Melissa realized. It was going to be hard enough to sleep tonight as it was. She hadn't eaten much in the last few days, and she would need her strength here.

Quietly acquiescing, she slid down from the bunk. Chloe stood a good head and shoulders taller, and the look in her eye revealed impatience and a low level of tolerance for Melissa's fragile state.

"So what'd you lie about?"

"What?"

"You said you were here for perjury."

"Oh. I kind of—I set someone up for a crime they didn't commit."

"Who was it? An old boyfriend? Dumped you, so you got him back?"

"No," she said. "It was someone who really had committed that crime earlier. He got off, and I just—I wanted him back in jail."

"Hmmm," Chloe said in that gruff voice. "Too bad you got caught."

"I didn't get caught," she said. "I confessed."

"Say *what?* You mean to tell me you in here because you confessed to somethin' you hadn't even been caught doin'?"

"Yeah, basically."

"Man, I thought I was dumb. How long you got?"

"Six months," she said.

"It'll be the longest six months of your life." She went to the doorway, then looked back, as if waiting.

Melissa looked beyond Chloe to the women streaming by. The looks in their eyes frightened her, and she wondered if they would be able to see her fear.

Chloe stepped out into the stream of women heading for the door, and suddenly Melissa felt even more vulnerable, even more afraid. Following, she stayed as close as she could to Chloe all the way to the dining room.

CHAPTER THIRTY-TWO

L arry didn't want to hear the doorbell ring that night. He didn't feel like company. He had sat alone in his apartment, with the shades drawn and the lights out, until dusk had fallen. Now it was almost dark in the apartment, but he didn't care.

The bell rang again, and he got up and headed slowly for the door. It was probably Tony, he thought, with some lame invitation to go get a pizza, trying to pick up Larry's spirits. But when he opened the door, Lynda and Jake stood there.

"We just wanted to make sure you're all right," Lynda said.

"Me?" he asked, turning his back on them and going back to his living room. They closed the door and followed him in. "It's Melissa who's not all right."

"She is, Larry," Lynda said. "I checked on her this afternoon. She's okay."

Tears came to his eyes, and he covered his face with his hand and plopped into his chair. Jake went to the couch and sat down, leaning his cane against the arm, but Lynda kept standing.

"Every time I picture her there, I just . . ."

"I know," Lynda whispered. "I'm so sorry. I did everything I could."

"I know, I know," Larry said, cutting her off. "Tony and I didn't help a whole lot. I keep going over and over the things I told the DOC, wondering if something I said tipped the scales, if I could have worded things differently. Maybe I could have said something better, different, at the sentencing. Maybe I didn't plead hard enough."

"You did the best you could, Larry. And as for the DOC, you didn't have a choice. You told them the truth. That's all Melissa wanted you to do. Nothing you said would have made that much difference."

He sighed, then leaned his elbows on his knees and looked down at his feet. "Sometimes it's just so hard to understand. I prayed and prayed, with all my heart. I felt God listening."

"He *was* listening."

"Then why did this happen?" he said through gritted teeth, getting to his feet. He walked to his window, pulled back the blinds, and looked down on the parking lot. The streetlights were on, making it seem even darker in the apartment, but he didn't care. "Why didn't God answer this prayer?"

Jake got up and went to stand behind Larry. With his hand on Larry's shoulder, he said, "I've asked that question myself, buddy. More than once. I'm not smart enough to answer it."

"I don't get it," Larry said. "Why wouldn't God intervene? What purpose could it possibly serve to have Melissa in jail?"

Jake's eyes misted. "I've never been to jail, Larry, but after the crash, when I lay flat on my back, not able to move from my waist down, that was as close to prison as I ever want to get. I lost my job, my friends, my looks . . ."

Larry glanced up at the scar on Jake's cheek. He hardly noticed it anymore.

"I asked over and over what purpose there could have been in that. For the life of me, I couldn't see any good in it. But there was a purpose, Larry. A big one."

"But she's in *jail*. There's *not* a purpose in that!" Larry cried, turning sharply away from Jake and marching to the darkest corner of the room.

Lynda and Jake said nothing. Finally, Larry shrank a little, as if the anger were draining out of him. He turned on the lamp and dropped back into his chair.

After a long silence he said, "I'm sorry, guys. I didn't mean to yell at you. It's just—you're the only ones here to yell at."

"Yell away," Lynda said softly. "It's okay."

He wiped his eyes, then looked at Jake. "I wish I could believe it'll all work out. That good will come of it. That there's a reason.

531

That it makes sense, somehow." He leaned back, studying the ceiling. "See, when I think about it, I do trust God. I do know that he's in control. It's just that sometimes it seems like things are so *out* of control. How can anything good come out of all this?"

"He's God," Lynda said. "He made order out of chaos. He created the universe. He also created Melissa, Larry. He'll take care of her."

Lynda saw Larry's Bible lying on a nearby shelf, picked it up, and flipped through it. "There's a verse in Psalms that I quote to myself, whenever I watch a battered wife go back to her husband, or whenever I have a client who winds up serving time. I didn't know this verse when I was going through all my trouble, but it's important to me now." She found the page, then handed the Bible to Larry. "There it is. Psalm 91. Read the whole chapter when you get time, but for now, just verses 11 and 12."

Larry looked down at the verses. "For he will command his angels concerning you to guard you in all your ways; they will lift you up in their hands, so that you will not strike your foot against a stone."

"That's what he'll do with Melissa, Larry," she whispered.

"Do you think so?" he asked, his pain arguing against this simple expression of faith.

"I know it. She's there because she decided to tell the truth. To right a wrong. God will honor that."

He studied the verses again, and slowly felt his tension and bitterness easing a bit, leaving him only bone tired. "Thanks," he whispered. "I'll hold onto that. I really don't have any choice."

They sat still for a moment, then finally, Lynda stood up. "Would you like to come over and watch a movie with us or something? I could make popcorn."

Larry shook his head. "No, thanks. I have something else I have to do. But I really appreciate you guys. You're good friends."

Lynda hugged him quickly, and then they were gone.

Quiet settled over the house. Returning to his seat, Larry read the whole psalm again, feeling the peace that it held. But behind that peace was a growing sense of guilt. Who was he to feel peace while Melissa was where she was? It was Melissa who deserved to feel peace, not him—not after the decisions he'd made.

He set his Bible back on the shelf, grabbed his keys, and headed out the door.

He hadn't lied to Lynda and Jake. He really did have plans. He was going to watch Pendergrast. As he had promised Melissa, he was going to catch him at something. And he didn't care if he had to give up sleep for the next six months to do it. Somehow, Pendergrast was going to pay.

With God's help—if he still had any right to expect God's help—Larry would be the one to *make* him pay.

CHAPTER THIRTY-THREE

The women spoke in low tones and sat where they were supposed to sit at dinner, unwilling to start trouble—and no wonder; guards were everywhere. Still, Melissa felt the eyes of some of the inmates on her, assessing her, testing her for that look of fear she knew she wore like a banner. Chloe sat next to her, saying little to those around her, just scarfing down her meal with a zest that Melissa had not seen in many others.

The food was bland but nutritious, so she ate. She thought back over the meals she'd eaten with Larry, when they had shared deep heart-to-hearts, with Melissa sharing parts of her truths with him and Larry probing for more. The memories of time wasted and time lost brought tears to her eyes, but she blinked them back, desperate not to let anyone here see her crying.

When she'd eaten all she could, she set her napkin back on the tray and waited to be told where to go next.

"They give you an assignment yet?" Chloe asked after she'd polished off her plate.

"Laundry," Melissa said.

"It's hot in there," Chloe said. "They got me in there, too."

Melissa looked over at her roommate. She was a brooding woman, and she still sounded gruff, angry, frightening. But she had made a stab at conversation; that was a hopeful sign.

"You watch TV? You can go to the TV room after dinner."

"No. I'll just stay in the room and read." She couldn't bring herself to call it a cell.

"Look," Chloe said, as if growing weary of the timid act. "Your best bet is to get a look at as much as you can this first day in. See what you're up against. Besides, if you stay in the cell by yourself, I can't promise you'll be safe."

"Well, I can lock it, can't I?"

Chloe grinned and breathed a laugh. "You *are* dumb. Girl, these doors lock from the outside—not the inside."

"Oh." She looked around, noted that more inmates had spotted her. A group across the room to her right were staring at her and whispering among themselves, and to her left others were wrenching their neck to see her. "Then I guess I'll go."

Chloe shook her head at her idiocy, and again Melissa stared down at her food, unable to make eye contact with any of the threatening eyes around her.

The TV room was a big room full of couches and game tables, and a television sat up high in the corner, in a metal box that kept anyone from vandalizing it. The biggest, most ominous inmates among them controlled the station selection, and the others sat around in clusters, talking.

Melissa watched two women get up as soon as they saw Chloe come in, and Chloe ambled over to the chairs they had abandoned and sat down, as if they were understood to be hers.

Melissa hung back at the door, trying not to attract any attention. But it was too late. Two of the women standing near her turned toward her, amused. "You new?"

"Yes," she said quietly.

"Hey, everybody!" one of them shouted. "Check this out!"

All eyes in the room turned to her, and Melissa shrank back against the wall.

"So what's your name, honey?" one of the women, with a pasty complexion and greasy red hair, asked.

"Melissa," she choked out.

"Melissa!" the redhead shouted. "Aw, ain't that pretty!"

"Look, I don't want any trouble." But that was the wrong thing to say. She watched as the COs turned their backs, allowing the harassment to continue, as if she somehow deserved it.

"She don't want no trouble!" the redhead said. "I'll bet a sweet thing like you never expected to end up here. Can't believe a jury would convict you, with that soft hair—" She grabbed a handful of Melissa's hair, but Melissa jerked back. "And them big eyes."

"It wasn't a jury," Melissa choked out.

"Not a jury? A judge then. Didn't you bat them eyes at him and tell him that you were just too delicate to be in here with all us criminal types? So what'd you do, anyway?"

Melissa didn't answer.

"Honey, I asked you a question," the redheaded woman asked, growing more agitated. "I don't sense a lot of respect from you. Didn't you hear what I asked?"

"She's in for child abuse, Red," one woman on the couch piped up. "I heard about her last week on the news. She left her children in the house, then burned it down."

"No, I didn't!" Melissa cried.

"I saw it, honey. That was you."

"Child abuse? Murder? Arson?" the redhead taunted. "No wonder even that soft blonde hair didn't save you."

Tears were coming to her eyes, despite her efforts to hold them back. "It's not true," she whispered. "Please."

Another woman grabbed a handful of her hair and jerked her head back so she was looking up at the ceiling. "Please what?"

"Let me go!" Melissa shouted through her teeth. "I haven't done anything to you!"

"We're just welcomin' you, honey," Red said. "Like we do all the girls." A round of laughter erupted over the room as others got up and started toward her.

"SHUT UP!" Chloe's voice cut like a chain saw through the room, and breath-held silence fell over them as the big woman rose to her full height. "Can't you see I'm tryin' to watch *Wheel of Fortune*?" she belted out. "Let her go so she'll shut up! I been listenin' to her whimperin' all day as it is!"

The inmate dropped her hair, and Melissa rubbed the roots where it had started to tear out of her scalp. She looked at Chloe, waiting for her wrath to fall.

The women scattered slowly, so as not to appear frightened by the big woman, but they left Melissa alone.

Melissa stood at the door a while longer, trying to catch her breath, trying not to cry, not knowing whether to go right or left. Finally, she sat down in an empty chair and fixed her eyes on the television, trying not to provoke anyone else, holding her hands clasped to keep their trembling from showing.

She hadn't expected God to protect her through Chloe, but it seemed he had. The next hurdle, she thought, was to stop being so terrified of her protector. Chloe had rescued her from the others, but she didn't know who would rescue her from Chloe. Maybe she could learn not to make Chloe mad, she thought. Maybe she'd be lucky enough not to be around when someone else did. Maybe she was just going to have to get used to living in abject fear.

Maybe not every day of her six months would pass as slowly as this first day was.

The noises of the jail kept Melissa awake that night, though Chloe had fallen asleep the moment her head hit the pillow. Melissa lay in her cell, staring at the ceiling, listening as doors opened and closed for reasons she didn't know and didn't want to know. Now and then, COs spoke to each other without lowering their voices, and the sounds of hard shoes clicked on the floor.

Somewhere, she heard the sound of someone crying, a sound that was sometimes audible, then muffled, then loud again. She wondered how many inmates lay awake as she was tonight, nursing broken hearts, missing family members, bitterly regretting their mistakes.

She wondered about the dead flowers Chloe kept in the vase on the cardboard shelf.

Her own tears couldn't be held back any longer, and she covered her mouth to keep from giving in to the despair. She didn't want anyone to hear her crying. She didn't want to incite the wrath of the guards, or of Chloe.

She wondered if Pendergrast was laughing at her, rejoicing at the way things had turned out. His crime against Sandy was still being played out, the ripples still rippling. He was still raping their family, and Melissa was one of the victims.

Bitterness swelled within her. Her hands trembling, she reached for the Bible that she'd put under her pillow and clutched it tightly against her chest, like a shield that would keep her from her wayward thoughts. There was someone in the world she hated, and before this ordeal was over, there might be many others.

She couldn't forgive—not yet. It was too hard.

Help me, Lord. Help me to do what I'm supposed to do.

Chloe's heavy breathing ceased for a moment at the gasping sound of her tears, and Melissa turned over and buried her face in her pillow.

"You cryin' up there, ain't you?" Chloe barked.

Melissa didn't answer.

"I told you I didn't want to hear no blubberin'."

"I'm sorry," she whispered. "I was trying to be quiet."

She waited, bracing herself, for Chloe to get up, but the woman didn't move.

"Least you ain't makin' all the racket that other one is. You'd think she lost her best friend. Probably killed her herself."

Melissa didn't answer.

"I find out who that is, she'll have a *reason* to cry tomorrow."

Melissa sat stone still, holding her breath to keep from agitating the big woman.

After a moment, Chloe's deep, heavy breathing returned.

She was asleep for now, and Melissa would do well to let her stay that way.

Lying as still as a log, and just as rigid, Melissa waited for the night to pass.

CHAPTER THIRTY-FOUR

L arry ate dinner in his car the next night. The minute he'd gotten off work, he had headed for Pendergrast's apartment complex. The man's Cherokee wasn't there, so he tried Pendergrast's office. The Cherokee was still sitting there on the gravel parking lot.

He parked behind a low-hanging willow tree and rolled down his window. A heat wave had come through, making temperatures hotter than usual for October, and now, as the sun went down, it seemed hotter than it had been all day. As he bit into the hot dog he'd brought with him, he tried to imagine what Melissa had eaten tonight. Was she still terrified? Was she able to eat at all?

His appetite left him, and he tossed the hot dog back into the bag it had come in and sipped on the drink that was now watery from melted ice.

Please Lord, let me catch him at something tonight.

It wouldn't get Melissa out of jail, but at least he would be able to see some justice being served.

He saw the front door to the office building open, and Pendergrast came out and got into his car.

Larry waited until Pendergrast was a block away and had turned right onto the main road before he cranked his Chevy. Staying back in traffic, he followed him across town to Highland Drive, a brand-new, just-paved road near the mall.

Pendergrast pulled into a site where a building was going up; men were still there working. Pendergrast got out, cut across the dirt, and shouted a few orders to the men around him.

Larry waited about twenty minutes for Pendergrast to go back to his car as the other construction workers split up and headed for their own cars. Larry let three trucks pull between him and Pendergrast, then followed them back to the main road. He trailed as Pendergrast went home, locked his car, and trotted up the steps to his apartment door.

Larry waited.

His cellular phone rang, startling him. He reached for it and clicked it on. "Hello?"

"I knew you were in your car." It was Tony, and Larry braced himself.

"Yeah? So?"

"Did you even go home?"

"I had things to do, okay?"

"Yeah, well, I just wanted to see if you'd want to go get a bite to eat."

"I've already eaten."

"Where are you, man?"

"What difference does it make?"

Pause. "You're at his place, aren't you? You're staking out Pendergrast."

Larry glanced up at the apartment. "I'm off duty. I don't have to account for my time."

"Look—let's go eat, and talk, and then you can go back there if you have to."

"No," Larry said. "I'm staying right here."

"He knows you're gonna be on him, Larry. He's not going to do anything this first couple of weeks. He'd be nuts."

"He *is* nuts."

"Man, you're asking for trouble. You're obsessing. You need to let yourself off the hook, man. Melissa doesn't expect this. She wouldn't want you to suffer just because she's in jail."

Larry rubbed his forehead. "Tony, if you don't have anything more constructive to say, I have to go."

"Look, just be careful, will you? I don't want to break in a new partner."

Larry clicked the phone and tossed it on the seat. Maybe Tony was right. Maybe nothing was going to happen tonight. But one of these days it would, and when it did, he would be there.

An hour or so later, Pendergrast came back out, got into his Cherokee, and pulled out. Larry followed, not optimistic that Pendergrast would commit a crime tonight, since Pendergrast seemed to do his prowling in the other car. Still, he followed him to the bar where they'd first arrested him.

He knew it was going to be a long wait as Pendergrast ambled in. To keep busy, he pulled Pendergrast's rap sheet and file out from under the seat. The two rapes they'd known about had happened very late at night, when the women were alone. It was clear that Pendergrast had known they would be alone, because both had been married, and in both cases he'd come on a night when their husbands had been working. Which meant he'd been watching them for some time. Then, on exactly the right night, he had broken into their homes and overpowered them.

Maybe there's someone he's watching now, he thought.

It was nearing midnight when Larry saw Pendergrast strutting out of the bar with a woman under his arm. Quickly, he cranked the car.

He watched as Pendergrast got behind the wheel and started the car, and thought how he'd love to slap a DUI charge on him. But that wouldn't help. That would keep him behind bars for about an hour.

He followed him to a neighborhood with small stucco houses, and hung back, several houses down with his lights off, as Pendergrast and the woman went inside.

Larry checked his watch. Maybe he should just go on home. This wasn't Pendergrast's typical MO. He didn't date the girls he raped. It was all done anonymously, cruelly, without any warning. He doubted this girl was in any danger.

On the other hand, he couldn't take the chance of leaving, just in case Pendergrast did hurt her.

He almost fell asleep several times, but shook himself awake, forcing himself to stay alert. It was almost three when Pendergrast came back out of the woman's house. He watched the man get into his car and drive off, and then he saw lights being turned off throughout the house. She was all right.

Cranking his car, he followed Pendergrast back to his apartment. It was nearing 3:30 when Pendergrast walked slowly back inside. Larry sat watching for a long moment, waiting for Pendergrast's lights to go off. When they did, at around four, he realized that the man was in for the night and wasn't likely to go out again.

Wearily, he headed for home and fell into his bed, praying that he'd be able to function the next day.

He fell into a troubled sleep, filled with dreams of Melissa being stalked and hounded by inmates and prison guards, being hurt or abused.

When the clock woke him at six A.M., he was soaked with sweat. He sat up abruptly. *God, help her*, he cried in his heart. *Please protect her.*

But the troubled feeling wouldn't leave him as he got ready for church—then changed his mind and decided to resume his stakeout instead. The obsessions he'd been accused of kept growing—more and more intense.

L arry's eyes were getting tired as he wove between cars on the interstate, trying to keep up with Pendergrast in the inconspicuous gray Toyota. He had followed Pendergrast home from work again tonight—as he had last night—watched as he went into a fast-food restaurant for dinner, then home. And just after nine, when Pendergrast had come out again and gotten into the gray Toyota, Larry's adrenaline had begun pumping. Maybe this was what he'd been waiting for.

He almost gave up when he saw Pendergrast turn into the mall parking lot and park outside a Dillards store. Was he going shopping just before closing time?

But Pendergrast didn't get out. Larry parked a few rows away and reached for the infrared binoculars he'd laid on the seat next to him. From where he sat, he had a terrific view of Pendergrast. The man made no move to get out. He was waiting for someone. And it didn't seem likely that he'd have brought the gray Toyota to pick up a girlfriend.

Larry watched as several families spilled out of the store near closing time, and he saw the manager of Dillards lock all but one of the doors as they prepared to close.

Group by group, employees walked out, escorted by a security guard, then dispersed in the parking lot, heading to their separate cars.

Pendergrast sat straighter now. He brought something to his face—binoculars? A camera?

Yes, it was a camera, Larry realized. Probably the camera they'd gotten from his apartment. He had, of course, gotten all of his confiscated things back after the charges against him had been dropped. The camera had a long lens on the front, and Larry guessed it was a night lens. He was taking pictures of the employees coming out. Larry moved his binoculars in the direction Pendergrast was shooting, and saw a young woman who looked about twenty, with long, flowing blonde hair a lot like Melissa's. She passed Pendergrast's car, unaware that she was being watched, and got into her own, which was two spaces down from his. By reflex, Larry reached for his gun and waited for Pendergrast to make a move.

The girl got into her car. The lights came on as she cranked it. Pendergrast did nothing as she pulled out of her space. The moment she was far enough across the parking lot not to see him, Pendergrast's lights came on and he pulled out in the same direction.

Larry followed, keeping his lights off, as his mind reeled. Pendergrast had targeted that young woman as his next victim. Larry's heart pumped triple-time as he followed both cars out into the light stream of traffic.

The young woman took an unfortunate route home—Highland Drive, the newly paved road where new construction was in progress during the day. The same road where Pendergrast had construction projects under way. Now, at night, the road was deserted.

From this distance, Larry couldn't read her tag number. He reached for his night binoculars again and held them to his eyes. Mumbling the numbers back to himself, he pulled the pen out of his pocket and scribbled the numbers on his arm. Tomorrow he could look it up, if it wasn't too late.

He followed as they came to an area of new housing at the end of the long road, and she pulled into an apartment complex only a couple of months old. He held his breath, waiting to see if Pendergrast was going to make a move. Pendergrast, too, pulled into the complex but continued on around the parking area, appearing to be just one more resident looking for his parking space. Larry pulled in near the young woman's car and cut his engine, waiting.

She got out and locked her door. Clutching her purse, she started toward her apartment.

Pendergrast's car came slowly around now, and pulled into a space. Larry watched him as Pendergrast watched her go up the steps and around to her apartment door.

"What are you doing?" Larry whispered as Pendergrast just sat there. Was he going to wait until the lights went off, then break in somehow and attack her? Or was he just watching, planning, for some other time?

After about twenty minutes, Pendergrast cranked his car and pulled out again.

Larry sat still for a moment before following. Then, staying far enough back not to be seen, he followed him back across town to Pendergrast's apartments. Pendergrast parked the Toyota at the far end of the parking lot, locked it, and walked over to his Cherokee. He pulled out, and Larry followed him to the bar where they'd arrested him. Was he done with the woman for tonight? Was he going back later?

Not willing to take the chance of missing whatever Pendergrast was up to, and risking the life of that young woman in the process, Larry decided he could make it the rest of the night without falling asleep. He had to.

Pendergrast was getting ready to make a move, and when he did, Larry would be there to catch him.

Larry's eyes were raw by the time he made it to the police station the next day. Pendergrast hadn't made a move; instead, he'd left the bar well after midnight with some other woman, and Larry had sat outside that house, waiting for some sign that there was trouble inside. At nearly four A.M., Pendergrast had driven home.

"You look like death warmed over," Tony said as Larry approached his desk. "Have you been sleeping?"

"Not much." Larry sat down and flicked on his computer.

"Are you sick, man?"

"No," Larry said irritably. He punched in the tag number of the car he'd seen the young woman driving last night, and waited.

"What are you doing?"

"He's stalking somebody."

Tony pulled up a chair and straddled it, looking over Larry's shoulder to the computer screen. "Who is?"

"Pendergrast. I followed him last night. He's stalking a woman who works at the mall."

Tony looked confused. "What do you mean, he's stalking her?"

"He's been watching her. He knows when she gets off work, what kind of car she drives, where she lives. He follows her home, and watches her go in."

"Well—does *he* go in?"

"No. He waits and watches, and then he just drives away."

Tony thought that over. "Are you sure he's not just pulling your string? I mean, maybe he realizes you've been following him. Maybe he's just trying to give you something to chew on."

"He doesn't know I'm there."

"How do you know? You've been watching him every night. How do you know he doesn't see you?"

"Because I've been careful, okay?" The name came up on the screen, and Larry sat back in his chair. "Her name is Karen Anderson. She's twenty-one. That's her, all right."

"What are you planning, Larry?"

"To get the captain to put somebody on her twenty-four hours. Maybe warn her what's going on."

"Larry, we can't spare that kind of man-hours. We have work to do."

Larry banged his fist on the desk and swiveled around in his chair. "That *is* our work, man! Keeping a woman from getting raped is just as much a part of our job as it is to clean up the mess afterward. Personally, I'd rather do it before."

Tony backed away slightly and lowered his voice. "But look at the logic, Larry. We know at least a dozen dangerous guys out there right now who are likely to commit a crime at any given time. It doesn't mean we can follow them around every minute of the day just to catch them at it."

"Then this whole system is twisted! If we can't prevent crimes, we might as well not even be here!"

Tony got up. "Look at you, Larry," he said, an edge of anger in his voice. "You're going to drop from exhaustion, and nothing's going to be accomplished. As a matter of fact, you'll probably make some terrible mistake and get yourself killed, just because you're not alert."

"I'm plenty alert."

"Oh, yeah? Your eyes look as bloodshot as a drunk's on Monday morning. And you haven't shaved."

Larry rubbed his jaw. He'd forgotten. "I'm growing a beard."

"In honor of Melissa? Have you taken a vow of self-deprivation until she serves her time?"

Ignoring him, Larry got up and kicked his chair out of his way. "I'm going to talk to the captain," he said.

Tony gave the chair a kick of his own as he went back to his desk.

Sam Richter was a no-nonsense captain who hated wasted time more than anything else in the world. He hated meetings and conferences and telephone calls that took him away from his work. Today, he was in a particularly bad mood because of a frustrating new case. And he was in no mood to listen to Larry's pleas to go off on some wild goose chase to get revenge for his convict girlfriend. The thought thoroughly disgusted him.

"Come on, Captain. I know he's about to strike. I have the name of the victim. We need to put a twenty-four-hour watch on her."

Sam looked at the ceiling, as if trying to find some patience there. "Millsaps, tell me something. When's the last time you slept? Or shaved, for that matter? Or took a bath?"

Larry thought of pleading the fifth, but instead he chose to remain silent.

"That's what I thought. It hasn't been recent." He leaned forward on his desk, his big hand propping up his chin. "Millsaps, I'm going to tell you this one time. Leave that man alone. You've caused him enough trouble. If you keep at it, you're going to get this police department slapped with another lawsuit, and I'm not in the mood to negotiate with that ambulance-chaser of a lawyer again."

"But Captain, you can't ignore what I saw! He's going to strike—I know he is. We can keep another girl from being raped."

"*Another* girl?" Sam asked on a laugh. "Millsaps, there wasn't a *first* rape. At least, not one that we can prove."

Larry burst out of his seat. "You're not buying into that innocence story, are you? How many times have you seen a suspect admit to what he's done? He's pretending he's innocent!"

"He may not be pretending." The captain stood up dismissively and took a file over to his file cabinet. "Millsaps, I know your girlfriend's going to jail really knocked you for a loop. Everybody in the precinct's talking about it."

Larry rolled his eyes and peered out the window to all the activity beyond it. "I should have known."

"But I don't have time to coddle you, man. I don't have any man-hours to devote to making you feel better. About fifteen minutes ago a jogger discovered a body washed up on Peretta Beach, and it turns out she was one of those two seventeen-year-old runaways from St. Clair. Now, I only have two detectives. You and Danks. I need you working on this, not going off on some hunch."

Larry couldn't accept that. "We can do both, Captain. Work on both cases. We can follow the girl, and—"

The captain leaned over his desk. "What part of 'no' don't you understand, Millsaps?"

Larry slapped at the chair he'd been sitting in, knocking it over.

The captain straightened with a look of quiet rage in his eye. "One more word—one more outburst—one more *anything* from you, Millsaps, and you're on suspension. Matter of fact, I just might put you on it, anyway. You're losing your edge, Detective. You're cracking up. I've never seen you behave this way in all the years I've known you. If you come in here like this tomorrow, you can look forward to a long vacation."

Not honoring that with a reply, Larry turned and slammed out of the office. As he bolted across the room, Tony looked up. "Hey, Larry. Wait!"

Larry didn't answer. He fled from the building as fast as he could.

CHAPTER THIRTY-SIX

Though the prison was air-conditioned, the huge room where they worked on the laundry was sweltering. Tiny vents at the top of the big warehouselike room blew cool air in, but the heat from the irons and the dryers and the steam from the washing machines all filled the room with a humid heat.

Melissa had been there only an hour, and already her hair was soaked with perspiration. Her clothes were sopping wet and sticking to her, and she began to feel dizzy, as if she might faint from the heat.

Behind her, women cursed at each other, but guards who had the misfortune of being assigned to this location didn't bat an eye. They were used to the foul moods and foul mouths of the women who worked here day after day.

She grabbed the next jumpsuit in her basket, laid it on the ironing board, and quickly reached for the iron. Her fingers brushed the hot metal, scalding her flesh, and she jumped back, knocking the iron over.

A CO was at her side in an instant, not to help, but to warn her against wasting time.

Quickly, she picked the iron back up, fighting back the tears in her eyes as her skin began to blister.

Where was the peace she was supposed to feel? Where was the comfort that would chase away the paralyzing, stomach-knotting fear? All she felt was the terror of messing up, the horror of making the wrong person mad, the fear of getting killed in this abyss where they had sent her to teach her not to lie.

She looked across the room and saw her big roommate, Chloe, folding towels with a slow, methodical rhythm. Each night, she lay awake, listening to the rhythm of Chloe's breathing, waiting for the woman to snap and decide that she was angry enough at Melissa to attack her.

But she hadn't. Chloe was a mystery. One minute, she was leering at Melissa as if she could snap her in two, and the next she was leering at the others who looked as if they might like to try. She couldn't decide if the woman was tormentor or protector.

She longed for ice to put on the burn to relieve the pain, but she kept working. She tried to shift her mind away from the pain by wondering where Larry was, whether he was working today, whether he would be coming to visit tomorrow.

She wouldn't be crushed if he didn't come, she told herself. It was best if he didn't. She didn't want him to see her this way.

Her parents would come, and that would probably be all the emotional upheaval she could stand for one day. That she had ever put them in the position of having to visit their child in prison gave her such shame that she wanted to die.

Her mind counted the hours she had been here already. Five days. That meant there were only 177 days to go. 4,248 hours. 254,880 minutes.

Only three days before she'd earn her first visitation privileges.

She needed something more constructive to occupy her mind and wished that she had memorized Scripture so that she could call on it now when she felt such despair. Maybe that's what she would start doing during her free time in her cell. Maybe it would get her mind off Chloe's bad moods—and her fears that the next moment she might explode like a ticking bomb.

CHAPTER THIRTY-SEVEN

The back door to his church was open, as it always was during the week, and Larry stepped into the big corridor, avoiding the choir director and minister of education who were conversing in the hall just outside their offices. Hurrying, he made his way to the small private prayer room at the back of the building and slipped inside.

It was dark, except for two dim little bulbs at the front of the room. There were four pews, and he slipped into the back one and looked at the small podium on which a big Bible lay open. His sister had gotten married here—it had been a quiet wedding, with just the families in attendance. Katie was shy, and she hadn't wanted a big production made out of something she considered so personal.

That had been a joyous occasion, an occasion when Larry had felt the Holy Spirit's presence so keenly that he'd felt he could reach out and touch his Savior. Now, it seemed like ages since he'd felt that.

He sank into the pew, covering his face, letting out the deep, dark misery on his heart. "Everything's out of control," he whispered to his Creator. "I can't help. I can't change anything. And now I can't even come to you."

The barren loneliness in those words hit him harder than anything else had that day, and he wept into his hands, desperate for some word that would somehow restore him. But there was a wall there—between him and God—a wall he had constructed himself. And he had made no move to break it down. Like Melissa, he'd decided that he wasn't worthy, that his own choices had rendered him unacceptable in God's eyes.

"I was going to lie for her," he whispered, propping his elbows on his knees and looking down at his feet. "You took it out of my hands. I didn't have to do it. But I would have. And I'm just as guilty as if I had."

He wondered whether he'd have felt repentant and remorseful if Melissa hadn't come forward and if he'd gone through with his plan to cover for her—

Yes, he thought unequivocally. He had been miserable about the choice even before he'd made it. It would have eaten at him, just as it did now. That was God's curse—as well as God's blessing.

He looked up at the ceiling, as if he could see God sitting there, judging him. "I don't even know what to say," he cried. "I want to pray for her, plead with you to change things somehow, to get her out of jail, to put Pendergrast away—but how can you hear my prayers when I've turned away?"

He leaned his arms on the pew in front of him and rested his head on them. "Nothing makes sense, Lord. He's going to do it again. To another innocent girl. And it's Melissa in jail instead of him. Help me to understand!"

A verse like an admonition came into his mind:

You do not have in mind the things of God, but the things of men.

He looked up, his face wet and twisted, and wondered why that verse, of all others, had spoken to him just now. It couldn't work to God's glory, he thought, for a beautiful, sweet, broken woman to be in jail. Or for Pendergrast to ruin another life. Those couldn't be "things of God."

Again, the verse played like a chant through his mind, and finally, he broke down and got to his knees. Maybe that *was* God's answer—that Larry *didn't* understand it, and that in fact it wasn't up to him to understand. Who was he to question the mind of God?

Suddenly, an overwhelming remorse fell over him, so deep and heavy that it almost flattened him. He had done exactly as Melissa had done. He had trusted his own solutions rather than God's. He had taken things out of his Father's hands, and with his own limited vision, had decided how things should go. "Please forgive me, Lord. Forgive me for not trusting you. Forgive me for making a decision to lie and cheat, for turning away."

He wept until he was exhausted. Finally, he got up again and sat on the pew, listening, waiting, hearing. His eyes fell on the open Bible, and he slowly got up and went toward it.

The book was open to Luke 22. Aloud, in a trembling voice, he read Jesus' words.

"Simon, Simon, Satan has asked to sift you as wheat. But I have prayed for you, Simon, that your faith may not fail. And when you have turned back, strengthen your brothers."

But he replied, "Lord, I am ready to go with you to prison and to death."

Jesus answered, "I tell you, Peter, before the rooster crows today, you will deny three times that you know me."

Jesus had known that Peter would turn away, that he would lie, and cheat, and run. And even knowing that, he had assured him that his relationship with God would not be ruined. *When* you turn back, Jesus had said. He had known he would. Just as he had known Larry would.

Larry felt that same forgiveness washing over him, cleansing him, filling him with the strength he would need to get through the days ahead. They were no worse than Peter's future had been—no more frightening, no more uncertain. But this was *his* future . . . and Melissa's. And he would need God to get him through it.

He sat back down, amazed and awestruck at the way the Lord had ministered to him, even when he hadn't deserved it—but then he realized that he had *never* deserved it. That was the beauty of grace. God was not dwelling on his past sin. God was looking ahead to how he wanted to use Larry.

"Strengthen your brothers."

Melissa would need strengthening. And he would be there for her.

"Peace I leave with you; my peace I give you. I do not give to you as the world gives. Do not let your hearts be troubled and do not be afraid."

More Scripture he'd memorized, never realizing how much he would need it one day. Now it came to him like an old friend, holding his hand, propping him up.

He sat there for a while longer, in his own private Gethsemane, soaking in the peace of God's love and forgiveness and hope.

And knowing that whatever was to happen in the next few hours and days, it was all in the hands of the Almighty God.

An hour later, as Larry and Tony drove in silence in their unmarked car to the beach where the runaway's body had washed up, Tony looked at him. "I took it from the way you burst out of the building a little while ago that the captain nixed your idea."

"He said what you said. Not enough manpower."

"I figured."

"So meanwhile, another girl is going to end up a victim before we act."

"Maybe not."

Larry was bone tired and didn't feel like arguing. But he couldn't let that go. "He's a rapist, Tony. We know it. And now he's stalking another woman. How long before we realize what's going on? What'll it take? Why is everybody so dead set on proving that Pendergrast is a saint?"

"History," Tony said. "We thought he'd done something before, and it turned out he didn't. Nobody else wants egg on their face." Tony looked over at his friend, as if deciding whether to say what was on his mind. "Larry, there are people on the force who think you're losing your edge. They think you snapped when Melissa went to jail. They don't give a lot of credence to your ideas right now."

Larry sat still for a moment, letting it all sink in. Too emotionally exhausted to fight back, he said, "I've been on this force for twelve years, Tony. I've always done my job with a clear head and all the energy and commitment I could give it."

"We know that, Larry. But look at you. You haven't shaved in days, you haven't slept, you're probably not even eating—it's hard to put a lot of stock in what you say when you look like you're about to go over the edge."

"Then ride with me," Larry entreated. "Ride with me tonight, after we're off duty. You'll see. I'll show you."

"Larry, you saw him stake her out once. That doesn't mean he does it every night."

"He might," Larry said. "Ride with me. Just come once and you'll see."

"Man, I need my sleep. So do you."

"All right. Just until the mall closes. Just give me that long, and I'll take you home."

"So what do you hope to accomplish? I mean, even if I come, and he stalks her tonight—"

"Back me up with the captain. Tell him I'm not losing it. Talk him into putting a tail on the girl."

Tony sighed. "I don't even know if he'd listen to me."

"That's my problem. Just come with me. Let me show you."

Tony moaned. "But it's Friday night, man. I have a date."

"Cancel it. Look at the irony here, Tony. We're heading out to the beach to investigate this girl's death—and at the same time, *another* girl's life is in danger, and we won't do anything to stop it."

The look in Larry's eyes was so haunted, so weary, so determined, that Tony found himself agreeing.

"No matter what we find, the girl on the beach is dead. We're not going to bring her back. But what if we had seen somebody preparing to kill her before she died? What if we could have stopped it? Would we have turned our heads and gone on with our other cases?"

Tony thought that over for a long moment. "All right, Larry," he said finally. "But just tonight. And that's only if we're finished with the work on this case by then. After the news reports on this girl's death come out, we might get some call-in leads on the girl who ran away with her. But if we don't have any strong leads on this case, I'll go with you."

The girl who'd been found on the beach was a young blonde who had apparently been raped and beaten to death before she'd been dumped into the Gulf. Larry and Tony hadn't spent much time at the site where she'd washed up; there was little evidence there to collect. Instead, they spent the afternoon talking to her shocked family members and friends. Her best friend, Lisa, who had run away with her and still hadn't been located, had been known to abuse drugs with her. The coroner said that the girl may have been dead for two weeks.

The trail of her killer was cold, and Larry suspected that it would take them out of their jurisdiction. She had probably been thrown in from a boat somewhere out at sea, and it had probably taken several days for her to wash up. They had already spent entire days searching for leads on the girls' whereabouts, and Larry suspected that they would have just as much trouble piecing together the facts surrounding her death.

Since they had no leads, and little information about what had happened to the girls since their disappearance, Tony agreed to ride with Larry that night.

They followed Pendergrast home from work, then ate their own cold burgers in the car, waiting for him to come back out. "I thought of going into the mall and finding her," Larry said. "Telling her to be on her guard."

"That would be a mistake at this point, Larry. You can't alert every girl Pendergrast looks at. The man has never been convicted of anything. If you start going around telling people to look out for this guy because he's a rapist and he's after them, you'll wind up losing your job."

The door to Pendergrast's apartment opened, and he came out into the darkness and headed quietly down the steps.

"He's going to the Toyota," Larry said quietly. "He thinks he's covering his tracks with his Cherokee parked at home."

He cranked the engine, and pulled out without turning on the lights. Across the parking lot, they saw the lights come on in the gray Toyota, and Pendergrast pulled out.

"What do you think?" Larry asked, pulling into traffic several cars behind him. "You want to go to the mall?"

Tony was silent as they followed. "Isn't it a little early? The mall doesn't close for another hour."

"I don't know. Let's see."

"He's turning."

"Going to the mall," Larry said victoriously.

They followed him down the streets that would take them to the mall, and Larry pointed to the Dillards store. "He'll go there," he said. "Watch him."

They watched as he pulled into a parking space not far from the Dillards entrance. Larry and Tony pulled in several aisles over.

"Now what?" Tony asked. "Does he just sit there?"

"Did last night. Just sat there watching and waiting."

Tony absorbed it for a moment. "Maybe it's not just her he's after. Maybe he's just waiting for anybody who looks vulnerable."

"Maybe," Larry said. "He was taking pictures. Looked like he had some kind of night lens on his camera."

"He took pictures of her?"

Larry nodded.

"Hmmm." The light came on in Pendergrast's car, and Tony leaned forward. "Is he getting out?"

"Looks like it." Larry grabbed the handle of his car door. "He's going in. I'll follow him. You stay here in case I lose him and he comes back out."

Tony nodded, and Larry got out and quietly mashed the door shut behind him. He walked several yards behind Pendergrast, several rows over, and waited to let him get inside before he made it to the door.

The lights of the department store assaulted him as he stepped inside, and he looked around to find Pendergrast. He was up ahead, walking through the cosmetics section.

Larry skirted the area, then rode the escalator upstairs. As soon as he got off, he went around to the rail that looked down on the cosmetics area in the center of the store. From here he had a perfect view, and Pendergrast wasn't likely to look up and see him.

He watched as Pendergrast seemed to be studying the men's cologne. After a moment, the girl he'd followed home last night finished with her customer and waited on him.

She was pretty, Larry thought, and younger than she'd seemed last night. She looked just the way Pendergrast liked them: blonde, small, delicate—like Melissa and Sandy.

Larry's stomach tightened into a knot as Pendergrast leaned on the counter, with that charming, drop-your-guard grin that was so deceiving. She was enjoying him, he thought. She was laughing at his flirtations.

After a moment, he paid for the cologne and, with one last comment that made her laugh again, he sauntered away.

What is he doing? Larry asked himself as he watched Pendergrast head back out the door. Did he ask her out? Was this whole thing nothing more than a man getting interested in a woman and pursuing her?

He waited until Pendergrast was gone, then rode the escalator back down and went to the same counter. He saw the display of men's cologne that Pendergrast had purchased and picked up a bottle, himself.

"May I help you?"

He knew by the information in the computer about her, based on her car registration, that she was only twenty. She looked even younger. "Yeah, I was just trying to decide if I wanted this. That guy who was here a minute ago, he bought some, didn't he?"

She smiled. "Yeah. He did."

"Is he a regular customer?"

She shrugged. "I've never seen him before, but he said the scent caught his attention. I tried to interest him in the bath products and shaving cream, too. I'll bet he comes back."

"Why?"

"They usually do. They get one product and they fall in love with it. Or they get such a response from their girlfriends that they can't help wanting all the rest."

Larry smiled. "Do you get many of them hassling you for dates?"

She giggled. "Occupational hazard when you sell men's cosmetics. Here, you want to try some?"

She sprayed the cologne on his arm, rubbed it in, then offered him the back of his wrist to smell.

He nodded. "I like it. But I don't generally wear cologne."

"Your girl will like it."

His grin faded slightly. "She likes me without it."

"Then buy *her* some. I sell women's cologne, too. Over here. You can try some of it—"

He held up his hand to stem her sales pitch, and leaned on the counter. "No, I don't need any today. But just tell me one thing. That guy who was here. Did he ask you out?"

She looked confused at the question. "No. Why?"

"I was just curious. He looked a little old for you."

She was irritated now. "I really don't think that is any of your business. Now, if you'll excuse me, I'm a little busy."

558

As she walked to the other side of the counter, he thought about telling her that the man who'd just bought cologne from her was a known rapist, that he was stalking her, trying to build trust, but that she couldn't trust him. The phone rang, and as she answered it, Tony's cautions raced through his mind. He couldn't panic her now. Not without more cause.

Sighing, he headed for a different entrance from the one he'd used coming in, and circled through the dark parking lot back to the car, praying Pendergrast would be watching the doors he was closest to and not see him.

The light didn't come on when he opened the door. The mechanics at the precinct had long ago wired his car to keep that from happening. He slid into the driver's seat.

"Where have you been, man?" Tony asked. "He came out ten minutes ago."

"Talking to the girl."

"Oh, no. You didn't."

"He bought something from her. Didn't ask her out, though. He's still sitting there?"

"Yeah. Getting close to closing time. Larry, you didn't tell her who you are, or who he is, did you?"

"Nope."

Tony breathed a sigh of relief.

"We just have to watch," Larry said. "Get a little more to go on. He's trying to establish her trust. Maybe so she'll go with him later."

"But that isn't his normal MO, is it? I mean, he didn't attack women who knew him. He uses the element of surprise, breaks into their homes—"

"Those are just the ones we know about. Besides, they identified him, didn't they? Maybe they had seen him before."

Tony grew quiet.

Customers began leaving, going to their cars, as a security car patrolled the parking lot.

They waited quietly for the employees to scatter.

"Here she comes," Larry said as the young woman came out of the building, along with several other women and a security guard. "Funny how they all have such a sense of security being with that guard, but the minute they pull out of the parking lot they're on their own."

"She has us," Tony said.

"Yeah. Tonight she does."

They watched her car start up, and just as Larry had expected, Pendergrast's lights came on, too. "Time to go," Larry said.

Keeping his lights off, Larry waited until she had pulled to the parking lot's exit. Pendergrast followed.

As they drove down the deserted street, Tony shook his head. "Unfortunate route home."

"Tell me about it. 'Course it depends on your perspective. From his, it's the perfect route."

After a few minutes, they reached the end of the road and she turned into her parking lot. Pendergrast followed, but Larry didn't pull in. This time, he stayed way back, on the side of the street, watching.

Tony brought his infrared binoculars to his eyes and watched her trot up to her apartment. Pendergrast stayed in his car, watching.

Her light was on for several minutes when Pendergrast pulled out of the parking lot and headed back the way he had come.

Larry's heart sank.

"Guess he's not doing anything tonight," Tony said.

"No. He's not ready yet. But I don't think he'll wait a whole lot longer."

Larry started the car but headed in the opposite direction from Pendergrast.

"Where we going?" Tony asked.

"Home," Larry said. "That was the deal. After the mall closes, I take you home."

Tony was quiet for a moment. "You're coming back, aren't you?"

Larry didn't answer.

"Larry, are you gonna stay up all night again watching him?"

"What do you want me to do, Tony? He raped Sandy at three A.M. What if I go home and get some sleep in my nice warm bed, and tomorrow morning the headline in the paper is that a nice, young, innocent blonde woman was raped by an unknown assailant during the night."

"Larry, you can't stay up all night and work all day."

"Then back me up on this," Larry said. "Tell the captain we need to be on this case for a while—then we can just work nights. Tell him what we saw tonight. Tell him I'm not crazy."

Tony sighed. "I'll try. But with this other case—"

"There's no case more important than this one," he said. "Not to me. There's a rapist walking the streets of St. Clair. You tell me what's more important."

Tony didn't answer.

CHAPTER THIRTY-EIGHT

The captain didn't come in the next day; he had meetings with the mayor all day long. Larry found himself torn between hurrying through his other cases to get back to Pendergrast and haunting City Hall, hoping to run into the captain. Giving up, he resolved to sacrifice another night's sleep to follow Pendergrast, just in case. Tony, afraid that Larry was about to reach the point of exhaustion, agreed to keep watch with him.

Pendergrast was getting bolder. Tonight, as Larry and Tony watched from across the dark mall parking lot, Pendergrast went into Dillards again. This time they both followed, watching him from two separate vantage points in the department store.

Pendergrast didn't go near the young blonde woman; instead, he watched her from a distance across the store. His fascination with her was clear. He watched her wait on customers, watched her clean the counter, watched her restock merchandise.

When she took a break and walked out into the mall, Pendergrast followed her, with Larry not far behind. She went to the food court and bought some French fries and a drink, then joined some friends at one of the tables. Pendergrast blended into the crowd at one of the vendors, continuing to watch her.

Tonight, Larry thought. *He's going to do something tonight.*

One by one, her friends left to go back to their jobs, leaving the woman alone at the table, and Larry held his breath, waiting, wondering if Pendergrast would approach her now. But he didn't. It wasn't his style. He had shown himself to her only once, so that he would be familiar to her, but not recognizable. He probably didn't want to be identified later.

Two women had identified him already. He had probably learned from those mistakes.

Finally, she threw away her bags and her drink and headed into the ladies' rest room.

Pendergrast followed.

The long hall leading to the rest rooms was dimly lit. Larry had long been aware of it because so many crimes had happened right there, and he had once tried to convince the management to either put an armed guard there or else to close the facility altogether and put a rest room out near the mainstream of mall traffic. But so far they hadn't listened.

Now, he felt helpless as Pendergrast gave her a head start to reach the ladies' room around the corner of the long hall, then started down it himself. Larry couldn't follow without being seen. All he could do was wait, and listen, and pray.

Five minutes later, he saw the woman coming back up the hall. Breathing a sigh of relief, Larry backed into the crowd, becoming invisible. After a few seconds, Pendergrast came back up the hall, his eyes intense as he followed her all the way back to her store. When she was behind her counter again, he headed back to his car.

Tony was already in the car when Larry made his way back. "See anything?" Tony asked.

Larry reached for his infrared binoculars. "He followed her to the bathroom. I thought he was going to act then, but he didn't."

"He's getting hungry," Tony said. "No question. Something's about to happen."

"Poor girl is walking right into this." Larry watched as Pendergrast settled back in his seat, watching the door. "So what did you see?"

Tony shrugged. "Same thing you did. When I saw you following them out of the store, though, I figured you had it under control. So I took the opportunity to take a look in that car of his. The door wasn't locked."

Larry dropped the binoculars and looked at him. "Find anything?"

"Nothing in the front. But when I clicked the release on the trunk, it came open. I found a shovel and a jumbo-sized garbage bag."

Larry's face went pale.

"Doesn't mean anything," Tony went on. "He could have been taking them to clean up a construction site or something. Just because it was big enough to put a body in—"

"You think he's a killer?" Larry asked.

Tony shook his head. "I didn't say that. We can't jump to conclusions."

But Larry already had. "Tony, we know that he's got an obsession. We know he's raped twice before, and my bet is that he's done it more than that. We don't know how many times, or how bad. He almost killed Melissa's sister. Could be that he's stopped someone from talking before." He brought the binoculars back to his eyes. "He broke into Melissa's apartment, wrote on her mirror, hid in her attic. He was probably going to kill her, too."

Tony peered toward the man sitting so inconspicuously in his car. "Yeah, well, you should probably be glad she's locked up. She's probably in the only place she could be safe from him. Hey, if somebody set me up for something I didn't do, I'd want to get even. Put that revenge in the mind of a man who's a maniac already, and you don't know what he's capable of."

"Then you're admitting it," Larry said. "He's a maniac."

Tony didn't answer, but he didn't need to. Larry knew Tony was convinced.

"As it stands," Larry whispered, "he's just going along with business as usual. Setting up his target, moving in for the kill . . ."

"Well, if you're right, he won't get away with it this time." Tony looked at his watch. "Mall closes in an hour."

They waited, watching, as Pendergrast waited, watching.

An hour later, when the employees began to come out, they saw Karen Anderson among them. This time, however, she wasn't alone as she separated from the group and headed for her car. There was a man with her. They watched as she got into her car, and the man got in on the other side.

"She's giving this guy a ride home," Tony said, cranking the car but leaving the lights off. "What's Pendergrast doing?"

"He's cranking up," Larry said, watching him through the binoculars. "He's going to follow, anyway."

They followed quietly as she took her usual route home. Pendergrast drove about a quarter of a mile behind her, and Larry and Tony, with their lights still off, followed a good distance behind him. When they reached her apartments, they parked on the street again. The man got out with her, and the two of them headed up to her apartment.

Pendergrast didn't wait. As if angry, he sped back out of the parking lot and headed back up the way they had come, past the construction sites. Larry and Tony struggled to keep him in their view as they turned the car around and followed. Halfway up Highland Drive, Pendergrast turned onto a dirt road and disappeared among the trees. Tony stepped on the brakes.

"Where's he going? Should I follow him?"

"No. We don't know where that road goes. Besides, there's only room for one car. If he turns around and comes back, he'll see us. Let's just wait."

So they waited, holding their breath, for Pendergrast to return. After about twenty minutes, he did.

They followed him back to his apartment. When his lights went off after twenty minutes, they assumed that he'd gone to bed. Quickly they drove back to the dirt road down which he had disappeared earlier. Tony started to turn the car into the little dirt road, but Larry stopped him. "Not a good idea," he said. "Let's park and walk. If he sees our tire tracks tomorrow, he'll know someone's on to him."

Tony pulled the car to the side of the road. They got out and hiked up the long, dirt road, shining their flashlights as they went, not knowing what they were looking for, but hoping they'd know when they saw it. They followed the tiny, broken road all the way to the end, about a mile into the woods, then around a curve and further into the trees.

"Do you think this is where he was going to take her?" Tony asked.

Tony nodded. "Has to be. But it's too dark to see anything tonight. We'll have to come back tomorrow when the sun comes up."

Larry agreed. "Even if we don't find anything, at least we can get familiar with it in case we have to come this way again." He gave Tony a pensive look. "It won't be much longer now," he whispered. "He's ready. I'm just worried about the girl."

"Well, we could tell her and stop the whole thing. She could quit her job, never go home alone again, move. It would divert this attack, all right, but it wouldn't stop him from the next one."

"I want to get him," Larry whispered. "I want to get him for good."

"Then this is the only way. She'll be traumatized and terrified, but she'll be alive. We won't let him hurt her."

Larry thought about that for a long moment. "I just wish I could be sure of that."

CHAPTER THIRTY-NINE

It was nearly nine in the morning by the time Tony and Larry made it back to the dirt road they had seen Pendergrast turn down the night before. They had watched his apartment for most of the night, then gone home for a little sleep before getting up and getting started again. Today, fatigued but determined, they made sure that Pendergrast was engaged at a construction site in another area before they checked out the road.

In the daylight, Highland Drive looked less threatening. Construction was going up in various places along the road, and the curb was lined with the trucks of men working. But the dirt road to which they'd followed Pendergrast last night was at least half a mile from the nearest construction site.

Again, they left the car on the street and followed the road on foot. After walking for twenty minutes or so, Tony asked, "How far do you think we've come?"

"A mile, at least," Larry said. "I didn't even know the woods back here were this thick. Where do you think it goes?"

"Nowhere," Tony said. "The next road is close to the interstate, but that's several miles from here. Listen." He slowed his step. "Do you hear that?"

Larry listened for a moment. "Water. Do you think there's a pond or something? Maybe people fish here?"

"Now that I think about it, there's a little canal that feeds into the Gulf. The road Highland runs into crosses it. It must cut through these woods."

They followed the road until they came to the canal. The Toyota's tire tracks turned onto a clearing there, and Larry muttered, "Bingo."

"This is where he came last night, anyway," Tony said, stepping into the clearing and looking around. "Well, one thing's for sure. If he's planning to bring her here at night, it's far enough back that nobody would hear her scream."

"And if he left her here, it's not likely that anybody would find her for a while, either."

He set his hands on his hips and looked around. The canopy of trees was so thick that little sun got through. It was hot, too, for little wind was able to sweep through the thick brush. He wondered how Pendergrast had found this place to begin with, then realized that the guy probably knew the land around here intimately, since his company contracted the clearing of it for new construction sites. Proffer Builders might even own it.

"What's this?"

Tony was across the small clearing, stepping through bushes and trees, getting closer to the water.

"What?" Larry asked.

"Oh, man." Tony turned back. "You've got to see this."

Larry hurried across the clearing and stepped through the brush. His breath caught in his chest when he saw what Tony was standing over. "Unbelievable."

It was a round hole about six feet deep, but the diameter of the hole was no more than three feet. The dirt that had been dug out of the hole was piled next to it, ready to be shoved back in.

Larry got down on his knees and peered into the hole. "Well, there goes the possibility that it's preparation for clearing the land. That shovel and bag you saw last night?"

Tony looked in and saw them at the bottom of the hole. "He's planning to kill her."

"Yep."

"He would have buried her here, and nobody would have found her. He could bury her in five minutes, kick a few leaves over the dirt..."

Larry sat down on the ground, resting his arms on his knees. "He might have buried Melissa here."

"Do you think he'll go after Karen Anderson tonight?"

"Could be. We have to be ready. Somehow, he's going to have to get her into his car, so he can get her here." Larry was beginning to look pale. "What if we don't make it in time, Tony? What if we get there too late?"

"We won't."

Larry rubbed his face. "This poor kid. She has no idea what's about to happen to her."

"We'll stop him before he hurts her, Larry."

"We *hope* we will." He looked at Tony, playing possible scenarios over in his mind. "What if we used a decoy?"

"We can't," Tony said. "Not if we want to catch him on something that'll stick. You can't really think he's going to drag some woman off and rape her without looking at her face."

"We have to catch him," Larry said. "But there has to be some other way."

"There isn't, man. She'll be all right. We'll be right there, and the minute something happens, we'll have handcuffs on that guy so fast he won't know what hit him."

"I don't like it."

"What do you mean, you don't like it? This is your case! You started the whole thing!"

"But this is somebody's life, Tony!"

"Hey, if it weren't for you, we wouldn't know anything happened until her mother reported her missing. You're saving her life, not risking it!"

"But there's a way to be more sure. First, we have to tell the captain, and get his support on this."

"Yeah, I'm with you. And then?"

Larry looked up at him. "And then we have to tell her. Maybe she can help us."

Despite Larry's absolute exhaustion, his adrenaline was pumping as he went back to the station. He was about to catch Pendergrast, and that was enough to keep him going.

It was midmorning when he and Tony finally were able to get in to talk to the captain about taking the Pendergrast case full-time until they caught him. Tony backed up what Larry had already said—adding credence to the story with his clear-headed, emotionless recitation of the things they'd observed—and the captain paced in his usual way, turning the facts over in his mind.

"Okay, I'll buy it—something's about to happen," he said. "And since we don't have any leads at the moment on the girl on the beach, I guess you can work on this for a couple of days. But if nothing happens in the very near future, I'm gonna have to take you off of it again."

Larry's relief was apparent, but he pressed on to the next question. "Thanks, man," Larry said, getting to his feet. "But there's one more thing. I want to let the woman in on it. See if we can convince her to cooperate with us."

Sam considered that for a moment. "You might blow the whole thing if she says no."

"I'll convince her."

"How?"

"I don't know," Larry said, leaning over the desk. "But her life is at risk here. If we tell her, arm her, let her know what's about to come down, she might be willing to go through with it. It's the only way we can be sure to stop it when it happens. Otherwise, something could go wrong, and she could get raped, or even killed."

The captain sat slowly down at his desk. Clasping his hands in front of his face, he gazed at Tony. "What do you think?"

Tony wasn't sure. "I'd hate to have her balk and run. Then we might never catch him. On the other hand, if anybody can convince her, Larry can."

"It might work," the captain said. "We can do a lot more to prepare if she's with us."

"All right," Larry said. "Then we'll go talk to her. But we're going to have to make some promises. Give her a sense of security. Let her know we won't abandon her."

"Let me know what you need," the captain said. "I'll make sure you get it."

Tony shook the captain's hand and started to the door, but when Larry reached for his hand, the captain held it a beat longer than necessary. "Sorry about the other day, Millsaps. I may have been too hard on you. I was a little stressed, what with this body washing up, and the mayor breathing down my neck about the drug problem."

"Don't worry about it, Captain. I have a tough skin."

"You must," he said. "How long've you been working around the clock now? A week?"

"I'll sleep when we get that jerk in jail."

"So will I," the captain said. "So will I."

CHAPTER FORTY

The crowd of inmates walking from the dining hall to cellblock C threaded into a single-file line that followed the yellow line down the hall and back to their cells. Melissa watched a group of correctional officers coming toward them, walking side by side. She had never realized how much she would miss the freedom to walk the way she wanted, where she wanted. Now, every step, every thought, every activity was monitored and controlled.

Some of the women talked as they walked behind each other, but most were quiet, for one never knew when the wrath of one of the "bosses" might be stirred. It didn't take much. One woman had been caught looking too long at a male officer, and it had made one of his jealous coworkers angry. She had dragged that woman out of line and put her in isolation for three days. So Melissa walked with her eyes downcast, never straying from that yellow line, for fear that she'd be cited for bad behavior and have even one extra day added to her sentence.

As they drew closer to the doors to their cellblock, instead of crossing diagonally toward it, they had to follow the yellow line to its corner, turn ninety degrees, and then follow another line toward the doors. It was degrading, humiliating.

As soon as they were in their cellblock, however, they were free to leave the line and mill about their floor. Melissa hurried toward her cell.

Something tripped her, and she stumbled, then quickly recovered her balance. She turned around. The redhead who had harassed her on her first day was walking behind her, grinning.

Melissa compressed her lips, determined not to be drawn into a fight. But when she turned to walk on, the woman tripped her again. This time, Melissa swung around. "What do you want?" she demanded.

Red shoved her then, and Melissa lashed out to defend herself. Before she knew what had happened, the woman flung herself away from Melissa across the concrete floor, slammed herself into the opposite wall, and screamed. She came up with her knee bleeding. "I'll kill you!" she shouted.

Realizing that she was watching an award-winning performance, Melissa backed away, hands raised, as the COs rushed toward them. "I didn't touch her," she said. "She was harassing me, and then she flung herself across the hall—"

"She's lying!" Red screamed. "She knocked me across the hall! Look at my knee! I think it's dislocated. I won't be able to work tomorrow because of her."

"All right," one of the COs said, grabbing Melissa's arm roughly. "I'm writing you up. You can spend a night in isolation, and see if you still want to fight tomorrow."

"But I didn't do anything! She set me up!"

But the CO didn't care. He dragged Melissa out of the cell-block and down to the isolation cell she had heard about but never seen. It was six feet by four feet; everything was metal and welded down. There were no sheets on the bed, just a two-inch-thick pad that served as a mattress on the metal bed frame. A metal sink and a metal toilet were welded to one wall. The room was sweltering.

"Listen to me, please," she told the CO. "I'm telling you—"

But the huge, sliding metal door slid shut behind him, and she was locked in.

"I didn't do it," she whispered, sitting down on the edge of the bed. "I didn't do it."

She sat there for hours, waiting for someone to come so that she could plead her case, but no one came. Unable to tell what time it was, but guessing that it was nearing midnight, she finally stretched out on the miserable excuse for a mattress and tried to sleep. Red was probably sleeping soundly in her cell, with her knee bandaged up from her self-inflicted wound, and laughing that she'd escaped a day of work at Melissa's expense.

Fantasies of revenge floated through Melissa's mind—fantasies of *really* dislocating the woman's knee—but in the wee hours of morning, she realized that she'd tried that before. That's what had landed her here. She wasn't going to become like the others here, she told herself. Even if it killed her, she would resist.

Tears ran down her temples and into her hair. *Help me to forgive them, Lord. I'm not very good at that.*

And as she finally drifted into a fitful sleep, she knew that she could trust God to answer that prayer, in his own time.

CHAPTER FORTY-ONE

Larry and Tony made sure that Pendergrast was working away in his office before they went to Karen Anderson's apartment. They had already learned from her license tag information her address, her name, and her age. Now all they needed was her trust.

They tried to be quiet and inconspicuous as they made their way up the stairs to her door. Larry knocked. After a moment, they heard footsteps.

"Who is it?" a woman asked through the door.

"Larry Millsaps, St. Clair Police Department. Can we talk to you for a moment?"

The door cracked open, and Karen peered beneath the chain lock. "What about?"

Larry glanced at Tony, and he stepped forward, flashing his badge. "We're detectives with the St. Clair P.D. Are you Karen Anderson?"

"Yes." She reached through the crack in the door and took both badges, read them, then peered up at the two detectives.

"We need to talk to you in private. It's very important."

Reluctantly, she closed her door, unlocked the chain, and opened it again. "You were in the store the other night," she said to Larry as they came in. "You didn't tell me you were a detective."

"No," he said. "I was hoping it wouldn't be necessary." He closed the door and glanced around the small apartment.

"Could we sit down?"

She led them into the small living room furnished with old furniture that had seen better days. A pair of shoes lay in the middle of the floor, and books and papers were scattered all over the couch and coffee table. "Excuse the apartment. I've been studying."

"You're in school?" Tony asked.

"Yes," she said. "I go to Jones College in the mornings."

Larry moved some library books out of a chair and sat down. "Don't clean up on our account. You probably have everything right where you need it. We just need to talk to you."

She stopped straightening and swept her hair behind her ears. "What's going on?"

Larry gestured for her to sit down, and finally, she did. "Miss Anderson, we're here because you're in danger. In the course of an investigation that we've been doing, it's come to our attention that you're being stalked. Were you aware of this?"

She frowned and looked from one cop to the other. "Stalked? What do you mean?"

"You're being followed by a man who has been arrested before on rape charges. He's been watching you. We believe he has every intention of making you his next victim. And soon."

"What?" The word came out in an astonished whisper, and she sprang up and went to the window. Peering out, she asked, "Is he out there now?"

"No," Larry said. "We made sure he was someplace else before we came here."

She kept staring out the window. "Why haven't you arrested him?"

"Because he hasn't done anything yet. Twice before he was arrested and got off on technicalities. We have to wait until we can catch him at something substantial enough to get him put away for a long time."

"How do you know he's following me? Maybe it's someone else."

"No, you're his target," Larry said. "He goes into the store, watches you. He's approached you once that we know of."

"Who? Who was he?"

"The one I asked you about that night. Do you remember?"

She came back to the couch, trying to remember. "No. I waited on a lot of men that night. I can't remember . . ."

"Well, that's just as well. He also parks out in the parking lot and waits for you to come out. For at least the past three nights he's followed you home."

Terror crossed her face, and she rushed to the door and turned the dead bolt, then hurried to the living-room window to see if it was locked. Desperately, she turned back to them. "The phone calls. Could he be the one making them?"

"What phone calls?"

"I've been getting a lot of hang-up calls. Like someone's just trying to see if I'm home. At all hours, day and night."

"It's him," Tony said, glancing at Larry. "Has anything else happened?"

"Well—no. I didn't know anyone was following me. I can't believe I didn't see him." She hurried around the apartment as she spoke, frantically checking window locks. "I've been taking the shortcut home, driving down Highland Drive all by myself. My mother warned me to take another route—" She swung around, confronting them. "What are you going to do about this?"

"We're going to catch him. But we need your help."

"*My* help? Are you kidding?"

"You're the only one who *can* help us right now," Larry said.

"But how? What can I do?"

"You can cooperate with us. Help us catch him."

She went back to her seat and sat on the edge. "By doing what?"

"Just what you've been doing," Tony said. "Keep going to work, driving the same way home, letting him follow you."

"Until what? He rapes me?"

"He won't rape you. We can protect you. We need for him to think everything is normal. But if you help us plan this out, we can trap him."

"So I'm the bait? Dangle me under his nose, and he'll strike?"

Larry looked down at his shoes. "I'm afraid you're the bait, anyway. We're just trying to protect you."

"No!" Beginning to cry, she shot up again. "I can't do this. I'll—I'll move. I'll go back and live with my mother."

"What about your job? School? Don't you think he'll find you?"

She thought about that for a moment. "There's a law. A stalking law, isn't there? You could arrest him just for following me."

"It wouldn't hold him any amount of time," Larry said, "if it stuck at all. He's smart. He's gotten off twice. We have to make sure that what we get him on is substantial enough to lock him up for a long time."

She shook her head again and began to pace. "Maybe— maybe he'll get discouraged if he can't find me. I mean, why is he after me, anyway?"

"He's sick. He's picked you out, Karen. He likes blondes. He's obsessed with you. If you change what you're doing, you could throw him off for a few days, but there's no guarantee that he wouldn't catch up to you eventually. By then he'll just be more desperate."

"I can't believe this!" she shouted. "I haven't done anything to anybody. All I do is go to school, work, and study. Why would this happen to me?"

Larry got up and took a couple of steps toward her. "You can turn it around, Karen. Go from being the victim to being in control."

She wiped her wet face with a trembling hand. "What would you do for me, if I did?"

"We'd have someone watching you twenty-four hours a day. We'd never let you out of our sight. When we think he's about to strike, we could wire you with a microphone so we would know what was happening every minute."

"But how far would things have to go before you arrested him?"

"At least far enough that there's no question that he was going to do you bodily harm."

Terror flooded her face as she shook her head violently. "I can't do it. You're asking too much."

"We realize it's asking a lot," Tony said. "But there's no other way."

"Karen, he's a threat to countless women out there," Larry said, getting face-to-face with her. "One woman is dead because of him. He broke into her house and brutally raped her. Almost killed her. She wound up killing herself. I don't even know how many others he's raped. But he's smart, so he's still out there on the street. We need to get him, Karen. Right now, you're the only one who can help us."

Her breath caught on a sob. "I'm twenty-one years old. I weigh 105 pounds. I can't fight him."

"We'll fight him. All you have to do is bait him."

"But I'm scared!" she cried. "Let somebody else do it, a policewoman or something."

"And what will you do?" Tony asked. "Move out of this apartment? Quit your job? Give up school? Are you going to let a maniac like this control your life?"

"I don't want to."

"Even if you did, would you ever know for sure that he wasn't stalking you again? As long as he's out there, he could come after you. He might find you, before we ever had the chance to catch him again."

"I can't do it!" she cried. "You'll have to find another way. I'll hide, if I have to. But I can't do this!"

"Then what *are* you going to do?" Tony asked.

She thought about that as she looked frantically around the apartment. "I guess I'll pack a few things and leave." She ran back to her bedroom, pulled a suitcase out of the closet.

Larry came to the door of the bedroom. "Karen, just trust us. We'll be there. We won't let anything happen to you."

"How can I know that?" she screamed. "It's my life that's at stake, not yours. If you mess up, let me down, it's no skin off your nose! I—can't—do it!"

Larry glanced over his shoulder to Tony. The look his partner gave him said this was hopeless. She was going to run, and Pendergrast would be thrown off. Sam would get impatient and close the case. On his own, Larry would have to haunt him night after night, waiting for another chance. Who knew when that would come?

Meanwhile, Melissa was sitting in jail, and Pendergrast was free, and the injustice of it all was overwhelming.

Larry leaned his forehead against the door casing as Karen ran around, grabbing the things she would take with her.

"Karen, this really good friend of mine—a woman I care a lot about—her sister was the woman who was raped and then killed herself."

Karen slowed her packing and looked up at him.

A tear stole out of Larry's eye, and he wiped it away. "He got away with it. Walked scot-free. My friend, Melissa, she's sitting in jail right now because she tried to set it up to look like he'd raped her. She figured she'd have all the evidence they needed this time. He'd never walk free again. That's desperation, Karen. She put herself in jeopardy, could have been raped or killed, to catch him. But it didn't work out, and she finally wound up confessing. She's in jail, Karen, and he's out there somewhere, terrorizing women like you. He's dangerous, and nobody's going to stop him."

She covered her face with both hands, and her shoulders shook with the force of her despair.

"If Melissa were here, she'd cooperate. She'd do anything, because she wouldn't want even one more woman to be stalked and raped like her sister was. Melissa loved Sandy. She was pretty and blonde, like you. She had a new husband, and everything was going great for her. And one night, when she didn't expect it, this man broke in and ruined her life. She couldn't live with it. And she's not the only one, Karen."

"I scream when I see a roach," Karen bit out as the tears soaked her face. "When the wind blows hard, I have nightmares. You're not looking at a brave person."

Larry took a few more steps into the room, his eyes beseeching. "Karen, the terror's not going away just because you run. Wouldn't you feel safer knowing that we're with you? Watching you?"

"No," she said, closing her suitcase and snapping it shut. "No, I wouldn't feel safer. I have to get out of here." She grabbed the suitcase up off the bed and dragged it into the living room. Leaving it at the door, she started gathering her schoolbooks. As she stacked the last one, she broke down. For a moment, she stood there with her books clutched in her arms, her eyes squeezed shut, and her shoulders rolling with the force of her sobs.

Larry touched her shoulder, but words escaped him.

"I don't want to quit school!" she cried. "I'm almost finished. It's not fair!"

"No, it isn't," he whispered.

"I like my job, and I like living here. How come he gets to ruin everything?"

"He doesn't," Larry said. "We don't have to let him."

She hesitated and looked up at him, and for a moment, Larry thought she might give in.

But instead, she opened the door and grabbed her suitcase. "I'm sorry," she said.

Tony and Larry followed her out, watched her lock the dead bolt with her key, and Larry carried her suitcase down the steps to her car.

She was still crying when she got behind the wheel and looked up at him. "I'm sorry. Call me a wimp. I just can't do it."

"I understand," Larry said. "Just be careful, okay?" He pulled a card out of his pocket. "If you need to get in touch with me, call these numbers. You'll catch me at one of them."

She took the card, looked down at it, then nodded and sucked in another sob. "I have to go," she said.

Larry backed up, and she closed the door.

She backed out of the parking space, and sped out into the street, leaving them standing there alone.

"Now what?" Tony asked.

Larry shook his head and sighed. "I don't know. I honestly have no idea."

"Maybe she'll change her mind."

Larry thought about that for a moment. Somehow, he didn't think so.

Slowly, he walked back to the car without saying a word.

CHAPTER FORTY-TWO

L arry was one of the first ones to show up Saturday for visitors' day. He waited outside for the group to be let in, and let his eyes sweep over the other family members and friends who were waiting to see loved ones. A young woman who looked no older than seventeen stood with a baby on her hip, a toddler at her knees, and a hyperactive three-year-old running up and down the sidewalk, refusing to heed her warnings to stay by her side. Larry wondered if she was the children's mother, or just keeping them while their mother served time.

A man who looked as if he'd just crawled out of bed sat on a step of the jail with two little girls—one on each side of him, holding his hands. Had they come to see their mother?

And then came a small, quiet man alone; and two women together; and more children.

Did they all feel as forlorn as he did, coming here to see what the justice system had done to the person they loved? Ironic, he thought, that he would feel like this, when he was often the one putting them behind bars. But he had never seen the pain from the other side.

The doors opened, and they all filed in. One by one, they were searched for items that were against the rules. Larry set the bag of books he'd brought Melissa on the table. As he waited for them to search him, his heart recalled the despair he'd felt yesterday when he had searched the stores for something that he could bring her—something that would lift her up, give her strength, help her to feel God's mercy and grace. He had sat in his car and wept because he'd been unable to find anything other than books—so impersonal, so benign.

"All right," the guard said, shoving the bag of books back across the table. "These are fine. Just go that way into the rec room."

Larry followed the flow of people into the big room. Since this wasn't a maximum security state penitentiary, there were no glass booths to talk through. They could sit at the same table, touch, hold hands, and he could hold her if she cried.

That, he supposed, was something he should be thankful for.

He waited with sweaty palms as one of the guards ran down a list of rules for visiting.

Most of these people were regulars, like he would be, he thought. Even the small children knew the rules and the routine.

The doors opened, and one by one the prisoners came in, some with hugs, others with cross words, others with a dull expression that said they didn't care who visited, because no one really mattered. He watched hopefully, expectantly, each time the door opened, and when Melissa didn't come right away, he began to wonder if she was going to refuse to see him. She had told him not to come. What if she'd really meant it?

His heart was sinking lower when twenty or more inmates had been brought in, and Melissa still wasn't among them. Abandoning his bag of books on the table, he walked over to the guard.

"If she didn't want to see me, would they come tell me, or would they just let me sit here and wonder?"

The guard's eyes fell on the door, and he asked, "Is that who you're looking for?"

Larry turned around and saw her at the door. She was wearing her orange jumpsuit and looking timidly around for him. He started toward her, noting how pale she was, how tired she looked. Her hair was pulled back in a ponytail and she wore no makeup— as some of the other inmates did. She looked like a fragile sixteen-year-old rather than the gutsy twenty-three-year-old who'd almost beaten Edward Pendergrast. But he'd never seen a more beautiful sight in his life.

She saw him and started toward him, and he met her halfway and threw his arms around her.

For a moment, he just held her and felt her body shaking as she began to cry. Then, quickly pulling herself together, she let him go.

"Let's go sit down," she whispered.

He led her to their table and set the books on the floor. Taking her hand, he looked into her eyes to see what he could read there. "You look great," he whispered.

"I'm okay," she said. "Really. It's not so bad."

"Are you getting along okay? With the others, I mean?"

She took in a deep, ragged breath. "Yeah."

She was holding back, he thought. She wasn't going to share much. "Do you have a cellmate?"

She nodded and looked around. Chloe was across the room with a man who must be almost six feet, but still shorter than Chloe. They were standing and talking quietly. "See that woman over there? She's my cellmate."

Larry's heart plummeted again. She looked like a linebacker— a linebacker in a bad mood. "Do you two get along okay?"

Melissa looked down at the woodgrain on the table. "I stay out of her way. Try not to make too much noise."

He was getting alarmed, and he cupped her chin and made her look at him. "Melissa, has she been harassing you?"

There was honesty in her eyes when she answered. "No. Thankfully, she's kind of left me alone."

"What about everybody else?"

Her eyes teared up, and she looked down at the wood again and tried to rub off a spot. "Well, I haven't met Miss Congeniality yet. I'm still looking for her. This isn't the best place to make friends."

He watched as she clasped her hands, and he saw the burn across her fingers. "What's this?" he asked.

She covered the burn and withdrew her hand. "I burnt myself on an iron. I work in the laundry. It's no big deal. I did it myself."

He wasn't sure she was leveling with him; carefully, he took her hand and examined the blisters. "Have you put anything on it?"

"I told you, I'm fine," she said. "Now, can we change the subject? Let's talk about you. You look tired. Are you sleeping?"

"Of course," he lied, though he couldn't remember the last time he'd had more than two hours' sleep at a time. Even though Karen had disappeared yesterday, Larry had followed Pendergrast last night to see what he would do. He had sat outside her apartment most of the night, waiting for her to come home. When she never did, Pendergrast had finally given up.

He rubbed his hand across his jaw and told himself he should have shaved for her. He had been so anxious to see her that he had only taken time to shower.

"Are you growing a beard?"

He tried to smile. "Looks like it."

She wasn't buying his "everything's fine" routine any more than he was. "Larry, tell me what's going on."

He sighed and decided there was no point in hiding the truth. "I've been following Pendergrast. Watching him."

Behind them, an inmate and her lover became embroiled in an argument, and their profanities were gaining volume. Melissa seemed not to notice. "Really? You're watching him?"

"Yeah." He lowered his voice. "He's been stalking another girl. I'm afraid to let my guard down for a minute."

"So what are you doing? Following him around the clock?"

"Something like that," he said, glancing over his shoulder at the loud couple. "But I'm thinking that may change pretty soon. The girl's onto him now, so she's kind of disappeared. As soon as he realizes it, he'll give up and look for somebody else."

"How do you know she's onto him?"

"I told her. I wanted her cooperation, so we could catch him, but she balked and ran."

Across the room a baby in a carrier wailed, and its tired mother ignored it. "What if you used somebody else?" Melissa asked. "Put another girl in her place."

"The problem is that it's a little touchy. He's watching her. We can't replace her at work, because he'll know. We could pull a switch as she gets into her car, but even then, the minute he gets close enough to see her, he could back off. I can't catch him and get enough to convict him until he does something. And if he balks and cans the whole thing, I may not be around the next time he tries this. No, the only way was to get her cooperation. Now I'm almost wishing I hadn't told her."

"You had to. You couldn't let her walk into this blindly."

"That's how I felt yesterday. Today, I'm not so sure." He looked up at her with a half-smile. "I was really hoping I could bring some good news in here today. I wanted so much to tell you he was in jail."

"Larry, I want him caught too. But I don't want you killing yourself to do it. You're exhausted." She folded both arms on the table and fixed her troubled eyes on him. "Don't let anything happen to you, okay?"

He nodded his promise.

The CO crossed the room and reprimanded the angry couple behind them. Melissa swallowed and looked around at the other inmates interacting with families she didn't know they had. The room was quickly filling up with cigarette smoke and more crying babies, and she wished she and Larry could go outside together, breathe the fresh air, feel the sunshine. But that wasn't possible. She moved her troubled, timid eyes back to his. "You know, I really didn't expect you to come today. I knew my parents were coming this afternoon, but you were a surprise."

"Why? Didn't I tell you I would?"

"I told you not to."

"Well, I had to."

"Why?" she asked.

He took her hand again and seemed to study the shape of her fingers. "Because I miss you like crazy. I've worried about you day and night. I can't stand the thought of you here."

Her lip began to tremble, and she struggled with her tears again. He hated himself for making her cry.

"I don't know how all this happened," she whispered, bending her head down to hide the tears. "I did something wrong to try and right things, and I wound up hurting so many people. I didn't want to hurt you, Larry, and the last thing I want is for you to keep coming here out of obligation. Six months is a long time. You'll forget about me. I hate to get used to having you come, and then start noticing that you're coming less and less. I hate for you to feel guilty about having fun when I'm in here, like you owe me some debt."

"That's not going to happen," he assured her. "Melissa, look at me."

She looked up, her eyes red and wet.

"I love you. It's not something I chose to do, but it happened. I really mean it. I've never felt like this about any other woman."

She sucked in a sob and covered her mouth. "I love you, too," she whispered. "But I'm so worried about you."

"*You're* worried about *me*? Why?"

"Because you're out there, and he's out there. And you're trying to catch him at something all by yourself. Larry, I've tried that. It didn't work."

"There's a difference. I'm a cop. I know what I'm doing."

"I knew what I was doing, too."

"But you manipulated what happened with you. I'm not manipulating anything. I'm just watching."

"Please don't get so tired that you get sloppy and let him see you. He might kill you, Larry. He's a vicious, violent man."

"I'm going to get him off the street. But I'm going to come and visit you on every visitors' day, too. Got that?"

She sat gazing at him for a moment, wiping her tears as fast as they came. "I have a lot to be thankful for."

"What?" he asked. "Tell me."

She tried to think. "Well, I have you. Not everybody in here has somebody. And I'm safe from Pendergrast. He can't get to me in here."

Larry smiled. "That's right. That's what Tony said. Thank God for small favors."

"That's a big one," she admitted, "and I do thank him. I thank him for other things, too. Like the fact that I'm learning to depend on God. Completely. Being this low makes me realize how high he is. But he's still here, too, even in this place. I feel him."

"I feel him, too," Larry whispered. "Sometimes when I think of you being here, and I get such dread, I feel his comfort. But I don't think I want to be comforted. I guess in a way I feel I'm doing some kind of penance by worrying myself sick about you."

"We have to have faith, Larry," she whispered. "This morning, I was reading the book of James. He said life wouldn't always be easy. He said to let your trials strengthen you. I intend to do that."

"Then I will, too," he said.

As the noise grew around them, and the chaos in the room continued, they put aside their doubts and fears, their worries and anxieties, their remorse and regrets, and lost themselves in the world they had in common.

But that night, as Larry sat in his car in the parking lot across the street from Pendergrast's, waiting for him to come out of his apartment, Larry began to worry again. Melissa had looked so tired. The burn on her hand might not have come from the iron at all. And that cellmate of hers would instill fear into the toughest of men.

He had a long talk with God, pleading with him to find her another cellmate, pleading with him to protect her with his angels, pleading with him to let something good come of all this.

And then he pleaded that he would be able to catch Pendergrast at something soon, so that he could lock him away.

But it wasn't going to happen tonight. Pendergrast didn't go out. Larry wondered if he'd realized he'd been found out.

He gave up around four A.M. and went home to get a couple of hours' sleep before he had to be at church. He needed to worship today, he thought. He needed to feel God's glory. He sure hadn't seen enough of it in that rec room at the Pinellas County Correctional Facility for Women.

CHAPTER FORTY-THREE

The prison chapel was filled with more women than Melissa had expected that Sunday morning. She had hoped it would be a sanctuary—a safe place in the midst of all this madness. But as she went in, she saw the red-haired woman who had harassed her sitting at the back, and some of the others that she feared scattered around the room.

Had they come to worship, she wondered, or had they come to break the monotony of their lives?

It didn't matter, she told herself. What really mattered was that she had the opportunity to worship here, and she was going to.

Her heart felt lighter as one of the women from the prison ministry began to play the piano and direct the inmates in some praise songs. Most of the women didn't sing, she noted, but some of them did, Melissa among them.

Next to her sat a tiny Hispanic woman with dark circles under her eyes, singing in a lovely, lilting voice, with tears running down her face. Melissa could easily picture the woman in a small evangelical church, with a cotton, flower-print dress on, and maybe a hat with a bow. Instead, she sat here in her prison-issue jumpsuit looking as out of place as Melissa felt.

The chaplain who gave his time to come here on Sunday mornings was a young man in his early twenties, probably someone who had never had a church of his own. His name was Doug Manning.

"If you have a Bible with you, please turn to John, chapter 4."

Melissa opened her Bible to John, and noticed that the woman next to her did as well. Few others had Bibles with them.

It was the passage about the woman at the well, and as he launched into his sermon about the woman with a past, the woman who stood before Christ with all her sins exposed, and was offered forgiveness freely and without cost, Melissa felt a renewal of hope.

After the sermon, the chaplain entreated the women to stay for a prayer time, but one by one, most of the women filed out. Only the woman sitting next to her, and four others in different parts of the room, stayed behind.

Melissa sat quietly, waiting for the pastor to lead them.

He looked disappointed that so many had gone. "Well— since there aren't many of us, why don't we come up to the front here, and sort of put our chairs in a circle?" As they came, he asked, "Do you all know each other?"

Melissa looked around. A couple of them knew each other, but she knew none of them. "No. I'm new."

"Then let's introduce ourselves. I'm Doug, and this is my wife, Tina."

The woman who had been sitting next to Melissa offered her a timid smile. "I'm Sonja. I'm in cellblock C. I haven't been here long, either."

The next woman, a heavyset, jolly-looking woman, spoke up. "I'm Betty. I used to be a choir director in a little mission church we belonged to."

The next one, a black woman whose Bible looked worn and used, nodded to Melissa. "I'm Keisha. In cellblock A."

And after her, the last one, another black woman with huge, almond-shaped eyes who looked like model material, said, "I'm Simone. Cellblock B."

Doug smiled, pleased, then looked at Melissa. "And you are?"

"Melissa," she said quietly.

"Do any of you have any specific prayer requests?" he asked.

Sonja spoke up as tears filled her eyes, and she groped for the tissue she carried in her pocket. "I need prayers," she said. "I don't belong here. I didn't do what they said I did."

Doug looked as if he'd heard that before, but he didn't voice it.

"I didn't know my husband was selling drugs," she went on in her heavy accent. "When he got arrested, they arrested me, too, because they had seen me driving him places and dropping him off

590

at places where he was making deals." Her face reddened, and she covered her face. "But I didn't know what he was doing." She stopped, sniffed, and tried to steady her voice. "I have three small children. Two, three, and five. I have to serve a year, but that's an eternity to them. They'll forget all about me."

The horror of that situation gripped Melissa, and by instinct, she reached out and took Sonja's hand.

"All right," Doug said. "We'll pray about that. Anyone else?"

"Yes," Betty said. "I'm due to get out in four weeks. I need prayers that nothing happens to mess up my release."

"All right." Doug looked around, waiting, for anyone else to speak up. "Anyone else?"

"Yes," Melissa said, almost in a whisper. "I'm not like Sonja. I did something wrong to come here. But I need prayers for strength. I need to see some sense in all of this."

"You may not ever," Doug warned her. "Sometimes you just have to trust God's sovereignty."

She breathed a laugh. "I'm beginning to realize that."

"Well, let's pray for these particular requests, and then I'll pray for each of you, that you'll be safe here, and that you'll be lights in this dark place. You know, a lot of those women who walked out of here just now are hurting. They need some Christian influence here. And you may not have noticed just now, but each of the cellblocks is represented in this little group. That's no coincidence. Each one of you has the power to change this whole facility."

"I don't feel very powerful," Keisha said.

"Me, either," Betty added.

"Well, neither did the disciples after Jesus died. But they didn't understand what was ahead. God saw their future, even when they didn't. He saw the reason, and all the purpose. Maybe you're here to work on the women in this prison."

"It's hard to care about them," Sonja said. "Some of them are hateful and wicked."

"Maybe they've never known any better."

"Maybe that's just an excuse," Sonja said. She brought her remorseful eyes up to Doug's. "I'm sorry. I just haven't been feeling much love for my fellowman—or woman—lately."

"Then we'll pray about that, too."

They held hands and prayed, earnestly, openly, with tender, broken hearts, and in doing so they created a bond that Melissa hadn't felt in years. She wanted to feel it more than once a week, she thought.

When the prayer was over, she felt empowered. "We need a Bible study," she said. "More than just once a week. Would that be allowed?"

"Of course it would," he said. "But I'm in seminary during the week, about three hours from here. I can only get here on Sundays. Would you be willing to lead it?"

Melissa's eyes widened. "Me?"

"Sure, why not?"

She looked around, surprised, and saw that everyone was looking expectantly at her. "Well, the truth is—I'm not real well educated on the Bible. I haven't really been walking with God for the last few years."

"Great opportunity to learn more," he said. "Just be available, pray about it, and God will lead you."

She hesitated and looked from one woman to another. "Would you come, if we had one? Say, three times a week?"

To a woman, they all agreed that they would.

"From this core group, other women can be reached," Doug said. "One by one, you'll bring them into the group, and it'll grow. I've seen it happen before."

"When?" Sonja asked. "You're too young to have seen much."

Doug only smiled. "My mother was in prison for several years when I was a boy," he said. "She was a battered wife, and she killed my father to keep him from killing me. That's why I feel such a burden to keep this prison ministry going."

"How many years was she in?" Sonja asked.

"Seven," he said. "But I had a loving grandmother who brought me to see my mother every time she could. My mother became a light in the prison. She built up a Bible study that started with three women and grew to about 200. And Sonja, I can tell you that, even from prison, my mother had a strong influence on me. I saw her making the best of the worst situation, and I saw her taking what had been given to her, and still being available for God to use. She wrote me a lot of letters, and read me books over the telephone at night, and rocked me when I visited. It wasn't the best situation, but she made it good."

"Wow. And look how you turned out," Sonja whispered. "Maybe my babies will be all right, too."

"And so will you. You know, some of these women were drug addicts when they came in here. Now that they're clean, they're different women. Regular human beings, with feelings, and regrets, and loneliness. Think of them as being like you, even the ones who act like monsters, and love them, anyway."

He knew, Melissa thought. He understood. And she felt so blessed that God had sent him to them.

As she went back to her cell, she felt called to be the light that God had sent for this dark corridor. And she decided that Chloe needed to be the first to see that light.

That afternoon, Larry came to visit again, and this time, Melissa was brighter. As they sat and talked and watched the other inmates with their families and friends, she noted Sonja in the corner with her children. The two babies were in her lap, and she was rocking them, while the five-year-old performed some little songs she'd memorized from a videotape she had at her grandmother's.

And then she saw Chloe again with her husband. The soft look on the woman's face made her look like a different person.

Later, when they were back in their cells, Melissa tried to make conversation as she straightened her things. "Your husband seems nice, Chloe."

"Yeah. He's a prince. He's stuck by me, too. Through thick and through thin. He'll be there when I get out. And you can bet I won't wind up back in here. This is my last time. I ain't like those other women, who don't know no better than to keep doin' stupid stuff—killin' and prostitutin' and sellin' and shootin' at folks. Man, if you could get the chair for havin' the stupids, they'd be killin' ninety percent of the women in this jail."

Something about that struck Melissa as funny, and quietly, she began to laugh.

"What's so funny?" Chloe asked.

Melissa covered her mouth with her hand and tried to stop.

She heard Chloe laughing on the bunk beneath her, and felt the bed shaking with it.

"Well, it's true," Chloe said. "You can laugh, but these girls—they ain't like you and me, with our little namby-pamby crimes. Some of these women did some bad things."

Melissa came to the end of her laughter and took a deep breath. The laughter had cleansed her, relaxed her. "What did you do, Chloe?"

The woman's voice got deeper and more serious. "You won't tell nobody?"

"Of course not."

"I'm in for forgery. Forged some checks. They belonged to the woman I worked for. It was stealin', but I never shot nobody. And I never shot *up* neither. I was clean, except for forgin' checks. Never thought I'd get caught. She had plenty of money. Didn't think she'd notice if a little of it was missin'. It was what they call a victimless crime. I never hurt nobody."

That was something to be proud of, in a place like this, Melissa thought. One person's sins were worse than another's. There was always someone whose sins were worse than yours. She supposed that was why the other inmates had tried to pin child abuse and murder on her, so they could all hold her up as an example of how far they would never go.

The thing was, she wasn't sure there was a big difference in God's eyes.

"Why don't you want me to tell?" she asked.

"'Cause," Chloe said. "Some o' them might have the impression that I'm in for murder. I might have given 'em that impression."

Melissa began to laugh again. "Why, Chloe?"

"It helps for them to be scared of you."

Melissa sighed. "You have an advantage."

"You got that right. Ain't nobody much who wants to cross me here."

They were quiet for a moment, as Melissa contemplated her size.

"You married to that honey who keeps comin' to see you?" Chloe asked.

"No," Melissa said. "How long have you been married?"

"Herman and me got married three years ago. He's my man."

Something about that made Chloe seem more human. "Does Herman come often?"

"Every weekend. Never misses a one."

Melissa turned over on her back and studied the dark ceiling again. "At first I didn't want Larry to come. I didn't want him to see me like this."

"You may not have a bunch of makeup, but you don't need none. You look fine. He'll probably just be glad to see you're in one piece."

"Will I stay that way, Chloe? In one piece, I mean."

Chloe didn't answer for a while. "It ain't gon' be easy, sister, but I'll do what I can."

After a few minutes, she heard Chloe's deep, heavy breathing on the rhythmic edge of a snore, and she knew she'd gone to sleep.

CHAPTER FORTY-FOUR

aren Anderson sat up abruptly in bed in her mother's guest room, and listened . . .

She could have sworn she heard a noise. But the trees outside the window were rustling too loudly, and the wind was blowing too hard—

What if he was out there?

She hadn't slept a full night since the two detectives had dropped their bomb on her. All night she heard things, and expected things, and imagined things.

She got out of bed, went to the window, and peered out into the night. There was no one there. At least, no one that she could see.

She thought of waking her mother and asking her to keep her company, but her mother would only think she was crazy. Karen hadn't been able to tell her mother about the man who was stalking her. She didn't want her to be afraid, so she'd just said that she'd had her heart broken and she didn't want to be alone. But now, in the middle of the night, listening for any and every sound, the loneliness and fear were overwhelming.

When would she stop listening? When would she be able to go back to school, or work, or anywhere, without looking over her shoulder?

Not until the man was caught, Larry had said. And he wouldn't be caught if Karen didn't help. Not until he picked another girl to attack—assuming that the police hadn't given up trying to catch him by then.

She went into her mother's room and stood in the doorway, feeling like a little girl who'd had a nightmare and needed her mother. Only the nightmare wasn't a dream—it was real. And her mother couldn't help her.

She thought of the woman who was in jail because she'd tried to get this man put away. And she thought of the woman who had killed herself. She could almost understand getting that desperate.

She went back to bed, climbed under the covers, and tried hard to go to sleep. But even with her eyes closed she saw the shadowy, mystic figure of a man who wanted to hurt her. He was still out there, even if he couldn't find her. One of these days, if he wanted to badly enough, he would. And then, just as she let her guard down, just as the police did, he would make his move. And there wouldn't be anywhere to turn.

Feeling sick, she closed her eyes and tried to sleep. But it was impossible to sleep when you were listening, waiting . . .

The steam of the showers hung in the air, wetting the concrete floor. Still in her stall, Melissa dressed quickly, her jumpsuit clinging to her damp skin. The thought of dressing in front of some of these violent women didn't appeal to her, so she tolerated a little discomfort for her privacy.

Hanging her towel over her arm, she pulled back the curtain and stepped out, her flip-flops squeaking as they slipped across the floor. She couldn't get out fast enough, she thought. Even though the showers were closely guarded, this was the most threatening room in the prison. She'd seen two fights break out here, for which several inmates—even the ones who'd been victims—had gotten isolation. It seemed that the high temperatures and the steam added up to boiling tempers.

She had just dropped her towel in its designated tub and headed for the door when she heard someone running toward her from behind. Before she could turn around, something walloped the back of her head, knocking her to the floor, facedown. Someone was on her instantly, her weight crushing her. She screamed as someone wrenched her arm behind her back, threatening to break it. The other inmates began to laugh and shout encouragement. "Let me go!" Melissa screamed.

"Not until you learn who's in charge around here."

"What do you want?" Melissa asked through her teeth.

"Respect. And I ain't been sensin' any from you."

The woman lifted Melissa's head by her hair, then banged it back into the concrete, bloodying Melissa's nose and scraping the skin off her forehead. She yelled again, but the guards weren't there.

She heard another set of footsteps coming, and suddenly the weight of the woman was jerked off of her.

She turned over, wiping the blood from her nose. Chloe was holding Red against the wall with her hand at her throat. Other inmates stood around, suddenly quiet.

"This is my cellmate, understand?" the big woman asked each of them. "*Nobody* touches her, or they answer to me. Any questions?" She looked around at each face in the room. When no one protested, she shook Red. "And you—I'd take great pleasure in cleanin' out the toilets with your head. If there's somethin' about what I'm sayin' that you don't understand, feel free to speak up any time."

Red didn't answer. It was clear that she feared Chloe.

Chloe let her go. "Get out of here now!" The woman leered at Melissa, silently promising to get her later, and headed out of the room.

When Chloe was satisfied that no one was going to attempt anything else, she turned on the water in the sink and began to brush her teeth, ignoring Melissa, who still lay on the floor. Melissa got to her feet and looked around at the others who were staring at her. Some of them snickered quietly. Others found other things to do. No one wanted to be the target of Chloe's wrath.

Bending over one of the sinks, Melissa washed the blood off of her nose. She fought back the tears as she looked up in the mirror. Chloe stood next to her, drying her mouth. "Thank you, Chloe," she whispered.

Chloe grunted and handed her a towel to stop the bleeding. "If it don't stop, you could go to the infirmary. Get out of a day's work."

"No, it's okay."

As she washed the rest of the blood off of her face, she wondered if God had provided this huge hulk of a woman to be the guardian angel who would protect her.

His grace amazed her. As she went back to her cell, she thanked him for disguised blessings like Chloe.

CHAPTER FORTY-SIX

T he light on his answering machine was blinking when Larry got home at four o'clock Tuesday morning, exhausted and agitated from watching Pendergrast watch Karen Anderson's empty apartment. A couple of times he'd seen another petite blonde get out of her car and trot up to another apartment, and he'd tensed up, expecting Pendergrast to go after her. But it seemed that he was waiting for Karen. For now, no one else would do.

Pendergrast had finally given up and gone back to his apartment at about 3:30. How he existed on as little sleep as he was getting, Larry couldn't imagine. He knew it was killing him.

He pulled off his shoes, sat down on the bed, and punched the button on the machine.

"Uh, Larry, this is Mrs. Nelson—Melissa's mother? We just wanted to talk to you and see how you think Melissa is doing. Please call us tomorrow if you get time."

He fell back on the bed in frustration as it beeped. What would he tell them? They wanted reassurances that she was all right, but he wasn't sure himself.

As a message from one of the guys at his church played, he tried to remember what day it was. Tuesday, he thought. Wednesday was the midweek visitation day at the jail. He could see Melissa tomorrow night. But first he had to make it through this day and the next.

The line beeped again, and the third message began to play. "Detective Millsaps," a woman's voice said. "This is Karen. Karen Anderson."

Larry sat up and lunged for the machine to turn it up.

"I—I need to talk to you. I've changed my mind. Please—no matter what time it is, call me at this number."

He grabbed the phone and dialed as she called it out. She answered on the first ring.

"Hello?"

"Karen? This is Larry Millsaps."

"Thank goodness." She breathed out a heavy sigh of relief. "I've been so scared."

"Why? Has something happened?"

"No," she said. "But I keep thinking something's going to. I can't sleep, I can't eat . . . If I help you, if I do what you ask, will this all be over soon? Will I be able to go back to my life?"

"Yes," he said. "Karen, it's really the only way to put this all to rest."

"All right, then," she whispered. "What do I have to do?"

CHAPTER FORTY-SEVEN

I t was the first time Melissa had found the pay phone in her cellblock not in use, and she hurried to it, jabbed her quarter in, and quickly dialed Larry's number.

His machine answered, and she left a tentative message that she was sorry she'd missed him, then hung up, feeling like an idiot. What made me think he'd be at home? she asked herself. Did I really believe he'd just sit around grieving over me?

Feeling that old anxiety and despair creeping in, she pulled another quarter out of her pocket and dialed the operator. "Collect to Pensacola," she said. "James Nelson. From Melissa." She wondered if the operator could tell that the call was coming from jail, if she was judging her . . .

Her mother answered the phone and accepted the call, and Melissa felt instant relief. Just to touch base with someone she loved, just to hear the voice of someone who loved her.

Her mother was telling her about the prayer chain she'd started, when Red rushed around the corner, making a beeline for the phone.

"Get off," she said. "Now!"

Melissa hesitated. Chloe wasn't around, and she knew better than to cross the woman without her. But her mother was talking, and she didn't want to frighten her by hanging up suddenly. Trying to compromise, she raised one finger, promising to get off in a minute, but Red didn't back down.

"It's an emergency," Red said. "I have to call my kid."

Melissa doubted that there was an emergency, even though she had seen emergency messages occasionally brought to the inmates. Still, there was an anxiety in Red's eyes that she didn't want to provoke. "Uh—Mom? I'll call you back in a few minutes, okay? Somebody needs to use the phone."

Melissa hung up, retrieved the quarter that had come back after the operator connected them, and turned around.

Red shoved her away from the phone, almost knocking her down, and grabbed the phone. "Give me a quarter," she said.

"I only have one," Melissa said. "I need to use it."

"I said give me the quarter!" she shouted. "Now!"

Gritting her teeth, Melissa handed her the quarter.

Red snatched it and shoved it into the machine, and Melissa thought about leaving. But something, some stoic, stubborn pride, made her stay. Maybe she was making a collect call, too, she thought, and the quarter would come back. Maybe she could still get it and call her mother back.

"This is Jean," the woman barked into the phone. "I got a message to call. Where's Johnny?"

She waited, then said, "I don't care. I want to talk to him. No, I don't want to talk to Carol. Where's my kid?"

Again, she waited, and her face began to redden. "What do you mean, an accident? Put Carol on the phone. Now!"

Something was wrong. Melissa looked up at her.

"Carol, where's Johnny?" Red yelled louder. "I want to talk to him! Put him on the phone!"

She cursed, then kicked the brick wall behind the phone, and let another curse fly. "You're lying. This is just some sick joke, isn't it? Put my kid on the phone!"

Melissa took a step forward. Red's face was twisted, and tears came to her eyes.

"He wouldn't do that! He knows to look both ways. I did teach him that!" Her voice broke and she began to sob. Letting go of the phone, she slid down the wall. The receiver dangled on its cord as Red buried her face in her knees and wailed.

Melissa stooped down next to her and took the phone. "Uh . . . they're still talking. Do you want to . . ."

Red just shook her head. "Hang up!" she sobbed. "They're liars."

Melissa slowly brought the phone to her ear. "Hello?"

"Where's Jean?" a brusque woman's voice asked.

"She's—she can't talk. She asked me to hang up."

"She thinks I'm lyin'," the woman said. "But I wouldn't lie about a thing like this. Her kid's dead. She's got to accept it."

"Dead?" Melissa looked back at the woman sitting huddled on the floor. "What happened?"

"He ran out in front of a car. It was bound to happen. He never listened to nobody. Wouldn't do nothin' I said. It wasn't my fault. And I can't pay for no funeral."

"I'll tell her to call you back when she's able." She hung up the phone, heard the quarter roll into the coin-return slot. Sitting down on the floor beside her, she tried to find the words to help her. It was strange, she thought, that until now she hadn't even known the woman's name.

"That witch. I never should have let her keep him. I should have let the state take him! He's not dead. She's a liar. Always has been."

Melissa looked around, wishing someone would come and rescue her from having to extend any compassion at all. But she was the only one here. Finally, as the woman's sobs grew deeper, she touched her shoulder. "You could have the warden find out for sure."

"No," she said. "I don't want to know. I don't want to know." Her voice got higher in pitch as she went on, until it was just a hoarse squeak.

"How old is Johnny?"

"Seven," she cried. "He's just seven. He can't be dead. He wouldn't be dead."

"If it is true, you could probably get out to go to the funeral."

"There's not gonna be any funeral for my baby!" she cried, getting to her feet. "He's not dead!" She looked at Melissa suspiciously. "You'd like it, though, wouldn't you, if he was! You'd think I deserved that!"

"No, I wouldn't," Melissa said. "I wouldn't wish that on anybody."

"Well, he's not! He's probably asleep in bed, and my sister just got drunk and thought she'd see if she could pull my string. He's a weapon she uses against me. She's always been like that."

She wanted to ask why Red was crying so hard, if that was what she believed. Instead, she watched as the woman ran back to her cell and closed herself in.

Melissa heard the soulful wailing late into the night, and when Chloe asked if she knew who it was, she didn't tell. Even Red deserved a chance to grieve her dead son.

By the next morning, word around the cellblock was that the news was true: Red was getting out that afternoon for the funeral but would be brought back right afterward.

Before she went to work that morning, Melissa wrote her a note and slipped it under her door. It said, "Please let me know if there's anything I can do for you. I'm so sorry about your son. Melissa."

Red didn't respond.

Melissa prayed for her all that day as she worked, and that evening, when Red came back to her cell, she saw the red swelling in her eyes, the purple tint to her lips, the pale cast to her cheeks. Her heart ached for her.

Again, before supper, she stuck a note under her door. "We're having a Bible study tomorrow at 4:00 in the chapel. Please come. It may be comforting to you. Melissa."

All that night, she listened to Red's wailing again, but the next morning, when she encountered the redhead at breakfast, she did nothing to acknowledge either of the notes she'd sent. Instead, she sat with the group of malcontents she usually sat with, her eyes cast down at her plate. She ate little and didn't speak at all.

That afternoon, when Melissa started to leave her cell to go to the chapel, Chloe looked up from a letter she was reading. "Where you goin'?"

"To the chapel. We've started a Bible study group. It meets at four."

"You gon' miss visitation?"

"No," Melissa said. "It'll be over by five."

"You ain't goin' by yourself, are you?"

"Well, there's another woman, Sonja, who's going from our cellblock."

"Sonja?" Chloe asked, astounded. "Goin' with her is like hangin' a rib-eye steak around your neck to swim through a school of sharks. They'll eat you alive."

"I'm going anyway," Melissa said.

Groaning, Chloe pulled her big body off the bunk. "Well, then, I guess I'll have to go with you. If I don't, you'll wind up mincemeat and I'll be stuck with another roommate. Probably one who's worse than you."

Melissa smiled. "You're welcome to come, Chloe, for whatever reason."

"I ain't got no Bible, though."

"You can look on with me."

"Whatever."

The woman followed Melissa out into the corridor, past the bubble—which wasn't really a bubble, but a booth where the guards sat—out of the cellblock and toward the chapel.

There were already three others waiting when they got there.

One of them was Red, sitting slouched in a chair with her arms crossed across her stomach.

Chloe took one look at her and said, "I'll handle this."

Melissa stopped her. "No, Chloe. I invited her."

"What? Are you crazy?"

"Her son died. She's in pain. I told her to come."

"Well, you're gon' be the one in pain, if you don't watch out. Abomination, it's a good thing I came."

Red looked up as they walked in, then quickly averted her eyes.

Both she and Chloe sat stiff and disinterested, not offering anything to the conversation about the book of John. But the group went on, each of the core members aware that a witness was being made here, that the two women, each here for different reasons, were hearing at least some of what was being said.

Red left before the meeting had entirely broken up, but as Melissa and Chloe went back to their cell, Melissa silently thanked God that progress had been made. She didn't fear the red-haired woman anymore. She'd had a glimpse into her heart, seen a little of her pain. Now she had compassion for her, and she knew that was a miracle. But she expected more miracles.

The next time she was able to get to the phone, Larry still wasn't home, and this time she left a message that she had called to see if he was coming to visitation tonight.

It was frustrating hanging up without talking to him, and she wondered again where he was. Was he still following Pendergrast? Was he getting any rest at all? Had anything happened?

When she started back to her cell, she saw Red hovering in the corridor. She tensed, wondering if Red had overcome her grief enough to go back to her old, threatening ways. Was she waiting for an opportunity?

Melissa kept walking until she was a few feet away from her. "I need to talk to you."

Red's words were clipped and angry, and Melissa was apprehensive. Choking back her fear, she said, "Okay."

Red stepped back into her cell, and Melissa tentatively followed, wishing Chloe were nearby, instead of in the TV room. She stayed near the door, but watched as Red sat down on her bunk.

"What's wrong?"

Red just looked down at her feet and shook her head. "I was just thinkin'. You know, about hell. Wonderin' if there's one for little kids."

Suddenly all the fear rushed away, and Melissa sat down next to her. "Oh, Jean." It was the first time she'd used her name and it felt strange, but she went on. "Little children don't go to hell. They're too small for God to hold them accountable for their mistakes."

The woman looked hopefully up at her. "Then Johnny's in heaven, you think?"

"I'm sure of it. Jesus had a special place in his heart for the children."

Red pinched the bridge of her nose, fighting her tears. "I never really thought much about heaven or hell before. I pretty much assumed I'd go to hell when I died, if there was one. But Johnny—I never counted on takin' him there with me, or sendin' him ahead of me." Her stoic face cracked. "I didn't take him to church even once. What he knew about God, he never learned from me."

Melissa took her hand, squeezed it.

"I just wish . . . that the last time he visited here . . . about a month ago . . . I wish I'd known I was never gonna see him again. I'd have read him that book he likes a few more times. He wanted me to, but I got tired of it and wouldn't. I coulda read it twenty times and he wouldn't have got tired. I should have read it just one more time." She dropped her face in her hand and wept harder. "I can't believe I'll never see him again."

Melissa touched her hair, stroked it, and began to cry herself. "You can see him again, Jean. You just have to make sure you go to heaven, too."

"Too late for me," Jean said. "Some things you can't take back. I done too much."

"God can forgive anything."

"Not what I've done."

"Try him."

Jean looked up at her and saw Melissa's tears. Frowning, she asked, "What are you cryin' about?"

Melissa sniffed. "The same thing you are. I'm just so sorry."

"Why?" Red asked suspiciously. "I would have beat you to a pulp the other day if Chloe hadn't stopped me. How do you know I still won't?"

"You might," Melissa acknowledged. "I realize that."

"Then why would you cry over my baby?"

Melissa wasn't sure, but she gave it her best shot. "Because I know how I would feel if I were in your place."

They stared at each other for an eloquent moment, a moment in which anything could happen. Then Red looked away, as if uncomfortable with the thought of truly connecting with anyone.

"What did a debutante like you do to get put in here, anyway?"

The question, designed to break the intimacy and put Melissa on the defensive again, didn't daunt her. "I lied to a grand jury."

"About what?"

"I told them I'd been raped when I hadn't."

Red began to laugh. "What was it? Revenge on some guy for dumpin' you?"

Melissa looked at her feet. "Yes, it was revenge. But I was never involved with him. It's a long story."

"Looks like the joke turned out to be on you."

She felt the blow, knowing it was aimed to hurt, but she didn't let it. "You're right. It backfired. But God's forgiven me."

Red thought that over for a minute. "Bet you never thought you'd wind up in here with us losers when you were sippin' wine with all your elite little friends, plannin' out your lives and doin' lunch."

Melissa realized where this was all going, so she got slowly, sadly to her feet. "Look, if you need to talk again, I mean if you really need to talk, instead of just flinging insults, you know where I am."

Red's eyes got a dull, thoughtful gleam as she watched Melissa leave.

CHAPTER FORTY-EIGHT

Karen Anderson's hands trembled as she buttoned her blouse back over the microphone and wires taped to her chest. "Are you sure they'll be able to hear me?" she asked Pam Darby, the lieutenant who was helping her.

"Positive. They'll hear every word."

"But couldn't I have some kind of ear phone so I could hear them?"

Pam shook her head. "Sorry. It might be too obvious. But as long as you're at work, they can reach you by phone."

"It's not the part at work that I'm worried about," Karen said. "It's the part where he approaches me." She raked her fingers through her hair. "See, I just can't believe that they could get to me soon enough. I mean, what if he has a gun? What if he has a knife? What if by the time they hear him hurting me, it's too late?"

"These are good cops, Karen. You have to trust them."

"Right," Karen said, flinging her hair back over her shoulder and leveling her eyes on the cop. "So you're telling me that you wouldn't be scared to death to walk into a maniac's hands like this?"

"Of course I would. It takes courage. Lots of it. You're a hero, Karen."

Karen wasn't buying it. To her, it just sounded like flattery to get her to cooperate. "Not yet, I'm not. And if I wind up getting killed in the process, am I just going to be one more statistic?"

"You're stopping the statistics, Karen," Pam said evenly. "That's why we need you."

Karen went to the window and peered out to the street, where cars passed by in a steady stream and pedestrians hurried to and from their offices. She wondered what she had ever done to wind up attracting Edward Pendergrast. Was it something she'd worn? The way she acted? Maybe it was her hair. He liked blondes, they'd said. Maybe she should dye hers after this was all over.

If she survived it.

Beginning to feel sick, she turned back to Pam. "Those other women he raped . . . do you have pictures of them?"

She thought for a moment. "Well, yeah. In his file."

Karen lifted her chin. "I want to see them."

"Why?" Pam asked.

Karen's eyes filled with tears as her face reddened. "I want to see what he did to them. I want to see what I have to expect."

Pam shook her head. "Karen, nothing like what happened to them is going to happen to you. Trust me. You don't want to see those pictures."

"That's what I thought," Karen said. "That bad." Her stomach roiled, and she set her hand on it. "I think I'm gonna be sick."

"Just take some deep breaths," Pam said, getting face-to-face with her. "In . . . out . . . in . . . out . . ."

But Karen only shoved her out of the way and headed for the bathroom. She bent over the toilet and wretched, making the tape on her chest pull with the effort, reminding her that someone was probably listening to every sound. She flushed, left the stall, and rushed to the sink. Cupping her hands, she caught some water, drank, then caught more and splashed it on her face. She looked up into the mirror, at the wet, pretty face that had caused her so much confusion over the last few years. She was too pretty to be taken seriously, and she'd fought that since high school. A woman who worked full-time and put herself through college deserved a little respect, she'd always thought. Now, that prettiness was more than a stumbling block. It was her enemy.

She began to cry as she stared past that face, to her hair, vowing to cut it off the moment this was all over, so that it wouldn't attract any more attention from sick rapists.

Pam poked her head into the bathroom. "Are you okay?" she asked. "I could get you something to settle your stomach."

Karen nodded. "Anything you have." She watched as the cop left her alone, then looked back into the mirror and began to sob. She would never make it. She would get sick the moment he spoke to her. She would throw up, ruining everything. She would slip up somehow, and he'd kill her.

Quickly, she began to unbutton her blouse, her trembling hands making it almost impossible to function. She grabbed the end of the tape with her fingertips and started to jerk it back, tear the microphone off . . .

But then what? Would she go back into hiding? Would she have to keep waiting?

She slammed both fists against the mirror, then spun around, trying to calm herself. She had to do this. She had no choice. It was the only way to find peace again.

She tried to breathe as Pam had told her . . . in . . . out . . . and slowly, she began to button her blouse again.

The door swung open, and Pam came back in. "Here's some Pepto-Bismol. Captain Richter keeps two or three bottles in his desk all the time. He has ulcers on his ulcers. Why don't you take it in your purse in case you need it while you're at work?"

Karen nodded and took it, opened the bottle, and guzzled a mouthful down. Then she shoved it into her purse.

"Do you think you're ready?" Pam asked.

Karen closed her eyes and tried to summon her strength. "I guess so," she whispered. "Ready as I'll ever be."

Is there anything we've forgotten?" Larry peered at Tony and the captain across the table in the interrogation room.

"I don't think so," Tony said. "I think we've covered everything. As soon as she's ready, we are."

"What if she loses her nerve?"

"She can't. We've gone over and over it."

The captain stood up and peered out the window. "The van's ready. And we have enough men on the case. We can't afford to do this again. We have to bring this to a head tonight."

"I think it would have come to a head without us, Captain," Larry said. "There's a hole dug with a body bag just waiting for her. I don't think he plans to waste any time."

The door opened and Karen came in, followed by Pam Darby. Karen looked pale and more fragile than usual, but she'd dressed as she usually did for work.

"Ready?" Larry asked.

She pulled in a shaky breath. "I guess so." Her hand trembled as she ran it through her hair. "You're not going to let me down, are you? You'll be close by the whole time?"

"I promise," Larry said. "And we'll be calling you in the store every step of the way, letting you know if he's waiting, where we are, everything. And when things start happening, we'll hear every word you say."

She closed her eyes. "This is the worst thing I've ever been through in my life."

"It could have been a lot worse," the captain said.

She wasn't sure about that. "So what do I do now?"

"Get in your car," Larry told her, "go by your apartment, take your suitcase in like you just got back from a trip, just in case he's watching. We need to let him know that you're home—that things are back to normal. Then come back out, head to work. I don't think he'll strike this early. The risk is too great. He'll wait until you get off work."

"I'm gonna be sick again."

"Can't," Tony said. "There's no time."

They started out of the room, but Larry hung back. "You guys go test her mike. I'll be there in a minute."

He waited until Tony, Karen, and the captain were gone, and then he sat back down and stared at the wood grain of the table. *This is it, Lord*, he thought. *Please help us. Don't let anybody get hurt.*

He wished he'd been able to talk to Melissa when she'd called earlier, to tell her to pray for them tonight. But she hadn't called back, and now he wouldn't be able to make visitation. She would wonder where he was and convince herself that he had already lost interest. It would be Saturday before he'd be able to tell her differently.

Maybe he'd have good news.

He felt a little sick himself as he pulled up from the table and started for the door. In all his years of police work, he'd never wanted to catch anyone so much. And he'd never been more afraid that something could go wrong.

CHAPTER FORTY-NINE

M elissa tried to look her best with what she had to work with as she waited to be called to the rec room for visitation. Chloe had gone over half an hour ago, as had many of the women from her cellblock, but Melissa's name hadn't been called yet. She tried to read while she waited, tried to straighten up her cell, but no one called.

Finally, she ventured out of the cell and went to the bubble at the end of the block, where two guards sat doing paperwork.

"Excuse me," she said. "No one's called me, but I'm pretty sure I was going to get a visitor tonight. Could you check the list and make sure there's no one out there for me?"

The CO scanned the list. "Sorry, honey. No enchilada."

Her heart fell, and she started back to her cell. There were still two hours left. Maybe he was just running late.

She climbed up on the top bunk and curled up into a ball. Whatever the reason he wasn't here, whatever it meant, it was his happiness that mattered. Not hers.

Closing her eyes, she began to pray for him, that whatever he was doing, God was with him. She prayed that he wouldn't feel guilty for skipping this visit, that he wouldn't be distracted from whatever he was doing or whomever he was with—that if God had another plan for him that didn't include her, that she could accept it.

But even as she prayed, despair washed over her. Loneliness as smothering as a gas seemed to suffocate her, and she began to cry. She cried for the next two hours, until Chloe came back.

"He didn't come?" Chloe asked.

"No," Melissa whispered. "He's a busy man. I'm sure he would have come if he could."

"Yeah, right." Chloe changed clothes and plopped onto the bed. "It's not a lot to ask, you know. That they come and spend a hour with us, just to break up the time."

Melissa didn't want to talk about it anymore. "I'm okay," she whispered. "Good night."

"Yeah," Chloe said.

The big woman was snoring long before Melissa fell off to sleep.

CHAPTER FIFTY

The surveillance van was an old purple van with no back windows, in which they had a wealth of equipment that could monitor everything that Karen said in the store, and everything that was said to her. She was nervous. Her conversations at the counter were short, brief, clipped. One of her coworkers asked her why she was in such a bad mood, and she told her she had a headache. When she spilled two bottles of cologne, then knocked another one off the counter while trying to clean them up, Larry and Tony began to wonder if she could go through with this at all.

Two rows away, they saw Pendergrast, waiting as usual for the mall to close. It was only fifteen minutes until closing time. Karen's voice was shaky, and her coworker suggested that she sit down and drink a glass of water. But she refused and tried to finish doing her job.

Tony sat in the front seat, watching with infrared binoculars through the windshield. "He's reaching for something in the backseat," he said. "What's he doing?"

Larry abandoned the tape recorder to John Hampton, their surveillance expert, who sat with headphones on in front of the tape equipment.

"He's getting out!"

Larry came to the window and watched as Pendergrast got out, looked both ways to make sure no one saw him, then sauntered over to Karen's car.

Larry grabbed his camera with the night lens and focused it. "He's got something in his hand." He clicked. "What is it?"

"Can't tell," Tony said. "He's bending over."

Larry snapped the camera again as Pendergrast stabbed something into Karen's tire, then hurried back to his car.

"Okay, this is it." Larry's heart beat wildly as he hurried back to the telephone. "I'll let her know. Tonight's definitely the night." He dialed the number for the men's cologne counter.

Through the binoculars, Tony tried to determine whether the tire was flat yet. It was hard to tell. "He's either going to try to get her into his car right here in this parking lot, or he's expecting her to drive off and not realize anything's wrong for a block or so."

"It's too risky to get her here," Larry said. "Too much could go wrong." He held up a hand to stem Tony's reply as Karen picked up the phone.

"Men's Cologne."

"Karen, it's Larry. You okay?"

"Yeah. We're getting ready to come out. I'm just waiting for the security guard who usually escorts us."

"Okay. Now, listen. He just did something to your front left tire. Looks like he punctured it—not real bad, so I don't think it's flat yet."

"What's he gonna do?" she whispered.

"We don't know yet. But get in your car like normal, and pull out, like you would if you didn't know. Stop a quarter of a mile down the road, and get out to see the tire."

"And then what?" she whispered viciously.

"He'll probably pull up behind you and approach you."

Dead silence, then in a high-pitched squeak, she said, "I can't do this."

Larry glanced back at Tony, who could hear her through the tape recorder. "Look, we're right behind you, Karen. We're not going to let anything happen to you."

"Where will he take me? What if he loses you? What if something happens before you can get to me?"

"You have to trust us, Karen. Now, just act normal."

He could tell she was crying. "The guard's coming. We're about to go."

"We're ready, Karen. Are you?"

"No, but that doesn't really matter, does it?"

Larry glanced at Tony again. "Karen, we can hear every word that's said. Remember, you're not alone. It's going to be all right."

"Here goes," she whispered, and hung up the phone.

Tony slipped into the driver's seat, keeping the binoculars to his eyes. Already, some of the employees were being escorted out. Pendergrast was sitting at attention, watching, waiting, for Karen to come through those doors.

Larry grabbed the radio mike. "All right, guys," he said into it. "We're almost to liftoff. Stand by."

The three men in the van held their breath as they watched the front door open again. Karen and a group of employees spilled out. Karen stayed with the security guard until she was almost to her car, then ventured out, as stiff as a board, and tried to jab her key into the door lock.

She dropped her keys, reached down to pick them up, then seemed to have trouble getting the car key into the keyhole in the door.

"She's shaking like a leaf," Tony muttered, watching through the binoculars.

She got the door open, then quickly slid in and locked it again. It took a moment for her to start the engine, turn on the lights, and pull out of her space.

"Is it flat?" Larry asked.

"It looks low," Tony said. "Won't last much longer, but it'll at least get her out of the parking lot."

"Here he comes." Pendergrast had cranked his car and turned on his lights like any of the other employees who'd just come out. Pulling out of his space, he took another parking lot exit, as if trying to be far enough away from Karen that she wouldn't know she was being followed. He waited until she'd pulled out, then slowly began to follow her to the barren road where he would carry out his plan.

The van pulled out as soon as he was far enough away not to see them.

"All right. She's having trouble," Tony said. "Looks like the tire's completely flat now."

"She's not stopping," Larry said as he slowed to stay far enough back to be invisible in the darkness. "When's she gonna stop?"

"She's riding on the rim," John Hampton said from behind them. "She's scared to stop."

"Well, she'll have to sooner or later. Pendergrast is getting closer."

They watched as her brake lights came on, and she pulled to the side of the road. "You guys had better be back there," she said in a hoarse voice.

"We are, baby, we are," Tony answered, though she couldn't hear him. "All right, he's pulling in behind her. Stop the van."

They stopped, and Tony watched with the binoculars as John monitored the tape. Larry began to sweat.

They heard the car door open, and saw Karen get out as Pendergrast approached.

"Hi." It was Pendergrast's voice. "You having some trouble?"

"Yeah," she said, so quietly they had to turn up the monitor to hear. "My tire's flat. Do you happen to have a jack?"

He took a look at the tire and whistled. "No, I sure don't. But I'd be happy to give you a ride somewhere."

She hesitated. "Do you have a car phone? Maybe you could just call someone for me, and I could wait."

He chuckled like anybody's big brother. "Sorry. Look, I don't want to leave a woman out on this road by herself. I wouldn't be able to sleep tonight. You never know who might come along. Let me just take you up to the nearest gas station, and you can call."

Again, hesitation.

"Come on, Karen," Larry whispered.

"Okay," she said finally. "Let me just lock it up."

She was stalling, and Larry looked over at Tony. He was sweating, too.

She locked the doors, then walked slowly back to Pendergrast's car and got in the passenger side.

Larry began to inch the van forward as he pulled the mike off its hook. "All right, boys," he told the cops who'd been planted at various spots in the woods where Pendergrast had dug the hole. "He's got her. Everybody in place. Let's not drop the ball now."

Pendergrast's car pulled slowly back onto the road.

"I can't believe it's flat," Karen said. "That tire was new."

"You probably ran over something." His voice had changed.

"I'm glad you were coming by. It sure would have been scary to stand out there alone. I've been meaning to get a car phone, but—"

From the van, they saw Pendergrast turn onto the dirt road.

"Where are we going?"

"Shortcut," he said.

Larry punched the accelerator, and the van flew toward the dirt road, its lights still off.

"On a dirt road?" she asked. "I don't think so. Look, stop the car. I'm getting out."

"You're not going anywhere," he said calmly.

The van reached the dirt road, and Larry pulled over to the curb.

"You can't go up in here with your lights off," Tony said. "Road's too rough. You'll get stuck."

Larry drew his gun and opened the van door. "I'll go the rest of the way on foot. Radio the others. Tell them not to make a move until I give them the word. As soon as you hear them get out of the car, pull in, and hurry."

Bolting out of the van, Larry took off on foot, following the dirt road. His heart pounded faster with every step, and he uttered a prayer under his breath that nothing would go wrong. He ran for what seemed an eternity, following the dirt road. He heard the water and knew he was getting close to the clearing.

A car door slammed, and he heard a blood-curdling scream, propelling him faster.

The road curved, and he saw the clearing. The Toyota was parked there.

Karen screamed again, but he didn't see her or Pendergrast. Holding his pistol out in front of him, he scanned the trees, but couldn't see where they had gone. Frantic, he followed the sound as fast as he could, into the thick brush. It was too dark to see where he was going, so he pulled his flashlight out of his pocket and almost turned it on. But he knew Pendergrast would see him.

He heard Karen pleading and crying, and he ran faster, pushing through bushes and around trees, feeling his way as he gripped the pistol in one hand and the flashlight in the other, while he groped for his radio to tell someone to intervene.

His foot sank into a hole, and he tripped and dropped both the radio and the flashlight. He reached for them frantically, feeling through leaves and dirt, but couldn't find them. She screamed again, so he left them and went on as fast as he could. He was getting closer—he could hear Pendergrast's voice, and Karen's screams were louder . . .

Karen struggled to free herself from Pendergrast's arms as he dragged her through the brush, branches and twigs tearing her clothes and scraping her skin as they went. With all her might she screamed, but he wasn't afraid. They were too isolated out here, and he knew they couldn't be heard.

It wasn't supposed to go this far! They were supposed to stop things before Pendergrast got her out of the car, she thought on a wave of terror. But here he was, dragging her off where no one could get to her, and she was going to be dead before anyone stopped him. Was catching him all they cared about? Did they need a dead body to get the conviction they wanted?

They reached another clearing where the moonlight shone through, and she could see more clearly now. If she could just break away—maybe she could run—

He grabbed her hair and flung her to the ground, and she screamed out again. They weren't going to come, she thought desperately. She looked up at him, saw the crazy look in his eye as he pulled a scarf out of his pocket and wrapped the ends around his hands. Was he going to strangle her?

Deciding her allegiance to the case wasn't as important as her life, she used the only weapon she had. "The police know you're doing this! They're all over this place! They followed us here!"

Pendergrast seemed amused by that. He grabbed her hair again, pulling her up, his fist in her hair almost drawing blood at her scalp. He crammed the scarf into her mouth, then wound it around her head until it cut into the sides of her lips, choking and cutting her at the same time. She tried to scream, but couldn't, as he knocked her to the ground again.

As the van made its way down the dark road, silence screamed through the headphones. Tony cursed. "Something happened. He must have found the wire."

"I don't know," John said, listening carefully on the headphones. "I still hear the struggle. Maybe he gagged her."

"Where's Larry? He should be there by now. He should have sent the others in."

John shook his head and clutched the headphones, as if it would help him to hear better. "Stop the van, Tony. We're getting too close. He'll hear us and we'll have a hostage situation. Maybe that's why Larry hasn't signaled us yet."

"We *already* have a hostage situation!" Tony said, continuing to drive. But as he reached the clearing, he saw the Toyota and realized he was going to have to go the rest of the way on foot anyway. "All right," he told John. "I'm going in. Get up here so you can drive if you need to."

"Negative," John said. "I can't monitor the tapes and drive the van at the same time. We need the tapes for evidence!"

"Well, we don't need a dead girl!" Tony hissed. "Or a dead cop. I'm going!"

Before John could stop him, he took off down the dirt road, desperately hoping that it wasn't too late.

Larry tried not to make a sound as he pushed through the brush toward the scuffling sounds he could still hear. He came to the end of the brush, at the clearing where they'd found the hole yesterday.

He saw the opening in the trees overhead, and moonlight shone down on a circle of ground.

Karen was on the ground in that circle, kicking and fighting with all her might, though she was gagged and couldn't scream.

Pendergrast's back was to Larry, and Larry inched closer as Pendergrast fought, struggling to grab Karen's hands to restrain her.

Larry lunged forward and shoved the barrel of his 9 mm to the back of Pendergrast's head. "Freeze!" he shouted. "Let go of the girl, step back, and put your hands behind your head!"

Stunned, Pendergrast froze, and as he let Karen go, she slid across the dirt out of his reach.

Pendergrast spun around, trying to knock the gun out of Larry's hand. He kept his grip, but Pendergrast lunged at him, trying to wrestle it from his hands.

The gun fired.

With a yelp, Pendergrast dropped, clutching his shoulder with one hand. With the other, he reached into his boot and drew his own small pistol.

"Don't even try it," Larry said through his teeth, pointing his gun between Pendergrast's eyes. "Drop the gun. Drop it! Now!"

Pendergrast looked up at him, evaluating him, testing him. Slowly, he raised the gun, holding it between his thumb and forefinger as if he were about to toss it toward Larry. But he didn't.

Instead, he flipped it up until his finger was over the trigger, and aiming it at Larry's forehead, he cocked the hammer.

"Drop—the—gun," Larry uttered through his teeth. "I'm giving you to the count of three."

Pendergrast smiled.

"One . . ."

He wasn't moving.

"Two . . ."

A *whack* split the night, and Pendergrast fell over. Behind him stood Karen, still gagged, but holding a fat branch. Pendergrast twisted on the ground, grabbed her legs, and pulled her down, shoving the barrel of his gun against her ear. "You put the gun down, Millsaps," he choked out. "Drop the gun, or she's dead."

"Killing her won't keep me from killing you, Pendergrast," Larry said. "I'll bury you in that grave you dug."

Karen bucked and twisted with all her might, making it hard for Pendergrast to keep the gun against her head. Grabbing a fistful of hair, Pendergrast slammed her head down.

He tried again. "The gun, Millsaps. Drop it, and nobody has to get hurt."

Out of the corner of his eye, Larry saw Tony stealing through the brush, the same way he had come. He knew that, by now, at least five other cops were hiding in the shadows. Slowly, he lowered his gun and dropped it on the dirt.

Pendergrast laughed out loud, letting Karen go long enough to turn the pistol on Larry.

The gunshot shrieked through the air, but it wasn't Larry who was hit. The bullet from Tony's gun hit Pendergrast in the hand that clutched the pistol.

He let out a high-pitched yell, and the gun went flying.

Larry dove for his own gun, but Pendergrast went for it, too, fighting for his life with his one good hand. His fist flew across Larry's jaw, splitting the skin, but Larry struggled to grab the pistol. Pendergrast reached it first, and Larry clamped his hand over Pendergrast's. On their knees now, each of them reached for the hammer, and both fingers grabbed for the trigger.

When the gunshot rang out this time, they both dropped to the ground, still entangled.

"Larry!" Tony shouted, and burst forward.

Sirens blared as a convoy of squad cars reached the clearing, shining their headlights into the trees.

Only then could Tony tell which one of them had survived.

Larry pushed Pendergrast off him and slowly stood up.

Tony rushed forward to the limp body lying on the ground. Turning him over, he felt his neck for a pulse. "He's dead."

Larry looked down at the gun as if it were a foreign thing. Opening his fingers, he let it fall to the ground. Then he went to Karen and untied her gag.

She was sobbing as he got it off, and she fell against him, weak and hysterical. As he held her, he looked back at the body.

Cops swarmed out of the trees, lighting the area with flashlights and headlights.

But the victory was hollow. Larry had wanted the man in jail. He had wanted him exposed, tried, locked away in a prison where he would endure the torment he deserved. He hadn't wanted him dead. That was too easy. That was too quick.

Shaking, Larry helped Karen up and walked her to one of the squad cars. Helping her in, he told one of the cops, "Get her to a hospital. Make sure she's all right."

He stood back, watching, as the car pulled away.

When it was out of his sight, he went to the hole Pendergrast had dug to hide Karen in. The shovel and bag were still there, as was the pile of dirt waiting to be pushed back in. He reached for his flashlight to better see the contents of the makeshift grave, but remembered he had dropped it, along with his radio.

The lights from the headlights made it easier for him to find his way back through the brush, and he spotted the flashlight. He reached for it, and his foot sank again, just as it had when he'd been running through earlier.

Turning the flashlight on, he shone it down on the circle of sinking dirt. It was loose and thinly covered with leaves. He stooped and brushed the leaves away.

It looked as if the dirt had been put there to fill a hole, and he scooped a handful out, then another, and another.

"Tony!" he shouted. "Over here!"

In seconds, Tony was beside him. "Get a load of this," he said. "Looks like we have another hole. Question is, what's it burying?"

They got a shovel and centered all their efforts around digging, until the beams of the flashlights revealed what was hidden there.

"Oh, no," Larry said. "It's a woman."

They pulled the dirt-encrusted body out and shone the light in her face.

"Ten to one this is Lisa," Tony said. "Our other runaway."

Larry dropped wearily down to the dirt. "So Pendergrast killed her. That means he killed the girl on the beach, too."

"Yeah," Tony said. "He must have dumped her in that canal."

"Her and who else? We might find others."

As the others photographed the hole and the body, and recorded all of the evidence they would need to close the case, Larry began to feel bone tired, sick with exhaustion. He got up and started to walk away. Tony followed him. "Look, man. I owe you an apology."

"For what?" Larry asked.

"For not taking all this as seriously as I could have. I mean, I did at the end, but in the beginning—it never crossed my mind that he was a killer—or that he had anything to do with the girl on the beach."

"Didn't cross mine, either," Larry said. He stopped and looked off into the night. "I just keep thinking. That could have been Melissa in that hole. He might have killed her, too."

"He didn't. And he didn't kill Karen Anderson. She was roughed up and traumatized, but she's in one piece. It could have been a lot worse. Karen and Melissa are both going to be fine."

"Yeah," he said. "You're right."

He walked back to the van and leaned on the hood as the flurry of activity went on around the bodies. He wanted to hold Melissa, and listen to her breathe, and thank God that it hadn't been her in one of those holes, covered with dirt . . .

Tony walked up behind him and slid his hand across his back. "Why don't you go home, buddy? It's all over. We can take it from here."

"No," Larry said. "The evidence. We have to make sure—"

"He's dead," Tony reminded him. "The evidence won't matter much now."

Larry realized wearily that Tony was right. There would be a rush of news reports, and friends and acquaintances of Edward Pendergrast would come out of the woodwork, providing glimpses of the dark side of the killer. Maybe even more bodies would be found.

But there wouldn't be a trial. Pendergrast had already been convicted. And he wasn't going to find a way to squirm out of this one.

"Come on, buddy," Tony said. "Go home. Get some sleep."

Larry didn't have the energy to argue as he got back in the van.

CHAPTER FIFTY-ONE

The depression that Melissa had gone to bed with had kept her awake for most of the night. She tried to tell herself that it didn't matter that Larry had skipped that visit, that she'd expected as much, that it was inevitable. But the bottom line was that she was already in love with him, and the worst part of her incarceration was that she was going to lose him.

Had God really forsaken her?

She forced herself out of bed early the next morning, dressed in the orange jumpsuit that she was beginning to hate with all her heart, and got her Bible. Chloe woke up as she opened the door that the CO had unlocked just moments before.

"Where you goin' so early?"

"Bible study," Melissa said. "We decided it would be a good way to start our day."

Chloe cursed and pulled out of bed. "Well, I guess I have to go, too, if you are."

"No, you don't. You can sleep some more."

"And let you get pulverized walkin' to the chapel?"

"Chloe, everyone's still asleep. Nobody's going to hurt me."

Chloe ignored her as she stepped into her jumpsuit. "Your blood ain't gon' be on my head."

Quietly, they started down the long hall to the door of their cellblock.

It was midmorning when one of the officers came to get her. "Put your stuff up," she said. "You have a visit from your lawyer."

"Lynda?" she asked, turning off her iron and taking off her apron. "Why?"

"Do I look like I know all the answers?" the woman barked. "She's waitin' in room B."

Sweeping her bangs back from her perspiring forehead, Melissa followed the officer out.

But it wasn't just Lynda who waited for her. It was Larry, too.

Her face lit up, and when he reached for her, she threw her arms around him.

"I missed you last night," she whispered.

"I missed you, too," he said. "But you know I wouldn't have skipped if I didn't have to, don't you? You knew that, didn't you?"

She let him go, and he saw from the look on her face that she hadn't had that faith at all.

"Melissa, something happened last night. Something really important. And Lynda agreed to get you out for an attorney's conference today so I could talk to you. She pulled a few strings to get me in."

Melissa gave Lynda a half-smile. "Thanks, Lynda." She realized then that she had no makeup on and was damp with perspiration. Her hair was pulled back in a ponytail, and she felt like a frump. But before she could apologize for her appearance, she saw the bruised cut on Larry's jaw.

"What's this?" she asked, touching his face gently. "Were you injured?"

"Melissa, Edward Pendergrast is dead."

She stared at him. "What do you mean, he's dead?"

"We were able to catch him trying to rape a woman—"

She caught her breath. "That one you told me about?"

"Yes. She cooperated with us, and we had everything we needed on him. I wanted to get him in jail, make him rot there. But things took a turn . . . and now . . ."

Lynda stood up. "There was a struggle over a gun, and—"

"And I shot him," Larry said.

She could see that they weren't easy words for Larry to utter.

"He's really dead?" she asked.

"Yes," Larry said. "He can't hurt you anymore."

She threw her arms around his neck, holding him for dear life. Together, they began to weep.

"I prayed he'd get caught and convicted," Melissa whispered. "Sometimes I didn't think God was going to answer."

"He did," Larry whispered. "He was caught *and* convicted. It just wasn't our court he was judged in."

"He's really gone," she whispered, awestruck. "When I get out, I don't have to be afraid."

"He's really gone."

Lynda smiled. "I've sent a plea to the governor, Melissa, as well as the judge who sentenced you. I've asked them to pardon you, or at least consider reducing your sentence to probation, given the circumstances surrounding Pendergrast's death. Now that the story's going to be all over the news, I think we may be able to get something done."

Melissa considered that for a moment. "When?"

"I don't know. It might be a few days. Maybe even a couple of weeks. But I'm doing all I can."

"Good," Melissa said, letting go of Larry. "I need a couple of weeks, at least."

Larry shot Lynda a look, and they both looked at Melissa as if she'd lost her mind. "For what?"

She wiped her eyes and smiled, the first genuine smile Larry had seen on her in a long time. "I'm not here by accident," she said. "God needed me here. We've got this Bible study going . . . and some of the people I was terrified of . . . they're coming now, and they're listening. If you get me out, I'm coming back as often as I can, to keep the group going."

Lynda's eyes grew tearful as she began to smile. "That's one of the most amazing things I've ever heard."

Dismissing that, Melissa looked at Larry again and wiped the tears on her face. "The girl—is she all right?"

"She was pretty shaken up last night," Larry admitted.

"Can I see her when I get out?" she asked.

"I'm sure it can be arranged. Until then, you could write her a letter. I'd take it to her."

"All right," Melissa said. "I want to thank her. For myself . . . and for Sandy."

CHAPTER FIFTY-TWO

Karen Anderson sat in her apartment the next day, curled up in her favorite chair with a blanket over her that covered the scrapes and bruises on her legs. The ones on her arms and face were more apparent . . . but it was the ones on her heart that she worried most about.

She had spent the first night in the hospital on a sedative, and though she knew that Pendergrast was dead, she'd been afraid to come home. Her mother had threatened to sue the police department for involving her in such a dangerous situation, and Karen hadn't known whether to support the suit or discourage it. Finally, she had forced herself to return to the apartment where he'd watched her, and try to get on with her life.

She had almost refused to let Larry in when he'd shown up at her door, but when he told her that he had something to give her from his girlfriend who was in jail, she had reluctantly opened the door. She'd had little to say to him, and he had left quickly, but not before telling her that she was his idea of a true hero, a gift sent from God, and that he would do anything he could to help her heal from her trauma.

Now that he was gone, she opened the manila envelope and emptied out the contents. There was a letter there, and several pictures of a beautiful woman, with blonde hair and bright blue eyes. Beneath the snapshots was a smaller envelope.

She unfolded the letter first and began to read.

Dear Karen,

I started this letter several times, trying to find the right words, but there just aren't any. How can I tell you how much it means to me that you would risk your life to save the lives of so many potential victims? How can I explain the closure I feel at knowing that he won't be waiting when I get out of here? How can I describe my gratitude to you?

There aren't words to do it, Karen, so I decided to send you pictures. Meet Sandy, my sister . . . at her graduation, and her wedding . . . with me, and with our parents. Losing her caused pain so deep in us that we thought it would never go away. But what you did has helped to relieve that pain so much.

Thank you, Karen, and if you feel up to it when I get out, I'd love to meet you and shake the hand of the brave woman who helped me wake up from my nightmare.

God bless you,
Melissa

Karen wiped her eyes and looked at the pictures again. The beautiful, happy eyes of the woman who had killed herself smiled out at her. In comparison, what had happened to Karen seemed mild.

She picked up the smaller envelope, and opened it. It was another stack of pictures, but this time, a note from Larry was stuck to the top of the stack.

Karen,

I thought you might like to see the two women we know Pendergrast killed, and some of the other women whose lives you may have saved. Some of these were pictures we recovered from Pendergrast's apartment.
Larry

She saw the two women on top, the one who'd washed up on the beach, and the one he had buried. She flipped further through them and saw the random snapshots of women who didn't know they were being photographed. Women coming out of their homes, getting out of their cars, coming out of stores . . .

She leaned her head back on the chair and looked up at the ceiling for a moment. What she'd done was a good thing. Maybe it hadn't been so terrible, after all. It could have been so much worse. For her. For all of them.

The telephone rang, but she didn't move. The machine picked it up, and she kept looking through the pictures as her voice played its message. It beeped, and a voice said, "Miss Anderson, this is Chip Logan with the *St. Clair News*. We'd like to do a feature story on you for our paper . . ."

She smiled softly then, but didn't pick up. She wasn't ready for that just yet. But maybe later, she thought. Maybe soon.

This hero stuff was just going to take a little time to sink in.

EPILOGUE

After the phone call from the governor the following week, and the *20/20* interview with Melissa about the Pendergrast case, Judge L. B. Summerfield, who'd sentenced Melissa, agreed to release her on probation.

She had a final Bible study with her group that morning, including Chloe, who had begun to read her Bible each day so she could "argue" intelligently with the others in the circle. Melissa promised them she would be coming back with Doug to worship on Sunday mornings, and that she'd start work immediately to get permission to continue meeting with the Bible study group as part of her personal prison ministry.

Before she left her cell, she sat down on the bunk next to Chloe. "You know something, Chloe?" she asked.

Chloe grunted.

"For most of the time that I've been in here, I've considered you my personal angel, sent by God. Did you even realize you were being used by God?"

"Me? God ain't *never* used me."

"He did, Chloe. Before I came in here, my lawyer, who's also a good friend, gave me a verse of Scripture that meant a lot to me. It said that God would protect me. And it was so true. God protected me through you. Thank you . . . for being there."

Chloe smiled one of her rare smiles. "So you think God was really usin' me?"

"I sure do."

She chuckled slightly. "I'll be. Didn't even know God knew I was here."

"He does."

"Thank ya, Melissa."

"Are you going to keep coming to the Bible studies, even if you're not having to protect me?"

Chloe shrugged. "Might."

Melissa stood up and looked around the cell. "Would you like to keep all these books?"

Chloe's eyes widened. "I never been much of a reader. But I have been a little interested. Maybe I will read 'em."

"All right. They're yours. And I'm going to visit you Saturday and bring you some groceries. How's that sound? I'll bring you a box of Snickers."

Chloe laughed. "Girl, you're a saint."

She leaned over and kissed Chloe on the cheek, and the woman looked embarrassed. "Thanks, Chloe. For everything."

Then, quietly, she left the cell for the last time.

Red was lurking in the hallway, leaning against the wall. "I knew you wouldn't be here long. What did you do? Flap those blonde locks in the judge's face? Promise him somethin'?"

Melissa just looked at her. "You know what happened, Jean. You saw it on the news just like everyone else."

"Yeah, but I know what goes on behind the scenes."

"And you know me." She extended her hand to the bitter woman, but Red only slid her hands into her jumpsuit pockets and started to walk away. "I'm coming back," Melissa said to her back. "For the Bible studies."

"Right. I'll believe it when I see it."

Melissa smiled. "You've got a deal." She watched until Red had gone back into her cell, then left cellblock C for the final time.

Larry was waiting for her at the warden's office. She ran into his arms, laughing and crying. "Am I really free?"

"Completely," he whispered against her ear, holding her as if she could be snatched from him at any time. "Free to do anything you want," he whispered. "Free to go back to the life you had before. Or free to go in a new direction."

"I didn't have much of a life before," she said, looking up at him. "For the last three years, everything has revolved around my obsession to get Pendergrast."

"Then it's time for you to start over," he whispered. He handed her the bouquet of roses he'd laid on the table, and as she buried her face in them, he added, "And maybe that new beginning could include me."

She looked up at him, her eyes soft with anticipation. "What do you mean, Larry?"

"I mean that I love you," he whispered. "And I want you to be my wife."

The fragile joy and hope in her eyes slowly faded. "What will your friends say? I'm an ex-con. You're a cop."

"They'll say, 'Congratulations, Larry. She's the prettiest ex-con we've ever seen.'"

A soft smile broke through her turmoil. "No, really. What on earth will you tell them?"

He thought for a moment, then framed her face with his hands and looked into her eyes. "I'll tell them that when God shows me a treasure, I'm going to take it every time."

She wiped her tears and stared up at him with soft eyes that seemed so innocent, but she'd experienced more than she'd ever wanted to. Larry was a gift from God, something she hadn't earned, but she wouldn't refuse, either.

Throwing her arms around him, she said, "Of course I'll marry you!"

He whisked her up in his arms then, holding her in a crushing hug. Melissa laughed out loud, and he joined her, and they each realized what a new, magical lilting sound the mingling of their joy produced. It sounded like grace.

And Melissa knew why they called it amazing.

AFTERWORD

I often think my life is much like that of a mouse in a maze. There's a plan and a path which is perfect for me, and it's not so hard to find. But I can convince myself that I have a better way—a shortcut, or a more interesting route to where I'm going. Sometimes, I even think the destination I choose is better than what has been ordained for me.

I picture God standing above that maze, urging me to take the turns and twists he's planned for me, luring me this way and that, showing me open doors and nudging me past the closed ones … but so often I ignore him and go in my own direction. Sometimes I kick down the doors that would keep me out of trouble, and I forge headfirst into what lies behind them. Those are the times when God groans and slaps his forehead in frustration. But then—always—he says, "I can still work with this," and moves to Plan B, C, or D, making another path for me. It might be less wonderful, because of my own careless choices, and it might be less useful to him, but he doesn't give up. He continues to work with me and guide me away from the dead ends in my life, and he opens the doors that will lead me to what he wants me to have. I have never strayed so far that he couldn't guide me back.

That's grace. That's the grace of a father who loved me—a poor, ignorant, rebellious, vagabond mouse—enough to send his Son to die so that I could get out of that maze once and for all. With my eyes on the cross, I don't have to bump into walls and turn in circles and backtrack through the corridors of my life. All I have to do is follow him. And trust.

Abundant life? You bet it is.

That's why they call that grace *amazing*.

Terri Blackstock

ABOUT THE AUTHOR

Terri Blackstock is an award-winning novelist who has written for several major publishers including HarperCollins, Dell, Harlequin, and Silhouette. Published under two pseudonyms, her books have sold over 5 million copies worldwide.

With her success in secular publishing at its peak, Blackstock had what she calls "a spiritual awakening." A Christian since the age of fourteen, she realized she had not been using her gift as God intended. It was at that point that she recommitted her life to Christ, gave up her secular career, and made the decision to write only books that would point her readers to him.

"I wanted to be able to tell the truth in my stories," she said, "and not just be politically correct. It doesn't matter how many readers I have if I can't tell them what I know about the roots of their problems and the solutions that have literally saved my own life."

Her books are about flawed Christians in crisis and God's provisions for their mistakes and wrong choices. She claims to be extremely qualified to write such books, since she's had years of personal experience.

A native of nowhere, since she was raised in the Air Force, Blackstock makes Mississippi her home. She and her husband are the parents of three children—a blended family which she considers one more of God's provisions.

TERRI BLACKSTOCK

#1 bestselling suspense author

TRUE LIGHT

a RESTORATION Novel

Be sure to read this sample chapter from Terri Blackstock's novel *True Light*

ONE

THE BUCK FELL WITH THE FIRST SHOT, and Zach Emory couldn't help being impressed with himself. From his deer stand, it looked like an eight- or ten-pointer. If the weather stayed cold, he'd be able to make it last for several weeks' worth of meals.

He climbed down from his deer stand and pulled up the collar of his jacket. It was so cold his ears were numb, and his fingers had begun to ache. But it was worth it. Even in the pre-outage days, Zach had spent many mornings sitting in a deer stand freezing to death, just for sport. Now it was a matter of survival.

He jogged toward the animal that lay dead twenty yards away. His brother Gary would be crazy with envy. They had a competition going, and Gary was two up on him. Zach hoped Gary had heard the gunshot and would come to help him move the deer. It would take both of them to lift it into their rickshaw.

He bent over the buck. Ten points. And a perfect shot right through the heart. His dad would finally be proud, and if he was lucky, his mother would drag herself out of bed to get a look.

He heard footsteps behind him and turned to see a man emerging from the trees, walking toward him. Zach squinted, trying to place him. He'd seen him before, but he couldn't remember where.

"Did I score or what?" he asked as the man came closer. "He's a ten-pointer. Got him in one shot, right through the ticker!"

The man didn't look like he'd come to celebrate. He stopped about thirty feet away . . . and raised his rifle.

Was he going to shoot? Zach's hands came up, as if that would stop him.

The gun fired—its impact propelling Zach backward, bouncing him onto the dirt.

TWO

THE BUILDING SMELLED OF MOTOR OIL AND GREASE
—A scent Deni Branning associated with progress. A symphony
of roaring engines brought a smile to her face as she rolled her bike
inside. Oh, for the days of noise pollution and hurry—of bumper-
to-bumper traffic, honking horns, blaring radios, and twenty-four-
hour TV.

All over the large warehouse, mechanics and engineers with
black-stained fingers worked at converting engines. The building
had been purchased by the feds a few months ago, when they insti-
tuted the draft. Instead of drafting soldiers, the government had
conscripted all of those with experience as mechanics. Later,
they'd added others to the conscription list: electricians, scientists,
and engineers. Many of them were allowed to live at home and
work in the local conversion plants, but others had been sent
across the country to serve where they were needed.

Pushing down the kickstand on her bike, she reached into her
bag for her notepad and looked around for someone in charge. She
saw Ned Emory, from her neighborhood, standing nearby with a
clipboard, instructing a group of mechanics with a disassembled
engine laid out in front of them. She headed toward him.

"Excuse me," she yelled over the noise. "Mr. Emory?"

He turned. "Yeah?"

She could see that he didn't recognize her, even though his
son Zach had been close friends with her brother for years. "Deni
Branning. Jeff's sister?"

Recognition dawned in his eyes. She reached out to shake
hands with him, but he showed her his greasy hands. "Better not
shake. What brings you here?"

"I'm writing an article about your work here. Do you have
time for an interview?"

As if he hadn't heard her, he turned back to the men, barked
out some orders that she couldn't hear, and started walking away.

Glancing back over his shoulder, he said, "I heard the newspaper is back up and running. They hired you, did they?"

She caught up to him and tried to match his steps. "That's right. *The Crockett Times*. They liked what I'd been doing on the message boards around town. This'll be the cover story for next week's issue."

He didn't seem impressed, so she pulled out her big guns. "You guys are like rock stars. Everybody wants to know what you're up to."

Pride pulled at the corners of his mouth, and she knew she'd struck a chord. "Sure, I can give you a few minutes. What do you want to know?"

He started up a staircase, and she blew out her frustration as she followed him. "Is there someplace we can sit down?"

"I don't have time to sit down." He reached the top of the stairs and headed across the concrete floor to an area where a dozen mopeds sat in various stages of completion. "Hey, Stark! I need at least four of these done by the end of the day. Get Bennett over here to help you."

Deni's gaze swept over the bikes. "Wow. How can I get one of those?"

"You can't. They're not for the private sector." He was walking again, but she hung back, unable to tear herself away from the coveted mopeds. She stepped toward one and touched the seat.

He turned back and gave her an impatient look. "Do you want to do the interview or not?"

She shook off her longing and forced herself to focus. "Of course."

He led her past a table filled with generators, and again, her longing kicked in. "Do those work?"

"They do after we harden them against the Pulses."

Her heart quickened. If they were making hardened generators here, it wouldn't be long until they actually had electricity. Could there really be lightbulbs at the end of the tunnel?

"When will those be available for the public?" she asked, catching up to him again.

"Our illustrious supernova will burn out before we can finish supplying the hospitals. They're priority number one for the generators right now. Without robotics, assembly lines—electricity, for that matter—we have to do everything by hand, one at a time. And even if we could produce enough for the public, there's one missing ingredient."

"Gasoline," she said.

"You got it." He reached a series of offices with glass walls, overlooking the work on the floor below them. "We can't get enough gas without operating tanker trucks, and once we get it here, we don't have electricity to work the pumps."

She was well aware of the chain of problems. "But aren't you guys all about creating work-arounds?"

"Right now we're just trying to help critical services operate. Like I said, the star will likely burn out before we get caught up with that. Then we'll shift our objectives from sustaining to rebuilding." He headed into one of the offices, dropped his clipboard on his desk, and motioned for her to take a seat.

As Deni sat down, something outside the glass caught Ned's eye, and Deni turned to follow his gaze. Someone was running up the stairs.

Ned frowned as his son Gary came running toward his door. "Dad, Zach's been shot!"

"What?"

Deni caught her breath and got to her feet.

"We were hunting at the Jenkins's place. I heard some gunshots and . . . when I found him .?.?."

"Is he dead?" Ned blurted out.

"I don't think so. I got help and somebody went to get an ambulance. They're taking him to University Hospital."

Ned grabbed his son's shoulders. "What condition was he in when they took him?"

Gary trembled as he raked his hands through his hair. "There was blood all over his shirt . . . front and back."

Deni's heart stopped. Her brother's best friend.?.?.

Ned raced out of the office and hurried down the stairs, Gary on his heels. Deni followed them as far as the top of the stairs, then waited there as they hurried through the building. All the engines went quiet, and everyone stared as Ned ran to a beat-up Buick. "The keys!" he shouted. "Where are the keys?"

Someone tossed them to him, and he got in and started the engine. Gary jumped in beside him. Two guys pulled up the garage door and the Buick rumbled out.

Deni muttered a prayer for Zach as they drove off—and then a thought struck her. Jeff, Deni's brother, sometimes hunted with Zach. Could they have been together? What if he'd been hurt too?

She had to get to the scene of the shooting. She ran downstairs, grabbed her bike, and pedaled out behind them.

THREE

"ZACH? ZACH, CAN YOU HEAR ME?"

Zach tried to open his eyes, but they were glued shut. Something was shaking and bumping him—and with each jolt, pain exploded through him.

"Zach, we're getting you to the hospital, okay, buddy? Stay with me."

Was he in an ambulance? How long had it been since he'd been in a running car? Weeks? Months? Years? His brain couldn't find the answer.

He tried to breathe, but something was crushing his chest. Drowning . . . choking . . . gurgling.

Something sliced through his throat. "We're gonna help you breathe, buddy. Hang on, we're almost there."

He couldn't breathe. Gagging. Smothering. Gasping.

The ambulance jerked to a stop, people all around him yelling, probing, pushing.

As they rolled him into the building, Zach knew he was dying.

FOUR

THE MEETING HAD BEEN DRAGGING ON FOR HOURS. Doug Branning shifted in his seat and wished they would take a break, so the attendees could dash outside to the Porta-Johns lined up around the Birmingham Jefferson Convention Complex. For weeks, he'd looked forward to the symposium of economic leaders in the area. His success as a stockbroker had gotten him an invitation, and he hoped to hear about when the banks would open and what the plan would be for infusing money into the economy.

Because the big complex was without electricity, chairs had been set up in the multileveled lobby of the big building, so they could take advantage of the light from the windows. He'd sat riveted for most of the day as financial leaders argued that opening the banks would have a destructive effect on the economy. Others countered that opening them would help. Doug wasn't sure which side of the fence he landed on, professionally. But as a victim of this disaster, he wanted his cash.

The government leaders who'd come in for the symposium and who had been conducting meetings like this in several major cities, were here to gather advice from local leaders and update them on the state of the economy. So far, all Doug had done today was listen.

"The banking systems lacked sufficient records of their account balances to open the banks a few months ago," Edward Freelord, Federal Reserve Chairman, said, his voice carrying over the crowd. "When the computers crashed, most of the banks had only a few current hard copies, and those have had to be reproduced by hand. Local banks now have the information they need for their local account holders, so it is feasible for them to open. We're considering instructing them to give account holders no more than 2 percent per month of their balance, to avoid a run on the banks."

They'd already established that the law would prohibit foreclosures on property during the Pulses, since no one was able to make payments right now, and the banks would not be allowed to loan money except to those involved in rebuilding the infrastructure and helping the government function.

Several of the audience members weighed in on Freelord's idea, offering pros and cons that Doug was sure the leaders had already considered. But Doug's mind was busy calculating the scenario's direct benefit to his family. He'd had about 15,000 dollars in his checking account at the time of the outage, and another 30,000 dollars in savings. His stocks and bonds and other investments totaled over a million dollars, but those were worthless right now.

He jotted the figures in the margin of his legal pad. With the government's suggested plan, his family would be entitled to 900 dollars a month. With the new rock-bottom prices, they would be in great shape.

Once again, the world would be separated into the haves and have-nots, and his family would rise to the top. It wouldn't help his friends in the Sandwood Place Apartments, most of whom hadn't had any money even before the outage. But maybe it would help them indirectly, as money spent in the economy trickled down to make their lives better.

Would it? That was a pipe dream, he feared. But he'd deal with it later.

Someone tapped on his shoulder, and he glanced up to see Jeff, his sixteen-year-old, standing over him. "What are you doing here?" Doug asked in a whisper.

"Sorry, Dad." Jeff looked upset, and Doug knew something was wrong. "I have to talk to you."

Doug got up and followed Jeff back up the aisle, to the front door. They stepped out into the cold. "What is it?"

"Dad, Zach Emory was shot this morning!"

"What? How?"

Jeff told him the little he knew.

"You weren't with him?"

"No, I was helping Mom set up at the swap meet. They said he was really bad, that he lost a lot of blood. Some people who were there when the ambulance came weren't even sure he was alive." His chin trembled, and he settled his misting eyes on Doug.

"Dad, I want to go see if he's all right, but Mom told me to come by and get you first."

"Of course," Doug said, glancing through the glass back up at the podium.

"You don't have to leave," Jeff said. "I can go by myself. It's just that Mom thinks I'm a kid who can't be alone in the city."

"I can leave now. Don't worry about it."

"But what if you miss something important? Like when they're opening the banks?"

Doug shook his head. "This is just a fact-finding mission. They haven't made any decisions yet."

They headed to the bike rack and unchained their bicycles. Getting onto his bike and pumping out into the street, Doug couldn't imagine what Zach's parents were going through. He looked over at Jeff as they rode. The boy's gaze was fixed on the road, but Doug could see the pain behind his eyes. Zach was one of Jeff's closest friends.

He prayed as they rode, but his prayers were selfish. As much as he wanted Zach to be alive when they got to the hospital, he wanted even more to protect his son from the pain of sudden and unjustified loss.

Only God could control that now.

Last Light

Terri Blackstock,
#1 Bestselling Suspense Author

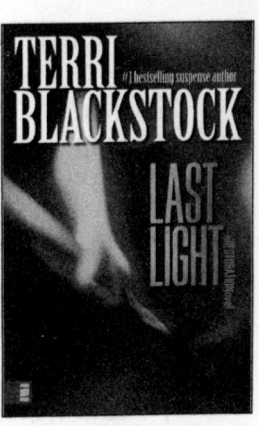

Today, the world as you know it will end. No
need to turn off the lights.

Your car suddenly stalls and won't restart.
You can't call for help because your cell
phone is dead.

Everyone around you is having the same
problem ... and it's just the tip of the iceberg. Your city is in a blackout. Communication is cut off. Hospital equipment won't operate.
And airplanes are falling from the sky.

Is it a terrorist attack ... or something far worse?

In the face of a crisis that sweeps an entire high-tech planet back
to the age before electricity, your family faces a choice. Will you
hoard your possessions to survive — or trust God to provide as you
offer your resources and your hearts to others?

Yesterday's world is gone. Now all you've got is your family and
community. You stand or fall together. Like never before, you must
rely on each other.

But one of you is a killer.

#1 bestselling suspense author Terri Blackstock weaves a master-
ful what-if novel in which global catastrophe reveals the darkness in
human hearts — and lights the way to restoration for a self-centered
world. *Last Light* is the first book in an exciting new series.

Softcover: 0-310-25767-0
Audio CD, Unabridged: 0-310-26880-X

Pick up a copy today at your favorite bookstore!

Night Light

*Terri Blackstock, #1 Bestselling
Suspense Author*

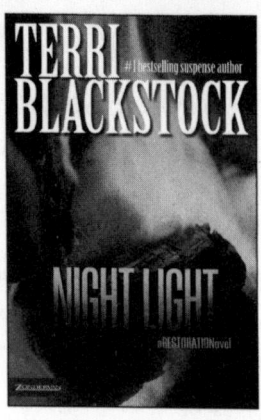

In the face of a crisis that sweeps an entire high-tech planet back to the age before electricity, the Brannings face a choice. Will they hoard their possessions to survive — or trust God to provide as they offer their resources to others?

#1 bestselling suspense author Terri Blackstock weaves a masterful what-if series in which global catastrophe reveals the darkness in human hearts — and lights the way to restoration for a selfcentered world.

An era unlike any in modern civilization is descending, one without lights, electronics, running water, or automobiles. As a global blackout lengthens into months, the neighbors of Oak Hollow grapple with a chilling realization: the power may never return.

Survival has become a lifestyle. When two young thieves break into the Brannings' home and clean out the food in their pantry, Jeff Branning tracks them to a filthy apartment and discovers a family of children living alone, stealing to stay alive. Where is their mother? The search for answers uncovers a trail of desperation and murder ... and for the Brannings, a powerful new purpose that can transform their entire community — and above all, themselves.

Softcover: 0-310-25768-9
Audio CD, Unabridged: 0-310-26921-0

Pick up a copy today at your favorite bookstore!

More great books from
Terri Blackstock

Sun Coast Chronicles

Softcover 0-310-20015-6

Softcover 0-310-20016-4

Softcover 0-310-20708-8

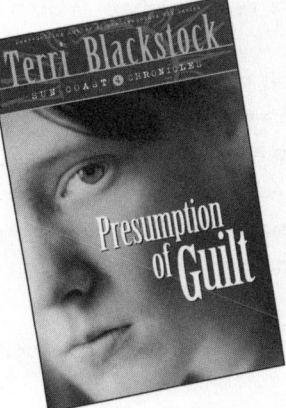

Softcover 0-310-20018-0

Pick up a copy today at your favorite bookstore!

Cape Refuge Series

This bestselling series follows the lives of the people of the small seaside community of Cape Refuge, as two sisters struggle to continue the ministry their parents began—helping the troubled souls who come to Hanover House for solace.

Cape Refuge
Softcover: 0-310-23592-8

Southern Storm
Softcover: 0-310-23593-6

River's Edge
Softcover: 0-310-23594-4

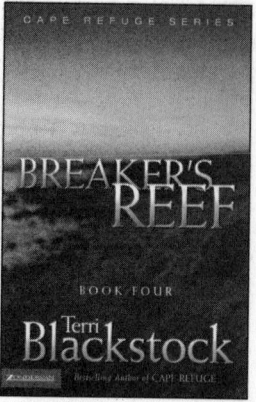

Breaker's Reef
Softcover: 0-310-23595-2

Pick up a copy today at your favorite bookstore!

ZONDERVAN®
.com

Three ways to keep up on your favorite
Zondervan books and authors

Sign up for our *Fiction E-Newsletter*. Every month you'll receive sample excerpts from our books, sneak peeks at upcoming books, and chances to win free books autographed by the author.

You can also sign up for our *Breakfast Club*. Every morning in your email, you'll receive a five-minute snippet from a fiction or nonfiction book. A new book will be featured each week, and by the end of the week you will have sampled two to three chapters of the book.

Zondervan *Author Tracker* is the best way to be notified whenever your favorite Zondervan authors write new books, go on tour, or want to tell you about what's happening in their lives.

Visit *www.zondervan.com* and sign up today!

ZONDERVAN.com/
AUTHORTRACKER
follow your favorite authors